THROUGH THE WILLOW

A PHOENIX QUEEN LEGACY

JADE JONES

CONTENTS

*To the women who always dreamed of being more than just a filler
in a story.
This is for you.*

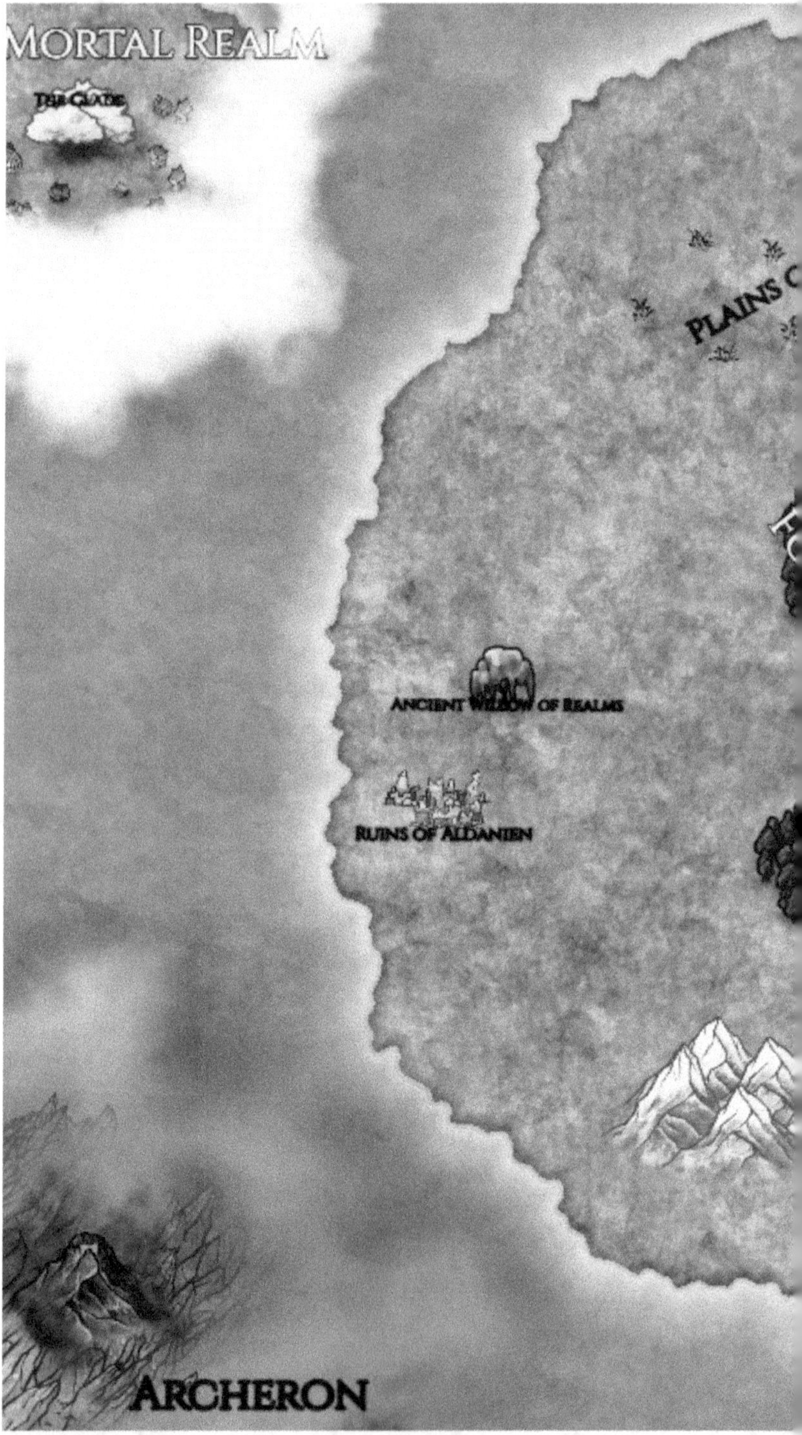

MORTAL REALM
THE GLADE
PLAINS O
ANCIENT WILLOW OF REALMS
RUINS OF ALDANIEN
ARCHERON

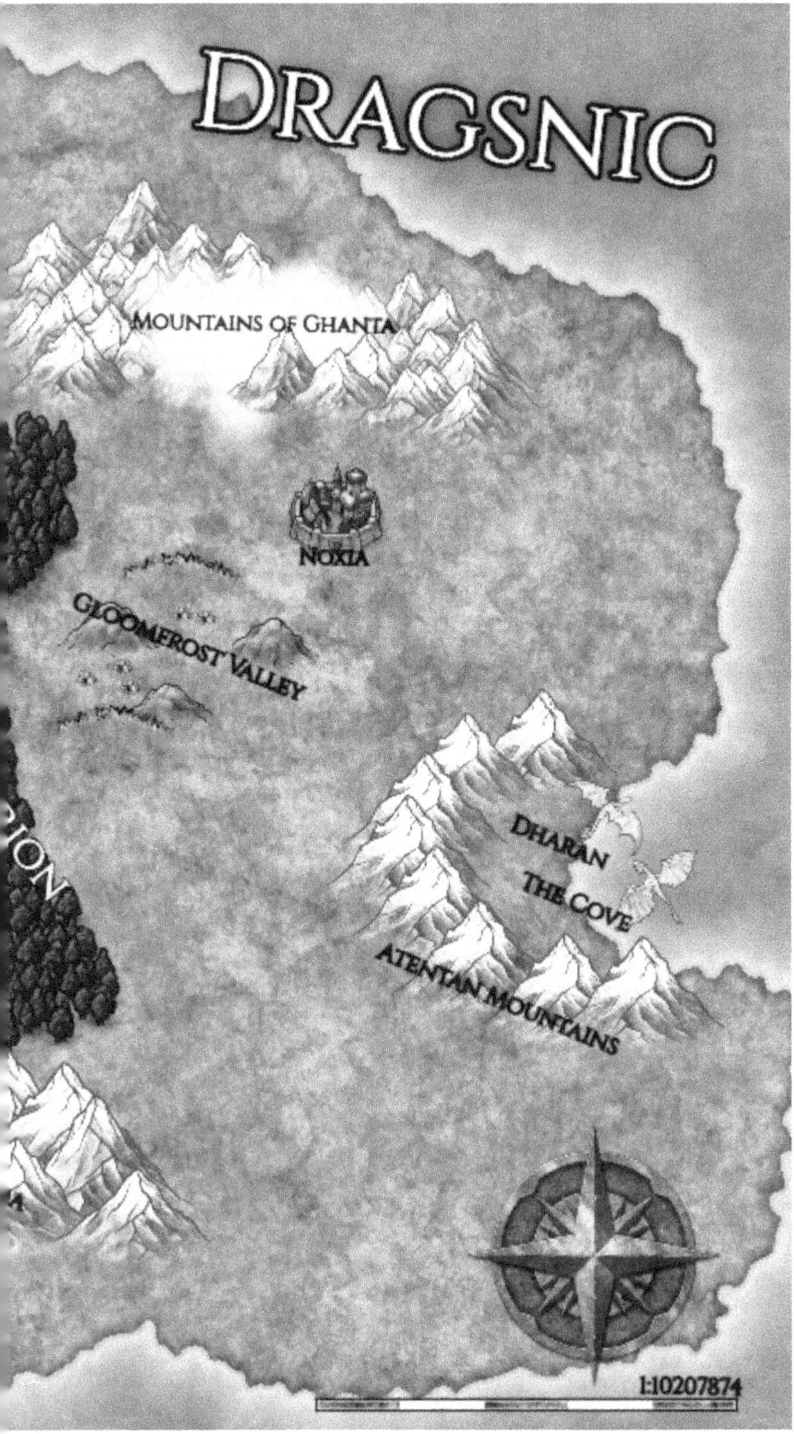

DRAGSNIC
MOUNTAINS OF GHANTA
NOXIA
GLOOMFROST VALLEY
DHARAN
THE COVE
ATENTAN MOUNTAINS
1:10207874

PROMISES MADE

The evening held a crispness that caused shivers to crawl down her back. The days were growing colder, and winter would soon be upon them. Which meant Audelia had to train harder. She didn't care that her tiny arms, which had grown some muscle in the year since Audelia had begun her training, were currently screaming at her to stop.

She had watched members of her Cadre push themselves to the brink. So, Audelia had decided she could do the same. She needed to. Audelia did not care that her uncle Bronn, the head of her cadre and her father's older brother, had told her that it would take years to reach the level he and the others had.

She had made a promise to someone. One, she intended to keep in more ways than one. Mathias, her most trusted guard, had laughed saying he was surprised it had taken her this long to even decide to begin training. After all, she was always on the pitch, watching the others over the years.

Audelia loved watching the knights train, especially her cadre. It was like a dance. Every move entranced her, and she knew it was something she wanted to learn. When she decided to tell her parents about her decision, Mathias taught her what to say; because she was nervous, they would laugh at her.

Mathias had told her if they did, he would make them pay; she had merely laughed. After all, a princess was supposed to be soft and demure, all the things Audelia felt she rightfully lacked. Which was no wonder considering her mother, Queen Naseria, was a warrior herself.

Audelia wanted to be like her mother. She wanted to be strong, not needing to rely on the men who protected her. Audelia loved each of them dearly; some like older brothers, others like uncles. They were her family.

When her father had asked why, every nerve in her tiny body had surged with a renewed strength, because the reason why, that was the very reason she pushed herself daily.

Because I want to protect the people I love, they defend me every day, and they deserve someone to protect them as well.

Audelia's father and uncle had just laughed at first; she thought it was because they had found her seven-year-old self, deciding she wanted to protect ancient warriors funny. She had almost begun to yell at them to stop making fun of her.

But then her uncle's large frame knelt before her with a smile that made his brown eyes look like warm pools of chocolate. Her uncle Bronn had told her that what she had said was one of the very reasons he had given up the throne when he was a boy. Because of the call to protect, it had laid with a blade, not a crown.

Audelia had heard that story before, parts of her wanted the same, to just become a warrior and forget the throne. The responsibilities of the crown terrified her. When she watched Mathias and the others train or heard them talk about their adventures, she yearned for it.

But it was her mother's words that had come next, that played through her head now as she swung the blade in her hands at the worn wooden dummy.

"My moonbeam, I know that the call of a blade is strong, for it sings in my own heart. But, my love, you must remember that you need to be both. The Blade and the Crown. You are our daughter. You have the call of both in your heart. Audelia, they burn brighter in you than you will ever realize. Become the blade, but as you sharpen your sword, sharpen your heart as well, for that will forge a new crown."

After that, they agreed that she could come as often as she wished to practice. To make her measure of things, but the first time her uncle had placed a blade in her hands, even with it being wooden, the flames that always sat curled dormant inside her had swelled, lapping at the edges of her soul. *This.* This was something she was meant to do.

From then on, she trained daily, slow at first because her small body screamed in protest. Audelia had been used to working her body, and she trained in magic with her aunt Mara daily and sometimes even with her mother.

Skye, another of her guards who was currently on the pitch working with her through drills, had told her that she had to build her strength before they could ever press steel into her hands. Luckily, she hadn't had to wait long before she was throwing daggers.

It was one of her favorite pastimes lately, much to the

horror of her lady's maid, because Audelia had a habit of throwing her daggers into the doors of her armoire, and recently, one of them may have accidentally fallen apart while Helen, her lady's maid, had gone to open it.

Today, however, she had chosen to focus on the short sword. It was the one she had been struggling with the most. She hated it. Mathias told her to be patient and that it would take time to master the heavier swords. Audelia merely shook her head at his statement. Part of her knew it was true, but something deep inside her told her she didn't have time. Not just to keep her promise but because lately, she had kept having these dreams.

These terrifying dreams had her waking up crying, clutching the stuffed dragon Mathias had gotten her, which looked exactly like his dragon Tadan. It brought her comfort, and if it didn't, she would read from the book that permanently lived under her pillow, another gift.

Lately though, even they didn't help calm the fear bubbling inside her, didn't chase away the insidious voice that had begun to chase her even into the day. She should tell someone; she knew it. Maybe Waldrom would know a spell or something that Audelia could use to keep the nightmares at bay.

It would be hard to get him alone, though. The wizard was usually with her mother or with the cadre, revamping the wards on their armor. Then, it would be a matter of whether he would tell her mother. They were as close as siblings, not that Audelia really understood that, as she was an only child. Well, for now, her mother was currently round with child.

That fact made her want to train harder, too. Audelia wanted to be a strong, protective big sister; she wanted to be able to keep her new sibling safe, as her cadre did her.

So here she was, pushing herself to her limit, as a storm began to howl into the early evening air.

Audelia swung against the dummy harder this time and grinned in triumph when the usually stoic dummy finally gave in and swung back in a slight bounce from the hit.

YES! If she kept up this pace, it wouldn't be long before she could start to learn battle magic along with her regular lessons. Mara had promised Audelia that if she could master the short sword, they would begin the new lessons.

"Very good! Now remember not every opponent will be standing stock still. You must anticipate their movements." Bronn called to her from his position at the head of the training field.

Audelia fought the urge to roll her eyes, and he always said that. She knew. After all, she had been watching the cadre for years since she was a tot. Audelia had heard their stories, and never once had any opponent just stood there, waiting for their end.

"Yes, uncle," Audelia replied demurely; she could hear the snicker from Skye near her. Anyone who knew Audelia knew that her tone would take on a more demure character if she was annoyed.

Most days, the pitch was full of trainees learning to become knights and guards for the kingdom. However, on nights like this, it was only full of her uncle and her cadre.

Audelia was the only princess she knew of that even had a cadre. Usually, a prince or princess, typically just the heir apparent, would have one or two loyal guards.

She herself had seven men sworn to protect her at all costs, and they had come one by one to express their fealty. They had all very quickly become family to her.

Many had told her parents it was far too many, but many in the kingdom did not know that it wasn't just because her parents cherished her and were protective.

Fate had played the more prominent role. Each member of her guard had come to her, and no posts had been issued for new guards. No, they each found their way to her.

The one that shocked the world was Mathias; Audelia had chosen him.

When Audelia was born, she had been blessed by the Phoenix Queen herself. Audelia held parts of the Goddess' fire within her. On her wrist was a mark she had been born with.

A phoenix's burning feather intertwined with the black wing of a dragon.

Waldrom had inspected it, and from what her mother had told her. The wizard had actually fainted; that part always made her giggle.

In the end, he revealed she was The Heart of the Phoenix.

Audelia still didn't fully understand what that meant, and every time she asked, she was told that everything would be revealed when she was older, just that she was an incredibly special girl.

The call to end training broke her from her thoughts. She did not want to stop. Audelia wanted to keep going but needed to. The flame inside her rose a little as she swung, which was perfect because the rain had begun to fall and caused her warmed skin to prickle with small bumps as the ice-cold water fell around her.

If she was The Heart of The Phoenix, she needed to do this not just because of her promise to a boy she missed with her entire heart.

A strong hand came down on her shoulder, and on instinct,

she twisted her body, with the blade still secured in her hands, slamming it into the side of the body belonging to that hand.

"Fuck!" A rasp and cough sounded; the voice was familiar even with the rasp. Audelia turned to take in her would-be attacker. Only to see Skye standing there, rubbing at his side, where she had used her strength to hit him.

"I am so sorry! Don't you know not to sneak up on someone with a sword!" She shrieked; she felt horrible and yet a little proud that she had hit him hard enough to cause discomfort.

Howling laughter rang out around them as the other cadre members exited the pitch.

"Your aim is getting far better, little fire." He chuckled, winking at her before his smile turned serious. "But it's time to stop for the evening," Skye spoke, his voice taking on its usual candor with a slight authoritative edge.

"I'll be fine." She huffed and turned back to the dummy; Audelia began to swing repeatedly, ignoring every word that Skye said. She pushed it away, casting a small, soundless spell under her breath. That unless he touched her again, she wouldn't hear his words.

So, she swung again and again, getting hit with water every time her wooden blade made contact with the now-drenched wooden dummy; every wet thump fueled her resolve.

"Little Fire." Skye's voice finally broke through the spell. She could feel the puff of warm air hit her cheek, and he reached around her and grabbed her arm to halt her swing.

She hated it when he used that nickname. It reminded her too much of... she shook her head, not wanting to think about it right now, she didn't want to start crying in front of Skye.

Instead, Audelia let fury flare inside her. "Stop calling me that!" She yelled. If he hadn't stood so close, her words would have been lost to the downpour and the growing thunderclaps around them.

Sorrow crossed over his eyes momentarily as Skye regarded her, which spurred the fury more. Audelia hated the pity people gave her when they knew she was upset about something like she was this delicate little thing that needed to be coddled. She didn't; she was brave, as she had promised.

Audelia would not cry; she couldn't, not here. Never here.

She watched Skye open his mouth, then shut it a moment later before she could give a retort and yell something foul at him. Audelia was plucked from the ground by large arms that had grabbed her from behind and hoisted over a muscled shoulder. "Let me down!" She yelled.

"Not happening, Shadow Flower." Mathias chuckled his warm, thick voice, an immediate slight balm on her temper. Audelia was still fuming, though, and kicked a little; she hated him for doing this. Mathias merely chuckled at her attempts.

"You are a brute, Mathias." Audelia huffed as they made their way across the remaining feet of the training pitch. She, of course, could not see the laughing faces of the rest of the cadre as they approached the large, doubled doors leading back into the annex that connected the rest of the castle.

A husky laugh broke through her brooding. "See, you caught yourself a little bird, did you?" Her uncle's voice greeted them as the warm glow of the torchlight warmed her chilled skin.

Gods, she was cold.

It did not, however, stop her from turning her petite body, still in Mathias's grasp, as if he knew she would bolt back outside if he set her down. Smart male. Audelia glared at her uncle, which was only met with an enormous laugh from him.

"Aye, I did. One that I think needs her bed before she catches a cold, and both Mara and Naseria have my hide." Mathias laughed; Audelia could feel the reverberation against her now chilled body.

Before she could protest that she had legs and could very much use them, she sneezed so loud that all those aches she had been pretending didn't exist came back to her in full force, making her wince in pain.

"You overdid it, Shadow Flower; you need not push yourself so much," Mathias told her as they made their way toward what she assumed was her chambers. The warmth from the braziers throughout the halls sent slight, merciful hints of warmth to her as they walked.

Mathias had, at least after the wince, shifted her to where he held her under her back and below her knees. As angry as Audelia was, she was enjoying the warmth that always radiated from him. Dragon's blood, he used to joke when she once asked him why he was always so warm.

"Did not," she mumbled before nodding off in his arms; she felt his chuckle rumble in his chest as they walked.

Audelia vaguely remembered being placed by him into her bed, the sound of him talking to Helen about changing her clothing after he left so she would not catch a cold and perhaps have some warm stew sent to the room later. She had felt the press of lips against her forehead before sleep, took her the rest of the way.

Audelia woke a few days later, much to her chagrin; she had indeed gained a cold from pushing herself too much, coupled with the freezing rain she refused to get out of.

Before she had fully passed out from the potions, every man in her cadre had been called to her room. Her mother and aunt had been very angry with not just her but the entire cadre, Bronn and Mathias taking the brunt of it as usual. If she hadn't been in such trouble herself, she would have giggled at the look of fear on each warrior's face as they were scolded.

Sitting up, she stretched her body, awakening all her muscles again; they ached, but not as severely as before. She felt far better than before. Audelia's aunt told her that the potion she had made would remove all the aches and pains. But, by Gaios, did it smell like the bowls of the Underdark and tasted just as vile.

Though, at least it helped, and Audelia shouldn't need it again anytime soon. Hopefully.

"*Et Fiero,*" Audelia whispered at the candle on the table by her bed. It flared to life, and she smiled. She never tired of its wonders, no matter how much magic she used. Audelia stood, her bare feet hitting the cold stone floor of her bedroom.

Moving to the spot by her bedchamber door, she pulled the worn bell pulley to let Helen know she was awake. Soon after, Helen stood behind her, placing her hair in a half-up-do with braids, and had her red curls cascading around her face. Audelia wore a simple dress of a velvety green, its long half-bell sleeves drooping well past her wrists, and the sash across her hips was embroidered in a gold filigree. It was beautiful.

A short time later, Audelia went to her mother's garden. She always loved coming here. It was like she stepped into an entirely new world. The smell of every flower her mother adored greeted her, and the soft flit of birds' wings as she walked the marbled stone path leading to the one place that brought her joy and sorrow.

The cherry blossom tree sat near a small spring in the garden. Audelia had spent the majority of her leisure time here when she wasn't in the library with Mathias or the vine and flower-covered pergola a few feet away with her mother on the mounds of soft velvet pillows—when she had time to lay about, of course.

With the clear blue sky above her, she took a deep breath and walked under the tree's boughs. And it had been a while since she last visited if she was honest. She couldn't bear to look at the tree for the past few months and refused to even go near the garden. So, she knew that Skye, who was with her today, and the twins somewhere in the shadows were more than shocked that she chose to come here. When she woke, something deep within told her she needed to be here, that it was necessary.

Audelia placed her hand against the tree's rough bark, wishing that somewhere in Morena's realms, *he* would hear her. "I miss you, but I promise, I am getting stronger."

Audelia sat down with her back pressed against the tree trunk and reached beside her into the hidden compartment just under a root that stuck out from the grass. He had told her they had made it ages ago using building magic, and it was their treasure box.

She smiled softly as she opened the small box under the root, its lid sticking a little from disuse, pulling out the book she had placed there months ago when the news had first arrived. He had sent it only a few months prior, but it had arrived the same day, as did the news of his death.

Audelia leaned back again, running her fingers over the book's leather; it was a copy of *Arteus the Dragon Lord*, a thrilling epic love story between star-crossed lovers and one of her favorites. The copy from the castle library had been destroyed by a rather horrendous feline that roamed its halls.

Audelia smiled. He had promised that he would send her one if he found a copy during his travels with his mother. What would she do to trade this copy with him? To have him back, her best friend and her first love.

She opened it like she had the night she had been told. The writing on the paper on the inside of the binding tear stained from her first reading. She could still make out his handwriting. The last words she would ever have of his.

My Firebird,

I miss you. Daily. I finally found a copy of Atreus the Dragon Lord in a shop today.

We're in a strange city, and I'm growing worried. Firebird. I promise I will come back for you. Keep my pendant on you. It will keep you safe.

Please be safe.

All my love,

Your Warrior

Something had him scared when he had written to her. Had he known? Tears welled in her eyes as she thought of how scared he could have been. Her fingers curled around the pendant, which always felt warm in her hand. Sometimes, she could pretend he was still alive and that he would come through the arches in the garden any day now.

Oh, how she wished she could have saved him.

Audelia felt her magic begin to rise. It unfurled, warming her skin. Sometimes, she wondered if the magic inside her was sentient, sensing when she needed it, not just for protection but as a form of comfort.

Placing the book she had yet to read again since that day on the grass beside her, she took out some of the little trinkets they had collected through the years. And placed them on the grass in front of her.

"*Cadalium nito,*" she spoke softly, watching the trinkets rise before her. It felt good to use magic, to let it stretch and curl.

"Ento Nito un," she flicked her fingers in soft movements, and the trinkets began to spin in little circles.

"Practicing? I am surprised." Audelia whipped her head up, losing concentration. The little trinkets fell to the grass in a thud. She watched her aunt Mara walk toward her; the woman was beautiful, in a soft pink gown that made the warm tones of her brown hair stand out in the waves of curls around her heart-shaped face.

"I always practice." Audelia protested, jutting out her chin in defiance.

"Oh, of course, I must be mistaking you for my other niece, who likes to milk it when sick." Mara's laugh was melodious as she came to sit beside Audelia in the grass under the tree. "Are you okay, my dove?"

Audelia only nodded. Her hand tightened around the pendant again. The warm stones sent that feeling of warmth through her—*his warmth.*

Mara opened her mouth like she was about to say something, then shut it again. Audelia looked at the trinkets on the ground before her. "How about we practice together?" Mara asked, her voice soft, comforting.

"Okay."

The pair worked on some of the spellwork that Audelia had learned recently. Audelia loved these moments when they just played with magic, and she adored Mara being her teacher, but those moments where they were just aunt and niece felt comforting.

A sudden tremor worked through the garden, causing them both to gasp in shock. Everything shook, and petals fell around them as the tremors grew. Mara reached for Audelia as Skye called for them. She could see him running for her before a flash of violent color coated the entire garden. She couldn't see, but she felt her aunt pulling her closer. "What's happening, Auntie?" she whispered, her voice shaking.

"It's alright, dove. It's okay," Mara kept repeating. The brilliant flash was gone, but Audelia's vision was still fuzzy; she suddenly didn't feel well.

She could barely focus on what was happening. She saw the shape of a man; no, it wasn't a man. It was some demon cloaked in shadow. Tendrils of it began to seep from its form.

They seemed to race towards her; usually, shadows didn't scare her. Mathias wielded them, and so had *he*.

But these. They felt *wrong*.

Mara screamed out a spell that Audelia hadn't entirely caught the words to, and a shield of white smoke formed in front of them, blocking the black tendrils and causing them to thrash against it. The shouts of guards coming from the edges of the garden, Skye and the twins among them.

"Audelia!" Skye shouted; his voice, which was always steadfast and jovial, was full of fear. It sent shivers down her spine as she watched the black tendrils.

Her eyes widened as the tendrils seemed to burn away the white smoke protecting them. "Stay back!" Mara screamed, pushing Audelia behind her.

She was terrified now as the last remnants of the smoke shield wisped away. Her magic was rising; she felt it warm her, but she didn't know how to use it to protect herself; she could release it in bursts, but those would knock her out for days for expending too much at once.

Remembering the blade stuffed into her boot under her gown, she reached down to grab it, and as she stood back up, her hand shook as she held the dagger aloft. She willed her hand to still; she was strong; she could do this. Audelia watched in horror as the demon stalked toward her.

The guards met the demon before it got too close, but it was short-lived, as with a swipe of his unnaturally long arm, the guards were sent flying in the opposite direction, landing with sickening thuds.

"Shit!" She heard Ezreal scream as he and his twin Micah sent bursts of blue smoke toward the demon, trying to draw it away. But the smoke merely leaped around the beast's form like it was nothing.

A moment later, the demon growled at them and sent them flying.

Skye was the vanguard, the last visage of protection for Audelia and Mara. Her aunt was just in front of her slightly, muttering incantations as fast as she could and sending magic hurling at the demon.

"Enough of this!" A voice spoke. It was harsh and screamed violence. Before Skye or Mara could say another word, they were both wrapped in tendrils of thick smoke, with specks of red slithering within the black.

The demon centered its focus on Audelia, stalking to her. As the creature approached her, terror coursed through her, making her shake worse; her knees felt like they were going to buckle. She could see its lizard-like face, its scales a sickly grey, eyes blood red and slit. She wanted to run, but she couldn't. Audelia was frozen in place.

Her own fear placed a tamper on her magic, and she could feel it thrash inside her, trying to claw itself out.

Audelia could do nothing as it reached up to drag a taloned finger against her cheek, and she watched a pink-forked tongue drag across its lips. "Pretty thing," It cocked its head.

She couldn't speak, so she could use simple magic, something to help those she loved. Every word came out as puffs of air, and it had to of used a silence spell on her. Then, she felt the tendrils of the black shadow twist around her body and squeeze.

Audelia screamed out in agony; her body felt like the tendrils were pulling it apart. She felt the mark on her wrist burn. Audelia wanted it to stop, needed it to stop. She fought back with every bit of magic inside herself.

She felt the moment; the fire that was always there burst free. It was like a weight had been lifted off her soul.

Fire exploded from her and burned away every thick, slimy speck of the black shadow-like tendrils until they were ash. Audelia couldn't stand anymore and fell to the ground, hitting her knees hard. Her vision was blurry, going dark around the edges. Audelia heard that voice again, the one full of malice. "I have come; you,—Princess of Fire— will be *mine.*"

Audelia fell to the side; all she could see were soft pink petals and ash around her. As her small body gave out, she watched Skye and Mara reach for her as her eyes closed, and everything changed.

PART ONE

FATE IS A FUNNY THING; IT
ALWAYS FINDS YOU IN THE END.

CHAPTER ONE

Audelia woke with a start, and her body was drenched in sweat, the echoes of a scream hanging on her lips. Her throat felt thick, like she genuinely had been screaming in her sleep. Gods, she hoped not. She had the nightmare again. The never-ending one.

She first had it when she first moved in with her aunt. She had woken screaming, and when her aunt had woken her, Audelia had been sobbing that a monster had killed her parents. Her aunt Mara had held her tightly, her hand working across her back in delicate sweeps soothing her.

She had seen a psychiatrist once after an outburst in school where Audelia had gotten into a fight with a girl. When asked why she had hit the girl, Audelia had said that she laughed at Audelia for having a nightmare about monsters killing her parents. Her response had the school stating that she needed therapy because she was not *coping well* with the sudden change in her life. That was the school's delicate way of expressing that they thought she was acting out because her parents were dead.

The psychiatrist had told Audelia and her aunt that the trauma of losing her parents at such a young age had caused her to blend fantasy with reality to cope.

Mara had been furious with the psychiatrist. Audelia never understood why, but she was grateful. She hadn't felt like she was mixing fantasy with reality, but she also couldn't fully understand why she kept having nightmares.

That was years ago. Luckily, Audelia had gotten better at pretending that the nightmares and strange dreams didn't bother her. They made for fantastic stories, though. Ones that her best friends, Lila, and Shawn, loved hearing about as they grew up.

Audelia was startled out of her thoughts by the sound of "Meltdown" blaring from her phone's alarm. *Time to get up.* Groaning, she sat up, the covers of her duvet pooling at her hips as she stretched, feeling her muscles loosen.

Audelia reached for her phone, turned off her phone alarm with a swipe, and silenced the phone as an incoming text alerted her. She couldn't help but smile when she saw the name on her screen.

Shawn. Audelia's heart skipped a beat at his name, and then she smiled as she opened the text from her best friend.

SHAWN

Morning Beautiful Storm! 😀

Audelia's cheeks reddened; it was silly she still reacted this way. He always sent morning texts like clockwork, and they had her heart racing every time. She knew he never meant anything by it; that's just Shawn. Audelia figured he probably texted Lila the same, just using her nickname *bubbles*. But it didn't matter that those texts had her for a moment every morning, pretending they meant *more*. She would never tell him *that*, of course. Audelia was too scared to ruin their friendship. But she was hopelessly in love with her best friend and had been for years.

Smiling, Audelia texted back as she swung her legs off her bed.

AUDELIA

Gif of Johnny Depp in Willy Wonka saying, "Good morning, star shine, the world says hello."

SHAWN

Your GIF game is getting better. *Gif of Mr. Miyagi shaking his head in approval.*

AUDELIA

Well, I do have an excellent teacher. 

SHAWN

And who is this magnificent teacher? Have you seen someone behind my back? *Gif of Micheal Scott saying "How dare you"*

Audelia laughed as she put her phone down to get ready for the day. The sweat from her nightmare was clinging to her skin, making it feel tight.

Audelia walked to her ensuite bath, reaching around the corner of her stone walk-in shower, turning the knob, the rush of water from the rain shower head above bursting to life. She quickly stripped from her babydoll tank and shorts and stepped under the curtain of water.

She twisted her neck in a circle, working out the tight muscles. She washed herself, and the smell of peony and warm amber hit her nose from her body wash. As much as she wanted to linger under the water, Audelia knew the nightmare would chase her all day if she did.

As she worked the conditioner into her curls with her slender fingers, she heard a knock on her bathroom door. "Yeah?" She called out, poking her head out of the water to hear better. Audelia moved enough that her head popped around the edge of the little wall that blocked the rest of the shower from the bathroom.

Her aunt's melodious voice broke through the rushing of the water behind her, albeit a little muffled still by the door that Audelia could see was now ajar. "I'm making waffles this morning; do you want some?"

"Yes, please. Oh, you might want to make extra. Lila and Shawn are coming over later, were going to see a movie playing at *The Little Theatre* later." Audelia said back.

Mara laughed loud and boisterously. "Oh, are they? Color me shocked!" Audelia smiled as she watched the door shut and heard her aunt's retreating footsteps, a chuckle still coming from her aunt, getting softer with each retreating footstep. Audelia returned under the spray, rinsed the conditioner, and finished washing herself, deciding to use a quick leave-in before she got out.

Shawn and Lila coming over early for breakfast was commonplace in their home. It had been since the day she brought them both home back in grade school. Those two had become permanent figures in the household ever since.

Turning off the shower, Audelia stepped out, grabbed the fluffy lavender towel from the hook, wrapped it around herself, and grabbed a cotton t-shirt from the stack of white cotton shirts she kept on the shelf by the shower, and proceeded to wrap it around her hair for plopping.

Walking over to the sink, she looked into the slightly foggy mirror as she began to apply her facial moisturizer and the other serums she liked to use. Audelia took in her appearance, eyes traveling over the peach coloring of her skin, accentuated by soft freckles across her shoulders and sprinkled across the bridge of her slight pixie nose. She had a love-hate relationship with her freckles, the love outweighing the hate most days.

Audelia had a heart-shaped face with soft, high cheekbones that gave her what Lila called a "romantic novel heroine face." She laughed every time she said that, though she supposed it was fitting of her features. If only she had a romance heroine's fate, then maybe she and Shawn could be together. Friends to lovers' style.

Maybe one day.

Pushing the thought from her mind, she applied a little makeup around her lapis lazuli-blue eyes. They were her favorite features and the only ones that gave her a clue about her mother. Audelia couldn't remember her parents' faces, another trauma response, but her aunt had told her that she had her mother's eyes.

Audelia had never seen a picture of her parents, and there were no family photos in the house, save for the ones of Audelia and Mara after she came to live with her and then pictures of Audelia, Shawn, and Lila. She had asked her aunt why they didn't have any of her parents, and her aunt said that she had a fire a year before the accident, lost all the photos, and had to move.

As for the pictures from her home, the one that Audelia

could never recall but liked to pretend was a little blue cottage-style house with white shutters surrounded by wildflowers, and Mara had claimed that when the house had been sold, everything within had been sold as well. She always thought it was weird, but her aunt would start crying, and Audelia would quickly change the subject.

Eventually, she stopped asking and pretended that the man and woman in her dreams were her parents. The woman in the dream's eyes matched her own, and she held on to that with a steadfast heart.

Audelia finished applying her makeup, enjoying the simple, classy look with the slight smolder to the eyes, making the blue hues pop. Pulling her hair from the shirt, she added the serums that would help keep frizz away since she decided to keep it down today, the lush flame-red curls framing her face, giving off Scottish warrior princess vibes.

Walking over to her giant walk-in closet just off her ensuite, she quickly grabbed a pair of cheeky royal blue silk panties with lace trim along her hip and pulled on her favorite dark blue stretchy jeans. She loved how they hugged her curves.

Audelia paired it with a sage green corset top with bell sleeves; walking back into her room, she grabbed her purse and a pair of retro sneakers because she knew they would end up walking around the village afterward.

She grabbed her phone, slipping it into her back pocket. Audelia quickly made her bed, pulling the soft, blue duvet back into place and affixing the pillows. Her phone sounded with a message as she went down the hall towards the kitchen, where she could hear nineties country songs playing.

Audelia swiped open her phone, opening a group text thread between her, Lila, and Shawn.

LILA

Picking up Shawn, then on our way! We are soo doing that new Romcom!

SHAWN

Really? Another Romcom? Can't we do an action movie, Bubbles?

LILA

Gif of Micheal Scott saying, "God NO!"

AUDELIA

I wouldn't mind that new one with Asher Kingsby. He is dreamy. *Heart eyes emoji followed by hot emoji*

LILA

You always side with him, Storm. It's not fairrrrrrrr. Ugh fine. But you're buying the popcorn, Shawnie boy.

SHAWN

Gif of Leslie and Ron from Parks n Rec hitting beer bottles, saying Deal in bold.

Audelia laughed. Maybe she did always side with Shawn, it wasn't intentional, but she did want to see that new Asher Kingsby movie. It looked so good; it was based on the novel of the same name, and she was excited to see the couple in it come to life.

Win-win, in her opinion.

In the kitchen, Mara was making blueberry waffles; the sweet smell filling the air made Audelia's mouth water; she walked over and kissed her aunt on the cheek. "Morning, Auntie." Turning away after grabbing a piece of bacon from a nearby plate to munch on, Audelia opened the fridge and grabbed one of her little bottles of vanilla chai tea protein drinks that she drank every morning.

"They are on their way?" Mara called over her shoulder as she added more batter to the waffle iron. The slight sizzle from the heated surface fills the air for a moment.

"Yup. Texted a few minutes ago, so I give it about five or so before we hear Lila bursting through the doors." Audelia laughed, taking a sip of her drink. The cool, creamy drink with hints of spice hit her tongue. She placed the drink on the table in the kitchen and grabbed plates and cutlery from their respective places.

The two of them settled into their usual cooking routine and getting the table ready. "Did you finish that new novel by Arista Stone yet?" Audelia asked after a while. She had been dying to get her aunt's reaction to the heartbreaking story of second-chance love after loss.

"I started it last night. You should have warned me how much it would make me cry!" Mara turned to face Audelia, where she stood by the table.

Audelia took in her aunt. Mara was a beauty with soft curves, usually in some sort of summer dress like she was in currently. This one was buttery yellow, with soft blue and white flowers and ruffles that accentuated her aunt's chest. Audelia hoped when she was her aunt's age, she still looked that amazing. Mara had a soft heart-shaped face, framed by delicate brown curls that fell in gentle waves, brightening her light green eyes, that reminded Audelia of the jade stones she had seen in a museum in the city as a child.

Mara volunteered at a local shelter most days, her hours sporadic, which, as a child, was perfect because Audelia was always involved in some activity, especially once she discovered the dojo and Alexander, the man who owned it. Out of all the activities Audelia had joined, that was the one that she enjoyed the most. She devoured every class, from martial arts to even sword fighting, and still did weekly. Every time she was there, it felt oddly like home to her.

Now, with Audelia in her mid-twenties, Mara used all the extra free time to bake or read. She worried that her aunt was lonely sometimes. In all the years she had been growing up here, Audelia couldn't remember a time when she had seen her aunt date. Flirt, yes, Lila and Audelia used to pretend as girls that her aunt and Alexander would get married. Yet, nothing ever came from it, no matter how much those two seemed to flirt. But still, she had never dated, and he had never made a move.

"I told you Arista loves to break your heart before she lets the couples have their happy endings. But trust. This one is beyond worth it. Declan makes my heart swoon. I wish I had a man like that." Audelia said dreamily. Her thoughts turned to Shawn, and she wondered momentarily if he would be as adoring as the men she read about.

The sound of the door opening and closing broke her from her thoughts as Lila's dulcet tones were calling out to them from the front of the house. "Honey, I'm Home!" Audelia and Mara laughed at Lila's usual greeting, either announced or unannounced.

"That girl," Mara shook her head, the curls bouncing about her face, as she turned back to finish plating out the waffles, which had finished a moment ago.

A moment later, Audelia watched as Lila, her petite friend with a pixie-like face and small nose, entered the kitchen. Her striking hazel eyes, flecked with grey, lit up when they two locked their eyes. "Hey, Storm."

"You're missing a person. Where is Shawn?" Audelia asked, bracing for his appearance.

"He's outside on the phone with Sobo." She jerked her chin toward the hall and walked further into the kitchen.

Audelia smiled as she looked at her. Lila may be petite, but she commands the room, not just because of her jovial nature but also because of her sense of fashion. It was as bold as her gaze, with a short leather skirt that fit her lithe form like a glove. The skirt was paired with black knee-high laced boots with a slight heel and a bright cropped sweater the color of cotton candy. Her spiky platinum hair in pastel hues perfectly complimented her vibrant outfit.

"Auntie! Did you make waffles?" Lila's pouty lips went into a wide grin as she rushed to plant a kiss on Mara's cheek before taking the two plates Mara was currently bringing to the table. "Thanks!"

Audelia went to grab the remaining two plates; she heard footsteps behind her as she reached the counter. She knew it was him, and she always seemed to know where Shawn was in a room. His warm breath tickled her neck as he reached around her for the plates. His minty, cool scent made her think of winter nights, wrapped around her, making Audelia's heart race. "Here, I've got this. Go sit." His husky voice made her knees weak.

"How about I take one, and you take the other?" She spoke, holding in the quiver that liked to make its appearance when she was nervous, and today, she was. *Maybe it's just from the nightmare.*

He gave her a lopsided grin, and she took him in momentarily, letting her eyes shamelessly wander over him, hoping he didn't notice her stare. Audelia took in his lean, muscular body, currently in a grey long-sleeved Henley, that made her mouth water to see him in. Shawn wore his usual dark-washed jeans with dark boots underneath. Shawn worked for his father, having started straight out of university, building boats.

She allowed herself one more look at his face as he turned to head to the table, hoping for everything she had that she didn't blush in front of him like a schoolgirl. Audelia couldn't help it sometimes. He was beautiful, with a strong jaw and olive skin from working in the sun. His Asian-Irish heritage never allowed him to tan fully, but it left him with a slightly darker tone than her peach complexion. Shawn had strong, handsome features on his face, and he could have been a model if he had wished with his almond-shaped dark green eyes that reminded her of the heather after a storm, thick dark brows, and short-cut black hair that always seemed to curl at the end, which made his current style of a quaff, swoon-worthy.

So many times, Audelia had wanted to run her hands through that lush hair. To feel his breath against her skin as she did so. To feel him against her, worshipping her, loving her. Audelia wondered what kind of lover he would be, with that physic, he had to be at least an attentive one, full of stamina, that would have her writing and panting with need. Her body pulsed with want of him, of wanting to know what his touch would be like. She yearned for it.

Audelia felt a hand touch her arm, and she jumped a little,

jarring her from her shameless thoughts. Shawn stood before her, plate still in hand. A look of concern knitted in his brows. "Hey, you okay, Del?" This time, she knew she had blushed all over her face and chest in embarrassment.

"What- yeah, of course. Just lost in thought, is all. Didn't sleep the best last night." She replied sheepishly, giving Shawn a sweet smile, and walked over to the table, setting her plate down. He sat beside her, and his knee brushed hers, and she could have sworn for a moment she heard an intake of breath come from him.

But it had happened so fast that she was convinced she imagined it. Audelia looked down at her plate of blueberry waffles, covered in fresh berries and whipped cream, home-made; of course, Mara hated the spray can stuff, so she always had some on hand. Mara had outdone herself again; she hadn't just done waffles and bacon but scrambled eggs with spinach and cheese. Which Audelia knew was Shawn's favorite.

"This looks amazing, Mara. Thank you so much for making extra." Shawn spoke, his voice polite and kind. He had always been like this, Audelia thought; she knew exactly what her aunt's response would end up being in this little dance of theirs.

"Thank you, sweetheart, but you don't need to thank me. I have been feeding you three since you were still on the playground. There will always be food here for all of you." Mara looked over the table at all of them, and they each gave her a grateful smile. Her aunt was too good for this world, with its cruelty. She belonged somewhere better. She knew she didn't need to look at her best friends to know they thought the same.

After that, they all ate breakfast, occasionally discussing

books, movies, and more books and their plans for the summer. That topic always gave Audelia a pang of guilt because she, Lila, and Shawn had scored a beautiful townhouse to rent together near Audelia's favorite spot in the village.

The Glade.

Their small village didn't have much, unlike most prominent towns and cities further from their little hamlet. They had a small movie theater big enough to host three movies daily and a small bookstore, where Audelia worked part-time when she wasn't working on her master's in literature.

But, the big draw that made her heart pound every time she saw it over the past fifteen years was the giant Weeping Cherry blossom wisteria tree. It was an arborist's dream. Because, in all the world, it was truly one of a kind. The tree was the size of the redwoods of California, and you could see the bright hues of blue, purple, and pink from miles away. It lured you in like a beacon.

Surrounding it was a small, lush forest with a singular path through it. The path led to the magical realm that was the little glade under the boughs of the magnificent tree. Audelia treasured it. The tree and the area under and around it felt like she was entering another world where magic and creatures of story and myth were real.

When they were little, Lila, Shawn, and Audelia would spend hours telling stories under the tree's boughs. Pretending they could see fairies sleeping in the buds of the blooms or that the lights under the boughs were lit with pixie dust.

The Glade brought such immense comfort to Audelia that she always went there when everything felt like it was too much. When she could not chase away the nightmares, a day like today, Audelia decided that before she came home tonight, she would go and read in her hiding spot in The Glade.

She would let the magic of the place wash over her, and hopefully, it would banish the ill thoughts.

Audelia stood grabbing plates, including those of her aunts, as they finished eating. "Don't even think about it. We have this, Auntie; go read your book and relax."

Shawn and Lila responded with "Yes, we do," which Prevented Mara from protesting. So instead, her aunt stood, grabbed her mug of coffee, and kissed her niece's cheek, thanking them before heading to the living room.

Sometime later, the three of them had finished cleaning all the dishes and wiped down the kitchen. The trio found Mara deeply engrossed in the novel. She had propped on her knees where she lounged on the couch. "Hey, Mara. We're going to head out for the movie. Did you need anything while we were out?" Audelia made sure to touch her aunt's shoulder, or the words would never register.

It took a moment before Mara closed the book and looked up at the three of them. "No, baby, I don't need anything. You three, *go* have fun. I've got my coffee and book. I'm set for the day." Mara shooed them away with her hand.

They laughed; Audelia and Lila grabbed their purses from the hooks by the front door and set out for the day. The front door clicked shut behind them.

CHAPTER TWO

As the trio stepped outside, the sounds and smells of early spring surrounded them. The scents of freshly blooming flowers and grass, finally getting a chance to peek out from the frost, made Shawn smile; spring was one of his favorite seasons. From the beautiful smile that crossed Audelia's lush lips, he knew it was one of hers as well.

God, he loved it when she smiled. It always made her brilliant eyes sparkle and stole his breath every time. Everything about this woman had his heart racing since they were kids.

"Movie first?" Audelia spoke, her voice sultry to his ears, made his pulse jump. He looked at her as the sunlight caused the hues of red in her curls to spark into a living flame. Audelia looked like a fire goddess come to life.

The outfit she wore clung to every curve; he bit his lip for a moment, stifling the groan that rose up as he thought of how he wished he could run his hands up and down those lush curves. He gave her his lopsided grin, which always made her eyes seem to dance. Shawn grabbed her hand, intertwining their fingers like he always did. He needed to touch her in whatever way she would allow. "Movie, that way, you ladies can set up camp in the bookstore, pretty sure Gideon has a

"

permanent sign up in your little corner window." Shawn teased as they began to walk down the sidewalk.

It was too lovely a day for them to drive around. He and Lila had only driven because she lives on the outskirts of town, and his home was on the way. It was going to be so much easier once they all moved into the townhouse this summer. Shawn could not wait for it, to be able to be closer to Audelia. He needed her like he needed the air in his lungs.

"Gideon is barely ever there. I swear in all the time I have worked there, I think I could count on one hand the amounts of times I've seen the man." Audelia said. This was true, and she had started working at *Once Upon A Chapter,* their sophomore year of high school; in those few years, the reclusive owner had barely been seen. Audelia let go of his hand, and his heart sank at a loss; the loss wasn't long because she looped her arm through his a moment later and leaned her head on his shoulder; the smell of her peony-infused conditioner filled his senses. "Besides, I work there, so why can't I have a favorite corner to relax in?"

"Of course, how silly of me." Shawn inched closer to her as they walked, holding her closer.

Her scent was maddening, and it took everything in Shawn to focus on the conversation the women were having as they walked the six blocks to the theater. Audelia smelled of peonies, the wild fruitiness of black currant, warm amber, and cherry blossoms. Some days, when he was extra cruel to himself, he would wonder if she smelled the same everywhere. Shawn could barely count the number of times he went to bed hard if any lingering hints of her were on him.

Audelia was not only his best friend, but she also held a much deeper place in his heart. He was profoundly in love with her, yet he felt like a coward, unable to jeopardize their friendship or risk losing her in the process. She meant too much to him. Still, he wanted her to be truly his, a longing that resonated deeply within his soul.

The walk was both torture and rapture for him, and he enjoyed every damn moment. The closer they got to the theater, the more animated his two best friends became; Audelia had let go to join Lila, and the two walked in front of him, giggling.

The trio got to *The Little Theatre*. Shawn took in the façade of the building; a few years back, someone had come in and rebuilt the old theater that had burned down before they had been born. The columns and their matching ornate large double doors had been the only things to survive the fire. When a new theater that held all the plays in town had been built by the ocean, this one had been left to rot until a decade ago.

"Okay, so plan of attack," Lila spoke, her voice taking on a determination that, to this day, terrified him. A determined Lila was a force of nature. "I'll get the tickets, Audelia and Shawn snacks. If you forget my red vines, I will hit you with my car later." As she walked to get the tickets, she winked, but Shawn knew it was a threat. One simply did not forget Lila's red vines.

"Well, shall we, my lady?" Shawn gave a cheesy bow that had Audelia giggling, the sound making his heart beat faster.

"Why yes. How gallant of you." She fluttered her eyelashes at him and smiled as she took his offered arm. As they walked, Audelia looked back at Lila, who was flirting with the ticket booth operator. "Hey, Bubbles! Don't forget it's the Asher Kingsley one, NOT the rom-com." Lila turned to them and stuck out her tongue in response; Audelia and Shawn laughed.

Shawn had the feeling he was about to watch a rom-com just because he knew that if Lila felt extra petty, she would do what she wanted, just to drive him crazy. It was not that he genuinely felt bothered by romcoms; it was more about how Audelia reacted that he struggled with. The more enraptured by the love on screen she became, Audelia would make little noises and movements, would have him itching to take her, and make her feel all those things and more.

The coolness of the theater greeted them as they opened the vintage double doors; the owners had done the original feel of the theater justice; it even boasted old play posters mixed with the latest blockbusters, making it not so ornate that it felt stuffy. Shawn and Audelia headed for the concession stand, and the smell of popcorn suddenly made him famished. It made him laugh that one could have eaten before a movie and still feel hungry the second that buttery, salty smell of popcorn hit one's senses.

They quickly ordered two jumbo popcorns, Lila's red vines, and a root beer for Lila. Audelia had gotten a cherry soda for the two of them to share. She never really drank much during a movie, so she usually took sips from his.

Lila met them a few moments later with a saccharine smile, which made her pixie features seem even more vibrant. She looped her arm through Audelia's after grabbing her red vines and drink, from Audelia. The two giggled the whole way to the amphitheater room. They took up their usual sitting arrangement with Audelia wedged between them.

The movie had been a triumph, and they had seen *Steel Fortress*; Lila had said he was lucky she had scored the number of the hot guy running the booth; Shawn thanked whatever god was out there that he didn't have to sit through the torture of a romantic movie. The movie was as action-packed as the book. Audelia had grabbed his hand at one particularly intense moment, and Shawn had refused to let go of it, running his thumb back and forth over her soft skin. They were currently in heavy discussion over which parts they loved more in the book as they walked down the breezy sidewalk toward the bookstore.

Once they arrived at *Once Upon A Chapter,* the bookstore was a restored Victorian townhouse. It was midafternoon, and the spring sun was warming their skin. Shawn had pushed his sleeves to his elbow on their walk over, and he could have sworn he had seen Audelia watch the movement, and had blushed. But that was impossible, and she couldn't feel the same. He was deluding himself, even if his heart pounded with hope.

"You coming, Shawn?" Audelia's sultry voice broke him from his thoughts. She had a brilliant smile on her face, one that made the freckles on the bridge of her nose crinkle a little. Oh, how he wanted to kiss every single one of them at that moment.

He pushed the thought away as he closed the distance between them and ushered her to go inside. The smell of tobacco, chocolate, and books filled the air. God, he loved that smell.

For the next few hours, the three of them walked up and down the aisles and had a little pile forming by the very window seat that Shawn had teased Audelia about earlier.

Finally, the women had given in and settled into the bench seat that was covered in pillows. It really was the perfect spot to read, hidden away from the rest of the shop, if he was honest. So, they stayed undisturbed while reading from the piles of books they had selected. Shawn had his back against the wall and his legs spread out before him, with Audelia relaxing her head against his thigh, her red hair splayed across his jeans in a fan.

He couldn't help himself and played with a few curls as he read; little moments made him reevaluate his fear of losing her. He wanted to take that leap and make her his so desperately. He was already hers, even if she didn't know it. He would burn the world for her—his *A Chroi.*

Audelia gave a soft sigh as she read, a soft smile playing across her pink lips, and it went straight to his heart, making it beat wildly. Shawn decided right there that he was tired of waiting. He would take that plunge if she gave him any indication of her feelings for him. He refused to accept that he would lose her. She was everything.

A few hours later, Audelia was making her way towards The Glade. Lila had made her way back to her car, which was still parked in front of Audelia's house. Shawn was her only companion at the moment. She had told him he didn't need to walk her to, but he insisted there had been reports of people acting suspiciously lately, and he didn't like the idea that she would be at The Glade alone.

She had relented because the look of worry that crossed his eyes made her heart lurch into her throat. So, here they were, walking arm in arm toward the place that brought her the most peace. It was not lost on her, that she was also with the man that made her feel safe.

"Shawn, you're being silly." Audelia teased after a while of walking. "I have spent so much time there that I might be part wood sprite, with how at home I am there. You know it's the safest place in our entire village." She playfully nudged him. He got like that sometimes, throwing himself into the title of her knight. Her protector.

If she could get over her fears of losing him, then maybe, just maybe, they could be what she dreamed of. His.

He sighed and turned to look at her, making them both stop at the top of the hill that overlooked The Glade, which was sprawled out in all its glory to their side. "Del, I know. But those reports have been running through my head all day. Something is going on, and the idea of something happening to you? That kills me." He reached up and cupped her cheeks then, his callused thumbs working back and forth motions that sent shivers of need down to her core.

If she could gain that courage and close the distance? Would he taste as warm and minty as she always dreamed?

Audelia leaned into his touch, willing for this moment to never end. As he watched her, the look in his eyes felt like so much more than a friend being worried about the other. She wanted it to be more.

"Come on, my *darling* knight, you know this damsel can easily kick someone's ass. Alexander made sure of it." She teased, pulling away. Audelia hated doing it. She wanted to remain in his hold forever, but the thought of losing him. It was too much. The thought was a balm to all the raging thoughts deep in her heart.

Audelia grabbed Shawn's hand and pulled him with her down the hill. She could have sworn he grumbled something, but it was lost as the wind picked up around them briefly. It carried the scent of the blossoms that permeated into her very skin.

The Glade.

It didn't matter how often she saw the beauty of this place; it would always steal her breath. Sprawled out just a way down the incline of the hill they had banked, was a small forest of greens, and in their center, was the largest tree she had ever seen. The Willow, at the center of the Glade, was ethereal in its hues of pinks, purples, and blues as the early evening sun beamed down on the blooms. Blooms that never left. They seemed to be in an eternal bloom that stumped every arborist and horticulturist that had come over the years.

She always said it was because magic lived there. Audelia knew it was probably childish, that she believed. But she couldn't help it; something deep in her soul told her that the feeling she got every time she stepped under the boughs *was* magic.

As the two of them walked, the hair on the back of her neck rose as they passed the few buildings at the edge of the small forest. Audelia grabbed Shawn's hand tighter, instinct telling her not to look to keep going.

It felt like something was coming up behind her, like the icy claws of some evil thing that lurked had come out to play.

Her breathing picked up enough that Shawn had noticed and stopped their pace again. "Del? You okay, babe?"

Audelia fought with herself, but those icy claws seemed to grip tighter. She let out one last shaky breath and looked up at him just as, in the corner of her vision, she saw the errant foot of someone being dragged into the alley behind them.

She used Shawn's eyes, which were vibrant with worry, making the hue of green more profound, to anchor herself, just like she had in the past when these small panic attacks had surged. Audelia tried not to think about the times in the past when she had seen the same odd occurrence. Like something in him was responding to her fear. But that was ridiculous.

Maybe it was just a trick of the eye? Brought on by the panic attack.

She chose to ignore whatever it was like she had every time. Instead, her focus remained on the man she loved standing before her. "I'm fine. Just a weird chill; someone must have walked over my grave." She teased him with a shrug of her shoulders, hoping he would take it at face value and not linger on it.

This time had felt *more*. Those icy claws had felt *real*, and Audelia was scared that if she lingered on them too long, they would return, and this time, they would never let go of her.

"Are you sure? You had gone very pale, and you're shaking still. Del? You know you can tell me if something is bothering you."

She smiled as big as she could manage, as she willed the shaking in her body to still. Audelia did not want him to worry; she didn't want to be a burden to him again.

Not again, *never* again. "It was just a chill; I am fine, I promise. Fox, I swear." Audelia used his nickname, the one she had been using since they met, knowing that he would drop it with the use of the name. It was like their little code.

If something was ever serious and they wanted the other to know it, they used their nicknames, Fox and Storm.

Audelia could see he wanted to say something back and deny that she was okay. But she saw in his eyes the moment he gave in. With a heavy sigh, Shawn spoke and briefly pressed his forehead to hers. "Fine. Storm, you better not be lying."

Then, he stepped away, not realizing that her heart was pounding in her ears at his words. They were normal, but somehow, this time, they had been said in a deep growl that had heat racing for her core again.

The rest of the walk to the path's entrance, which would lead straight under the boughs of the Willow itself, was uneventful as they walked hand in hand.

As they arrived at the path's opening, still stuck in darkness, the lights had not come on just yet to light the path. Shawn's phone rang. He grumbled and went to reach for it in his back pocket.

He grabbed it out and showed her the screen lit up with *Mom*. Audelia just smiled and waited. She knew what was about to happen; his mom had only ever called if she needed him to come home for something. "Sea Mam?" The Irish Gaelic, in his words, sounded like a dark lover's caress against her skin as Shawn pulled her closer to him.

Audelia could make out some of his mother's words as she rested her head against his chest. Mrs. Fintan had the tendency over the years to switch between her native Japanese, to Gaelic when on the phone with Shawn. Sometimes, she was on the receiving end; luckily, having known Shawn for fifteen years, she had learned a few phrases in both.

Tonight, however, his mother was speaking so quickly, jumping back and forth, it was a surprise Shawn could even pick up the words. Shawn gripped her tighter as if he couldn't help but need her closer. Audelia was okay with that; she soaked every ounce of his warmth and woodsy mint smell she could manage. He ended the call and dipped his head against the top of her own.

"Everything okay, Fox?" Audelia's words were soft.

She felt the reverberation against her exposed skin as he sighed. "Yeah, Storm. Mam said Sobo is coming for a visit, and I need to go home and help clean. It is a surprise visit, so clearly, it's an emergency." He laughed and kissed the top of her head, his arms wrapping her in a tighter hug—one she did not want to end, ever.

"You mean like every time? Remember the time she came unexpectedly, and we accidentally broke that vase? Gods, I have never been so scared of your mother as I was that day." Audelia laughed, recalling how his sweet, quiet mother had turned into a raging storm at the sight of broken red porcelain pieces on the carpet.

"Gods, that visit was… terrifying." He chuckled and pulled away to look at her, his eyes shining with mirth and something… deeper. Consuming.

Audelia just looked at him, sighing longingly, as the lights beside them began to glow, bathing them in a bronzed radiance, making him look like a god standing before her.

"Well, go. I'll be alright here. Give your parents my love." Audelia wanted to get to the safety of the boughs; her heart was beating so fast at the look he kept giving her. She wanted him to kiss her so badly that her body was vibrating with the need. Audelia couldn't risk being around him much longer, or she would burn everything to the ground to feel his lips on hers, just once.

His gaze turned into a dark storm at her words. "Like fuck you are. Storm, it's getting late. I'll walk you home. You can come back in the morning, when it's safer."

Audelia pulled up short at his words. *What the hell?* Shawn had never treated her like this, as if she couldn't bring a man to his knees in pain. "What did you just say?"

"You heard me, Del. There have been reports of strange things happening in the village. I can't risk you." His eyes were pleading now, unaware of the storm building inside her.

"Yeah. I heard you. Shawn, I'm not some helpless damsel. You have been to every class I have ever taken at the Dojo. You know I can handle myself, better than most." She sneered. Her skin felt warm, like a flame inside her fanning into an inferno.

Yes, she had heard the reports, and they had scared her because they reminded her of *him*. But she had promised herself she would *never* feel helpless again. Shawn had helped her. Hel, *he had been the one to remind her that she was fearless. To Fly and burn the world in her wake.*

Yet now he was acting like this?

"Please, Storm. I know you could kick my very ass right this moment. But I'm worried. Those reports didn't seem like the regular run-of-the-mill thing. Whatever is out there is danger-ous." He gripped her shoulders, like he wanted to shake sense into her.

But she was stubborn and wouldn't let some unknown scare her from the place that brought her such peace. She needed it today; Audelia did not fully understand the deep-rooted need. It beat like a drum in her soul, begging her to go to her spot.

Audelia sighed, stepped closer to him, and placed her hands on his chest; she could feel his heart beating hard. She smiled at him. "Shawn. I will be fine. I need this. Please."

"Storm, I know you do. I know you need this place. But I need you to be okay." His words broke her heart. He had never sounded so defeated before.

"I will be Fox; I will call you the second I feel unsafe. Alexander's house is two blocks away. I can run there if something happens." She caught the panic in his eyes, and to ease that, she added, "which, nothing will. I promise. Now, *go*." She pushed him a little for emphasis.

Audelia saw the anger and reluctance in his eyes, and it broke her a little. She hadn't meant to upset him. She just needed this. Needed him to see her as strong, she never wanted Shawn, of all people, to see her as broken. Even if, in her heart, she felt she was.

"You call the second something happens. I swear to fuck, Del. If you get hurt, I will punish you myself." He growled the last words, and she tucked *that* away for later, when she was alone and could lose herself in the promise those words provoked. Shawn pulled her into his arms one last time; before he pulled away, he placed a lingering kiss on her temple.

Audelia's breathing had become rampant as she watched him trudge away, as if every step was painful for him.

Pushing that away from her thoughts, Audelia turned and walked into the now-lit path leading to the inner sanctum of The Glade.

The path was roughhewn, as she walked, the roots of trees trying to reclaim the path for themselves. Audelia felt like she was being watched as she walked, but it didn't send shivers of fear down her spine. No, this feeling she had felt every time she entered the copse of trees leading to the willow. As a girl, she and Lila would pretend that the little folk were watching them from behind moss-covered rocks and thick tree trunks.

The lights ahead of her shown across the small, stone bridge that crosses a small brook, and into the inner sanctum. The deeper she walked, the more at peace she felt. Every sharp edge that had dug at her all day seemed to dull and ease away.

Audelia pushed away the flowery boughs that acted as a curtain, keeping the magnificence of the inner sanctum from direct view. Their floral scent filled her even more calm as she walked through them and under the great boughs above her.

Great they were indeed, for the lowest branch was still fifteen feet above her. Those low-hung ones were wrapped in large fairy lights that looked like Japanese lanterns floating above. They burned all day, for if not, the inner sanctum would be so deep black that a person would never find their way out of the canopy of blooms.

Audelia took in everything before her. The flowing branches cascaded in a waterfall of blues, purples, and pink blooms, lining the inner Glade. Some descend over the open area. It was magnificent.

Under its branches, it was like entering an entirely different world. Benches of stone and moss, some carved out of more extensive roots stuck up from the green grass, laid here and there. It was one of the many mysteries of this place—no one had placed them here. It was as if the little folk had come and set up places for them to gather. Small vine-like swings hung from lower branches. Sturdy enough to hold two people at once. As a child, she spent every second she could under this tree. Few liked to remain under the branches, even as magical as it felt. Many would just come and look and then quickly leave like something told them not to linger inside. However, anytime Audelia was inside the branches, it was like the tree called to her. Soft whispers on the wind soothing her, like it did now as she made her way toward the great trunk of the tree.

Audelia loved the whole sanctum, but the part that seemed to call to her every time was deeper inside, through what looked like a part of a root that had lifted and created an arch. The opening was covered with vines, so many did not venture to this back place. But it was her safest harbor.

She pulled back the curtain of ivy, stepping into the small arch, and into the darkness of the small cove. By memory, she walked a few paces to where she knew a Shepard's hook lantern was in the ground. Feeling the coolness of the wrought iron, she reached for the pouch tied to his pole. Inside, there was a metal matchbox. Audelia quickly pulled out the box, struck a match to life, and reached up the tiny flame, her only guide. She opened the face of the lantern and placed the match against the inner wick. She and Lila had been the ones that would replace the large candle that sat within the glass panes of the lantern.

As the flame caught, Audelia took in the small space around her. It wasn't very large, only a dozen or so feet wide on all sides. This was the only spot that man hadn't obstructed throughout The Glade.

It was nestled among a lattice of vines and smaller willow blossoms. Mossy boulders dotted the area, providing cozy seating areas amidst the verdant greenery. In the corner rested a small wooden bed swing, seemingly supported by larger vines. Over the years, Audelia, Lila and sometimes Shawn had adorned the swing with fluffy pillows and warm blankets, making the small sanctuary theirs, but the area remained untouched, almost magical. The soft scent of soap and fragrant blossoms still lingered, a testament to the enduring beauty of this hidden nook.

Audelia walked toward it now, struck a second match, and lit the other Shepard's hook inside, lighting the whole place in a glow that warmed her heart. She placed the matchbox inside its little pouch on the first hook and returned to the swing.

She removed her shoes, even her socks, and curled her bare toes into the earth at her feet. Audelia felt some of that growing heat from before melt away. She sighed and grabbed the book she had bought earlier from her bag before placing it on the ground beside the swing. She sat back and curled up in the swing, the pillows forming the perfect cocoon. Her world narrowing into the tale of thrilling romance with dragons, magic, and forbidden love.—not knowing how true those stories could become.

Audelia lost herself in the pages, her mind occasionally drifting between Shawn and the dream that had haunted her steps that day. She didn't even fight it as her body felt heavy, and she was pulled into sleep, the book in her hands falling to the soft floor of her harbor.

CHAPTER THREE

Everything was dark, and she didn't know where she was or what was happening. Audelia's heart pounded in her chest; at least, she thought it was her heart. Nothing felt real. Not her body. Not the movements her brain told her she made. Something was.... wrong.

This must be a dream, she thought. *It was a logical thought; she was falling asleep one moment, and the next, she was here. That was logical and sane. This was just some sort of strange dream.*

Right?

Taking a step forward, she hoped that there was something in the dark abyss that seemed to swallow everything. All she knew was that she desperately wanted to get out of it. She wanted to wake up warm in her bed. Maybe text Shawn, depending on the time, he was usually still up to talk to, when she couldn't sleep. Yes, that's what she would do, force herself awake like she had done in the past when the dreams turned dark and far too real for comfort. Audelia would force the wake, she'll feel like shit after, but it was worth escaping this... whatever this was.

Audelia willed herself to wake, pinched her arm, and thought the words wake, *but nothing happened.*

Fuck.

So, she walked.

Audelia walked for what seemed like ages, or at least she still hoped she walked. She had thought of walking, but she wasn't entirely sure if she was walking in this deep, chasmic space. She tried to steel herself, but with every minute and every hopeful step, she felt even more worried. Her darker dreams had never been like this before. The dark seemed to feel alive around. Darker than darkness. Audelia wanted to leave. She called to whatever great god watched over her; she had never been overly religious, but she believed there had to be something out there—watching over everyone.

Hopefully, they will listen.

As if some being had finally listened to her for once in her life, the world around her seemed to convulse. She only knew it did because one moment she was in the terrifying quiet of the dark, and the next it was like wave after tumultuous wave slapped against her body. Audelia held her position against the assault, hoping it would soon stop.

As suddenly the waves had crashed, the eerie calm returned. But all was not lost because she saw a beacon of light as she looked up again. It seemed far, but she hoped that, like in most dreams, as you will things to happen, you move toward things faster than in life.

So, she rushed toward the light. Hoping that whatever the light was, it was good and not something worse than this crawling dark around her. Which, as she ran, seemed to press and pull at her like it was trying to stop her from reaching the light.

Within a moment, the beacon that had been so far still was suddenly so close that the searing bright of it, made her eyes water as they adjusted to the sudden onslaught. Audelia pushed past the pain and walked into the light. As she crossed the threshold hold of what could only be described as an archway of sunlight, the dark behind her seemed to scream in an eerie, bone-shattering wail.

Before she could even contemplate whether that wail was at the loss of her escaping or in warning, the world seemed to pull her forward, and her body felt stretched like every molecule of herself was being ripped and put back together and stretched again. She tried to hold in the scream that rose to her throat, but even that was pulled and ripped, muffled by the warping. Her whole being felt off and dizzy as she was finally deposited. At some point in her fear and pain from whatever the fuck that had been, Audelia had closed her eyes.

If she was honest with herself, she hoped that the minor warping she just went through was her being deposited back into reality, but some deep-seated part of herself knew. Knew that whatever was going on in this dream was not done with her yet.

"Hello, my puppet." A chilling voice said from somewhere nearby. The maliciousness in the voice sent dread coursing through her. She shook her head, praying and begging that this would end. She didn't want to see what belonged to that voice. Something with such hate could only haunt her.

"Your fear—it is truly delicious. Open your eyes. Open them." Audelia merely shook her head at the command. She didn't want to. Everything in her wanted her to run, but she was so deeply rooted in fear and dread that a shake of the head was all she could do.

"OPEN THEM!" Audelia's eyes snapped open; she had fought the movement with everything she could, but the words and the threat in them. She was more terrified of what this voice would do if she did not obey.

Gods, she should not have opened her eyes.

Before her stood a thing of nightmares; the creature was covered in gray scales, and grotesque horns steeped in a deep crimson seemed to adorn its body, but the face, the human-like features, terrified her more than the demon-like body. The face was beautiful, ethereal even with the deep crimson eyes. It was meant to trap, to lure one in. Audelia had seen it before, not in a creature but a normal man, one that lured her with sweet promises and vicious hate. But this creature held more evil in it than anything Kage had ever done. His hate and viciousness would be child's-play for this being before her.

"Come, my dear. Join me. Come now, and I shall spare you the pain for running from me the first time." Its voice was penetrating, like a spurned lover's caress. Audelia felt herself take a step back as the way it had tried to lure her with its honeyed words had finally broken the spell on her. She needed to run, to get away from this thing.

Her heart pounded as she threw all caution to the wind, turned on her heel, and ran as fast as her body would take her. She had to get away from this creature. She had been under the claws of one monster before. Audelia had promised herself she would never be taken in by another. She made her way through the sudden greenery around her. Gone was the bright chasm, and in its place was a valley of flowers like the creature thought she would believe the lies here, that it was just a misunderstood beast, her savior, but monsters never hide long.

A roar behind her echoed, her blood chilled as it screamed, "RETURN TO ME!!! YOU ARE MINE!!" The honeyed words of before were gone. The searing hostility had returned to new levels. As she ran, she felt something pull her back, like some invisible force was trying to stop her escape.

She wouldn't let it; she thought of all the good in her life, of Shawn and his green eyes, which brought such comfort to her. She needed to get back to him. Audelia would bear this. She would get back to him. To Lila and her aunt, to Alexander. Home. She thought. Audelia saw the edge of a cliff before her. She would jump, hoping that the jolt of almost death would wake her.

Audelia screamed as something clawlike grabbed ahold of her ankle and yanked her back. She gripped the ground around her, the feeling of the soil digging into her nails as she tried to keep the thing grabbing her from fully taking her. She kicked with everything she had, but it was fruitless; all she managed to do was kick the air. The thing was dragging her back toward the creature, which was invisible or not even there. Audelia couldn't decide which was worse.

"Help!" She sobbed out to the ether, hoping that something or someone would save her from the nightmare she was being dragged closer to her. The depraved look on the demon's face stopped her heart. It would kill her. She knew it deep in her heart, and she would relish it.

She heard the flapping before she saw the deep green of leathery wings. Her heart raced again, not in fear. No, it was strange. The sight of the wings brought her a sense of relief. Audelia watched as the wings tipped and revealed the body of a large dragon. Its enormous head swung toward her scream, its eyes a deep tourmaline caught on her body being dragged. They were so kind, as they met hers. That kindness turned to abject fury and turned back toward the demon behind her. The dragon turned in its flight to face her fully; Gods, this dragon was gorgeous.

Its enormous jaws opened in a roar, and a second later, an arrow of flame shot out like a fireball toward whatever was dragging her. She felt the looseness a moment later, and it was gone. The force that had been dragging her back toward untold horror, Audelia jumped quickly to her feet and stood between the nightmare and the beautiful green dragon before her. Its jewel-like eyes met hers, and in silent command, it turned its body again and swung itself around, its body hanging in the air just off the cliff, its wings beating in time with her heart.

Did it want her to get on it? *Audelia looked behind her to see the demon stalking toward her snarling.* Fuck it. *She thought, turned back toward the dragon just beyond the cliff edge, and ran.*

Audelia ran and leaped toward the body of her savior as the demon screamed, "YOU CAN RUN, BUT I HAVE ALREADY FOUND YOU PUPPET!!" *Its words weighed with promise. One she hoped would never come to fruition. She was within moments of landing on the dragon's spine when thunder broke through the sky.*

Audelia jolted awake, falling from the swing she was on as another shaking boom broke through the area. *Fuck, that was terrifying.* The scenes of the nightmare worked their way through her. She had never had such an intense dream before. Yes, they always felt real, but this felt different.

Audelia wiped a hand over her face and felt the wetness then. She had been crying not from tears but from the ache in her eyes. No, this was different. As if the world decided to answer for her, the downpour began again, the roar of the rain louder than even the thunder that beckoned a moment later. Even in the thick canopy of her secret spot, rain this heavy would find its way in.

Standing on shaky legs, she took in her soaking wet clothes. The nightmare had been so intense that she hadn't even woken from the rain that had been drenching her.

Well, fuck me, this is going to be a lovely walk home.

Audelia quickly grabbed her bag and the now-soaked book, and she mourned for a moment at the ruined tome. She shoved it into her purse; luckily, she hadn't taken too many things with her for the movies, so her bag was relatively empty except for lipstick and a hair tie, and she was pretty sure an old granola bar. Her phone was still in her pocket, thank God for waterproof phones, or she would be utterly fucked.

Wanting to get home as fast as she could, she didn't even bother to pull it out to check for the several messages from her aunt and probably Shawn. So, instead, she threw the sloping bag onto her shoulder and began to walk through the darkness of her little alcove. The rain must have seeped into the lanterns enough to extinguish the flames. That was fine. One less thing for her to have to do before she left.

Why had she? She hadn't been tired when she came here; on the contrary, she had been enthused by the prospect of reading here and enjoying the sounds of nature around her. It was odd, and she hadn't fallen asleep like that in years.

Shaking it off, Audelia quickly made her way through the arch that led to the rest of The Glade. It was dark, little shadows of light still twinkling from the lights in the boughs above her, but even it couldn't eliminate the fear the dark gave her. It reminded her of the pressing dark from the dream and the creature that had stood in the brightness, more horrendous than that crushing dark.

She quickened her pace as the thunder broke again, this time followed by the crash and crack of lighting somewhere high above her. Just as she reached the curtain of hanging bloomed branches, she heard a whisper above the din of the rain. It started soft and then rose as the warning in the tone turned her blood to ice.

Audelia...... Audelia......

It was a woman's voice, familiar though she could not

place it. It didn't bring fear, but the warning in it, as it said her name repeatedly, had her running toward the curtain. She didn't even bother to move it aside; she quickly brushed through it, the soft caress of the blooms barely registering against her cheeks.

As she raced, the dark began to press in on her, like in the dream, but more. Audelia gripped her bag tighter as she ran with everything she had. She squeaked as she slipped in mud along the path, crying out in pain as her knees slammed against the uneven cobblestoned path.

Willing herself to move again, she stood, her legs threatening to give out again, and she ran again. Luckily, she had walked this path so often that she could make it to the street even in the dark with only bursts of lightning to give her bearings.

AUDELIA!!

The voice was a banshee's cry on the wind as she ran. Something was warning her. But from what?

Lightning lit up the trees again, casting eerie shadows around her, and she swore for a moment those shadows moved. It was not just a simple trick of the mind either because the next flash revealed shadow-like figures approaching her. Gods.

She saw the opening to the path before her and sobbed at the freedom from the dark trees calling to her. She heard the voice yell again and looked back, seeing several figures with red eyes stalking her.

In her blind dash, she ignored the opening of the trees and ran smack into a hard wall of flesh. Thick arms caught her before she could fall, heart racing, bracing for an attack. It took a second to register that the arms holding her were full of comfort, not malice.

"You alright, Miss?" At the kindness that seeped in his warm sweater voice, Audelia looked up, taking in the man before her. A small gasp broke through her. The fear that seemed to seep from her dissolved as the piercing blue of the ocean looked down at her, his eyes full of such comfort that she felt the adrenaline waver.

The man was tall, so damn tall that he seemed to block the rain from her face as she looked up at him in the din of the street lamps. The man had a kind but ruggedly handsome face, a deep scar that was almost white crested along his sharp, scruff-covered jawline. Lightening flashed again, casting a soft hue on what seemed to be a bright, sunny blonde head of hair clinging to his face from the downpour.

He gave her a small smile that, if she weren't riding off the fear of the trees, would have melted her panties from her body.

"Miss?" He asked again, a hand reaching for her face, but she flinched away, still riding everything from the past few minutes. His thick brow furrowed momentarily before he waited for her to respond.

"Please.... Don't hurt me..." Her voice sounded foreign and broken. The man must have picked up on the fear in her eyes.

His eyes turned soft, full of concern, as he let her go gently, ensuring she had her footing before he let go, and took a small step back. "Ach no. Don't worry, little one. I couldn't even hurt a fly, let alone a crying girl." He laughed softly. She nodded, her body shaking from the cold of the rain and the adrenaline crash.

"Sorry."

"No worries. But I'll ask again, are you alright? Do I need to call someone for you?" His eyes flicked behind her, and the hairs on her neck stood up. Was whatever had chased her still there? Had anything chased her?

Suddenly, feeling silly for acting like the hounds of hell themselves were at her heels. She looked at him again. Hoping her face gave the confidence she was trying to muster. Audelia felt so damn tired suddenly. "Yes.... yeah... Sorry, I must have spooked myself walking in the trees."

"Are you sure? You look a little more than spooked, darlin'."

"I'm alright. Thanks for your concern. You have a good evening, sir." She straightened herself more, adjusting her bag over her shoulder from where it had dropped in the collision.

Audelia walked away before he could say more, even though parts of her were screaming that she should remain near the man. For a stranger, he was oddly comforting.

She could have sworn she could feel his eyes watch her as she walked, like a guarding angel keeping her safe from harm. She clung to that as she walked a little quicker. The rain had let up some, so it wasn't that bad of a walk toward home.

Her mind still raced over everything that had happened.

What was that?

Whose voice had that been? Why did it sound familiar?

Why her? Why was this happening to her, of all people?

Why did it have to be in The Glade of all places?

As she walked home, the same questions played in her head, and then she added in the stranger who seemed to have saved her from whatever had lurked in the shadows of the trees. Gods, she was going insane.

Audelia had been alone tonight. That late, no one ever

came to sit and admire the magical world under the canopy of branches and blooms.

The beats of her ringtone made her jump. Heart racing, Audelia paused her walk and pulled her phone from her pocket. The illuminated screen showed her that Mara was calling.

Audelia picked up, willing her voice not to sound wobbly, and she answered. "Hey, auntie."

"Oh, thank goodness! I've been trying to get you to answer for over an hour, dove!" The worry in Mara's voice had guilt twisting in her gut. She hated making her aunt worry.

"Sorry, I fell asleep on the swing in The Glade. I only woke a few minutes ago, and my phone was still on silent from the movie."

"Where are you? This storm is supposed to turn worse; I know you enjoy storms, but they make my poor heart race."

"Just a few minutes from home. About halfway from The Glade. Should be home in maybe ten minutes, fifteen if the rain picks up again." Audelia threw as much apology as she could muster into the words.

"You better. Just be careful, dove. I worry." Audelia winced as she quickly told her aunt she loved her and hung up.

She picked up her pace, not only because she wanted to get out of these wet clothes desperately but because she didn't want to have her aunt worry more.

Thinking about it, she glanced at her phone again, noticing her aunt's and Lila's missed calls. Her heart was sinking more at the number of missed calls from Shawn. Audelia didn't want to open her messages app to see what he said. She was sure it would make her switch routes and head to him instead of home. As much as she wanted his comfort, she knew her aunt's worry would be worse.

She would text him when she got home. As she got closer to the house, the storm had indeed begun to take a turn for the worse. The wind howled against her skin and pushed her even harder.

Audelia raced the last several feet to the front door of the craftsman-style house. Unlocking the door quickly and rushing inside, she rested her back against the door, catching her breath.

"Oh, good, your home." The relief in her aunt's voice was palpable, as she stood at the end of the entry hall, Audelia took in her aunt, clad in her pajamas with her curls falling freely about her face. Her green eyes reminded Audelia of the dragon from her dream. She thought about telling her aunt about the dream for a moment, but something made her stop.

She merely nodded; her aunt's eyes turned warm, and she gave her a small smile. "Go change, take a hot shower, and I'll have some nice hot tea on your nightstand when you get out." With that, her aunt turned on her heel, heading toward the kitchen.

Audelia kicked off her soaked shoes and socks, the latter making a splattering wet smack as they hit the rug before the door. Her toes were like ice as she raced up the stairs to her room, straight for her ensuite.

A nice long steaming shower later, Audelia was sitting in her bed surrounded by her pillows and thick duvet, and she had put on her warmest pj's to chase the last vestiges of cold from her. But even with the warmth, she still couldn't shake that dream or the race from The Glade.

She had texted Shawn a while ago, letting him know she

was okay and that she was sorry about worrying him. He hadn't responded, but given all the cleaning he had probably done in prep for Soba coming to visit, she figured he had passed out. Plus, it was almost midnight.

Audelia was still reeling from how long she had been asleep in the swing, reeling from the nightmare and what it could mean.

Wait, could mean? What the hell?

It was a damn nightmare, that's all, one so terrifying it had briefly transferred into reality; she felt childish the more she put that logic to the task. That had to be what it was. This was reality, *not* a fantasy novel.

Deciding that was that, Audelia curled deeper into the warmth of the covers and picked up her Kindle from beside her on the covers. She had bought the eBook of the one she had sadly destroyed due to her falling asleep in the rain.

She quickly got lost in the world of second-chance romance and knights sworn to protect their queen, their lost love. It was a beautifully tragic read, and she adored it. Audelia loved using fiction to chase away the nightmares and the hard days in life. Book therapy, as Mara called it.

Before long, Audelia had discarded the book beside the empty mug of tea on her nightstand; she curled into the heat of the blankets and fell into a dreamless sleep.

CHAPTER FOUR

The next morning, Audelia woke up groggy, her head pounding, making her wince. She uncovered herself and began her trudge downstairs to the kitchen in search of Tylenol and maybe some nice hot coffee.

Audelia could hear the soft singing as she reached the edge of the kitchen. It brought her such comfort after the events of the night before. Luckily, she had slept dreamlessly, but the remnants of that nightmare still lingered. Walking on silent feet, she reached her aunt, where she stood already dressed for the day in a soft purple sundress with bell sleeves. Audelia wrapped her arms around her aunt like she used to do as a child when a nightmare had chased her from sleep, and she needed the warmth of the woman before her.

Her aunt squeaked and dropped her spatula back into the pan of eggs she was currently scrambling. "Goodness! Dove, you scared me." Her aunt patted her hand and freed herself to turn away from the hot pan and look at her niece. Her shock turned into worry as she took in Audelia's pale face and haggardness.

"What happened, my love?" Her aunt pulled her into a deep, comforting hug, her hand stroking up and down Audelia's back.

She didn't speak at first, just soaked in the warmth and love that always radiated from her aunt. Mara was pure sunshine, even on a cloudy day. Audelia hoped one day she would be as strong as her to be the anchor in a storm.

Her aunt pulled away for a moment to meet her eyes, her soft hands came to cup Audelia's cheeks, and the love and worry that mixed in the emerald depths of her aunt's gaze finally broke the damn inside her.

Taking a deep breath, Audelia told her aunt everything. Well, almost everything; she didn't tell her about the small fight with Shawn or how she could have sworn she was being chased in the trees. Not even the stranger with the kind ocean eyes.

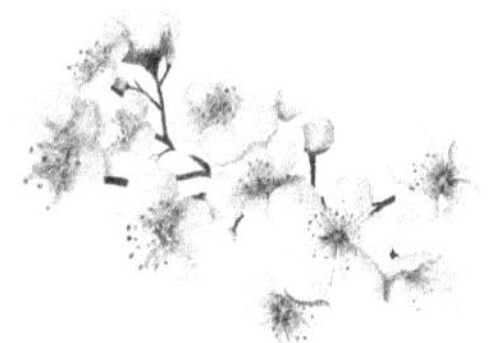

The rest of the day passed in a blur; Audelia didn't really want to talk to anyone. Even after talking to her aunt about the dream, its grip on her didn't lessen. It felt like something had shifted in her. Something profound, and it terrified her. So, she shut herself off.

As the evening rolled in, Audelia found herself curled on her loveseat in her bedroom, a cup of tea on the small table beside her, her favorite comfort show playing for background noise, and the book she had started the night before. Sadly, the paperback of it was indeed destroyed even after a night of drying in the bottom of her bag, forgotten in her rush home. So, she curled up with her Kindle propped on a little bean pillow she used when Audelia wanted to be extra lazy with the reading. Her favorite warm cashmere blanket in pale blue draped around her body.

After some time, she must have fallen asleep on her spot on the loveseat because she woke to her room shrouded in darkness. Aunt Mara must have come in and turned off everything for her. She sat up from her spot on the loveseat, rubbing the sleep from her eyes. She was still tired, but a chill seemed to linger in the air. Audelia moved the blanket off herself and stretched out a little.

She made her way to the kitchen for a quick cold drink before she would curl into her bed and hopefully wake having shaken off the last of this ache.

The house was dark, except for a few nightlights she and her aunt had placed throughout the house for ease of night-time movement. She used these to guide her around the edge of the open living room, which was cast in shadowy darkness, to the kitchen. The rain had stopped sometime in the early evening, and the breeze coming in from the open windows was welcome as Audelia grabbed a bottle of water from the fridge.

She leaned against the counter and took a deep drink, relishing the cool feel on her throat.

The sounds of voices coming from outside had her pausing. She glanced at the clock on the microwave, which read two in the morning. Her aunt's door had been dark when she walked by it on the way downstairs.

Curiosity got the better of her, and, like a thief in the night, Audelia crept quietly toward the wall closest to the sliding door that she now noticed was open; the only part closed was the screen to keep out the bugs.

Tilting her head around the corner, keeping herself in the shadows. Audelia finally beheld who was on the deck, the soft glow of the citronella torches lending the only light. In the soft glow of the flames, she could barely make out the soft browns of her aunt's curls and her petite frame, and Mara was turned away from her, leaning over the rails of the semi-hexagonal deck. The angle placed her aunt in the closest view. What shocked Audelia, however, was that her aunt wasn't alone.

Because, next to her petite aunt was another, the two of them currently leaning toward each other.

Obviously, she knew she hadn't been from the voices, but it was a shock to see her aunt currently leaning into the substantial, very man-shaped form next to her in the semi-dark and from the slight touches the flames revealed in their dance. Very intimately close together.

The wind picked up briefly, making the flames nearest the two shift, revealing bits of the man's profile. Strong jaw speckled with reddish fuzz, and intense, familiar eyes that swam with deep-seated love for… *holy shit.* For Mara.

Did her aunt have a secret lover? Why? In all the years

growing up Mara had never even dated that Audelia could recall. As a teen, Audelia had asked why her beautiful aunt had never married. Mara had simply said it wasn't for her that she was content to lose herself in fictional men and take care of Audelia.

She had never, of course, bought that for a damn second. She and Lila had speculated that Mara was probably hiding a harem worth of secret lovers. No one that beautiful and kind didn't have someone on the hook somewhere. Lila was going to flip whenever Audelia found the time to tell her about this.

The man's thick and husky voice broke through her thoughts as he spoke. "Are you sure everything is okay, my love?"

Why does he sound so familiar? Audelia racked her brain for it. She knew she had heard it before, and the way he said *love* rang like a bell in her. Between the eyes she had caught and the tone of him saying love, she could have sworn it was Alexander out there, which made no sense. Why would they hide their relationship from her?

Maybe she was less awake than she had thought; that had to be it. Because if Mara and Alexander were hiding this from her. *Fuck*, she didn't even want to think of how much that hurt.

"Besides the dream she had. No, handsome. Though I do worry greatly about her lately." Mara's voice sounded so defeated.

Wait? Why are they talking about me?

"I know, and I do as well. It's been too long. Too quiet. I fear something may befall us all soon." Audelia watched as the man pulled Mara into an embrace.

She should go. Obviously, Mara had kept this a secret for a reason, but she couldn't bring herself to move.

Audelia watched as the two embraced in the quiet of the evening before the man spoke again. "I do have some news, and the men said they have seen her being followed more by unsavory-looking men. Though I believe one to be Shawn from the description." A small chuckle radiated from him.

Shawn? How much of her life did this man know about?

Mara laughed. "I can only imagine which of the men describe that sweet boy as unsavory. But are you all surprised? She is a beautiful young woman; of course, she has men clamoring to be near her."

"Yes, but some of them, my men said, seemed to truly have ill intent toward her. That last time. We don't want to risk that happening again." The man's voice had filled with such raging anger that Audelia sucked in a breath.

"It's what lingers near her in the shadows we must worry about it. She is older now. He will be more insistent in trying to grab her. That's why I fear the dream she had. What if it was him finding a foothold here?"

"I know. I have the twins keeping an eye on such things. Have you heard any whispers from him?" From the tone, Audelia had the feeling this *him* was not the former they were speaking of.

"Nothing. I go daily to see if maybe if I am close enough, he will speak. It's been almost fifteen years, and still silence." Mara's voice was thick with sorrow and longing.

The man stepped closer to her and pressed his forehead against hers; Audelia watched as the man cupped her aunt's cheeks. The gesture made Audelia's heart begin to race. "I miss him, Bronn. So much…. But mostly, I miss you."

The pang deepened in Audelia's heart. She should go. It felt wrong to hear these words.

"Oh. My lady, my love. I am here. I will always be here. Not even a great cataclysm could keep me from returning to you." His voice was rough with need so much that Audelia blushed.

She watched as he tilted Mara's chin up and crushed his lips to hers. She heard her aunt sigh into the kiss. Audelia turned from her spot to hopefully creep back toward the stairs while the two lovers were busy.

"What will we do with Audelia?" Her aunt's words had her stopping in her tracks. The tone had changed again, back to that deep-seated worry that crushed her very soul.

"That girl is as brave now as she was as a child. Whatever happens next, I have every confidence she will handle it with grace. And what she cannot handle, my men and I will do the rest." The man spoke with such confidence and knowing that Audelia was utterly thrown.

Did she know him? His voice did sound somewhat familiar, but nothing in her memory really pulled at her. How could he know her in that way? Better yet, what the fuck did he mean by whatever is to come?

"I do as well, but Bronn— I fear that day. I love her so much; we have all lost so much already, and the idea of losing her as well... I don't think I could handle it."

Did she know a Bronn? The name didn't sound familiar, but the glimpses of him and his voice, they were. *Was it someone from when she was a kid?* A lot of her childhood was a blur; perhaps that was the reason she couldn't place this man. It added to her questions of why her aunt kept him a secret like this. It stung that she kept this from her.

"My Mara." He pulled her back into a tight embrace, and

Audelia could hear the ragged sobs break from her aunt. It took everything in her not to run out to the deck and hug her aunt. Tell her that nothing was going to happen, but she couldn't do it.

She couldn't ruin this moment, even if she was burning with questions.

Another voice spoke so softly, she couldn't make the words out, but the man had turned toward the backyard. "I must go. I have already tarried here too long. If any saw me, I don't want to find out if they were alerted."

Her aunt sighed heavily. "I know... I wish we didn't have to hide; I miss sleeping in your arms." The couple kissed again, this one slow and full of regret at parting. "Tell the boys I said hello. Oh! Don't forget the basket on the counter; just be quiet while grabbing it. I baked you all your favorites."

At those words, Audelia hurried back to the steps. Halfway up, she heard the sliding door click back into place. She quickly and, as lightly as she could manage, got back to her room. Shutting the door quietly, Audelia leaned against it.

Audelia didn't dare move even as she was burning with questions. She debated texting Lila or maybe even Shawn. But she knew the latter had work in the morning, and she didn't want to bother him with this. Lila would answer, but something kept her hand from grabbing it. Instead, she walked to her bed and got under the covers.

She had almost fallen asleep when she heard the door to Mara's room close, and the soft sounds of crying drifted into the quiet of the house.

Audelia slept in the next morning; her body and mind felt dragged down still. She needed to get out and do something. Maybe go visit Shawn and see Soba. She loved his grandmother. But she also slightly feared seeing the woman. She was all-seeing. Soba could see what lingered in one's soul from thirty paces.

It was still early in the day, not quite noon. So, she still had plenty of time before she was due at the dojo tonight.

Making herself get out of bed, Audelia walked to her ensuite and stripped out of her pajamas. She opted for a bath, hoping a good soak would soothe everything. She would switch to a fun, romantic audiobook while she bathed.

That sounded perfect.

Walking to the cabinet by the sink, she grabbed salts and a milk bath she had gotten a few days ago. It smelled like cherry blossoms and vanilla. Audelia started her claw-footed soaking tub, turning the temperature to that perfect amount of heat. She poured in the salts and emptied a generous amount of the milk bath—the blend filling the room with a relaxing scent.

After throwing her hair into a high bun and selecting the new romcom that Lila had told her about on her Bluetooth speaker, Audelia sank into the warmth of the tub. She leaned against the pillow, suctioned against the edge, and closed her eyes.

She stayed in for over an hour, and by the time she got out, her muscles had felt lank and loose, but her mind was still swirling with unease; it had waned a little, but not enough.

Audelia decided she would dress for a run. If the luxurious bath hadn't done the trick, then a run the day after a good rainstorm always did the trick. Something about running, when the smell of ozone still lingered in the wind, always settled her. Almost as much as a storm did.

She grabbed a bright pair of lavender stretch running pants that clung to her curves and always made her ass look amazing. Audelia paired it with a soft pink athletic bra and a lavender racer tank that said *I work out, So I can carry more books.*

Audelia was working her hair into a high-braided ponytail when her phone went off. Hope raced in her; maybe it was finally Shawn texting her back. She hadn't heard from him since the day before when she told him she was okay; she had just fallen asleep early with a headache.

Walking toward her bed where she had left her phone before the bath. Every step felt wrong, though. Something chilled inside her as she stepped toward her phone, like a sense of foreboding screaming at her to walk away. To not look.

Shaking it off, Audelia grabbed her phone from the duvet. She was being silly; more than likely, it was a text from the group chat between her, Shawn, and Lila. They planned to go to the theme park in three towns this coming weekend. So, knowing Lila, she probably wanted to hammer out the last-minute details for the trip.

With that playing in her, Audelia clicked the button on the side of her phone to see what Lila was about to go full rant on. *Because she would, and it would be days of it*, Audelia mused.

Just as the screen turned on, another message came through. The screen read an *unknown number,* causing her to furrow her brow. Who would be texting her that she didn't already have on her phone? *Maybe it was someone from the bookstore?*

That sense of unease crept back in as she perched herself on the edge of her bed and clicked into the message thread.

Everything in her stopped as she looked at the first message.

UNKNOWN

Your cries of fear the other night made me so
very happy.

Another came in shortly after.

UNKNOWN

I wonder how you would sound as I tied you
up and made you bleed.

Scream, cry, beg. Gods, just the idea of you
begging for me to stop makes my cock hard.

Would you cry more if I tied up that pretty
friend of yours?

Maybe I'll cut her up for you. Make a pretty
bouquet.

I should kill that boy of yours. Wear his face
when I fuck you.

MMM....I like that idea.

She could barely keep up with the messages as one after
another came in, each more vicious than the last; the threats in
them held a dangerous promise. The world around Audelia
began to spin and blur as her heart began to race.

This had to be some sick joke. It had to be. Who would talk
like this to a stranger?

Audelia felt sick as she closed out the chat after silencing it.
She needed to talk to Lila or Shawn or just someone. But the
idea of touching her phone right now, she couldn't bear it.

She tossed it across the room where it landed with a thud
on the round rug by the sitting area in her room. Laying back,
she curled into herself and cried.

Audelia lay there wishing that she had never seen the messages. That it was a nightmare. Yet, the reality of them refused to leave.

As those messages played over and over in her head, Audelia bolted to her ensuite and barely got the toilet seat up before the contents of her stomach gave way as it finally clicked; who could have sent messages like that?

Who had sent ones like that before?

She would have preferred some crazed stalker to the true sender of the messages.

Kage.

CHAPTER FIVE

Audelia wasn't quite sure how long she had remained in that spot, but she hadn't fully trusted herself to stand as the initial shock and fear finally began to wane.

She had rested her back against the cool tile of the bathroom wall, letting the feeling ease the heat coming from her body. She felt like she was burning up. Not with a fever; this was different, strange.

Why was he texting her? How the hell did he even get her number? She had changed it the next day after Shawn had come to get her from that hotel, where she had barely escaped with her life. It was the most she could do. Shawn had pressed her to file charges against him, but Kage's daddy had his hands in a lot of big pockets. Anything she filed would just disappear even if the rape kit came back positive.

She didn't want to go through that; she didn't want her

aunt or the people she loved to have to know what she had truly gone through. Shawn only knew because when the world had fallen around her, and Kage had beaten her so severely that she had three broken ribs and a fractured wrist. Audelia had wanted Shawn. She had *needed* him.

The blocking of his number and the fact she had stabbed him after one of his most violent outbursts when she had told him she was leaving him. Somehow, it had kept him away from her for the past few years. So, why was he suddenly trying to mess with her again?

She tried not to think about the *why* too much. *Borrowed time.*

That phrase played in her head from the moment she ran out that hotel door. Kage was never going to really let her go, even if she had wished for it so badly. In her darkest moments, she had even hoped that either the drugs and bleeding had done him in or that he found someone new. Both left a bad taste in her mouth.

The former she knew hadn't happened because she and Shawn holed up in a hotel, an hour from the one he had picked her up from after he made her go to the hospital. Audelia had checked the news and even downloaded one of those police scanner apps just to see if he was dead or taken to a hospital. Nothing had come up, so while she healed, she and Shawn came up with an excuse for why she looked like she had gone several rounds with a champion boxer.

The whole time, she had been worried Kage would burst through the door and take her away forever. It never happened, but that feeling of borrowed time lingered.

For the past few years, she had learned to live with it. To enjoy what she did have, and to hope that maybe, just maybe, one day Shawn would see her, and the two of them could run off into the sunset.

The loadstone of texts in her phone proved she would never get that. She would need to leave before he got his claws in her again. Maybe she could time it with the trip this weekend; it would be last minute, but she had enough saved and enough from the life insurance from her parent's death.

Audelia needed to think.

She did not want to leave the people she loved; she would be fucking damned if she allowed that monster to steal more from her than he had. She should take her life back, but could she risk her family? With a wavering resolve coursing through her, she stood from the bathroom floor and went to the sink. Audelia rinsed her mouth with some mouthwash before looking at herself in the mirror.

Audelia could see the war in her eyes. The scared young woman and the fierce one at odds with what she should do next. It was draining but at the same time, that burning inside seemed to uncurl from itself.

She had felt it before years ago, the night she had finally said *enough* and got herself out. To center herself, she took a few deep breaths. Audelia decided she would go on a run.

Running always helped when her mind was at war with too many thoughts and outcomes playing out. If the run didn't work, she would bake. Over the years, she had learned she was just like Mara and used baking and its need for order as a beautiful way to sort through everything by placing it in its own equally measured place.

The more complicated the dessert or bread, the more patient you needed to be, and the more you had to truly settle everything inside.

She thought. *Yes, if the run didn't help, she would bake, maybe a soufflé.*

Audelia splashed her face with water and applied a little concealer to hide some of the red puffiness from her eyes. Mara should have gone to work already, but just in case she was still home, she didn't want her to notice.

Throwing on a pair of sparkly pink running shoes and socks to match, Audelia made her way down to the kitchen to grab her running water bottle from the fridge. The house was quiet as she reached the arch into the kitchen. The only sound was the breeze drifting in from the open windows. It cast little designs of dancing light all over the house from the gauzy curtains.

Audelia grabbed the holder for her bottle, secured it to her waist, and tossed her phone and keys into the little second pouch. She grabbed the bottle from the fridge and added one of her hydration pods to it. There's no telling how long she may run, so she might as well make sure she had the extra boost.

Securing it to its holder, Audelia made her way to the front of the house to run. Her gaze caught on the sliding door, and her mind drifted to the night before. All the mess from this morning had made her forget the other loadstone in her life.

The secret lover Mara had. The one that looked and sounded like Alexander. She had called him Bronn, and the name didn't ring a bell. But maybe Alexander had a twin? One he never bothered to tell them about for the past decade that she had known him. Top that off with the fact that her aunt kept this person from her, a person her aunt trusted so damn much that she felt it was okay to talk to him about the fucked-up dream she had.

Audelia threw her earbuds in as she walked outside; more questions kept plaguing her. Who were these other men? The one Mara and this Bronn character said they kept an eye on her. What was she, some secret mafia princess that needed shadowy bodyguards? But the more significant issue was, why did they decide to hide all of this from her?

That betrayal stung.

She didn't even know how to broach that without entirely losing it. Shaking the thoughts away, she locked the door, turned on her *heartthrob boybands* playlist, and began to jog. Audelia decided she would head toward the coast; maybe the salty ocean air would do her some good.

Audelia let everything roll over her like a storm brewing. It's what she always did. Let her soul soar with every step she took, build that storm inside, and then ride it out.

She could feel it under the surface of her skin as she ran. That pulsing beat, it raged inside like some primordial power stretching out and opening its eyes. She welcomed it, and as her feet slapped on the pavement, she felt like every step left behind a burning mark.

Everything was thought, eddied, and then built again. Like a maelstrom, she felt the power rise to the challenge. She didn't even question it, never had. She let herself become the storm, become the inferno.

Audelia felt aflame with it. It crawled over her skin with purpose. It was a whisper of ancient promises. It was her, and she was the flame.

Her fingers felt odd, numb, and tingly, and she looked down at her hands for a moment and gasped as she took in the flames that flickered there. She was so lost in trying to figure out how the fuck her hands were on fire, and it didn't hurt that she crashed into someone walking on the sidewalk.

She barreled into them hard, knocking them and herself down in a heap. "I am so sorry!" Audelia pleaded as she stood, offered her hand, and then held in a gasp again as the flames that had been there before were suddenly gone. All that was left was her regular hand and the look of pure annoyance for the suited man scowling at her.

He ignored her hand and stood, brushing off the nonexistent dirt from his suit; he fixed her with a glare with his deep grey eyes. "Watch where the fuck you are going, little girl." He spat at her and knocked into her shoulder as he stalked away.

She winced at the contact, her skin felt oversensitive, but it didn't stop her from turning toward the man's back and knocking her wrists together twice at the man in an age-old *fuck you* gesture. "Rude ass."

Audelia rolled her shoulders and started back up into her usual gait. After that, she didn't even really pay attention to her direction; she just ran. Letting that power build again, and with every spark and every fear those texts had given her, started to ease. Logic began to weasel in, reminding her it could be a wrong number or some poorly placed joke, even at most, a completely new stalker.

She hoped any of those were the tangible outcome, because it would mean Kage was finally out of her life. *Gods, I have lost it if those options were preferable.* She thought.

It had been years, and if he had been that obsessed with getting her back, surely he wouldn't have waited this long?

Besides, last she knew, he had moved to some country with his daddy when he got a new ambassador position. The icing on that particular cake was the fact that the father of such a monster was allowed to have a say in anything remotely important.

Audelia wasn't sure how long she ran before the need to stop began to scream at her, so she eased to walk as she crested a hill, fully intending to have a drink of water and maybe sit for a few minutes. Then, she would stretch out again and finish the run.

She didn't want to be too exhausted; as much as she had enjoyed the comfort this run had given her, she had class tonight at the dojo.

She was excited for class, as it was covering armed self-defense. Perfect timing with how her life was going. However, she was not looking forward to seeing Alexander like usual.

What if she was wrong? What if that was his last night? How would she face the fact that the two adults in her life, the people who felt like her parents, had been lying this whole time?

Audelia didn't want to dwell on that. If she did, she would cry. They were her two biggest pillars, and then learn that the foundation of those pillars was a lie? One that didn't even make sense to her. It would *crush* her.

Coming to a stop, she closed her eyes. After taking a centering breath, Audelia opened them again and finally rounded the hill before her, where The Glade stood.

Chuckling to herself, she made her way down to the tree. Of course, when her world seemed to spin out of control, she would lead herself to her personal Meca.

The Glade was the epicenter of everything for her. As she looked at it, the sun shone like a glowing halo over the greens and blooming colors of the trees. She knew that if any peace was to be found, it was here.

She wouldn't even let the events of the other night sully it. It would never hold that kind of power of her love, *no,* her *devotion* to this place.

Logic played in her head as she walked. Maybe it was just the grogginess of the dream she had. The man who had stopped her from falling hadn't seemed alarmed; yes, he had looked behind her with slight worry. But logically, that could be because she was running like she was being chased, and he was checking to see if she was really being chased.

She felt her cheeks heat with embarrassment at the kind, gorgeous man who had helped her. Audelia must have appeared so foolish to him. Hopefully, she never saw him again, as much as she would love to thank him.

It was busy today as she neared the entrance to the path that led to the heart of this beautiful place. She wouldn't go into the main area. The idea of being around so many people right now made her skin crawl. So, instead, she wandered into the trees that made up the little wooded area around the mammoth willow tree.

The dark never scared her, and shadows had always been her friends. Audelia could not remember much of her childhood before Mara took her in, but she did remember bits and pieces. None made sense, though.

It was like flashes of some jumbled puzzle; she had told Lila about it once when they laid under the boughs of the willow in the heart of The Glade. She knew Lila would understand; they had dreamed of similar things. Growing up playing in the fairyland that the blooms and vines had provided.

For them, make-believe was as real as the scuffs on their knees from learning to ride their bikes, so she told her. Told her every crazy fantastical thing she remembered, the petals in the ashes she mused to Lila.

It was all crazy, of course, two little girls deciding that Audelia's parents hadn't died in some accident but had been killed by some creature lost to legend. Joked that Audelia was a lost princess; after all, that's what the dreams and the little moments of memory she held seemed to tell.

With how the past few days had gone, *maybe,* she thought, as she wandered among the spears of light that made its way into the trees, casting a glow in the dark. Perhaps those two silly little girls were right that she was more than just filler in a story.

Smiling, Audelia walked back toward the edge of the trees, her little walk in the radiant dark clearing more of the thoughts.

With each step, she felt like she was that beacon of light, an ever-burning flame. One that, if she wanted, could set everything ablaze like a phoenix and rise from the ashes. With that playing in her head and the power that still seemed to buzz just on the edge of her, she began the trek back home.

Audelia slowed her pace as her phone started to buzz again and again. Somehow, she knew it wasn't Shawn or Lila. Both would have called if it was urgent if she hadn't responded right away. So, she gave it another moment, and then her phone buzzed repeatedly. Audelia knew. She knew with her soul it was the unknown number.

With that resolve, she ran a little faster, not liking how exposed she felt that he could come up to her at any moment. As much as she hoped, Audelia knew she would relent. Fear would take over, and all that training over the years would go out the window. Her thoughts would only linger on one regret:

Shawn. The fact she would never get the courage to be with him. That she would give herself to a monster to make sure he and her family, Lila, would remain safe.

Above all, she wanted them all safe. Kage was a loose cannon. Audelia would never risk them.

The sounds of her neighborhood shook her from the spiraling thoughts, the ones that disgusted her, the ones that made her seem weak.

Looking up at the small porch of her house, her heart froze. There, sitting on the little bench they had for packages and food delivery, was a large bouquet of white petunias and orange lilies.

No.

The word echoed in her head over and over as her breathing became erratic, her heart racing so fast it felt like it may very well burst free any moment. Audelia fought back tears as she stared at her front door, and the flowers that sat there, a calling card.

The honk of a horn made her jump, turning to the sound, terrified of who was behind the wheel of the car. *Was it him? Was this it?*

Relief flooded her as a man approached the car, which was pulling over to the curb a distance from her. The two seemed to exchange a few words, and the man rounded the front of the car and jumped into the passenger seat. Several more buzzes came from her phone, one after another, over and over.

Audelia let out the breath she hadn't realized she held as the car and two men drove away, none the wiser to the young woman about to burst into tears on the sidewalk. On numb legs, which seemed to know what to do, Audelia walked across the street and ran up the steps. She hoped her demeanor gave off nonchalance even as her body shook. It was a miracle she was able to get the zipper open to her bag and grab the house keys out.

It took a few tries before she could get them into the slot, a few stagger breaths to calm her enough. She prayed that Mara wasn't home or that Lila hadn't deemed to show up randomly and was waiting in her room. Audelia needed time to collect herself as much as she wanted her people.

The moment the keys clicked, releasing the lock's tumbler, a small sob broke free from Audelia. Letting the door open a little, Audelia grabbed the flowers, and just touching them had tears streaming down her face.

Braving it all, she tossed them into the neighbor's open bin from its spot near their porch. She didn't want to bring them into the house. Scanning the surrounding area quickly, seeing no one watching, she slipped inside, locked the door immediately, and armed the security system.

Fearing that she would soon hear a body jolt the door, trying to find entry, Audelia backed away slowly. Her eyes never left the door, even with it locked and the system on; she didn't dare it. Not until she was at the foot of the stairs. Then she shot up toward her room. Once in her room, she closed even that door and locked it.

Her heart was racing still. *Would he get in? Was he even out there?*

As if in answer, her phone buzzed again, over and over. This time, in the safety of her room, she dared to look. *Maybe I'm just going crazy; it's probably just Lila or Shawn, possibly even Alexander, to see if I'm coming in early to help set up the dojo.*

As the screen lit up in her palm, she knew she was so very

fucking wrong. Text after text from an unknown number. She caught a few in the notification bar.

UNKNOWN

Mine.

Mine, my pretty. MINE.

Mine MINE. Are you listening WHORE! You cannot escape me.

I wonder if you will look as good running from me, or will you look better bleeding as you run?

She couldn't read anymore. Quickly, she blocked the number. Hoping it would stop the texts. She didn't want to look at the others that had kept flooding until she stopped it.

Walking to her window, she peered out to see if anyone was outside or watching from the little park across the street. When she saw no one, she let out a breath of relief. Audelia decided to take another shower. Maybe the heat of the water would wash all of this away.

Two hours later, showered and redressed in different workout clothes, Audelia was ready for the dojo. She needed this. Taking the classes, Alexander gave at his dojo and small gym that was connected to it, they had helped. When she was a kid grieving her parents and adjusting to a new life with Mara, she needed something to put all that upheaval into.

Shawn, who had become a fast friend in school, had told her about Alexander and his junior classes for karate. The more he had talked about it the more she had craved it. So, after begging Mara, Audelia enrolled in the next class that she knew Shawn would be at so she wouldn't be alone.

From there, it spiraled into an obsession that even stints in ballet and piano and a horrible experience with cheerleading could never shake.

As she grew older, she devoured all the classes he would let her enroll in, and when he wouldn't let her because it was for adults, she begged and then proved she could handle them. Alexander relented and started to teach her and even Shawn privately, with the occasional Lila, from karate and boxing to even a local favorite, sword fighting. Audelia took them all. Her biweekly classes were her personal haven.

Checking herself over in the stand-up mirror, Audelia took in the royal blue cheetah print leggings and plain matching racer back with the built-in support bra. Her bright, flaming hair was pulled back into a Dutch braid with smaller ones within each strand. Even with the slightly red and puffy eyes, which she decided she would wear as a badge. She had survived the day.

Audelia felt like a warrior as she stood there. Closing her eyes for a moment, she took a deep breath, and when she opened them, she banished everything from her mind. All the fear from earlier was gone. Her phone had been silent except for a few texts from Shawn asking if they were still meeting early at the dojo and one in the group chat from Lila saying that she just got the bug's oil changed, so they were a go for this weekend.

The messages sat there still, several still unread, but during her shower, Audelia had decided she would tell Shawn about it. That together, they could brave those messages, and he would be the voice of reason for what she should do. The idea of showing him terrified her, but she needed him.

She was a damn warrior. Audelia had used that phrase a lot when she felt like she would break under the thumb of Kage or when life felt too much. At ten, she had learned about Viking Shield Maidens and fell in love. From that point, it was her mantra.

Audelia and Lila had even had shield maiden runes tattooed along one of their ribs just below the side of her breast. So, the power of fierce women would always walk with her.

Reciting it over and over in her head, Audelia walked downstairs, preparing to head to class a little early. She wanted to get there before it got too dark.

"Is that you, Dove?" Mara's voice came from the living room. Audelia detoured to tell her aunt goodbye for the night. The sight of her aunt in the big oval chair by the fireplace, a blanket draped over her petite frame, her hair pulled into a high bun, book on her lap. She suddenly wanted to tell her aunt everything, but then the sight of her aunt at night with a strange man who could genuinely be the twin of Alexander. The truth kept from her, stilled her voice.

"Yeah, just heading to the dojo early. Figured I would see if Alexander needed help setting up, Shawn is meeting me there." She kept her voice steady, even as last night played over and over in her head.

"Okay, be careful. Tell Alexander I said hello." Audelia had to fight the gasp that was fixed to escape at how her voice caught with saying, Alexander. *Was it true? Was it him? Why the lies?*

Before she could begin the onslaught of questions, she merely nodded and spoke as she turned to leave. "I will. Night, Auntie."

Audelia left quickly after that, the echoes of betrayal hanging in the air.

CHAPTER SIX

As Audelia stepped out onto the front porch of her home, everything felt heavy. She didn't know if she could take this anymore. Parts of her wanted to turn back inside and confront her aunt. Yell, scream, cry, but she knew if she went back inside right now, she would destroy everything.

The lies, the threats, and the betrayal that seemed to linger on the edge of a blade brought forth again by seeing Mara tasted like iron in her mouth. Audelia wasn't proud of it, but she had a temper. If she was pushed enough, it was as raging as the inferno that seemed to hum deep inside her lately.

She was ripe to explode, but she would be damned if the people she loved got caught in the shrapnel of it. Even if right now, they seemed to be the ones digging the blades in.

Why the lies?

That was the one thing that didn't make sense. She and

Mara had always been honest with each other, even when things started to get more complex. Even when she was asking questions, Audelia knew Mara wasn't ready to give the answers, too. Mara still told her. They always shared everything; no boundary was off-limits for them.

So why now? For how long?

Tears threatened to spill, but she fought them off as she began walking down the house's steps and turned toward the ocean. She would take the long route today.

Needed extra time to think.

She was still nervous about walking alone, thinking about the texts and who was behind them. The probable answer was Kage, and the wild card was that it was someone else. It was funny as she walked; if she really thought about it, she would take the latter over the former.

If it was Kage, he would have three years to build his anger and plot and put everything into focus again. That, above all, terrified her because he was terrifying enough on a whim, but to have had time to plan? The idea had her blood turning to ice.

Audelia came up to the sea walkway, the salty breeze greeting her as she turned to walk its path. Off in the distance, she could see the beginnings of another storm brewing off the ocean. It painted a picture of her life, she thought, and she paused to lean against the metal railing of the little boardwalk. Seeing nature capsulate the pain and beauty going on in one's life was truly beautiful.

She took in the hues of blues, candy pinks, and soft hues of yellow from the last cast of the sun before Twilight truly set in and how it seemed to push in vain against the dark pressing in, not from time, but from something more potent. Something that spoke to her soul. This dark was its own force; a herald riding in on waves of deep cobalt blues, crushing midnight dark, and there were little echoes of pure white as lightning crashed like a god going to war. It sent a shiver down her spine as she thought of the contrast to her own life again. Audelia realized as she watched the oncoming storm she was the light dying out. No, she *was* the storm, that the light for her wasn't true light, but a falsity, that she was the light, and sometimes the dark needed to devour first for a new dawn to begin.

Together, the image built inside her, and she welcomed it. Somehow, seeing what she felt inside before her cast over the water-centered her. That lonely feeling she had fought in her room earlier, the one that had her almost deciding to run, to be a coward and not the damn warrior she was. Audelia was able to push it back and silence it.

She would talk to Shawn tonight. Tell him what was going on; he was her rock. If anyone in her life would know what to do, it was him. God, she loved him. As each day passed, Audelia increasingly realized that her love for him was past friendship. No, she loved him with a deep passion and need of having him by her side for everything. She was his.

Tipping her head to battle over the water in thanks, Audelia pushed off the railing and began to walk again. A little taller, a little straighter.

Audelia loved the path she took, the quiet and serene feel as the salty breeze moved around her with every step. Usually, this time in the evening, not many took this path to the shops downtown off the wharf, and given that it was still early spring, most kept from the water once the sun left for the day. *All the better*, she thought.

She still felt slightly broken, a little more durable now, but it was still under the surface. Audelia walked toward the seawall tunnel that created a walkway under the more extensive boardwalk that started further inland and reached out toward the seaways; during the summer, it would be filled with carnival rides for the summer festival. Now, as she looked up, it was deserted and eerily quiet. Audelia turned back to her thoughts as she walked.

Maybe she should talk to Mara? Ask her about the man who looked like Alexander, or she could ask the man in question. The thought had her stomach rolling. What would she do? If what she was questioning was true? Could she handle it?

Yes, she was a warrior, but even the fiercest shield maiden had a breaking point. Would this be hers? She faced a monster and survived it, but the idea of the two people who, to her, felt like her parents or what her parents could have been. The idea that they had kept this lie. Built a foundation for their lives on it?

Audelia wasn't sure she could survive the damage.

The buzz of her phone had her jumping, breaking her thoughts. Suddenly, everything felt too much, her skin too thin, and her heart raced as she pulled the phone from her pocket. *Was it the unknown number again? Had he found her? Was it Kage? Oh, gods, was this it? Would she never see Shawn, Lila, or her aunt again?* Her breathing hitched and then became sporadic as she turned to the front of the phone to face her.

Shawn, one message waiting.

Audelia's legs felt like they were going to give out. The relief that rushed through her was palpable. She leaned against the wall of the little tunnel she was walking through. The feeling of the cool cement felt terrific against her suddenly burning skin.

Maybe she wasn't as okay as she had thought if a simple

incoming text had her spiraling into a panic. She leaned her head against the wall for a moment, closing her eyes; she let everything settle around her.

The sound of waves echoed in the tunnel, and she used that to center her and ease the tension inside. Audelia pictured every thought, every fear, as the waves against the cement wall of the seawall tunnel echoed as a roar. As every wave receded, she let go of another worry. With each of these little mantras she used her shield maiden one to replace each wave.

She didn't have much further to walk now, and the Dojo was only a few more blocks from the tunnel. Just another twenty feet, she would have the cool ocean breeze against her skin again and the clarity it offered. Even in this cool tunnel, she felt fevered.

Taking one last deep cleansing breath, Audelia looked at her phone again and swiped to open the message from Shawn.

SHAWN

Hey Beautiful 😊 We still on for class tonight?

Audelia couldn't help but smile, even when the world was crashing around her when she felt like she could break for good. Something about Shawn always pulled her back. He had this way about him that was intoxicating, so much so that even a simple mundane text like this was enough to help move past everything, to cast this glow around her, one that had that fiery power that she felt again, purring in answer.

AUDELIA

Of course! Headed there now.

SHAWN

gif of brother from Napoleon Dynamite going YES. See you soon, babe.

Smiling, Audelia pushed off the cement wall and began walking toward the tunnel's end. She could see a few of the shops facing the sea in the distance. Once she reached the end of the tunnel, she knew she would see the red neon sword that she would be steps from one of her havens. She remembered when Alexander had gotten it made, and he was so damn giddy like a schoolgirl that day. Audelia had taken a photo of him standing by it doing the Vanna White showcase move, and she gave him a copy for his birthday that year in a sparkly frame that she had made with the words *World's Biggest Dork Award.*

Alexander had displayed it on his desk like a badge of honor and would tell anyone he could about how much he loved his award. A twang of heartbreak crept back in at the thought of Alexander, of the memory of her and Mara laughing as she glued the words to the frame.

Gods. What if they are lying? What the fuck would she do with that? It would taint everything. Was it all tainted? If this was from the beginning all a lie? Fuck.

The heavy crunch of rock came from behind her, and Audelia whirled toward the sound, her heart thundering. She sucked in a breath, preparing to fight, to get away. But she was met with nothing.

Nothing was there, just an empty tunnel. Whatever had made the noise had already left, whatever it was. Which was odd. The sound was as if someone of great weight had stepped on the bits of gravel and sand in the tunnel. She took a timid step, still unsure if what she had heard was in her head.

Heart in her ears, Audelia decided not to walk toward the sound and whatever had caused it, even if she was curious on some level, so she turned back toward the other end and the dojo blocks away.

Only the tunnel wasn't empty. Ice and dread traveled down her spine, and her knees shook as she took in the silhouette blocking the entrance. It was nearly ten feet tall and broad.

Oh, gods.

Audelia started to back away, not daring to turn her back on whatever the fuck that thing was. It loomed there, waiting.

Then it shifted as she took one step, then another. Its arms, at least she thought they were arms, moved outward like it was reaching; the thing had no visible shape; it was like a giant— giant— *Shadow.*

It was a fucking giant monstrous shadow.

The silhouette of claws, because its hand was not a hand but a damn claw. Fuck.

She was so damn fucked.

Audelia stepped back again; her body shook, begging her to turn and run. But she couldn't look away. Didn't dare to.

It stalked forward.

As it did so, the air around her became unnaturally thick, like mud. Suddenly, she couldn't move. Something was keeping her movements. Audelia struggled to shift and take another step as the thing prowled toward her with predatory intent.

It had no eyes she could see, just fathomless black before, but she caught whisps like the creature wasn't fully corporeal. Audelia was terrified now. How could she fight that?

If she could move again, how would she fight back against something that wasn't solid?

Could she?

If she couldn't fight or move, she would try to scare it off and try to get help. With that in mind, she took as deep of a breath as her lungs would allow; she prepared to scream to get anyone's attention; surely someone was out. Close enough to help her. *Please...*

Audelia screamed. Or she would have if the very scream that could have saved her died in her throat. She tried again to no avail.

The creature paused, and a screeching keeling noise echoed around her. *Was it laughing?*

Audelia took this chance, and even as the sound continued, chilling her to the bone, she shoved her weight into another step.

Yes!

She broke free of whatever was holding her and took another step, twisting to see behind her—everything in her stilled.

The tunnel behind her was gone. No, not gone, blocked. Where once was the sight of the ocean and the rest of the sea walk, now was a fathomless black hole.

Her knees threatened to buckle again. *No. No. No. No.*

She was trapped.

Tears began to form in her eyes as she turned to face the thing in the tunnel with her. She would die here. This was her end. Not at the hands of her ex-boyfriend and whatever revenge he had to keep her as his plaything forever. No, it was here in a sea tunnel, by a fucking Shadow.

She took a step back again, if this was her final stand, like hell would she give it a fair chance, she would fight, she would fuck, she didn't know what she would do, but starting, she wouldn't let it reach her easily.

A shaft of light caught her eye then, the last vestiges of

twilight casting their final applause. She hid her gasp of relief as Audelia watched it dance along the tunnel wall as if light was getting in. Then...then that meant...

There! The tunnel where the creature had come from, the exit it, was still there if she could somehow get around it. She could run like hell. Audelia could run and hope that she could reach the dojo or maybe the closest business to her that was still open. This early in the season, some closed early. But maybe. Just maybe someone would still be open.

Hope surged inside her.

Audelia took a stealing breath and moved; she had a plan. She would dash around as wide as the tunnel would allow her and hopefully skirt around the creature. That bulky thing shouldn't be able to shift as quickly, even if it is half-corporal. With it to her back, she would run full tilt toward the end of the tunnel and whatever freedom she could find.

She had just skirted the creature, the wall she had just been leaning against before, to her left as she ran, only for something to slam into her right side and shove her against the wall. Audelia screamed in pain as the bite of cement slapped her skin. She gasped for air as the force that had shoved her pinned her in place.

Biting back another whimper, Audelia fought against whatever held her to the wall. Looking down, she could see whisping bands of black that stretched around her body and pinned her, every moment had her screaming in pain and fear as the band tightened like a python.

Oh gods. She had been so close. Freedom had been *right* there....

Ice.

Pure biting ice brushed over her face, and she looked up at

the creature's whisping black form hovering in front of her. With it closer now, she could see two deep bloodstone eyes staring at her. They seemed to float in the swirling abyss of black. Evil.

This thing was pure fucking evil, and it had her in its grasp.

She was going to die. Oh gods. Tears began to fall as the heavy grief of never seeing Shawn, never telling him how she felt. Never telling Lila how much she had cherished their friendship, Mara and Alexander. They would never know how much she loved them like they were her parents.

It was gone.

Everything was gone.

"Please…. please…don't hurt me…" She whimpered—one last plea before the end.

The bands tightened, and then a voice filled her head. It was like a lover's caresses dipped in poison. *You will be mine.*

Her body shook in pain, in fear, in heavy grief that burned deep in her soul. Her breathing was harsher now, as if she couldn't get all the air in her lungs.

Then she watched in horror as a clawed-whisped hand reached toward her; it curled, and then she was screaming again.

Pure agony coursed through her body at the brittle frost on her skin as it brushed its claw along her cheek. Gods, it hurt. She felt the skin on her cheek blister, and the coppery taste of blood filled her mouth. She choked on it.

The power inside her unfurled in response. It snarled and snapped at the ice, threatening to destroy her. The inferno rose. She could feel the fever all over her body as invisible flames surged around her.

Her body felt so damn drained and weak, even as the

raging tundra of flames built inside her. If this creature didn't kill her, then this fire, power, whatever it was inside would. It felt like raging death.

She closed her eyes as the pain became too much. Then, a voice filled her head. Not the poisonous dell, but a voice warm as chocolate. *Open your eyes, my star. It's okay.*

She shook her head; she didn't want to see the creature again. She wanted her family; she wanted Shawn's strong arms around her. Audelia didn't want to see the dark of the death to come. Tears streamed down her face as she felt a phantom touch against her cheek.

The pain was suddenly gone. Where there was biting unbearable pain, now was nothing. *Open your eyes.*

This time, she obeyed.

All the air rushed back into her lungs as Audelia stood where she had been moments before in the tunnel. *What the fuck?*

Turning in the spot, Audelia could see through both ends of the tunnel. Everything looked exactly like it had before. Even the last vestiges of twilight were still making their last bow of the evening. She reached a hand to touch the cheek the creature had touched.

Instead of bubbled, painfully marred skin, all she felt was smooth skin. She lifted the arm that had slammed into the cement, expecting to see red and bits of broken skin from the uneven cement. Nothing.

She was unmarked. Even that feverish feeling was gone. That strange primordial power vanished as if it had never been. Nothing was wrong with her. It didn't make sense. The thing had shoved her, banded her to the wall, and then touched her with a burning, icy touch that she thought would kill her.

Yet, she stood where she had been, just before the noise from behind her had triggered whatever that had been.

What the actual fuck?

Was she going insane?

Had she imagined it?

No, there was no way.

She had felt the pain, felt the fear and grief of loss viscerally. Shaken by everything, Audelia walked toward the end of the tunnel, wanting to get the fuck out of this place as quickly as she could.

Even though her legs felt like jelly, she made it out of the tunnel and paused as the wind picked up a little and drifted over her skin. It carried the smell of ozone and salt. The storm was closer now. It probably would make landfall by the time class was over. She used the monotony of a spring storm to calm the rest of her racing thoughts and thunderous heart.

She was a warrior, after all. She wouldn't let whatever that thing had been, real or not, tear her under. She would rise above. She would conquer it just like she had other monsters in her life.

With that renewed sense of bravery, Audelia made her way to the red glow of the sword in the dojo window a few blocks away.

CHAPTER SEVEN

Audelia felt like she had control over herself as the front of the dojo came into view. *Hoped* was probably the better word for it because that sleeping fire inside seemed to stir under her skin. But she could do this, and she had to.

If she could pull herself together after Kage had beaten and raped her to the edge of nothing, she could rally after being attacked by some shadow creature. She was a warrior.

Looking up at the soft colors of the white stone face of the dojo and its adjoining main gym, she recalled the feeling of safety this place gave her. Even the deep glowing neon of the sword was a comfort, and it was the beacon in the dark.

Audelia remembered the first time she walked through those glass doors. She had been eight and still grieving the loss of her parents and the upheaval of her life. Everything had felt so sharp that she kept getting in fights, and then Shawn.

She suddenly realized that Shawn was the reason for everything good in her life. Even as an eight-year-old boy, he had reached out a hand and given her what she needed to heal. Audelia didn't know what she would do if he weren't in her life.

He had been the one to tell her of the class, and she begged Mara to take her. When she walked through those doors, it was like every hard edge suddenly dulled. Even now, it was hard to describe the sense of peace that being there had brought her.

Over the years, she used this place as her balm for life. Yes, The Glade was a more significant part of that balm, but here, she could let everything out.

For an orphan who never really fit in, this was a place where she was normal. Where she fit. Alexander was a big part of that, too. He was the father she had always craved. Even in her mid-twenties, she still could not recall her father.

Was he a good man? Would he have taught her how to ride a bike? Read her stories at bedtime? Held her when she cried?

Mara never really liked to talk about her parents, so after a while, she stopped asking. It hurt more to ask anyway. So, instead, she focused on the parents she had. Mara and Alexander.

Walking into the cool air of the dojo, Audelia realized that was one of the biggest reasons why she was so upset about what she had seen on that porch. That if the man was Alexander--doubt was still there, because Mara had called him Bronn--if they had been lying this whole time, carrying on a secret affair. Audelia didn't know if she would handle that well.

Audelia tore her thoughts from it and was so tired of thinking of the possible betrayal. It was becoming too much.

She took in the space around her. Audelia helped a few years back when he updated the space. Alexander had pulled the cool blues and warm creams from the main gym into the dojo. She had come over every day to help, at least once it reached the point where Audelia *could* help. Still, it had been a lot of enjoyable, eventful months.

The memory had her smiling as she walked along the path that led to the locker rooms. It had taken weeks of remodeling, especially when the tatami mats on the floor had taken an entire month longer than promised. The mats were worth it, and Alexander had designed them so that every few feet were blocks of deep blue amidst the buttercream primary mat color. It had been a genius move, but she remembered how frustrated Alexander got when he was called by the company, telling him that it would be just another week. That had become a *weekly* occurrence until, finally, these beautiful mats arrived.

Walking into the small dojo locker room, she recalled more of the memories of the remodel. When the mats finally arrived, that had been a fun week of installing; she recalled as she skirted the edge of one of those blocks, the bonding agent for the mats to install them had refused to cure in the time frame, and that smell. *Oh, gods.* She laughed as she walked to the locker she usually used. That smell had clung to them for *weeks*, and not just them; the gym next door also had a heavy dose. Audelia remembered helping make several apology fliers to customers, and she and Shawn had pranked Alexander by making this bright pink basket full of clothes pins, with a sign done by Lila saying: *For your convenience, take one. We know we smell, sorry.*

Alexander had burst out laughing when a customer had

come up to him and thanked him for the plug, but complained that it made it hard to breathe through reps. One of her best pranks yet, she thought as she opened her locker with a smile and grabbed her dojo shoes.

Audelia sat down humming, and the memory had brought some of the remaining shadows of the day from her. She switched her shoes for the deep blue of martial arts shoes. She didn't always need to wear these, but from what she knew of tonight's class, they would be more practical than going barefoot.

With them on, Audelia grabbed her outside shoes from the floor and stood. She placed them in the soft grey metal locker, along with her bag and her phone. Thinking about it, she quickly shut the phone off. The last thing she needed tonight was the distraction of her phone ringing during class. So, having it off worked best.

Audelia worked out some of the tension in their shoulders as she walked into the main dojo. The smell of cypress and white lily wafted through the air from the burning incense on the small Shinza altar placed against the east-facing wall. The subtle undertones of the lemon verbena cleaner used on the mats added to the aromatic ambiance. She always enjoyed the smell here; it brought this sense of home to her—a belonging.

Audelia headed toward the back wall where the hall to the office and the main gym were. She stopped, taking in the last change from the remodel—the mural.

Once the painting and the flooring had finally finished, Alexander had asked Shawn if he could do something for the back wall. Alexander knew that Shawn had been itching to make a mural somewhere in town, but no one had wanted one at the time. Audelia still recalled how excited Shawn was that he would get the chance to show the world his art.

The ending result was fantastic; Shawn had taken the dojo and gym's names to heart and created a giant flaming sword along the wall; even years later, it looked brand new, the swirls of oranges, reds, and brilliant yellows that made up the flames. They looked so damn real that if you touched them, it would burn you. Shawn had poured his heart into the work, and it showed.

Just below the mural beside the open hall was a white folding table; Alexander must have set it up earlier. Sitting on top of the table were a dozen prop knives; Audelia picked one up. She liked the weight of it, how it felt like a small extension of herself, flipping it a few times, catching it by the hilt with the precision of years of practice. Smiling, she placed it on the table again and turned toward the lit hallway to Alexander's office.

The glint of metal caught her eye as she walked past the equipment room just inside the hall. Audelia paused to look at the wall of different training blades for the more experienced classes. Over the years, Alexander upgraded those as well. When he first started teaching blade classes, it had just been daggers and short swords, but as its popularity grew, it ranged from halberds to small daggers. Audelia even remembered a class taught by Shawn's uncle. She recalled that he had been visiting from Japan on one of Soba's many visits over the years. Shawn had been bragging about his uncle's skills from the temple he worked at, and Alexander convinced him to teach a class on Katanas.

Audelia wondered, idly walking away from the glint of the blades, if maybe sometime soon they would do another class on katanas; Shawn's uncle had said they barely breached the surface of what they could learn. Or perhaps she and Shawn would finally take Soba up on her offer and go to Japan and learn there.

She walked toward the office door, noticing it was slightly ajar and the light was on inside. Taking a few steady breaths, Audelia gathered the courage to go inside. She knew he wouldn't mind if she just walked inside, but she was suddenly nervous. *Could she handle being around him right now? Should she have even come to class with all this going on?*

The sound of grunts coming from the cracked door to the main gym just down the hall that connected both buildings made her attention waver from opening the door the rest of the way. *Odd*, the gym is closed right now. Changing her mind from seeking out Alexander, she made her way to the end of the hall, opening the connecting door to the main gym. Like some invisible tether was pulling her toward whoever was on the other side of that door. Not many would get access to the gym through this hall.

The sound of grunts grew louder as she pushed the door open. There was Shawn going at a hanging bag near the door she had just opened. He was shirtless, his muscles glistening with sweat and bunching in delicious waves as he hit the bag repeatedly in seamless strikes.

Her mouth dried out as she leaned against the door, watching, mesmerized by his lethal beauty. The movements brought her attention to the tattoos on his upper shoulders and upper arms. Audelia noticed a few new ones on his left shoulder as the skin pulled taut in a thrown punch. She couldn't quite make them out, but they were certainly new. She recalled him saying he had been working on his sleeve again. It was like watching a tapestry of art roll with every motion of his upper body.

It was taking everything in her not to go and touch those ripples. To feel the weight and sheer force in every movement. So, like a damn creeper, she stood and watched him. Her racing heart still beat like crazy, but it had changed from the panic and fear of before to a raging lust as Audelia enjoyed the view before her.

Thud, Thud, Thud.

Audelia held back the gasp as he increased his speed and the power in his hits as if he was trying to get something out. She wasn't sure which he was going for, whether to beat it out or it into submission. She had never seen him put such force into his moves before. The focus he was holding was intoxicating.

Clearing her throat to get his attention, that she suddenly very much wanted on herself, even if she was very much enjoying her voyeurism. Not that it mattered because he was still beating the bag harder and harder. It was swinging like a wicked pendulum and was starting to worry her; it would smack him in the face if he didn't slow down.

Audelia decided he needed to see her because either his music was too loud, as she noticed the black bud in his ear upon better inspection of the rest of him, or he was in such a hyper-focus of those hits that nothing else registered for him. She supposed it was probably both, so she walked into the gym and went to a bench press near the bag; it would place her in his focus.

She sat down and waited, watching. And because she was only human, she enjoyed the new angle of watching him. Another benefit to this view was the added to the sight of his muscles as they bunched and released with every swing. From this angle, she noticed that he had more than just the new tattoos on his arm and shoulder because they were revealed in small moments. It was on his chest over his heart; it looked like a phoenix and a dragon, but he was moving back and forth too much to really see it.

It took all of a minute for Shawn to notice she was sitting there. She knew the minute he had because his face had gone from that bunched focus to a giant grin as he caught the bag on the swing back and settled it. "Hey beautiful, when did you get here?" He reached for his towel sitting on a nearby bench and wiped the sweat from his face and neck. *Pity,* she thought; she really was enjoying the look of him covered in sweat.

Still slightly speechless from seeing him like that and lingering on what had occurred in that tunnel, Audelia couldn't put it into words. She wouldn't even touch the rest of the day with a ten-foot pole if she could help it. If she even thought of it, she would fall into a puddle of tears because of all the fear and unknowns in her life. Audelia wanted to stay as strong as she could manage, especially in front of him. It wasn't that she thought he would judge, but she didn't want him to see her as this broken thing. It was her biggest fear every time she leaned on him.

That resounding *would this be it? The moment he decides she isn't worth it?* She didn't like that she even had insecurity with him. Shawn had never given her any indication of that ever, but it still lingered.

So, she merely nodded and looked down, and she knew if she looked at him, her cheeks would be as red as her eyes had been earlier. A shift of movement in front of her, and then Shawn was there, his fingers under her chin, making her look at him. She was met with her bright emerald eyes and the slight red hue from his working out. He was fucking breathtaking.

Audelia watched as his face went from joy at seeing her to pure concern as his dark brows bunched and concern crept into the edge of his eyes. "Del? What's wrong?"

"Nothing. I'm fine." She didn't want to talk about it, so her eyes glanced at the still softly swinging bag. "What has you working out before class?" She tried to deflect. It may have been childish, but she didn't know if she could handle this conversation. That tip of the blade balancing act was starting to form before her again.

"Just needed to let some shit off my chest. Now stop deflecting Storm." He tipped her chin up again; she had tried to look down again. His eyes had gone darker as she took them in again. "What happened?" His voice had even dropped to a thick velvet tone.

"I told you. I'm fine. Just a long day." She felt so damn defeated. That tipping point coming toward her like a bullet train.

"Bullshit." Audelia flinched slightly at his harsh tone.

He moved closer to her, kneeling in front of her now. Shawn's movements were gentle as he pulled her to him. Audelia slipped from the bench to kneel on the floor with him. Their knees touching. She shook her head, trying to fight the tears threatening to fall. Shawn cupped her cheeks then, his thumbs working soothing back-and-forth motions across the arch of the bone.

"Audelia, I know you're not okay. My girl comes into this gym and the dojo with the biggest smile on her face *every* time. This place and the Glade are your happy places." *Fuck.* He was right. She always was smiling here. Yes, she smiled in the bookstore, but it was different here. Even at the Glade, it was different.

These were her *axis mundi*. If someone were to crack her open to find where her world revolved, what pulled the parts of her gravity, it would say *The Glade and Swords of Flame.* Her family and Shawn, Lila, were important, as were books; they filled her soul. Moored her. But *these two places* pulled her into the orbit of her life. Without them, she would shatter. Her ability to weather a storm would be gone.

Shawn's voice pulled her back from her thoughts; it was soft and warm, and she leaned into it. "Storm, baby girl, *talk* to me. I can see it in your eyes; something happened. I can't help if I don't know what happened." His thumbs worked back and forth; she focused on their comfort. She used it to fight the rising tide inside her.

Audelia leaned into him wanting to hide her face, burying it in his chest. Her resolve began to break, and every carefully laid brick crumbled from the wall around her. It took only a heartbeat before Shawn pulled her closer and wrapped his arms around her to hold her; for a few minutes, she just leaned into his touch, her fingers digging into his back.

He kissed her hair and cupped the back of her head to his chest as he spoke softly, so full of love that it obliterated the remaining bricks. "I've got you. I promise I will always have you."

Audelia broke down in his arms; she didn't talk, just let the emotions of the past few days wash over her again and again. Shawn held her through it all, not saying another word; he just held her, giving him all his love and strength. One hand on her back, working back and forth in soothing motions, while his other hand gently cupped her head as he kissed her hair ever so often.

Her breathing was harsh as the torrent of tears and emotions started to ebb, and all that was left in her was a soul-deep numbness.

She pulled back, knowing she probably looked a mess, with tears falling slower now. Audelia looked at Shawn, whose eyes swam with unspoken emotions and worry for her. She gave him a small, broken smile. "Sorry...for crying on you." Suddenly feeling ashamed of how she was acting, Audelia looked away, focusing on a spot on the rubber mat-covered floor.

"Hey, don't do that." Shawn gripped her chin again, his touch gentle and firm. He guided her to look at him. "Don't hide from me."

She took a deep, shaky breath and just looked at him, at a loss for words. Her throat hurt from crying so much. Audelia just leaned her forehead against his, using it to center herself.

"I'm sorry." She whispered again.

"Storm, you're worrying me. This isn't like you. What happened, baby?" Her eyes flicked to his as they leaned together, never breaking the contact of their foreheads.

"I'll tell you later, okay? We have class." She started to stand, her legs shaky again. All that resolve she had gained after the tunnel suddenly disappeared, leaving Audelia with a deep ache.

Shawn stood with her, his body still wrapped with hers like he couldn't bear to let her go entirely. She took advantage for a moment and leaned into his warmth. "Del? Are you sure you want to go to class? We could cut, go grab a pizza, and do a movie marathon or something at your house."

"No, I need this. I need the class. We'll talk after, I promise." Audelia simply smiled and kissed his cheek, then turned to head back to the dojo. She needed the class, not just to re-center herself but because she was growing more worried about things to come. Between the shadow stuff and the threats from very realistically Kage, she had to be ready.

Even if the idea of just going home with Shawn and pretending everything was okay sounded like a dream, Audelia was a warrior, and warriors kept going even when the world weighed them down.

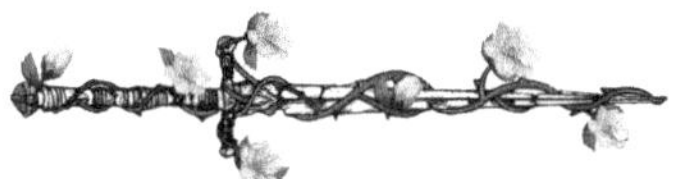

Shawn watched Audelia walk away, and all he wanted to do was run after her, pull her back into his arms, and guard her from whatever was making her look like the world was ending. He couldn't stand it. When he had seen the redness around her gorgeous blue eyes and the tears fighting for release, it had shattered him.

He felt so helpless when it came to her. The balancing act of being just her friend when he wanted to be everything for her. If he had let her keep with the deflecting, he knew without a shadow of a doubt. He would have told her, and she was the reason he was hitting that bag so damn hard his knuckles ached.

Not out of anger, never anger. No, it was that all-encompassing need for her. To make her his, as he was hers. Always would be. It was getting harder to maintain the friendship line.

Too many times since the movie, he had debated on texting

her, going over to the house, and just telling her it all. Laying himself bare for Audelia. But she had seemed listless lately, and he didn't want to burden her.

No, that was wrong. He was too scared of that beautiful creature telling him she only saw him as a friend or, worse.... a *brother*. So, he had come in earlier than usual, got the key from Alexander for the gym, and started in on the bag. Shawn had briefly considered asking Alexander to spare and have someone lay him out. But that would have resulted in very likely injury because, in his current state, Shawn wouldn't have backed down. He would have kept going till he could no longer stand.

Shawn walked to the locker room in the main gym and jumped into a quick five-minute shower. He knew he would be covered in sweat again soon, but he needed a moment to cool down after Audelia. Changing into his usual outfit of a muscle shirt, athletic shorts, and martial arts shoes. Shawn headed back to the dojo, locking the gym behind him.

He tossed the keys back on Alexander's desk, finding it empty. Shrugging it off Shawn went to put his bag into the lockers upfront. He felt the tension in the air. Looking around as he reached the locker room. Shawn took in the odd sight of Alexander and Audelia keeping their distance.

Something had happened.

Tossing his bag into the locker next to the one he knew Audelia always used, Shawn stepped back into the dojo and walked to her.

"Everything okay?" He whispered as people started to file in from outside and to the locker room to change shoes.

"Yup," Audelia emphasized the *p* with a loud pop. *Shit.* That couldn't be good. He knew her enough to know that it was her. *If you fuck with me right now, you'll end up on your back and your balls aching.* Not in a good way, either.

So, Shawn just nodded and started to stretch out for class. Helping her with some of her own stretches when she asked for help. He used the touch to center himself. To make sure she was okay enough to be there. Not that he would make her leave. No, he just needed to know how much to prepare for. Making sure she was okay, in whatever way she needed, that was what he would be, what he would do.

Shawn watched Alexander on the other side of the room; the man was huge and imposing, with broad shoulders and muscles that rivaled Greek heroes from mythology. Clearly, whatever had gone down while Shawn had showered had made the man nervous. Alexander kept moving back and forth on long legs like he had no real direction when he would pause to look at something and then pulled at the blonde hair he kept in a bun with the sides shaved. Shawn looked at Audelia, who seemed so damn lost that he was debating his earlier thoughts of making her leave with him. But he knew no one would keep her from what she had set her mind to. Gods, help them all.

A short time later, Alexander called everyone to attention for the beginning of the class. Everything seemed fine, except that Shawn could tell Audelia was just going through the motions. The usual glow that came from her during class was gone.

The longer Shawn noticed the lack of the spark in her and that growing tension every time Alexander got closer or weighed in her stance or her moves. The closer it seemed to him that Audelia was going to snap.

Shawn was watching her go through the motions of the newest combination with her partner and wincing as she kept aiming the blade for his balls or throat every time she took him down. When Alexander walked over to watch Audelia and her partner go through the moves, giving instructions as they went. Turning Alexander cut Shawn with a look of *get back to your own task.* As he turned, he saw Alexander call Audelia and her partner, whose name Shawn honestly couldn't remember; he wasn't a regular.

Over the din of everyone else doing their moves and the shouts of takedowns, he didn't catch the words that were said. All he saw was Alexander pull her to the side and make some sort of comment that had Audelia bunching her nose in disgust.

Then, the pair were shouting at each other, causing the entire dojo to go stalk still and turn to watch.

"Like you have fucking room to talk! I know your fucking lying!" Audelia was shouting and shoving at Alexander now. *What the fuck?* Shawn started to run to them. He didn't like this. Didn't like the storm that was breaking; he could have sworn flames were licking at her arms.

"You need to knock it the fuck off right now." Shawn had never heard Alexander raise his voice in all the years he had known the man, let alone at Audelia. Shawn was sure that the man loved her like a daughter. Then again, the daggers they were currently giving each other it was the nail on the head.

Father and daughter fighting just more intense than most fights people would see. Shawn wondered if the two would start trading physical blows.

"I'll knock it off when you grow a fucking pair and tell the gods damn truth." As if his thoughts had manifested it. Shawn watched as Audelia launched herself at Alexander, landing a decent right hook straight into his jaw. He could hear the crunch of the jaw from where he stood.

Fuck.

"My office now! Shawn, make her go." Alexander turned toward Shawn then, his eyes were dark flames of anger and what looked like small amounts of despair. Then, in clear dismissal of Shawn. Alexander went to stare at her again.

Shawn bowed his head and walked to the woman he loved. He placed a gentle hand on her arm. "Come on, Storm, let's go get a drink from his office cooler." Her eyes met him, the tears there, the utter defeat that had crept back again, making her blue eyes a turbulent storm and him wanting to turn back to Alexander. The man who he respected with everything he had, Shawn wanted to fucking punch him for whatever had just fucking happened.

Shawn pulled her to him as they walked toward the office, with the whispered words of the other patrons trailing them. As Shawn and Audelia walked into the office, he heard Alexander's voice echo through the hall. "That's it for the night. I am sorry for cutting the class short, but I will gladly give refunds and call you all for a reschedule." He shut the door after that, turning back to her.

Audelia turned to Shawn, her tears streamed down her face, and she looked so gods damn haunted; Shawn had his arms around her instantly as she fell apart in his arms again.

CHAPTER EIGHT

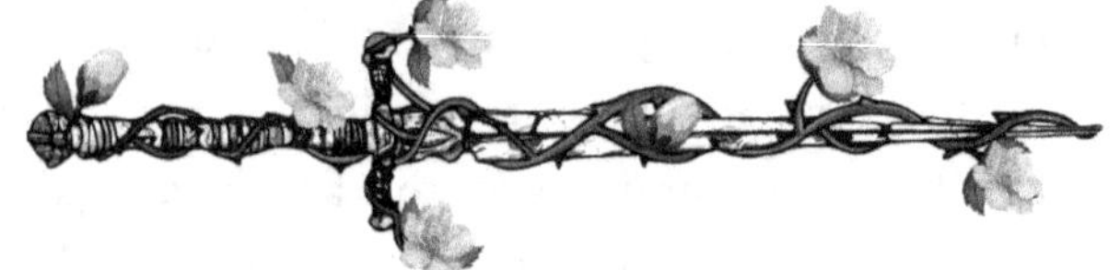

How had everything gone so wrong?

He wasn't still entirely sure what had happened. When he had walked into the dojo and seen Audelia, she had looked antsy, and her eyes were puffy like she had been crying. Bronn had immediately gone to her, his baby girl. His niece. It still killed him that because of a cruel twist of fate, he had to pretend like the young woman crying wasn't his own blood.

Bronn had tried to soothe her, but every word seemed to bounce off of her and made her even more agitated, so he had relented and begun to do checks for the class. They were unnecessary; Bronn had a system that ensured everything was in order far before the beginning of a class.

Even when Audelia's best friend Shawn had come in from the locker rooms, the air still felt tense. Bronn could tell that the man wanted to question him about why Audelia was so upset; he had the feeling it was more than just because his best friend was upset. He knew that look, the look of a man in love with a woman he was scared to lose.

But Bronn would bet all the gold in the halls of Astorian that Shawn would never lose Audelia.

As the class had gone on, the tension had gotten worse, Bronn had even sent a quick text to Mara asking if something had happened that day. She had replied that nothing she knew of. That had caused Bronn to do the stupidest thing he could have done. He had approached her as she was getting a little too rough with her sparring partner.

He should have fucking known better. She was so much like her father that Bronn had forgotten…. So, when he had pushed just a little too much, she had exploded.

Fuck.

Bronn had lost his temper with her, yelling until it became too much, so he made her go to the office, sending Shawn with her. Shortly after, he dismissed the class. He hated canceling a class, but he was still seeing red and needed time.

So here he was, grabbing his phone and keys from the locker up front, like a thief in his own damn gym. Thank the gods that he didn't leave them in the office like usual. Maybe the fates knew this was coming, and they had decided to spar him from further scorching of his niece's wrath.

Bronn sent a quick text to Shawn asking him to please lock up the dojo before they left. Shawn knew where the spare set was kept in the office, so he said they should take their time. He was going to clear his head.

He was halfway down the street when he realized his greater blunder. It was meeting night. *Fuck me.* In the chaos, he had forgotten.

He pulled his phone back out and sent it out to the group chat, saying that they needed to change the meeting spot. Mathias would be pissed. He fucking hated not getting to see her from a distance. If this whole damn situation was challenging on anyone when it came to Audelia, it was him. Their bond was unlike anything Bronn had seen apart from a mating bond.

That's why Bronn ensured that most of the meeting nights happened right after a class. So Mathias and the rest of the knights could see her. To know she was truly okay.

Ten minutes later, Bronn was pounding on the back door of a reconstructed Victorian house. A moment later, the door swung open to reveal the tall, lanky figure of Gideon Fedare. "Well, well. What did the illustrious general do to fuck up this time?" Gideon leaned against the frame, his heart-shaped mouth pulled into a cocky grin, making his pale grey eyes sparkle. *Smug bastard.*

"Cut the poor man some slack, Gid. Not all of us walk around as perfect as our asses." A second man stood slightly behind Gideon, and he was a foot taller than Gideon and as broad as Bronn was. His strong-jawed face was all smiles as he wrapped a tattooed arm around Gideon's shoulders. "Hey, boss."

"Alaric." He nodded to the blonde-haired, blue-eyed jokester of their unit. "You two going to fucking move? Or are we going to keep standing in the doorway as the storm finally hits?" Bronn snarled; he wasn't really in the mood for those two and their respective antics.

Both men laughed and shifted to let Bronn inside—the space's warmth spread over him as he closed the door behind him. Stacks and stacks of books of varying ages covered the shelves in the room. The group made their way through the storage room and into the central space of the bookstore. It was currently after hours, so no one but them was inside, but still, it felt like all eyes were on him.

He nodded toward the stairs he knew led to Gideon's apartment above. "Let's go where no one can see us here."

"What's wrong, Bronn? Scared someone will see you know how to read as well as punch?" Gideon snickered as he made his way up to unlock his door. He was currently clad in dark slacks and a dark blue oxford sweater; Bronn always found it funny when his best friend dressed like he was purely a scholar. Though, he guessed it fit who Gideon pretended to be here, the quiet bookstore owner. No one would know that Gideon was one of the fiercest warriors their realm had ever seen.

"Fuck off, when are the others getting here?" He growled as they walked through the door into the apartment. Gideon's home was all dark woods and deep greens, with books on every available surface. Just like he kept his keep back in their realm. The thought of going back home had grief making its way back into his heart.

They had lost so much over the years, and he thought as he took a spot on one of the tufted hunter-green couches in the open-spaced apartment, not just their homes but their sense of self. Here, they all had to pretend they didn't know the most important person in their lives. Audelia.

She was to be protected at all costs. So, they kept their distance, even though he hated to. Sometimes in the darkest moments, especially like right now, Bronn wanted to damn it all. Damn, every carefully laid protection that Waldrom had made to keep her safe and go to that blue craftsman with the wrap porch and pull *both* his girls into his arms.

Because it wasn't just Audelia; Bronn had lost, but Mara as well.

His wife.

His mate.

His gods damn everything.

They had to pretend to be strangers; for almost fifteen fucking years, he had seen and held his wife in his arms for mere moments. When they had landed in this world all those years ago, they had nothing. No memory of what had happened after the attack just flashes, and then Waldrom, his brother-in-law, speaking in their heads, telling them that Audelia would not remember them. She would know Mara but no others. They could not be near her for too long, only small doses. Nothing long enough that if agents of Lefrain gained a foothold, they would be led directly to her.

Their princess, his niece, his fucking goddaughter, and according to Waldrom, the sole person who could one day save their realm.

So here they were, hiding away in Gideon's apartment doing the meeting they did once a week. That was another thing about the rules Waldrom had placed. They could be around each other as much as they wanted. But not Audelia, and not Mara, because she was the one raising Audelia alone. That last part fucking gutted him daily.

His beautiful mate had to raise their niece alone and had to navigate this strange world alone. The moment he saw Waldrom again, he was punching the damn wizard.

His thoughts were interrupted when the loud bang of a door slamming against a wall echoed in the apartment. Looking away from the window, he hadn't even realized he had been staring at, in his revelry, to see the two figures coming through the doorway. The younger of the two had his russet-red hair pulled back from his lean face; his matching russet eyes were glassy with apologies. Apologizes Bronn knew were meant for the larger of the two, who was barreling toward him with rage on his face.

Mathias was not just a large man but a god's damn giant. All thick corded muscles and lethal power. Bronn had only moments before he was hauled off his spot on the couch and thrusted painfully against the wall. If it had been anyone else, Bronn would have laid into them, beaten them down into submission. But there was no taming the dark fire that was Mathias.

"What the fuck did you do!" Mathias's voice cut through him like the edge of a knife. His russet eyes swirled with shadow. Even here in this strange world bereft of magic, those shadows that lived in his very blood had refused to leave. Bronn knew the male could not use them, but they still answered his call on occasion, and the strength in his fucking pinky could still lay waste to the strongest.

Defeated, Bronn hung his head as best as he could manage in the hold Mathias had him in. His voice echoed it. "I don't know."

"Brother, let him go. We all know you're pissed, but please don't break him. I don't want to deal with Mara and her wrath if her precious love monkey is broken." Skye spoke from somewhere near them. Bronn didn't keep his eyes off Mathias. Mathias was big, but he could strike like an asp if he needed to.

Mathias seemed to debate momentarily before he sighed and let go of Bronn. "Fucking idiot." He snarled before stalking across the room and taking up a spot leaning against a bookshelf. It made him seem even larger and more vicious, leaning like that before all those books. Bronn rubbed at his throat before he looked around the room at his men. The only ones missing were the twins. "Where are Micah and Ezreal?"

Skye spoke as he plopped down on one of the hunter-green tufted couches. He was the picture of nonchalance. "They texted saying they were running on a lead, something about Shades being spotted a few counties over."

Shit.

Bronn pulled his phone from his back pocket and looked over the message from the twins. Shit. Shit. If Shades were only a few counties over, then they'd found her.

"I don't wanna be the bearer of even worse news, but I think they are already here," Alaric spoke from his spot on a stool at the kitchen island across the room. His usual jovial countenance was gone, replaced by wariness.

Bronn collapsed into the nearest chair; the world spun around him for a moment. Mathias growled. "What does that mean."

He was right. Maybe Alaric was wrong, maybe just maybe it wasn't a shade. Then Bronn thought about how Audelia looked today; it wasn't just upset, under the yelling and the tears of hate toward him. Bronn had seen fear there, too. Not just fear of angering him, but something else.

"Two nights ago, I was keeping an eye on our girl. She had gone to The Glade like she tends to do. Her and that guy, the one that hangs around her all the time, the one that is clearly in love with her." Mathias growled at that, making Skye and Gideon snicker. "Anyway. It was late. She hadn't come out for hours, so I was going to go in there, check things out."

"What happened?" Bronn knew if he let Alaric go when he was nervous like this, it would drag forever before they got what information they needed. He needed to know. Needed to know how bad shit was about to get. *Fuck, had they come near Mara too?*

"She came running out when it was storming pretty bad; Audelia looked terrified. Her magic was riding her a little, but not enough. She slammed into me, and fuck. I have never seen her so shaken." Alaric's voice broke as he was lost in memory. "I held her for a moment; I know I know against the rules, but she was scared and almost fell, and fuck, I needed a moment to know she was okay. But, behind her, in the woods behind her, I saw them."

"How many?" Mathias spoke, and Bronn could have sworn the shadows in the room shifted.

"Six."

"Are you sure? It was storming pretty badly the other night; maybe you counted wrong with her there and the low lighting." Gideon asked Bronn, who could see him working from every angle, taking in the variables.

"Positive. I wouldn't slack on this. Not when it comes to her; they remained in the dark, and none followed her home. I'm unsure if it was because I was there or she was riding her magic that night. But I followed her home, and none followed either of us."

"Damnit!" A loud crash boomed through the room as all heads turned to Mathias, standing with his fist through the wall beside a bookshelf, the contents of which were now around him in a heap. Mathias didn't even notice he was bleeding as he stood there heaving, anger radiating off him in waves.

He turned toward them all; the look on his face was beyond murderous; it was the face that haunted many. A beautiful monster, that's what Eudora and Mara used to joke about when talking about Mathias. Standing there now, his features sharper in his rage, the way shadows seemed to stretch around his body in whispers. He was both.

"Could you not destroy my home, please?" Gideon spoke and crossed to begin picking up his books from the floor, not even caring that Mathias was radiating malice that made people cry when faced with him on a battlefield.

"Fuck off. I told you not to trust the damn wizard, Bronn. I fucking told you. If we didn't have to keep our distance, those gods damn Shades would have never gotten even close to her." He prowled closer to Bronn then. In those steps, he became Death's Shadow. The nickname was given to him in jest but spoke true to all that faced him. "Where is she now?"

Bronn knew not to keep that from Mathias, especially now, and if Shades were here, Mathias was the perfect person to keep near her. "Probably still at the dojo with Shawn. After we fought or whatever the fuck happened. They remained while I came here; I was going to talk to her. But I couldn't bring myself to cause more pain than whatever was going on with her. Shawn will make sure she makes it home." Bronn still felt defeated thinking about the pain swimming in her blue eyes. It shattered him.

"Fuck that damn pup. I'm going now. Let me know when you pull your head out of your ass long enough to realize we're fucked; if she gets hurt, I swear to Morwena, I will fucking kill you, Bronn." With that, Mathias stormed out of the apartment. A few moments later, the echo of the back door to the shop slamming shut greeted them.

Those remaining sat in silence; they all agreed, even Bronn, that they shouldn't have taken everything Waldrom had said as fact. Yes, it had been to protect her, but Mathias was right.

All the distance did was eat at their hearts and put her in danger.

Standing, Bronn started to pace the room. His mind was running like crazy; every scenario played through him, and all ended in the same conclusion. Before he said it, Skye beat him to the catch. "We need to keep closer to her, and if this is the beginning, maybe we should keep a patrol at The Glade. If I were a betting man, that would be the easiest way to grab her."

"Agreed. Alaric, why didn't you say something to us sooner?" It was nagging at him. Alaric was usually quick to let them know when things happened. Hell, they had a growing list of pictures of the guys he had dragged into alleys and beat to a pulp for getting too close to Audelia.

"Sorry, boss. At first, I thought I was seeing things. Then, when no one else reported seeing anything off with her, I thought maybe I had imagined it. But then the twins sent in about sightings counties over..." He trailed off then, the guilt thick.

"It's fine. She was okay, and she was home last night." Last night......*Fuck*.

Had she seen them? He only went over when it was in the middle of the night, and Audelia's light had been off. Did she come down to talk to Mara? Bronn suddenly couldn't breathe again.

"I'm just going to add to the flames, but we fucking failed her," Alaric spoke, his voice taking on a deep edge to it. "She can't even go to the place that brings her comfort without being hunted by those fucking demons. What the fuck was the point of this?"

"Seriously, if they were going to find her anyway, why did we need to keep from her? I miss my little fire." Skye stood and walked to the fridge. It seemed so mundane, but Bronn knew Skye needed to keep his hands busy, and he didn't have his blades on him. Skye was like his older brother Mathias in that way, always needing to keep busy and having a deep kinship with Audelia.

Bronn slightly agreed with him, saying what the point was until Waldrom's voice filled his head. *The peace will not last; I cannot see the when, but eventually, Lefrain's Shades will find purchase; this spell is just to ensure it is harder for them to find Audelia.*

"We didn't fail her, Skye. Yes, it has sucked, and yes, they found her, but Waldrom knew it was only a matter of time. Us keeping the distance as hard as this shit has been, it was to keep her safe. Lefrain knows us, knows what we look like, and we would have been a beacon to her."

A resounding fuck went through the room as the men all hung their heads in defeat.

After a pause, Gideon spoke again, his voice sure and strong, "Bronn, it's time. You have to tell Mara, and the two of you must figure out how to tell Audelia. If the Shades are here, then it's time. I'll send word to the Druids; they'll know what our next steps are."

"No one tells my brother. He'll lose his damn shit if he finds out our way home is Druids. Not that I blame them, I don't fully trust them either after—well, you know."

"Agreed." Gideon, Alaric, and Bronn said in unison.

Bronn gave orders to the others before he began his journey to the other side of town to the blue craftsman with the wrap-around porch that held the two women he loved most.

His phone buzzed when he was a block from the house, and as he pulled it out, he saw a text from Mathias.

MATHIAS

They are still at the dojo; Audelia seems to be telling the pup something. I don't like the look he is giving her.

Bronn rolled his eyes at the overprotectiveness and responded before walking up the steps of the quiet house.

BRONN

Leave the boy alone. He loves her, and he protects her just like we do.

In more ways than them, he thought, as he unlocked the front door. The house was quiet as he made his way into the house. The living room was dark and quiet, but the soft notes of music drifted from upstairs. She must be in her room.

Moving up the stairs, Bronn prepared himself for how he would tell her. Gods, this was going to destroy her. He hated it.

Mara was a strong woman, but when it came to Audelia and everything that had happened, it was a toss of the coin on whether she would fall apart or become the fierce warrior he knew she could be.

The closer he got to her bedroom, the stronger the scent of eucalyptus, rose, and citrus filled his senses. His mate. His heart ached at the thought of seeing her soon.

Bronn knew what he would see when he opened her bedroom door, and the idea of her had him quickening his steps. Bronn enjoyed the view before him as he eased open her bedroom door.

Mara was curled up in a soft green blanket thrown over the cream duvet she was under, a book was propped up on a pillow, and in her hands was a bright pink mug with the words *This is my emotional support mug.* His heart ached at the memories of coming home from journeys, where he had to bring her a new book from whatever faraway place he had been. Preferably romance at her insistence. It was their ritual, one he missed dearly.

Just as he missed her dearly. Gods, he hated that to see her; he had to be a thief in the night. He missed hearing her laugh and seeing how her jade eyes lit up when she found a new book.

They had talked about it a few times over the years, dating in this realm. It would make sense here, a beautiful woman like herself falling for the man who her niece looked up to. Hell, even Audelia had hinted several times to both of them that they should just get married.

But even as they both craved each other, they didn't want to risk her.

They would never be able to live with the guilt if they found her too soon. Audelia had deserved a childhood before all the weight of their realm and kingdom were slung over her shoulders.

Mara shifted in her reading as Bronn continued as a silent voyeur from the doorway, still unnoticed. His breath caught as she shifted, and the blankets around her fell as she sat up, grabbing the book as if the spot she read had needed her to be closer. Her brown curls fell in graceful waves around her face.

The movement had always made his vision zero in on her sleep attire, and his mouth watered. The thin straps of the soft blue babydoll nightgown she wore had fallen off her shoulder a little, revealing more of her perfectly round breasts beneath. Bronn watched as a heavy sigh escaped her, and between her delicate brows were three little creases he desperately wanted to kiss away.

Mara was a beauty, but reading Mara was his favorite. When she was so caught up in the world between those pages, she began a damn goddess-given flesh. His body ached just looking at her. Gods, did he need her. To worship her body and forget all about duty, danger, and the looming death that probably awaited them back home.

"Gods, you're beautiful." He whispered when he could no longer remain quiet.

She gasped and dropped her book, knocking over the mug she had precariously placed on her bed. A look of pure joy and shock broke over her face as she launched herself at him.

He moved quickly to hold her in his arms. She was warm and so damn deliciously soft. Her slender, tanned arms wrapped around his neck as she hugged herself to him.

Bronn held her tightly, breathing in her scent. There was so much to say tonight. But, for just a moment. He needed just to be Bronn and Mara.

The rest could come later. So, he took the moment and pulled back and kissed her. He threw everything into that desperate kiss. She opened for him eagerly, a moan escaping her mouth as she kissed him back. For a moment, everything left. All the worry, the uncertainty. It was gone. As long as she was here in his arms, everything would be okay.

Sadly, she pulled back to look at him, her jade-green eyes searching his, her voice a whisper. "Bronn...my love? Why are you here?" Her questions were like a death knell, ending the fantasy that played in his head.

She knew.

He would not risk all of this for a moment of weakness. Gods, if only he were that sort of man. But duty. It always outweighed everything, especially when it came to protecting his niece. His Queen, now with his brother gone.

"Things...have occurred." He sighed, pulling her down to the bed with him. He held her hands tightly. Trying to use the touch to anchor him for what he was about to tell her.

"What things?" Her voice was barely a whisper. He hated the worry he would place on her, but she needed to know.

Taking a deep breath. He told her. Everything Alaric had told her. The suspicions the twins were following. And, how Audelia had seemed off today during class. He told her everything.

After, they sat in silence. The words seemed to echo around them. Taunting the fragile peace they had held these past fourteen years.

Maybe they had done this wrong. Perhaps they should have remained closer. Did they mess up? Did they already fail Audelia?

"I see." Mara sighed heavily. Her words sounded wearisome. She leaned her head on his shoulder.

"Did... Did your brother ever say what we should do if this occurred?" He hated asking. Hated the pain it would bring his love. She missed her brother. They had been close, and having to leave without knowing if he was alright had nearly killed her.

"No. Just that we would know, know when the time was right." Her eyes weren't focusing like she was searching her inner memories for anything that could help.

"If...If he did send someone or something here. Then, we will have no choice. She is in danger here. Without magic. Without her memories...." She trailed off as silent tears began to fall.

"My love...It's alright. We will do this. I have the men preparing. Someone will be following her daily now. And Skye is setting up by The Glade." He reassured her, pulling her into his lap as silent tears began to fall.

"Bronn...she is still so young. This will break her..." Mara whimpered and buried her face into his shoulder.

"No. She is strong. You have raised her to be strong. And she won't be alone. She'll have us." He held her tighter. Pulling her down onto the bed. He just held her as she cried.

Come what may, they will be ready. They would ensure she was safe even if the truth caused her to hate them. They would remain.

They would see her home at last.

Their Kingdom.

To whatever awaited them.

To Fate.

CHAPTER NINE

Audelia cried in Shawn's arms for what felt like hours. After Alexander had yelled at her, and demanded she go to his office, she had debated for a moment in causing a bigger scene and storming out into the night. But she had felt that if she left the dojo in that moment, she would use her upset to dictate her actions in such a way. Audelia worried it would destroy everything. She didn't want to lose the people she loved again.

So, she relented, feeling her body turn numb as she fought the tears welling in her eyes and let Shawn pull her to Alexander's office. She had watched the worry cross Alexander's face, and it broke a part of her.

The walk to the office felt like a lifetime, even with Shawn's strong arms around her. When the door closed, she felt everything uncoil, and she fell into his arms and wept.

In a fluid motion, Shawn grabbed her under her knee and

pulled her into his arms. he had moved them to the loveseat in the corner that, through her childhood, she had spent hours reading in whenever she came here to just be. When they sat, she had crawled into his lap and just cried more, his arms banded around her, with a hand brushing through her hair.

She must have fallen asleep for a moment because she opened her eyes to see she was still curled in his lap, but that heavy feeling was gone. Her eyes ached from the crying, but she felt a degree lighter than before. Shifting, she sat up, and her heart pounded as she looked at Shawn. He gave her a small smile, his arms still banded around her waist.

"You, okay?" His voice was soft and raspy. Still needing a minute, she just nodded.

"I need more than a nod, babe. What happened?" His eyes searched hers as he moved a hand to push a loose strand of her red hair that had fallen into her face. The soft touch made her body shiver.

She closed her eyes for a moment before she looked at him again. Audelia wanted to tell him everything she had planned on it, but then she saw Alexander, and everything had gone red. Audelia had lost it, but she felt so damn tired carrying everything around with her. It was becoming too much to bear alone.

"I—I need to tell you something." Her voice was a rasp as she tried to swallow the ashy feeling in her throat.

Shawn shifted closer to her and placed his palm on her cheek, his callused thumb rubbing across her cheekbone. "You can tell me anything, Storm. I promise."

His words were like a levy breaking inside her. With a calming breath, she stared into the depths of his emerald eyes and told him everything.

The odd dreams, the shadows that seemed to chase her, Kage texting her, the flowers, the man on the deck with her aunt, that she suspects is Alexander. It all came pouring out of her, and as every word passed her lips, she felt lighter and just a little braver.

As the last of her words spilled from the ether of her mind, silence weighed on them as they sat in the office. Her heart was pounding as she watched him take it all in. The silence was killing her, though.

It was eating at her as the clock on the wall ticked away; this would be the moment he left. Everything she had said was insane.

Shawn was so quiet, his eyes contemplative; when she could no longer take the silence, she stood, trying to hide the shakiness in her voice as she spoke. Hoping that her legs wouldn't give out, she started to walk to the desk where Alexander kept the key.

"If you want to leave, it's okay. I can lock up."

"Wha—" Before she could take another step from him, her words seemed to be the final tether on whatever he was thinking because he stood and pulled her to him. Shawn twisted her to face him again, and her heart hammered in her chest at how close they stood, at the sheer intensity in his eyes.

"I'm not going anywhere, Del. Never. I told you, I have you. I meant that."

"Oh. It's just you were so quiet, I thought...I thought maybe it was too much. It's all insane."

He laughed then; it was rich and full, and it made heat pool deep inside her. "Oh, it was definitely insane, but—but it fits. Yeah, it fits." He smiled at her and leaned forward to kiss her forehead before gripping her hands in his, lacing their fingers together.

"Fits? What part of all that fits? Fits what?" She pulled back to look at him better, and he seemed so, so damn calm it was unnerving. Here she was freaking out, and he was standing there like she told him the sky was blue.

"Fits you. You are extraordinary, Audelia; you always have been. Even my Sobo could see it when she first met you. She told you your destiny was dancing on flames that the very wind takes a breath when you do." He pulled her into a tight hug, and she settled herself into his warmth. She remembered that visit and the story of the Phoenix Queen and her Dragon Knight. She recalled how she cried as the words of the story had seemed to crack her open.

Remembered Shawn holding her afterward as she cried that time, too. It had changed both of them that night. It was the story of not just the Phoenix Queen and her mate but also of Shawn's family and how they saved a being from another realm. He had been more protective after that night. It was when her feelings had started to grow even more.

It was a story that constantly played in her head, one that even Shawn would talk about occasionally. His voice broke her from the memory playing out. "Maybe this is fate finally coming for you. If it is, I plan on being there every step to see how bright your flame sparks. If you will have me." He pulled back, smiling with an intensity that for a moment, she thought that he was going to kiss her.

He leaned forward, closer to her, their faces so close to each other it would take one final moment, and their lips would touch, and their entire relationship would change. She watched his eyes look to her lips and then back at her, seeing the heat in them.

Audelia thought he was about to close the gap between them when his phone went off with a call. They jumped apart, her head swimming and her heart fracturing just a little at how fast he had pulled from her.

Shawn pulled his phone from his pocket, looking at the lit screen. "It's mam. Give me a second, yea?" She nodded, unable to speak; her heart roared in her ears as he smiled at her and swiped to answer the phone call.

Audelia walked out of the office to give him some privacy. It was dark and quiet here; Alexander must have turned the lights off before he left. She was still so angry with him; she knew in her gut that he *was* on the porch that night. She felt it in her soul.

But where did that leave her? Why did they lie? She couldn't wrap her head around it; the anger, the deep-seated hurt, she wanted to scream to hit something. Moonlight cast into the dark dojo, illuminating the dummy that stood in a corner by the window. Growing up, Alexander would let her and Lila dress the dummy in costumes for the holidays. Every Halloween, they rotated which character they would pick. This past year, they had dressed the practice dummy as *Lord Farquaad* with a sign Shawn had painted asking about the muffin man. Alexander and her aunt had laughed so hard, and he had joked that she and him should dress as *Shrek and Fiona*. It had been funny at the time watching her aunt blush at the suggestion.

Now, it made her see red. They had been hiding it from her and had the gall to play flirt in front of her? Audelia stomped over to the dummy and grabbed it knocking it as hard as she could to the floor. It landed in a resounding smack that felt fucking good as she screamed in frustration.

She screamed over and over and dropped to her knees as the grief filled her again. She barely registered Shawn running to her and pulling her to him again. As the tears she thought were gone, she found purchase again.

"Let's get you home a chroi." Shawn's voice was soft as he pulled her to a standing position, and they walked to the lockers. She moved numbly as she grabbed her shoes from the locker and sat down. Everything was playing through her head again.

"Shawn... Why is this happening to me?" She felt the tears well again as she looked at him again.

Shawn kneeled in front of her then, and she focused on the intensity of how he looked at her; her heart skipped a beat as she thought of the almost kiss in the office. If he tried to kiss her again, she would give him. Even if her life was messy, she wanted him, wanted to be with him. She was already his. She just wanted to have him as hers.

He grabbed her shoes from where they dangled in her hands and worked on switching them for her. His touch was gentle as he removed her dojo shoes and changed her back to the lavender sneakers she had worn here.

When he finished tying her last shoe, his hands glided up her calves, and he squeezed for a second to get her attention again. She looked down at him, kneeling between her legs, a look of love and warmth on his face. "I'm not sure, but Audelia. I am not leaving. I have you. Always." He squeezed her calves again and stood, towering above her.

He smiled and extended his palm for her to take; she took it and pulled her to stand. "Now, let's get out of here, head to your place, order a ridiculous amount of pizza, and watch something."

She nodded, and they walked back to the main area again. They talked about what they could watch as Shawn ran back to grab the keys to lock up. She tried to smile brightly when he came back, twirling them around his finger.

Audelia couldn't shake the feeling of everything changing as they stepped out into the cool night air. Shawn locked up and pocketed the keys. Without saying a word, he grabbed her hand again and interlaced their fingers as they walked into the night toward her house.

They walked quietly, Audelia leaning against him with their hands still entwined. Every step back home brought a sense of relief. Especially knowing he was there with her.

She could deal with whatever fallout everything held. Because she knew he would be there to hold her hand and protect her.

As they got closer to her house, a distant rumble could be heard in the distance.

A storm was brewing.

She smirked; the relaxing feeling that came from storms worked its way through the stress of the day.

"You and storms. It never changes." Shawn smirked. She hadn't even realized she had made a noise; he knew her so well.

"What?" She asked, raising a brow at him. She could see something blazing in his eyes in the street lights—a sort of need and admiration.

"Nothing... It's something I've always loved about you. Since we were kids, you always seem to come alive in a storm."

He nudged her shoulder, smiling that hundred-watt that makes someone's legs turn to goo kind of smile.

"Thanks, I think." She shook her head as they came to her front door.

Unlocking it, she and Shawn stepped through. The house was quiet except for the sound of violin music filtering through the closed bedroom door for Mara's room as they made their way up the stairs, Shawn's hand never leaving hers. Mara must have decided to read in bed tonight, which, let's face it, they both loved doing, especially on nights when a storm loomed in the distance.

"Quiet. Mara must have decided to go to the room early tonight." Audelia put her finger to her lips and motioned to her bedroom door with her chin. But, for a moment, she stopped before making her way to her room.

He was watching her. It was odd how he was watching her. Like, had she ever seen him watch her like that? It was this sort of intense gaze that made her cheeks redden before she dragged him to her room.

Maybe she was going insane.

It would be fitting after the day she had, had today.

First, shadows trying to do gods knew what, and now Shawn was looking at her like he wanted to kiss her or something. She shook her head as they stepped into her darkened bedroom. She reached over and turned on her ceiling fan light, and he closed the door behind them.

Suddenly, her room felt tiny.

Audelia made her way to the loveseat in the corner of her room and turned on her TV on the wall, trying to find something for them to watch. She felt antsy. Like the world around her was in this haze, something between her and Shawn had shifted. She didn't like the feeling of being so off-kilter. Though, if things with them changed, Audelia would gladly let the world around them explode if it happened.

So, as she searched through *HBO* for something, Shawn sat on the edge of her bed, looking through his phone to see where to order pizza from. It was always like this with them. They didn't always need to talk constantly. If they had a plan for something, they just got to it.

Tonight, though...she felt like everything was on pins and needles, and she really needed someone to just talk or do something at this point, or she was going to explode with nervous energy.

Just as she decided on *Game of Thrones* for them to watch, something they had both seen a million times before, so they didn't need to pay attention fully, but it was still something they loved to just cuddle and watch. She was so nervous, and she wasn't sure why. They had done this dozens of times growing up. She and Shawn cuddled on the couch under a blanket, watching something on TV.

Yes, she had times when her heart pounded when he would play with her hair or rub her arm casually. So why this time?

Shawn was her person. Lila was her sister in all ways. But what her and Shawn had? It moved past worlds when everything turned to shit around her; she turned to him. He would never judge, and he would be there to pick up the pieces while making her feel so damn loved.

It was why, that horrible night when Kage hurt her for the last time, she knew without a doubt she needed him to be the one to come get her. Without a single mark of hesitation, he came. If anything, it took more to get him to not go back into that hotel room and kill him than it did to get him to come rescue her.

"Pizza should be here in like twenty. I even got you the stuffed breadsticks you love." Shawn smiled at her, putting his phone down on the sage green end table by the couch; he then slid into the spot by her on the loveseat.

"You're a god. Thank you." She leaned over and kissed his cheek in thank you.

His cheeks instantly heated as soon as her lips left his cheek. That's new. Had he ever blushed when she did that before?

"I know what my girl likes on a bad day." He boasted with a false bravado. Instantly focusing on the slaughter of the night watchmen at the beginning of the first episode.

Trying to think of a change to the subject, she came up blank except for one thing. The texts from the unknown number, her phone had gone off repeatedly when they had been walking. A new unknown this time, but it had been an onslaught as they walked here.

"Can you hold my hand while I open the text from the number?" She gulped in a breath, trying to settle the shaking in her voice. It may be an unknown number, but by the feeling in her gut and the look of anger on Shawn's face, they both knew it was Kage.

"Del... Of course. But love, are you sure you even want to read whatever he wrote?" Concern laced his usual strong, warm voice. She loved how much he cared about her wellbeing.

Taking a deep breath, she squared her shoulders and looked over at him. Just hearing him sound so loving and caring steeled her nerve. With Shawn by her side, she could face whatever new horror was in those texts.

"Yes. As much as I so fucking wish, I could just delete it and move on. I know if I don't, it'll burn forever in my brain. I know nothing good will come from reading whatever the bastard wants to say...But I am also terrified that if I don't read it and something happens, it's like I was just begging for whatever comes to hurt more than necessary." She was fighting back tears at the thought.

"I know. But Audelia, babe, you need to know. I will. Never. Let him. Hurt. You, again." He grabbed her hands in his large ones and looked into her eyes with every word.

She felt so damn safe with him when he spoke like that. Even now, with the fear radiating through her body, she felt so safe with the warmth of his hands and the conviction and promise of his words.

"I know you won't. You always make me feel so damn safe. But I'm still terrified, Shawn. For fucks sake, he sent the flowers today." The tears were starting to flow in warm drops down her cheeks. If she never saw those flowers ever again in her life, it would be too damn soon.

Before she processed it, he was pulling her into him. His strong arms wrapped around her body, pulling him as close as possible as if he was trying to shield her very soul from anything happening.

They sat like that for so long that it seemed like the world just paused around them. Just him holding her, letting her cry out the fears that raged inside her. No judgment, just love and warmth.

CHAPTER TEN

After a time, he pulled back just enough to rest his forehead against hers; the simple movement was grounding for her. She focused on her breathing and the feeling of him holding her. Audelia opened her eyes to look at him.

Their foreheads were still resting against each other; she expected his eyes to be closed like hers had been. But, instead, his were open, and swimming with emotions. She noted with a shaky breath that it was worry that lingered in his eyes. His eyes showed her so much love, worry, and adoration that the last had her swallowing a small gulp—lust.

Something warm pooled deep inside her at that last emotion. She felt her own lust rising as she looked at the man she had loved from afar for so long. How had she been so blind? Audelia could tell by how deep that lust seemed to echo in him that this wasn't new.

Shawn looked from her eyes to her lips, and she watched his tongue poke out for a second before his eyes flicked to hers again. Her breathing hitched again as he leaned towards her again. They both jumped as his phone went off. Audelia could have sworn he cursed as he pulled away from her to grab it.

Audelia's heart was pounding. Was he about to kiss her before his phone went off? Or was she just an idiot who was so messed up emotionally that she was hoping her best friend would kiss her?

But she would truly be lying to herself if she hadn't wished he would. When had the lines between them blurred so much?

"Pizza's here. I'll be right back." He smiled and kissed her forehead quickly before getting up and leaving her room.

She was blushing as she grabbed her phone and pulled up Lila's message chain. Ignoring the six unread messages from the unknown number.

AUDELIA

Girl, I am freaking out.

LILA

Everything okay? Do I need to come over?

AUDELIA

No. No. But Shawn is here.

LILA

And? Why would you be freaking out if he is there?

AUDELIA

Because….

LILA

?? Girl. Do I need to come over there and kick someone's ass?

AUDELIA

LOL, no.

LILA

Then WTF.

WAIT.

GIRL, DID HE FINALLY TELL YOU?!?

AUDELIA

Tell me what?

LILA

NVM. Why are we freaking out, baby girl?

AUDELIA

I thought he was about to kiss me. But then his phone went off because pizza is here….and now I think I misread things because it's been a long-damned day.

LILA

Misread what exactly?

AUDELIA

Well….I was crying (totally okay, I mean I have things to tell you later but I'm okay) and he held me……and then he shifted, placing his forehead on mine…all romantic like they do in Arista Stone novels….and I thought he was going to kiss me….but I think I'm just being an idiot.

LILA

Bitch, first off, you are far from an idiot. And I totally think he got that tattoo because of you. I also have seen how that boy is with you. And girl, it is far more than what a brother-like best friend would act like. It's more heart-stealing love for someone like a knight looks at his lady love.

AUDELIA

I doubt it. Let's face it. Who would want to be with a weirdo like me?

LILA

Him. Shawn fucking Montgomery would. And I bet he has wanted to for much longer than you realize. Just. ASK. HIM.

Before she could respond, Shawn walked back into her room, and the aromatic smell of pizza and her favorite cheese-filled sticks of orgasmic awesome. Audelia quickly shook off the nerves of what-ifs and focused on the food and the man in her room.

He placed the food down on the little ottoman puff in front of the loveseat and handed her the small box of her cheese sticks. Her mouth watered as she opened the box, pulled one of the pillowy bastards of the cheese gods, and took a bite.

"Mmmm. Soo damn good." She mumbled through the bites as she inhaled one of the cheese sticks.

Shawn audibly cleared his throat at the moan that she had given the damn cheese sticks.

"Good?" He chuckled, looking at him with a mischievous grin.

"Always." She spoke through the mouthful of cheese and bread. Gods, she was awkward.

They ate in silence for a while; the only noise was the current drama unfolding in the lands of *Westeros* on her TV. It felt like they had just settled back into their normalcy but for the two things held in the air like Bran before he was pushed from the tower.

The texts and the charged energy around the possible or she was as batshit in the head kiss that *almost* incurred.

After they were both satisfied and just watching the tv leaned into each other. Audelia finally pulled her phone from the table beside them and handed it to him. Her hand had only slightly shaken as he took it from her.

"Open the texts. I'm too scared to open it, but I do want to see it." Her hand shook as she released it into his open palm. Terrified, didn't even begin to explain the feeling of turning the food she had inhaled into lead.

She shook more as soon as the phone's weight left her hand. The ones this morning had been so horrifying that she had almost run. What if these were worse? Would she have to leave him? Her safety, her everything?

"Del... Look at me." Shawn curled his finger under her chin, forcing her to look at him. She darted her tongue out a little at the look he was giving her.

Seriously, what is going on with them? Whatever shifted tonight, it was big, that was for sure. Maybe she should ask him, as Lila says. She has yet to be wrong.

"It's going to be alright. No matter what that fucker has to say, I am here, and I will remain here until you no longer need me." His voice was like velvet death as his words. Shawn was usually protective of her, but this new alpha male protective he was being? She may be terrified of what those texts say, but damn it was fucking hot.

"Okay. Let's look." Her voice was still shaking, so she pulled herself into him more, seeking his warmth. He quickly obliged, pulling her tight to his side.

Cocking her head slightly so she could see her phone screen, she watched as he pulled open the text thread.

The air left her lungs in a great rush as she took in the words.

UNKNOWN

Little Lamb, little lamb. You will be mine again soon…So very, very soon.

Tears were starting now, burying her face into Shawn's warmth, and she used the feeling of him holding her tighter now to ground herself.

It was Kage, and there was no doubt now the use of Little Lamb was his favorite nickname for her. He used it when he was angry, usually when his fist was making contact with her stomach over and over.

Audelia couldn't look, not after seeing the nickname, but she knew they were terrible. Shawn cursed and gripped her phone so tightly that she was sure it would snap at any minute. The ones earlier today, she had a feeling they paled in comparison with the new ones.

She caught the last message before Shawn could move it from her line of sight.

UNKNOWN

I'm coming soon, and I will kill him. He has touched what is mine. I warned you before. When I get you again, you will watch as I kill him slowly; I'll keep him alive long enough to make him watch as I fuck what is mine. Then, I will end his life, and I will fuck you on his corpse so you learn to never leave again.

Audelia was thoroughly shaking now; every cell in her body screamed *at her to run.* To leave and never look back. Nothing good would ever come from this.

She hadn't felt this terrified since the night she finally left. That night was still a nightmare for her. Every hit, cut, and the several times he forced himself on her, her finally fighting back, calling Shawn to get her.

"FUCK!" Shawn growled out as he threw her phone toward her bed. He pulled her entirely into him and just held her, his hands working soothing motions across her back, both for her and himself, she thought.

She coveted the warmth of his body wrapping itself around hers in comfort. Here, this is where she felt safest. His arms.

Always.

"He...is never going to let me go, is he?" She choked out against his chest. Audelia was scared to look into Shawn's face. If she had been stronger all those years ago then maybe, maybe Kage wouldn't be threatening her yet again.

"Audelia..." He sighed and pulled back just enough to look her in the eyes. He pulled his arms from around her and placed his warm hands against her cheeks. Cupping them gently, he worked his thumbs back and forth; each swipe eased her fears.

It did not, however, stop the tears from flowing more

freely; he always knew all the right things to do to bring her the most comfort without using his words.

"I'm scared...Shawn." She managed to get out in soft, broken words.

"I know, baby. And I wish you didn't have to go through all this again. But I promise you this. He will. Never. Touch. You. Again." He kissed her forehead, pulled her back into his arms, and just held her tightly. She could feel every hammering of his heart. She focused on it, on him. He kept whispering it was going to be okay.

Audelia snuggled into him as much as she could manage. She never wanted to leave his embrace.

"We need to tell Alexander about this, and I know things aren't okay with you two right now. But Del. He needs to know Kage is threatening you." At his words, she went stiff and pulled back from him. She stood instantly.

No, she can't tell him. Gods no.

She may fear Kage, but she feared the look of disappointment in Alexander's eyes when he learns of everything. She never told him the full extent of what that monster had put her through. Even now with their relationship in an upheaval by the secret of what she had seen, what he was hiding from her. She still loved him like a father and still looked up to him.

She was pacing now. She couldn't sit still; her mind was racing, looking back at every mistake she made concerning Kage. Audelia had been trained for years in how to protect herself. Yet, that fucker destroyed everything she had. Next to him, she was just that pathetic little girl who couldn't defend herself—the little girl who failed everyone in her life.

Maybe that was why they kept things from her, and they saw how fucking weak she was.

"Del...talk to me. What's wrong?" His words were pleading, full of worry. But she couldn't hear him above the noise in her head.

"I can't tell him.... He'll be so *disgusted* with me." She whispered. She was flexing her hands now, needing to move more than the pacing was affording her.

Shawn was suddenly in front of her, halting her pace. He rested his palms on her shoulders, trying to steady her. "Why do you think that? Alexander loves you; for all purposes, you are his daughter in his eyes."

"Exactly! He taught me for years how to protect myself. And in a short span of time with that MONSTER, I lost it all. Everything. It was gone when he was around." She was crying harder now.

"Shh...Del... breathe. It's okay. I promise. He could never be disgusted with you." He moved his hands from her shoulders to cup her cheeks again, swiping the tears away with his callused thumbs.

"But...what if he is? I never... I never told him what happened..." She tried to look away from him, utterly ashamed of herself.

Shawn sighed and forced her to look at him again. His eyes were swimming with such affection that her heart broke more. Why couldn't it have been Shawn she had been with back then? Then, none of this would be happening.

Gods, she was a fool.

"It doesn't matter. He could never hate you, just like I could never hate you. That monster took from you. *He* is to blame. Never you. I won't allow you to think that way." Determination swam in his eyes as he looked at her.

Something was changing. She could taste it in the air. It terrified her and thrilled her.

"Why? How could you even stomach to be around me after I let all that happen? After I was sullied by him. I'm trash, Shawn. Maybe I deserve whatever fate is trying to deal me." She choked out every word.

"Audelia, let's get one thing straight. You, my love, are not trash. You are not sullied. Nor are you damaged. Or whatever silly notion is currently swimming in that brain of yours." He growled out the words. Not in anger at her, but that someone had made her feel like this. *Did he call her my love?*

Her breaths were becoming shallow as her heart started to race. The look in his eyes was burning her alive as he held her there in the middle of her bedroom.

Thunder boomed in the distance, and soon, the sound of a downpour pelted against the windows in her room.

"Why don't you see me like that? You have seen me at my worst throughout the years...why do you still view me as anything but broken?" Her voice wobbled, but she never took her eyes off him. She couldn't, even if she wanted to.

It was like a pull. Like the one when his Sobo told them that story or when she was in The Glade.

Ancient and waiting.

He laughed then. It was quiet and full of an unanswered promise. Shawn shook his head softly, carefully debating his next words. His eyes flicked to her, the emerald dark and heavy.

"Because... Audelia" Shawn seemed to pause like he was struggling, then his eyes intensified, and she felt herself holding her breath as his voice turned thick. "I am in love with you. To view you as anything but the strong woman I have seen you become would be like telling the stars that they do not shine brightly every night. Pointless and blasphemous."

She had never heard him speak with such reverence before.

Her heart was racing as she looked at him.

But, before she could speak a single word to his confession, one that was sending her world into a tailspin, she might add.

He slammed his lips onto hers.

CHAPTER ELEVEN

The kiss destroyed her and rebuilt her again in one singular movement.

She couldn't think past the feel of his warm lips on hers, the heat of his tongue seeking entry greedily. Audelia let him. Gods did she.

One moment, the kiss was soft and gentle; the next, it was a claiming. His hands moved from cupping her cheeks to wrapping around her waist, pulling her into his heat.

She pushed herself into him, one hand gripping his shirt, feeling the soft fabric bunch under her trembling grip, and her other hand wrapped itself into his hair.

Audelia's breath was labored, her chest rising and falling in a heavy staccato beat. The kiss continued, his lips and tongue dancing with hers; small whimpers came from her throat as the intensity increased with every thrust of his tongue in her mouth.

She had never been kissed like this before.

Audelia felt adored and worshipped by every caress of his hands on her body. Why had they never done this before now?

Gods, they were idiots.

She *was* an idiot.

And he was *everything.*

He always had been.

Shawn's grip on her lower back was punishing. Deliciously punishing. He pulled her into him tighter, like he was trying to meld their bodies together forever.

She didn't know when but somehow, he had begun maneuvering them to her bed. They were all tongues and teeth as she felt the back of her knees hit the edge of her bed.

Audelia gasped into his mouth at the contact as they fell backward onto the soft blanket she kept on her bed for reading.

Them, falling to her bed seemed to give him pause, for the kissing stopped, and Shawn pulled away to look down at her. His corded arms caged her in where they rested by her head.

Their breaths were ragged, both of their chests rising and falling at a labored pace.

Audelia was struggling to find the words as she looked up at him. His green eyes were glassy with a lust she had never seen before in him. But it wasn't just lust she saw there; it was a wanton undoing of finally giving in to whatever had been plaguing him this whole time. She knew if she were to look through his eyes, she would see the same on her face.

She had wanted him for a long time, but the fear of ruining their friendship terrified her, so she never said a thing. Instead, she stupidly went into the arms of a monster and almost lost everything to that monster. Yet, Shawn had always been there, waiting and loving her in whatever way she needed.

She didn't deserve him.

"Audelia…I'm—I'm sorry… I—" The look in his eyes had shifted to panic. Panic that he had done the wrong thing, panic that in a moment of giving himself over, he would lose her.

Instead of words, she merely reached up a shaking hand, gently placed it around the back of his neck, and pulled him down for another kiss. This one was a reassurance that she wanted this just as much as he did. Shawn sighed as she claimed him this time.

As they kissed again, this time soft and sweet, Audelia smiled as he gave in to her demand. The weight of his body on hers was everything she could have ever wanted.

She felt *safe*.

They rolled slightly until they lay side by side, kissing. His warm palms exploring gently over every curve of her body like he was memorizing everything about her. All the new parts he had never touched or noticed before.

After a while, he pulled away again, making her whimper at the loss. Shawn placed his forehead against hers, staring deeply into her eyes as he held her. Audelia's heart soared at the love in the deep emeralds.

"I… can't believe I finally did that." His voice was raspy and sent shivers of pleasure down her spine.

She smiled at him and gripped him at his back, where her hands had finally settled in their exploration.

"I'm honestly glad you did." She blushed, like a girl who had never been kissed before.

In truth, that kiss had knocked every kiss away from

memory, they didn't matter anymore, every touch of Shawn's lips were the only ones that mattered.

He laughed softly and reached to brush his knuckles against her reddened cheek.

"You are beautiful; you know that?" Shawn's eyes were dancing in the lights from her room.

Audelia bit her lower lip at his compliment. She didn't feel that way most days. The echoes of Kage's abuse and her just feeling out of place most days tended to haunt her steps.

So, she leaned into him and kissed his cheek in thanks.

Shawn pulled away from her, then stood and pulled her with him before he turned and sat on the bed. He pulled her back down to him, where she collapsed slightly into his lap.

He pulled her closer and scooted them to her headboard, where he sat with his back against the cream-tufted headboard, placing her head on his chest. She could feel his heart beating in his chest, heavy and sure.

Audelia snuggled into his warmth, enjoying the comforting feel of him. They had snuggled like this before, watching movies or shows or just seeking each other's comforts on bad days.

Yet, this felt different. Everything for them had shifted on its axis, and she wasn't as scared as she had thought. It felt right. Inevitable.

They sat in silence, just holding onto each other, their hearts beating in tandem, Shawn trailing his fingers up and down her arm until she broke the silence with a question she needed to ask.

"Shawn, you said you loved me?" Her words were barely a whisper. She wanted to hear it again, but she was still scared. Scared that if it was put out into the universe, it would become real, not some dream she conjured because she was frightened of what was going on with Kage and the shadows that seemed to haunt her.

Scared that maybe she misheard him, that it wasn't love, that this was just a moment, gone and fleeting, and if she voiced it, everything would shatter, and she would be more broken than she already was.

She could not lose Shawn. It would destroy her to lose him.

"Yes. I did." His voice rumbled against her ear, which was against his chest. She didn't want to look up. Didn't want to dispel this moment.

Shawn had other ideas.

He pulled away slightly enough for him to bring his long fingers under her chin, gently forcing her to look up at him. It was in his eyes again that deep love and adoration, so deep it made the emerald color burn. It made her breath catch; her heart stuttered in its rhythmic beat.

"Stop doubting whatever you are doubting. Del. I know you, and I know a million little doubts and questions are thundering through that brain of yours." He smiled at her and continued with words that made her heart soar as he touched her lips delicately.

"I love you. I have loved you for years. Remember when you first met Sobo?" She nodded in response. Audelia would never forget that visit, the story under the willow in The Glade, how it made her soul feel complete, or Shawn holding her while she cried.

"I had called her to visit then. I wanted her to meet you. Not just because my parents have always considered you a daughter, but because I wanted...No. I needed her to meet the girl I was so impossibly in love with. Audelia, I have loved you for so long that every beat of my heart has been yours since we met. You control every beat, every breath I take. It's yours. It will always be yours for as long as you'll have me. And even after you no longer want me in your life, it will still beat for you. I will still protect you from whatever you need, even if you don't see me. I will always be there. Forever."

Her breath caught. Everything in her seemed to pause and listen. Then, every beat slammed back into her. Like her body needed to catch up to this declaration.

Her chest heaved in every heavy breath. She didn't know how to fully speak to what he had just said.

Didn't he know? Didn't he see she would never send him away?

Because most words were currently failing her, which was a pity because she was usually fucking great at words. Audelia's brain, however, had stopped functioning at a declaration that would make Mr. Fitzwilliam Darcy fall to his damn knees.

"Shawn, I could never send you away. I love you. You have been my rock for years. I don't think there could be anyone else. I've just been scared. Scared to lose everything we have." She closed her eyes as she spoke. She felt ashamed to have been scared, to still be scared. "But even when I was scared, I have loved you. You are my person, my other half."

Everything she touches seems to become tainted.

She could never live with herself if the same happened to Shawn.

His response was to silence her train of thought with another searing kiss. This one was a claiming, one of all he had said and her telling him she loved him too. It was possessive and intoxicating, and she felt herself leaning into the flood of emotions.

His tongue teased the seams of her lips, and she opened for

him greedily. It became a dance of tongues as he pulled her closer to him. She was soon straddling his lap, her thick thighs on either side of his, wrapping both her hands into his hair, trying to get closer.

He sought the same as a growl forced its way into her mouth, and he gripped her hips, pulling her closer to him as the kiss became a savage want of heat and need.

She felt him then. Between the heat of their bodies, she felt his arousal, his need for her. He ground himself into her with every lash of his tongue.

Oh gods. He was huge.

If the thick heaviness currently pulsing against her clothed center was any indication. She wasn't sure he would fit, but she felt herself growing wetter at the prospect of trying.

Audelia ground her core against his length on instinct. The feel sent shivers of need down her spine, and a soft moan escaped her lips.

He growled into her mouth again and rocked his hip into a rough upward motion into her. Everything was ablaze at that moment. She had never felt such a need in a long time. It filled her with an emptiness that needed to be filled desperately.

Gods, did she need him.

She hadn't had the need for sex with someone in forever, and her only companion was the purple rose currently sitting in a box in her nightstand behind the chocolate she kept there *because we all need a little chocolate after we rock out to our book boyfriends in our head.*

"Del..." His voice was husky as he broke their kiss, his eyes searching hers to see if what was happening was okay.

She rolled her hips in response and went to kiss his throat, dragging her teeth against his skin, relishing the smokey citrus smell to his skin.

Outside, thunder boomed, and lightning crackled against the sky, filling her room with echoes. She loved storms, but she could only focus on the man who said he loved her and the feeling of being in his strong arms.

Her response was all it took for him to grip her hips and flip them. She felt the soft plush of her pillows against the heated skin exposed through her tank top.

They had too many clothes on still. She thought.

To remedy that, she reached up with hungry fingers and began to pull his shirt over his body, exposing the lean lines of his muscles; her mouth watered as every inch of tattooed muscle made themselves known to her. She wanted to lick every line and commit them to memory.

"Gods, your fucking delicious looking." She spoke, her voice somehow husky.

He chuckled as he helped her remove his shirt. Her eyes zeroed in on the tattoo of a dragon and a phoenix swirling together on his chest, just like in the story Sobo had told them so long ago. She reached forward and kissed his peck over the tattoo. She would ask him about it later, but from the heavy breathing and the soft I love you as she kissed every line, she knew he had gotten because of her as a hope for what they might one day have.

For now, she needed him. She felt so achingly empty.

She sat up slightly and began to pull her tank and bra free when his warm hands stopped her.

"No, let me." He breathed and reached for the fabric; he pulled the clothes free from her in such a sensual way that she was stunned for a moment. *When did having her own clothes removed by someone feel so fucking amazing?*

She felt a cool breeze as the air nipped at her fevered skin as she laid back to expose herself to him. Audelia watched his eyes roam over her in fevered motions.

His breath hitched as he took in the swell of her breasts, the toned yet soft lines of her stomach with the bit of pudge she was insecure about but couldn't fully be helped because gods did; she loved food. No amount of working out and fighting could ever tame. Shawn looked at everything she saw as a flaw, like it fueled his desire, and the heat pooling low in her belly turned to lava.

She was breathing heavily as he traced a finger over each breast reverently, loving the trail of heat they left behind scorched her very soul. "Gods, you are perfect baby." He spoke in velvet tones and leaned down, taking the swollen peak of her breast into his mouth and laved his tongue around her nipple. She moaned and arched her back at the touch.

She was burning alive with need, and they had barely touched. Goosebumps broke out over her skin as he sucked on her breast and began to twist her other nipple with his callused fingers. She moaned again and gripped her hands into his hair.

She could feel herself building with every touch.

Audelia rocked her hips against him, seeking the need for friction. She still had her leggings and panties on, and she felt as if she would die if he didn't take them off her soon. She needed to be filled, so she chased that ache with the roll of her hips against him, the need growing to a peak.

Gods, she would come before he even touched the apex of her body.

"Patience, love, I want to take my time with you." He sounded so authoritative with her, and it sent another shot of arousal coursing through her.

She whimpered, fucking whimpered, as he thrust his erection against her thigh as he continued the methodical onslaught of pleasure his very talented tongue was giving her breasts. Because he was switching back and forth now between them. He would work his tongue over one and suck and nip and wring pleasure from her while his hand would tease and twist her other needy breast.

This was torture, blissful fucking torture. She moaned and writhed beneath him, gripping his hair as she chased the first peaks of orgasm, and he hadn't even touched her aching core yet.

He gave another bite to her nipple and sucked and laved as the first orgasm raged through her, and she tossed her head back as she moaned in pleasure. "Fuckkk..."

He smirked, like the devil he was, at what he was doing to her as he sat up and began to remove his shorts and his boxer briefs.

Audelia watched as his thick glistening cock sprang free from his shorts. He was fucking huge, fuck. How was that supposed to fit inside her? Her mouth went dry as she took in every thick, corded inch of him; need coursed through her again, and she felt another orgasm start to rise at the thought of him inside her, stretching her deliciously.

She reached forward to grip him; fuck, she couldn't even fit one of her slender hands around the girth. He hissed and thrust his hips as he felt her fingers close and pump around him as much as she could. She felt powerful as he moaned and gripped her legging-clad thigh.

Audelia bit her lip at his response. "Fuck, baby, your hand feels so damn good around my cock." She grinned and pumped him again, but he stopped her. Shawn reached for the band of her leggings.

"Not right now, baby. This is about you. Not me. And I am for damn sure not done learning every inch of you, not done tasting you." Lust swam in the words he spoke in that velvety growl of his.

She pouted her lips at him, as she eye fucked his length, she wanted to taste him. See if that length could fit in her mouth. Wondering if she would choke on the veiny thickness of him.

He gripped the bands of her leggings and her underwear tighter, tugging slightly, and she lifted her hips for him as he yanked, fucking *yanked* them off her in one fluid motion like they were nothing and tossed them to the floor with a soft slap as the fabric hit the hardwood.

Fuck that was hot as shit.

Shawn paused then, his chest rising and falling, making his dick jump with every movement as he drank in her naked body before him. He looked at her like a starving man, and she was the feast he was finally being rewarded with.

And fuck, if that didn't make her pussy weep and clench with need.

Heat rushed to her cheeks as he continued his lazy perusal of her curves. She felt insecure and powerful as his eyes swam with heat, lust, and devotion for her, insecure because she hated her stomach and thighs, the stretch marks there, and the scars she prayed he didn't see from the many nights she had been with that fucking monster.

Audelia suddenly wished she had turned the lights down before they started their binge-watching. He would see them.

She didn't want him to see them. Her cheeks heated, she wanted to move, didn't want him to see how broken she was.

She squirmed then, trying to hide herself from him; she moved a hand to block his view. Audelia fought the tears that threatened to fall. Shawn stopped her, his touch gentle as he went to move her hand from where it blocked several of the thicker scars.

"*A Chroi*, you don't need to hide from me. You are perfect." He smiled down at her, and it made her heart hurt because she was scared if he saw, that he would leave after seeing the proof of how broken she truly was.

His gaze fell to where her hand had been.

Shawn paused then; she watched a muscle tick in his jaw. As he knelt down closer to her legs and looked at the scars on her inner thighs, the jagged edges of blade cuts. His eyes changed then; the lust was replaced by pure anger. "Audelia, where did these come from?" His gentle touch caressed every hurt along her thigh and at the ones below her navel.

Tears sprang at the corners of her eyes, and she looked away from him. She wanted to curl into a ball. She didn't want him to see or have to explain how bad things had been. "It's nothing…. just ignore it…please." She pleaded with him, still unable to look him in the eye.

"My love, it's not nothing." His voice was soft as he shifted his body and leaned down closer to her thighs, to the ugliness.

"Don't look, I'm ugly and ruined. Broken." Each word was a rasp.

"No. Not broken." Shawn began to press his lips to every jagged scar and every inch of them. With gentle kisses, he whispered, "beautiful." Another soft kiss on another scar, "Perfect," Shawn kissed them over and over, repeating the words until she was softly crying at how safe and loved he was making her feel.

She felt the bed shift as she came to pull her into his arms, cradling her naked body to his. He rubbed his hands up and down her arms, soothing her as tears fell.

"It was him, wasn't it?" His voice was a growl, the anger coursing through his every word.

She couldn't speak; she just nodded and buried her face into his chest.

"I'll fucking kill him. Fuck, baby. I am so damn sorry." He kissed her forehead tenderly, lovingly.

She didn't want to talk about it. She didn't want to dwell on it anymore.

She felt safe here in Shawn's arms.

The darkness couldn't hurt her here.

Kage couldn't hurt her here.

She wouldn't allow him to take more from her.

CHAPTER TWELVE

S o, she steeled herself, sat up slightly, and crushed her lips to his. She kissed him with everything she had, every word she wanted to say, and gave herself to him. Shawn answered in kind. The kisses were slow, as he made sure she was okay, then when her tongue darted across his lips, and she dug her nails into his chest.

Shawn devoured her. The kiss turned passionate, and it refueled their lust. She needed more. Needed to forget the horror. Audelia needed Shawn to fill her and replace everything.

"Shawn….Fuck me…please," she whispered into his mouth as she tangled her tongue with his. Her heart was racing, and she needed him desperately.

He groaned and rocked his cock against her and flipped them again. His grip was somehow gentle and possessive, and she craved more of it. She was below him as he looked into her eyes, searching, trying to see if she was truly okay with what was happening.

So, she responded by reaching between them and ran her thumb over the mushroomed tip of his cock and squeezed as she ran her palm down him. He closed his eyes as her fingers trailed down his shaft, a soft moan escaping his lips.

"Please...I need you..." She whimpered to him; in response, he claimed her mouth again and thrust into her palm.

He reached down between their bodies and ran his fingers along her needy cunt. She bucked her hips into his touch, reveling in the rough calluses of each finger as he began to work over her clit, in smooth circles bringing her to the edge again. She gasped as she felt two of his fingers slip inside her and started to pump in and out in fluid motions.

Fuck, his fingers were goddamned magic.

"Fuck baby, your pussy is so damn wet and so fucking tight. I can't wait to feel you around my cock." Shawn's voice was a growl of need as he pumped her again and again.

She pumped him again and gasped as she felt those two fingers curl inside her, hitting just the right spot that had her body exploding with every sensual touch he gave. She was writhing beneath him, becoming an undulated mess of need for him. She screamed his name as the second orgasm rocked through her body.

"Such a greedy pussy, baby. You like when my fingers fuck you, my love?" He leaned down and claimed her mouth as she cried out in pleasure again. He pulled away again as he rubbed her clit with the heel of his palm in swirling motions as he watched her come undone again.

She needed more.

So much more.

"Shawn…I need you in me." She whimpered, claiming his mouth again in a rough kiss. She felt his breath hitch at her words, and he growled, kissing her harder; as he removed his fingers from her sopping core, she whimpered at the loss.

She watched with lust-filled eyes as he brought those fingers to his mouth and tasted her. His eyes darkened as he sucked every last drop of her off his fingers. "Best dessert I could have ever asked for."

He moved her hand from his cock, and soon, she felt the velvet thickness nudge at her wet entrance. Her heartbeat was pounding in her chest, making her supple breasts rise and fall as she gripped her nails into his back and moved to wrap her legs around his. He teased her for a moment as he rocked his cock up and down her soaked folds, and she whimpered with need.

Then, without warning, he thrust into her in one fluid motion. He seated himself to the hilt, stretching her in such painful, delicious ways. Gods, she was full. He swallowed her cries with his mouth again in a searing kiss while he let her adjust.

"Fuck…your pussy feels so damn tight and warm. Like it was made for me." His voice was husky and dripping with lust.

Audelia bucked her hips into him, urging him to move again. She needed more.

And fuck did he oblige.

He started to piston in and out of her in long strides. Every time he plunged back into her, she felt herself free-fall into the next orgasm fast. He continued his relentless movements. He moved his lips from hers to her throat, which she angled for him, giving him better access; he kissed and sucked her skin into his mouth in a ravishing claim.

It was relentless; his every thrust into her had her body shivering in pleasure; her breasts were rubbing in all the right places against his chest, sending euphoric pleasure through her body as she began to crest that next peak of pleasure.

She moaned and worked her hips in time with his thrusts. Then, he stopped the long thrusts. He gripped her legs, bringing them to rest on each shoulder, and pulled out.

Audelia whimpered, trying to push him back into her wet core with her hips. Before she was about to demand he take her again. He thrust home again. Audelia cried out his name in a scream of pure ecstasy.

She felt her whole body jolt in the movement. And he sat up from her so he could push deeper inside her. He thrust in deep and began to rock his hips, the feeling of his balls hitting her ass as he thrust in deep motions. He claimed every inch of her in his movements.

Branding her with every delicious movement he gave her.

Her breast tightened and ached as she felt her pussy walls clench against his thickness, as the wave of an intense orgasm ravished through her body. She cried out, "YES!!"

He picked up his pace at her cries and continued into a punishing rhythm, making her come again quicker this time. Audelia had lost count of how many orgasms he had wrung from her. Her body felt spent and on fire with need at the same time.

"Fuck baby, you feel so damn good coming all over my cock, like a good girl." His voice was thick with lust.

He released her legs and, in a fluid motion that shocked her, flipped them again. Audelia landed on top. She cried out as her body slid down his length, as her legs squeezed his hips. She began to ride him, moaning at the new, deeper angle.

Fuck, she would never tire of this. Of him.

Audelia moved in slow, punishing rolls of her hips against him as he gripped her thighs, his fingers digging into her skin, *fuck, she would have delicious bruises later*. She reveled in it as she chased her pleasure.

"That's right, baby. You take your pleasure from my cock, like a good fucking girl. Fuck you're perfect."

She began to lift up and down along his shaft. Reveling in the feel of her body sinking over every thick, delicious length until she felt him fully inside, filling and stretching her over and over. Audelia continued the movement adding a roll or swivel of her lips with every movement, his cock brushing every sensitive part inside her. The friction of his pelvis against her clit, making another orgasm build quickly.

Shawn thrust up in unison with her, increasing the friction and fullness. She moaned loudly, entirely giving over to the sensations. His grip was punishing as he started to buck up into her.

"Fuck, your pussy is gripping me tight." His moans grew louder with every roll and lift of her hips along his shaft.

Fuck, did he feel good.

She picked up the pace as he reached forward and took her breast into his mouth, and sucked as he thrust up into her in one punishing movement. She cried out louder this time.

He fucked her harder then as she wrapped her legs around his hips. As they came together deeper, harder, she cried out in pleasure more and more.

There was a sound in the background like heavy footfalls that neither of them registered as he fucked her hard. He flipped them again, sinking into her deeply, his hips rearing back as he pulled back for another thrust. Her heels dug deeply into his toned ass, begging for more.

But before he could thrust home again, his cock, half inside her from his movements. Her door was thrown open with a loud bang that rattled the hinges and the bookcases against that wall.

They both froze.

Eyes wide, they both looked toward the door and who they saw there was not who they had expected.

Instead of the flushed, embarrassed face of Aunt Mara.

Alexander stood there, his face red with rage as he took in the scene before him. And fuck did he look pissed.

CHAPTER THIRTEEN

The air seemed to still in that moment. Then, in a flurry of movement, one second, she was in Shawn's embrace, and next, he was gone, being thrown across the room into her bookshelves by Alexander.

Audelia quickly grabbed Shawn's shirt and threw it over herself. It covered her to her knees. She was in shock. So many questions ran through her head at what was unfolding before her.

Alexander had Shawn pinned by the throat against her bookshelves, causing several to fall to the floor from the impact. "What the fuck do you think you're doing?!?" he roared in Shawn's face.

From where she now stood on shaky legs, he squeezed Shawn's throat tighter. So tight she heard the harsh gasp for air from Shawn. The scene broke her heart. The two men she counted on most in her life were suddenly at odds with each other over her.

"Alexander, stop it!" Audelia shouted, finally gaining her feet. She grabbed at his muscled arm that was holding Shawn by the throat and pulled, trying to break his hold. She felt flames building inside as her heart roared in her ears.

Gods, he was going to kill the man she loved.

"What the fuck is your problem!" Shawn spits back at Alexander, trying to break free of the vice grip hold that Alexander had him in.

Alexander seemed to ignore her protests and only grew angrier as he looked over at her, At her kiss-swollen lips, now ratted hair, and Shawn's shirt on her. That seemed to set him off even more because he pulled away from Shawn only to swing a meaty fist at him.

Hitting Shawn center mass and making his body crumble to the floor.

"How dare you lay your hands on her!" He bellowed, going in for another punch, this time to Shawn's jaw.

She could hear the crunch of bone as the knuckles connected with Shawn's jaw.

"Fuck! Alexander, I didn't hurt her! I would never!" Shawn tried to block as Alexander kept throwing blow after blow. Luckily, all those years of training with Alexander prepared him for this moment, and Shawn was able to block a few blows.

"Alexander STOP IT!" She cried. Why was he acting like this? She went to pull him away, this time using a disarming move he had taught her. Hoping to hell it would break him out of the rage he seems to be running on.

What the hell was happening?

"Alexander! Stop! I LOVE HIM!" She cried, still pulling at him to let go and get off of Shawn.

She was starting to worry he would actually kill him.

At her words, he seemed to pause his onslaught.

He turned his face to her, his big brown eyes taking in the tears in her eyes. As if realizing he was hurting her by hurting Shawn, he pulled away.

Standing, he reached for Shawn's hand to help pull him up. The second he was back on his feet, she grabbed for his shorts so he could be clothed since, in all the hustle, he was still naked.

Audelia reached for him and curled into him for his warmth, positioning herself in front of him to block him and to know he was okay. Because fuck, Alexander just almost killed him.

The sound of soft footsteps greeted them as Mara, wrapped in her robe, illuminated the shadowed hallway. She looked disheveled and had a soft pink to her cheeks as she took in the scene before her.

Audelia took in her aunt's appearance and then swung her eyes to Alexander.

Alexander, who was standing in her bedroom, late at night, in his.... boxers?!?

And he was shirtless. WHAT. IN. THE. FUCK.

"It looks like we all have a lot to talk about. I'll make tea." She sighed and backed away as her eyes flitted to Alexander; she disappeared into the dark hallway.

Yes, you do. As the shock wore off of actually seeing the proof, what she saw in the dark the other night wasn't in her head. They really had lied to her. At that moment, she didn't know what to do about it. But she would get answers.

"Why are you here, Alexander? It's pretty *late* for a social call." She sneered. Her eyes were still simmering with anger that he had hurt Shawn and for the lie burning in her heart.

He bunched his hands into fists and took a deep breath; his voice was lethal. "We'll talk about...." He paused, his nostrils flaring, and pointed to both her and Shawn. "this... In the living room," At that, he turned on his heel as if he hadn't just pummeled Shawn within an inch of his life.

"Are you okay?" She whispered to him as she watched Alexander's fleeting form leave her eyesight.

He coughed painfully. The sound made her wince. He pulled her closer to him. "I'll be okay. Are you okay, though?" His eyes searched her face, taking in the tears still falling from the scene she had watched.

"Yea...I think so. Was it just me, or was he in just his boxers?"

"Yeah...and I thought me being naked was weird for the moment...but that was...I don't know what that was." He laughed, wheezing a little.

"It was me not having imagined him on the deck last night." She laughed, and it felt hollow. She felt hollow.

She quickly shut her door to give them some semblance of privacy. The sound of the kettle being turned on, cups being pulled out of cabinets, and the grumbling of what sounded like Alexander crept down from the kitchen.

Good, he could be annoyed cause she was livid.

She pulled off Shawn's shirt and tossed it to him, and he put his boxer briefs on and got dressed again. She smiled when she caught the lust in his eyes at her naked curves. Walking to her dresser, she opened the drawer that held her night clothes and picked up a pair of silky shorts and a tank with lace trim around her breasts.

As she was tying her hair back into a less messy ponytail. She felt Shawn come up behind her and wrapped his arms around her waist. "I'm sorry...it ended like that...But I am sure as hell not sorry, *us* happened." He kissed her cheek and just held her in his arms.

She leaned back into his warmth, breathing easier with every second he held her in his strong arms.

"I guess we have to go out there...Or Alexander might drag you out of here by your balls." She laughed, twirling in his arms. Resting her hands on his chest, she looked up at him.

He certainly looked a little worse for wear. She could see the discoloration already forming along his jaw; she reached up and kissed the ache there.

"Yes, I would rather only you gripped my balls." He smiled, pulled her tighter, and claimed his mouth on hers. They kissed, tongues dancing, and then sighed as the kiss ended far too soon. They would have time later, she promised herself.

"Always." She giggled, kissed him, and grabbed his hand to leave the room.

A short time later, they both made their way towards the kitchen, Shawn's hand laced with hers. It was a normal thing for them, but now, after what just happened, it made her heart soar.

Of all the things they expected to find as they rounded the corner to the kitchen, Alexander held Mara in an intimate embrace that made even Audelia's knees weak. Was sure as fuck not on the list. It made her feel a war of emotions after the shock of seeing them like that: anger and love.

She could do this. She could be mature and lighthearted;

maybe this was just a recent thing, and they hadn't had a chance to tell her. Reasonable, she decided before she smiled widely, hoping it came off as genuine. She wanted them happy. It was the lying that was causing the hurt—the omissions.

"Do I get to punch him for doing that? Like he did, Shawn?" Audelia snickered. She was shocked by the sight, but it felt like a long time coming. So, as angry as she was, she was excited by this change of events.

They broke apart like two teens getting caught making out on the porch. Shawn laughed under his breath, but not loud enough for Alexander to hear, *wise move.*

"There will be no punching in my kitchen, Audelia Elide James," Mara smirked and raised a brow at her.

Audelia cringed a bit at the use of her full name. It was rarely used. It always felt so off when it was said allowed. Yet, she could never pinpoint why that was.

Alexander cleared his throat. His eyes might as well have been filled with flames, with the anger rolling through them as he stared Shawn down.

Rolling her eyes at him, Audelia went to help her aunt with the tea.

They placed everything on a tray, and everyone made their way to the living room.

Audelia pulled Shawn by the hand, not skipping a beat, and they plopped down on the loveseat by the fireplace. She pulled her legs up onto the seat and curled towards Shawn.

Shawn, poor thing, was stiff as a board as if he were waiting for the executioner's axe, which was not helped by the growl that came from Alexander as he sat down next to Aunt Mara.

"Calm down, my love," Mara whispered to Alexander. The

turn of phrase shocked Audelia. Not because of what was said, *well* maybe a little. But the fact that her aunt said it like she had said it every single day for years to the man next to her. Audelia's heart began to race.

I want them to be happy. I want them to be happy. She repeated in her head over and over, but then the betrayal crept back in.

But why did they hide this? Why hide that kind of love?

The air around everyone was tense. Very fucking tense.

Everyone seemed on edge, everyone but Aunt Mara, that was. She acted like this was normal as she poured tea into everyone's cups and, to Audelia's fucking surprise, added sugar and cream to Alexanders like she knew exactly how he took it.

She couldn't take the questions in her head anymore. She needed answers. Shawn gripped her hand and squeezed in reassurance. He knew how much she was struggling with this.

"So, how long has *this* been going on?" Audelia pointed her finger at Alexander and Mara, swinging it back and forth for emphasis. "Don't even think about lying either because I *saw* you on the deck last night." Alexander and Mara flinched at her words, but she watched as Alexander dismissed her accusation and glared at Shawn.

At least that had been some sort of acknowledgment, though she still didn't understand why Mara had called him Bronn.

"That is not important. What is important is why the fuck was *he* in your bed." Alexander growled.

"Because I am an adult, and I have needs?" She took a sip of her tea. It tasted perfect, and she knew Shawn had added everything she liked while talking to her aunt and Alexander.

That was clearly the wrong choice of words because

Alexander was up again and had moved so unnaturally fast, pinning Shawn against the loveseat with his arm across his throat.

This time, Shawn was prepared and broke the hold, shoving Alexander back. "What the fuck is your deal tonight, Alexander?" Venom laced Shawn's words. It shocked her; Shawn had always held Alexander in such high regard.

"My problem? My problem is I told you years ago when you started sniffing around her, to stay the fuck away from her. Clearly, it did not stick." Each word was spewed in Shawn's face with vitriol.

She was just his student; yeah, she always viewed him as family, but this was intense, even for his usual protectiveness. But to tell the man she loved to stay away from her? The fuck.

"When the hell did you tell him that?" Audelia looked between the two of them incredulously.

Ignoring the growls and literal steam coming from Alexander, Shawn shifted, looking at her with that smile of his that made her thighs clench.

"About four years ago, at the dojo BBQ. He noticed how I looked at you while you and Lila hung out in the pool. And well, he put two and two together...then he..."

"He what? Please tell me what was being said on my fucking behalf like I can't make my own damn choices." She was pissed now. First, he deflected about what she had seen, and now that he had the nerve to treat her like he had the right to a say in her life. Setting down her mug of tea so she wouldn't break the ceramic, as she felt the rising heat from inside again. She took a deep breath, waiting for the answer.

"He and a few of his buddies pulled me away from everyone and told me, in no uncertain terms, that if I were to do anything *untoward*, they would personally put me in an early grave."

"The fuck!?" Audelia couldn't believe what she was hearing. Why the fuck would he threaten Shawn?

Shawn who has always been everything but unkind toward her.

Shawn, who was her fucking rock.

Shawn, the boy she had loved for longer than she realized. Alexander threatened him?

It was her turn to push as she shoved Alexander away from Shawn. It hurt her wrists because he was a damn boulder, but she pushed, nonetheless. He moved, probably because he was shocked at the motion. Or possibly, the fire currently burning in her own eyes.

"Who gave you the fucking right to do that? Is it because you have obviously been with my aunt for gods knows how long in secret? Just because you are with her doesn't mean you deserve a fucking say!" She yelled at him. She stood between Shawn and Alexander.

The air shifted, and suddenly, she was standing at the crossroads to something big. Audelia knew everything about to happen in this room would change the foundation of her life. It didn't feel like it was entirely because of the man she finally chose to take to bed.

Alexander paled at her words. She expected to hear something along the lines of *Because I know better than you do, and he is just a stupid boy that doesn't deserve you.* Or something about how much he loved her and Mara, so he did have the right.

But him going pale? Nope, she never would have guessed that in a billion fucking years.

He looked from Audelia to Mara and back again. His eyes

danced like he was at literal war with himself on how to answer her.

That's a new one.

It was like all the tough exterior that was. Alexander was beginning to crumble as he took several steps back and fell back into the accent chair by the fireplace.

He looked lost. So incredibly fucking lost in this moment that Audelia found herself walking backward till she felt Shawn pull her down against him on the loveseat. Audelia almost felt bad for yelling and blowing up at him earlier, but that anger and betrayal still tasted like ash on her tongue.

Everything was quiet in the room as they all waited for what would be said next. Outside, the storm raged on the occasional booms and cracks filled the palpably silent room.

"So, why did Alexander find you two together at this late hour?" Aunt Mara asked with a raised brow; she gave them a mischievous smirk.

"He came over after class, and we finally told each other that we loved each other," Audelia smiled through every word. "... I love him, Auntie. So damn much, I was an idiot for not seeing it sooner."

Audelia leaned back into Shawn's warmth and felt his lips graze her temple. "And I love her."

They noticed Alexander perked up at their words in the corner, but he still looked torn between what he wanted to say and what he should say.

Why was he fighting his words so much?

"Lila owes me fifty then." Mara laughed and sipped her tea. She looked over at Alexander with such longing that Audelia's heart clenched.

"Wait....You guys BET on how long till we finally confessed

to each other?" She couldn't believe that her aunt and best friend were talking about them like that.

"Of course we did, sweet girl. Everyone could see how you two looked at each other. It was just a matter of *when* for the both of you." She laughed; it was soft and beautiful. It reminded Audelia of her childhood after she lost her parents; she remembered Mara always made sure their home here was filled with laughter, good food, and even better books.

She felt Shawn laugh behind her as he nuzzled her neck. That brought the first words from Alexander in what had seemed like ages.

"Could you not molest her in front of everyone..." He growled out under his breath.

"I'm sorry? He can do whatever he pleases to me because I allow it. What is going on with you?" She sneered at him. She loved the man, but how he was currently acting was really making her want to punch his fucking face.

He merely huffed and stood, beginning a series of pacing around the room. Whatever was going on in his brawny head was truly turning him into a basket case. Audelia had never seen him so on edge like this.

"Alexander. Sir, I know you don't trust me at the moment. But I promise you this. I love her, and I will protect her with everything I have. No one and nothing will ever harm her while I am beside her." Shawn's voice was strong and filled with love with every word he spoke.

"Hmph," Was all that Alexander gave in reply. He continued his stalking of the room because, at this point, the pacing seemed more predatory than just trying to get his bearings.

"So, Auntie, how long have you and Alexander been

together?" She asked, trying to sound amused about it, but she was raging inside. Audelia watched as her aunt blushed and folded in on herself shyly.

"I....um...we...awhile..." She barely managed to get out.

"Mara....don't say anything more." Alexander had stopped pacing and seemed to stare around the room like he was searching for something lurking in the shadows.

She wouldn't lie and say that that didn't scare her. The shadow from earlier was still very much in her mind, riding shotgun to the Kage danger.

"Why can't she say more? Are you fucking ashamed of being with my aunt? Because I may be tinier than you, but I will cut your damned balls off if you hurt her." Every word she spoke was laced with cold venom. She certainly was fucking pissed off now.

"Gods. Never. I love her. I have loved that woman for a very long fucking time. And it will take everything in the fucking world and then some to tear me from her." He spoke with such devotion that tears formed in Mara's eyes, echoing the ones now forming in Audelia's at the declaration. She wanted to be pissed still, but damn that thawed some of the anger.

"Then, why can't she say more than what she did?"

"Because there are things, little one, that we can't tell you yet. But know this; I love Mara with every fiber of my soul." He stopped moving, sat beside Mara, and clasped her hands in his.

Mara merely nodded and leaned into his warmth.

CHAPTER FOURTEEN

This whole night was dizzying.

A humming had started inside her head as Alexander had spoken at Mara's confession that they had been together for some time, from everything that had happened that day. Something deep-seated inside her thrummed to life.

Her head suddenly felt like a stabbing, burning ache was trying to burst free. She groaned and gripped her head in her hands.

"Del? Are you okay?" Shawn's worried tone echoed through the growing pain in her head.

"My head is killing me." She whispered through the growing roar that was coursing through her head.

Gods, everything hurt.

"Shit." It was all that came from Alexander as he grabbed his phone from his jeans pocket and texted someone.

Weird time to text someone randomly, what with the love confessions and the aching pain in her skull that was going on tonight. She thought, but even that felt foggy and painful to think.

Shawn pulled her into him tighter, curling her body as much as he could. He began to run his hands lovingly through her hair, massaging her scalp here and there, hoping to soothe the ache.

"I'll get some medicine for her," Mara said softly, leaving the room to grab Tylenol.

Audelia felt nauseous, and her whole body felt like it was slowly being engulfed in flames. The feeling deep inside her uncurled just a little.

"Fuck Storm, you're burning up." Shawn cursed as he felt her now flushed and feverish skin.

"I don't feel well…" She mumbled as she curled tightly into a ball in his lap. He felt so much cooler to her right at that moment.

Which told her a lot because he was usually very warm.

"I think you have a fever, love." He spoke softly, kissing her sweaty brow.

"Here, take this, dove." Mara handed her a small dose of some amber colored liquid that smelled like honey and something citrusy. She vaguely remembered it growing up but still didn't know what it was. Right now, blindly taking something felt wrong.

"What is it?" She asked as she gulped it down in one swallow.

"Something that will help." Her voice was stern and assured in a way she hadn't heard from her aunt in a very long time.

Immediately, Audelia felt better. It was like something cool worked its way through her whole body and eased away all the ache and heat that had ravaged her body a moment ago.

"Woah, what did you give me? I feel like I was fucking reborn with that." Audelia gasped as the last of the heat ebbed from her body.

"Just an old family recipe for pains." Mara shrugged her shoulders in response.

Some recipe. She could make a fortune on that cure-all.

"What the hell just happened? She was burning up one minute, and now she feels like her normal tempt again." Shawn asked; his voice wavered a bit like her sudden sickness and recovery had scared him some.

"Nothing at all. Like I said, it was just a simple cure-all. It's just been a long night for everyone." Mara told him in a voice that spoke of utter finality.

Audelia couldn't recall a single time she had ever seen Mara use such a tone with anyone. Something was undoubtedly going on.

It was time for answers.

"What aren't you telling me?" Audelia accused them. She knew bullshit when she saw it, and whatever game they were playing wasn't going to fly tonight.

"Nothing, little dove. You overheated, that's all. Your body has been doing that since you were a child." Mara spoke.

"Overheated? She was on fire a moment ago. I've never seen someone go from normal to burning up like that." Shawn sneered, holding her tighter. *He actually sneered about how normal Mara was acting about this.*

"Watch it, boy." Mara snapped at him. *That was surprising.*

Audelia sat up, keeping her hand intertwined with

Shawn's for support because she was about to say something, something she hadn't said to her aunt or Alexander before, but for some reason, it felt like it needed to be said tonight.

Maybe it was the storm giving her strength like it did earlier when she finally gave in to her feelings for Shawn or read those damn texts.

Either way, she was done with being told half-truths.

"Mara, I love you, Auntie, but please tell me what is going on? You both are acting odd. First with, hiding that you seem to have been in this long-term relationship for gods knows how long. And then today, with fucking Kage texting me. I can't take lies and half-truths tonight." Tears welled up and fell as she spoke every word.

"What about Kage texting you? Why is that psycho texting you?" It was Alexander's turn to speak, and his voice was laced with anger at mentioning Kage.

He had never liked Kage and didn't like that she had stopped going to classes as often when she was with him. Mainly because if she did, he would have seen every bruise she hid under her baggier clothes.

"Because he wants me back...." Her voice was shaky with that confession. She looked to Shawn to continue for her. She couldn't bring herself to say the words. So, she nodded to him.

She was tired. So very fucking tired. All that previous energy and strength was starting to seep out of her very bones.

"It's not just that. There are *things* Audelia didn't tell you about when they were together." Shawn spoke softly, pulling her closer to him like his touch to protect her from the horrors of her past.

"What the fuck do you mean by that?" Alexander growled.

Mara sat there with tears in her eyes as if she knew the words that were about to be said, and it broke her heart.

She knew her aunt suspected something more had happened with her and Kage, but she never said anything about it.

Audelia flinched at the angered tone Alexander used. It wasn't that she was frightened of him, she could never be scared of him. It was that it brought back memories of her time with Kage into a stark reality that was ready to engulf her again.

Alexander must have noticed because he shifted and reached for her knee, squeezing it in comfort. "I'm sorry, little one, what happened? Did he--did he hurt you?"

"Yes...every day for the entire time we were together and then some...." She cried every word out and then turned to bury herself in Shawn's chest.

"Fuck...." Alexander spoke softly, but his voice was filled with rage.

"Why didn't you tell me little one? I would have helped you, protected you. That's my job." He pulled her from Shawn only to engulf her in his warmth as he held her tightly.

"You're my teacher. You taught me to be strong and to protect myself.... How—how was I supposed to tell you...that I failed." She cried into his chest. Her heart broke to tell that truth finally. All her anger at him faded away into the safety that was Alexander and the love he had for her.

The shame that filled her soul, that she had failed Alexander, that when push came to shove, she let a monster take the reins and almost kill her.

He held her tighter at those words like he was trying to take away all the pain that asshole's hands had dealt her.

"It was bad, Alexander. He almost killed her. I was there the night he tried, and she finally got away from him. I should've killed the bastard while I had the chance." Shawn's voice was thick with anger as he spoke somewhere behind her. She felt his hand reach her back, running in soothing circles as Alexander held her.

"Fuck. Kid, you should have come to me and said that she had been hurt like that. I would have ended him right then and there." Alexander growled at Shawn, the words vibrating against her face where it was buried in his shirt.

"Don't....don't be mad at him. I made him swear to tell no one. I didn't want anyone to know my shame. Or look at me like I was this broken thing...." She still felt like a broken thing. Even with Shawn always there, always comforting her, she felt broken.

So damned broken.

And tainted.

"Audelia...." Alexander pulled from her, only to cup her cheeks in his large hands. His eyes begged her to believe all the words he was about to say. "Let's get one thing straight right now. You, my darling girl, are not fucking broken. That bastard may have made you feel that way. But I know in my very fucking soul, you little one can never be broken." Tears were swimming in his eyes as he looked at her like she was every-thing to him, like a father's love for his little girl.

Trying to lighten the mood, she teased because she could never deal with things in a mundane way. "You are only saying that because you're banging my aunt." She giggled through her tears.

That seemed to shock him still, and then the whole mood

changed. Again, for the second time that night, everything seemed to teeter on the edge of a needle.

Something monumental was about to occur, and all they could do was hold on and kiss their ass goodbye.

Alexander looked over at Mara, who was crying, and she nodded her head to him.

He let her go, gently pushing her back into Shawn's waiting arms; she could see it in his eyes. Whatever he spoke next, he knew she would need him more than she needed the man who was like a father to her.

He stood and paced again before the fire as he seemed to come to terms with the finality of the words he was about to utter.

Mara stood then and walked to him, grabbing his hands; she stood before this giant of a man and spoke to him softly; a sad smile played on her face as she spoke.

Then, when she turned, eyes still brimming with tears, Alexander spoke. His voice was full of regret, anger, and love as each word fell like a bomb. "Because, little one, I am more than your teacher, more than the man who loves your aunt. I am your uncle, sweetheart."

CHAPTER FIFTEEN

ER, UNCLE?!

"I'm sorry? What the fuck did you just say?!" Audelia yelled; she was shaking now.

Her brain had heard the words he had just told her, but for the life of her, it felt like some sick joke. Her uncle?

"Audelia, I know it's a lot, but I am your uncle," Alexander spoke gently; his voice wavered a bit, the usual strong bravado; it came out meek and slightly broken.

She laughed, just laughed; this was ridiculous. This had to be some fucking prank him, and Mara decided to mess with her because of what he walked in on.

"Very fucking funny, Alexander. You are not my uncle. I know I love you like family, but if you were my uncle, then you, sir, are a fucking asshole for keeping that from me all these years." She snarled and stood up. Shawn grabbed her wrist, trying to pull her back down to him to calm her.

But there was no calming her right now. So, as much as it hurt her to do—because she really needed his comfort—she pulled away from his warmth and began to pace much like Alexander had been doing.

"Little dove, please. Listen to what he has to say." Mara spoke this time. Audelia could hear the heartbreak in her aunt's voice, but she didn't care.

"Listen to what? More lies? Utter Bullshit?" She spat back. She felt like she was on fire again. Everything felt like she was looking through the smoke.

Her uncle? Why?

Why would they keep something like this from her?

Tears pricked at the back of her eyes; she willed them not to come. To not break down here like a small child.

That was it, though. All she could think of was when she was a small child and had just lost her parents. She had no one, just Aunt Mara. Gods, she had spent night after night wishing for more family. Wishing everything could go back to normal.

Then, she met Alexander when she walked into his studio one day. Only having gone because she needed an outlet for all the anger and sense of loss that was a constant inferno to her soul.

He became like family pretty easily; she would come to him when she needed a dad. She loved her aunt, but sometimes, a girl needs her dad. So, she looked to him.

This hurt.

"Little one. Please, let me explain." Alexander's voice was pleading now. She could hear the anguish in it.

She didn't stop the pacing; everything was racing for her.

She needed to move. She needed something because right now, all she wanted was to punch him in the damned face and then run to The Glade.

"Fine. You have five minutes. Talk." She laced each word with vitriol.

"I know how angry you must feel right now. I am sorry for that. But it was to protect you."

Protect her? What a crock of fucking shit.

"I'm sorry? To protect me?! How the fuck, does lying to me for YEARS...protect me? How does hiding that you are, in fact, my uncle *protect* me?" The tears were going to burst forth soon; she didn't know how much more she could take.

It was Mara who spoke this time. "Audelia, my sweet girl. You need to listen to what he needs to tell you." Her voice was surprisingly close. Audelia hadn't realized that during her pacing into madness, her aunt had gotten up and walked to her.

"Are you kidding me? Why? Why should I listen to a damn thing either of you has to say to me? Is my whole life a fucking joke to you all?" The tears were coming now; they felt cold against her warmed skin.

"I know. I am sorry we kept this from you. It is not something we took lightly. And it has killed us constantly to lie to you. Especially for Alexander." The sympathy in her voice made Audelia pause. She could see them now. The tears her aunt was shedding.

The sight broke a bit of the storm brewing in her soul. Just enough to temper it, it still crashed like waves in the back of her aching heart.

"Fine. Speak, I'll try not to constantly call you a dick as you speak. No promises..." She sighed. Moving to sit back beside

Shawn. He was the only one in the room where she could seek comfort because he was the only one who hadn't lied to her for fifteen years.

He quickly wrapped her in his arms and gently kissed her temple. The movement and warmth grounded her.

"First off, I am sorry, little one. This was not something I ever wanted. You have always been the brightest spot in my life. The day you were born was one of the best moments in my life. I knew the moment I held you in my arms that I would protect you at any cost to myself." His voice was laced with love and regret. Mara had returned to his side and held his hand tightly in comfort.

"You...you were there the day I was born?" Audelia's voice was soft, barely a whisper.

"Yes. Your father is the one who placed you in my arms. I had never seen my brother so ridiculously happy except when he married your mother."

"My dad.... he is your brother?" The tears were coming harder now. She didn't know why, but knowing that Alexander was her uncle not only by blood but that he was her father's own brother hurt more. That he had cast her aside so damn effortlessly, yet she was his brother's child.

Why?

Why did everyone keep this from her?

She felt the waves of anger start to thrash more and more against the wreckage of her heart at every word.

CRACK.

"Yes, he was my baby brother, and he was my king. That is the other thing: you are a princess Audelia, well now queen, I suppose, with your parents gone."

CRACK.

A laugh escaped her now. This was beyond a joke. It had to be. "What is this the fucking *The Princess Diaries*? I mean, you certainly have Joe vibes. Seriously, this is such a fucking joke." That anger she had been holding on to was breaking through the walls she had thrown up when she had seen her aunt's tears; it seeped into every word.

"Audelia...you are a princess; it's not some joke." His voice was serious, and it expressed so much.

She was too lost to anger to give a damn. This had to be a joke. Her a Queen? Ha!

"Yes. It is. Instead of being honest with me. You concoct this ridiculous straight out of a fucking *Disney* movie lie to what? Make me grateful that my father's brother chose to leave me behind? Chose to lie to me when we did meet? Treated me, his *niece*, a piece of his brother, like she was just some random girl that walked into his Dojo that day?!" She couldn't breathe. This was such shit.

SHATTER.

They lied to her. The humming in her very bones was returning.

Every day for fifteen years, they fucking lied to her.

She lost her parents, parents she can't even really remember anymore, and then her uncle had cast her aside like trash, with some excuse that it was for her *safety*.

"Then who are you to me, Mara? Should I even call you my aunt?" Mara flinched at the words. "Are you actually my aunt, my mother's sister, like you told me years ago? Or are you just a lie, too?" She laced every word with the betrayal she was feeling.

That anger had raged back through her, seeking an outlet,

something she could destroy with it. The buzzing was back. Growing this time at a terrifying rate.

"Don't talk to her like that, Audelia. I know you are hurting right now, but Mara has done so much for you that she does not deserve you speaking with such hate." Alexander growled at her, pulling Mara to him like he could shelter her from the hate that Audelia was throwing at her.

"I honestly don't fucking care right now!" She was on her feet again. Her hands were shaking as she balled them into fists.

"I am sorry, little bird. But I am your aunt." Her words were sure, but the look of utter heartbreak was on her face as she continued. "By marriage, I am married to Bronn, whom you know as Alexander; he had to change his name, and we had to pretend we weren't married or knew each other. So, if they found him, he would not accidentally lead them to *you*." She was crying heavily, but every word she spoke was strong.

"You've got to be kidding me? So, it had been you on the deck, with your real name? The one you cast aside like you did me? What the actual hell?" She couldn't stop the hateful laugh that escaped through the sobs.

Her whole world had gone to shit.

She had been so scared before with the threats from Kage or the strange shadow...but this was worse.

So, much fucking worse.

"You know what? I don't even fucking care anymore! You can all go to hell! Fuck, I'll take the fucking shadow from earlier being real over this whole bullshit!" She yelled and stormed off to her room.

As she stormed away, she didn't notice the look of pure

horror on both her aunt's and now apparent uncle's faces. All she could see was that she needed to get away from them.

As she reached the stairs, planning on locking herself in her room, she changed her mind and ran out the front door instead. She didn't even notice that she was still barefoot and dressed in bootie shorts and a Cami that her breasts were practically falling out of.

She barely heard Shawn yell after her as she barreled down the empty street. Barely noticed the rain pelting her skin. It didn't even feel like rain. She was so damned warm from the buzzing and the growing inferno unfurling within.

She knew the one place she needed to be.

The Glade.

So, she ran.

Ignoring everything, ignoring that Kage was out there somewhere, probably watching her, that there was a strange shadow creature of nightmares that had tried to kill her or ravage her that could be hunting her this very moment.

All she could think was *good.* She was raring for a fucking fight right now. Let them try. She would burn them to the fucking ground if they came anywhere near her.

The sound of thunder and lightning strikes were like the beat of drums, keeping her moving forward as she made her way to the Glade.

Her feet hurt, she was pretty sure her soles were bleeding from running barefoot all this way, but she didn't give a shit.

Why? Why did they all have to lie to her?

How could they?

She was just a little girl who had lost her parents and then lost her uncle all in one swoop.

It was worse that he was always there, loving her, protecting her. But he refused to tell her who he truly was.

It hurt. It all fucking hurts.

She was burning.

Everything felt on fire again. Like fire crawled over her skin as she ran. Audelia could have sworn she felt steam as every drop of heavy rain hit her skin. Even her tears felt like they just turned into it.

So, she ran, the Glade finally coming into view. And she felt relief at the site of the large pink and purple blooms of the large Weeping Willow that lay at its center.

She felt like she heard someone behind her; it was probably Shawn still chasing her. She knew he would follow her but give her the needed space, never venturing far enough to have harm befall her.

Audelia ran harder as she hit the first line of trees. It was so dark here tonight. The usual lights strewn about the trees for anyone who wanted to come at nighttime were gone.

The small cluster of trees was dark. Even the shadows had thickened in the rain.

The hairs raised on the back of her neck; she was being watched. Something was out there. It felt evil and dark.

She kept running; she knew these trees; she didn't need light to find her sanctuary.

Audelia was feeling weak. Everything was beginning to feel sluggish, and it felt like her mouth was full of ash. She coughed and stumbled.

She was burning alive.

Her body was starting to give in to the burn she felt. It lulled her into a painful stupor that she fought with every step.

A branch snapped nearby. Sluggishly, she moved toward

the sound, preparing to take on whatever made its way out of the shadows.

Something was for sure coming out because she could see a darker shadow in the dark; it seemed to cleave the darkness from itself, and a pair of blood-red eyes were watching her.

The shadow.

It was back for her.

Her breathing was heavy, like syrup running through her lungs. She was getting dizzy from all the heat.

But, as much as she fucking hated him right now, Alexander, no... Bronn...he had taught her to fight. To stand her ground, no matter what. She would not yield to whatever this was.

She was strong.

She was a force of nature.

She was so fucking tired. Fuck. She was going to pass out soon.

NO.

She would not give in. She would fight even if it killed her. Even if her body gave out, she would not yield to this.

The shadow was growing closer, and everything felt heavier. Like the shadow was sucking the very air out of the area, her breath came in shallow hard bursts.

She was dizzy and felt like each breath was through a needle.

She wanted to call out. But her voice was gone. She couldn't speak even if she wanted to; between the burning in her body and the breath being sucked from her body, she was stuck.

She could move still, sluggishly. But it was at least something.

So, she did probably the stupidest thing she could right now.

She began to run.

She ran as fast as her burning body could take her, hoping without hope that she would reach The Glade and maybe, just maybe, she could hide in her secret place.

Audelia could have sworn she heard someone call her name, but she couldn't hear past the pounding in her heart echoing in her ears.

The shadow, she could see from the corner of her eyes, was chasing her. Gaining on her for every two feet, she carried herself.

Fuck. It was going to get her before she could reach the safety of The Glade. And she knew she would be safe there. Something about the inner sanctum of The Glade always had this heavy protective presence.

She cried out in her soul. For something, anyone, to save her from whatever that shadow was.

She was scared. For the first time since the night Kage had almost killed her, she was terrified. She had been scared the first time she saw that thing, whatever it was.

But it was different this time. She was feeling weak and vulnerable, easy prey for whatever was hunting her.

But she kept running. She ran and ran, stumbling here and there; her knees were surely bleeding at this point, for she felt the sting every time her knees slammed into the graveled path under her feet.

Her vision was beginning to haze. It was already dark as hell here, but it was like even the dark was starting to blur.

She was going to pass out soon. Just a little farther. Please. Just a bit farther, she kept crying to herself.

She could barely see the glow of the lantern lights that were always on in the sanctum of the boughs.

It seemed so far away.

Audelia pushed herself as fast and hard as she could. She was burning more. It felt like, before long, nothing would be left of her body. It would be the same as the ash she tasted on her tongue.

The lights were getting closer. She was almost there!

Only a few more feet and she would reach safely. Then, she would hide or fight whatever ended up happening until Shawn could find her.

She knew he *would* come. And probably Alexander—Bronn. They had to.

A screech bellowed through the blackness around her. Causing her to halt her steps, as she did, she pitched forward at the sudden halt.

But, before she could fall, strong arms wrapped around her; she tried to scream in panic, but a large, callused hand bound itself over her lips, blocking the sound.

She pulled against a thick, muscled chest. Fuck, whoever had her was huge!

Definitely not Shawn or Bronn.

She fought; whatever energy and strength she had left, she pushed into every movement. She tried to wrench herself free.

Audelia had been taught how to get out of holds for years. This was child's play.

Well, it would be if her body wasn't burning up and she wasn't dizzy as hel.

Still, she gave it her all and managed after a few moments to somehow free herself. She bolted.

A renewed stamina, probably fueled by adrenaline, she gave chase from whoever had grabbed her.

Hoping she wasn't headed straight into even more danger, she ran.

Audelia hadn't gotten far before those same arms bound around her again and tackled her to the ground.

Holding her there, the hand worked itself over her mouth again. This time, she felt warm breath caress her ear as a gravely velvet voice spoke.

"Quiet…You need to be quiet little flower…. Please, little one…" His voice was so gentle and laced with worry.

Who was he?

She didn't feel malevolence about him. His hold, now that she thought about it, was angered. It was gentle and calming. Something about his voice stirred a familiarity in her.

Audelia stopped trying to break free then. As she did, she felt him pull her up gently. She let him one because her body felt like it would give out any second now. And two because she felt safe with him.

She didn't even know this large giant of a man, but something in her very bones told her. Safe. Audelia chose to lean into the instinct instead of fighting anymore. She didn't have the energy left anyway.

He turned her to face him. His face was etched with worry as he seemed to look her over for any wounds. A growl seemed to seep from him as he took in her bleeding hands and knees from her constantly falling.

She blushed in embarrassment. And then as the light from the nearby glade shifted, she blushed again as she took in his features.

Holy fuck, he was gorgeous.

Even in the dark and shadows, she could see his chiseled features, the strong jaw, and the face that would make a Greek god weep. His eyes were expressive, and she could have sworn glowed a bit in the dark around them. She could barely see the braids that were tossed throughout his hair.

She just stared at him. Dumbfounded. And dizzy.

Fuck, she was still so fucking dizzy right now, even looking at the handsome man currently holding her in his thick tree arms.

"Who....who are you?" She whispered, her words slurred. Her eyelids were getting heavy, sleep sounded so good right now.

But no, that shadow was out there somewhere.

And Shawn was looking for her.

She knew it in her bones he was.

"Someone that is going to protect you, my shadow flower." His soft words were a caress.

All she did was nod.

Nodding was a bad decision. It made her head feel like it was going to explode.

The burning was back and so much worse.

The safety she had found in this stranger's arms had ebbed all the adrenaline, and her body was giving in to the pain quickly.

"My....head......hurts..." She cried out barely a whisper.

"Shit...I've got you...they will be here soon." She could barely hear his words; they sounded underwater.

She felt him pull her into his arms, holding her close, and she clung to him. Still, not understanding why she trusted him so much, she didn't care.

Darkness was creeping into her vision.

"It's....still.... here...run.... leave me." She begged. This kind of man didn't need to be taken down by whatever horrors were currently trying to harm her.

"The fuck I will. Hold on to me." He growled as he shifted her into his arms and stood holding her tightly. She wrapped her arms around his neck, and he began to run.

The movement jostled her and made the buzz she had heard earlier return.

She was losing feeling in her body, and everything was beginning to go numb; all she felt was fire.

And tasted ash.

Audelia hadn't realized just how fast this guy was running until the edge of the trees was in a blurry view, and she could see the streetlights.

The relief of it was short-lived as she went limp in his arms, her arms falling from his neck.

She heard him scream her name.

How did he know her name?

Before she could ask, everything went up in a burning inferno of darkness that swallowed her whole.

CHAPTER SIXTEEN

All she saw was darkness. Darkness and fire.

She was being pulled in so many directions she was going to fall apart.

Through all that, she could hear voices; they were loud, and it made her head hurt more.

She very much wanted to wake up to tell them to shut up. But she couldn't speak, she couldn't *move*.

So, she did the only thing she could while everything was burning flame and darkness around her; she listened.

For a moment, everything was quiet, like the darkness and flames she had felt before had stopped—a *small reprieve*.

One she was thankful for. Her body felt light, practically non-existent, like she was a waif in the current land of darkness that still eclipsed her entire being. She felt lost and hurt like she would go insane if the darkness didn't relent, and gods, what if this was it? What if she was dead?

What about Shawn? They had just come together and finally admitted what they had felt for years. She wanted years with him. She wanted to see their love grow from the friendship they had to the epic love story that it could be.

She wanted that. She wanted to forgive Mara and Bronn for the betrayal because, at the end of the day they were the closest thing she had to parents.

She didn't want to die.

She wanted to go back. To undo it all, to tell them she loved them all.

Audelia stood in this strange place of darkness that seemed to go on for ages; she just walked over and over, hoping for something.

The end of the tunnel like in the movies? Or for anything else but the flames that had seemed to lick her body at the beginning.

As much as the voices had hurt, they had been a grounding, and now that she was here in this lack of sound darkness, she was growing scared.

Scared of what this meant, what was happening.

Did that man kill her?

No.

He was saving her, Audelia didn't understand much of what was happening, but she hadn't felt anything violent from that man. He had held her so protectively, so almost lovingly. There was no way he could have killed her.

But, still, one moment, she was burning up and dizzy, and in his arms as he ran, and then it was just this.

The dark and the flames that had finally crested over her body.

She still felt a buzz of their heat, but they were momentarily gone. She walked for what seemed like hours, trying to hold herself together.

But she was becoming more and more hopeless.

Audelia was never leaving whatever sort of hell this was.

She was so very fucking tired of walking on end in this void. So, she sat. Her waif-like body felt heavier as she did. Like all, the hope was draining from her, leaving a heavy dread in its wake. It came in tears, sobs that ravaged her body, making it convulse with every tear that cascaded down her cheeks.

She missed them. She missed their laughs and voices and wanted to go home. To see them again. To live, to stop whatever this was from continuing.

Just as she had given up, the flames returned. They ran up her body like whisps. She screamed as they danced across her body, leaving not a single inch of skin free from the blues and reds of the flames. She was nothing but the flames anymore.

And just as soon as they arrived, they were gone. The last flame licked out as if it had never been there before. She was finally free of the less dark void she had been crying in.

Before her was the edge of the trees; she was back in the forest before—before The Glade!

She was alive!

Up ahead, she saw three figures standing around, and she rushed to them; she didn't know why she did.

It seemed stupid to do, considering all that happened, and she didn't quite understand how she went from being in that stranger's arms to just standing there with him nowhere nearby. But she didn't care. Something told her it was safe to go over to those figures.

As she got closer, she could hear their voices; they were

fighting. One man was bigger than the other two gods; he was a tall fucker. She giggled a little because his height reminded her of a giant from old fables she had read as a child.

It was probably not the best time to giggle, considering she was pretty sure she had just almost died and had been chased by shadows again. But she couldn't help it; something about the sight before her made her laugh.

A voice cut through as she made her way closer to the three men. For they all three were for sure men by the broad muscled shoulders.

"Where the fuck were you?!" The tall one yelled.

He sounded pissed....and scared? That was odd for a big man; she thought nothing would scare him except something larger than him. But what the hell would be bigger than him? That thought sent a shiver down her spine.

"Calm down. Mathias, what happened?" The other voice spoke, smooth like velvet and oddly familiar to her. But her brain was still fuzzy from whatever happened in that void.

"Calm down?! Are you seriously asking me to calm the fuck down, Bronn?" The tall man growled; she could practically hear the chomp of teeth as he snapped the words at Bronn.

Wait? Bronn? As in, her uncle?

Audelia picked up the pace as she realized it was indeed the man she had known as Alexander standing there going toe to toe with the giant beast of a man.

She was both happy and angry at the sight of him.

"We got here as fast as we could. She ran out of the house so damn fast; I could hardly keep up with her." Bronn's words were laced with regret.

She was surprised; she was a pretty decent runner, but she

didn't think even her fastest strides could outrun his tall, framed ones.

She was so confused she walked faster, getting pretty close at this point; she took in the scene before her. She could see the massive man better now; he was huge with thickly corded muscles and russet-colored hair currently loose about his shoulders, with small braids dotted throughout. She could see the outline of the jaw she saw earlier, which was as chiseled as she remembered.

The giant man, Mathias, still had his back to her and appeared to be holding something, but she wasn't sure. Whatever it was had Bronn looking terrified. Next to him stood Shawn. He looked disheveled and out of breath like he had been running for a while, his clothes drenched from the rain and probably sweat.

The look in his eyes stopped her dead in her tracks. He was pale and had this heartbreaking look on his face, like he couldn't quite believe what he was seeing. Her heart was racing, taking in the look on both their faces.

Audelia wanted to call out, but something told her to remain there. But surely they could see her? She wasn't that far from them. Even in the rain and dark of the night, with the pale glow of the streetlights around them, they should be able to tell she stood there.

Mathias moved so fast that she was surprised she had even seen the movement. One second, he was about three feet from Bronn, and the next, he was snarling in his face like he very much wanted to rip Bronn's very throat out.

"You should have been here fucking sooner! And what the fuck is this little shit doing here?! He has no fucking business being here!" He roared in Bronn's face and then turned to Shawn.

From how pale Shawn's already sheet-white face had gotten, the look was probably terrifying.

She didn't like that this stranger was scaring Shawn. She didn't like the look of terror and heartbreak on his face.

It spurred her into moving, even though a voice in her head told her to STOP! DONT GO! She was never really good at being told what not to do, especially if it involved the people she loved.

Before she reached them, Shawn spoke in a voice she had never heard before it was velvet-laced death as he looked the man in the eyes and snarled. "The same could be said of you! Who the fuck even are you? Let go of her!"

Her?

What the hell was going on?

Just as she got closer to them, the scene before her dropped her to her knees, and all air left her body.

As Shawn reached for the bundle in Mathias's arms, the man delivered a kick to his solar plexus, knocking him to the ground with a sickening thud. But it wasn't seeing the man that she loved with her whole heart be kicked to the ground like a rag doll. No, it was what, no who was currently being held with reverence in Mathias's arms.

Audelia.

Her body was somehow in his arms.

Everything stilled for her. As it did, she looked at herself. Everything was coming into a stark clarity for her. Her current body was firm, but it felt light and featherlike, like the waifish feeling she had of herself in the darkness.

Was this some new level of hell?

Was she truly dead, and some god had decided it would be a hilarious fucking joke to let her see her dead body being held before the two most important men in her life?

But no.

She felt her heart beating. It felt distant, like it wasn't currently in her body, but perhaps it was in the one in Mathias's arms?

She leaned into the sound, the thrumming beat, and lured herself to well *herself.*

As she got closer, her body felt lighter; it felt like, at any moment, a decent breeze would whisk her away.

Mathias's shouting brought her back to what was happening before her two selves.

"Don't you dare even fucking think of touching her!" He seemed to hold her body closer to his like he could protect her even more, like he would give his very life to keep her limp body safe.

"The fuck is your damn problem!" Shawn yelled as Bronn helped pull him to his feet begrudgingly. Time had not endured him to Shawn quite yet.

"Mathias...calm down, brother. Shawn here would never hurt her. Ever." Bronn's voice was calm as he raised his hands placatingly at Mathias.

Why was this man so protective of her? Was he family, another member of her family, kept from her all these years? She didn't recall seeing him before, but his face was familiar as if he were from a dream-given flesh.

"Are you seriously going to let this psycho keep ahold of her? He will probably kill her the first chance he gets!" Shawn yelled at both of them.

"Shawn! I'm here! I'm okay! I promise..." She cried out to him, hoping against hope that he could hear her. She reached out a hand to his shoulder, but he didn't react to the touch, and the usual warmth she felt wasn't there.

"This psycho is the one that just fucking saved her from the godsdamn shadow wraiths that were hunting her!" Mathias barked. She then noticed that he was rubbing her shoulder with one hand in a soothing gesture as if trying to wake her and comfort her simultaneously.

CHAPTER SEVENTEEN

S hadow wraiths?--What the fuck are you talking about?" Shawn stuttered, his eyes wide as he looked behind Mathias' back at the tree line like something could slither out at any moment.

After the night she had, honestly, it wouldn't surprise her.

"Like I am going to explain to a child like you. Now, get the hel out of my way so I can get her somewhere safe." He pushed past Shawn, almost knocking him to the ground again.

Audelia stood there in shock. She didn't understand what was happening or why she was here but was also in Mathias' arms. The wind shifted as the rain picked up again, and she suddenly realized she was dry. *Why didn't she feel the rain still pelting everything around them?*

"Take her to my house. You know where it is. I'll call Gideon to grab Mara from her house. She'll have everything we need." Bronn immediately jumped into action and quickly matched the strides Mathias was taking.

"Better fucking hurry with that shit. She was burning the fuck up, still is, but now I can't get her to wake at all." Mathias' angry tone was laced with worry.

"Fuck!" Was all that Bronn said as he reached into his pockets and grabbed his phone.

Audelia, who had been frozen to the spot since they started moving, finally ran after them when Shawn broke out of his own similar spell of shock.

"Wait! Shouldn't we take her to the hospital? She is covered in blood, and if you can't wake her, what if she hurt her head?!" Shawn cried out after them as he ran to catch up to the two men's long strides.

Being as light as she felt, Audelia was struggling to keep up with them. It was like every step toward her body became heavier and heavier, and she couldn't tell if that was a good thing or not.

"A mortal hospital isn't going to do shit for her. They couldn't fix her if the goddess of life herself appeared before them and told them how to do it." Mathias laughed at Shawn.

Mortal hospital? Goddess of Life?

Who the hell talks like that?

Luckily, they ran not that much farther; Bronn lived not that far from the Glade. Audelia was always jealous that from the upper balcony of the house, you could see the whole of The Glade and the small forest that surrounded it.

Audelia had barely caught up with them as they were opening the house's front door. It was a beautiful little house, a two-story craftsman style in a bright sunny yellow with cream shutters; its delicate looks did not match the roughhewn man who owned it. She always found it so contradictory that he owned this tiny fairytale-looking home that was better suited to Mara than him---well, that made sense if they were married; he had probably gotten it with her in mind.

More and more things just did not make fucking sense to her.

She had just enough time to make it through the door of the house before it closed behind the men.

Mathias was racing up the stairs to one of the spare rooms she had never seen before.

"Put her on the bed in there. I'll go get some water and towels from downstairs," Bronn spoke as he began to disappear down the hall and towards the kitchen.

Audelia followed closely behind Mathias and Shawn as they took her limp body to the room in question.

The room was colored in pinks and purples, with white furniture and light wood throughout the space. It was very much at odds with the man who lived in this house. Everything in this room screamed her. He had painstakingly made a room here specifically for her at some point in the past fifteen years.

Which was odd because she had stayed here plenty of times and had no recollection of this space. She was usually in the guest room down the hall across from the master bedroom. Wonder why he kept this from her?

Audelia watched as Mathias gently laid her body on the violet quilt of the bed; she watched in awe as this giant of a man, who looked like he wanted to murder people for fun, laid her hands gently over her frail-looking body and placed her head on two pillows to lift her just a bit. It was so loving that it warmed her heart in ways she didn't quite understand.

All the while, Shawn constantly tried to get around Mathias to be at her side. She just placed herself on the bed by her own head, leaning against the headboard. She felt so drained as if she could sleep forever. It was strange looking down at herself resting on the pillows.

In a daze, she just watched as everything happened around her.

Shawn finally managed to get by Mathias when he had briefly moved to get a chair to place by her side just as he had softly brushed his knuckles over her cheek lovingly and whispered to her. "I am so sorry, my love...gods Del, please.... don't leave me..." His voice broke with every word, full of love and terror that she may never wake again.

"I'm sorry, the fuck did you just say?" Mathias growled, pulling Shawn from Audelia's side. She was slightly amused by how the man acted towards Shawn's declarations of love to her.

Gods, she was tired...

Mathias had Shawn by the collar and was snarling in his face.

"Get your hands off me asshole! I need to be by her! She is fucking hurt!" Shawn roared back and tried to kick his way free from Mathias's grip. The sight would have been hilarious if she was not so very fucking tired at the moment.

Mathias took his unoccupied hand and landed it into Shawn's stomach again, making him grunt in pain. "I don't give a single Fuck. Stay. Away. From. Her." And at those words, he tossed Shawn like a rag doll to the floor and took his spot by her bedside.

She tilted her head in curiosity; the look on Mathias's face was not what she expected from how he constantly snarled at everyone. He looked—broken.

Like his entire world was in jeopardy, and he couldn't do a damned thing about it, and that world at the moment was her.

Seriously, who was this guy?

She felt like she had seen him before, but she still couldn't place him, and at this point, she was just too fucking tired to even try.

The buzzing was back in her head, but it seemed to jump back and forth between her body and herself.

Shawn was back up, and his face was twisted with hate for the man sitting by her side. "I don't know who the fuck you are. But you will not stop me from being by the woman I love." In defiance of the current look, he was receiving from Mathias. Shawn sat on the bed beside her and took one of her hands in both of his.

She couldn't feel the movement of his fingers caressing her knuckles. Fuck. That probably wasn't good.

"Get your fucking hands off her. And don't ever say those fucking words again." Mathias snarled and ripped her hand from Shawn, bringing it to his own hands.

She seriously wished she wasn't so damn tired so she could ask questions about what the fuck was happening. And why was Mathias, whom she had no recollection of, acting too protective of her?

"The fuck is your problem!" Shawn was on his feet again, reared his fist, and punched Mathias.

Seriously guys? Fighting right now while she is lifeless in a strange bed. How cliché.

She rolled her eyes with a smirk and closed her eyes as the two men snarled back and forth, and Mathias tackled Shawn to the ground and had him in a headlock. Audelia was about to close her eyes when she heard the shattering sound of foreheads smashing together.

She looked just in time to see Shawn smack his forehead into Mathias. Both had blood currently streaming down their faces as they stood facing one another.

"Really, brother? Fighting children now?" Another voice said this one was jolty and lyrical but very masculine. She lifted her heavy head to see another man enter the room and take in the scene before him.

He could be Mathias's twin. Just younger and leaner. The man who walked into the room had the same russet-colored hair as Mathias, just shorter and better trimmed; his hair was shaved off one side and left long on the opposite side. They had the same russet eyes, but Mathias, she saw now, had flecks of emerald throughout his eyes and a large twisting scar that fell across his left eye down slightly past his jaw.

Both men were handsome in their respective ways. The younger was *Apollo* to his brother *Hades*. The new man wore a rain-soaked blue t-shirt that hugged his every muscle and jeans that hugged the thighs that could shatter a watermelon. If she could right now, she would be drooling at all the delicious men at her bedside.

Mathias scoffed as he wiped the blood from his face with the back of his palm. "I wouldn't have to if he would stop trying to touch her and spouting bullshit about being in love with her." Every word was laced with a promise of blood.

"Wow, getting soft in your old age, big brother? Surely words like that would have left the poor boy dead by now." The younger brother laughed.

"Skye, can you not try to rile your brother up right now?"

Bronn's voice cut through the room. He sounded as tired as she felt.

Gods, she needed a nap.

"But its soo fun!" Skye laughed as he made his way into the room; as he claimed the opposite side of the bed his brother and Shawn were currently on, he let out a loud hiss. "What the fuck happened?" As he took in her bloodied body, unmoving on the bed, his jovial tone changed to thick death.

"Shadow wraiths in the forest by the tree. They were.... hunting her." Mathias spoke softly.

"Fuck..." Skye sat down on the bed beside her, looking down at her prone form; if she was in her actual body and not whatever this waif-like existence was, she could reach out and touch him.

"What is fucking going on? You all are talking nonsense meanwhile; she is still burning up to the touch and won't wake up! She needs a fucking hospital." Shawn yelled from where he stood; he balled his fists and looked at each man in the room like he wanted to end them all and take her from this place.

"Shawn...son, you have to calm down. Trust me, none of us in this room is remotely okay with how she is right now. But we must wait for Mara. She has what will help Audelia." Bronn spoke gently, reaching out to place a hand on Shawn's shoulder.

Shawn shrugged it off, stomped over to her body, and retook his place on the bed next to her; he reached over her and gently kissed her forehead, whispering. "Please.... Del....wake up...don't...leave me." His words broke her damn heart.

All three men snarled at Shawn, who ignored it and focused on her, willing her to wake up and return to him.

Gods, she wanted to wake up. Why couldn't she wake up?

She reached over to touch her own body, hoping that maybe just a touch would be enough to bring her back. But as she barely skimmed the skin of her forehead. The flames were back.

They scorched her body again, and she screamed out in pain. As she screamed, her prone form began to convulse. Everything felt like it was spiraling at that moment.

She couldn't breathe; the air in her lungs became ash again, and it was suffocating her; everything was going black again. Audelia could barely hear the shouting of all four men as they frantically tried to get her to wake up to stop shaking like she was; there was foam frothing at her mouth.

She could have sworn she heard all four men crying as they pleaded with gods that this wasn't her last moment and that she would come back to each of them.

If she weren't in so much damn fucking burning pain, she would feel warm and loved in that moment.

She couldn't take much more. Everything hurt so fucking much.

The world spun around her as darkness began to creep back in.

Just before everything went dark again, she could have sworn she heard her aunt's voice and another man's break through the current buzzing in her head.

The dark swallowed her whole again.

This time, it felt heavier, and the flames felt greater like she was reaching a whole new level of pain and loss.

She was in that dark void again. Audelia just laid there screaming out in pain as the dark licked about the flames that scorched down to her very soul.

Suddenly, everything went quiet; the buzzing was gone; even the sound of her agonized screams stopped, though she could still feel the screams around her lips. But she was voiceless.

Everything was soundless.

Then.

A voice.

It started out soft, like they were calling through a small hole somewhere far away. Then it grew like a thundercloud rolling her way.

She closed her eyes, hoping whatever it was would leave her alone or end her misery.

The feeling of someone standing by her caused her to open her eyes.

Then, the voice spoke again, this time gentle and warm. She curled towards it, for it soothed the pain. She craved the comfort it brought her, like a warm sweater on a cold winter morning.

"I am so sorry, my little star. I wish it wouldn't have to come to this.... but he has found you. It is time to come home. Come home and find me. Let this guide you." Suddenly, a bright light in the figure stood before her hands. He had no actual shape; the voice was male, that's all she could tell. Even the brilliant light of the glowing small star in his hands gave no clue as to who this man or being was.

Audelia reared back as he moved his hand, holding the small burning star that reached for her. She couldn't move, though she was frozen; whether it was in fear or pain, she couldn't really tell.

The next thing she knew, another searing pain engulfed her body as the star in his hand plunged into her chest. She cried out in surprise and terror.

"Shh....little star, do not fear. This will help. To guide you home."

"Home?" she barely croaked out; her mouth was full of ash, and it hurt to talk.

"Yes, little one, it is time to return to the land of your birth."

With those parting words, everything went quiet again, and then a thumping noise filled the air until it roared around her.

With a shout of pain, Audelia opened her eyes again.

CHAPTER EIGHTEEN

The first thing she noticed was that everything *HURT*.

Like not just a simple ache, she still felt like she was on fire and that her body had been beaten to the point of death.

The second was that she was not in the same clothes she had been running around in. Gone were the silky lacey Cami and shorts, and were replaced with the soft cotton of a t-shirt and what felt like sweatpants two sizes too big and most assuredly *not* hers.

She looked around with her eyes, not daring to move, else she would make the pain even worse than it currently was for her.

Even though she had seen it all in her waif form, seeing it truly through her own eyes was a different creature itself.

The colors seemed softer, more toned down than they had last night. Wait, had it only been last night?

It was dawn; she could tell that much as the soft orang-ish hue of the early hours of a new day seeped in through the closed curtains.

Everything hurt.

She would've preferred dying to the pain she was currently feeling. It was as if she had been taken apart and haphazardly put back together with new pieces that didn't entirely *fit.*

Her breathing was shallow and felt tight, but not as tight as it had felt last night before she had passed out in Mathias's arms.

Mathias.

A part of her was anxious and curious to see her savior in the light of day, and not when she was on the brink of death or whatever the hell that was last night.

Audelia started to move slightly; she didn't especially want to, but she also didn't just want to lie there in her uncle's house when so much had happened. Fuck that's right, she has an uncle now.

That whole fight felt like forever ago, replaced by her attack in the trees of The Glade and then having that out-of-body experience, and—

She was forgetting something.

She couldn't quite tell what; it was like it was there up front, but it was all blurry, and she could not make out its shape.

It felt important.

No.

Important didn't seem like the right word.

It felt monumental. Life shattering.

But what the fuck was it?

A grunt came from beside her; it was then she felt something other than the pain, a body curled against hers.

She didn't even need to look to know exactly who had been holding her probably all night.

Shawn.

After everything that had happened, she was honestly surprised he was even allowed in the room with her, let alone in the bed with her.

She shifted slightly, trying to curl herself into his warmth. Audelia wished she could stay like this. Forget all the craziness happening in her life and lie here with Shawn.

"Del… please… come back to me…" His voice was barely audible and sleep-filled.

But those words. She had heard him plead to her over and over last night. Her heart broke for him because he was worried about her, even in his sleep.

Ignoring the spasms in her body, she shifted to face him, and she took in his sleeping face. She had seen him sleep plenty of times throughout the years. Yet now, it felt instantly different, now that they both gave in to their feelings for one another.

His sleeping face was beautiful and heartbreaking. She could see every worry line etched there, showing that he hadn't slept well. She reached up with a shaking hand and brushed some of his wayward black curls out of his face.

"I'm here. I am going nowhere. I promise." She whispered back to him.

His eyes snapped open at that moment, and she was greeted by the intensity of the emerald with gold flecks throughout his eyes as he looked at her.

Like he couldn't believe she was speaking, that she was okay, that it wasn't just a dream.

"Are....are you really here?" His words were quiet and broken, like he was scared to voice them out loud.

All she could bring herself to do was nod and give a soft, pained smile.

"Oh god, baby!" He suddenly yelled, sitting up and scooping her body into his arms to hold tightly.

"Don't you ever do that to me again...please, Del." He kissed her forehead, and then he looked at her, his heart pounding in a beat that matched her own sporadic rhythm.

"I'll try not to." She laughed and stopped as a cough worked through her body in a spasm, with everything tightening; she winced.

"Shit...I'm sorry. I shouldn't have moved you like that." Shawn gently placed her back on the bed. His eyes shining with regret for causing her pain.

"Hey... Look at me. I'm okay. I'm here." She tried her damnedest to hide the wince that time.

"You're still hurt...God, Audelia, it was terrifying...I thought.... I thought..." He was crying then and looked away like he couldn't bear to let her see him break.

She reached for him then and pulled him down to her. She fought the pain it brought; it was worth it because she couldn't stand to see him cry. So, she did the only thing she could think of to get him to stop.

She kissed him.

It started out as gentle and salty from his tears. Gods, she had missed the taste of him. Chai spice with a hint of mint and citrus. She opened for him the second she felt his tongue work back and forth against her lips.

At the entry, their kiss went from gentle to needy and claiming. Like they were never going to get this moment again, like they were starved for each other, she clung to him as the kiss deepened, and she moaned at the fire it ignited deep in her core.

She needed more.

So much more.

She reached her hands around and gripped his shirt, trying to pull him closer to her. He resisted a bit, like he was scared he would hurt her, but when she snaked a leg around his hip and urged him to her, he finally relented.

The feel of his firm, warm body on hers eased some of the pain, and she craved it.

Craved the way his kisses and his now roaming touch grounded her, pushed away everything the pain, the uncertainty, the crazy fucking shit that was the past day.

It all disappeared while she was in his hold.

Replaced with safety and love.

And she craved it like the air in her lungs.

"Del…" He spoke softly into her mouth as he broke the kiss, and they both collected their breaths. She could feel his need for her against her core, and it sent lust-filled aches of warmth into her core.

"I need you…Please, Shawn…" She pleaded with him, reached towards him, pulled his bottom lip between her teeth, and playfully pulled.

"A Chroi….I want you too…but we can't, not now." His voice of reason angered her. She could give a fuck less what was currently going on. She just needed him.

She needed to feel him inside her.

Right now, them. It was the only thing in her life that made sense. Maybe that wasn't the healthiest coping mechanism, but she didn't fucking care.

Audelia felt his stiff cock pressing against her. "That says otherwise…" For good measure, she rolled her hips up, causing his hardened length to glide against her needy flesh. His own hips rolled in response.

"Fuck—You don't know how to play fair, do you?" His voice was raspy and husky. "We have so much to talk about."

She smiled, tilting her head, wrapped her other leg around his hips, and used them both to grind into him more for emphasis. "We have time to talk later, first, I need you."

He groaned and let a small moan escape his lips before he pulled away from her. Every inch apart seemed to be agony for him. He sat back on his heels and gripped himself, hissing slightly as he readjusted himself before fully sitting down and looking at her.

His eyes were heavy with desire as he looked over at her, but that quickly changed to worry as he took in the bandages on her hands and over her knees.

"Audelia….it's been a week since that night…."

Her entire world tilted.

A week?

No, it was just last night.

There was no damn way it's been a week.

But then she looked at him again. Noticing what she had barely noticed before, the dark circles under his eyes, the weeks' worth of stubble over his jaw.

Oh shit…

She sat up, sending a course of pain throughout her body and making her head swim. "How….all I did was faint. Yeah….I cut myself up pretty bad…but…a… week?"

"More... happened after you passed out, baby." He looked away from her as he spoke the words softly, like he didn't quite want her to hear them.

"Like what?" She grabbed his chin to make him look back at her.

"They will explain. I'm still processing it myself, and I don't think I'll be able to really tell you everything." Shawn began to roll over to his side again, preparing to stand up.

"No! Don't go, please. I am so confused by what is happening to me. I....Don't want to be alone.... Please." Her voice was a weak whimper.

"I am just heading downstairs to get Mara. I promise I will never leave you, my love." He reached over and cupped her cheek, his thumb sending shivers of warmth through her.

She nodded; she trusted him. Even if, at this moment, she didn't entirely trust the world around her, he remained her constant axis.

A short time later, she heard the clatter of several footsteps running up the stairs near the room. She braced herself for questions, both from them and the ones she very much planned on getting answers about.

The first through the door was Bronn. She wanted to still be angry with him for all the lies, but that all died as she took in the disheveled look of relief as he took in her form. Tears were brimming in his brown eyes, highlighting the bits of amber flecked about his irises.

"Hey..." She spoke in a broken whisper.

"Thank the fucking gods." He let it out in a relieved breath. Rushing to her side, pulling her into a tight embrace, causing her to wince, just as two other men pushed their way into the room.

Mathias and his brother…. Skye? She vaguely remembered from her weird dream-like state, but wasn't entirely sure she could trust what she had seen.

Both looked as worn out as Bronn did. It warmed her heart and confused her. She didn't know these men, yet…yet they cared about her like they had known her for her entire life.

More secrets.

Will she ever be done with them, or is this her new reality?

She just watched as the men all filed in like she was the entirety of their respective worlds.

Bringing up the rear were her aunt and Shawn. Mara entered the room, her eyes filled with tears as she looked at Audelia and then at the men who loomed at the edge of the room, watching on like pillars of strength and protection.

"Men…" Mara scoffed, shaking her head as she brushed past them and went to Audelia's bedside, her eyes on her niece as she pulled her into a tight embrace.

"Little dove, you will NEVER scare me like that again," Mara spoke in a mix of worry, relief, and anger, not toward Audelia but because she couldn't protect her niece from harm.

"I'll try not to?" She gave a feeble smile, trying to lighten the omnipresent mood, with all eyes on her.

Mara scoffed at Audelia's little joke and began to check her over, looking at the bandages all over Audelia. It was odd seeing her aunt like this.

Mara was always such a caregiver and had been a nurse for a bit when she was younger, but had never really felt like it was what she wanted to do with her life. So, seeing her act like this again after so long was like fresh air on the balminess of the past few days.

"You're healing nicely. But. I still want you to remain in bed for a few more days; you...you went through a lot and overexerted yourself that your body needs time to catch up." Audelia could tell by her aunt's tone that she wanted to say more but didn't know how to say it.

Audelia looked around the room as she rested against the headboard, her hand resting firmly in Shawn's grip like he was scared to let go; honestly, so was she.

She could see the worry on all their faces. She understood her uncles and aunts and even Shawn's look of worry, but she still did not understand the looks coming from the two men standing at the foot of the bed.

Though she did want to smile at the look on Mathias's face, he looked like he wanted to push everyone away so he could be by her so badly, but by the look her aunt had given him, he was doing his absolute best not to do that very thing. Instead, she watched as he kept both hands in a tight fist; she was sure that blood was probably pooling in his palm.

"What happened? I don't.... I don't understand. Who are they?" She gestured at the two men in the room and continued. "I don't.... what is happening to....me? Am I going crazy?" She felt panicked by everything.

She was grasping at too many straws, and her body was trying its damndest to catch each edge of them and couldn't quite get them.

She wanted to cry, scream, and go and duke it out with anyone. Instead, her body ached, and she felt like she was still forgetting something...

Something important.

Something bright and warm.

She felt it then, like a little ember uncurling itself deep in her chest. She wanted to reach toward that warmth and hold onto it forever.

Come find me, little star—a voice like a warm sweater called to her.

Her whole body went rigid at the voice; she had heard it before...right?

"Del? Are you okay?" Shawn spoke softly; his hand was on her cheek, his thumb working back and forth, soothing her; she was vaguely aware of a growling sound coming from somewhere in her room. She must have made a sound or something to draw attention.

Shaking her head, she looked at him and gave a small smile. "Yeah... Fine... just a little tired." It was only half a lie; she was tired. But that voice was as warm and safe as it felt, and she was frightened by what it meant.

"Maybe this should wait, then. You need your rest." Mara spoke softly, and she gave a small smile. Audelia looked at her, noticing Bronn stood beside her with his hand on her shoulder.

It was still odd to refer to him by his real name. Odder still, that he had a different name than the one she had known for her entire life.

So many lies.

She didn't want to be angry again. After last night, she wanted to move on. She wanted to forgive, but it still hurt. Hurt that everyone except Shawn and Lila had lied to her.

Gods, Lila.

How was she going to explain this current craziness to her best friend?

Wait... didn't Shawn say she had been out for a week? She and Lila were supposed to get together the day after her class.

What did they tell her? Did they lie about where she was or what was happening? Wait. Of course, they did; they had zero qualms over lying to their niece for the past fourteen years, of course, they would lie to someone important to her.

"If it's been this long, Lila must be worried. We were supposed to get together the day after class." She spoke softly to Shawn. She needed to hear from him about what had been told to Lila.

"She...she has been so worried about you, Del.. She has texted me every day. Mara told her you had fallen after class and had hurt yourself. But that you were fine..." He reassured her. At least it wasn't a total lie.

"She shouldn't have been told anything, that little druid..." Mathias growled out. He had spoken more, but it was all under his breath; she had barely caught the word Druid. Why would he say that?

"*She*, is my best friend, Lila deserves to know what's going on with me more than you. A total fucking stranger." Audelia snapped at him. She was thankful for him caring about her that night, but she did not like his tone about Lila.

Audelia expected a snarky retort from him, but instead, he threw her for a loop and laughed.

He fucking laughed.

What the fuck.

"I didn't want her to worry too much about you. So, I only told her about you falling. I know how much Lila means to you, little dove." Mara reached out and gripped Audelia's hand, pulling her attention from Mathias and the smirk he was giving.

"Thanks." She couldn't genuinely say too much. She was still twisted inside.

Relief and anger still warred inside her over everything going on.

Follow me home. The voice came again, and she felt that little ember grow just a fraction.

She wanted to ask more. To ask the voice what was going on and who they were, but she suddenly felt tired again.

With heavy eyes, she curled herself into Shawn. She knew everyone was watching her, but she was just so tired, like something was forcing her to sleep.

She gave in to falling into a heavy slumber. She felt Shawn tighten his arms around her, and her name being spoken as a dream pulled her under.

CHAPTER NINETEEN

Everything was chaos around the sleeping princess. Shouts and screams seemed to echo around the chamber; even the barred door could not hold back the noise.

Worry lay thick in the air; one could almost choke on it.

And anger, anger that the men currently standing guard over the frail form could not prevent this from happening. That they had, on some crucial level, failed her.

Soft whimpers came from her tiny form, and Mathias rushed to her side. He was always with her. They all were, but he most especially. They had such a tight bond that it took a lot to keep them apart. She was everything to him—his little shadow flower.

And right now, he hated himself so damn much because he couldn't protect her from what had happened, and he didn't know if he could protect her from what was to come.

So, he did the only thing he could, he stayed by her side, took her *tiny hand in his and held onto her. He hoped that his strength would lend her some comfort as she lay in the sleep that Waldrum had placed her under.*

Screams came from just outside the door, the sound followed by the clang of swords crashing against each other.

"Fuck. What are we going to do? We can't just stay here and let them come to her!" Yelled Gideon from his spot close to the door. The usually calm and collected man was disheveled and on edge, his short brown curls were sticking at odd ends as if he had been pulling them in his frustration.

"You heard the wizard; we have to stay by her. If any of us leave her side, the spell he cast will break, and they WILL find her." Alaric's rough voice broke through the noise from outside the room. He gripped the hilt of his blade, keeping his eyes on the door, waiting for anything to come through.

"Thank gods she is sleeping through all this," Skye spoke softly from beside his brother, leaning against the wall, his sword also out, waiting for what happens next.

"Small blessings," Mara said. It was the first time she had spoken since Bronn had brought them all to this room where the girl they all loved and protected lay in a magical sleep.

She sat at the foot of the bed in Bronn's arms. He was armed like the rest, but his blade was away as he held his mate, who had been crying when they first closed the door, but had gone silent as the screaming had begun outside these walls.

The only two not currently in the room were those who possessed their own magic and could return at a moment's notice; a talent that even if he could do, it would take Morena herself to pry him from her. The twins had shadowed themselves to follow the king and queen as they returned to the throne room to lead their people. Their return would spell the worst and would summon Waldrom, who had gone to his cave to seek answers.

Damn wizards, *Mathias swore in his head.*

He ran his thumb back and forth over Audelia's tiny hand, hoping the movement would stop the whimpering.

"Mara...can't we do something for her? I hate seeing her like this." His voice was weak, the only thing betraying his fear of something happening to Audelia.

"No, I wish I could do something, but Waldrom used a blood spell to put her into that sleep. Only he can break it or tamper with it. If I tried. I could.... I could end up alerting them where we are." She cried.

"Damnit...." He went back to focusing on the precious girl lying before him. He would burn the entire world if it kept her safe. He had never cared for anyone like this, yeah, he loved his little brother, and he even had a sister who had disappeared years ago during the last war, along with her child. But. Something about this little girl spoke to his very soul. He knew the first moment he saw her that she was his to protect forever.

It felt like hours had passed since they had been sequestered to her bedchamber to await whatever fate deemed to occur next. From the looks that each of the men in the room kept giving each other, one thing was for sure. The world would burn if it meant keeping Audelia safe from Lefrain.

A sudden shudder ran through Mathias, and the air in the room shimmered; all hands went to blades, even Bronn had stopped keeping his hands on Mara and stood ready for whatever was to happen next.

But, instead of danger, there stood the two shadow twins of her guard. Fucking hel, he hated when they did that.

"What happened? Why aren't you with the king and queen?"

Bronn spoke, his voice laced with anguish. It was as if he already knew the answer but was scared to say it out loud.

Neither spoke, not that they ever really did. Instead, Mathias let out a shuddering breath as his vision changed, and suddenly, he wasn't seeing the room anymore.

Instead, he was in the War Room looking at their beloved queen and the king whom they had known since childhood. Both looked worried, yet they still gave off this regality to them as they were giving out orders and deciding the very fate of their people. They were born to be this.

They couldn't hear the words being spoken. It was mainly just a flurry of movements of what had happened. Mathias felt his hand tighten its hold on Audelia's little hand, as if holding her like this could somehow mask the pain that was about to happen.

There were several guards, and General Fartail stood by them, pointing at spots on the model map before them. From the glimpses Mathias could see using the twins' vision, things weren't looking good. Lefrain had taken quite a lot of the kingdom in such a short time.

How the hell did he manage that? They had the best legions in the world, and their Shadowlance legion was the best at having their hands in every pot out there. They always knew when an attack was coming. Yet, this, this moment, they did not see.

Did they have a spy in their midst? How could Lefrain gain such a foothold so suddenly?

In the vision, a loud crash boomed as the large double doors behind the king and queen burst open in an explosion; they merely swung in loose clumps that still somehow managed to remain on the hinges.

Darkness crept into the room; it crawled like a viper in the grass.

Mathias felt the hairs on his neck stand on end, watching the scene unfold.

As it settled, in sauntered a tall man, he was sinister and regal as he stalked toward the guards who had surrounded the king and queen. He merely smirked and waved his slender hand, and the guards standing before him withered away into husks.

Mathias felt the twins move closer to the king and queen, rallying their power to sweep them away the first chance they got. They would not let them die here.

Lefrain laughed again, it was like nails scraping against marble. "You really think your pathetic efforts will stop me?"

"Leave now. You do not belong here. You will not have her." The king, Garrik, growled and pulled his blade. He pushed the queen slightly behind him, protecting her and the babe in her womb.

"Ha! Like you could stop me? I am darkness itself. I cannot be stopped. I am infinite." Lefrain raised his hands; he held no blades, but as he lifted his hands, tendrils of black crawled away from his hands. The twins seemed to recoil from the tendrils. They felt wrong, which was honestly saying something because the twins loved shadows.

So, whatever this was....it wasn't good.

"Cal dara ut mirama!" Queen Naseria yelled, and billows of sunlight seeped from her outstretched hands, washing over herself, the king, and even the twins felt the warm embrace of the light.

In a twist of movement, the dark lashed out at the light coming from the queen, both seemed to clash and twirl as they battled each other for supremacy.

Lefrain barely seemed to move, only little twists of his hands and a snarl as he controlled the black that was trying to engulf the light. The queen twisted herself, and from this distance, the twins could see she was struggling to keep the dark at bay.

This would be her final stand.

Mathias felt the tears beginning to form in his eyes. Not Naseria. Not her.

"Give up. Perhaps ill spare you and make you my whore. You can watch as I take your daughter over and over and then have you for leftovers." Lefrain sneered.

"Fuck you!" Screamed the king, and he lunged, his sword coming down in a blinding arc of steel as he tried to take Lefrain down.

Laughing, Lefrain merely raised a hand and gripped the blade as if it were simply a fly he was swatting away. Garrik groaned in pain as he fought against the resistance from Lefrain holding his blade. He twisted, breaking free for a moment, only to be sent flying by a tendril of black smoke. He crashed to the floor some feet away.

A scream echoed from the queen as she sent another blast of light toward Lefrain. "Don't you fucking touch him!" Naseria moved in a flurry of skirts and had her own blade in her hands, swinging in arcs of light that seemed to blast from her blade as she began to engage Lefrain.

That had finally given pause, and he unleashed his peculiar blade of sharp, jagged edges, his own black smoke billowing off the edges.

They began a dance of light and dark and the din of clashing steel, over and over, neither truly landing any blows to the other.

Until a cry rang out as Garrik had resurged again and ran at Lefrain, his blade raised, aiming for his neck. Lefrain barely even looked in the direction of the king coming at him with a killing blow. He merely flicked his wrist and sent a blade of red and black toward the King, piercing him in the heart. The King's body writhed in pain, his cries of agony piercing through as the red and black seemed to engulf his body.

No, not his king, his brother in arms, not Garrik. How would he tell Audelia?

It lifted his body off the floor and seemed to seep into his body, and then slowly, the world stood still in those ensuing moments. It began to seep out of his eyes, and his mouth had opened in a scream as his body was pulled apart by the raging black and red that tore through him. His parts were thrown around the room in heaps, and blood seemed to rain down as his head rolled toward the queen, where she was battling Lefrain.

Holy fuck.

"Garrik!!" She screamed as she watched her beloved die and turned her anguish into her power; the light seemed to crescendo as she threw everything she was into the blows.

Lefrain laughed as he threw more of his magic into his movements. As he did, Naseria's light seemed to sputter. It was the mating bond. It was fracturing as Garrik's soul sprang forth from his head, and he called out her name one last time before a red wraith appeared from the black smoke that had killed him and tore apart his very soul, eating it.

She faltered then as the last moments of the bond broke. His soul was gone. Truly gone, for that was no ordinary wraith; it was a soul-eater. Without his soul going into the Nightlands, their bond would be no more, and her own soul would wander for eternity when she died. She would never know peace. Gods, Naseria.

Lefrain took advantage of her falter and grabbed hold of her arm. The twins tried to move closer, but could not move. She had frozen them to the spot.

Fuck, she knew this was the end.

Her voice echoed in their heads. "Leave me. I am lost, but Audelia is not. Tell this to Waldrom. Protect her, get her away before he gets to her too...... and.... tell her we love her very much.... and that we are so very proud to be her parents.... Now go!"

As she gave the final order, as they gathered their shadows to leap from the room, they watched in horror as Lefrain took her lips to his and sucked the very light from her body as he plunged his blade into her belly. As the last of their shadows began the leap, they watched her body crumple to the floor.

Mathias sucked in a startled breath as his vision returned to the room before him. It was then that he noticed the blood covering both of the waif-like twins. No one spoke as they all took in what they had seen.

They were gone.

Queen Naseria...beautiful, kind Naseria.... She was gone.

King Garrik, a man who was like a second brother to him,.... gone.

He turned to look at Audelia asleep in her bed, and his heart shattered. How would they tell her? How do they come back from this?

As if she had sensed his questions, Audelia stirred, and her little eyes opened, taking in him standing beside her bed. "Mama...where is Mama?" She cried out.

That seemed to wake everyone from their daze. Shit... she shouldn't be awake yet. Fuck. How the fuck do they tell her? Before he could say anything, Mara was by her side. "I'm sorry, my little dove..." Mara pulled her niece into a tight embrace and cried, her hand gently brushing fingers through Audelia's hands.

"I want Mattie....Mattie, where is Mama??" She cried, reaching for him. Fuck. Fuck. Fuck.

He couldn't find the words, so he merely sat beside her in bed and pulled her into his arms and held her as Mara and Bronn told her that her parents were gone. Everything was a blur; he could hear everyone talking at once about what to do next. Questions about where Waldrum was and what they were to do.

But he barely registered the words, his world slowed and centered around the little girl, who was tough as dragon scale and sweet as flowers. He held her, feeling her little sobs wrack through her tiny body, he would burn Lefrain where he stood the moment, he had a chance for what he had done to the king and queen and for the pain he was causing his shadow flower.

Shouts rang outside the door, and a large boom rattled its hinges. They were here—Lefrain's men, and probably the bastard himself.

He held Audelia tighter and pulled Mara closer to them both as Bronn and the other flanked them in a protective barrier. Mara was calling on her magic, and he could taste the tang of it in the air. He began to call his own and to call the dragon that was paired with his soul.

"Tadan, I need you." He spoke down the bond they shared.

He knew Tadan had heard him for a mighty roar rent through the sky outside the bedchamber window. Mathias was prepared to jump through the window the second he could, with Audelia in his arms, to get her far from here.

Before he could, the door blasted open, and black smoke began to billow in through the smoke of the blast, but it seemed to stop. Everything stopped.

The hell?

He looked around and noticed they all were moving, but the figures at the door he could see through the smoke had stopped, as had the smoke, like everything had frozen solid.

"Mara...was that You?" Bronn spoke softly, afraid to converse too loudly in case this was not his mate's doing.

"No...it wasn't..." She said, her voice wavering.

Before another could speak, the tang of magic ran through the air, and a soft pop gave way to a figure standing before them.

Waldrom stood before them in the small space between their grouping and the incoming black and gray smoke. He was a thin, tall man with lithe muscles that poked out through the bright blue tunic he was wearing. He wore beads around his wrists, and rings adorned several fingers on his hands; he held them up as if he had just cast a spell and forgotten to lower them. Perhaps he was still working the spell?

"Sorry... I am late, it appears..." His velvet voice was solemn as he took in those gathered in the room. He locked eyes with his sister, and the grief shone in his eyes. They went full white, momentarily, as he saw what the twins had seen happen.

They knew he had seen it because the usually jovial man was now crying. He felt the loss strongly because he had been closest to the queen. They had been childhood friends from the moment she found him wandering in the Whispering Woods one day.

"Fuck..." he paused for a moment looking over at Audelia curled into Mathias's arms. "I am sorry I failed you, little star." He finished speaking as he walked closer to Audelia.

She didn't look at him; she just buried her head further into Mathias, who growled at Waldrom. He could feel the magic from his dragon seep further into himself. The feeling of the wings he had only when the bond was strongest were beginning to form, he ignored the pain of them, focusing on his primary goal. To protect his princess at all costs.

Waldrom noticed this and held his hands up in a placating manner. "Sorry, I am afraid that as much as you do not wish me closer, I must be to perform what is to be done."

"Don't you dare touch her." His voice was barely human. It came out as a snarl and a huff.

Waldrom merely tsked and froze Mathias still with a flick of his eyes on him.

Fucking wizards.

"He'll never forgive you for that." Muttered Skye to his left. Damn straight, he wouldn't.

"I am aware, hopefully, we will all live to see that day."

Mara spoke then, her voice was broken as she fought back more tears. "What are we to do? Lefrain is here...he killed Naseria....He'll come for her...brother...please, what do we do?"

"What we must. I am sorry, but things are about to become very hard for all of us. This is the only way." He knelt before Audelia, who turned to him as if in a trance.

"Little star...you won't remember this... I am sorry, but you won't even remember them. I am sorry for that. But this is the only way to keep you safe from Lefrain." Waldrom spoke softly to her and reached out to touch her cheek, as he did, her body went limp in Mathias' arms.

"What the fuck?" Mathias snarled.

"She is fine. Only asleep. But I am sorry, I do not have time to explain everything. I will entwine it in the spell that when you all wake, you will remember and know what to do. However, I must tell you, you cannot tell her who she is, and you cannot tell her who you are. Her magic is tied to who she is, if she knows the block I have placed will end. Mara, you will be the one to take care of her, and I'm sorry, but you and Bronn cannot be together; it will lead them to her."

Before anyone could say another word, a bright blue light engulfed their bodies, and they knew no more.

Audelia woke with a start, but she wasn't in bed anymore; she was in the blackness again. Like she had been the day she fainted after being chased by those shadows.

"Hello?" She called out to the dark around her. She was scared again. The dream she had was terrifying, and her heart felt like it had broken anew.

Were those people her parents?

Why was she in Mathias's head?

She didn't want this. She just wanted to be a normal girl who loved stories and could spend her day reading or practicing her fighting skills and being held by the man she loved.

Sabo's words echoed through her, *"Aye. Destiny comes for us all in the end. My girl, yours seems to dance in flames around you. Like the very winds, take their breaths when you do. It will come for you one day."*

Destiny could go fuck itself.

A warm laugh echoed around her. "So much like your father. He always hated destiny, too."

"Who...who are you?" Her voice was shaky.

No words came, but suddenly, a figure began to walk towards her. He was still cloaked in the dark like the other day when she was in this raging darkness.

"It is time to come home, little star." A sudden piercing light engulfed her again.

She sat up in bed with a start. The first thing she noticed was the startled looks on the faces around her, a mix of shock, awe, and relief. The second thing she observed was the faint glow in the center of her chest.

Mathias let out a curse, and she noticed he was on the floor with his brother crouched beside him.

"Fucking wizards."

CHAPTER TWENTY

She was glowing.

Holy fuck, she was like a goddamn light bright.

She could hear Mathias from the floor, he was on a nonstop rant about how much he hated wizards and their bullshit of entering people's minds. But it barely registered. All she could focus on was the glow and the buzzing in her ears that seemed to start softly and were now ringing like a fucking bee was permanently in her damn ear.

Audelia reached up to cup her ears, hoping to relieve the sound. She curled into herself a bit, trying to get it to stop. She was going insane.

That had to be it.

The glowing, the whatever the fuck that dream was, this buzzing in her ears, this whole fucking thing. It had to be insanity. She was just an ordinary young woman, as well as any woman who loved learning sword skills and firmly believed fairies lived in the trees of The Glade. But, as *Grandma Aggie Cromwell* once said, *"Being normal is vastly overrated."*

But still, it was the principle of the fact that she wanted to be an average young woman, who just found out her best friend of forever loves her, and she loves him back. That's what she wanted.

Not....whatever is happening to her.

She wasn't worth this crazy, life-changing, monumental thing. Shawn would see that anytime now, and he would leave her; they all would.

Audelia was shaking; she didn't know when she had started to, but she could feel the little tremors working their way over her body.

She can't breathe. *Fuck, is this a panic attack?*

"Del.... *A Chroi?*... It's okay... breathe, okay?" Shawn's voice broke through the buzzing, shaking, and cataclysmic shaking of her very life.

She zeroed in on his voice and his touch. Because he was touching her, she could feel that now. Why didn't she notice he was rubbing her back in soothing motions? She felt herself lean into the warmth of his hand, using his voice to ground her in the now again.

Trying her damndest to forget about everything and purely focus on him. He was here, and he was real. She could hold on to that.

As she did, she felt everything that the buzzing had pushed out come to her. Everyone was talking, Mathias she could hear was still very pissed about whatever had happened to him. Skye was on the floor, teasing him about it, making it worse, that man took nothing seriously. Bronn was trying to get Mathias to shut up and talk about what he was even saying, with glances towards her to see if she was okay. So clearly, that was going fucking great.

Mara was on the bed beside her, and Shawn, the look of worry and fear on her aunt's face broke her heart. She didn't like worrying her so much. Some of her may still be angry about the lies, but she still loved her aunt, and the last thing she wanted was to worry her even more.

As she focused on everything around her, especially Shawn's touch and voice, he kept telling her to breathe and that it would be okay. The buzzing started to lessen; it was slipping farther back to the buzzing of the other day when she ran.

Like a power was sitting like a viper waiting to strike. As much as it frightened her, that feeling also grounded her more. A part of her was reaching out, telling her it's okay, we got this.

It oddly soothed her.

"Little dove? What happened, baby girl?" Mara's voice was soft as she reached out and touched her knee gently.

"Is....this....is this really happening to me?" Audelia's voice was rough and raspy, like she had been screaming for an extended period of time. Hell, maybe she had been. After all she had seen in that dream and the culmination of everything else, screaming like crazy sounded reasonable.

At her words, everyone seemed to go quiet; even Mathias had stopped his growling about wizards. They all seemed to turn to look at her.

It should have made her uncomfortable having all these eyes on her. But it didn't; she felt safe here, with these people, even the two strangers whom she had only just barely met; she felt safe with their caring eyes full of worry and mixed with love.

She took those looks and bottled them away to use later when she felt she might need them.

Shawn was the first to speak, his voice calm and full of reassurance. "Yeah, babe, you are for sure lit up like a Christmas tree right now. Past that, I am not entirely sure what is happening. But you're safe, I have you." He pulled her closer to him, then held her in a tight embrace for a moment, and kissed her forehead before pulling back enough so she could still look at everyone.

"I'm not fully sure what that was, little bird. One moment you were talking, and next, you were asleep, and then you started screaming...and shaking so much." Mara's words were shaky. Audelia could hear the fear in them.

"Well, that explains why it feels like I swallowed nails." She laughed softly. It felt good to joke just a little bit.

Obviously, no one else found that funny—*tough crowd.*

"Yeah, you scared us shitless little one. Do you remember what happened?" Bronn's voice was like rough velvet as he came to stand behind Mara, placing his large hand on her shoulder. Audelia watched as her aunt raised her other hand to entwine with his.

"I'm....not sure...One minute I was asking about Lila, and the next...I was in this strange dream." Her thoughts slammed back to the dream.

Had those been her parents? She felt like she knew them, and the queen in the dream sounded like her mother from the few memories of her voice. Then, there was the fact that on that bed had been her—the eight-year-old version of herself.

No. It was just a dream. Yeah, they had told her that everything she knew wasn't what she knew. But, come on. There had been magic in that dream, and Mathias, or the dream version of him, had called on a dragon.

A *Fucking* dragon.

And then there was the fact that everyone there had pointed ears. She didn't have pointed ears, reaching up, she felt the tops of her very rounded ears. Even those around her had rounded ears.

It was a dream. A Fucking crazy dream. But it's still a dream. Right?

But if it had been just a dream, why did she now know who Skye and Mathias were? Or at least the semblance of who they were. Before falling asleep, she still didn't know who they were. Yeah, she recalled from her waif state that she had heard their names, but now it was different.

She felt like she knew who they were. They didn't feel like strangers anymore. At least not entirely, they were no longer these odd men in her room. No, they were her protectors if the dream had shown her anything.

That fact scared her a bit, but it was also kind of comforting.

This was her life now, wasn't it?

What if...what if Shawn didn't want to be a part of all of whatever this was? She couldn't blame him if he ran for the fucking hills. This was a lot.

"It wasn't a dream, little flower." Mathias stood then and came to stand at the foot of the bed. His face was solemn as he looked at her, his eyes gleamed with unshed tears.

Then, she remembered, he was on the floor when she woke up, which seemed odd now that she thought about it. He was a strong man; he didn't seem like the type to fall over or trip. Could whatever had happened to her happen to him, too?

"What do you mean?" Her voice was barely above a whisper.

"What you saw wasn't a dream. I know because I saw it too, and I had lived that day fifteen years ago." His voice was laced with anguish as his eyes went distant, like he recalled all they had both seen.

"What do you mean you both saw it? Saw what?" It was Skye this time; he looked at his brother like he couldn't quite believe what his brother was saying.

"I'm saying that when she and I both passed out. It was because someone got into our minds and linked them, showing her the worst day they could have ever shown her." Mathias spoke each word, laced with venom, at whoever had done this to them.

Audelia could feel the tears welling in her eyes as she looked at him. It was real.

Everything she saw.

It had happened.

Which meant.... oh gods.

"What is happening? Why was I shown that? How could that have been a memory? You all had point ears--like you were--like we were fae?" Her mind was spinning as she spoke. Each word was like this finite moment in time, and she was crashing into the boulder that would spell her entire life into a work of fiction.

"Fae? What do you mean, Del?" Shawn spoke to her softly, with a look of concern in his eyes, and broke parts of the dam she was trying not to set free.

"Everyone...everyone in this room, including an apparent

eight-year-old version of myself...had the pointed ears of the fae, just like the old stories we used to read." She whispered the words. She could hardly believe she had spoken to them out loud.

Fae? Was she fae? How the fuck was that possible?

"Yes, little dove. What you saw if it was a memory of Mathias's, then you saw the truth of who and what we are." Mara spoke as she squeezed Audelia's knee in support.

"But that doesn't make sense. We don't have pointed ears, and everyone looked different; they were more feline in their facial structures, not this." She gestured to everyone in the room.

"That is because my brother, Waldrom, cast a spell on all of us; we are still fae, but as long as we reside here in this land. We will appear as the mortals do; all be a little stronger."

So, they were fae......what in the actual fuck.

The room felt like it was spinning as she took in everything they told her and what she had seen in that memory.

Her life was truly just a lie. But why? Why did they lie to her? Just why?

The tears were begging to set themselves free as she thought back to the king and queen from the memory, if she was the princess in that bed.

Then....

Those were her parents, weren't they?

Oh gods, they were dead.

She watched them die.

It wasn't just a sad twist of fate that took them from her, no, it was a brutal death at the hands of the most terrifying being she had ever seen.

She couldn't breathe.

Her skin began to crawl with heat. She felt like her every cell was on fire. She couldn't suck in a breath, and when she tried, all she tasted was ash.

Oh gods, not again.

Was this going to happen to her constantly from now on?

Was she just going to burst into flames one day out of the blue?

She felt a touch on her back, which was cool compared to the heat that was coursing through her body at the moment. So, she latched onto it. Pulled her entire being into that touch, grabbed hold of it, and used it to pull herself out of the inferno that was still raging inside her.

Everything slammed back into her in one large gulp of air as she let that touch ground her and be the bridge she needed.

"Del? Del, my love, are you okay?" It was Shawn; everything felt fuzzy, like she was looking at everything through a film, but she knew for certain that the touch on her back, the one that brought her back from the flames, was him—the man she loved.

He was always there for her.

"Ow...everything hurts..." She groaned.

She heard shifting to her right and looked over. Her vision started to clear a little, and it cleared enough to see Mara pulling little vials out of a bag on the end table by the bed.

"What is all that?" Both Shawn and Audelia asked at the same time.

"Little bits of potions, things that are simple in their workings, that they can go unnoticed in this realm. Things...we thought we may need one day for you or Mathias." Mara spoke as she began to pour little bits from a few different colored vials into a small clay cup she had also pulled from the bag.

"Me and Mathias? Why?" Audelia tilted her head and looked over at Mathias, who blushed. The giant of a man blushed with...embarrassment?

"Yes, you see, some members of the fae produce large amounts of magic. I, myself, have a meager amount, mainly for potion making and small bits of protection. But fae like Mathias and you have an untapped amount of magic that, even with the spell in place, will sometimes seep through and cause.... issues." Mara looked over at Mathias, who, even more to Audelia's surprise, turned beet red and looked away.

"It's not my fault. How was I supposed to know if I got upset enough that my magic would start to leak, and I would *accidentally* cause a few random tornadoes...It's not my fault this realm is so.... *delicate*." He grumbled and raked a hand over his face.

"You caused tornadoes to appear?" She couldn't help it, but a laugh burst from her, and she kept laughing as she saw his face go even redder; her whole body shook with laughter.

Gods, that felt good.

Before she realized it, several of the others, even Shawn, were laughing at how embarrassed Mathias, the giant of a man who gave off this air of strength and stoic anger, was blushing!

"You are all assholes...." He growled, but she could see it when he looked at her, a tiny little smirk in the corner of his mouth.

"Yes, he did...thank goodness he had gotten so upset during a bad rainstorm that year, so it wasn't as unusual to the people here. But still, things like that can happen. They happen with you, too, just not like that." Mara spoke, her voice was light from the laughter, even she had given with the others.

It brought a small smile to Audelia, seeing her aunt laugh and smile like that made her feel a little bit better.

"What---what do you mean? I have leaked magic? When? How?" She looked at the faces in the room and then at her aunt.

She had leaked magic? What the hell?

She tried to think back to all the times in her life when she sometimes felt more. Yeah, she had felt like something was brewing inside her a few times throughout the past fifteen years, but no glowing, nor any flames, or anything *odd*.

Right?

"Nothing, like what occurred with Mathias, but you usually would run high fevers, like your body was burning alive, they have terrified me. But, as far as I am aware, it's only ever been in the form of you not feeling your best. I think it is because my brother ensured that your end of the spell was stronger to safeguard that your true magic never came out."

Her true magic?

So not only was she fae, which holy fuck balls, but she had magic?

Then, she remembered the woman from the memory; she had wielded magic, very powerful magic, from what it had seemed.

Did she get it from her?

Her....mother?

Gods...she died, died and the words.... she told the twins to tell her.... oh gods.

The tears burst forth anew, great, raging sobs that stole her breath and made her whole body curl in on itself.

"It was them.... wasn't it? Mathias? What I saw--that was them?" Her voice was barely a whisper; she needed to know anything but the words, she didn't want to say them. Didn't want to think that it was true, that she had watched her parents die.

"Was that who, baby?" Shawn asked. He reached and gripped her hand as if he knew whatever was said next, she would need him more than before.

"Mathias? Was that...." Gods, she couldn't say it. Couldn't voice the words; this was too much.

Her parents, she knew in her heart that it was them, —but she *needed* to hear it.

Needed someone to tell her it was them.

"Who did she see in the memory, brother?" It was Bronn this time. His voice was unusually soft.

"I'm sorry, shadow flower, that was your parents you saw." His eyes were sorrowful as he looked at her. he took a step toward her, like he wanted to hold her and tell her everything would be okay. But, as much as she could see it in how he carried himself, he didn't reach for her. Instead, he sat at the edge of the bed, seeming to need to be closer to her.

"Naseria and Garrik?" Skye spoke.

She began to scream in anguish as what she saw fell to the forefront of her mind. She watched it over and over.

Their deaths.

The brutal way they died.

The loss of her parents, and then, as the memory showed her, the loss of her entire self.

She truly had lost everything that day. She had always felt that when she thought about her parents dying. It always felt more significant than what she had been told.

"What's wrong, *A Chroí?*" She felt Shawn's warm hands cup her cheeks and bring her to look at him. She could barely see him through the tears. Her heart was breaking so damn much.

"My...my parents.... I saw......saw...." She choked out every word.

"Sweetheart? Saw what? It's okay, I've got you.... You can tell me. What happened?" His voice was gentle as he wiped the streaming tears from her cheeks.

She couldn't say it. She couldn't.... couldn't tell him that she watched her parents die...

They died...

Gods, what was her life?

"It's okay, shadow flower, it'll be okay," Mathias spoke, his voice was thick with sorrow and bits of anger that she didn't think were directed at her or even Shawn. Her guess was whoever had pushed the memory through them both and made her watch.

Shawn swung his head to Mathias, his touch still on her in comfort, but he growled. "You don't even know her. Don't act like you have any right to say those things to her. It was your memory she was forced to somehow see. It's your damn fault she is in pain like this!" Mathias flinched.

His words cut like a blade into Mathias; she could see it in his eyes. They went from sorrow for her to regret and shame.

"Don't...Shawn...It's not his fault.... he didn't force me to see.... see..." She reached out to his arm to stop him from doing whatever he wanted to do. She still couldn't get the words out, but could say that bit because it wasn't Mathias's fault; he didn't do this to her.

"Okay. Okay, let's all calm down a bit. What was in this memory, brother?" Skye broke the brewing tension in the room; his voice was a force.

Mathias's shoulders slumped then. He looked to her to see if it was okay for him to talk for her; she found it comforting that he wanted to make sure she was okay with it.

She merely nodded and braced herself for the words he would say.

CHAPTER TWENTY~ ONE

Audelia thought she could handle hearing someone else say that it, say the words that would truly damn the life she knew and rebuild it on bones of heartbreak and, of all things she could have ever thought, magic.

She gripped Shawn's hand as she focused on the words Mathias spoke.

"The memory that she and I were forced to watch was the day she was marked. It started when we were in her bedchambers, guarding her as all hell broke loose around us." His voice was a rasp, like he was trying to fight back tears at what he would need to say next.

An audible gasp worked its way through everyone in the room.

"I don't understand, so it was a memory of you all in her room protecting her, why is it such a bad memory?" Shawn spoke, but his words were unsure. "Del?"

"It wasn't just the memory of us guarding her. It was also the vision that the twins showed us." Mathias spoke softly, and Audelia could hear the heartbreak in his every syllable.

"Twins? There are more of you?" Shawn asked.

"Yes, boy, there are four others, two of which are the twins Micah and Ezreal, who can speak to shadows and project memories to others. They were with the king and queen that day, so we would know what was happening outside the room. In case Waldrom didn't return, we could plan a way to fight out and get her to safety." Mathias snapped.

"Calm down, brother, the mortal is merely asking a question." Skye placed a placating hand on his older brother's shoulder.

"Go on, Mathias, what happened in the room she saw?" Bronn spoke, but his words seemed to waver; the look in his eyes told Audelia everything she needed to know. He couldn't remember, at least not entirely.

Audelia braced herself. She scooted closer to Shawn and leaned into his warmth, wishing he could make it all go away, as she heard the screams in her head.

Her heart was beginning to shatter.

Mathias took a deep breath, seeming to ground himself. "She saw us in the room, felt how I felt watching her in that bed, and how worried we all were in the room. Waiting for Waldrom to return. Fearing what would happen to her and our king and queen. Then the twins arrived, and she saw the vision they gave us…… she watched her parents die, every single moment down to the moment the twins appeared in the room." His words were garbled as the tears he had tried to hold back began to flow.

It was them.

Her parents.

Oh gods.

Her mind was reeling as the scene that she now knew was a memory, all she saw was the brutal way her father and mother had died.

It just played over and over, like her mind had decided that it wanted to rub her face in by playing the scene repeatedly.

She was vaguely aware of the others crying and people talking, but the buzzing was starting to come back.

It started up slowly but held a sharper edge than it did before. Almost *violent*.

But the mild way it had crept into her mind did not last long before it blocked out all other sounds. It was like her magic, or whatever this really was, didn't want her to focus on anything but those images.

The sacrifice her mother and father had made for her.

She didn't deserve it, not the sacrifice, not this adoration she could feel flowing from everyone in the room.

She was tainted.

Weak.

She was the cause.

If she had been stronger, if she had been enough. Then her parents wouldn't have had to die, and the people around her wouldn't have had to give up their whole lives to protect her.

She was just this weak girl; yeah, she could fight, but when it came down to the moments that counted, she was *nothing*.

The shadows, Kage. She had been so weak with both.

How was she going to stop this darkness, this omnipresent being that had shattered everything? How was she going to do that when she couldn't handle an ex-boyfriend raping and almost killing her?

You cannot. A voice whispered in her ear; it was a soft purr. It felt sinister and sent a trill of dread through her.

You are weak.

You will fail.

They died because you are weak.

You always will be.

She felt it then like a shadow had overtaken her vision. *When had that happened?*

Had she been so caught in her grief that she didn't notice the shift?

Yessss. It hissed.

The voice, so eerily similar to the one she heard in The Glade, kept taunting her, and she felt stabs of pain hit her body like she was being stabbed over and over.

Her body convulsed as the voice laughed.

She cried out in pain. But no words had left her throat. Audelia clawed at her own throat as she continued to scream for help.

The voice just laughed more, and she felt it then. Claws tore down her cheek, and the sick wetness of blood licked her skin.

She wanted to vomit.

You are so beautiful. I will stop if you let me have you. Little pet.

Her body merely convulsed and rocked as the stabbing ebbed into this pulsing force of hate and pain. She was crying, and she could feel the tears mixing with the blood racing down her cheek.

No. No. No.

She didn't want this; didn't want to give in to whatever this was.

She just wanted the pain to stop.

Poor weak thing. The voice taunted; she could feel a warm, vicious breath in her ear. The more it spoke, the more it reminded her of the demon from her nightmare in The Glade.

Oh gods.

She had to stop this. Whatever this thing was, she wanted no part.

She reached inside herself, to the warmth in her chest, hoping against hope that it would be enough to stop whatever this was.

You can't stop this. I will have you. My pet. Pretty.... little sad pet. You shall be MINE!

The buzzing was back, and it roared in her body, so that she felt it then. That warmth, but it wasn't the light from Waldrom. No, this warmth was a flame, a brilliant red flame that swept over her body in soft tingling sensations. She felt the pain start to ebb away, destroyed by the fire that now fully engulfed her body.

She cried out. But still, no words came. Her voice. It was still gone.

It won't be long, my pet. I will find you. And you will be mine... you cannot stop fate.

She was getting tired of being told she belonged to someone she did not want. Tired of it all, she would not cower, not from another controlling being or whatever the fuck this was.

You can go fuck yourself! She finally screamed as the final vestiges of this dark hate that had been encasing her were burned away. She felt powerful as she banished the dark from her and felt everything lighten.

As her eyes opened, she could have sworn she heard a

woman's voice tell her something, but she could not tell what it was.

When Audelia opened her eyes again, she found that she was on top of Shawn and had him by the throat.

His eyes were wide, not in terror but worry for her. She also noticed several other hands trying to pull her from him.

What the fuck?

"I... I'm sorry..." Her words were a whisper as she pulled away from his throat and scurried away from all the hands on her and him.

Oh gods, she had almost killed him.

Why?

She buried her face in her hands, too ashamed to look at anyone. She was still burning up; she could feel the heat as it caressed her skin in an embrace. She didn't understand what was happening.

All she could remember was hearing Mathias say the words that it had been her parents she had seen slain—next, that voice and the pain.

Had that been...... Lefrain?

An audible gasp broke through the room. Had she said that last part out loud?

"What—what did you just say?" It was Bronn, who had moved to her right and placed a gentle hand on her back, she couldn't bear to look at him. At any of them.

But one thing she did need to know right now was if Shawn was okay. "Is....is Shawn okay?" Her words were a broken whisper to her uncle.

"Mara has him, and he'll be okay. But, little one, I need to know if you are okay. What happened?" Worry laced his tone.

"I think.... I think Lefrain was talking to me...." Just saying his name brought a cold chill over her body.

"What the fuck do you mean?" It was Mathias this time. She felt the bed dip, and a shadow passed over her as he loomed.

"I... mean...one second, I was thinking about how it had been my parents I had seen. And the next I felt a buzzing, and then this thick darkness crept over me, and there was......a voice. It was taunting me... Telling me I would be his.... calling me their little pet and that I could not avoid fate."

"What else did you see or feel?" Bronn spoke. He sounded like a general trying to assess the threat lurking in the shadows.

So, she told them. Everything she had felt, the pain, the fact she couldn't talk, her body convulsing, and then the fire that swept it all away from her.

When she finished, everyone was quiet. She still couldn't bring herself to look at them all. Or to face whatever she had done to Shawn.

What if he never wanted to see her again?

Suddenly, she felt a hand under her chin, forcing her to look up. But she clamped her eyes shut. She couldn't look. Couldn't face what she had done.

"A Chroi. Look at me, please?" Shawn's voice sounded hoarse, but she could hear the usual warmth under it. She blinked through the tears she had been shedding, and his face came into focus.

"I'm sorry.... I didn't know it was you...." She threw herself into his arms, seeking his warmth and forgiveness and hoping he would not forsake her. Audelia felt his arms hold her tightly, looking to soothe her worry.

"It's okay. I'll be fine. I'm more worried about you, sweetheart." He pulled back just enough to look at her, swiped the tears away from one eye with his thumb, and smiled at her. He kissed her forehead and pulled her into another embrace.

She relished in the safety of his arms, his love, his support.

"It does sound like something Lefrain would do," Mara spoke from behind Shawn.

"But, how? He should be locked away in our realm; that was the whole point of us coming here." Skye spoke.

"It seems he found a way in," Mara spoke, and the words echoed around the room like an albatross.

Lefrain. He had found them.

Found *her*.

"What does that mean then?" Audelia spoke softly. She pulled a little from Shawn's embrace but kept herself close to him, grabbing his hand to keep herself anchored.

"It means it's time for everyone to come to the fold. It means our time here is up." Bronn spoke his words, sealing their fate.

"I'll call the others," Skye said as he stood from the spot he had knelt on the bed when he had been trying to pull her from Shawn. He gave her a weak smile and left the room.

"Let's give her some time to rest, shall we? I'm sure it will take some time to get the twins back here, knowing them; they are far from here." Mara softly said as she stood from her place behind Shawn and began to rush Bronn and Mathias out of the room.

"If I have to leave, then so does he," Mathias growled, pointing at Shawn.

"I am not leaving her. Not after all that." Shawn pulled from Audelia and stood till he was in Mathias's face.

Well, their friendship is obviously off to an alphahole start. She smiled to herself at that.

"If you two are done swigging your cocks around." Mara chided. Audelia would never get over hearing her sweet, kind aunt talking like that.

Maybe this was how she always was.... before.

"Mathias, she is safe in this house. We will all be right downstairs. Besides, you know Audelia can handle herself. We all saw to her training throughout her adolescence." Bronn spoke, pushing at Mathias to finally get him to leave.

Mathias huffed and looked directly at Audelia. "I am sorry that you had to see all that, princess. Call out if you need me for anything, and I will be there." His words brought a blush to her face as he walked begrudgingly from the room.

"Well, come get you both when the others arrive, and we'll talk more then." Mara squeezed Audelia's shoulder reassuringly.

Audelia and Shawn nodded as Mara and Bronn left.

Audelia stood on shaky legs as the door closed and threw herself at Shawn. He caught her quickly and held her tightly as she cried.

She didn't remember the last time she had cried this much.

But it was starting to feel like it would never stop.

"It's okay, my love. It's alright, I've got you." He stroked her hair lovingly and guided them to the edge of the bed where they sat, him still holding her tightly.

"It's not alright. All of this.... It's a lot....and then my parents, how they died..." Her voice broke as she said the words out loud; it was the final nail in the coffin of her growing reality.

"It is undeniably a lot. But Del, I have always known you

were more than all this. This small town, this world, honestly." Shawn brought a hand up to her chin, making her look into her eyes. His eyes were brimming with this sense of awe and devotion.

It made her knees weak and her heart pound.

"What do you mean?" She was curious because she had always been a young woman who just loved stories and learning how to fight. Yeah, she loved the magical feel of The Glade, but that was the most she indulged in something that felt bigger than her.

The warmth in her chest seemed to give a little nudge when she thought of The Glade.

"I mean, there have been times throughout the years where I don't know how to describe it, but you just seemed *more* than just you. Especially when we are the Glade, during a storm, and then when we were at the studio doing fight moves." As he spoke, she thought back to all those times and places.

She had felt *more*; those moments gave her a sense of purpose, of *power*, like she was this infinite thing, and she had held those moments like they were her strength.

Audelia had never realized someone else had noticed those things, too.

"Thank you." It wasn't enough; she wanted to say so much more, but she felt so very drained by the day. The last forty-eight hours had been so life-altering that she felt like she was no longer herself.

Maybe that was a good thing?

"You don't need to thank me, love. I love you, Audelia. I will stand by your side in whatever way you need. Maybe I can be your sexy right-hand knight." He winked at her, giving her a reassuring smile.

"You are such a dork." She laughed and leaned in to kiss him. Grateful that he was here, that he loved her enough not to run.... when she had hurt him.

"Are...you sure you're okay?" She asked softly, her hand reaching up to touch the harsh red lines of her fingerprints, Gods she had held him tightly in those moments.

"Yes. Del, I was more worried about you than myself. Your eyes...they had gone distant and cold; it was like you were there. It...it scared me that I had somehow lost you." He pulled her again into an embrace, this one felt like he needed to reassure himself that she was here.

She felt his worry, and her heart broke more.

"Tell me everything that had happened that I don't remember." She asked.

So, he told her how Mathias had finished telling them that she had seen her parents die in the vision, the people known mainly as the twins had shown them, and had told them the rest of the memory, and had told them of her interaction with whom she now believed was Waldrom.

She hadn't realized Mathias had seen that part. She also hadn't known he was along for the ride down memory lane either.

Shawn spoke about how everyone, including himself, had cried, and that he had noticed she had gone quiet. At first, he thought she was crying, the way she cradled her face in her hands and shook a little. But then, when he had tried to get her to talk to him while the others had consoled each other over the freshly opened wound of their sovereign and friend's deaths. She hadn't moved, and then she had let out this scream and had everyone jumping to their feet, and then she was on him.

Audelia felt like she was going to puke as she listened to him talk about how she had hit him and straddled him and wrapped her hands around his throat and had just been this shell of herself, choking him. He said she was crying through it, though, but no one could get her off of him, and then all of a sudden, he had felt her loosen her hold slightly, and then the lights were back in her eyes.

The rest she remembered.

Gods...she could have killed him.

Whatever that being had made her do while it had trapped her in that dark. It could've caused her to kill the man she loved.

What if it happened again?

She couldn't think. Everything was swimming through her head.

"Audelia? *A Chroi*, are you alright? Do I need to get Mara?" Shawn spoke softly after what had seemed forever after he had finished telling her everything.

"Will....will you just hold me for a while?" Tears swam in her eyes as she begged.

"Of course, my love." He scooped her up and pulled them back down amongst the pillows on the bed, pulled her face to rest on his chest, and curled around her body protectively. He kissed her forehead and stroked the back of her hair softly.

They just lay there in each other's embrace as the beginnings of a new dawn crept through the windows outside the room.

CHAPTER TWENTY~TWO

Sometime later, there was a knock on the door, and Mara poked her head in, a small smile lighting up her face. "The others are here if you feel up to it to come down. Bronn ordered Chinese for lunch, figured we could eat and talk."

"Yeah. We'll be down in a moment." Audelia sat up from where they had been lying in bed, rubbing the sleep from her eyes. She hadn't even realized she had fallen asleep. The rays of sunlight were spearing through the closed curtains, billowing in the open window breeze.

How long had she been out?

She turned to look at Shawn, who smiled at her as he sat up and kissed her shoulder. "How are you feeling, love?"

"Like I've slept so long, my life ended and began anew without me knowing it." She gave a small laugh. Stretching out her arms, she reveled in the feeling of all the sore muscles loosening; she still ached around the bandages, but it wasn't as bad anymore.

Though if she was honest with herself, the ache was welcome because it meant she was still fighting somehow. Maybe, just maybe, she wasn't weak, and she could do this.

She wouldn't let Lefrain win.

She still didn't understand what was happening to her, but she was done having controlling men try to make her what they wanted. She would be stronger.

Audelia stood, walked over to the dresser at the far side of the room, and noticed a pile of neatly folded clothes. Her clothes were not from the other night, but clothes that Mara had probably brought.

She wondered if they would stay here from now on or if Bronn would live with them now.

The idea made her smile. She could have a family again.

Not as broken as before, but maybe a little fuller.

She began to strip out of the oversized shirt and sweatpants she had been wearing. Her skin felt thick, like it was covered in something. Looking around, she noticed a bathroom peeking through a half-closed door on the wall near the window.

"I'm going to shower, I feel gross." She told Shawn. Grabbing the clothes, she walked into the small ensuite bathroom. It was simple, with light blue walls and marble tile on the floors. It held a single claw sink with a matching mirror and a gorgeous two-person stand-up shower with the design of a rushing wave in the tiles.

Turning the water on to the highest heat she could stand.

She looked for a brush in a little stand by the sink, and finding it, she began to run it through her knotted hair. As she felt the steam of the shower start to stir the air, she stepped in.

Relishing the burn of the hot water, she tipped her face into the stream and just stood there, letting the water wash everything away.

All the lies, the pain, the new things that scared her.

She just let it burn and renew her.

Audelia was vaguely aware of warm hands that brushed along her midsection and pulled her against a broad back. "Hi." She spoke softly as she kept her eyes closed and leaned her head against him.

"Is this okay?" Shawn spoke, uncertain if he had just crossed a line with her. She smiled, turned in his arms to face him, and reached on her toes to kiss him.

"This is perfect. You are perfect." She deepened the kiss, enjoying getting lost in his taste. She reluctantly pulled away and rested her head on his chest, letting the water wash over them both.

He kissed her forehead and pulled away to grab the bottle of body wash from the little alcove in the shower. "Can I wash you?"

She nodded, watching him as he began to lather the soap in between his hands. Closing her eyes, she enjoyed the feeling of his hands moving over her. It wasn't a sexual moment, but it was beautifully intimate as he washed her body. Taking gentle care over her bandages, he kissed her here and there as he washed her.

Just gentle, tiny kisses, but with each one, it was like he was banishing away every dark thought she had had since the night Bronn and Mara told her the truth. He gently made her turn so he could get her back.

As he washed, he kneaded her shoulders. She let out a soft moan as he worked through all the tight muscles and whimpered when she felt his hands leave her body.

She needed more.

Needed him.

Not just the sex, the sex had been mind-altering, but it was these simple, loving touches he gave her. They brought her this sense of peace and grounding. Something she had always craved.

She gasped as she felt his fingers in her hair, and a shiver ran down her spine as he worked his hands over her scalp and through her curls. It was so euphoric having the man you love wash your hair. She couldn't fully explain how damn perfect that feeling was.

Shawn turned her again so that her hair was in the stream of water from the rain shower head. He leaned in and swept her into a heavy kiss as the soap rinsed from her body and hair. "I love you." He whispered into her mouth as he pulled away to help her finish rinsing.

"I love you, too." She spoke back softly. She reached over to grab the soap and began to wash him, too. Enjoying the sensation of all his strong, lean muscles rolling under her hands. She placed kisses here and there on his chest and then again on his back as she washed him.

They finished rinsing each other and giving kisses here and there. But they never went farther than the kisses and gentle caresses that promised more later.

Shawn reached over to turn off the shower and stepped

out, wrapping a towel around her waist. He reached for her hand to help her step out of the shower and pulled her naked body into his and kissed her again.

"I'll never tire of that." He purred to her as he wrapped a towel around her.

"Me either." She smiled and began to dry herself. They both quickly dressed, and she looked at herself in the mirror as she worked the brush through her damp hair.

She looked the same; her freckles were still delicately around her nose and cheeks, and her eyes still held that same starkness they always did. As she brushed her flaming curls, they felt the same.

But she knew she wasn't the same. Not everything had changed. She may look like the woman she had been a few days ago, but she hadn't even been that woman either.

Somehow, deep inside, she always knew it. Knew that she was more than just who she thought she was.

Reaching into the drawer of the little cabinet by the sink, she found other hair supplies waiting for her: hair ties, different masks, and mousses for styling. Like, Bronn had truly planned on this being her room one day. It made her blush that he had put so much thought into what she would need or want.

She picked up a styling mousse and worked a bit through her curls so they wouldn't frizz in the humidity that always seemed to last after any storm in the late spring. Taking one final look in the mirror, she ran her hand down her throat to the necklace she had there. She had worn it since she could remember; it had been around her neck. It was a simple design, delicate gold wrapping around two stones, one a pearl color with a tiny cherry blossom encased, forever in bloom, and just below a dark blue crystal that she had sworn she had seen something inside shift around every so often. But she loved it.

Audelia now wondered if it was something her mother had given her; she wanted so badly to remember them. To know what they were like. To know what her childhood had been like because she didn't remember anything past the first morning she woke up at Aunt Mara's house after they had died.

Shawn came up behind her then and wrapped his bare arms around her waist. She placed her hands over his and leaned against his chest. Audelia took in how they looked together. Shawn was almost a foot taller than she was, wearing a blue polo shirt that hugged his muscles in all the right ways. He looked huge compared to her curvy, slightly petite frame.

She had rounded hips and thighs that clung to the fabric of her jeggings, her full breasts were currently resting in the plums of the sweater she had on that went into a deep v hugging her breasts, it was a soft lavender color with mixes of pastels strewn here and there and it capped off at her elbows. The soft colors brought out the hues of red in her flaming locks that were curling tighter about her face as they dried.

"What are you thinking, a chroi?" Shawn's warm breath tickled her ear as he bent his head beside hers and gently kissed her cheek.

"That, I want just to stay here and not leave the little bubble of this room. Does that make me a coward?"

"No, my love, this is a lot. You are handling this gracefully, and I'm pretty sure a coward would have run from the hills by now." He laughed and turned her around and kissed her deeply.

She sighed as she pulled away from the kiss that had made her knees weak. Wishing she could stay here, but knew she couldn't. So, she raised to her toes, kissed his cheek, and left the bathroom.

Shawn reached for her hand as they reached the top of the stairs and laced their fingers together. They descended the stairs together, and it felt like she was crossing some unknown barrier with every step. She felt it in her bones that everything she had been would be gone once she stepped down that final step.

Audelia took a long breath as her foot settled on the first floor. She felt shaky, not just from her injuries but from everything that was going to happen from now on.

So many questions kept playing on a loop in her head; she didn't know which to settle on first.

But she did know that she wanted more answers and to learn about everything they could tell her. She also wanted to meet these other men—the ones from the memory. Audelia especially had questions for Gideon, who she fucking worked for, but above all, she wanted to see if she felt that same sort of *knowing* that she had when she met Mathias and Skye.

Would they be like they had been in the dream or different?
Would they hate her?

Voices broke through her spiral of questions as they approached the archway to the living area. She looked around at Bronn's home and felt like she was seeing it for the first time.

She had been here countless times for barbeques, parties, and just hanging out because he was one of her favorite people. But now that she knew he was her uncle, she could see certain things now. Little knick-knacks here and there, color choices, ones that before just seemed like his taste, she now could see it was touches of things she and her aunt liked.

Her heart broke a little. He had painstakingly decorated this beautiful, cozy home with her and Mara in mind, and he had to live here alone, separated from them, seeing all these small things that would have brought them such joy. She fought back the tears at the image of Bronn sitting here, alone day after day.

The couch came into view, as did the head of four men she had never seen before, and yet had. It was hard to believe that she did not know them but had seen them and felt the emotions Mathias had tied to each person when he had looked at them.

It was all very confusing.

All conversation stopped as she walked into view. She gripped Shawn's hand as all heads swiveled in their direction.

She was suddenly very nervous to be in this room, to have all these eyes looking at her.

"You've got this, *A Chroi*," Shawn whispered in her ear, guiding her to the oversized chair by the fireplace.

She sat down, never letting go of Shawn's arm as he perched on the arm of the chair; she really wanted him to sit with her so she could lean on his warmth.

But she also didn't want to appear weak to these new men.

If she was a princess—*now queen*, like they kept telling her, then she was their leader for all intents and purposes, a fact that made her knees shake.

Audelia looked at the four men sitting across from her on the large sectional that occupied most of the living area. The one closest to her she recognized was Gideon, the reclusive bookstore owner and her boss, with his sharp features and soft green eyes that seemed to calculate everything. Like he was taking in every detail about her and how Shawn acted towards her, she noticed a tick in his strong jaw as he noticed their entwined hands.

Evidently, it was mutual for all the men as they all seemed to hone in on how friendly Shawn appeared to be with her. Granted, it wasn't like how Mathias practically growled whenever he saw Shawn overly affectionate with her, but it was still there.

It made her happy a bit, not that they seemed so territorial over her, but the fact that they seemed to care so strongly about her that they were acting like a bunch of big brothers, about to give the "You hurt her, and I'll kill you" speech.

Next, she took in the blonde-haired man, whom she recognized from the memory as Alaric, she believed his name was. He was barrel-chested and beautiful. He had these bright, intense blue eyes that brought a sense of awe when you looked at them. But something about him nagged at her. Not in a bad way. But, like she had met him before, but she couldn't seem to place *where.*

Maybe he just had one of those faces?

Then, she looked at the two men who seemed to shrink back into the shadows as they awkwardly sat in the bright, cheery living room. They seemed so out of place with their dark clothes and black raven hair; they had pulled back their hair in man buns. They were identical down to everything; the long nose and thin face reminded her of a young Keanu Reeves. They were well fit, but in that lithe way, you see in dancers. But the hardened looks in their dark eyes as they kept watching Shawn made her feel like they shouldn't be underestimated.

"Audelia, this is Gideon at the very end, whom you know

from the bookstore, then Alaric, and the twins Micah and Ezreal. They are the last of the Cadre sworn to protect you." Broon spoke, his words taking on that authoritative tone again.

Gideon and the twins merely nodded their heads in her direction. Visibly, they were the stoic ones of the group, but for different reasons, she imagined. She could still see the wheels turning in Gideon's eyes. *What was it that she saw in Mathias's memory? Right, he referred to him as the scholar of the group.*

She took that little kernel back for later. If anyone could give her more information about the fae realm, her bet was on him.

But it was Alaric who shocked the hell out of her, getting up and yanking her out of her seat in a bear hug, as his booming voice echoed in the room. "Welcome back to the fold, Princess!" He twirled her a bit; he was like a happy child, which was refreshing after all the sober talk of the past day.

Growls came from Shawn and Mathias at how he was holding her and moving back and forth like she was a toy he won.

"Put her down, you idiot, she is still injured," Skye spoke, his voice raised in a slight laugh mixed with concern. "And remember, she is our *Queen* now, Alaric."

"Oh shit! Sorry, your majesty. Are you alright?" He placed her back on the floor carefully, and it was the way he spoke then and the way he held her gently in his arms that she real- ized why he seemed familiar.

"It was *you*." She spoke, looking up at him like she had that day in the rain. His striking blue eyes, strong jaw, and a smile that could melt your damn panties off. It had been him that day when she heard the voices.

"What, was him?" Shawn spoke from behind her, and she

felt his hand on her back in silent support, which was good because Alaric's twisting made her dizzy.

Alaric stood there and raked his hands through his blonde hair. "Yeah, that was me. Sorry, I couldn't say who I was that day." He gave her a sheepish smile as he turned to sit back down on the sectional.

"He was the guy I told you about the day I heard voices in The Glade." She turned towards Shawn as she went back to sit down.

She felt so awkward with all these eyes on her, so she reached towards the coffee table full of Chinese food and grabbed an egg roll, munching on it to give herself something to do.

"Oh. So, you knew who she was that day? What were you doing there?" Shawn asked, his tone held suspicion towards Alaric.

"Boy, we have always known who she was." It was Gideon who spoke then, his voice was soft and melodic,—the kind of voice that you picture when you are reading a romance novel that has that stoic love interest.

"I am not a boy. And I still find it pretty shitty that you all knew who she was and just ignored her for the past fourteen years. Especially Gideon and Bronn, who pretended not to know her while still being around her."

"Ha! I like you, kid. Got balls. But you're wrong, and we didn't ignore her for fifteen years; we were always there watchin' and keeping her safe as best we could, given the circumstances." Alaric gave a saccharine grin at Shawn.

Audelia thought back to the past fifteen years. There were so many times she felt like she had been watched, like someone was keeping a constant watch over her. The only times she hadn't noticed were when she was with *Kage*....Gods, did any of them see her with him? See how he treated her when he thought no one was looking? He had always been good about not showing *that* side in public places.

"Well, you all did a shit job, as did I when it came to Kage." Shawn spat out, but she could hear his hate for himself with those words. He felt like he had failed her when she was with Kage.

But the truth was, Kage was damn good at letting people see what he dictated they see.

It's what made him dangerous.

"Kage?" Gideon spoke. Audelia could see his mind working, Kage had come into the bookstore several times, usually pissed she had taken an extra shift. She saw the moment when he placed the name with a face and was instantly angry.

"Yeah....he is my ex...." Audelia spoke softly and hated even acknowledging he had been anything to her.

"I think it's time we all cleared the air. Us and you as well, my little dove. I know you don't want to speak about what happened, but you told us he is threatening you. It may be linked to everything else." Mara spoke, her words were kind and gentle, like she knew how hard it would be for Audelia to speak about certain things. But she was right.

It all needed to be said on *both* sides.

"If we are to speak on all that has happened. Then it is best if the boy leaves. This has nothing to do with him. He is an *outsider*." Gideon spoke, his words felt like blades.

"I am not fucking leaving her." Shawn spat out at them. "I am not the outsider here. All of you are, as far as I'm concerned."

He was right in a way. Besides Mara and Bronn, Shawn had always been there. She wanted him here.

"The fuck, we are little boy. I may have respected how you have been the past few days. But I don't fucking care when it comes to all of this. She is precious to all of us in this room; we have been with her for her entire life. She is the air we breathe, and we have all pledged to fall on our own blades if we fail her." Mathias spoke then, standing in front of Shawn, his teeth bared.

Not this again.

"Well, then, it looks like you'd best get on that, because from where I am standing, you all failed her, again and again. I am not fucking leaving the woman I love with people she doesn't know. Hell, as much as I love *Alexander* and Mara," She saw Bronn flinch at Shawn using his fake name to dig the knife deeper. "I don't want to leave her with them either because they have lied to her about too many things." Shawn's words cut through everyone; Audelia heard a soft sob come from Mara at Shawn's words. He had always been so kind to her, to Bronn, but hearing how he thought of them right now broke her heart a little.

But he was right again, and she began to think her mind racing, the noise of Shawn and several others arguing seemed to fall to the wayside.

They had lied to her. Yes, it was to keep her safe, but that lie had made her feel so alone in the world, so alone that when a cruel man was telling her all the things she wanted to hear, she fell for it.

Because he had made her feel seen when she felt like she was so unbearably alone in her life.

So much so, she hadn't seen the monster lurking beneath the surface.

She had been so lost in thought that she hadn't even noticed that Shawn had gotten off the arm of the chair at some point. She gasped when everything came into focus to see that Shawn and Mathias had begun to fight and were on a heap on the floor, trading blow after blow.

What the hell? Seriously with this shit?

Audelia watched as Shawn and Mathias traded blows, and fuck, Mathias was strong as shit. She had fought Shawn before, and he was a pretty skilled fighter, but Mathias was taking the hits like it was child's play to him.

She winced when she heard the crack of bone in Shawn's jaw. She leapt to her feet then, as the other men in the room seemed to have decided just to let them wail on each other, but she wasn't going to let this continue.

Audelia waited for the pause in the punches and found her spot; she moved in with a low swinging kick to Mathias's kneecap. Audelia hit him at just the right place that sent him to the floor. Taking that opportunity, she threw her fist back and slammed it into his jaw. She felt the crunch in her knuckles as she made contact, but she didn't care. This needed to stop now. Mathais must not have seen what was going on because he snarled and twisted his body to send her slamming to the floor.

She hit with a loud exhale of air; Mathias's eyes went wide as he realized what he had just done. "Shit." Someone spoke.

The apology was screaming in his eyes as he was pulled away from her by Bronn and Skye. Audelia stood, a little off-kilter by all the movement, and walked on shaky legs over to

Shawn, kneeling in front of him where he cradled his jaw. "You, okay?"

"Yea...fucker has a good punch though," Shawn smirked but then noticed her pale face. "Are you okay?" He spoke softly, helped her up, and moved them both to the oversized chair again. This time, he decided he wasn't keeping his distance. He sat and pulled her next to him so that she would be cradled against him.

It was very alphahole of him, but right now she didn't care.

"Well, now that... That is over; you all need to get over this. Shawn is staying. He is her boyfriend, and it is more than that. He isn't as much of an outsider as you all think he is." Mara spoke, her voice taking on an annoyed edge. She had apparently left the room at some point because she handed an ice pack to Shawn for his jaw.

Audelia could see the bruises beginning to form under the blue of the ice pack as he placed it on his jaw with a wince.

"What is that supposed to mean, Mara? He isn't one of us. I don't care if he thinks he has some sort of hold on her, but he isn't one of *us*; he is a child and shouldn't be a part of any of this. He won't be able to protect her." Mathias spoke, and Audelia could hear anger lacing every word.

"He can. Bronn has trained him since those two were children. He handled you decently, which is saying a lot. But it's the core of who he is that means he isn't just some outsider."

Audelia looked at her aunt, confused. The core of who he is? She appreciated her aunt coming to Shawn's defense, but that part made no sense; Shawn was Shawn. Right?

"Shawn is an Ito. His family has been loyal to the Phoenix Queen for centuries, so not only is he loyal to Audelia because of his love for her, but also because of who his family is. It's ingrained in him to be there for her. Just as it is for us."

"He is an Ito? How? I thought that clan died out ages ago in the mortal lands?" Gideon spoke, his voice was eager, like he was trying to gain as much knowledge as he could before he made his judgment. Past the original, he had clearly given at the beginning.

"Yeah. My mother's side is from the clan Ito. What does that have to do with anything?" Shawn spoke.

Wait. Did her aunt mention the Phoenix Queen? Like the story Sobo had told them?

"Wait, you said the Phoenix Queen? Like the story?" Audelia asked, her mind racing.

"That isn't just a story, my queen. That happened with the Goddess we call The Phoenix Queen Eudora. She was trapped in the mortal realm, and a clan led by Ichiro Ito had given her shelter and protection. We all grew up on that legend." Gideon spoke.

A goddess? It was true? All of it? That means Shawn's ancestors had sheltered an actual *goddess.*

Holy shit.

"That was real? I mean, a part of me always felt like it was real, but to actually hear from someone other than Sobo.... It's unreal. So, Ichiro really did do all of that." Pride seemed to swell in Shawn's words.

"It's why you were named after him, that's why your grandmother thought it was destiny that you happened to meet Audelia." Mara smiled at them.

"So, this kid is the ancestor of Ichiro Ito? Holy shit.... Badass." Alaric grinned.

"Yes. Which is why he deserves to be here, so stop trying to get him to leave her." Bronn spoke then, his voice held that finality that a general would give his soldiers the final command.

They all nodded, though Audelia could see Mathias was still not happy about it.

Such a *grump*, that one.

Mara clapped her hands together before she spoke again. "Well, now that is settled, Audelia, my dove, can you tell us about Kage and anything else you can think of that seemed strange lately?"

Audelia nodded. She told them about Kage, the abuse, the raping, which earned several growls, and she felt Shawn tightened his grip on her hand. She told them everything that had happened in their relationship and about how Shawn had been there to help her. She told them about the times she had heard voices or seen strange shadows, but the one that stuck with her was the one from over a week before she had gone into the studio.

How it felt different from the other times. More menacing, and as if it could actually harm her. To how, after almost two years of nothing, Kage had left those flowers on her porch and sent those messages, sent them the same day she saw the Shadow.

By the end, she was exhausted, but it had felt good getting all that off her chest. She even made sure to tell them that she had dreams, little flashes of a life that felt real.

She leaned her head on Shawn's shoulder as she finished. He wrapped his arm around her, holding her close.

"I am so sorry. I had no idea all that had happened." Mara's words were garbled as she cried. She stood and pulled Audelia into a tight embrace.

"It's over now. He can't get to me. I won't let him." Audelia spoke. A part of her feared he could get to her, but she wanted to believe she would be stronger this time, that he couldn't do those things to her again.

As she looked at the faces around her, seething with rage over what had happened to her, she knew at least that these men would not let Kage get near her.

"I think, possibly, this man Kage, that he may be taken over by one of the wraiths Lefrain uses." It was one of the twins who spoke, startling them all. His voice was like worn leather.

CHAPTER TWENTY~THREE

"Taken over? Like possessed?" Audelia spoke, her words barely audible.

"Yes, he may have entered a bargain in order to get you back. From what you said, he was very possessive of you. It would not be a long shot to think that Lefrain's agents would have seen that and used it as a way to keep a foothold in this world." The twin with the voice like worn leather spoke, she honestly couldn't tell which twin was which.

Kage was possessed?

She couldn't even bring herself to feel sorry for him for whatever trick this agent may have used. Just fury. Fury that the bastard thought, entering into some sort of pact with a demon would give him an advantage over her.

Wait, would he have one now?

She was mortal right now, according to what they had told

her so far. Whatever, magic, she clearly had a mind of its own. So, she couldn't entirely rely on that.

Shit.

"Okay, so I think it's time you all explained things to me. Because if he is taken over by this agent, I need to know what all that means. And I need to know who I truly am. I am so lost right now in what is real and what still feels like fiction." When Audelia spoke, it took on an authoritative tone, one that surprised even her.

"Of course, little one. Again, I am very sorry that we had to keep this from you. I know at this point, it just feels like an excuse to you." Bronn stood and walked to kneel before her at her spot in the oversized chair, his eyes were shining with truth and regret. "But I promise you I truly am remorseful for what this is causing you."

Audelia reached out to him and placed her hand on his cheek, giving a small smile. "I know. I can see it in how you all have been the past few days. I won't lie and say that this all hasn't broken my damn heart, but I will say, as long as you all are honest from now on, I think I can move past the hurt."

Bronn leaned into her hand and gave a small smile. "I understand." He stood and returned to his seat beside Mara, who grabbed his hand and entwined their fingers.

"As we told you the other day, we are family, I am your uncle, my younger brother Garrik was your father and our king. I hadn't wanted to be a king, I had always wanted to use the blade to protect others, I was always hot-headed when it came to dealing with people. But your father--He was everything. He could calm a raging crowd with a few well-poised words. It was--Magical to watch. He was always more fit to be king. And then he met your mother, Naseria. She was the spring to his world. My brother had always been about books and people. But when Naseria came into his world, I had never seen my brother so damn happy. They married a year after he officially became king after our father had passed. She was crowned shortly after, and she was so well-loved by our people, that people would constantly come to the capital to catch glimpses of her. Your parents were always outside the castle. Which was such a pain to make sure they remained safe. Granted, both were very skilled with a blade, and your mother."

"She was the most talented sorceress of the age. Many believe she was descended from the Goddess herself, with how she commanded magic. Honestly, I don't know who was more powerful between her and Waldrom. But I still worried. Lefrain had been gaining followers by the decade. We always knew that eventually, the time of peace that had been in the kingdom would come to a stark end. Praying we would never see that day come to pass. Even if that felt like a fool's hope, I never wanted to see the pain in their eyes when it felt like the world around them was in flames." Bronn paused like he was looking for the right words.

What he had said so far was painting a picture in her head of the people she wondered about. *Her parents.*

She wished she could see more of them than just those horrible final moments of their lives.

They seemed like wonderful people. Audelia wondered if one day she would get the memories of them back. She wished with everything she had, that she would.

She felt Shawn's hand working its way up and down her arm in soothing motions.

"You were born about two hundred years into their rule. It

wasn't that they didn't want to have children, but conception is not an easy thing in the royal line occasionally, sometimes it's a few years and sometimes it takes several hundred. We aren't entirely sure of the cause for such a long period of time that it takes. Naseria always said the goddess wanted them to be fully set in their roles as king and queen before adding on the care of an infant. We knew, though, that it had constantly saddened your mother when she struggled to conceive. She always held such strength, though. Able to find a silver lining to whatever heartbreak she was dealt. I always admired that about her."

"When you were born, you caused quite the stir, from the flaming red hair to the mark on your wrist." Audelia immediately checked her wrists, there was nothing there, why?

"But I don't have a mark on my wrist?" She found herself stroking her right wrist, though Audelia remembered from a few of her dreams the raised edges of a mark on her wrist.

"Yes. That is because Waldrom spelled it away. We honestly don't know if it will ever come back." Mara spoke then.

Audelia nodded but kept rubbing her thumb over that spot. Like something inside her kept yelling at her that it was there to not lose hope.

"But, the part that caused the most stirrings in the kingdom was the prophecy that came shortly after your first birthday. We only know parts of it because either the oracles didn't give us the proper one or because the gods and goddesses above find it hilarious not to reveal everything. I have always assumed the later."

"My money's on Flontis, that damn trickster always did

find it funny to fuck with all of us." Alaric laughed slapping his knee.

"Flontis?" Shawn asked, though Audelia wondered as well.

"He is one of our many gods. There are several, and it would take longer than we have to go over them all. But he is the one that likes to play tricks and sends messages to the oracles." Gideon added.

Audelia nodded, planning on asking a lot more questions about the gods and goddess from Gideon sometime in the future. She had been right that he was the one to go to for information.

"Anyhow, the prophecy states that a child born with the heart of the Phoenix, would one day defeat the Darkness and bring forth a new age of Gods and Goddesses however if the Darkness was to take her as his bride, then eternal dark would rain down across all the realms. That a union of Fire and Shadow was absolute. We never understood that final part, considering the darkness uses shadows, we fear it meant that there was no stopping Lefrain from taking you as his bride. He had learned of it as well and began his ruthless pursuit of you."

Audelia found herself curling tighter into Shawn, who had brought his arm to pull her to him as if he could protect her from what could happen. She felt him kiss the side of her forehead in comfort. Her heart was hammering in her chest.

Were they right, was this just going to always end with her in Lefrain's clutches?

Was that all she was? Just a place mark in some fucked up prophecy?

How the hell was she supposed to destroy a powerful being like that?

She was going to be sick.

"It's okay my love, I have you." She felt Shawn's warm breath on her ear as he whispered to her. She merely nodded. She couldn't talk.

She merely leaned more into his warmth as her thoughts began to spiral again.

Her mind was reeling from everything.

"Luckily, he went quiet for years, well as quiet as an evil fuck like he could be, we still had wars, mainly from his followers, but nothing from him. It was like he had gone underground, just waiting for the right moment to strike, gladly letting his followers do his dirty work. It was decided that I would become head of your own Knights, being the General of the armies it was the proper choice, that and I would not allow another to be in charge of your safety, I could not trust others to make the right choices on assigning others to guard you. So, the Flaming Swords began their watch. At first, it was just myself, and Gideon. We were still at war, so finding the right males or females to pull from the lines to guard you was hard. You, however made that choice for us when you were about four years old." Bronn grinned as his eyes swam with the memory.

Audelia tilted her head, wondering how the hell, at four years old, she had chosen one of the people to protect her. That didn't seem like a smart decision.

"You trusted a four-year-old to make the decision on someone to guard her? What the fuck? Were you an idiot? Is that why things went south because you trusted a four-year-old to make that kind of choice?" She didn't mean to sound that accusatory, but it seemed asinine that they had let a four-year-old, even if it was her choose someone for this big of a thing.

A loud laugh came from Skye and Alaric at her words, and it made her blush, maybe that was a dumb thing to say.

"Careful little fire, or you'll break my big brother's poor cold heart." Skye gave a big grin as he patted Mathias on the shoulder.

Mathias, to his credit, tried to hide the redness in his ears at the embarrassment. But something in his eyes says it wasn't because of what she said but for something else. "Fuck off, Skye." He growled.

"Aww is my big bad brother embarrassed that he fell to his knees and begged to be the guard of a small child?" Skye laughed clearly, missing the murder in his brother's eyes. "Big Ol' Mattie boy, who knew you were such a teddy bear?" Skye grinned like a cat.

Mathias, quick as lightning, grabbed Skye by the collar of his shirt and tossed him to the floor like a sack of flour. *Oh goodness, that was kind of hot.* He stood over him with a glare, placing one foot on his brother's chest to keep him on the floor.

Skye merely laughed, like the threat from his terrifying brother was the highlight of his day.

"I told you to fuck off, *little* brother." Mathais spit back at Skye. There was menace in his eyes but also just the tiniest hint of...*amusement.*

He was amused?

The idea of the stoic, slightly terrifying Mathias finding his little brother teasing him amusing made Audelia feel warm all over. It was sweet seeing this tiny sliver of brotherly affection.

"Knock it off, you idiots." Gideon snarled, clearly annoyed by the interruption to Audelia being told everything.

Right, he is definitely the no-bullshit type.

"Aw, come on, Gid, let them fight it out. It's always hilarious when Mathias whips Skye's ass." Alaric boomed out a laugh.

"Such children..." Mara murmured; her tone giving a motherly tone, one that showed, she was clearly annoyed by their outburst. "Will you two stop for now or take it outside so you don't destroy Bronn's home." She scolded them, with a tsking sound.

It made Audelia laugh, a full belly laugh. Gods that felt good.

She felt Shawn begin to laugh behind her, she knew why, it was rare to see Mara get strict or angry and when she did, it was like watching a cinnamon roll get angry.

"Sorry, Mara." Both Mathias and Skye spoke at the same time, their voices taking on the tone of a child getting scolded by their mother. Audelia noticed that their ears were red in embarrassment.

It warmed her heart.

She desperately wanted to remember them, to see for herself how she fit into their lives.

"Yes, I know it sounds stupid that we let a four-year-old dictate a new member, but the circumstances, well, we couldn't not say yes." Bronn's tone took on an amused tone.

"You see, it wasn't that you told us, it was more, after what occurred, there was no other option but to appoint your chosen person."

"I don't understand?" She asked.

"One day, Mathias came back from the front lines, being general of the Dragonlance legion, he needed to report of any new...missives per say. Well, as you can already tell Mathias, does not...*play* well with others. So, he had gone to the gardens, a place in which you were constantly at with your mother or with Mara. You found him there that day. Most children are scared of him, especially considering he had currently been covered in blood from the war, but not you. It was quite a sight. Your father and I had gone searching for him, when he hadn't turned up in the war room, to our surprise, we found him a crowd of people yelling at him, what shocked us was the reason why."

"It was shocking because those people were a bunch of fucking twats, is what," Mathias grumbled.

"Indeed, they honestly were. We came upon the group to find you in his arms and him looking rather angry at the people who were yelling at him. Guards were pointing blades at him, demanding he let you go. They thought he had come to kill you." Bronn spoke.

"Kill me? Why?" Audelia asked, yes, she had noticed Mathias to be rather gruff, but the interactions so far had proven him to be very protective of her, like an older brother.

"Because they were gods damn fools. I still don't know why you let those idiots remain as guards for the castle if they couldn't tell the difference between hostile and protective." Mathias growled.

"You see little dove, the people in the court viewed Mathias and his dragon as brutes beneath them. They could never see past his demeanor to see that he is just a giant teddy bear." Mara giggled, reaching over to pinch Mathias's cheek.

"Yes, but I knew, it took one look to see you had claimed him as yours that day. I even joked that I had lost, that you had chosen a new favorite. In all honesty, you did that day. You clung so tightly to him that I took a bit to get you to let go of him so he could at least go clean himself off. It was quite the sight, seeing the Warrior of Death cradling the tiny four-year-old princess in his arms like he was ready to destroy the very kingdom if it kept you safe. It's been that way ever since. He swore fealty to you that day. And shortly after, Skye and Alaric joined us in the Cadre, but you were always closest to Mathias. You two have a bond similar to what he has with his dragon, but they are different. If you can trust any of us right now when you feel like everything has been a lie. Then Audelia trusted *him*. Mathias would rather fall on his own blade than bring you any harm."

She merely nodded. She felt Shawn squeeze her hand as if he needed to let her know she could always trust him, but she was never in doubt of him. Never would be.

Bronn continued. "The twins joined us when you were about six, completing the cadre. For a time, it seemed all of our fears were going to go unfounded. You were always with one of us, even if you were in the castle or with your parents or Mara, one of us was always nearby. Though you did tend to follow Mathias around like a shadow." Bronn laughed at that, his eyes swimming with memory.

She so desperately wanted to remember.

"Will I ever get to remember?" She whispered, her heart pounding, scared of the answer.

"We believe so. When the day happened, the one that ended everything and brought us here. You were with Mara in the gardens Skye was nearby, it was a normal day, you were practicing magic, we hadn't heard anything from Lefrain's minions in years, and everything was in a state of peace. War had ended the year prior; we should have known it was too good. Too quiet." Bronn's words began to hold an ominous feel to them.

Audelia could feel the buzzing in her blood, the magic that

she held, the one that lit her up, she could feel it there at the surface, like it was ready for the next words.

"We were in the garden practicing when suddenly, everything shook, and a blast of dark light in violent shades appeared in the garden and attacked. It blasted the both of us back. A shadow wraith appeared before us. Skye tried to fight it off, but it attacked so quickly. It was different than other ones we had seen before, stronger. It had come for you. We heard.... Lefrain spoke through it, saying he had come for you. It killed several guards, only the small amount of magic Skye held kept him alive. But, before we could get you away, the shadow touched you, grabbing you by the wrist. It.... marked you that day. A wing like a dragon lies on your other wrist, it has shadows that seem to creep from it. Waldrom was able to get it to recede, but the mark remains. We don't know why it's there; you already have your mark from birth, the one that tells us you have the blood of the Phoenix Queen in you." Mara finished speaking. She had tears streaming down her face, as she looked at Audelia.

"I'm sorry we could not protect you better, my dove." She whimpered, and Bronn pulled Mara into his arms and stroked her back as she cried.

The room was quiet for a bit after that. It felt surreal that all that had happened to her. That she was fae but not fae because of a spell. That a dark lord with unfathomable power was out to kill her or make her his bride. That fact made her shudder.

Audelia looked down at her wrists, they were bare, but she felt this needle-like pricking just under her skin like they were calling to her.

But what they wanted, she didn't know. Didn't know if she truly wanted to know.

Then, she recalled the dream she had had the other morning. As Mara talked, she felt like she knew what her aunt would say next, as if she had seen it before. Maybe she had.

You did, little star. That voice spoke again, this time like warm honey.

"So, I was attacked, then what happened? How soon after was the memory I saw?" She needed to know. Needed to hear if she had even seen her parents one last time before they had been forced apart.

Was she scared? What had they said to her? Did they tell her to be brave and that they loved her?

Tears were beginning to well in her eyes as her mind raced with questions, all the uncertainty was breaking her heart again.

"Not long after. You appeared in Skye's harms, barely conscious with Mara beside the both of you, all three of you looking worse for wear but relatively unharmed thank the gods. Waldrom appeared a time after and looked after you as the rest of the Cadre appeared. We took you to your room, where Waldrom placed you into a magic sleep, hoping that it would prevent Lefrain from using the mark to track you. The king and Queen were there to see you were okay. But they were not able to linger, and we sent the twins with them as Waldrom created a barrier in the room, to further protect you as everything happened. It was then that we received word of Lefrain and his forces appearing out of nowhere and had taken the capital and surrounding cities in a fraction of a moment. We still don't know how. The rest, you saw in the memory.

Except the spell. Waldrom placed one of each of us. For us, it blocks certain memories, and the ones we don't even realize are gone. But they are all memories that could lead to Lefrain and his agents finding us. Trust that we don't know the full scope of this spell. But we do know that your memory, your faeself like ours, was locked away. It should return once we are back in Dragsnic. That is at least what Waldrom did tell us. Mara was assigned to be with you permanently, being Waldrom's blood relative, he could use old rare blood magic, to hide her, and with you well hid as well, Lefrain would not find you."

So, she hadn't been able to talk to them one last time, to be held by them. They were just there one moment and gone the next. She felt the tears flowing now. Her heart was shattering.

"Us, remaining apart and pretending that we don't know you, it was part of the spell. To ensure, if he somehow did find this realm, and found us, that we would not be a beacon to you." Bronn told her.

"But we interact all the time? You have been a part of my life since I came to live with Mara. I don't get how that works." Audelia asked. That part, even the other night when he had mentioned it, still bothered her.

"It was the one thing I told Waldrom, I needed, you are my niece, my now queen, my blood, and Mara is my mate, that is a union that cannot be severed. I told him that I cannot live my life constantly in the shadows, I needed to be able to see that you both were okay. That I could ensure you remained able to protect yourself if we somehow failed you. He relented. So, an addendum was added that I could be apart but not fully apart of your lives. Throughout the years, Mara and I have met in secret because to be apart from your mate for too long. It is torture, and it is death. Our souls are one. That is a law higher than the gods themselves." Bronn placed a kiss on Mara's forehead and looked at Audelia.

Her heart was racing. This was *a lot*.

"So.... I'm your Queen?" Every word felt like a heartbeat in her throat. The tears had yet to stop flowing from the heartbreak, from just everything. Her entire world was on a tilt, running full speed into an unknown void.

"Not just our Queen, you are our salvation from the dark." It was Gideon who spoke then, his voice like night.

CHAPTER TWENTY~ FOUR

The words Gideon spoke seemed to still the air around her. It felt like he had summoned something phantasmal with those words.

It was like an *awakening* to her soul.

But it fell short. She expected to feel this rush of power at those words. Instead, she felt pain and an emptiness begging to be filled.

It had been an awakening, but not entirely; it was like something was stopping everything from coming forth, like she was stuck in neutral.

Audelia's bones ached from her toes to her teeth. Her body shuddered.

"Del? You okay?" Shawn's voice was laced with concern as he twisted to look at her better. His hand reached to her face, his thumb rubbing soothing motions back and forth.

"Yeah...My body just aches. It's like something is wanting

to burst forth, but something is stopping it." She gritted out through her teeth.

Fuck it hurt.

"It's possibly your magic, being told all this, it could be trying to trigger everything before it's ready," Mara spoke, as she rose to place a delicate hand on Audelia's forehead. "You have a small fever. Let me make another potion, and you should be all right. Make sure you eat. Everyone should eat." Mara spoke that last bit to everyone in the room.

Audelia watched her aunt leave the room. Something was different about her aunt. She seemed more at ease. Like a heavy load had been removed, one that Audelia had never noticed Mara had before.

It suited her.

She watched as the others seemed to begin to eat. She was hungry, but the idea of eating a lot of food right now made her stomach turn.

Movement beside her made her notice that Shawn had gotten up and was back with a small plate of her favorites. "Here, you need to eat. Even if it is not everything, you have been out for a week, you need fuel. Especially if we are about to face some big shit." Shawn gave her a small smile. She grabbed the plate from him.

"Thanks, handsome."

For a while, everything was in this relaxed silence. She took a few bites of noodles and some orange chicken. It tasted so good.

Mara returned a short while later and handed Audelia a small cup, telling her to drink it. She obliged; it tasted sweet and lemony.

"Thanks, auntie.' She smiled at her aunt as she handed the

cup back. Tears welled in Mara's green eyes, so much emotion was swimming in their depths.

"You okay?" Audelia reached out and touched her aunt's arm gently.

"Yes, my dove, I just.... I never thought I would hear you call me auntie again...After everything that has happened." Mara gave her a small smile before placing her hand over Audelia's on her arm.

"I'm still mad and hurt by everything; I understand the reasons why, even if it breaks me a little. But you are still the woman who has raised me, you are still my auntie always." Audelia gave her aunt's arm a little squeeze of comfort.

Mara pulled her quickly into a tight hug, making Audelia almost spill her plate of food, if not for Shawn grabbing it before it fell. Audelia wrapped her arms tightly around her aunt; there was something about being hugged by the woman who had been like a mother to you that just soothes everything in one's heart. She relished the moment, begging the universe to give her more of these moments. Merely so she does not have to fall entirely apart.

"Okay, my love, let the girl breathe." Bronn was there, placing a firm hand on Mara's back. His smile was warm as he took in the sight of his crying wife holding on to Audelia.

"Sorry, I don't know what's wrong with me." Mara pulled away and wiped the tears from her eyes. Audelia realized she had been crying too and wiped the cool tears from her heated face.

"It's okay, Auntie. It's been a few emotional days lately." Audelia smiled at her aunt.

Mara nodded and walked back to her spot on the sectional

with Bronn. Then, she started grabbing food from the containers on the coffee table.

Shawn handed the plate back to Audelia and pressed a chaste kiss to her cheek before he went back to his food.

For a while, they all sat around eating and making small talk. Shawn was enthusiastic, asking questions about anything and everything he could about the fae realm. Audelia listened to every word. She had wanted to ask, too, but she felt off. Like, too much had been going on, so she just listened.

Glad that Shawn always had such a love for lore that he was always ready for more information about anything. The summers his Sobo came from Japan, or his other grandparents came down from upper Ireland, he would ask for stories, any they could think of. Anything that you couldn't find on the internet or in a library. He always craved knowing more.

It made her laugh that they were always so similar about that. She was always right by him, asking as well. When they would play computer games or console games, she always went for the ones with the best lore. It was like reading a live-action book.

It always made her feel happy, and she wondered if, soon, all these small memories from this place would be all she had left of here.

Would she want to return here after all is said and done?
What if they cannot even get back?
Wait...How do they get back?

Audelia placed her plate down on the small table next to the chair. She looked around at everyone, laughing and talking like this was just a regular night. She desired it could be. Wished that she had so many more nights like this.

With this feeling of being well-loved. Family.

Because that's how these people all felt to her, like family, even the two extremely quiet twins who barely spoke still felt like family.

"How…How do we get to the fae realm? How did we get here to begin with?" She felt every face turn to her as she spoke, and she shrank back a little.

"So, to answer the second question. We are not entirely sure how we got here, but we all woke up in the places we live in now, we assume that was how Waldrom worked the spell. First, we needed to ensure as little contact with you as possible, which would have been hard if we arrived close together. So, Mara believes that her brother placed it into the spell to send us to the places we live, with identities and money, and the spell extended just enough that it was not odd to people that we all just appeared one day." Bronn spoke first.

Mara added. "It was a lot, us waking up here. This world was strange to us at first, so it took a while for us all to find each other again. And I knew my brother had to have been planning this backup for a while, with how much he had ready to go." She squeezed Bronn's hand before finishing her thought.

"I think with how this house is set up, the first plan was not to fully separate us. But I think at the last minute, he did not see a choice when it came to your safety. My brother, like everyone else here, loved you. He and your mother were best friends. He, regardless of magical prophecies, would have made every effort to ensure you survived."

That gave her so many more questions, questions she didn't even know how to voice.

She wanted her memories so damn badly, but another part

of her, the one that had been here for the past fourteen years, didn't want to know.

Because what would it mean for her? What life would she lead if she just buried her head in the sand and gave up on the world that seemed to call to her?

It was all fucking terrifying.

"I see...and the part about how we get back....to our world?" It felt weird saying the word; her tongue felt all gummy, and it sent tingling sensations all over her body.

Including that spot in her chest, where that tiny light seemed to stretch out like a cat inside her.

"That we have no clue, nothing in our individual spells tells us anything about how we get back. Just that we will know when it's time." Mara spoke softly. Audelia could hear the defeat in her aunt's voice.

"Fucking wizards. Why can't they make things simple for once?" Mathias growled.

"When I was in that weird dark place, after that memory and then before when I had been unconscious, that voice, who I think was Waldrom, he said to let this guide me home." She pointed to her chest, in the same spot that light had glowed earlier.

"Possibly, but I don't know how we implement that into finding our way back. We need to do this soon. If your powers are awakening and shadow wraiths are here in the mortal realm, then we must leave. Soon." Bronn spoke then, his voice was like thunder.

"What if we ask the druids?" Alaric broke the silence. All heads seemed to whip towards him.

"Druids? Can't we avoid dealing with them? Pompous assholes." Audelia expected those words from Mathias, though by the look on his face, he highly agreed with the sentiment. However, it was Alaric who spoke then.

"Pompous or not, they are the key players in this realm," Skye added.

"Wait, Druids are real? Like in *Outlander*? Or are we talking more of the *Dungeons and Dragons* variety?" Shawn asked.

Shaking his head, Gideon answered Shawn. "A little of both, I will give you mortals that much credit, you all tend to get things surprisingly right, just in the wrong places."

"Wow." Both Audelia and Shawn spoke in unison.

A small part of Audelia wondered what else here that had to do with legends and myths had also been correct.

She pushed that part away. There was no reason to really think about it, considering she would probably never see this place again.

Her heart ached at the thought.

Oh gods. Lila.

Would she ever see her best friend again?

Wait. Would Shawn even be able to come with them?

As if he were reading her thoughts, Shawn spoke. "If we do find the way back to your realm, will I be able to follow? I don't want to leave Audelia's side."

He said it as such a matter of fact like there was no question of him coming. It made her heart soar, but also ache as another thought pummeled into her.

But what about his family? Audelia couldn't do that to his parents, to Sobo. They were always so kind to her and treated her like family. She couldn't take their only child from them when there could be a chance he never came back.

"No. Shawn, as much as I want to have you with me. I can't let you leave your family. What about Japan? You always wanted to visit there, to see the old clan lands, the temple. You can't give that up for me. I won't let you." As she spoke, she felt the tears welling in her eyes.

She wanted to be selfish and demand that he come with her. She couldn't do that to him. Make him choose.

Shawn turned more towards her and placed his plate down on the coffee table. He took both her hands in his and brought them to his lips, placing a tender kiss upon them. Then he spoke his words like soft midnight.

"Audelia, *A Chroi*, I could never leave you. *Ever*. I don't care what we face in your realm. This is a part of you, and that means it's a part of me too. My family will understand; they always knew I would go wherever you went. Sobo always told me to stay by your side; she is wise, and she'll know why we just disappeared. She would make sure my parents understood." He paused and gave a small laugh.

"Hel, if she can't get them convinced, she'll call up my grandma Maggie, and the two of them will convince my parents I am okay. Between two wise women, I'm pretty sure my parents will yield any worry."

"Shawn....no, I can't let you do that. I am not worth that. What if you die? What if there is nothing left of my realm, and we are stuck, never to return?" She searched his eyes, searched for any doubt in them, and she hoped for something, as much as it would hurt. She didn't want him to give up everything.

"Not worth it?" Shawn shook his head and gave a small smile as he let go of her hands and placed both of his large palms against her cheeks. "Audelia, you are worth EVERY-THING to me. If I die, if there is nothing left of your realm, it won't matter. All that will matter is that you are safe and that I am with you. The rest is background noise. I love you, Audelia.

I have loved you for a very long time. Who knows, it's probably destiny that we met. I mean, you have the blood of this phoenix queen goddess in you, and I am the great direct ancestor of Ichiro Ito, the man who literally saved and protected a goddess. What were the odds you ended up in the same little town as me? If not, it is because we were meant to be. Even if we aren't, I will be honored to be by your side until you tell me to leave it. Even then, I'll remain as close as I can." He reached forward and placed his lips delicately against her own in a tender kiss that made her knees wobble.

Could she really be that selfish and say yes? To let him come?

As she looked into his eyes. She saw nothing but love, determination, and stark honesty. He wanted this. He wanted to remain with her.

It made her heart beat fast.

Gods, she loved him so damn much. The idea of leaving him behind, of him not being beside her through everything, killed her.

As much as she didn't want to be selfish, maybe fate, destiny, whatever had allotted her this one moment of self-ishness.

She *clung* to that hope.

She pulled herself into his arms and kissed him hard, her tears falling like crazy. She clung to him. Only breaking apart when she heard a clearing of throats.

"Sorry..." She spoke softly to the room, her face turning red. She didn't know why she was suddenly embarrassed. It wasn't the first time they had kissed in front of everyone, but for some reason, having all their eyes watching Shawn give this extraordinary declaration and them kissing felt more intimate than the others.

"It's fine, little dove," Mara spoke through a small giggle.

"So? Will I be able to follow?" Shawn spoke again, his words sounded stronger than before, and it made her heart squeeze in delight at the love she heard there.

"As long as it is a common portal, which there are many in this realm, if you know where to look. You should. However, as much as our Queen wishes you to come with us, I do not see that as wise. You are young and untrained. Our world is not for the faint of heart, especially for a mortal." Gideon spoke, his words held no malice, just brittle truth.

"I am stronger than I look. Bronn has trained me throughout the years. I know I am not as skilled with a blade as Audelia is. But I don't care. I will fight with you all if I need to. I'll swear a damn oath if it makes you feel better. My gran always told me the fae hold oaths sacred." Shawn looked at each man, each warrior in front of them, and he did not balk. Did not flinch anytime they took their turns to size him up.

Audelia looked to Bronn. Her uncle, the man she viewed as a father for all these years. His eyes seemed to find hers and made contact, and she gave her most to the look she gave him. Hoping he would allow it, no, *imploring* him to allow this. To make them see that Shawn was strong.

She wanted to say it herself, and maybe she was a coward for imploring her uncle to do it for her, but she felt in this moment, having his woman defend him probably wouldn't go well over with the others even if she was apparently their Queen.

Men were men, after all. Especially when all the men currently in this room exuded alpha energy, even the two very quiet twins gave off the feeling; it was in their eyes.

"Shawn is capable of a lot more than you realize. He is

right, I have trained him for years, and he has taken every class I have. He has immense talent, but I think if we start a more intense training leading up to us leaving our realm, he will do well in protecting her." Bronn spoke, his eyes leaving hers to pace over every one of her guards in the room and landing on Shawn. "However, if you are serious about the oath, I know the men here would greatly appreciate knowing that if you break it, they get to dole out the punishment. It is our law, after all."

The men around them grunted their approval. Mathias still held his glare at Shawn. He would for sure not be so easily swayed by a simple oath. However, Audelia thought that he was perhaps the same, with all the men here. He would trust no other but himself with her safety.

It made her heart skip a small beat at the magnitude of that thought.

"Fine, when and where do I need to do this?" Shawn's voice was eager, steadfast in his resolve. His want to remain at her side.

It was quiet for a moment. Then Bronn spoke again. "Soon, the moon should be up here shortly, and it must be done outside. Mara will have to make the elixir that you must take. Do not take this oath merely to show off. This oath is binding. In doing so, you bind yourself to her and bind yourself to us. If she dies. WE all die. If you dishonor the oath in any way, we will know you have done so. And we who hold the oath will dole out your punishment, which is usually death or intense pain."

"Well...that's... intense," Shawn said.

"You don't have to do it, Shawn, I won't think any less of you, I want you with me forever, no matter what, oath or not, that doesn't matter to me." She squeezed his hand.

"I wasn't saying I don't want to, Del, it's just more intense than I thought it would be, is all." He smiled and raked his hands through his hair. "Let's do this!" He gave another grin to the others watching.

Mathias chuffed, "Come on, kid, I wanna see what all you can do if you are going to be one of us. I need to know if you truly can protect her." He stood and walked to the sliding door into the early evening air.

The others stood as well, following closely behind. The food was all but forgotten as Shawn stood and kissed the top of her head and followed the men. He was grinning from ear to ear in delight.

"Is he going to be okay? Like this whole oath thing?" Audelia asked when it was just her, and her aunt and uncle left, she could hear the raucous of the men outside, beginning to do whatever it was they planned on doing.

"He'll be fine, little one. I promise. I would not have suggested the oath if I didn't think he could handle it or handle the men." Bronn spoke as he stood, gesturing with his hand to help Mara stand.

She merely nodded; her nerves were turning, making the food she ate sit like lead in her belly.

The sound of the men outside grew louder, a laugh here or there permeating through the closed screen door.

She sat there, at war with herself, over how she should feel about everything going on. As she sat there thinking, she noticed Bronn and Mara leave for the kitchen, the sound of cabinets opening, and bowls and other things being placed on the marble countertop of the island.

She should go outside, right? Or should she go help her aunt? How would a queen handle this situation?

Which began the thought process of what kind of Queen she would be? Her mind was reeling at everything, *Gods she wished her mom were alive.*

How would she handle this?

She did not want to disturb what they were doing, but she was also very curious about what was going on out there.

It would not be in their way if she were truly their Queen, right? Shouldn't she be there to see if the men sworn to her are to par? Not that she really knew what up to par would be in the case of immortal fae warriors.

At least she could find out if she went to watch.

Audelia stood and walked to the door; her mind made up. She still felt slightly weak on her feet; her legs were like rubber, but she fought through it and walked out into the cool night air.

The sight before her stole her breath.

CHAPTER TWENTY~ FIVE

She had expected to find that the others were picking on Shawn or being too hard on him. Since he was an outsider in the group, they didn't trust him. Wanted to be there to support him and maybe get the men to see he was worthy of being there.

But instead, she found the men all broken into groups of sparing partners, and Mathias seemed to be leading them in rounds of instruction. Skye and Shawn had been paired together, and gods.

It was beautiful to watch.

She had seen Shawn fight with others before, but this was different. It was like this coordinated, deadly dance; every move was like the grand thing, the twists and turns they each made to avoid one another, or as they laid a punch or kick or grab here and there, it was like she was watching this grand ballet.

Audelia felt like the unknown voyeur into this moment; maybe she shouldn't have come out here to watch them.

She felt so out of place, watching the men spare, watching how Shawn seemed to blend in with them seamlessly. Everything she knew had shifted on its axis, she thought as she watched them spar.

Up was down, and down was up.

She couldn't wrap her head around the scene before her. It was like destiny had reached out a hand and said, "Hey, here, catch a break."

It made her so unbelievably happy that these men, who seemed to be important to her, had, in one swift change of the breeze, decided he was important to them, too.

They weren't cruel, and they were supportive, each catching moves he made and correcting him or praising his natural raw talent.

Even Mathias had a glint in his eye that looked like approval if you looked really fucking close.

She felt ashamed that she had judged them so. That she had decided that they would be cruel to the man she loved, just because.... Because, well, honestly, she didn't know why she had thought that.

These men had been so kind to her, so protective, and had tolerated Shawn in their own ways, mainly because of her, but it seemed maybe she had judged even that.

They treated him like one of them.

Gods, she was horrible.

How was she expected to run a fucking kingdom if she was here judging these men who, from what they said, are sworn to her?

"He seems to fit in perfectly with them." A voice said from

beside her, and she jumped, having been so lost in her damn head she hadn't even heard Bronn approach.

"Yeah, he does." She moved to sit on one of the loungers on the deck, her legs were still like Jello, and she didn't want them to really notice she was here. Didn't want Shawn to feel like she was keeping an eye on him.

Gods, she was really being horrible. Maybe she should have stayed inside with Mara.

That was short-lived, as Mara herself, as if summoned by her thoughts, walked outside with a large tray full of little jars and bowls and a mortar and pestle on it. "It has to be made outside before the moon rises to her height." She said as she placed the tray down on the table nearby. Bronn had also placed a few things he had in his own hands down and gone to join the rest of the men.

She watched the men for a while longer, watching how seamlessly Bronn joined them, and how he and Mathias started to spar with one another. A part of her itched to join them, like she should be down there sparring as well.

It made her heart ache.

Instead, she decided to look over at her aunt, who seemed so lost in what she was doing, like the rest of the world had fallen away, and all that she saw was what she created before her.

It reminded Audelia of when her aunt would bake or when she made really elaborate dinners that Audelia, Shawn, and Lila would devour in seconds.

The thought made her laugh inside a little.

But then the thought of leaving Lila behind, of just disappearing on her, sobered her again.

Would they let her talk to Lila first? She wanted to tell her best friend everything. They shared everything.

As if conjured from her thoughts, her phone vibrated in her pocket. She hadn't even realized she had her phone. Maybe Shawn gave it to her at some point.

She shook off the thought and noticed Lila had texted her.

LILA

Hey, babes, how are you feeling? Auntie told me you weren't feeling the best.

AUDELIA

Yeah, feeling a lot better now. Miss you, girlie.

LILA

Up for visitors? I need some girl time…. plus, a certain naughty girl owes me deets on what happened with Shawn!

AUDELIA

Maybe soon? I know I've been such a flake. It's just been a lot…this week.

Before Audelia could see if Lila had responded, she heard a yell of triumph come from the yard and turned to see Shawn take Skye down in an overwhelming twist of a move that had him down by the throat.

The men had stopped and were cheering at the display. A smile played on her lips; she was glad that the men were so excited by Shawn proving himself like that. She watched as Shawn looked at her briefly and winked as he held Skye's head between his arms, waiting for a tap-out.

Skye seemed to be still trying to get out of the hold he was in. Yet, despite his movements, Audelia could see from here that there was no getting out of that hold. Shawn had taken a few years of wrestling in high school; holds were his bread and butter.

Poor Skye, she thought.

She watched as he tapped the ground three times, indicating he was yielding to Shawn.

Cheers rang out through the backyard as Shawn let go of Skye, stood, and reached a hand out to help the man up. Skye took it with a grin. "Well met, brother. That was surprising indeed."

Shawn gave a wide grin. "That was great, and you're a great sparring partner. But I was wondering, Mathias." He turned toward the man in question, the grin still there. "That move I saw you do on Bronn, could you teach me that?"

"I suppose if you were able to take down my quick shit of a little brother, then I don't see why not. If you can handle me, that is." Mathias smirked but nodded for Shawn to come to him. The men switched partners then.

Shawn laughed as he and Mathias began to spar. Audelia watched dreamy-eyed. She loved watching Shawn spar in the past, but something about watching him now that they had confessed their feelings for each other felt...more.

Audelia was sure she probably looked like a dreamy-eyed schoolgirl watching him learn the moves he had requested. Frankly, she didn't care because, damn, did he look hot with all those rolling muscles as he and Mathias seemed to move in a dance of twists and grunts.

The whole scene was making her drool.

What would it be like to be between both those rippling strong bodies.....

"Would you like to help me make this?" Mara's words

broke Audelia from her daydream, making her jump. Her face instantly heated as she turned to her aunt.

"It looks...." Audelia stood and walked over to the picnic table, where her aunt had everything sprawled out. It was a hodgepodge of different herbs, dried flowers, and little vials of different colored liquids. It looked like a chemistry set from an apothecary from the early Victorian age. "Complicated. I wouldn't want to mess anything up."

Mara merely laughed and gave Audelia a little bump with her hip. "Nonsense, my love, you used to do this all the time when you were little. You actually had quite the affinity for it." Mara wrapped an arm around Audelia's shoulders in a tight hug.

Audelia's stomach dropped.

Maybe she should be over it by now, given that everyone here are wonderful, loving people. But it ached in her very soul that whole parts of her life were gone. That, someone decided that the best way to keep her alive was to take everything she was or could have been away from her.

She could feel tears blur in her vision.

She fucking hated this.

Hated that she was trapped in this hel of not truly knowing herself.

Hated that the people she cared about had been the ones to keep this from her.

Gods, she was tired of lies. Tired of not knowing who she was. Tired of this ache in her heart.

Shaking off all the doubt that kept wanting to creep back into her life. She smiled, doing her best to hide the sadness in her heart. "I did?"

Mara gave her a sad smile as she grabbed a few of the items

they needed next. She handed them to Audelia along with a blue stone pestle and a medium-sized mortar bowl. "Oh yes. You were always quite keen to learn new recipes, granted, a few were to pull pranks on your guards." Audelia giggled at the idea. She wished she knew what the pranks had entailed.

Who had been her targets? Was it just her doing the prank, or did she and another guard do them? Did she have friends?

Do they mourn her? Should she mourn them?

Lila. Gods, she can't do this. She didn't know how, but she would let her best friend know what was really going on. She couldn't let another friend mourn her.

"Though you did spend the majority of your time training with Skye and Mathias." Mara continued as she added bits and pieces of dried herbs and flowers and a small white vial of milky liquid to the bowl in front of Audelia. "Mash that softly."

Audelia began to do the task. Her mind swung back and forth with all these questions: Who had she been before? Her friends? How did she view her life? So many questions made her heartache, and her brain hurt.

"Did....did I have other friends?" She asked quietly, her focus kept on the mashing of the ingredients, the din of the men in the yard hooting and grunting as they egged each other on.

Mara stopped what she was working on, a half-empty vial of thick red liquid in her hand. "Yes, little dove. You had many. But you mainly kept to the guards, and there was this one boy, whom you played with quite a lot. He was Mathias and Skye's nephew. Before their sister disappeared, he was always around you. Sweet boy." A sad look crossed over Mara's face, and Audelia wondered what had happened to that boy.

A part of her ached deeper, more intensely than before, at the thought of this boy.

Was it just because of what she felt for Skye and Mathias? Was she heartbroken not only for herself but for these two kind men?

"Do you know what happened to him?"

"No, sadly. It's something that has worn on both of their hearts for the past fifteen years. He disappeared a year before everything happened. Their sister, too." Audelia could feel the tears welling in her eyes, and she had to look away for a moment.

She felt a single tear fall down her cheek as her heart broke for them.

Maybe when everything was said and done, she would try to help them find him. If he were still alive.

"Auntie...I don't want to leave without telling Lila. I can't do that to her. My heart aches for everyone that I don't even remember, and those who possibly mourned my loss. I cannot do the same to her. She deserves to know why I just disappeared." She was shocked by how strong her voice was as she spoke.

She couldn't do that to Lila. She would be damned if anyone here stopped her from talking to Lila first.

"Little dove. I know how much you love her, but it isn't safe. As much as I wish you could tell her. I'm not sure it would be wise." Mara reached a hand over to squeeze Audelia's shoulder. "Now, take that bit there and add it to this bigger bowl, and as you stir it, think of all the love you have for Shawn. It helps strengthen the potion. It's not a needed thing. But since we are doing this with rudimentary magic. Every bit helps."

She merely nodded. She knew it would be a fight to get

them to see that she had to talk to Lila before they left, whenever that was. But she would not relent.

Audelia poured the concoction into the bigger bowl; whatever it was, it smelled good. Like winter fresh bubble gum, and something fruity. Like blueberries, maybe?

She started stirring, her mind wandering to Shawn. She thought about the past fourteen years she had known him; he was always there in the beginning. When they first met, he had this big, toothy smile that was just adorable, considering he had been missing his top front teeth at the time.

But he was endearing, and he didn't call her weird or make fun of her for crying so much. He just scared away the jerks who did and would bring her sweets from his parents' bakery. Shawn had never once made her feel lonely or scared. That's why, as they grew up, she leaned on him. Yes, Lila was her best friend, and she told her almost everything. But with Shawn, she felt so safe, no matter what she said to him. He wouldn't run or laugh. He would just be.

She loved him so much. So, she poured all that into the mixing. She found herself humming a song. She wasn't entirely sure what it was, just that it spoke to her.

Calmed her. Sent a buzzing through her body.

Made her feel warm inside, like a warm fire in the middle of winter.

A soft gasp from her left made her jump, and she almost upended the whole bowl. "Shit!" But when she settled the bowl, she noticed a light was reflecting off it. Weird.

"Audelia. You're glowing." Mara's voice was a whisper.

"What?" Audelia gasped as she looked down and saw that she was indeed glowing again.

She felt it more then. That warmth seemed to reach out

from her chest and spread over her whole body. She felt like she was being embraced by a lover.

Like home.

"Why....why am I glowing again?" Audelia's voice was a little shaky. She wasn't scared, but she did feel overwhelmed.

She was feeling too much at once. It was that feeling again. Like everything she needed, everything she was, was right there to grab. But when she reached out to take it, it wasn't really there. All that was left was this yawning portal of nothingness.

Something was still preventing her from accepting everything she was.

Her power.

Her memory.

Her life.

It was just on the other side. If only she could reach out and grab it, but try as she might, each attempt resulted in a pain that spread through her. "Fuck that...hurts."

"Del?" It was Shawn's voice breaking through her thoughts. She must have said that aloud.

She looked up to see that all the men were standing nearby, the look of concern etched on all their faces. Shawn was at the head of the group, closing the distance, his hand was on her cheek before she fully realized he was there.

"Are you okay?" His words were soft and comforting as she looked into his eyes. They seemed to search her, to see if he could see what was wrong. She could feel the warmth in her chest was still there, and it set a soft glow on his features in the dying light of the day.

"I'm okay. I promise. It hurt for like a moment. I was

trying.....I was trying to recall my memories." She felt like her world came crashing down as she spoke those words.

Shawn simply pulled her into his arms and held her in his hands, rubbing her back in comfort. "I'm sorry, my love. I wish.... I wish there was more I could do for you."

She squeezed him in response and just let him hold her for the moment. Soaking in his love. It helped calm the quaking storm in her heart just a little, and she even felt that warm light that had been radiating from her start to dim to just a low hum within her.

He pulled away enough to look her in the eyes, leaning forward, he kissed her forehead gently, making her eyes close, she felt his finger on her chin, lifting her to face him. "Are you sure you're alright, my love?"

Audelia gives Shawn a small smile and nods. "I'll be okay. Go back to your sparring; it looked like you were having fun."

"I'll be right over there if you need me, okay?" He looked over her like he was trying to see past everything, all the pain she was trying to hide just under the surface.

Luckily, he didn't see it, or he would have demanded she tell him honestly how she was feeling. But right now, she didn't even want to acknowledge how much she was genuinely hurting.

If she did, she didn't think she would ever have the strength to carry on. Nor to do what must be done for the people she had left behind all those years ago.

CHAPTER TWENTY~SIX

Sometime later, as the sun had finally set, Audelia watched the men start to light the tiki torches that Bronn had throughout the yard. Mathias set ablaze the fire pit in the corner of the yard. She remembered many nights in early and late summer sitting around that fire after parties. The way everything felt so carefree those nights.

How she, Shawn, and Lila would sit around singing off-key pop songs and would make s'mores, while the adults would talk about whatever it was they usually talked about. Everything back then had felt so new and perfect, safe. Now, as she watched those flames spring to life, she felt more of that shift.

The shift that told her there was no going back to those lazy summer nights around the fire.

She watched as her aunt brought the vial of what they had made together back to the table. Mara had left sometime before to finish the final vestiges of it. Audelia still wasn't entirely sure what it was that Shawn was about to drink. But something deep inside told her that it would bring no harm. The men around her also drank something similar.

Suddenly, a soft drumbeat seemed to appear out of nowhere as she watched Bronn bring out two wicked-looking daggers from the house. She looked around and didn't see anyone with a drum. But it seemed to ring about the air in an intense, pulling way.

It made her heart pound in unison; her body shook a little at the beat.

It felt *powerful.*

Primal.

Magical.

She noticed then that her aunt was chanting, as Mara brought the remaining items to the spot by the fire pit. It was so low that she had barely noticed it at first. But the words seemed to resonate and grow in strength.

It sent shivers down her spine.

Audelia watched as the men seemed to form a circle around the fire pit. She watched as they all took their shirts off, exposing rolling muscles, and her mouth went dry at the sight.

She found herself wandering closer to where Shawn was currently standing, watching everything unfold. Her fingers brushed against his in a comforting way.

"You, okay?" she asked. She could feel the nerves rolling off of him.

Meanwhile, her blood was beginning to pump with every beat that seemed to ring out into the night. She noticed even the air around them seemed to pause to listen to the beat.

It was *ethereal.*

Shawn clasped their fingers together and brought her hand to his lips, placing a gentle kiss there.

"I'm alright. A little nervous. Did you see those blades?" He gave a small laugh, but his voice wavered a bit.

"You don't have to do this. I meant it, Shawn; I won't think less of you. You are the owner of my heart and soul, and I don't doubt you; this isn't necessary to me."

"I know, A Chroi. I love you, Audelia, but, strangely, there is this part of me that is pulling me towards needing to do this, something...primal. Not just to prove to these men who look at you like they would rip their hearts out if it meant to protect you. I think it's in my own blood that I need, *no,* I want to do this. Prove with everything I am that I will lay down my life to keep you safe." The wavering had stopped in his voice; all she heard was utter devotion.

Before she could say another word, Bronn cleared his throat. "Tonight, under the witness of the moon and the flames, the keeper of magic. In front of our Queen, the woman we have each in turn pledged ourselves to. We offer to the fates another to protect her. Shawn Ichiro Montgomery, step forward into the light of the flames. Offer yourself to fate and flame."

The world seemed to pause at those final words. Audelia's heart was pounding, and she could feel the flames in her own body, which seemed to pause and listen.

A growing hunger seemed to stretch inside her, waiting.

The drum continued to grow.

Thump.

Thump, thump.

THUMP.

Shawn stepped forward into the light of the flames. Audelia watched, mesmerized by how the light seemed to give this otherworldly glow to the green in his eyes.

It was beautiful. He was beautiful. Standing in the light of the flames, with little pinpricks of moonlight etching into his black hair.

Mara stepped forward with the vial in her hand. She gave a small smile to Shawn. "Remove your shirt, son. Audelia, little dove, come closer."

Audelia obeyed. Her heart thrummed, and her breath felt lodged in her throat as she watched Shawn take off his shirt, exposing his rippling muscles and lean torso, and there was the tattoo over his left pec of a dragon and phoenix locked in an embrace.

He looked like a god bathed in the light of the moon and flames.

"Now I explained to you earlier everything that will happen. Do you still wish to do this?" Bronn asked. His tone soft.

"Yes. More than anything." He looked at Audelia and smiled. "I want to protect her, always."

Bronn nodded, and Mathias stepped forward, holding the two blades that Audelia had seen Bronn bring out earlier.

"Audelia, we will need you for this as well. I know you don't remember, but you did this with all of us. It will hurt a little, but not much. I need to slice your palm, and then I need you to place your hand over his heart when I tell you to, alright?" Audelia nodded in response; her nerves were surprisingly not at the service.

The drumbeat seemed to breathe into her, giving her strength.

Bronn took one of the blades from Mathias, it was as long as her forearm and curved at the end, it reminded her of a raptor claw, the way it was fat at the hilt of the blade and slimmed out like a flame. It had intricate designs on it in some runic language she didn't know. Its hilt was rose gold, with the etching of a phoenix taking flight. It was dangerously beautiful.

"Your hand, my Queen." Bronn's words were like a warm flame. Her cheeks heated at his use of *my Queen.*

Audelia stretched out her palm for him to take, his skin was warm as he held her palm open.

Before she could register it, Bronn took the blade and sliced it across her palm. She gave a small cry at the sting of the cut and then watched as blood began to well at the surface. "Just keep your palm closed for now, it's alright if it drips, we need it to drip into the grass as he speaks the words. Don't freak out at this next part." It was Skye who spoke to her softly. He had come to stand beside her.

She tilted her hand a little and closed her palm, and she felt the warm blood start to seep off her skin into the grass below.

As each drop fell, she could feel the drumming beat faster, like a war cry now. Felt that fire within her reach out and curl around each falling drop of blood.

"Kneel before me," Bronn said in a voice like thunder to Shawn.

Shawn kneeled in the grass, and the men closed in tighter around Bronn and Shawn. Skye placed a hand on her lower back and nudged her closer with them. Coming to a stop beside Bronn, slightly in front of Shawn.

"Repeat after me, I, Shawn, the great ancestor of the great Ichiro Ito, pledge my fealty to Audelia Elide Ferelith, Queen of

Dragsnic, Bringer of the Flames of the Phoenix Queen. My sword is yours; My soul is yours. May I never waver from you. May my sword keep you. I pledge to be your blade, to be your shield, to be your hearth. I shall fall on my blade and bask in flames and darkness if I should ever cause you folly. I shall protect you from now until darkness and the flames of death take me to the After."

Audelia held her breath. Those words seemed to echo through her, and the power in her rose with each word. Calling to her. Begging for her.

Her head ached as she tried to recall the times she had heard this before. She shook it off, trying to focus on the man she loved kneeling.

She watched as he took the blade Mathias offered him; it was the twin of the one Bronn had used, except this was blood red, like bloodstone.

Audelia watched as Shawn took the blade and sliced his hand open; with his other hand, he drank the vial that Mara offered him, then turned his face to look at her.

All the air whooshed from her lungs at the look on his face. The utter love and devotion that was written there. It made her knees tremble.

The words he spoke next made her eyes well with tears. "I, Shawn, the great ancestor of the great Ichiro Ito, pledge my fealty to Audelia Elide Ferelith, Queen of Dragsnic, Bringer of the Flames of the Phoenix Queen. My sword is yours; My soul is yours; May I never waver from you. May my sword keep you. I pledge to be your blade, to be your shield, to be your hearth. I shall fall on my blade and bask in flames and darkness if I should ever cause you folly. I shall protect you from now until darkness and the flames of death take me to the After."

She nodded, not sure what to say. But she felt the tears falling now, pride and love echoed in her soul, and the power within her started to glow again. Soft at first, like it was building for what would happen next.

Bronn stepped closer to Shawn now, holding the blade he had used on Audelia firmly in his hands. She watched as he placed one hand on Shawn's shoulder, leaning over Shawn's heart just above that tattoo. Mathias stood behind Shawn, now lending support to him.

She gasped as she watched Bronn begin to carve a rune into Shawn's very chest. "Oh, gods." She whispered. Shawn grunted in pain but did not call out.

She didn't know how he was standing the pain.

After a few minutes, Bronn stood back and gestured for Audelia to approach. "Audelia, place your sliced palm upon the rune. And say these words. I, Audelia Elide Ferelith, Queen of Dragsnic, Bringer of the Flames of the Phoenix Queen. Accept your oath of fealty, and I bind my soul to yours. May you never break this binding. I will never ask of you what would bring dishonor, Beatiu Unti Pateounce."

She nodded and, with a shaky hand, placed her bleeding palm against the ragged edges of the freshly carved rune on his skin. She looked him in the eyes as she spoke the words. Her voice strong and sure. "I, Audelia Elide Ferelith, Queen of Dragsnic, Bringer of the Flames of the Phoenix Queen. Accept your oath of fealty, and I bind my soul to yours. May you never break this binding. I will never ask of you what would bring dishonor, Beatiu Unti Pateounce."

She and the others gasped as she and Shawn were suddenly engulfed in a bright light that had begun from her chest. It seemed to strike out suddenly, and then it slammed down into the rune on his chest. The sudden rush and loss of power made her knees begin to give out. Shawn was there to catch her as she fell to her knees. "I've got you, a chroi."

Audelia watched as he winced, as the last of the light seemed to heal and scar over the rune on his skin until all that was left was soft pink raised skin.

CHAPTER TWENTY~ SEVEN

Audelia could barely move; she just continued to stare at Shawn. Taking in everything about him. It was odd, he was still the same man that, scarcely a week prior, she had finally told him that she loved him. And he, her.

Maybe it was the glow of the flames and the sparks of moonlight on his face and body. But at that moment, he seemed different.

Not for the worst. No, he seemed stronger, more confident than he had just moments prior.

He had this smile on his face that spoke volumes; there was so much there that Audelia thought it would take years for her to get to the bottom of everything truly etched there in the firelight.

She would enjoy that immensely. The thought of having years to figure out everything he truly felt in that moment, forever. Yeah, she really liked the fucking sound of that.

Shawn reached out and caressed her cheek, and she closed her eyes, leaning into his warm touch. Wishing that this would never end.

That they could be happy forever, that fate wouldn't pull them apart. She would destroy fate if it came to that. Her love for this man knew no bounds.

"How do you feel?" She asked, her voice soft, as she took in the now miraculously healed scar over his chest.

She reached out with gentle fingers and felt his muscles flex at her touch as she traced with warm fingers over the swirls and delicate lines of the rune. It was complex, and she had never seen anything like it before. Shawn placed his hand over hers, halting her ministrations.

"Good. Shocked as all hel that it's healed. But, good. I am honored to be bonded to you." He looked up at the men around them, and Audelia saw it. Each man bore the same rune in the same spot. "I am honored to be counted on as one of you if you all will have me."

Audelia watched as all the men gave smirks and watched as Skye and Mathias helped both of them stand. Mathias lingered close to her side, his hand on her arm, like he still couldn't fully trust that she wouldn't disappear at any moment.

She really fucking wished she could remember everything. Remember how she felt about each of the men. For now, she would settle on the fact that she did trust them and was angry at the lies, but still, she felt safe and loved with each of them.

Bronn stepped forward and embraced Shawn in a manly hug. "We are honored to count you as a brother."

To that, the men all chanted, "For Flame and Shadow!"

Sometime later, they were all around the firepit, Audelia

was in the swing by the flower garden, the one she remembered her aunt putting in a few years back, because she told Bronn, then Alexander at the time that even the manliness of men need to have a beautiful garden for the women in their lives.

Two weeks after that, Bronn had shown up at their doorstep asking for help from her to put the garden together, his vintage Chevy truck packed with soil, flowers, and lumber. The latter ended up going towards the swing she now relaxed in, snuggled into Shawn, which was covered in fluffy outdoor pillows that both she and her aunt had chosen.

Throughout the years, it became one of her favorite places to be whenever they were over here. She could relax apart from everyone, but not so apart that she felt alone. Now, it served as the perfect place for her and Shawn to hold one another as they listened to the men tell war stories from their lands.

It made a part of her ache. They were all stories of their homeland. Yet, it should have felt nostalgic to hear the stories, but instead, she felt empty and wanton. Like she could reach out to touch those memories, those little moments of the place that held her birth, the death of her parents, and her heritage. But anytime she tried, she was met with despair and pain.

She wondered if she would ever get that feeling again. *That feeling you get when you meet someone from your home and hear all those little tidbits that are unique to that place. To where you feel that happy sense of longing because you know one day you'll go back there. That it will always be a part of you.*

She wished she could have that. Instead, she had the taste of ash.

She sighed happily as she felt Shawn kiss her neck, as they listened to Skye tell a peculiar story about the time he fought a legion of Orcs by himself. To which Mathias slapped him on the back and said to him that he remembered that time because it was him and his Dragonlance legion that had to come to his sorry excuse for an ass's rescue.

Everyone laughed as they bickered back and forth about the details of that particular adventure.

She was craving his touch more and more as the night wore on. She desperately wanted to get lost in him. To have him bring her to the brink and let her forget all about the troubles that seem to shadow over everything in her life currently.

Shivers went up her spine as she felt his hand work its way up and down her thigh. He worked at a leisurely pace. One that was driving her crazy as his large, warm hand worked its way closer and closer to where she desperately wanted him.

She gave a slight moan, scooting herself closer to him. She didn't want him to stop. She wanted more and more. Turning her head slightly to get a better look at him in the firelight.

His gaze met hers. His eyes were dark and hungry. It made her mouth go dry, and the ache between her legs grew more fervent.

"Are you well?" His whispered words against her ear sent shivers down her spine. He was teasing her if that gleam in his eye was any indication.

"Very. Take me to bed, my love." Her voice was husky. She watched his eyes dilate with hunger for a moment before he gently moved from behind her and stood.

He reached out his hand to her, helping her stand. She gave him a warm smile, and she blushed when she realized everyone was watching them at that moment.

But Shawn only seemed to notice her as he entwined their

fingers and spoke over his shoulder to the others. "Goodnight, everyone. I think it's time our Queen got some rest."

Her heart thumped heavily in her chest at him calling her his Queen.

The others simply nodded, except for Mara, who raised an eyebrow at her niece and gave her a conspiratorial smirk.

It made her blush even more as Shawn pulled her from the backyard.

They quietly walked to the room they had been sharing for the past week. Yet, it felt different this time. Yes, they had been sharing the same bed, but she had been healing, so it had been more snuggles and comfort than anything more intimate.

Besides, the other morning when she had woken, they hadn't touched each other in that way. Nothing more than needy kisses.

She had been craving more.

It was a raging hunger in her since she watched him in the firelight, pledging himself to her.

It was becoming a claiming need.

As they got closer to the room, she became nervous. What if he didn't want her that way anymore? Yeah, he had that hungry look in his eyes. But. Her insecurity seemed to want to barge in and take control. It was making her more wary. More worried. Because he was honor-bound to her now, it changed things.

Gods, she hated her head sometimes.

Hated who had placed those doubts in her mind.

Despised that he somehow still held power over her.

Hated that when she wanted to forget, wanted to become wrapped in the embrace of the man, she loved; that *he* was there in the shadows.

She had barely even registered that they had reached the room; her thoughts, which had been full of lust and need, had begun to turn sour, and she was so lost to the darker thoughts that she hadn't even heard the door close behind her.

Audelia felt Shawn's finger under her chin as he made her look up into his eyes. Worry shone there. "Del? A chroi? What's wrong?"

She tried to look away in shame. She hated herself for the way her thoughts had turned, and couldn't bring herself to really look at him. So, she tried to look away. But he wouldn't let her. "Del... Look at me." His voice was a growl of a command. Enough so that it snapped her out of her thoughts.

Audelia looked into the eyes of the man she loved. He could see through her. See that she was being tormented about something and was worried.

She took in his emerald eyes, and it helped steal herself. Gaining the courage to speak what was burning in her heart. "I'm worried.... worried you don't want me like that now. That, things have changed. That I am not enough. It's stupid...."

"My love." His tone was soft and so full of love that her heart leaped. She clung to the love she heard in it. Willing those dark thoughts to go away and let her have this moment. Let her have all the moments before she might not be able to have them again.

She felt her body and her heart pause. Like she needed to prepare for whatever words he was about to tell her. She leaned into his touch as he placed both his hands on her cheeks, his thumbs working back and forth in soothing gestures.

"Audelia, I love you. I have loved you for a very long time. I just finally got you the way I have been dreaming of for years.

Nothing has changed in that regard. It will NEVER change. I took that oath because I wanted to. Because of the notion of being bound to you for eternity? Gods. I do not think I could have expected how much that made my heart soar and drove a primal need in me that frightened me. I get to remain by your side while you face everything you are about to. I get to keep you safe. I get to love you not from afar but right there beside you. But getting to call you my Queen? Fuck, baby, that was just.... icing on the cake of it all. I want you a chroi, I always will. Do you understand?"

She was at a loss for words. She felt every doubt that had been trailing her the whole way to this room disappear like smoke. All she could do was nod and whisper. "Kiss me then."

His lips slammed down onto hers in a punishing, claiming kiss. His hands moved from her cheeks to one, threading into her hair in a tight grip that sent tingling down her spine in abandon. He wrapped his other arm around her waist and thrust her closer to him.

The brutal kiss had her heart pounding, and that need between her legs grew to a crescendo. All those thoughts she had before, his lips and tongue and claiming grip, silenced every single one of them.

They were a war of tongues and teeth; her moans filled the quiet room. She gasped as his hand moved from her hair, trailing tingles of lust down her spine, as it cradled her ass, his other gripping her leg in a fast move as he hoisted her up, her legs wrapped around him eagerly as he slammed them with fervor against the wall, as they continued to kiss. It was an unleashing as her core throbbed at his touch.

Audelia gasped as Shawn thrust his hips into her. A moan

escaped into his mouth as she felt the hard, thick length of his arousal pressing in tantalizing strokes against her core.

"Do you feel how much I want you? How much you drive me crazy with need?" His voice was husky as he pressed his forehead against hers, their mingled breaths working in tandem.

She flushed and nodded, rolling her hips into him in response for more. Words were failing her.

She felt his hand slip from her hips to snake in agonizing, slow movements as he worked his way to the skin under her clothes. She whimpered when she felt him press against her clit through the lace of her underwear.

"Mmmm, so wet for me already?" His thick voice sent shivers down her spine as he began to work in small, harsh circles over the throbbing bud. Gods, his touch was magic.

She could feel the rising tension in her body. He moved to her neck, kissing her there and biting down to mark her, her hips rolling against his hand, seeking more friction. She needed their clothes gone, and she needed more of his touch.

She merely whimpered as he moved the lace aside and began to stroke through her wetness; the groan he gave against her throat nearly made her come right there.

"That's it, baby, come for me. Show me how much you love my touch." As she spoke, she felt two thick fingers delve into her in a quick thrust.

"Oh, gods!" She cried out as he began to work his fingers in and out of her in quick, hard movements. She felt the pressure within her reach its peak. She tried to hold on, to let it build more.

She couldn't anymore when she felt the heel of his hand press against her clit as he added a third finger. The blissful stretch and the pressure sent her reeling over the edge as she cried out in pleasure.

Her whole body was burning with need, even as she rode out the orgasm, she craved more, rocking her hips as he continued to piston in and out of her with his fingers, she moaned as she felt him curl the middle finger and began to hit her in all the right spots, making her breach that edge again.

"Fuck. I don't think I'll ever get enough of your pussy a chroi. It's damn magic." His words panted as he lifted her off the wall and began to walk them to the bed. His fingers continued their assault on her. Making her writhe with each motion.

He let go of her, causing her to whimper in protest, as the loss of his touch and the fullness had her throbbing with need, feeling empty. But she didn't have to wait long, his lips slammed back onto hers, and they became a mess of need and movements as they began to undress each other the rest of the way.

It felt so much more this time. Like they had a barrier they didn't even know was there, and it had been lifted. That him making this commitment to her had eased all the worries that plagued her. She knew without a doubt she could trust him. That he would never leave.

Her heart was pounding, and she moved away from him briefly and crawled onto the bed, lying back in its center, spread before him. She watched as his eyes darkened with hunger again. Her mouth watered as she watched him stroke his considerable, thick length in agonizingly slow motions.

"You're gorgeous like that. All spread out for me. Do you want my cock, baby?" his voice was thick and husky, his eyes devoured her as he looked at her.

It made her blush, which at the moment felt silly considering she was naked, panting, and impossibly wet for him.

Her eyes glittered with need as she nodded, biting her lip to contain the moan that was lingering there as he prowled towards her; the bed dipped as he got onto it and leaned over her; she flushed, taking in the heated desire in his eyes. She reached out, working her fingers into his hair, wanting more, needing it.

More touch. More of the delicious friction only he could provide her.

Her heart was pounding ferociously as she felt him nudge at her entrance. She felt her need rise again, that deep need of desire, building, waiting for him.

He leaned down and devoured her in a passionate kiss of warring tongues as he slammed himself to the hilt in her, making her gasp and cry out in pleasure into his mouth.

The sudden pressure and stretch made her come again in a flash of brilliant pleasure.

He worked into her over and over in quick succession. With each thrust, he would fully leave and make her whimper, only to thrust into her again and again.

Her eyes felt blurry as she rode the ecstasy that was him. She reached up to grip his back and dug her nails, trailing them as he continued to fuck her. Gods, this was heaven.

She never wanted to leave their bed. Wanted to remain here, entangled in him as he brought her to pleasurable bliss over and over again.

"I love you." His words were a whisper in her ear as he lifted away from her and grabbed her legs, putting them together, never letting up on his strokes, as he hooked her legs to one side of his shoulder.

His grip on her calves was tight; she was sure it would bruise, and she really couldn't care if it did. The only thought she had was the desire and the feeling of him inside her.

"Shawn!" She called out in a moan as she came again. This new angle was hitting all the right places as he began to slow his strokes. Taking longer, more lazily slow strokes as he reached down and worked her clit between his fingers.

Bringing her to another crescendo. She felt it build again and again.

Audelia couldn't remember the last time sex had felt this good. She had always dreaded sex with Kage. It was always pain, never this. Never this feeling of love and adoration that each stroke from Shawn brought.

She felt the tears well in her eyes; she didn't mean to cry, didn't mean to bring herself to that place again. Not now, not here. Not with Shawn.

He noticed right away and stopped his ministrations. "My love?"

"I'm okay. I promise. Come here, kiss me, don't stop, please." She steeled her tone; she wanted him to continue, wanted him to finish his final washing away of her past because she knew in this moment that her thoughts would never turn back to *him*. That Shawn would be all she saw from here on out.

He moved her to her side, pulling out briefly to cradle her against his chest on the bed. He slid back into her softly and lovingly in a single thrust. "I love you." She spoke softly.

Their ravenous lovemaking soon turned into slow, adoring strokes as they finally reached their climaxes together. They lay there entangled in a mess of limbs, and she never wanted to move again.

She felt him pull out of her sometime later, the bed dipping as he stood. She felt him leave the room for the bathroom. She closed her eyes, wishing the last tears would end so she could move on.

She gasped when she felt a warm cloth work its way across her as Shawn began to clean her up. She just lay there, letting him take care of her. He left again and came back in boxer shorts and was beckoning her to sit up so he could slip a shirt over her.

His shirt, she realized as the scent of him engulfed her, bringing her relief and safety the way he always did.

"Come here, my love." His voice was soft as he pulled her into his arms, and she curled into his warmth.

She felt the covers over her a moment later. "Get some sleep, a chroi." She felt him work his hand up and down her back in soothing motions as she rested her head on his chest.

She fell asleep shortly after, wrapped in the safety of his arms.

The flow of the next two weeks felt strange to her. It was like her old life just ebbed away as the days wore on.

Slowly, she was starting to come to terms with who she was. It still brought pain to her every time new things were mentioned. Like, whatever spell had been placed on her really did not want her to even think about who she truly was.

It scared her, and it really pissed her off.

For the past fifteen years, she has wondered who she was. What her life had been before she lost her parents. Wondering why she couldn't remember them, why even recalling her life before the day she arrived at Aunt Mara's had been, was met with nothingness—a *void*.

Hel, now that she thought more about it, she didn't even recall how she got to her aunts and began living there. It was like she was just there one day, and that was all she wrote.

As a child, she never questioned it and eventually forgot. Now, she realized it was the spell Waldrom had placed.

If she ever met that sorcerer, she was going to punch him in the face for putting her through all this shit. For putting these amazingly kind protective people through this.

Her and Shawn's days had been filled with learning more fighting styles in preparation for whenever they found a way home. It still felt surreal, the idea that her real home was such a truly foreign place.

The sheer fact that the Fae were real still filled her with this sense of wonder. Joy.

Their evenings were filled with talk around the fire, more war stories, and the occasional lesson from Mara about making smaller potions if she was ever to need them.

Every time her aunt told her how to identify plants or how to make things properly. A new light seemed to shine from her aunt, and she was in her element talking about these things.

It made Audelia happy. She knew her aunt had been struggling over everything that had happened lately. She was glad to see that her spirits were improving.

Audelia's, however, weren't.

Even nights being in Shawn's arms and making love to him could not relieve the ache in her heart every time Lila would text her.

They had barely talked, just small texts here and there, Audelia growing more and more worried about what to say to her. No visits. Try as Lila had, asking to come over or for them to have a girls' night. Audelia would either feign an illness or just ignore the text altogether.

She felt like such a horrible person.

Her guard would not let her leave the house. The threat of whatever Shadowed agent sent by Lefrain held too substantial a risk. It was irritating.

She could fight. She faced them before, yeah, she passed out the second time. But there was no guarantee it would happen again. Even Skye, who had been training her lately, said she was getting stronger. Shouldn't that count for something?

Audelia didn't know how much longer she could keep this from Lila. They told each other everything, and keeping this big of a secret was breaking her. She felt like she was betraying everything.

The need to tell her friend that she could leave at any moment was dire.

She had to tell her.

That's why that night, she decided that she would make them *see*. Make them realize she needed to tell her best friend that she was leaving and that she would probably never come back.

She owed Lila that much.

They owed Audelia that much.

CHAPTER TWENTY~ EIGHT

inally, after days, it seemed with Audelia constantly telling her uncle how badly she needed to see Lila. He finally relented. Of course, it wasn't a simple moment; she still couldn't leave the house. Or, as she liked to call his home—her fancy gilded cage.

For gilded, it was. Bronn had set this place up like Fort Knox and the Vatican's love child.

Except, where those places merely had skilled military guards, and maybe a few black ops personal hiding in the shadows. Here, they had elite Fae warriors with hundreds of years' worth of battle, strategy, and willpower behind them.

For males, as they preferred to be called, as she had found out after one too many times of grumbling about "typical men alpha bullshit." that calling them a man was an insult, that they were far better than the mortal men that liked to play at war.

Still, sounded like Alphahole bullshit to her. Though she relented because they were right, throwing them into the category of every man on the planet felt wrong. Even Shawn who was born and bred in this world, seemed to not even fill that quotient.

Daily, she watched him grow to be stronger and more resilient than she thought he ever could be. Not that she had doubted his ability to rise to the occasion, but it seemed like something greater than the lot of them was showing; it's cards with Shawn.

She was damn proud of the male he was beginning to be.

Most guys, she had decided, besides those in her books, which she had read so many during their days of seclusion here. She had realized most would have run in the other direction when faced with the decisions he had to make.

He wasn't just deciding to be with her.

No, being with her came with so many more things now. Obligations, danger, possible death, regret. The last two clanged around her head daily.

She worried he would wake up one day and regret everything. That she wasn't worth not ever seeing his family again, that he may not survive whatever awaits them in her realm.

She wanted to ask him. But, like the coward she was, she couldn't voice it. She needed to talk to Lila to see if this was all just in her head, the anxiety that always seemed to lap at the surface of her life, the voices left there by a sadistic rapist who was stalking her every move.

Luckily, nothing had happened here, but small things had been happening around town. Strange deaths, odd occurrences, that the twins brought to them daily.

They were the only ones who really left the house. Mainly

because spy work and gathering of intel were what they did best. Even here in a realm without magic, they had adapted quickly to using tech to grow their network.

Audelia had watched them a few times; they had set up a station in the living room, and occasionally, she was in there reading while both twins worked their magic. It was crazy.

She hadn't seen people work like that with tech except in movies.

It was like she was witnessing her own little Jack Hunt movie. Their spy work was above tier compared to those movies, plus those two were far hotter than even Ethan Pierce in his Golden Dawn days.

Seriously, besides really missing her best friend, she could not wait for her friend to see all the well-toned, hot as fuck men that were here.

It was like living in a reverse harem novel, except without all the sex. Well, without the group sex, because she and Shawn seemed to be constantly jumping each other's bones like the world was going to end tomorrow.

Granted, for them, it very much could.

Whether it be from the sadistic asshole currently being a puppet for some ancient shadow dickface, or the unknown that awaited them in their home realm.

Time seemed to be an unrelenting bitch that was getting her jollies off on torturing her.

The unknown was very much not like the song from *Ice Queen 2: The Spirits Return* movie. It was becoming more and more terrifying by the day.

But she shook that all off. The fears that liked to creep in the middle of the night when she couldn't sleep. Shook them away so that she could focus on the fact that Lila was coming here.

She was going to see her best friend in person for the first time in a month. *FaceTime* had not quelled the ache she felt at not being able to see her best friend.

That would end today.

Aunt Mara had set the deck out back up with a small feast of all of Lila's favorites. It was clear to Audelia that even her aunt was missing her, which made sense. She had always joked that Lila was like a daughter to her.

Still, it warmed her heart that her aunt was on board with Lila coming over.

That made three of them in the house.

Even waiting by the big bay window of the living room, waiting to see Lila's red bug pull up, she could feel the eyes of several very annoyed alphaholes boring into the back of her skull.

The broodiest of them all was Mathias, and he lingered the closest to her; she could feel the contempt wafting off of him in droves.

One day, she would get to the bottom of why he seemed so angered by the idea of her best friend coming over.

For someone who seemed to care a great deal about Audelia, she found it odd that he wouldn't view her being able to see the friend she missed to the point of depression as a good thing.

Maybe it was the idea that her coming here was like lighting a match without knowing if someone turned off the gas on the stovetop.

Will things explode, or will everything be okay?

Whatever it was, she would get him to tell her.

The warmth of a large hand rested against her back as Shawn came to stand beside her at the window. He leaned toward her and placed a soft kiss on her cheek. "You know, just standing at the window isn't going to make her car appear any faster, love."

"Hey, you never know. I apparently have magic somewhere in me. Maybe I can make things appear with willpower. And won't you look silly for doubting me?" She giggled and wrapped her arms around his, which had circled around her, cradling herself in his warmth.

"Well, if I am wrong, and you can do so, then I will do whatever you want me to..." He leaned in closer to her and whispered, sending tendrils of pleasure racing to her core. "With my hands, tongue.....cock. Your choice, my love."

She gasped and nuzzled his neck. "Say that any louder, and I'm pretty sure certain alphaholes in the house may kill you before I get to decide."

His only answer was a chuckle.

Before more words could be said, the sound of blaring music seemed to echo throughout the house as a familiar red beetle with fuzzy pink horns attached to the top pulled into an open space in front of the yellow house that had served as her home for the past month.

"Lila." They both said in unison.

Audelia was out the door faster than the males in the house could stop her. Shawn and Mathias following on her heels. The growls from the latter told her that she would hear it later about being so reckless with her safety.

She didn't give a damn in that moment as she watched her

best friend cut the engine to her devil bug as she called and climbed out, nearly jumping over the hood to reach her.

"Del! Bitch where the hel have you been woman!" Lila yelled as she launched herself at Audelia. The two women giggled and hugged, latching onto each other as if it had been years and a war that had kept them apart.

In some ways, it truly felt like that. But the second, she had her arms around her best friend. It was like everything felt normal again. Yes, Shawn quelled a lot of her uncertainty, but Lila was always her person.

The other side of her coin.

They just understood each other in ways no one else probably ever would.

"I've been here. It's a very long story. Let's go in, Mara, made all your favorites. It's like she loves you more than me." Audelia laughed as she kept one arm slung around her best friend. Shawn embraced Lila for a moment, kissing her forehead like he always did as kids.

"Hey dorkface, finally vagged up and got our girl, did yah?" Lila teased him as they all made their way to the house. The early summer air breezed around them, ruffling the smells of cookouts and flowers.

"Of course. Also, vagged up? Really, Lila?" He laughed.

"Hey, she has a point. Vaginas are tough, babe. They take a beating and still beg for more. Yet, your delicate bulge down there, one tap and you males cry out for your mommies." Audelia laughed.

The grumble from behind, which sounded like both a laugh and a hint of annoyance, brought Mathias's attention toward Lila. Audelia had never seen her best friend's eyes go so big before as she took in the tall, thickly muscled, green-eyed Greek God behind them.

Lila leaned closer to Audelia as she whispered as they ascended the stairs. "So, what's with the real-life combo of Hercules and Adonis? I mean, yummy, but what is going on?"

"I'll explain while we eat. Just wait. There is more man candy inside, as promised." Audelia whispered back. Apparently, Shawn heard her because he huffed out like he was annoyed with her assessment. It only made her and Lila giggle.

They made their way to the backyard, where the smell of brisket going in the smoker made Audelia's mouth water. Bronn, or well, *Alexander* as he needed to be called today, decided he would make this a small cookout.

"I still cannot believe you guys are living at Alexander's house. So, did he finally ask your aunt out after all these years?" Lila asked her between mouthfuls of rolls and artichoke dip. Of course, her best friend had wasted zero time in beginning to devour the food Mara had made.

Gods, she had missed her best friend.

"Yup. He finally vagged up." She answered. Her words brought forth a sound of several male coughs coming from the guys over in the yard sparring. Even with Lila, here they refused to not work on their skills.

As Skye had told her the other day while they played cards. They needed to be ready for whatever awaited them back home.

Which is why even Audelia made sure to brush up her individual skills. Including her skills with a blade and a bow. Her arms ached something fierce that even the multiple massages she got nightly from Shawn before they fell into their love-making could end the ache that had set in her bones.

"So, I got to know what is going on here? Like, is Alexander in the mob or something?" Lila waggled her brows at that. Looking around, Audelia took in how everything probably looked to someone who didn't know what was going on.

Maybe the mob would be a good cover? All the men were armed. Mathias was literally standing nearby with two pistols strapped in holster straps around his shoulders.

Looking at all of them, toned and burly, they did look like enforcers for some sort of mob. The cameras were everywhere. The way Audelia and her aunt were suddenly on lockdown.

"Shut up, weirdo. You're acting like we're in some dark romance novel, and you're wondering which man will be the brooding, tattooed man that just can't get you out of their mind." Audelia threw part of a blueberry scone at Lila. It was neither an omission nor a lie.

So maybe her friend would buy it.

Even if needing to lie to her, it made Audelia feel sick to her stomach.

"Well, we can't all get to fall in love with our childhood best friend. Some of us have to hope for fiction to become reality. My money is on tall, dark and broody over there......" She stole a quick glance over at Mathias and quickly turned back, leaning closer to Audelia, she whispered. "Never mind, maybe he *is* dorkface's competition.... like the man has yet to stop looking at you, girl."

Her words brought a blush to her cheeks. "Shut up, he is old enough to be my uncle. He is just very protective. Besides, no one could ever replace Shawn."

She meant that with her very soul.

Shawn was hers, and she was his.

As if he sensed precisely what she was thinking, he reached over and laced his fingers with hers.

"Ugh, fine lovebirds, but seriously though, is that Gideon over there?" Audelia nodded, but before she could say more or try to get to the bottom of that heated look, Lila suddenly had while looking at Gideon. Or the one he was giving her.

"There is, my darling girl!" Aunt Mara's voice rang out into the early evening air as she and Bronn came out onto the deck. Bronn was carrying a tray full of various meats that he had planned on cooking along with the brisket that was currently in the smoker. It seemed like a lot of food, but then again, they were feeding elite warriors. Audelia had gotten used to seeing the males eating half their weight in meat.

Even Shawn had begun to eat more and had actually added on a few pounds in muscle since they started living here. Not that she would ever complain, especially when she was wrapped around those thick muscles at night.

Lila jumped up and ran to give Aunt Mara a giant hug. She hadn't seen her Aunt smile that big in a while. "I missed you, Auntie!" Lila giggled; since they were nine, Lila had also begun to call Mara auntie, and it stuck.

After that, everything went back to how it always was; it was different, but the same. Lila fit in so well among the males here. The only one who seemed to be utterly annoyed with her being there was Mathias.

He seemed to sneer anytime Lila said a word. Occasionally, Audelia heard the words "Fucking druids".

Otherwise, the world felt normal again.

Like everything that happened had always been there, and she supposed in a way that was true. It had been, but she just wasn't informed of all the pieces.

They talked about everything.

Well, mostly everything. Every time Audelia thought about telling Lila about what was really going on here, the threat of Kage. That she was a freaking Fae Queen from another realm, she would freeze and bring up something else.

She felt like such a coward. She needed her friend's advice, yet she didn't want to break this thin bubble around them of normal.

So, she fed it into this fantasy that everything that had been happening wasn't. That her life was ordinary, that she wasn't about to embark on the craziest of things in her life. That she might die. Might never come back here.

She couldn't do it.

The evening was dying down. Audelia felt tired as she and Lila had curled together, talking about any and everything they could.

It all began to feel like something was coming to an end. Like they both knew that tonight would be the last.

It made her heart ache. She didn't want to lose this.

Fate was a fucking bitch.

It was close to midnight when Lila finally made her way back to her car to leave. Both women hugged each other tightly, and Audelia felt tears brimming as they hugged.

Would she see her friend again?

Is this the last time?

"So, I won't be back in town for a while and probably won't be texting much in the next few weeks." Lila's words broke Audelia from her spiraling thoughts.

"Why? What's going on?" It was Shawn who spoke then.

"My great aunt is sick. And the whole family is heading up

north to see her. Like, straight up, every family member is going."

Great aunt?

That seemed weird. Audelia racked her brain for a memory of Lila ever mentioning a great aunt who would cause the family to leave town.

She couldn't remember one.

She shook away the thoughts of betrayal that ran through her head and smiled at her best friend. "That sucks, I don't remember you having a great aunt still alive?" She didn't want to ask, but every instinct in her was screaming to ask.

Maybe it made her a horrible person for doubting, but after everything that had been going on lately, she didn't know if she could take another hit like this.

"Girl, you and me both! Mom got the call earlier today. Apparently, it's my great-grandma Aggie's baby sister. I didn't even know she existed until mom told me that the family was going to all go, and I mean like ALL the family. Apparently, she is super rich and powerful or something, and her passing would be a major shift in the family." Audelia couldn't sense a lie, but the story sounded insane.

She remembered Lila's mom's side of the family; there were rumors that they were tied to the Irish mob, but no one ever really talked about it.

Lila used to joke that the reason she was so boisterous was that she was secretly a mafia princess; it always made them laugh.

"Well, if it turns out you are a mafia princess, I expect you to come back with some tattooed, seven-foot-tall, muscled enforcer on your arm." Audelia winked, laughing as she hugged her friend again.

"But why won't you be able to call or text, though?" Shawn, who had apparently barely been listening to the conversation or was annoyed with what Audelia had just said, a part of her hoped it was the latter because she saw his jaw tick in a way that made her insides turn to fire.

"Yea, she lives like up in the mountains, and service there is shit. I had to download a bunch of books on my *Kindle*, just in case, so I don't go insane from lack of internet. Eli is pissed as hel. I won't be able to call or text." Lila rolled her eyes. "I told him I would be over after seeing you guys, so he could see me before I left in the morning. I'm sure he will be a delight about it."

Audelia giggled. "Well, it will suck not getting to talk to you, but it just means you will have tons of stories to tell when you get back!"

Part of Audelia was sort of happy her friend would be out of touch for a bit, yeah, she was going to miss her like crazy. But maybe because she'll have so much going on. She won't notice when Audelia eventually disappears.

"Love you, Li." She squeezed her best friend one last time, stepping back, and she felt Shawn's arms wrap around her in support.

"Love you too! Remember, everything will be okay," Lila called out as she got into her car. Audelia took in her best friend's face one last time.

Audelia felt the tears begin as she watched the red beetle drive away. She turned back into Shawn's embrace, burying her face into her warm chest. "It's okay, A Chroi. I know. I am so sorry that you couldn't tell her we were leaving. I promise I will try to find some way you can see her again when everything is settled in your realm. We will find a way back here so you can tell her it all. And maybe have her come visit? You two used to dream about all this being real. Magic exists, and I am fairly sure if we got her to your realm, she would probably never leave." His hand worked in soothing circles over her back as she cried.

He was right, though. If they could find a way to come back here, to have Lila visit her realm. It would be perfect.

She loved that he knew how much this hurt her and that he knew how much she would love the idea of Lila being able to come to see her.

Wait...he said, visit us.

Did he.... Did he plan to remain with her after everything?

She pulled back and looked at him. Her eyes shimmered with tears, and she leaned into his touch as he worked his thumb across her cheek, removing the offending tears.

"What is wrong, my love?" He tilted his head, his eyes searching hers.

"You said, visit us. Does that mean you want to remain there with me after everything is done? After, I am queen?" Her heart was pounding as she searched his eyes.

He smiled at her and brought his lips down to hers in a claiming kiss. His hand worked its way around to her hair, tugging just a bit. She opened her lips at his demand and deepened the kiss. She felt everything he poured into that kiss: his love, devotion, passion, and his promises.

Everything, and she gave it all back as they claimed each other, as the early summer night around them seemed to curl about them, and still, as if it stood witness to everything they were, all their hopes and dreams. Their enduring love.

He broke the kiss first, and they both panted, their breaths erratic as he leaned his forehead against her own. "I love you, A

Chroi. I will always love you. And even if you do not want me to remain by your side, I will always be there, the shadows protecting you. I promise you. No matter what, I am not going anywhere. Maybe, one day, you will no longer want me like this, but it won't matter. I will be by your side in whatever way you need. It might break me if one day you no longer want me. But I will endure because, my love, you are it for me. You are everything. I will go into hel with you. Always."

CHAPTER TWENTY~NINE

Audelia couldn't sleep.

She had tossed and turned constantly, anytime she had managed to fall asleep, it wasn't long before she was torn away from the safety of a dream to feel flames begin to lick up her arms.

Eyes of deep emerald with flecks of midnight in them.

She saw them every time just before she felt the heating scorch of the flames rise within her from that spot in her chest.

It felt foreboding, sending shivers down her spine, as she finally sat up. She tried to be as quiet as she possibly could as she shifted out of Shawn's hold of her.

They had fallen asleep talking, like they used to as kids, telling stories and telling each other their hopes, dreams, and fears. He had known something was bothering her, but he didn't want to pry, knowing she would tell him when she was ready.

This is how their little game of rambling started, he had done it when they were nine as she had been bullied by a group of older boys from school, they had teased her about being an orphan, and one boy had even pushed her off the edge of the play equipment causing her to twist her wrist when she landed.

Shawn and Lila had begged her to tell them what had happened, but she didn't want to say, not because she didn't want the boys to get in trouble, but because she felt weak and cowardly that she hadn't stood up for herself. But, in those days, she curled into herself anytime someone called her an orphan, called her trash, and unlovable. She had believed it.

It had eaten at her for days every time, no matter how much Shawn and Lila would try to distract her, or she buried herself in days at the studio at Bronn's. Those acid words wounded her on levels she didn't fully understand back then.

Levels that, later, as a young woman, she realized were still there, and Kage had found them and dug deep, sinking his claws into her. Till she almost died.

But the rambling game was her saving grace when it came to trying to get herself out of those moments. Shawn would start just talking about random things, shows he had seen, and stories from both sides of his family, and within each ramble, he would bury a question to her.

It was brilliant, and it got her to relax enough that he could find out what had happened without her feeling even more vulnerable.

Gods, she loved him.

Tonight, though, the game hadn't worked. She wished it would have, but she was such a mess of emotions and questions that every time she tried to voice one of them, her throat would feel like someone had shoved sand down her throat, and she just couldn't tell him.

So, he ended the game with slow kisses until they both fell asleep in each other's arms. But it all still plagued her, tore into her, making her feel like she could drown at any moment.

The tide was coming, and she didn't know if she would be able to stop it when it finally made its way.

Or if she wanted to stop it when the waves crashed over her.

She could feel it in her bones as she leaned down and kissed Shawn's forehead, leaning back, taking in the man who loved her.

He really had grown so much in the past month, not just physically but in all the ways she loved most about him.

He grew to be more caring; he seemed to know when she needed something, but he was never pushy about it. He would watch her in this way that made her heart race like he was telling her that if she needed a moment or whatever it was she needed, he would move mountains to make sure she got it.

No man had ever treated her like that before, never made her feel like she was the most important person in the world to them, that their world revolved around her needs, not the other way around.

It wasn't that he had never been like that before, but she had just never noticed it before, and there were these moments when she wished she had magic to send her back in time and slap her past self for not seeing this beautiful man lying on her bed.

With his dark hair that was a little longer than he usually wore it, to the point he was having to push it out of his eyes, or she would tease him and put it in a spare scrunchie she usually wore on her wrist she he could keep doing his training without hair in his way.

She adjusted the blankets over him a bit more so he wouldn't get too cold. She reached for a baggy sweater that she sometimes used as a nightshirt and slipped on a pair of leggings. The early summer evenings were chilly. She desperately wanted to sit in the cool air and let nature curl around her.

Audelia was quiet as she made her way down the stairs, no lights were on, so hopefully, she would be alone for the most part, she knew at least one of the males in the house was probably on guard duty making their way around the property here and there, enough to keep everything safe but not enough that the neighbors would notice that something was up.

She decided she would make some tea, hoping that the soothing feel of it would ease her mind enough that she could go back up and curl into Shawn.

Reaching up, she grabbed a mug from the shelf, smiling to herself, she had noticed over the past few weeks that not just her clothes, some books and little bits of home had made their way here, but also bits of her and Mara's home had made it here, including one of her favorite mugs that had pictures of fictional men from her favorite smutty books in all manner of dress or lack thereof for several, Lila had gotten it for a gag present a few Christmas's ago and it had quickly become one of her favorites. It was dirty and just plain funny.

Audelia frowned as it dawned on her that she wouldn't be able to celebrate Christmas here anymore. Did they even celebrate in her realm?

As she turned on the electric kettle that was always filled with water, she sobered a little, thinking about the fact that she really didn't know anything about the world in which she had been born, not just because she had no memory of the place, but because no one really told her about it.

If she were to be queen, shouldn't she know about these types of things? Not just how to rule or lead armies, she wanted to know about her people, what they loved, and what traditions drove them. History had always been something she loved, and she felt that old love awaken in her, wanting to know everything she could.

Audelia made a reminder to herself to ask her aunt or Gideon about it; the male was a walking history book of information on their world; surely, he would indulge her curiosities before everything changed.

She kicked herself that she hadn't asked more. She had been so caught up in the sudden turn her life had taken and finally being with Shawn that she had neglected to learn about her people.

Tomorrow, she would learn, and every day until they left, she would set aside more time to learn about her world so she wouldn't just be this untried queen coming to save everyone; she would be worth it.

Something, daily, she felt like she wasn't.

Her thoughts were interrupted as she quietly opened the sliding door to the back deck and took in the towering male currently perched on the top step, his russet red hair was unbound and curled in waves that made her slightly envious.

But that wasn't what had made her heart skip a beat as she took him in. It was how he held himself, like the weight of the world was starting to bear down on him. From the looks of the two empty bottles and the one he was currently nursing of whatever ale he preferred, something was eating at him.

He wore a soft grey Henley that hugged every inch of muscle, leaving little to the imagination. He had it rolled up to his elbows, exposing the expanse of tattoos that seemed to swirl and cover almost every inch of his tanned skin.

"Sorry, I didn't think anyone would be awake right now." Audelia apologized quietly as she closed the door to the house. She wasn't sure if she should remain here.

Maybe he needed the quiet of the middle of the night just as much as she did. She didn't want to be the one to end that for him. The male was kind to her, a bit overprotective at times, but even if she couldn't remember him, something about him always calmed her, and she tended to feel drawn to remaining near him.

Audelia decided that she would just go to the living room while she thought through everything, racing through her mind. But, as she turned to go back inside, Mathias's velvet voice broke through her roaring thoughts. "You don't have to go." Something about the way his usually so sure voice cracked a little had her softening.

She didn't speak; she just nodded and made her way to sit beside him on the steps. Audelia knew she should probably give the male some space, but something about the brokenness in his eyes, when he turned to watch her sit, made her steel her nerves and sit next to him.

She placed her mug of tea with honey and a splash of milk next to her on the deck. "You sure? I mean you seem to be in some heavy thoughts, and I don't want to intrude on that."

He merely shook his head with a soft smile that curved on the edge of his full lips, and he had days of beard growth on him now. She hadn't noticed that before. It looked good on him. But it also seemed to add to the sadness that seemed to cast a shadow over him.

They sat like that for a while, both just breathing in the night air around them, but she could feel it.

Something was wrong. She didn't exactly know what, but she knew something was bothering the usually stoic male.

So, before she could second-guess herself, she snatched the beer from his hands and took a swig of it. It burned a little, and she could taste the yeast in it. She was definitely not a beer person, but the look on his face made her smile a little.

He had not been expecting that.

"That was mine." His voice, usually gruff and velvet smooth, sounded slightly amused.

"Well, too bad." She stuck her tongue out at him and laughed at the look he was giving her. She had seen it before when his brother or one of the others teased him about something.

It made him appear softer and younger. Right now, it made her heart swell because it took away some of the sadness that seemed to press on him.

"Trouble. You are pure trouble, Del." He laughed slightly and stretched out his long, thick legs. In front of him on the steps.

Wait? Did he just call her Del? None of the males had used that nickname; they always used others.

"Did you just? What happened to calling me little flower or my shadow?" Her voice shook a little just thinking of those nicknames.

"I stopped calling you that because.... I didn't like the look that you had whenever one of us used the nicknames we have used for years." He reached over and grabbed the beer from her hands easily, her grip had loosened when he called her Del.

He simply took a swig and looked out into the yard like he hadn't just dropped something like that.

"What look? I don't care if you all refer to me as little, whatever you each have chosen for me. It's just a stupid nickname." Even saying the words felt like sand in her mouth.

"That would be a lie, girl. You see, I have known you since you were a toddler. I know when you are lying and when you are trying to act like you are stronger than people view you as. Which you are. Which is how I know it bothers you when we use nicknames because it's all tied to things you don't remember, and it reminds you of what you've lost. For that, I am sorry." He gave her a small smile, one that seemed genuine for him.

Before she thought more of it, she threw her arms around him and gave him a tight hug. She smiled when she felt his large arms close around her, and his warm scent surrounded her. It was calming.

"Thank you, Mathias." She kissed his cheek and took her seat by him again, leaning against him a little, enjoying his warmth and ease.

He felt like a caring uncle in that moment. Maybe that's how things had always felt around him, in those memories, she wished for more than anything she could remember.

"You don't need to thank me, Audelia. It has always been my honor to keep you safe, and part of that is also keeping your heart safe. I won't call you my little flower or my shadow anymore as long as it still hurts you." He nudged her a little and took a swig of his beer.

"I wish, I wish I could remember. Not just because of my

parents, but because I see how you all are with me and each other, and I want that back. I want that bond back." She sighed and continued. "Ever since I was told the truth, it's like a piece of myself I had always felt was missing was back, but it's *still* blurry. Like I can't quite grasp it even with it in my hands." She held her hands out in front of her, grasping at the air.

Like if she tried hard enough, she could bring it back.

"I am sorry, it's a part of all of this I hated the most for you. I have never trusted Wizards and their fickle ways. I get that it was to protect you, but I don't think Waldrom realized how much this would hurt you in the long run." Mathias's voice took on that hinge of a growl of annoyance she had begun to associate with him.

"Or druids, it seems. Don't think I haven't heard you growl that out every time they bring up needing to use the druids to get us back." She smirked a little around the rim of her tea. She swallowed a little, letting the warmth hold her, letting it ease some of the words in her heart that never seemed to find their way out.

"You caught that, did you?"

"Well, if you were going for subtle, I hate to break it to you, my good friend, you suck at it." She laughed, one that didn't feel forced for the first time in a while. It was funny how someone who was still such a stranger to her, but wasn't, seemed to bring back a side she thought was shattered that day she learned the truth.

"Yeah, well..." The words seemed to die on his lips as he stared out at the cool summer night around them. The stars were out, casting them in a brilliant blaze of dancing lights, and the moon held itself proud and glowing like a goddess.

It was the perfect night.

CHAPTER THIRTY

"I know to you I'm still just this little girl, but I have been told I am an *excellent* listener. Plus, I can see something is causing you hurt, and well, I don't quite like that." She reached over and wrapped her hand around his large, callused hand resting on his knee.

They sat quietly for a while, the only sounds around them were crickets and the breeze that had picked up just a little, wisping through the bushes and trees. She felt him squeeze her hand and took a deep breath.

"How much has your aunt told you about me?" His voice was quiet, like he was afraid to speak too loudly.

"Not much, just that you have always been very protective of me and that you also had a sister and a nephew who used to live in the castle."

"I also had a mate." His voice was dripping with grief, and

she knew whatever he said next was going to take a lot for him. So, she merely squeezed his hand in reassurance.

Mathias took a deep breath. "I lost her. Her clan killed her. She was a druid, one of many different clans within the druids. Hers were healers and a small group of dragon hatchers. That's how we met."

Audelia leaned her head against his shoulder, whispering, "I am so sorry."

"She was the one who was handling my dragon, Tadan. I was assigned to bond a dragon since I had shown aptitude for it, and it's in our family line. Dragon riding was second nature to us, next to battle. Many believed it was because our line descended from the Dragon Knight himself. Even if his name and truth have been lost for generations, one thing that remained was that my family line was once his."

"The Dragon Knight? Like the mate of the Phoenix Goddess? Really?" Audelia felt her heart start to race. Something deep inside her stretched, waiting.

"The one and the same. I had dreamed as a kid that maybe I could be like The Dragon Knight, so when I was thirty-five, which in human terms, I was just a teenager, I decided that I would train to become a dragon rider, and I quickly rose through the ranks and was tasked to go bond, which is tricky. If you have ill intentions as to why you wish to bond, they will burn you to a crisp." He laughed at that.

Audelia wondered what it would be like to come face to face with a dragon; the thought both terrified and excited her.

"That had to have been terrifying to go do. I kind of want a dragon now." She giggled, she felt like a little kid listening to her uncle tell crazy stories from his childhood, she supposed he technically was. However, something was different about how this story made her feel at her core.

This was *important*. What he would tell her would change her. Her very soul stretched out to reach for what would be said next.

"It was and wasn't. When I got there, I was told to talk to one of the hatchers about where to go in the heather that surrounded that area of the Atentan Mountains. I decided I didn't need a guide; I could find it myself. That's when I met her. My Neya." The way he spoke the female's name had Audelia's heart racing. There was such reverence in his tone that it shocked her a little.

"That's a beautiful name. What happened when you met her?"

"She knocked me on my ass for not waiting for her escort." He chuckled; it was the lightest thing she had ever heard from him before.

"She sounds like someone I could get along with." She gave a small smile, leaning her head on his shoulder again.

She was enjoying just being here with him, listening to him talk about his past.

"You do remind me of her in that way. You're as strong-willed as she is, even when you seem to doubt yourself." She felt his arm wrap around her shoulders and squeeze in reassurance.

"So, she knocked you on your ass. Which, by the way, had to have been hilarious to see."

"It honestly made me smile. I had not been expecting her to take me down like that. It was the first and only time I had ever underestimated her."

There was a beat of silence when he spoke again, his voice

took on that reverent tone again. "After that, when she finally let me up off the grass. She took me to the hatching grounds, telling me all about the dragons she had helped welp, the stronger ones, the ones she said held the most personality. The more she spoke, the more I felt this pull deep inside of me, drawing me to her. Her words, her entire being, were like this radiant light that held me captive. It was.... unsettling at first. Mainly because no one had made me feel like that before. Nor had someone looked at me like a person for a very long time. I was always seen as the Lord of Death, the killer. She saw me as more. She saw *Me*."

"When we got to the dragons, she stepped away from me, and the world felt cold and empty again. Until Tadan. I could sense him almost immediately; he was all brooding and sarcastic, even from a distance. As much as I did not want to walk away from Neya, scared that if I did, I would never see her again. I also knew I needed to get to Tadan. That he held a part of me that I hadn't realized had never been there until that moment. We bonded almost immediately, which is rare. It usually takes days for a dragon to decide if they wish to bond; they are very picky beings."

"Are they as amazing as I have always dreamed of being? I've been dreaming of dragons since I was little." She leaned away for a moment to take in his face.

She had truly dreamed of dragons for years. One in particular that seemed to always lurk in the background. It was like a dark blue, almost black, with purple eyes that always seemed to watch her, waiting.

"They are. When I first saw Tadan, my heart raced. His eyes were this deep red with flecks of green in them. And then I took in his size, which was like a small mountain. He was this deep grey with these red scales here and there. It was a rare scale, Neya told me later. He had lost his mate when he was young and had suffered from a heart sickness that left his grey scales sparked with blood scales, it made him stronger. He told me once it was his mate leaving her mark upon him so he would never forget her. I know now he was right. Losing a Mate......it marks you forever."

She squeezed his hand again. "I am so sorry Mathias. I cannot even imagine." Her heart broke. Would that happen to her if she lost Shawn? She wasn't sure how mates worked, but she wondered some nights lately if maybe he was hers. That they met for a reason, and felt what they did for each other, because it was *fate*.

She also told whatever fate if that listened, she would come for them if they took him from her.

A shiver ran up her spine.

"I hope you never have this happen to you. I know I don't quite care for the mortal. But he is a good mortal, and I hope you both have many years of happiness. I would not trade the days I had with Neya for anything. Nor would I change how things ended. As much as I wished, it hadn't come to pass. It gave me my son."

His *son*?

He *has* a son?

WHAT.

"Your son? Mara never said anything about you having a son. I mean, I didn't know you had a mate, but a child, if he was alive.... oh gods...I'm sorry." She realized she was babbling and that she may have said something she shouldn't have. But this revelation had stirred something in her. Something potent.

"Mara wouldn't have. She knew, as did your mother, and... and my sister Elarian." At his sister's name, she heard his voice break again. She remembered her aunt saying something about his sister and nephew, whom Audelia had been friends with, who had disappeared.

Her heart broke for Mathias; he had lost so much and still found ways to fight. To protect, when she knew in his heart, he felt torment. She had felt it in that memory they had been forced to share. She felt his pain.

But hearing the reasons for it? To give it a form? That broke her on all new levels.

"What happened to them? Your mate and son?" The words felt bitter on her tongue, but she also couldn't fight the feeling in her that was screaming that she needed to hear this.

To know the costs.

"I trusted the wrong beings. The druids. Her *own* gods damned people. I shouldn't have. They cost me *everything.*" Every word tasted like venom as he spoke. He stood suddenly, shaking free from her hand.

Mathias began to pace in front of her, and she could see all the anger, betrayal, pain, and utter devastation that seemed to play across his features over and over as he trailed his thick hands through his russet hair.

"I'm sorry. I shouldn't have asked." The words tumbled free in a mad, desperate attempt to ease some of what he was feeling.

But, from the piercing gaze that swung toward her, she knew there was no taking it back. The very earth around them seemed to call out to them both, begging for the words to be spoken. To tell the story that had brought such anguish to his warrior.

The thrum in the air seemed to ebb and flow as a battle waged in those eyes that watched her like a predator sizing up its prey. She didn't fear him, though. She knew it wasn't her he was seeing, but those whom he had trusted that had rid him of Neya's light, rid him of mate and a piece of himself.

"Don't be. To not speak of her, of them. It does a great dishonor to their lives. And.... Neya would want me to tell you her story."

Audelia merely nodded. The air in her lungs had tensed, and all she could feel was the pounding that seemed to come from the ground around them. The air had settled and stood to hear this story. To hear of the fate of Neya.

"As I told you, she was a druid. One of a healing clan and dragon hatchers. She was both. And she was fierce and bold. As strong as the dragons whose lives she helped, her heartbeat was like that of a dragon... And because of it. Her father...he feared what her life could become. Feared more the child that was growing in her womb. My child."

Audelia's blood chilled.

"When Neya was pregnant, we could sense something was different about her pregnancy. My sister was studying to become a healer and had been staying in the valley where the dragons were and where my mate spent most of her days. We had a small home there, a cottage. It was my safe haven when I wasn't on the battlefield. Neya had gotten sick. The babe he was pulling more magic from her by the day. His own was.... gods. He held so much power, and he was still in her womb. To protect them both, her father placed our son into a stasis. It was to keep them both safe. To keep his magic from over-whelming them both." Mathias's eyes were beginning to glisten.

She couldn't breathe. She knew what was coming. She knew it in her bones, but she prayed to whatever gods had existed in their realm that she was wrong.

No one could be that cruel.

"It was a lie. All of it. The stasis, the protection. I....I didn't.... I didn't know. Not until Tadan was sent word through Neya's dragon. That something was.... was wrong..." His breathing was becoming erratic, and he dropped to his knees as he spoke the next words. "The bastard......her father had been magically poisoning her and our child. He feared what our son would become. The rumors of my line. The magic that was buried in my line. He feared it would be the harbinger of our world. His ignorance brought about Neya's death. By the time I arrived.... she was *gone......*I couldn't feel her in my soul anymore...." He was crying now, and Audelia flew from her spot on the steps and wrapped her arms around the large warrior.

As she worked her hand in soothing motions over his hair, he continued. "Tadan was roaring as I walked into that cottage. Her father stood over her, not a single drop of remorse or heartbreak on that bastard's face. My sister was in the corner crying, my son in her arms. I could feel it, his magic. It felt off. Like whatever had been done had placed something on him. It was harming him. And then I saw her.... My Neya...my beautiful mate, covered in blood and still as stone on the bed. I shoved her father aside and brought her into my arms. And that's when he thought it was a wise time to tell me that he did what was needed and that my child was an abomination that needed to be—to be culled."

Mathias pulled back from Audelia, gently, but she could see the traces of anger in his face. She was crying now. Crying for what had happened to those Mathias had loved, crying because she knew Mathias was important to her, so his loss...it was like it changed her whole world, knowing this.

"He claimed that my child was dangerous and should not be allowed to live. That Neya and I should never have been together. Never have had a child. That her death was *needed*. As would my son's death." Mathias clenched his fists. "So, before I could let him get another hateful word out, I ripped his throat out, and I tossed his body outside for Neya's dragon. You see, he had not just been blocking my son's magic and poisoning them both, but he had been blocking her dragon, Farais, from knowing what was happening. Her death had set that block free, and Farais had felt EVERYTHING that my Neya had been feeling."

"Oh, gods."

"I went to my sister, and she let me hold my son. He was such a beautiful babe. Waves of dark curls reminded me of my brother when he was a toddler. I knew, in those moments, holding my son. That no one could know he had survived. Whatever Neya's father had feared. Others would know it was well, and he was a High Druid in the clan. My sister, my sweet, kind sister, she was the one who came up with the plan while I cried, holding my sleeping son, sitting next to my dead mate."

A spark of awareness crept up Audelia's spine.

"She told me she would raise him. Her husband had died in the war, the one I had been so caught up in that I hadn't noticed something was amiss with my own mate and child. We wouldn't tell Skye. It would remain between us and mine and Neya's dragons. Farais would help keep my sister and my son safe. I would be his uncle. We would keep this from him. So, that's what we did. That night, Skye arrived to meet our new nephew and to help me perform the right of the moon for Neya. We told him there had been an accident that had claimed both her and her father's lives. He never questioned where her father's body had been. Sometimes, I think he suspected we were lying. But we had never told anyone besides my sister that Neya was with child."

Mathias was quiet for a while as he sat back down in the grass. Audelia sat beside him. Remaining close, hoping having someone there by him would be a comfort, for all he was feeling in retelling their fates.

In a whisper, she spoke the question that seemed to echo through her. "What was his name?"

Mathias flinched. "I....I don't remember.... It was one of the things taken from me when we fell under this lovely curse, Waldrom thought, that would protect you. I'm not sure *why* my son's name can't be told. I know it, in my soul. But the words cannot come."

"Oh...I'm so sorry. Do you know if he was still alive before we were sent here?"

"No. He and my sister.... they died. You won't remember, but when he was six, you were about three. He and my sister came to live in the castle. I hadn't wanted her to. I had managed to bury myself in battle after battle after battle after I lost Neya and him. Because I had lost him. Not being to be able to see my son....it killed me. But it was the only way to keep him safe. I had become a shell of myself...until I met you and became your sworn guard. Well, she had gotten herself into trouble. Trusted the wrong man and ran to me, hoping that she and my son could remain there. Mara and your mother imme- diately agreed. They remembered my sister. They remained at the castle until a year before we left. Then.... they disappeared.

Farais, she had searched for them. She could sense my son because of the bond she had with Neya, but she searched for months. His scent was just *gone*. Which means they were dead. My sister, the last we knew, had sought sanctuary with the druids of Neya's clan. I believe they betrayed her. And killed them both."

CHAPTER THIRTY~ONE

Audelia was stunned.

Everything he had just told her. It crashed into her. Gods. He lost not only his mate but also their child and his little sister.

All because he trusted Druids. His mate's own kin.

Druids, a clan that was here, that Bronn and Mara had said, needed to be able to get home. They held the magic in this realm. Without them, unless her magic was able to open a portal home, they needed.

Gods.

How could they trust them? How could she ask Mathias to trust them?

The two of them sat in the grass for what seemed like ages in silence. She didn't know what to say to him. How do you tell someone who has lost so much that you are sorry? Would that even be enough?

She did realize something, though. The boy Mara had told her about was *his son*. Her friend, whom she didn't remember, was the boy that this male in front of her was never able to raise, all because of the magic that the boy had.

She felt a kinship with the boy. She may not remember, but she felt it. It was like they were two sides of the same coin. It made her feel ashamed. So much had been done for her, for the magic, that she didn't even know how to use. To protect her. Yet, this boy, for equal measure, had just as much, yet he was damned for it.

It didn't sit well with her.

She moved before he could and wrapped her arms around him again and tightened her hold. "I promise that once we get back to our realm and things settle enough, I will help you find out if they are truly gone. I will help you find them. No one should spend their life without knowing if two people they loved, especially their own child, are alive or dead."

She felt him tense for a moment before she felt his strong arms pull her closer. "Thank you, Del. That means more than I think you will ever realize. But I will not burden you with that. You will have a realm to lead when we return. The fate of one female and a child, you don't need to trouble yourself with it."

Shocked by his words, she pulled away. Staring at him, she took in the broken look on his face. The one he carefully keeps from the others. The one she had a feeling he only showed those whom he trusted with everything he had.

"Mathias. I know you don't really know me anymore. But I will tell you this. If I say I am going to do something, there is nothing in the world or now *realms*, that will prevent me from doing so. I will help you find your son and your sister. What kind of Queen would I be if I let one of my most trusted live with such pain? It would be a disservice. From what Mara has told me, you have been by my side since I was two years old, and you have protected me time and time again. Well, I am alive. I am protected by several people, but who protects *you*? Who helps you?" She gave him a look, one that brokered no response. "I'll tell you; I do. And I will do the same for each of you. You have sacrificed enough for me. It's my turn to help you."

And she felt every word in her soul. She would help each of them. Whatever they had sacrificed, she would ensure they found it again. *No matter what.*

She could feel him about to protest. She placed a hand over his mouth, speaking firmly this time, "Don't even fucking think about telling me that it is not needed, that you knew what you signed up for. Well, I don't give a damn. I didn't deserve you all giving up everything you knew to keep me from some sadistic bastard. So, I will ensure you find your closure, whatever it may end up being."

He nodded.

Good.

They remained like that for a while longer. She welcomed the warmth and the safety of his arms. It helped chase that pang that seemed to linger whenever she thought of her past or lack thereof.

She started to doze off sometime later. Her head rocked back and forth against him as she fought the sleep that was finally starting to come.

"Del?" Mathias's voice was soft, and she felt his warm breath trail against her neck. It was soothing.

"Hmm?" She mumbled, sleep starting to claim her a bit more.

"You're falling asleep, dear one." He chuckled softly.

She sat up then. Her body felt heavy, relaxed.

"Shit, sorry." She really hoped she hadn't drooled on him. Audelia quickly checked his Henley for any drool spots. Thanking whatever gods there were that there wasn't a single spot, she began to stand.

Mathias was right there to help her stand and pulled her into a strong hug for a moment. "Thank you again, Del.., for listening, for what you said after. It's not something I am able to talk about; it's my greatest shame that I failed them. I never wanted you to know it, but at the same time, it felt like something you needed to know." His cheeks heated as he gave her a small smile before stepping away and making his way to his discarded beer bottles.

She merely nodded, not knowing quite how to respond to that and realizing at the moment that maybe he didn't really need words. As she made her way back inside the house, she grabbed her teacup from the deck. She thought that perhaps she hadn't been able to sleep, not because of everything going on.

But maybe because someone had needed her. They needed to be able to voice what had been ailing their heart before everything changed again.

She felt that in her soul. Audelia was glad she had been that comfort for Mathias. That he was able to tell her things that he hadn't been able to voice aloud. Knew how rare it was to have someone like that, and that you never forget that kind of kindness.

It reminded her of Shawn and how he had been the one she was able to lean on and tell about all the horrible things Kage had done to her.

She placed the mug in the sink after dumping the remaining tea, just as Mathias came inside with his empty bottles, putting them in the bin. She turned and smiled at him. "Goodnight, Mathias."

"Goodnight, princess."

By the time she got upstairs, Audelia was exhausted. She shrugged out of the sweater, down to the tank and leggings she wore, and curled into Shawn's side. Soaking into his warmth, she fell into a deep sleep. Her mind wandered to the boy she had been told about playing with as a girl. The boy she now knew in her heart to be Mathias's son.

The evening air was thick, with the scent of storms brewing on the horizon. He knew he should have come on a better night. But something about storms made him think of her. Of the way, she seemed to brighten every time the summer rains came. Plus, with the cloud coverage, he was able to sneak into the cemetery more easily; no one would be out with a storm on the horizon, even if it were late at night. It was a risk he was willing to take. Lately, he couldn't shake his thoughts of her. Sometimes, they were so real his heart would leap, and his mind would forget.

Forget that she was gone. That he had failed her.

Coming here, as much as he did, was a risk. It was his way of reminding his heart of his failure. That even though he had promised her, he hadn't been there to keep her safe.

All these years, all the training, the bloodshed, the whispers about him. They were all for one reason. Her.

He would do everything in his power to end the bastard who took her from him.

He knelt before the grave as the last vestiges of moonlight sought out the cool, marbled stone. He had paid for the stone himself. None had been made in her honor. No, the fucker that killed her had deemed that she didn't deserve the sacred rights of the dead. No, he had told him that... that her body had been fed to the demons that were in the man's legions when he stormed the castle.

He clenched his hands tightly in anger, so tightly he could feel the sudden sting and rush of blood as he broke skin. Shaking out the pain, he knelt before the stone, placing a callused hand against it. He could feel the tears beginning to well.

He was a stone-cold killer to the world. But here.

Here, he was just the boy.

The boy who lost the girl who held his heart.

Held his soul.

She took it with her that day.

The day he lost her forever.

Any day after that, he became what his father wanted him to be.

Death.

Shadow.

A Harbinger.

Here though. He could mourn her. He could remember everything about her. Closing his eyes, he could see her.

Bright red hair that looked like a living flame, wrapped in tight ringlets about her face. Eyes. Gods, eyes that to this day still haunted him. Soft freckles over her nose. He used to count them when they would play in the gardens. She was ten the last time he had seen her. He could still hear her laugh. Gods, he wished he could hear it again.

She was beautiful even at seven years old. She was his entire world.

He had pledged to her to be her knight. To be the one to guard her side. He was only eleven and not yet even a squire. But still, he gave her the knight's pledge one day under the shade of the blossoming willow.

Regret seized him then. As it always did. It was his unfailing companion.

"I'm sorry." He choked out, placing his forehead against the cool marble of the tomb that didn't even hold her body.

"I'm so sorry I failed you. That you were scared and alone, and I wasn't there to hold your hand and keep you safe. I am so fucking sorry." His fist pounded the ground, causing it to quake. "It's been two hundred and fourteen years since I lost you. Yet, every day feels like the first. You have my heart, you know? You always had. I was so in love with you, yet as a kid, I didn't understand what that meant. But now, I know. I know what I felt for you. It was cosmic. I know that now. Too late. Too late to save you. To be there for you. I am so sorry for failing. But I promise my love. I promise I will end him. I will rip the heart out of the one who stole you from me. Stole all you were. I promise, even if it costs me my life, I will end him. Then, we can be together again. I will find you again. I promise."

He moved then, taking out the dagger his uncle had gifted him years ago. He sat up some, he undid the buttons of his tunic over his heart, and plunged the dagger into his chest, just enough to carve a rune there. Closing his eyes, he relished the pain. Taking a deep breath, he spoke again, his voice deep and husky. "I promise that I will find you in the afterlife. I will scour every inch of the beyond for you. If you are not there, and you have been granted a new life. Then

I shall sell my soul to the fates to bargain to be joined there with you. I will find you again. And this time.... This time, I will not fail you."

He felt the drumming in his soul hum in answer to his vow.

Audelia woke with a start. Her heart was pounding through her whole body. It wasn't just the dream that had startled her, though. No, it was the yelling coming from downstairs. She turned to nudge Shawn to rouse him. Only to find she was in bed alone.

She quickly jumped out of bed, slightly stumbling, and grabbed her sweater from where she had thrown it in the early hours of the morning when she had come back in from outside. Stretching her arms into the sleeves, she made her way downstairs, taking the steps two at a time.

The closer she came to the bottom, the louder the shouting was. It sounded like everyone was in the kitchen, so she quickly leaped off the railing, landing with a soft thud on the hardwood floor of the hallway. Her heart raced with every raised shout.

"We need to leave now!"

"We don't even know if we can go home that way!"

"It doesn't matter anymore. They have made their moves known. They will come here next. We must leave now." Bronn's was the loudest and most authoritative as Audelia rounded the corner to take in the scene before her.

All the men looked ready to attack at the slightest wrong move. What remained to be seen was whether it was the enemy or each other. She would have laughed at how the scene looked to her if not for the terrified look on her aunt's face. That made her heart slam to a stop.

"What happened?" Her voice rose, breaking through the volley of arguments running rampant in the country modern kitchen that looked so very out of place with all the giant Alpha males yelling. Powder blue and checkered prints did not exactly scream war room.

All heads swung towards her. Shawn was the first to reach her, bringing his arm around her like she was going to need his strength for what was going to be said next.

She turned to face him, taking in his stricken features. He was worried, but he was trying his best not to show it.

Shit. That wasn't good.

"Shawn?" She spoke again, her eyes searching every corner of his dark green eyes. What she saw there had her heart pounding; she knew what he would say before he spoke the words aloud.

"This morning, Alaric went to check on your house, and the entire place had been ransacked... and a message was left." He looked down then. She could feel the anger emanating from him.

What kind of message? Was it the Shadow that had been haunting her? Or was it the more disturbing option, Kage?

It was Gideon who spoke first. His voice startled her out of her spiraling thoughts. "They took many of your things. Like they were preparing for a journey. And written in what we assume was someone's blood. Whoever left the message said *She is mine. Soon, pretty one. I know who you all are.*" Though, his voice was usually like warm sugar wrapped in night. The words he spoke made her feel ill.

The room spun. She felt her body fall, but the impact never came as Shawn had caught her in his strong arms. Placing a kiss to her temple, he moved her to a chair by the table. His hand never left hers again as he worked his thumb back and forth in a soothing manner.

"What else?" She could feel it in the air. It was more than things missing, a message in blood, and the house trashed. They *knew* who did it. She could see it in every murderous expression of rage around the room. "What else was in the message. Tell me."

Skye spoke as he came to sit down at the table, the others following suit. "The house was covered in white petunias and orange lilies. Mainly all over—over your bed, Del." She was so shocked by his words that it barely registered that he had called her Del. Probably at the behest of his older brother to help ease her discomfort.

"Kage." She whispered his name. Hoping that if she didn't say it loud enough, maybe, perhaps, this wouldn't be happening.

Nods from all around the table.

Her aunt's face was covered in tears as she placed food around the table. It went untouched, but she knew her aunt. She cooked most when she was upset. This was the easiest way for her to handle what was happening.

Gods, their house.

"I'm assuming you took pictures?" She spoke, surprising herself with how calm her words came out.

On the inside, she was a raging mess of anger, fear, hate, disgust, and sorrow.

It was Ezreal who nodded at her words. He was the quietest of the twins. But he had a kind smile and had been showing her how some of the tech stuff worked.

She swallowed the bile that was threatening to rise. "I want to see the pictures. I need to see it."

Shawn squeezed her hand, drawing her attention back to him. His eyes swam with worry. "Are you sure, my love?"

"Yes."

Bronn nodded at Ezreal, who ran to the kitchen island to fetch the laptop that she hadn't noticed was open on the counter. He placed it in front of her and, after a few clicks, pulled up the pictures.

She began to look through them, at the hundreds of white and orange flowers, at the bloodied message written on the living room wall. As she did, she felt the power in her begin to yawn open. Felt it take its stretches.

Gods. Their home.

The safe place she and her aunt had created over the years was ruined. Tarnished. Sullied.

Her heart raged and broke, and every stitch that rebuilt over the damage was fueled by the fire she felt beginning to burn inside her. She knew by the gasps around the room and the tightening of Shawn's hand that her body was probably glowing again.

She didn't care. They would pay. That was her home. That was the place where she cried herself to sleep after losing her parents, where Mara made her brownies and started waffle Sundays, where she learned to love, and discovered that sometimes love is broken and wrong.

It was the place where she and Shawn had finally spoken the words that had been burning inside them for far too long. Where he had set her body aflame with his touch.

It was ruined.

Her sanctum. That bastard took it from her *AGAIN*.

CHAPTER THIRTY~ TWO

P ower was radiating from her, she could feel every pulse of it coursing through her blood, feel the weight of it as that ancient feeling inside curled and stretched, preparing for what awaited her next.

Each image that had been on the laptop in front of her was burning into her. Fueling the fire that was now always simmering just beneath her skin.

He had taken her home from her.

Taken her innocence.

Broken her, bled her, made her feel like she was less than.

Now, this? Her home?

Her heart was racing; she could hear voices around her, but nothing registered as she just stared at the final image —the one of her bed covered in those gods-awful flowers that made her very skin crawl.

She needed to leave.

Needed air.

Needed to do something.

No.

What she needed to do was hunt that fucking sadistic fuck down and end him like she should have done that night in the hotel all that time ago.

Warm, strong hands gripped her, pulling her back. She barely registered who it was as she just kept walking, heading toward the smell of the mid-morning summer air through the open screen door.

The hands gripped her harder this time. On instinct, she shifted her weight, bearing down on the person in front of her. She could feel that now, whoever was trying to stop her was directly in front of her. She shoved hard and placed a kick with her entire body. She heard a loud thud, a curse, and kept going.

Rage filled her blood, mixing with the fire in her, she could feel the warmth. Relished in how it would feel to kill Kage. To finally end his torment.

She wanted it so badly.

It blinded her.

Pulled her.

Shouts again. Someone told another to stop. Not to try whatever they were planning on doing.

Good, no one. Nothing was going to stop her from destroying Kage.

"Del! Stop my love!" A voice was behind her, close.

How did they get so close to her?

It didn't matter. She made her way across the yard. *Wait? When did she get outside?*

Everything felt blurry.

The voice called again, even closer, as a gentle touch placed itself on her cheek.

She stopped. The fire in her screamed at the intrusion on its mission.

Destroy. End.

She began to move again, this time, though, even as she tried to disengage from this person, object to whatever that was trying to stop her from killing. They refused to relent even as she screamed.

"Come back to me. Audelia. Please come back." She *knew* that voice. It lived in her soul, called to her, made her heart race in pleasure, in *love*.

The inferno within started to calm as if it, too, was trying to decide what to do next.

This voice held something over her.

No.

She needed to end Kage. So, she shoved again, but this time, she was met with her own back hitting the ground, a body pressed above her. Before she could move again, lips pressed to hers in an urgency.

The kiss was hard and unyielding, but it was also filled with such love that tears began to fall down her cheeks. It ended, and a voice spoke again.

No, not a voice. It was Shawn—her love.

"A Chroi?" His voice was both a plea and a question.

The warm, gentle hand from before touched her cheek again, as everything came into focus again.

She was in the backyard, on her back, and Shawn was above her, his eyes filled with tears, his face full of worry. *How did she get outside?*

Shaking her head, she felt the last of the fog in her mind

lift, the last vestiges of her power slam back into the coiled ball that lived in her chest. "What..." She could taste ash on her tongue. "What happened?"

"Oh, thank Gods." She heard her aunt exclaim from somewhere nearby.

Shawn stood quickly and pulled her up with him in a fluid motion her body was pressed against his. "Are you sure you're okay?" He gave her a quick kiss, his hand caressing her cheek as his green eyes searched hers, checking to ensure she was truly okay.

She nodded, still confused by all that had just happened.

"Let's go back inside and get you something to eat," Mara called from the open door of the house.

Shawn held her close as they made their way inside. As she walked into the kitchen dining area, she gasped and saw Mathias. The male had a large purple bruise on his jaw. "Okay...what happened seriously?" She spoke again.

Alaric laughed. His bellow was rich and full, sending a blush to her cheeks. "Well, princess, you punched our dear delicate Mathias here and put him on his ass." Snickers from the others around the table at his words.

"I'm...sorry, I did that?" She gestured to Mathias and was shocked not to find anger in his features, but, shit, was that pride? Pride that she beat his face and took him down?

"You did well, Del.. Granted, I could've done without the bruise to both my face and ego, but I'll take it because it means you can handle yourself," Mathias spoke, his voice rung with the pride she had seen in his features, but also traces of humor.

Nodding, she took her seat at the table again, noting that the laptop she had been looking at was now gone. Before she could ask where it was, a plate of waffles with a decent amount of bacon was put in front of her. "Eat. You are going to need it after an expenditure like that."

She nodded at her aunt as she realized she was indeed starving suddenly. She took a few large bites, barely registering that everyone at the table was watching her.

"Feel better, little one?" Bronn spoke finally.

Still not finding it in herself to speak, she nodded as she continued to eat.

"So, besides you taking Mathias to the floor in such a way that I'm pretty sure everyone in this room is still shocked. You were letting your magic ride you. You can't let that happen again; you could have killed him." His words felt like a dagger to her heart.

But then she felt anger rise at his words as well. *Let it happen?* She only just found out a month ago that she had magic, magic that was still locked inside her and seemed to choose when it wanted to come out.

But. Sure, don't let it happen again.

"I'm sorry, Bronn, but how is she supposed to control something she barely understands?" Shawn spoke, his words were accusatory as he stared Bronn down.

Damn, she wanted to kiss him right then. Not just for voicing exactly what she was thinking, but having trouble speaking out loud, but for the fact that he was staring down her uncle, a male he greatly respected.

A whistle noise came from the backyard as Ezrael's twin, Micah, made his way across the yard, eating the distance up quickly. She hadn't even realized that he had been the only one not in the kitchen when she came down earlier.

"They are ready. They told me to—" His words fell flat as he took in the room before him. "Clearly, I have missed things."

"Indeed," Spoke Gideon.

In a clear dismissal of what Shawn had said. Bronn turned to give Micah his full attention as Micah leaned against the wall by his twin. "So, what do the druids say?"

"Duncan said they are gathered at The Glade, beginning the rituals that awaken the magic in the tree from its slumber. We are to proceed there soon before it alerts other magic wielders in this realm."

"Then I think it's time we all pack up and leave to head home." Bronn stood, clearly deciding that this conversation was done.

She understood the urgency, but then her eyes sought out Mathias, and the look on his face had her heart dropping and a renewed sense of herself forming quickly.

"Wait. Should we really even trust the Druids? What if they are lying to us? We could be walking into a trap. We need a different option."

With a heavy sigh, Bronn turned towards her, but she saw his eyes flick to Mathias for a second. "We can trust these ones. I know not all druids can be trusted, but this clan is an exception. I have been in contact with them since we arrived, as has Gideon. They are our *only* option. We do not have the luxury of time anymore." His tone wasn't harsh, but it was unrelenting.

"It only takes one bad apple to spoil the pie." She quipped, a little spark formed over her hand for a moment before it was gone, leaving only a billow of smoke behind.

She knew she was being petulant. But she also didn't like the torment in Mathias's eyes.

Bronn's fingers came to the bridge of his nose as he pinched there, clearly fighting his irritation. "Yes, I am aware, trust me, Audelia. I know. However, they have something we need, something that can't be corrupted. They have The Wood Sprite. The Keeper of the Portal."

"*Fuck.*" Mathias swore. His eyes grew, and he turned to look at her briefly before taking a deep breath. "You're sure?" He looked between Bronn, Gideon, and Micah.

All three nodded.

"Can you tell me what the fuck the Keeper of the Portal is?" She ignored the part of her that was giddy at the idea of wood sprites being real. She still didn't want to trust the druids. What if they were like Mathias' father-in-law?

"It's exactly as it sounds, Audelia. This wood sprite is a being of ancient magics. They usually protect certain magical trees. In this case, this sprite is the only one who can open the portal to our world using the Willow in The Glade. That tree is a maelstrom of magic, linked with one in our own world." Gideon spoke, his eyes glinting with his usual mirth anytime he talked about knowledge.

"Why can't they be corrupted?" That was the part that worried her the most. *What if this sprite, what if they saw more merit in the dark being trying to kill her?* She thought.

It was Mathias who spoke to her then, his eyes swimming with a determination that was drowning out the torment for once. "Because they are of the purest forms of magic. Darkness does not call to them as it does to others. They only see purity. And they have attachments. Not only to the trees they protect, but sometimes to certain people. Usually those of a pure heart."

She wanted to argue because she was still worried, but she could hear the voice, that of the wizard Waldrom, speaking to her from the source inside her.

Trust in The Sprite, little star. You have known her for a long time. Every time you ventured to the tree, she was always there.

"I still say that even if you all trust these druids, we stay on our guard." She spoke and then stood, her legs felt a little wobbly, but only slightly.

The group broke apart, each member going to the rooms they had been occupying or to the living room, where several had left behind a considerable amount of their weapons.

Before, she and Shawn could make their way to the room so they could change into clothing that was more suited to the movement they might need. Mathias pulled them both outside onto the deck.

"Everything okay, Mathias?" Shawn asked, his gaze jumping back and forth between her and the tall, muscular male.

"No. I still don't like this. But that threat, him knowing who we are? Even I don't want to risk it to find another source home. If they have The Sprite, then I will trust them, for *now.* But I promise, Del, I will do everything in my power to make sure that nothing happens to you. To either of you." His last addition made her heart warm; it was his way of acknowledging that Shawn was important to her and that if something were to occur to him, it would hurt her.

"I know, thank you. But are you sure you're going to be okay with all of this?" She still worried the male might be tough as nails, but still, he lost three people important to him because of druids. Her pledge to avenge them for him coursed through her mind again. *Soon.*

"Yes. I *have* to be. Getting you home, keeping you away from that sadistic bastard is all that matters right now." He gave her a small smile, and his gaze swung to Shawn. Audelia watched as those bright, russet eyes of his drilled into Shawn. "Promise me, Shawn, promise that even if you see all of us fall, you will give everything to ensure her safety."

"I promise, Mathias. I will never falter from her side as we go forward." Shawn reached out his hand to clasp Mathias's forearm, which he extended and gripped back. The two males stared at each other, seeming to reach an understanding.

Mathias nodded and reached over to place a gentle kiss on her forehead, then walked away to arm himself.

Everything passed in a blur as they dressed upstairs. Audelia had changed into a brown pair of thick cargo pants that hugged her skin like leggings; she paired them with combat boots. She changed into a peasant top in a soft blue-green that cinched at her elbows and hugged her curves. Over it, she placed a tactical corset that Mara had given her a few days ago. It was a brown-bronze color and had spots like a baldric for her to place daggers. It gave her plenty of move-ment, deciding that she wasn't entirely sure what they would come across in her realm. So, she threw on a cream-colored light summer sweater, which was baggy and hid the baldric corset.

She threw her hair into a thick braid to keep it out of her face. She looked into the mirror, taking in her appearance. Audelia looked so *different* than the young woman she had been just a month ago. Still freckled with wild red hair, but stronger than she had been a month ago.

Turning to the sound of Shawn's booted foot coming to the floor as he switched up, bringing his other foot to him on the chair by the bed as he laced his boots. She took in his change as well.

Gone was the lithe, muscled man she had kissed for the

first time. Before her sat the man she loved; he had gained some muscle weight over the past month of training with the others. As he stood, she took in the thick cords of muscle that seemed to stretch against the fabric of the tunic he wore. He had a baldric of his own now laden with daggers; the males must have given him some.

That made her smile, and he returned it as he walked toward her. His stride sure as his powerful legs made their way to her, each movement made her mouth water. He smirked. "Are you eye fucking me right now?" His voice was husky as he leaned in to press his lips to hers in a gentle kiss.

She wasn't having that, cause yes, she had been eye fucking him. Because he was standing before her looking like a warrior, it was doing something to her. So, she kissed him back harder, he relented easily and kissed back just as hungrily.

They were like that for a while, kissing with a passion that made her knees weak but also made her heart ache because it felt like a *goodbye*. Felt like they knew things would change today. So, they held each other, taking comfort from one another. Neither spoke of the fears they both held on to.

The moment was broken when a sharp knock called out to them from the door. They broke apart but didn't fully let go, their foreheads leaning against each other as they caught their breath. "Yes?" Shawn called. His eyes were still fixed on her.

"Audelia, can I see you for a moment, little one?" It was Bronn's voice.

"Yeah, I'll be out in a moment." She called. There was no reply, but the sound of footsteps heading down the stairs could be heard softly a moment later.

Audelia brought her arms around Shawn, holding him to her, never breaking eye contact. His snaked his own around her as well. "I love you, Audelia. It's going to be okay. I can feel it in my bones. Today will be fine."

"I love you too, Shawn, so damn much." He leaned down one last time to claim her mouth. This kiss was soft, and she felt his love for her pouring through each gentle push and pull of their mouths.

They broke apart, and she grabbed the twin daggers that Mathias had given her a week ago after a sparring session. She sheathed them to her thighs and, with one last glance at Shawn, she made her way downstairs in search of her uncle.

She found him in his office at the back of the house. He was standing behind his desk, staring at a blade that sat on his desk.

She had been here so many times over the years. She always loved the light colors he had chosen for it. It was bright and filled with books, books she now realized were all the ones her aunt loved. That thought had her smiling. How had she never noticed that before?

She walked closer to his light walnut desk, one that was filled with pictures of her and her aunt, even one of her, Shawn, and Lila when they were—what looked like twelve? Taken in the backyard at one of the little bonfire parties, their missing teeth and the chocolate smears from the s'mores in their hands make her heart clench. Would she ever see her best friend again? Would she even survive all this to have a peaceful night like that again?

He must have noticed what she was looking at, because his gentle voice was back—the one that soothed her when she had fallen during a karate competition, and she was upset at having failed him. "You will, little one. I know everything seems so out of reach and like you will never know a good night of just peace again. You will. I know it in my heart."

"How can you? You didn't seem to like my judgment all that well earlier. I am to rule a realm. If I can't even make a decision that my battle-worn uncle doesn't like, how can I have any hope of coming out of all of this?" Audelia hated how she could feel her voice wobble.

He simply smiled and came around his desk, and pulled her into a tight hug. She wrapped her arms around him. Reflecting on all the times she did this as a child. She always loved his hugs; they had felt fatherly to her.

Now, with the truth of her life in the open, she realized why they had always felt that way. He was her father's older brother.

He pulled away and cupped her cheeks in his big hands. "I know because you remind me so much of your parents. Bull-headed, fiercely protective of those they love, and clever. So damn clever." She watched as the smile he gave her reached his eyes; it was the smile that she wondered if her father had as well.

"Do you think I will ever get to remember them?"

"Yes. As soon as we return to our realm, the magic that suppresses our memories should lift. If not, then we will seek out Waldrom's cave. It will have answers and hopefully him as well."

She nodded, her eyes catching on the hilt of the beautiful small sword sitting on his desk. "What is that?"

He smiled and reached over to grab it from his desk. She took in the details of it, still in its scabbard. It was a little shorter than a standard short sword, and it was a dark violet-black with gold etchings of what looked like *runes* on it. They were beautiful.

As he brought it between them, she took in the hilt; it was the same violet-black, except for the end of the pommel, which made her catch her breath. It was shaped like a phoenix head. She saw then that along the edges of the hilt were the flaming feathers of it, in a deep shade of indigo. Runes or whatever, those intricate linework worked their way around each feather.

"Here, take a look at it." Bronn handed it to her then. Her breath caught as she held it in her hand.

It felt *right*.

As if it were an extension of *her*.

She looked at her uncle, who merely smiled and nodded at her to remove it from the scabbard.

She stilled her hand, which had begun to shake at the feeling of rightness, taking a deep breath, she gently pulled the blade free. Bronn quickly took the scabbard from her, as she took in the beautiful blade in her hand.

She brought it closer, the blade tip facing toward the ceiling, as she took in the silver-greyed blade, what looked like rivers of that deep indigo worked their way around the blade in swirls that caught the light. Each time she did, she felt the power inside her awaken.

"Gods. It's beautiful." She merely just stared in *awe* of the blade.

It was a work of art.

"It was your mothers." Bronn's voice was like soft velvet. Yet, those words. They had sunk deep into her soul.

Her mother's blade? She stared down at the blade in her hand, her heart pounding.

"It was?"

He just nodded as she moved to grab the scabbard to place

the blade back into it. She didn't deserve to hold her mother's blade. Not when she didn't even remember her.

He halted her movements, shaking his head. "No, Audelia. She wanted you to have this sword one day. It was hers, yes. But little one. She had it crafted for you. It is both hers and yours."

Audelia looked down at the blade, tears beginning to well in her eyes. *Her mother made it for her?*

"Try it. You know the moves to ensure a blade has the proper balance." He stepped away from her then.

She nodded, willing the shaking in her hand to stop. As it eased, she took a breath, centered herself, and began to swing the blade in arcs, testing how it moved. Gods.

It felt like an extension of herself. Not only that. She could feel the magic that she still couldn't fully control, which seemed to reach out to the blade as she moved around, arcing in strokes.

She was crying now. The tears seemed not to want to stop as she finally reached for the sheath and placed the blade back. She hugged the sheathed blade against her chest.

Bronn stepped closer then. "Audelia. They would be so immensely proud of you. I know I am. Every day, I am in such awe of you. You have taken what was truly thrust upon you with such strength in grace. In such an Audelia fashion that I am so beyond proud of the woman you are and the Queen you are starting to become."

She looked up at her uncle then, tears falling down her cheeks as she looked into his chocolate-brown eyes. His eyes have always made her feel so seen when he looks at her.

"You doubt yourself; I can see it in your eyes. But my dear girl. You think I didn't see how you protected Mathias today?

You questioned today not for yourself but because you did not wish to bring harm to someone you care for. That, my darling, that is the makings of a great Queen. One I cannot wait to see one day." He smiled and pulled her in for another hug, and she gripped his tunic around the sword, still in her arms. She felt him pet her hair in soothing motions and pressed a kiss to the top of her head.

"Thank you, Uncle." She spoke softly, wiping away the tears with her hand as they pulled apart. She gave him a small smile.

CHAPTER THIRTY~ THREE

It was early evening as they made their way toward The Glade and *home*, she guessed. It was still weird to think about. That this place she had known for the past fifteen years was only a stepping stone in her life.

Not that it didn't feel like home; it had, but honestly, if she was being honest, she had never truly felt like she *belonged* here. It was why her head was always lost in books or daydreaming while in The Glade. The places where she felt most at home were with her friends, her aunt, and when she was at the studio with her uncle. Lately, though, spending time with her guard at Bronn's has also begun to feel like home.

But the one place where she went when she needed to ground herself, when she needed those moments where her world felt at peace? It was always The Glade.

It felt fitting that the next step in her journey would involve it.

She laughed a little at that thought.

"What's so funny?" Shawn asked from her right side. He looked so different, fully strapped with weapons, which were currently hidden underneath the light jacket he wore. They all had something keeping the weapons concealed, even though the small sword, like some of the others' larger swords, strapped to their backs definitely stuck out.

She smiled at him, walking a little closer grabbing his hand. They had been holding hands off and on during the walk to The Glade. "Just finding it funny that the one place in this town that always brought me peace is the very place we need to go in order to return to my realm."

"*Our* realm." He corrected. His words made her heart pound wildly. He had been doing that lately. Anytime she brought up the realm of her birth, he would immediately lay claim to it as well. It made her beyond happy that he viewed this new place as his home, too.

Still, a part of her felt horrible that she was taking him from his parents. He had called them earlier today, before she had gotten up to talk to them, they had been understanding that he wanted a new adventure, that she had been called by a distant family member on her mother's side, and that they were proud of him for deciding to be with her during such a change.

Part of her wondered if they knew what was really going on. Shawn said they had seemed slightly sad and proud as they had told him those words, and that they sent their love to both him and Audelia. It made her want to cry again that they had said that.

She would miss his parents and his Sobo greatly.

"I love it when you say that. *Our* realm. But yes. It just feels a bit like fate, you know?" Audelia giggled softly.

It was Skye who piped in from his spot, slightly behind her to the left. All of her guards were near her, either closely like Skye and Mathias, who were just ahead of her, or a bit farther away from her, like the others. The plan was to travel together, but a large group like theirs would draw too much attention, so they decided on smaller groups spaced out to look a little less conspicuous.

"Of course, it would be fate. The Glade is where we came into this world from, after all. It was brief, but I do remember us landing in a small grove by the tree. Before I could say a word, I was suddenly in the one-bedroom apartment I had called home in the past few years." He smiled, and it was such a boyish smile that, until he did smile, she often forgot just how much younger he was compared to the other males.

He had told her one day that he was only in his early thirties when everything happened. Most of her guards had been well over a hundred when they joined the Cadre.

Before she could question it more, a call of an owl worked its way through the quiet night. It sent a shiver down her spine. *When did they get so far into the trees?* Usually, she knew when she was in the comfort of the forest before the main willow. They enveloped her in safety. Yet, she hadn't even noticed this time, not until the sound of the little brook broke her thoughts. They were before the stone bridge that led into the main sanctum of The Glade.

"Dear gods," Shawn whispered beside her. She felt it then.

A drum beat.

It was becoming louder and louder as they made their way to the bridge. They stopped for a moment as the other group, which had been ahead of them, Alaric and the twins, waited by the railings of the bridge.

Here, they shed the jackets that blocked their weapons from view. Adjustments were made, as the blades of each one came into view; they each had a small pack on their back filled with supplies.

Hers had a few things from home she couldn't part with. A romance novel that she had always adored, it brought her a sense of comfort to have it with her; she knew it wasn't a necessary thing and would probably get ruined, but she couldn't be parted from it.

As she adjusted the daggers on her baldric, the lights of lanterns hanging around them caught on to the beaded Jade bracelet she wore. Shawn had run home a few nights ago and returned with it. He told her he had been planning on giving it to her for a while, but he really wanted her to have it for their journey.

She worried it might break, but couldn't bring herself to put it away in a pocket, and she wanted it against her skin. The words from that night played through her head as she grazed her fingers over the beautiful beads.

It was beautiful. She couldn't believe he had gotten her this bracelet.

"Audelia, I Love You. I have for a very long time; I know everything has been so beyond insane since we finally told each other how we felt. But I will never tire of telling you how much I love you. I truly believe you are my soul mate. My other half. You planted yourself so damn deep in my soul I don't plan on ever letting you leave again. I know it's not a ring, and one day, I will get you one if I am able. But I want you to know that this. Us. It's forever for me. One day, I will make you my wife. I don't know if I will make a good King, but I promise to try. I will love your realm, as I love you as fiercely as I can."

She was crying then as he reached her and pulled her into a deep kiss, one that felt like a promise, one larger than the one he had just given her. "I love you, too, Shawn, and I would be honored to be your wife one day. Us it's forever for me too."

They had made love that night. Staying up late to talk about just little things. About her fears about what would happen, about her parents, and how much it broke her very soul that she didn't remember them. That she didn't remember all those wonderful people who loved her.

He had held her, letting her cry and making a promise that he would do everything he could to help her get that back.

She had told him that her aunt had told her that she already had a piece of her past with her. The necklace she always wore was from the boy she had known as a child; he had made it for her using his magic.

The boy she now knew *was Mathias's son*, she thought. As she reached up to touch the necklace there, she told Shawn about him in the quiet that day as they had dressed. He agreed to help Mathias exact his vengeance and find answers about what had happened.

Shawn smiled at her then, taking notice of her playing with the beads. She gave him a smile that made him blush.

Soon, the others arrived, and everyone had shed their jackets and fixed their blades and bags. Her aunt came to stand by her and wrapped her arm around her waist. "I know you still don't trust the druids, I know why." Her eyes shifted to Mathias, who was talking to his brother.

The two shared a smile about whatever the younger brother had said. "I'm glad he told you. I hate that he keeps it to himself; he needs more in his corner. But my brother had worked with The Sprite here; he trusted The Sprite enough to ensure our safety in this realm." She gave Audelia a quick side squeeze before making her way to stand beside her mate and husband.

Shawn stepped closer to her, placing a kiss on her temple, and resecured his hand with hers. "I love you, A Chroi."

"I love you, too." Her words were soft, but she felt their weight. Felt it as the drumbeat seemed to beat in answer to their words to each other.

As if it was telling them—*he was hers, and she was his.*

The group began to walk across the rocky bridge, which she had walked over too many times over the years.

Yet, this time, it felt ominous. Final.

She paused for a moment before letting herself cross, her hand squeezing Shawn's.

As they came to the edge of the branch line. She felt her heart begin to beat in time with the drum. It grew louder with every step the group took towards the hanging branches of the inner sanctum. The purples, pinks, and blues of the flowers glowed in an ethereal way from the lights of The Glade.

She gasped as the branches parted of their own accord as if the tree itself was greeting them, letting them know that it was *ready* for their next journey.

Shawn glanced at her, and she nodded as they both walked through the arch the branches had made.

The sight before her made her breath still.

There were people everywhere. She had never seen so many people inside here at once. Usually, only a small handful came inside this area, not because it was small, but because it always felt so powerful that some people never ventured this close; they stayed just before the bridge in the little dips and valleys along the branch line.

But now she counted over a dozen people dressed in gossamer gowns of different colors, who were dancing and chanting. And the very air around them seemed to shimmer as if they weren't really there. Some that weren't dancing were standing around smaller groups of dancing, chanting in a deeper tone while holding shepherd-hooked lanterns that seemed to glow brightly.

It didn't seem real. The scene before her was magical. Pure magic, she could feel it pulse and pull with every step her group took into this sanctum. Turning toward the tree, she heard her uncle call her closer, but she honestly couldn't hear him over the hum of magic that seemed to wrap itself around her like a cat. It purred, sending shivers down her spine.

She had always felt a sense of magic here, but before, it had felt like it was in her heart and mind. Now, it *thrummed* with life.

"What did they do to the tree?" Shawn gasped beside her. She swung her head at him, his dark hair shimmering in the light of the lanterns all around them.

"It's runes to awaken the ancient magic," Gideon whispered to them as they continued to walk.

She looked back at the great tree whose branches they were currently seeking refuge in. It was stunning, it seemed to glow as if one of the gods had set it alight with their magic. Perhaps one had.

Bronn had said the Tree Sprite was tied to the tree and possessed godlike magic.

Perhaps that was what was at play here as she took in the runes that seemed to float just barely off the bark of the great willow tree.

"Over here, little one," Bronn spoke again, this time closer to her, as he pointed to a large group standing around someone before the tree.

She could hear the chanting around them change. It was

beautiful. Like every fantasy story she had ever read, came to life under the boughs of the tree.

Audelia had come to a stop; she barely registered Shawn, and Mathias stood beside her as she tilted her head up. Something had sent a pulse of magic through her. It had shocked her.

Shocked her because it felt familiar. She turned in a circle as she watched tiny floats of lights dance around above them. It was ethereal as she watched them move in patterns,

She had dreamed of this once, on one of the days she and Lila had spent lying in the grass in this sanctum. It felt like the tree was telling her a story. Maybe it was that day.

"Son of a bitch." Shawn swore beside her, breaking her from the magic lights dancing above her. She looked at him, taking in the fury on his face. It confused her, why was he so angry when this place was so fucking beautiful right now that she wanted to cry?

She noticed then that the large group ahead of them, which had been gathered around someone, had gone quiet. Well, not exactly quiet because several were still chanting, but an old crone had stopped and was looking at Shawn.

Beside her was a petite young woman, still turned away, with vibrant multi-colored hair in a curly pixie cut. Audelia still didn't understand what was going on, the pull of beating drums drowning out every bit of reason.

That was until the young woman, whose very skin was covered in blue, glowing runes, dressed in a gossamer gown more elegant yet fairy-like than the others, but paired with a pair of tanned leggings, turned around.

When she took in the woman's face, Audelia felt all the blood drain from her body as she whispered, "Lila."

What in the fuck?

Audelia stared at her best friend of the past fourteen years.

She couldn't breathe.

This couldn't be happening. *Not Lila.*

No, she couldn't have also been lying to her this whole time, too.

No.

Lila must have said something because Shawn was yelling at her. Audelia could hear the betrayal thick in his voice.

Audelia moved away from the woman she thought was her best friend. She needed to leave.

Needed to be away from this.

Not another person, not Lila.

She had been so preoccupied with her thoughts by the shouting of accusations from Shawn to Lila that she had run smack into Mathias's strong chest.

"It's okay, Del.. I've got you. Just *breathe.*" His voice was soothing as he wrapped his strong arms around her, and she pushed herself as close as she could get.

They stood there as Audelia's world crashed around her again.

She felt those new patches of her broken heart, the ones that had been healing as she grew to know the males in her life and learned more about how much they had gone through and loved her, she felt those reformed cracks start to break again.

"Del….Please, I didn't mean to lie to you." It was Lila's voice; she could hear the heartbreak in her best friend's voice.

"She doesn't want to hear it, *druid.*" Mathias spat as he stroked Audelia's hair. The way he spoke it made her wonder, had they all known? Was him saying, "Fucking druids" all the time around her, him hinting at her betrayal? Had he been lying to her after the confession he told her the night before, she doubted he would have kept that from her.

Things were quieter for a moment, and someone must have finally stopped Shawn; the only noises were the chanting druids around them and the beating drum of the magic coursing around them.

Finally, she felt Shawn beside her, felt Mathias let go of her briefly, only for his arms to be replaced by Shawn's. She breathed in his scent, letting the mint and bergamot of him soothe her. Ground her.

She nodded into his chest; Shawn kissed her forehead as she began to turn to face her best friend.

Audelia took in Lila for a moment; she was standing there in a gown that was like gossamer, but a little thicker now that she looked closer. Still, the same dark, tanned leggings and the same brightly colored hair in its curly pixie cut.

Yet, as she looked into the tear-filled eyes of her best friend, she seemed different. Audelia felt the magic seeping off of Lila then. It felt older, stronger. But it was *magic* she felt.

"*Why?* You are my best friend; you are like a sister to me! Why would you lie to me like this? What reason is there to lie about who you are?" Audelia yelled; she felt the tears begin to flow as she flung every word at her best friend.

She leaned against the warmth of Shawn's chest as she stared down at her friend.

The stranger before her. Because it was one thing for her family to have lied, for her guards, but she couldn't quite understand why Lila had lied.

Lila looked grief-stricken and looked around her like she was trying to find the words. As she did, Audelia noticed that her guards and aunt had all gathered closer to her. They all looked angered, hands on the hilts of their swords at their hips.

They hadn't *known.*

That sent a prickle of unease down her spine. If they hadn't known? What did that mean?

Oh gods, had she been trusting the wrong person these past fifteen years?

"I wanted to…gods did I want to tell you so many damn times, Del. So, fucking many. But I couldn't. It would have put you in danger. Please, believe me, Storm." Audelia flinched at the use of her nickname. "I would never hurt you." Lila pleaded.

Audelia's heart was breaking. *It all came back to that, didn't it?*

Back to the stupid spell Waldrom had put on all of them. *Always* back to that.

"Really, Lila, you're going to use an excuse for having lied to her. To your best friend? A stupid *spell.* Was that worth more to you than her? Fucking hels, Bubbles. Why would you do that to her?" Shawn yelled. Audelia flinched at the same time Lila did at the use of Lila's nickname, which they used as kids. It felt like another knife to her heart.

"So, to *protect* me, you never told me you were a druid? Is this because of the spell the others and I are under? Because Lila, that is fucking bullshit, and you know *it.* This world has druids, yeah, no one knows they are like *this.* It was an old Scottish folklore that the daughter of a daughter would be caught praying to standing stones and seeking out fairy hills. You could have told me you and your family were druids." Audelia spat. Her aunt had told her that if it were a cultural norm, the shadows wouldn't think twice about it.

So why? Why had she lied?

Audelia pressed tighter against Shawn as she felt his arm snake around her. She was grateful because, without him, she was sure she would have fallen to her knees from heartbreak.

"It's not...." She took a deep breath. "It's not because I'm a druid that I have to lie. Or a spell." Lila spoke, and Audelia could see her chest rising and falling as Lila fought back more of her own tears.

"So, you lied because you *wanted* to? Not because of a spell to protect me? What kind of shit is that?" Audelia spat at her so-called best friend.

"It was to protect *you*. Knowing who I am. It would put you in more danger than you knowing who your uncle was or your cadre." Lila's words were sure and strong this time.

More danger? What the hel?

"Lila, no. You cannot tell her." Audelia startled as she took in Lila's mother, who was standing near her. She hardly recognized Sorcha; gone were the pristine pencil skirt dresses of the lawyer. She wore a similar garb to those around her, complete with blue runes.

"Sorcha, I am far older than you are. You cannot tell me who I can tell; besides, it's pointless now. She is in danger regardless, and she is about to see the truth. I cannot lie to the only person who has ever been my truest friend any longer. I never should have listened to you or Callum. You have been good parents to me, but no longer, *young one*."

As each word fell, Audelia felt the magic that was around them shimmer and seemed to settle around them.

Lila had spoken so differently then, every word seemed ancient. She called her mother young one, for fuck's sake. *What was happening?*

"Who are *you*? Don't lie to me anymore. I am so fucking tired of lies. You say you can't lie to me anymore. Then tell me the truth for once in your gods damned life." Audelia's heart was pounding in her chest now.

The power inside her seemed to stretch a little and open a single eye as it waited for the next words to be spoken.

"Knowing me would have been more dangerous because I *am* The Tree Sprite. I am the Keeper of the Portal."

CHAPTER THIRTY~FOUR

Audelia moved in a fugue-like state as she and the others were moved to a seating area near the little alcove she had used for comfort so many times through the years. It seemed fitting that now, faced with this new development, she would be close to it.

She could feel the magic coming off the tree more now that they were closer to the trunk. Sorcha, Lila's mother, or rather *adoptive* mother, said that Lila needs to be as close as possible to the tree while they finish waking the ancient magic up.

Sitting there, all Audelia could do was stare at her best friend. She didn't know what she should say to her. Couldn't find the words to tell her how she felt. So, all she did was lean against Shawn's shoulder.

She felt so drained.

She felt Mathias sit next to her, and she soaked in the warmth coming from the male. She had the two males in her life that right now she felt the closest to; she cherished the support she felt pouring out of them in droves.

"So, I am sure you have tons of questions." Lila's voice trailed off as she stared at the ground. Like she couldn't bear to see the heartbreak she knew she would find in Audelia's eyes.

Grunts that sounded a lot like *no shit* came from everyone around her.

"How about you start where you decided to lie to the woman you have treated like a sister this past decade?" Audelia spat out her words like venom, making Lila flinch.

Good, she should feel horrible for doing this.

"Maybe I should go back a little bit before that. Not that what I did…doesn't need to be explained. It's just that. I'm sorry, this is a lot. I am not used to all of *this.*" Lila's words were wobbly, like she was fighting back tears.

"Well, that's tough shit Druid. Or I'm sorry, should I call you, *oh great Tree Sprite?*" Mathias hissed.

"Mattie!" Mara yelled from her spot on another bench nearby, her hand firmly clasped in Bronn's.

"No, he has a point, Aunt Mara. Lila has been lying to Audelia all this time. I get your reasons." Shawn gestured to the group around them. "It was for Audelia's safety because they would find you first, and you could be a beacon toward her. I am grateful for that. But Lila. There was no spell, nothing truly binding her from telling Audelia the truth or a fragment of it." Shawn's gaze swung from Mara back to Lila.

Audelia swore she felt a power beginning to hum from Shawn.

"No, Shawn is right. What I did was wrong. I see that now. I am so terribly sorry to both of you. You—you are the first friends I have ever *had*, and all I did was fuck it all to hel." Lila sounded so sincere.

First friends?

"Tell me. I will give you five minutes because we don't have the luxury of added time when shadow demons in the form of my abusive ex-boyfriend, could you know, *find* us and *kill* me. So, five minutes. Five minutes, and I may forgive you. But we will *never* be friends again." Audelia felt the tears fall as she added those last words. She couldn't take this; it wasn't *like* the others. They truly could not tell her. Lila had *made* a choice.

Shawn's hand gripped hers tightly, his thumb working in a soothing motion across her skin.

Seriously, she could feel something coming off of him. Her own magic seemed to purr at whatever she felt from him.

Maybe it's just the magic in the sanctum of the boughs. She could feel it caressing her skin like a lover as the chanting around them began to change tones, growing *louder and stronger*.

"Okay, that's perfectly fair. Though I will hope with everything I have that we will still be friends." Lila swallowed and took a deep breath, stilling herself.

"So, as I said, I am a tree sprite and the keeper of the Gate, or Portal, depending on who you talk to. But I wasn't always here in this realm. I lived in the forests of Insidor for the first thirteen hundred years of my life. About a hundred years ago, I was tasked by the elders of my family to open a portal to this realm for the first time in hundreds of years." She looked at Shawn before she spoke again. "It was *your* ancestors, Shawn, they had been given a gift for what your ancestor Ichiro had done for The Phoenix Queen, they were given a choice to come to our realm in safety or remain in this plane. Many of your clan had moved into the fae realm after that, except for a small group that remained. Your pregnant ancestor, Kagome, Ichiro's widow, remained to keep the spirit of the land alive. I was only a young sprite when that happened, but I was actually there when the old ancient trees opened, welcoming several hundred from your clan to our realm." Her eyes were sad as she spoke, and it made Audelia's heart ache.

"Wait. You're *fourteen hundred years old?*" Audelia spoke; she hadn't planned on it. Her mind was still reeling from everything, and the magic in the air around her seemed to throw her into a half-trance, like it was trying to feed her with more magic.

"I'll be fourteen hundred and twenty-five next year." Lila gave a small smile.

"Yet supposedly we are your first friends? That doesn't make sense." Shawn spoke; his voice was hoarse, as if he were battling his own emotions.

Audelia leaned against him a little more, lending him some of her strength. He gave her hand a squeeze in response, telling her he was thankful for her support and that he was there for her as well.

"Yes. Tree Sprites, we are ancient beings—Godlike in our magic. We don't... mingle with mortals or lesser immortal beings." Lila wrinkled her nose at that. "What I did broke so many rules. I am sure when we return to our realm, I will surely be punished for what I have risked. I did break our most sacred law." She said that last bit so nonchalantly that it startled Audelia.

"Why don't you—*mingle?* You are clearly very good at being around people." Audelia gestured at herself and the others.

"I wasn't always. The point is, it's very dangerous to be around lesser beings because they can influence us without us knowing. Meaning we could be tempted to do something unthinkable that would destroy too many lives. Our corruption could cause catastrophic things to occur and destroy the balance of magic." Lila took a deep breath again. "But I didn't care once I saw you, Audelia."

"Me? Why?" Her heart was beginning to race.

"I became curious one day, about fifteen years ago, a wizard sent a message through the magic of the tree, using the one in our realm as the communion point. He told me that he might have to send several from our realm to live in secret and safety, and that he might have to call on me to open the gate at a moment's notice. I had met him once long ago when I was still young; he is different from other beings and can be trusted, according to the ancient gods at least." She gave a small smile.

"Living in this realm was boring. Magic isn't exceptionally strong here, so I mainly slept inside the tree. Occasionally, I would come out and explore and recast some of the runes on the tree itself. *This* Willow is the first bridge between our realms ever created. It's older than the stars in the night sky. She is *special.*" Lila looked up at the tree, her eyes glazed with a sense of wonder and respect.

She seemed so different here. Still Lila, *yet not entirely.* It reminded her of when they were kids and would play here, how sometimes Lila talked differently; Audelia always assumed it was just that Lila had a better imagination than the two of them.

Wait. If she is over fourteen hundred years old, how is that possible? They grew up together.

"How had you been a child with me? We grew up together, Lila, I don't get it."

"Because I *chose* to take upon an immortal body. My *real* body, the one that will return when we cross the gate, is of a minor god. I am eternal. I was born from the celestial body of a cosmic goddess. But my body cannot handle a realm cut off from the source of my being. The Mother Tree. Idrisil. Without her magic fueling my body, I *cannot* be in my true form, far from the safety of the magic of the tree. The tree that I put to sleep fifteen years ago when I chose a mortal form to be your friend. It was taxing to do, to seal my being into the tree and such a small form, but it was worth it."

"Holy shit," Skye swore from a spot nearby. Others grunted in agreement.

He was right, though. *Holy shit.* She had been friends with a goddess? Minor one, yes, but still a damn goddess? *Fuck.*

"Why would you risk putting the tree to sleep?" Gideon asked. From the corner of her eye, she saw him leaning forward; the look in his eyes told her he was devouring all this new information. Something else was there in his expression, the way he seemed to soothe her with his voice. *Interesting.*

"Because for the first time in my existence, I found someone that fascinated me, that I yearned to be around. The day you first came to this realm. *I had been here.* None of you remember, but I am the one who finished the spell Waldrom set, sending you to the vestiges you would wear here to keep the princess safe. You were so young, Del. Gods, it broke my heart to see you that day. But I brushed it off. I am an eternal being. Everyone was young to me." Lila looked at Audelia again. The look in her eyes had Audelia starting to doubt her decision never to be her friend again. *She has risked so much to be her friend. How can she turn away from that?* She thought.

"But I couldn't stop thinking about you. Then, by the luck of the fates, you came here one day. You looked a little better than you had the day I first saw you. But still, there was such sadness about you. I had never seen one so young be so greatly sad, and it broke something in me. So, I watched you. For days, you kept coming back and would just lie in the grass, looking into the boughs of the tree, and you would talk. You told stories. *These* fantastic stories of warriors, dragons, elves, and magic. *Our realm.*"

Audelia's breath hitched; she could remember those days. They were fuzzy, but she remembered running off from Aunt Mara's house, crying, and would end up *here*. She would lie down and tell stories, ones that Mara had been reading to her nightly. It helped calm her. Kept the tears away. She always felt lighter after.

"You were imbuing this place. Your magic had been shut off from you. I remember Waldrom telling me you would not *have* your magic because the shadows would find it. Yet. *Here you were*, daily, seeping out little bits of magic as you spoke, slowly trying to wake the tree. I had begun to weave extra runes to protect anyone from noticing the change in the tree. Because *your* magic, Del? It's *eternal*. Even Waldrom, with his godlike magic, couldn't fully put a stop to your magic. Eternal magic can't be just shut off. It's *always* there. But your magic is clever, too. It knew your mortal body could not handle *too* much. So, when you came here to rest, it let itself *seep*. Keeping you safe the moment you *left* my barrier." Lila smiled, smiled so softly, like she didn't just drop a fucking bomb on them.

Her magic was eternal? What? How was that possible? Why her? Does that mean she is a goddess herself as well?

"That's why I had to keep making those potions." Mara gasped. "I never could figure out why she was *constantly* fatigued when she was little; it reminded me of her when she was first learning magic, but I never thought it was because of *that*," Mara whispered, just loud enough for Audelia to hear. Lila nodded.

"So, I decided that I couldn't stay away from you. So, occasionally, I would appear before you. I took on the form of a girl your age and spoke to you. Then, before I realized it, we were constantly playing here. You would come and tell me stories, and I would tell you some I had heard from others, stories from the druids that came here. Then, I decided I *wanted* to spend more time with you. I didn't want to be confined here anymore. I wanted to be a child like you. I wanted to be your friend, and friends with the sweet boy who came to play sometimes. I went to the elder of the druid clan here. I told her I wanted to become a mortal girl, that I would be there to keep you *safe*. No one would question you having friends; they fought me on it. But I am their *true* elder, after all. They didn't have a choice, especially when they arrived one day, and I had put the tree to sleep and become a small mortal girl." Lila laughed at that.

Audelia couldn't help but smile and laugh a little, because that was just such a *Lila* thing for her to have done.

"They relented when I refused to go back and undo what I had done. I wanted something for the first time in my existence, and I wasn't going to let them tell me I couldn't. I know I'll face trouble when we return, *my* elders will not be happy that I broke the cardinal rule, but. Del, it was worth *everything* to get to be your best friend, to be your sister." Lila smiled at Audelia, her blue-green eyes sparkling from the tears she had been shedding. They sparked now with a sense of loss and hope.

Audelia, as angry as she was, was starting to cling to that hope. After everything she faced, she didn't *want* to lose another person.

She realized Lila's reasonings, they were *ancient* and *strong*, and if she was being honest with herself as much as she believed in magic as a child, she felt like if Lila had told her, that a part of her would have doubted and pushed her away, for taking their imaginings too far. It would have been born of jealousy, and it would have destroyed their friendship.

Her heart was broken from the lies, but she still loved Lila so damn much. Just as Shawn had helped her in his own ways, the days they spent playing here and just imagining, and as they grew? They still came here to talk to just be. Lila helped Audelia heal from losing her parents, from the pain of what Kage had done to her.

Could she really toss that away?

Lila's voice broke her from her thinking. "Every time over the years, we came here. The days we daydreamed, talked of the books we had found and loved? We always came here to do so. It was a place I knew you found strength within these boughs; I may have been a little naughty when we would come here."

"What do you mean?" Audelia asked.

"When we came here, I would redo some of the magic that protects the tree, even while the tree sleeps, she still needs the runes, I still need magic to maintain this form. So, I would slightly wake her, just enough to strengthen our bond. We will always be bound, but Audelia, you are *also* bound by this tree. Not in the same way, but she watched you, *too*. Saw how you were struggling, and when you came here, with or without me, she gave you some of her magic, just little bits here and there. She told me once, when I came here alone, that you needed it, that something was coming, and she wanted you to be prepared. She *knew* this was coming. And what awaits on the other side? From what I feel from her now, she is waking up. *It's bad.* Really bad. She can't fully see what is going on, but she can *sense* it. Her sister is the tree we will travel to, and they can sometimes send feelings toward each other while the gate is closed."

Audelia looked up at the great trunk of the tree, which was almost entirely covered by the shimmering blue runes that seemed to float just around it. The tendrils of magic that seemed to seep from the tree, creating what she assumed was the barrier Lila had spoken of, wavered slightly. Just barely.

Then, that pulse was there again. *Waldrom.* "Fuck." She whispered, she could sense him like she did just before he pulled her into one of those dreams, the ones that left her reeling and feeling like she was covered in flames. Her hand went slack in Shawn's grasp. He spoke to her, but she didn't hear him.

Suddenly, a pulse of magic shook her, and everything in her vision went black.

She stood then. Taking in the pitch black that seemed to shimmer slightly as she looked around. "Waldrom?" Her voice seemed to echo through the empty space.

This place always unnerved her.

Yet, at the same time, she felt safe here, even as she felt the magic in her chest begin to yawn open. She let it this time, trying not to fight the building pressure of its movements.

"Hello, little star. You've grown so much." A voice came from nearby; it was stronger than usual. She took in the light timber of his voice, the baritone notes that seemed to lift with every word.

"Have you been watching me again? Which is creepy as fuck, by the way. In case you didn't know that." She watched as the figure came closer; she still couldn't see him, as if something was preventing her from seeing him.

All she could tell still was that he was tall and slender, but he held himself with a deep strength, whether it was from true raw strength, like the rest of her cadre, or knowledge. Even his shadow seemed beautiful.

He merely chuckled, it was deeper than she thought it would be. She didn't know why she was picturing his laugh, but it seemed at odds with his stature.

"Yes, I have, and you sound so much like your mother. She would be the first to let me know that my behavior was *odd*. I am still not used to interacting with others." He chuckled.

"Noted. Why am I here, Waldrom?" She was beginning to get annoyed with this little trick of his. *Plus, she knew that currently she was probably on the ground scaring the fuck out of the people she loved. And there was a fucking sadist doubtless on his way to kill her. Good times.*

"We will see each other soon. Remember, follow that home." He pointed to the soft glow on her chest. He seemed to still, suddenly, as if something had occurred wherever he was during this little chat of theirs.

Wait, where was he anyway? She really wanted to ask him,

but before she could say a single word, she was thrown back, and his voice echoed in her ear. "*They* are coming."

Who was coming? What the fuck?

She felt herself slam back into her body a little harder than she had in the past. Audelia was indeed on the ground, her head currently nestled into the safety of Shawn's lap. She gave him a weak smile; she could taste ash on her tongue again.

That was kind of getting annoying.

"*A Chroi?* My love?" Shawn spoke from above her; she took in the tears that were in his eyes. *Fuck. She hated that she scared him again.*

She sat up slowly, feeling his hand on her back to steady her. She twisted on the spot, so she was on her knees in front of him, reaching out. She placed her hand on his cheek, feeling the beginnings of stubble scrape against her palm. "I'm okay, my love. I'm sorry for scaring you. I promise I am going nowhere."

He nodded and pulled her into his arms, holding her tightly. He kissed her, and she moaned into this kiss. It felt different; it was more desperate, fueled by his worry that something had happened to her again and that next time, he may not get her back. She leaned into the kiss and wrapped her arms around his neck as they met each other stroke for stroke of the kiss. Shawn gripped her hair, yanking her closer to him as he intensified the kiss, making her moan around his mouth again. He claimed her as his hands dug into her scalp and her lower back, where the others rested.

A voice broke through the frenzy of their touches. "If you could stop for a moment. The druids said that the tree is awake and it is time." Gideon spoke his deep voice holding a hint of amusement to it.

Audelia felt her cheeks redden as she took in the faces around her; some held the same amusement, while others, *mainly* her uncle and Mathias, held anger. Then there was Lila, who was practically holding back tears as she tried not to laugh at the situation.

Mathias rolled his eyes and extended his hand to help her stand, and she took it, smiling as she stood. Her legs felt slightly unsteady, but the sensation was returning to her. It was then she noticed it.

Looking around her at the tree, she could literally see the magic flowing around them. She found herself reaching out to touch one of the tendrils nearby; it felt warm and cool at the same time. It wound itself around her wrist like a snake, then let go and moved on. "Wow." She whispered.

"It's amazing, isn't it?" Lila spoke from beside her. She had such a wonderful smile when she was truly happy, and Audelia could see it now; like *this*, standing around all this magic, Lila looked truly happy for the first time in what had seemed like a very long time.

"It is. Lila, you seem happy. It's this *place*, isn't it? The magic waking up." She nodded at her best friend. Because yes, she was horribly angry with her, *but this was Lila*; she was like a sister to Audelia. And from what she had told them, she had truly risked *so much* to be friends with her.

"This place will always make me happy. But what is truly making me happy is that you're here. I know you're angry at me, Storm, and I'm sorry for that. But it also feels damn fucking good that you know the truth now." Lila gave a small smile before she walked away toward the alcove near them.

Audelia could feel the magic thrumming stronger from that area. Before she realized it, she was walking into the alcove.

The whole area was bathed in a kaleidoscope of colors coming from the base of the trunk. It was *magnificent*, making her heart stir.

She heard footsteps come to stand beside her and felt Shawn's warmth before he spoke, that odd hum coming from him still. "Wow....that is fucking amazing."

"It is." She turned toward him, then placed a hand on his chest over his heart. His heart seemed to beat faster than usual, and his skin was *warmer*, too. "You okay, my love?"

"I mean, I feel a little off. But I think it's just the adrenaline and the awe of everything going on. I promise I am okay. Are *you*?" He nodded toward where they watched their best friend weave runes into the air, sending them flying toward the beginning of what she assumed was the portal. Gideon was standing nearby, watching Lila.

"Yeah. I'm still so fucking angry. But I think I was wrong to say I would never be her friend again. I still love her; she is my sister in my heart. I don't think I can easily toss that aside." She confessed softly so only he could hear her.

She felt Mathias come to stand in the archway of the little grove she liked to read in all these years—her personal sanctuary from the world.

It was not lost on her that this was the place where she would return to her realm. She felt the warm glow start to seep from her chest. *Like a whisper.*

"You are glowing again, Del," Mathias said, his eyes constantly scanning the area. The others, she assumed, had taken up spots throughout the sanctum to keep an eye on things.

That made her remember what Waldrom had said. *Let the light guide you home.*

Fuck. How had she forgotten that?

"I need to go find my uncle. I forgot when I passed out, Waldrom said someone was coming." She looked at Lila for a moment. There was still so much she wanted to say to her.

"Go, Del. They need to know what Waldrom said. Besides, it's almost time to leave; I can feel the gate opening the rest of the way. We can pass through the portal in a few moments. *It's time.*" She smiled, then turned her focus back to the magic she seemed to weave in the air.

Turning quickly, Mathias, Audelia, and Shawn made their way back into the central area of the sanctum. Everything felt the same. The thrum of magic was thick in the air; druids were dancing while chanting.

But she could feel it just as she saw her uncle standing by the crone she had seen with Lila earlier. Something shifted in the air. Something *foul and heavy*.

Before she could get a word out, a loud screech filled the air. All the chanting stopped, and an eerie quiet worked its way across the clearing. Audelia reached for Shawn and Mathias's hands, needing their strength, their hands curled around hers, offering her what she needed.

She knew what was coming; she could feel it in her soul. And it terrified the fuck out of her.

A dark and sinister laugh broke through the silence, and her blood went *cold*. She felt both males stiffen beside her.

"Well, it looks like we came just in time for a party." Her heart was pounding as the voice that haunted all her nightmares came from the shadows of a man entering the clearing.

She heard the swish of metal being removed from scabbards beside her. They knew who it was as well as she did.

Mathias had let go of her hand to remove his, but remained tightly beside her, his body shifting slightly in front of her.

The air felt thicker, darker, *vile*.

There, coming into the light of the lanterns, was Kage. Audelia gasped. Not because it was him, but because of how he looked.

His usual pretty-boy-next-door blonde locks, which he always kept neat, had become disheveled and stark white, as if all the color had been *drained* from them. Same with his skin, he was pale; his usual light tanned skin had turned pale, the only color about his sharp features, which were gaunt, was the black veins that seemed to *shift* just under his skin. His hazel eyes were gone; they were *always* lifeless at his worst moments.

But now they were this ice-cold blue, and held such terrifying malice that she felt her stomach turn as his gaze swept the area and settled upon her.

When it landed upon her, she swore she felt her heart stop, and ice-cold fear was thrown over her as he smiled. It was twisted and *inhuman*, as inhuman as the two shadow-like wraiths that stood beside him.

"Ah. There you are. It's time to come back with me, *Audelia*. Time to become *MINE*, my pretty." His voice was not his own. It sounded distant and like it fed on the nightmares of children.

Before anyone could do anything, the entire sanctum was plunged into darkness. All she could hear was screams and growls as chaos ensued.

CHAPTER THIRTY~FIVE

Her heart was pounding as Audelia reached behind her, removing the beautiful blade her uncle had given her only hours earlier. Her hand shook as she felt the soft leather of the hilt against her fingers.

She couldn't see a gods damn thing, the sanctum had been plunged into midnight, all she could make out were the vague outlines of Mathias and Shawn remaining at her side, each making a flanking formation to protect her best.

Otherwise, the only thing she noticed was the sounds of screams, both men and women, and the sound of snarls and tearing flesh. It made her stomach turn.

But worst of all was the other sound cutting through all the chaos, Kage was screaming her name. Calling out to her, demanding she come to him, or he would kill everyone here. It froze her blood.

"Don't you dare listen to him, my love. We will cut him down before he can manage that." Shawn spoke from somewhere close by. Gods, she wished she could see his face, see that he was alright. Occasionally, she heard a grunt from him or Mathias as they fought off whatever horrors were snarling around them.

She felt so damn useless. She wanted to fight, but Kage's constantly screaming her name in that inhuman voice was causing her to freeze in panic, in utter fear.

Suddenly, there was a snarl close to her. She turned in her spot and swiped out in an arch with the sword in her hand, hoping all those years of simple swordplay would ensure she made it out. She felt the contact as the blade cut through the flesh of whatever creature was just about to attack her. She was hit with a rotten stench as she arched the blade back to herself, the thing screeched, and she was suddenly shoved backward.

Audelia hit the ground hard, the air whooshing from her lungs, but she didn't have time to think on how much that hurt because whatever had knocked her down was thrashing against her as she used her blade to keep what sounded like chopping teeth from getting at her face, slime hit her face as she grunted pushing with all she could.

She screamed out as she felt claws tear at her forearm. It stung, and she could feel the warmth of blood start to drip down her arm onto her chest from the angle she was holding her arm, still trying to get the thing off her.

Taking a stilling breath, she launched her weight at the thing and managed to flip them, so its body was below hers as she moved quickly and, using both hands, brought the blade down upon its chest. It let out a wet gasp and went still.

She was breathing heavily, still straddling whatever had attacked her, when suddenly light filled the area. Someone had managed to get some sort of light spell to fill the air. *Small mercies.*

She blinked, clearing the fog from the sudden change in light. When her eyes adjusted to the sudden brightness, she looked down at the creature below her. Every thought eddied out of her head as she took in the masticated body below her.

It had at one time been human, but now it was disfigured, replacing hands were gnarls claws that looked like they had forced their way out of this person's skin, the flesh on its body was in a state of decay, but instead of muscles below the flesh, was bits of what looked like some sort of black shell casing, of gods knew what. The face was even more twisted, the jaw was loose as if it had screamed in such agony that the jaw had broken and just hung thereafter, its teeth were razor sharp. Whatever this thing was, she knew it would haunt her dreams for a very long time.

She pulled herself up as the chaos reigned around her; she didn't have time to dwell on what horror she had killed, for the sanctum was full of them, attacking druids and members of her guard.

Mathias was beside her in a second. He easily kicked away one of the creatures. As he did, Shawn was there, plunging a dagger into its chest. They seemed to move as one person, in *perfect* sync with each other, like *magic*. Shawn joined her side a moment later, taking her face into his hands, which were covered in the ichor-like blood of the creatures.

"Are you *okay*?" His eyes searched over her entire body, checking before settling on the blood now dripping heavily from her arm.

"I'm okay. It hurts, but I'll be fine. Are *you* okay?" She did her own perusal of his body, taking in similar cuts from the claws; he was covered in blood, both his and the same ichor she had noticed on his hands.

"Now that I can see you and know you're okay? Better, but we need to get out of here, they just keep fucking coming." Shawn looked away, taking in what she had seen; for every creature that everyone cut down, *more* managed to find their way into the sanctum.

Mathias circled them, protecting them and keeping the creatures away. He was drenched in blood, but aside from a few cuts, he seemed to be okay.

Where were the others, though? Panic settled in her heart. She swung her head around, trying to catch a glimpse of someone.

"Do you see anyone else? Where are Mara and Bronn, the twins? Skye? I only barely saw them before the lights went out." She was rambling, her voice shaking as she started to scan the carnage around them again, willing someone she loved to show themselves. Blasts of different colors aimed at the creatures, some managing to end the things, others only maiming them, but the fuckers kept coming.

Mathias answered her, "I can see Alaric and Gideon, they are twelve feet from us, currently battling more of these ghouls. The others I am unsure, but trust in them, Del, they have faced worse odds."

She nodded, gripping her blade, and leaned up to give Shawn a quick kiss, using the feel of him to ground her as they both turned and began working their way together, trying to find the others in the chaos.

As they moved, Mathias close to them, they turned and shifted as a group, working in tandem, they twisted and tore their blades through the masticated flesh. If one got too close for them to swing correctly, they kicked the body toward whoever was closest to make the killing blow.

"I see them!" Shawn called as he took down two ghouls with the twin daggers he had switched to briefly, having sent them into their faces. He quickly tore the blades from the creatures and returned to Audelia's side.

He pointed with one blade toward an outcrop near the base of the trunk, twenty feet from them.

Kage could be heard again as they made their way towards her guards and her aunt, where they seemed to have gathered to continue their fight.

He kept droning on and on about how he would take her, that she was his. As he walked toward them, he was flanked by two large shadows that, now that she could see them better, resembled writhing black flames with deep red eyes. That seemed to devour anyone it encountered.

It sent shivers down her spine to watch.

Kage had barely done a thing, letting the shadows beside him do most of the work; his job was to apparently talk, using that inhuman voice. "Oh, *Audelia*, my sweet pretty one, why don't we stop this so that you and I can have real *fun*? I have missed you."

"I will. *Kill.* that motherfucker." Shawn growled as he turned toward where Kage was heading toward them. He wasn't far anymore, maybe thirty feet, and gaining as he and his shadows took down people.

Before she could respond, three of those ghouls charged at her and Shawn. She swung her blade, tearing one in two in one large swing, but the other was on her in a second as Shawn battled the third. These two were larger than the others they had fought previously. As if the humans they had been before had been huge.

She screamed as it clawed at her leg, almost tearing it down to the muscle. She was breathing heavily as she fought the thing off. Before she could land another blow, it was torn from her, as a large sword pierced it through the chest, and Skye was there grinning like a madman. "You okay, my queen?"

"I am now, thanks." She grinned, but the smile fell from her face. Because, standing there twenty feet away was Kage, his arm wrapped around a woman, a blade of black and red against her throat. Sorcha. Lila's mother.

"Mother!" Lila's scream broke through the chaos; she was still standing by the alcove where the glow of the portal shone more brightly. She made to run toward the woman who had been her mother for years. But she was stopped by Gideon, who appeared at her side, holding her from moving closer.

The sanctum seemed to go deadly quiet, the sounds of the battle around them still raged on, but it was like all the sound in the world had gone out as Audelia stared at the woman she had loved as a mother figure, a woman who had taken in a goddess in a mortal form and loved her as her own child.

Sorcha. Oh gods, he was going to kill her.

Audelia could feel the tears welling in her eyes as Lila's anguished cries broke through the sudden silence.

This only made Kage laugh. It was cold and broken. It made her stomach turn at how inhuman it sounded.

"This can all be over, my dear. All you must do is come with me, be my bride, and all of this ends." His voice, cold and utterly void of any emotion, trailed over her body like venom.

She couldn't let Sorcha die. She would never be able to live with herself if Lila lost her mom because of her.

Audelia looked around at the people she loved the males who had wormed their way into her heart, and they were fighting tooth and nail to keep the ghouls back, she could see them all moving closer and closer to where she now stood frozen, staring in horror at the man she had once thought she loved.

"Come, Audelia, you know you are weak without me. Let me guide you like I used to. Come, and I will let this woman live." He pressed the blade a little harder against Sorcha's throat, and a trickle of blood worked its way down her throat.

She took a step toward him. She could end this. If she could get close enough, maybe, just maybe, she could kill him. She promised herself that she would *never* give in to his words again. But she couldn't let Sorcha die.

Strong arms pulled her back, and she was pressed against a chest she knew so well. Shawn.

"No, a chroi, don't listen to a word he says, you know he will kill her no matter what you do. Please, my love, stay with me. I have you—I have you, love." He whispered against her cheek. She felt the tears fall now, he was right, no matter what she did, Sorcha was as good as dead if they didn't do something, but if she went to Kage now, he would kill her, just because he knew it would haunt her.

She nodded, her grip on her blade tightened as she stared Kage down. "I will never go to you again. You are a monster, always have been, and now your madness is finally reflected on your skin." She gestured to the tendrils of shadow that moved under his skin.

"Oh, but you will, pretty one. You are going to be my bride, and then we shall have lots of fun like we used to." Kage laughed, sending another shiver down her spine as she remembered what he viewed as fun.

"You are *never* touching her again, you bastard!" Shawn yelled, his voice a thick growl; she felt the pulse of magic from *him* again, raising the hairs on her arms. Something was happening to Shawn; she could feel it in her soul. Her own magic seemed to reach out, as if it wanted to see what this new feeling was.

"Oh, but I will. She is mine, she will never be yours, Shawn. Have you tasted her yet? Felt how her body bows when she is on the brink? I, for one, cannot wait to *taste* her again. To make her bend to my will again. Don't you miss it, my love?" Kage tilted his head, and his eyes held such malice that the icy blue of his gaze seemed to shift like something was moving just below the surface.

She was going to be *sick*. The idea of his hands touching her again filled her with such fear and raging anger that she was starting to shake. That ancient fire inside was beginning to open its eyes. *Preparing* for when she needed it most.

"No. Go fuck yourself, Kage, you and your small dick go to hel!" She yelled, mustering all the strength she had left.

"That's *my girl*." She heard Mathias and Shawn both whisper.

She could hear yelling behind her, the others making their way toward the alcove where Gideon still held onto Lila as she raged to unleash herself upon Kage. Somehow, Gideon kept her subdued.

But she knew it would not be much longer until even he wouldn't be able to hold her back. Audelia could feel the magic radiating from Lila. She was ready to burst. Audelia's magic was rising to greet the pull from Lila's.

"Oh, my pretty one. *You are mine*, it's quite sad that you still keep denying this. *Denying* ME. Don't worry, I'll punish you for it. Perhaps, some time strapped to *my* bed will bring you back to heel. Maybe if you behave, I'll let your little puppy there watch as I fuck you." He sneered, licking his lips.

Mathias and Shawn both growled and took half a step forward, both preparing to charge forward to kill Kage.

"You even think about touching her, Kage, and I will fucking kill you. She is not yours. She is *mine.*" Shawn growled, his grip tighter on the blades in his hands. "I will never let you harm what is *MINE.*" The last word came out as a claiming snarl.

Everything happened so fast. One second, Kage was standing there, laughing at the declaration that Shawn had made, and next, he swiped the blade across Sorcha's throat and charged forward. He and his shadows grew in speed; the shadows reached them first, and Mathias began to engage with one of them. Each traded blows back and forth, the shadow moving like a living flame, dodging moves and preventing Mathias from landing any real, damaging blows.

The second came straight for her, and she recognized it then; it was *the same one* who had stalked her in that alley a month ago. But before it could get its tendrils around her, it was sent blasting back by a force.

They all did, both shadows, Kage, and the remaining ghouls, who were blasted back by wave after wave of pearlescent light. Audelia whipped her head around to see Lila standing there, her hands outstretched, her face stricken with *grief and agony.* Gideon seemed to still be holding her, but now it was more like he was trying to hold her still, whispering something to her.

"Get into the alcove!" He yelled at everyone as one more blast of light sent tendrils of it, holding Kage and his creatures to the ground even as shadows began to fight against the light.

Audelia was stunned, turning, she stared at Sorcha's body there on the ground, the blood pouring from the cut across her throat.

She was dead.

It was her fault.

"We have to *go*, my love. I'm so sorry, we must go." She felt Shawn pull her away, his arm around her waist, as she just stared, her eyes jumping from Sorcha's body to Kage lying there, being held by the tendrils of light, screaming that he would make her pay.

Everything felt like a blur as Shawn bent and scooped his arm under her legs and carried her away. She felt like she was slipping. It was too much. Her power pulsed as the man she loved carried her away from another person she had failed to save.

First, her parents.

Her kingdom.

Now, Lila's mom.

She closed her eyes and let the sorrow sweep her away.

CHAPTER THIRTY~SIX

She woke to the sounds of pounding against what sounded like a wall, muffled voices just beyond it. Audelia shook her head, fighting the pounding in her skull. She tasted ash again.

Turning toward the sound, she saw that there at the entrance to the alcove was Kage, one of the shadow creatures, who was still alive, and both seemed to be beating against something. It took a moment of focus to see that with every hit, a shimmer of blue light seemed to ripple away from the pressure.

The hatred in Kage's eyes sent shivers rushing down her spine. It held promises of pain, of her being stuck under him again, of being broken again till she would never leave *him* again. She felt like she was going to be sick.

"It's okay, my love. He can't get through." Shawn's velvet voice startled her. It was then she noticed he was holding her.

Her back to his chest, his arms cradling her, almost like he just plopped down with her still in his arms when they got inside the alcove.

Turning herself, she took in his face. He had flakes of dried blood all over his face, his beautiful green eyes looking at her like he was so damn relieved that she woke up. But there was sadness in them.

Her thoughts swung back to Lila's mother, Sorcha. Lila's anguished screams played through her head.

"Lila, where is she?" She immediately began to stand, and her legs wobbled. But she didn't care; she needed to comfort her best friend, no matter how angry she was by the lies; this was her mother who had died.

"Over there, don't worry, love, she is *well* cared for at the moment." He gave a small smile and gestured toward a spot behind her head.

She looked around the alcove, then, taking in the men around her, it looked like all her guards had made it, a little worse for wear but still alive, thank the gods. She smiled, seeing her aunt cooing over an injured Bronn. He had a cut across his cheek, and her aunt was currently dressing it. His eyes just watched her. Following his mates' movements like, he was more mesmerized by her than the bleeding cut on his face.

Near them were a few druids, no faces that she recognized; she didn't see Callum, Lila's father, among them; Gods, did they lose him too?

Her thoughts turned to Lila, and she searched for the brightly colored hair of her best friend. What she saw had her turning back to Shawn for a moment, and he merely gave a knowing smirk. Audelia turned back and took in the sight of Gideon cradling a crying Lila to him. He was sweetly petting her hair, his cheek resting on the top of her head as he whispered to her. She clung to him, and he, to her. Audelia noticed that the way they held each other was not just a kind man comforting a crying woman. No, even in the fog of the battle and heartache, she saw for what it was.

The beginnings of love.

A powerful one.

The same look Bronn was giving Mara—the look of a mate seeing his own mate.

Gideon turned his face just enough that he and Audelia locked eyes for a moment. He nodded and pulled away from Lila for a second, only to reach up and cup her cheeks, brushing his thumbs across them to wipe away the tears. He spoke to her.

Whatever he had said had Lila turning a tear-streaked face toward Audelia.

Audelia was up on shaky legs, Shawn behind her to steady her, and she ran to her best friend. They met in the center of the alcove near the base of the tree that was sending a kaleidoscope of colors across them both as Audelia pulled her dearest into her arms.

"I am so sorry Lila." She choked on the words, and she tightened her hold on Lila. She felt her friend begin to sob as she let go of whatever strength she had been holding on to, and the women fell to the ground as they just held each other. Both cried in each other's arms.

Mourning everything.

The lives lost, the shattering of the carefully cultivated life they had both been clinging to for almost fifteen years. They held each other as wave after wave of grief settled around them. The magic seemed to settle around them, giving them comfort like a mother would.

"I'm sorry too. For keeping this from you. It will always be my greatest regret." Lila whispered between sobs. Audelia didn't respond; she just pulled her friend, her sister, closer. Deciding that the lies didn't matter anymore. That they hurt, but she would put them away and lock them, never to think of them again.

It would hurt too much to dwell on them.

Too much was at stake, she understood that now. She just wished it hadn't come to her as she watched the woman who was like a mother to her die at the hands of the sadistic bastard that she thought she had loved at one point.

Audelia didn't know how long they held each other on the grass before the portal to another realm. But she felt a gentle hand on her shoulder, and both women turned to see her aunt's tear-streaked face. Audelia quickly looked her aunt over, taking in the blood of those ghouls on her, but didn't see a mark on her, *thank goodness*.

"My darling girls." Her voice was soft, the voice that Audelia had heard any time when waves of grief would hit her whenever she thought of her parents. It made her heart race as she looked at her beautiful aunt. "We don't have much time. I don't know how long Callum can hold that barrier; he is very weak already."

It was then that Audelia saw Callum, he was leaning against a rock, several surviving Druids huddled around him, a palm resting on some part of his body as they all chanted. Her heart stilled as she took in the wound on his stomach. He had been eviscerated, was slowly bleeding out, but he was still chanting, his palms outstretched as tendrils of the blue light traveled from him to the entrance to the alcove.

"Oh gods." She whispered, her face turning to Lila, who watched her father with such sorrow. This would be his last stand.

"I know. The portal is almost done. Just a few spells left, I had only stopped because—because—" Lila stopped talking as she began to cry again. Audelia *knew* why she had stopped because she had felt her mother's fear.

"Lila, you should tell him goodbye." Audelia made her best friend look at her. She knew Lila would not be able to live with herself if she never said goodbye to her dad. They had always been close throughout the years. Audelia could barely count the number of times that he had declared daddy-daughter dates throughout the years, which somehow ended up including Audelia each time.

Tears welled as Lila nodded. "Come with me. *Please*, I can't do it alone." Audelia nodded, her tears beginning to well.

Shawn was there to help the women stand. He walked with both as they reached Callum. His hand was holding hers, sending her his strength. A pulse seemed to emanate from where he lay.

God, how was he still alive? She thought. As she took in the man, she had known these past years, she noticed *it* then, the other druids that were around him. It was *them*; she could feel it pulsing from them, different from the magic coming from Callum. This was *soothing*. They were the ones keeping him alive. Keeping him from bleeding out because he was the strongest of them, the only one who could keep the barrier so Lila could finish the portal.

His gaze shifted from the alcove as Lila and Audelia knelt

beside her, a few druids having shifted to grant them some room, their hands never leaving his body. He gave them his signature lopsided smile, and her heart lurched as drips of blood broke free from his lips. "My girls."

"Papa...I am so sorry." Lila cried, laying her head against her father's chest. Audelia could sense it then; Lila was beginning to pour some of her magic into her father. She could see it working as some of the skin started to knit together.

Callum shifted, groaning in pain, and pushed Lila *from* him. His eyes filled with tears. "No, my darling girl. Please do not *waste* your precious magic on me. You must fully open the portal and escape from here. I cannot hold on for much longer." His words were firm, but Audelia disagreed. She didn't *want* to lose another person.

"No, Cal....please let her heal you. She can't *lose you, too*. We *need* you." Audelia begged, the tears coming harder now as she reached out to grip his hand. It felt so damn cold to the touch.

"My sweet princess, Sorcha and I were so glad that Lila had found you. That you had found each other. It has been an honor to see both of you grow to be such wonderful women. I wish we could be there to see what more you both will become. But if I know my girls, you will blow the realm away with what you manage to accomplish together. It's always been the two of you against the world." He gave them both such a loving smile. It broke her.

"Papa. No, please, I couldn't save Mama. Let me save you, and then I'll open the portal, and—and you can come with us. See the realm I was born in. *Please... don't leave me*." Lila sobbed, and Gideon was there pulling her back into his arms; she still had a hand on her father's chest even as Gideon held her, rubbing his hands up and down her arm in a soothing motion.

"My girls. Let me do this. Let me give my last stand to save you both. Let me *go*. I'll be with my Sorcha. I love you both so much." He gave one last, final weak smile and closed his eyes.

He wasn't gone, she could tell, but she knew he was in his final moments. They didn't have long before he truly would be gone. She brought his cold hand to her lips and pressed a gentle kiss there. "Thank you, Callum, for everything." She whispered before letting go.

Sobs wracked through her, she quickly turned and fell into Shawn's embrace as she cried for the sacrifice of Callum.

"Love, you must get the portal open. I know your heart is breaking. But we must get through now, or their deaths will have been for nothing. I am so damn sorry, Lila." Gideon spoke to her as he pulled them to their feet, still cradling Lila against him, who had reluctantly let go of her father to curl further into him.

Lila nodded. Giving herself one last moment in the safety of Gideon's arms, she turned back toward the shimmering portal.

"Bubbles, you sure you can do this?" Audelia asked quietly, her body slightly turned toward her best friend while still in the comfort of Shawn's arms.

"Yeah, I was almost done. It just felt a little off, but I'm sure that was just because the tree was sending me signals that something wasn't right out in the sanctum, that you all needed help." Lila gave a weak smile and took a deep breath.

Audelia watched with fascination as Lila began to weave her fingers in the air, with every twist, bits of shimmering light formed and were sent toward the portal before them. It was like she was conducting her own symphony as she made rune after rune of magic, sending them to join the others.

Her own magic seemed to open as the magic from the portal grew and wrapped around them. Her heart was pounding, and that glow in her chest came back.

She felt the others of her guard and her aunt come to stand around them, keeping close. The twins, she noticed, were keeping their eyes trained on the entrance to the alcove, where Kage snarled and banged against the blue of the barrier, which *faltered* again for a second.

They wouldn't have long before Callum was gone, and she had the feeling he would take the other druids with him. Their final stand. To send a lost queen home. Her heart broke at the cost of this moment.

As she took in the faces of her guards, she wondered if they were all thinking about the things they had been made to forget. If they were eager to get those back. Then, her thoughts turned to Mathias at her right. *Soon,* he would remember his son's name. She would too. Something about that thought sent a shiver up her spine.

She would get to remember her parents, of the life she had before this. Would be able to tell Shawn stories of them, to be able to tell him more about her realm. That this missing part of her would finally be *back.* Audelia would be *whole* again.

She looked at Shawn, leaning toward him, and placed a chaste kiss on his cheek as they watched Lila work.

It was then that she saw Lila's face turn in confusion. She continued her working of the runes, but she turned to Gideon, who was remaining close to her, and she whispered something. Like she was too scared to voice it out loud just *yet,* but had the strength to tell him.

His gaze flicked to the portal before them and then back at her. He nodded.

Lila turned then. Her voice was shaky. "Something is wrong. I'm not sure what exactly, but it feels off."

"What do you mean off?" Bronn spoke, his voice terse.

Mutters of agreement worked their way through the group. Audelia's heart was in her throat. Was the portal not opening? What was wrong with it?

Oh, gods, what if they can't get home? Her gaze swept back to the alcove; they were trapped in here. She had been in this place so many times throughout the years she knew every crevice of this space, *that* was the only way in or out. The brambles that created this space were too thick. They wouldn't have the time to cut through.

"Lila, my sweet girl, you have to *tell us* what is wrong?" Mara spoke, her voice urgent and a little sharper than usual, as she stepped closer to Lila, placing a comforting hand on her shoulder to calm Lila, who was currently freaking out by whatever she was feeling.

"It feels.... I'm not sure I can put it into words... just feels *off*.... I'm not sure what that means. It's our realm, I know it is because I can feel bits of Idrisil reaching out to greet me, and she is strongest in our realm." Lila's gaze swept over the group, landing on Audelia. "I'm not sure what we will be walking into."

Audelia tried to swallow the lump in her throat. The warriors around her each removed their blades, just in case they met with hostility on the other side.

Before anyone could see another word or decide on their next steps, a crack rang out. All faces swung to the alcove as fissures began to form on the shimmering blue of the barrier.

Time was running *out.*

They had maybe *minutes* from how those fissures were moving. Kage knew it too, for his snarl had turned to a sinister *smile*, and he yelled, "Soon, my pretty! Little Lamb!"

The twins pulled their blades from where they had them and took up a protective barrier between the alcove and the rest of her guard.

"We don't have time for this. When that fails, we are fucked. We are trapped here. Do you want him to take her? Because, at this point, he has more with him than we do. And I will be fucking damned if I let that fucking prick get her again." Shawn swore, his voice like the growl of a wolf.

"He is *right.* We don't have the luxury of time." Mathias agreed, his eyes fixed on the alcove, the grip on his sword tightening to the point that Audelia could see the veins on his exposed arms pop a little from the strain.

Bronn nodded and turned his gaze back to Lila. "Finish getting it open, Lila. We will take the risk. Alaric, Gideon, and Skye will head in first. Mara and I will follow. Then Audelia, Shawn, you, Mathias, Micah, and Ezreal will follow in the rear. The second you see them, you shut the gate *down.*"

Lila nodded and reached to grip Gideon's hand as she turned back toward the portal. She began to chant, "A sheanairean nan còmhnardan, fosgail do chridhe do na rìoghachdan, agus thoir air ais sinn gu rìoghachd teine agus sgàil." She repeated it over and over, outstretched her hand, and a whirlwind shot from her palm to slam into the shimmering surface.

Audelia's heart raced as a great surge of magic washed over them in a brilliant light. It reminded her of the light that had been holding Kage down to the ground. It felt like home as it caressed her skin. Her magic reached out to dance with the light as it sank back toward the portal.

Lila leaned against Gideon. "It's open." As the final word left her mouth, a great shattering rent the air. They all turned to see the barrier fall.

"Go now!" Micah yelled as he and Ezreal charged toward Kage and the shadow that had been beside him on the other side of the barrier; snarls could be heard from the shadows of the alcove, and more were coming. *Too many.*

The group sprang into action, Alaric and Skye running through first, as they all rushed closer to the portal. She could vaguely see them reaching toward a brighter edge of the portal. Skye yelled back, "Oh gods. You all need to get here now!"

The panic in his voice stilled her heart. "Gideon, go!" Bronn yelled as he and Mara began to enter the portal. Mathias and Shawn stood closer to her, flanking her on either side.

Gideon looked at Lila, his eyes full of torment. "Go, I'll be right behind you!" She yelled at him, shoving him toward the portal.

Audelia watched as he walked backward, as if terrified to let Lila out of his sight. As he entered the portal, she gasped. Gideon changed before her. His features became sharper, and his ears, *oh gods*, his ears elongated, coming to a point.

Before she could say a thing about it, Bronn shoved Gideon further in, his other hand gripping Mara's tightly.

Lila was at their side in an instant. She had yelled a final chant into the air. "We need to go! The portal will not remain open much longer."

As they ran into the portal together, a cry rang out behind them, and Audelia turned to see Micah and Ezreal skewered by the arms of the Shadow creature. Kage gave a sinister laugh as he walked toward the portal.

"No!" she screamed. Her heart was hammering in her chest, the magic within her was burning brighter as she watched the gasp for air, both making eye contact with her. "GO!" They rasped as blood spewed from their mouths, and their bodies went limp. The shadow tossed their limp bodies aside. Their hearts were in that, *things,* hands as it began to eat them.

"Fuck!" Mathias yelled as he dragged Lila with him. Audelia and Shawn gripped each other's hands as they ran.

The portal washed over them as they ran through it. She thought it would feel like passing from one place to another in an instant, but instead, the portal was like a long wind tunnel. The magic raged around them, shoving at their bodies as they ran.

She couldn't dare look back. She just kept running as fast as her feet would carry her, the feel of ash climbing in her throat as the glow on her chest pulsed the closer they got to the end of the tunnel.

She could see her aunt, uncle, and the others gathered on the other side, waiting. Something was *off,* though, because they looked panicked.

The magic around them began to *change.* It felt welcoming and warm, and smelled of pine, salt, and snow. She felt a change radiate through her body, and her heart surged with emotion. *Was* she about to *remember herself? Her parents?*

A small joy tore through her, but a grunt of pain and the loosening grip of Shawn's hand had her swinging to look at him.

Her heart *fell.*

Because coming out of Shawn's chest was a dagger, and blood was beginning to pool fast against the cool colors of Shawn's tunic. Shawn looked at her, fear and pain in his eyes, and she felt everything start to crumble as she saw Kage there holding the blade. He yanked it from Shawn, and he began to fall forward.

How had they not heard Kage coming up behind them?

"No!" Audelia caught him, screaming for help, as she felt Shawn's warm blood splattered on her blouse. "I've got you, my love. I've got you." She spoke over and over as she tried to drag Shawn's body away from where Kage stood manically, laughing at her.

She could hear the others shouting and felt a hand on her shoulder. *Lila.* She was crying as she looked at Shawn's wound.

Anger filled Lila's eyes as she locked with Kage in battle and sent a blast of pearlescent light toward him.

He shouted in anger as he was thrown away from them.

Suddenly, the tunnel wavered and tilted, sending them tumbling to the ground. Audelia *refused* to let go of Shawn; he was still breathing.

He had to be okay.

He couldn't die.

This couldn't happen.

Not him.

They screamed as the magic of the portal surged. Everything began to spin as she held onto the man she loved and prayed that when it stopped, she hadn't just lost him.

"I love you, Audelia." Shawn gasped out before everything went fuzzy.

PART TWO

DARKNESS FALLS

CHAPTER THIRTY~ SEVEN

She was still holding onto Shawn, she knew that much was certain. She could smell the mint, bergamot, and leather that always soothed her. It was the smell of heavy iron hitting her nose that made her heart lurch.

All she remembered before things went fuzzy and the entire portal seemed to spin was Kage plunging a dagger through Shawn's shoulder.

She opened her eyes, taking in the scene around her. She was outside the portal, Shawn still in her arms as they lay side by side, his breathing shallow, the wound in his shoulder bleeding heavily. *Fuck.* Sitting up quickly despite the ache in her head, she saw Lila on the ground next to her, staring wide-eyed at the sky above them.

Much to her dismay, she saw Kage a ways away, beginning to push to his feet. He looked solely unharmed but covered in what looked like blood. Her thoughts turned to the twins.

Micah and Ezreal. He had those fucking monsters *kill* them. Taken so much yet, he was *fine?*

Fuck, couldn't he just die already.

Looking around for the others hoping to the damn gods that they were alive. That what they had seen before every-thing went to shit hadn't been some fabrication.

There, currently battling what looked like more fucking ghouls, were the others. She could make out Mathias and Skye working in unison, back-to-back, taking on the grotesque crea-tures that seemed to have been waiting for everyone.

Just beyond them, on a hill, looked to be the ruins of some small settlement. That she was not expecting to see, from what Gideon had been telling her in her studies of her realm, there were no ruins near where the portals would let out. Because what portals were in use for other kingdoms, those were usually trading towns, fully abundant in rich cultures. Yet, the area here seemed to feel desolate, like something had sucked the life out of it,

Yet, that was for sure a ruin.

A wet cough from her side broke her from getting her bearings in what little time they had before Kage was ready to engage again. Which, from the malicious smiles he gives as he works his hands in strange patterns, is probably not long.

"Shawn?" Her heart was racing as his eyes slowly opened. *Oh, thank the gods, he is alive.*

Lila was at their side; her hand was immediately on Shawn's wound. "It'll be okay. I can heal him, but it won't be perfect because something is wrong with my magic. I think I'm drained...which is weird. But we can figure that out later." She noticed Lila looked different. Sharper, yet more delicate, her ears had shifted to a rounded point, and her skin seemed to glow a little.

"I'm fine, honestly." He rasped, trying to push Lila's hand away from the wound. Yet even that little movement had the wound seeping again like a faucet that won't turn off. Her heart plunged at the rate he was bleeding. He was going to *die* if Lila didn't heal him.

"Shawn, please..." She pleaded as tears began to form. She couldn't lose him, least of all to his own stubbornness.

The sounds of fighting grew louder; it was as if everything had been underwater for a minute, and now everything was coming into stunning focus, including the fact that an odd shadow was beginning to form in the distance, like a wall coming up just behind her guards, uncle, and aunt.

What the fuck is that?

A raspy, wet cough sounded from Shawn, breaking her from her thoughts. *Fuck, that sounds really bad. She turned to see the dark crimson of blood drip down his chin.*

"Shawn, let me heal you. Because from the smell of that wall over there, fucking Kage is cutting us off from the rest of our group. Audelia *needs* you to be okay. Got it?" Her tone was sharper as she began to murmur words, and a small amount of light formed over the wound.

Audelia watched as the skin began to knit together, just as it had when Lila tried to heal Callum.

Callum.

He was *gone*. Audelia could see it in her best friend's face; she was trying not to focus on the fact that both of the people who loved and raised her had just died for them.

Shawn groaned, and her focus snapped back to the man she loved. "You, okay?"

"Yea, now let's go *kill* that fucker." Shawn gave her a lopsided grin that didn't quite reach his eyes.

The three of them stood. Shawn reached for her cheek, the rough pad of his thumb tracing small, soothing circles over her skin. "I promise, A Chroi, I am okay. I am never leaving you." He kissed her quickly; she could taste the iron from the blood he had coughed up; it made her heart fall. It felt like they were saying goodbye, she felt another tear fall down her cheek.

She wished they had longer, knowing he was okay, she wanted to wrap herself around him and not let go for a very long time.

Later, she thought.

"Oh, how *sweet*, you decided to kiss what is mine. Now be a good dog and die." Kage laughed. His gaze narrowed on Audelia, and she felt sick as the predator he was zeroed in on her.

"I was *never* yours, Kage, I was *always* his." She yelled back, reaching down, and quickly grabbed her sword, which had luckily landed right by them. The hilt hummed in her grip.

Shawn did the same, and even Lila had a small dagger somehow. *Probably from Gideon,* she thought.

Kage sneered, shouting, "Ut Tala Nach!" At the final word, the ground around them shook, and that shadow-like barrier she had seen before? It was glowing, pulsing with power.

A growl resonated in the air, and Audelia turned to see a red-faced Mathias trying to get through the barrier that was preventing him and the others from reaching them.

New, smaller shadow beasts began to grow from the ground around Kage, and in quick succession, they began to run toward the trio.

One launches at Shawn, who batted it away with a swing of his blade. He arched it quickly, stabbing the creature.

Several more aim for Lila; they quickly overtake her, but before Audelia can move a step, the largest of the beasts lunges at Audelia.

She dodges just enough to miss the swipe of the creatures' massive claws.

It snarls, trying to get at her, but she parries and nicks its side, and a small yelp is heard as she kicks it away. Hoping it will stay down, she turns towards her best friend, who, to her shock, is faring better than she thought she would.

Lila trading blows with four beasts, using bursts of magic and what little blade-handling skills she has. She had taken a few classes with Audelia and Shawn throughout the years, but not as often. *Luckily*, they seem to be working for her, or perhaps it was something to do with the magic she possessed.

Audelia turned quickly back toward the beast that had attacked her; she had heard its growl again a moment before it launched itself back at her. This time, she was ready and plunged the blade into its chest.

It goes limp, the surprising weight of it causing her to stagger slightly.

She compensates with her left leg and pushes forward, sending the beast off her blade.

She moved toward Shawn, who was now battling five of those fucking things. While Kage just laughed at the carnage around him. A glance toward Mathias and the others tells her their battle is far from over.

Her heart pounds as she grabs one of the beasts and swipes the blade across its throat. That is the only one she gets the advantage on because a second twists towards her and clamps down on her forearm, causing her to scream in pain as she wrestles out of its grip.

She feels the flesh tear away, and she kicks and twists, plunging the blade of her sword through its neck. Only then does it go limp enough for her to remove her arm from its jaws.

Fuck, that hurts.

Shaking away the pain, she gets closer to Shawn, and they begin to fight back-to-back. Each step they took in unison. Two halves of one whole.

It's then that she notices those pulses of magic she thought she felt from him earlier have seemed to have grown.

She could feel it forming branches that extended away from him and ran toward the barrier, keeping them from their friends.

Audelia catches it a second before it disappears. But one of those tendrils she just saw coming off of Shawn managed to get through the barrier. Like it squeezes through a pinhole in the armor of the barrier.

Which meant that it wasn't as *strong* as they thought.

Perhaps, if she can get Lila away from those beasts, Lila may just be able to use her magic to blast the barrier apart while Audelia and Shawn engage Kage.

"This could all end, you know! Just give up and come back to where you belong, little lamb!" Kage calls out as Audelia and Shawn fight off the last of the beasts that had converged on Shawn.

For *fucks* sake.

"You sound like a fucking broken record Kage! She would never join you!" Shawn yells, his voice is still wet, and she can hear how labored his breath is becoming.

Fuck. The wound must have been worse than they thought. Lila had only healed enough to get him up and moving.

He needed to be healed again.

Her gaze swept for Lila, who was starting to falter in her steps, the beasts were far stronger than she was. Even her magic was beginning to fail on her.

Shit.

Kicking at the beast beside her, she brought down her blade on it quickly and raced over to help her friend.

She reaches Lila in time to pull a large shadow beast from her friend. She begins to toss it and feels heat course through her hand as her magic finally decided to join the fight. Audelia watches as the beast becomes ash a moment later.

Okay, I can work with that, she thought.

Lila is breathing hard as she gets to her friend's side. Audelia arcs her blade, taking out the final beast that was on Lila.

"You, okay?" Audelia asked, her voice slightly shaky from the racing of her heart, the taste of ash on her tongue again.

Lila nodded.

"Do you think you can get that barrier down?" She searches her friend's weary face, hoping that she can get the barrier down before things get worse.

She can still hear Shawn fighting off more of those beasts that just keep fucking coming.

Another surges at them and is quickly blasted away by pearlescent light from Lila.

Lila takes a deep breath, her gaze swinging around them, taking in the barrier and the cadre just on the other side of the barrier, the ghouls they were fighting seem to have barely even let up.

"I'm not sure...My magic...I don't know if I'm just not recovered from opening the gate or...... I'm not sure, Del, I can *try.*"

Hearing how unsure Lila sounds has Audelia's heart lurching into her throat.

Before she could say another thing, two more beasts came at them. Both women began to engage with the beasts, kicking and twisting, forcing them back. Audelia's magic didn't surge again, but she could feel it there, inside her, like it was waiting.

But what was it waiting for?

Shaking the thought away, she plunges her blade into the nearest beast, and a spray of black blood hits her in the face. It feels oddly cold, turning her stomach.

"Lila, we need to get closer to Shawn; that way, we can fight together and use each other to guard our backs." Audelia wheezed out; she could feel her own body starting to wane in strength.

Lila nodded, and they got back-to-back, even with her unsure movements, Lila handled herself as they slowly made their way back toward Shawn.

The three continue to engage with the beasts as Kage laughs, going on and on about how she is his.

Rage fills her, and she takes a dagger from the baldric on her chest and flings it at him.

It hits its mark, landing in his chest just above her heart. She smirks.

However, that slowly falls as she watches him remove the blade as if he were merely picking a piece of lint off his clothes.

"That." He sneered and began to stalk toward them. "Was not nice, little Lamb."

In a quick movement, he reared his arm back like he was about to throw something, and the next moment, a lasso of black and red stinging shadow was wrapping around her thigh, and he yanked.

Audelia felt the world shift under her as Shawn screamed, "Del!" She clawed at the earth, the gritty dirt digging under her nails as the shadows dragged her; they bit into her leg, causing her to cry out in pain.

Despite her best efforts, every tug and pull of her trying to break free, the strange magic Kage was using seemed to grip her tighter, sending a searing pain through her body. Her magic seemed to rage inside her, trying to break free, but it was like some barrier was preventing it.

Audelia tried to twist to get one of the blades free from her baldric, but couldn't manage to get one free. Panic was beginning to rise in her throat.

Oh, gods.

Kage just kept laughing as she was dragged. Before she could even brace herself, she felt his cold hand wrap around her throat from behind.

Her heart was beating so hard she thought it would burst soon. She felt so fucking cold with his hands on her.

She was still facing Shawn, who was fighting his way with everything he had towards her, shadow beasts fell as if some force inside Shawn was beginning to form. Audelia could feel the magic pulse from him again as he screamed in rage. He looked like fury born anew.

It seemed to blow from him, like a sonic wave, that pushed

her and Kage back. But Kage just tightened his grip on her throat, blocking the flow of air.

"Let her go!" Shawn snarled out a scream, and it sounded so animal. His eyes held such malice as he stared Kage down, but she also saw bits of fear there, too. As if he were terrified, he would be too late.

As his scream bellowed out, she saw it then; the others had stopped fighting, and it was like the entire valley had gone quiet. She saw Lila standing there, tears streaming down her face, and Mathias was beating on it with everything he had to get through the damn barrier.

She was going to die. This was her last moment. She could feel it in her heart, in her very soul. Kage would kill her just to see how much pain it would cause Shawn.

Lila shifted her footing like she was getting ready to make a run for it toward Audelia, but before she got ten feet, several tendrils of thick black and red shadows sprouted from the ground, they formed around her wrists, keeping her bound.

Gideon could be heard, his voice full of anguish as he shouted, "Lila!" He, too, had begun to beat at the barrier blocking them from the rest of her guards and aunt.

Shawn looked at her, and she began to cry. She had so much she wanted to say to him. She had wanted more time. More of those small moments she cherished so much.

"I love you..." She whispered to him.

Shawn's gaze met hers again, with such sorrow that her heart broke.

"Always..." He spoke and then launched himself at Kage.

He threw his whole weight into Kage, making Kage release her from his grip. But she was still trapped; the stinging shadows that had grabbed her kept her bound now.

She had to watch in horror as Kage drew a blade of midnight and what looked like blood in intricate patterns across its shining surface, his movements like he had held a blade his whole life.

Which was strange, Kage had never once taken a single lesson with Bronn, nor had he ever found interest in fighting like this. He preferred his fists being used on a woman. Particularly *her*.

The thoughts were gone as she watched Kage swipe and cut into Shawn's side, making Shawn stumble, and blood began to seep from the cut, staining the light-colored tunic a deep crimson.

Her heart was in her throat as she began to sob.

This was *worse*; being killed by Kage would have been easier. *This,* watching the man she loves with her entire being, battling against Kage. She didn't know if she could take it.

She reached inside herself, feeling for the sphere that was always there, waiting. She could feel it, that raging inferno that it was becoming, like it sensed the danger Shawn was in and was trying to answer her call. But the shadows on her were blocking it from coming out.

Every pull she gave to the magic deep in her, trying to work it free, made her stomach lurch and sent a sharp pain through her body.

She could only lie on the ground, trapped, as both traded blows back and forth. Kage never seemed to tire as he manically laughed with every swing of his blade.

Her heart was pounding, her soul felt like it was going to fracture as she watched Shawn begin to falter.

His steps were becoming more and more haggard as he

barely managed to block each blow. The wound on his shoulder was bleeding heavily again.

He was bleeding so fucking much.

No, please, she couldn't lose him. She begged and begged to whatever god was listening if they would save him.

Please....

Howls filled the air. Each one sent a shiver down her spine.

CHAPTER THIRTY~ EIGHT

More and more howls filled the air around them. Each one filled her with worry.

Were they there at Kage's command? Was there another enemy that had been lying in wait? Perhaps sent by Lefrain?

She didn't dare hope that *maybe*, just maybe, they were there to *help* them.

Seeing the blood dripping from Shawn's exhausted form had her too scared to even wish that they were there to help.

Fighting the grip of the black and red shadow magic still holding her captive, it had bound her legs, arms, and across her chest and torso. She twisted in time to see dozens of large wolves descending from a nearby hill.

They were fast and fucking *huge*.

Everything seemed to briefly pause as the large wolves

began to plow through the lines of ghouls and shadow creatures that her guards and aunt had been battling.

It was nothing but claws and large teeth, destroying everything in their path. But not a single wolf made to attack the cadre.

Thank the fucking gods.

"You fucker, you called them, didn't you?" Kage sneered in Shawn's face. He swiped out again, knocking Shawn down to his back.

Audelia screamed as she watched Shawn stagger to stand. *No.*

"I don't know what the fuck you're talking about." Shawn spat blood on the ground. He finally managed to stand; his legs wobbled, but he seemed to muster all his strength as he lifted his blade once more.

The snarls of the wolves seemed to grow closer, and the sound of the ghouls' high-pitched, gasping moan had started to lessen. Audelia briefly tore her gaze away from the love of her life, fighting for his life.

Her gaze caught sight of the wolves laying waste to the ghouls and shadow beasts on the other side of the barrier. Barely any were left, and the wolves and her cadre were gathering along the barrier, trying to find a way to break through. She caught sight of her aunt's weary face, the sorrow there.

But it was not the dozens of wolves standing around her cadre, trying to break the barrier; no, her gaze shifted to the white and silver wolf stalking to a place close to her.

It was gigantic, far larger than the other wolves; this one, *gods*, he was the size of a large bear back in the mortal realm. It was as white as snow, but had tufts of silver, like moonlight, in patches, and its eyes, *gods*, were the deepest violet. If the size didn't give it away that this was no normal wolf, it was the color and the knowing that seemed to sit in those depths.

His gaze watched her, and then swung to where Shawn and Kage were battling still, the wolf reached the barrier about ten feet from her.

It gave a great howl, and as it did, a great wave of what felt like magic, which she had felt coming from Shawn earlier, pushed at the barrier. Like before, only a small amount seemed to get through, and she felt it brush over her gently. It was warm and familiar.

She felt the shadows holding her seem to squirm as if in fear of the wolf nearby and the magic that moved over her body. Audelia tried to shift again, trying to break free of the hold it had on her.

Nothing, even that slight squirm it had given, it refused to budge.

Mathias's voice broke through the sounds of wolves pounding at the barrier, including the larger one by her. She swung her gaze at him to see him pointing to something near her.

She cocked her head for a moment, confused, then she looked, and there, a few feet from where she was on the ground, was the sword her mother had made her. The one she had dropped when Kage was choking her.

Audelia started to shift her weight to her knees as best as she could; she began to worm her way toward the sword, and every movement sent more agonizing pain through her body. She gritted her teeth as she got closer to the blade.

Shawn gave a great shout, making her pause, her heart racing. Her gaze swung to where he and Kage had been fighting. There, a bluish light like the one that had just caressed over her exploded from him, sending Kage flying and encasing him,

Content that it was holding Kage for now, Shawn turned toward her and ran to her, his steps sluggish, his beautiful face growing paler and paler by the second.

They *needed* Lila. He needed to be healed *soon*.

"Del!" Shawn fell to his knees beside her, his hands reaching for the shadow bindings that kept her from moving properly. As his fingers connected with them, he cried out in pain as the shadow magic surged and seemed to spark at him.

"The...Sword." Her voice was weak, the longer she was under this binding, the more he body felt heavy. Like it was *draining* her.

Shawn swung his gaze to where her sword lay a few feet away. He reached for it, grabbed its hilt, and brought it back toward her. "What do I do?" His voice was shaky, the blade shaking slightly.

"I think you need to cut at the shadow, I'm not sure, Mathias was yelling my name and pointing at the sword.... Just try it." She coughed, and her lungs tightened; the magic around her pulsed and squeezed, as if it were trying to latch on tighter to keep from being removed.

Shawn nodded, gripped the hilt tighter, and moved the blade parallel to one of the bands of shadow magic. He began to saw at it, and with each stroke of the blade, the shadow seemed to give a high-pitched squeal, squeezing her harder. It grated her ears, but she sighed in relief as the bands started to recede a little as he continued to cut at them. It was painful, but she bore the pain, knowing it was working. But she could feel the cold sweat breaking out over her body from the pain, and she didn't know how much more she could handle.

It was going to break her.

Her heart was pounding; he had managed to cut three of the bands holding her still. he was on the final one when he paused. It was the closest to her heart. One wrong move and it could easily kill her.

"It's okay. We're almost done. Just cut it. I *trust* you." She breathed. Audelia could move a little now and reached for his knee. She rested her shaky hand there, moving her thumb to soothe the worry in his eyes.

She nodded at him again, and he looked at her, his eyes full of tears. "I'm so sorry, my love." His voice full of remorse as he began to saw at the last binding.

She screamed as the binding seemed to tighten like a boa constrictor, trying to hold on to her with every last thing it had. Her scream echoed across the valley, and she could vaguely hear Mathias and the others yelling her name in fear. The large wolf nearby had upped its assault with every syllable of her scream.

Gods, it was going to *kill her.*

She could feel her magic trying to surge to the surface, clawing its way through her, trying to get out. To free itself from the slimy grip the last band held on her.

Shawn continued to cut, whispering how sorry he was and that he loved her. It all started to sound like white noise as the pain began to make her head swim.

She closed her eyes. The light hurt, everything hurt. *Gods, she wanted it to end...* Shawn was screaming in frustration at how the last band seemed to solidify, trying to hold on to her like it would take her with it before it let go.

Then, a voice. It was soft and melodic, and then it was beside her; she tried to lean into the warmth of it. *"It's okay, my sparrow, it's okay. I am so sorry this has happened. It was never supposed to be this way. Don't worry, my darling, he will be with you soon, and you will know safety."*

As quickly as it came, it was gone, and she mourned the loss of it. She didn't understand why it had felt so comforting. She kept her eyes closed, not wanting to forget the voice, *who had that been?*

"Del? My love? *Please*—please wake up, baby." It was Shawn's voice; he was pleading with her. It made her heart ache.

She was scared to open her eyes, scared that the band was still there, that he had stopped, and that's why the pain was suddenly gone.

"It's *gone*, it finally gave way.... please come back to *me*." His voice pleaded again, and she could hear the fear now, the utter hopelessness in it.

"Give her a moment, Shawn, it's okay. I can sense her. She is still here." That was Lila's voice. *Had it been Lila who had talked to her? Was that who the warmth was?* No, *that voice had felt familiar, but it wasn't hers, it was—was someone else.* Audelia wanted to hear it again, to see who was calling her "*sparrow*" and why it made her want to *cry*.

Audelia cautiously opened her eyes. Her whole body ached, but the searing pain was gone. Shawn hadn't been lying. He had gotten the final band free. She blinked a few times, trying to clear the fuzzy aftershocks of the pain. Could have sworn she felt the caress of a delicate hand move down her cheek.

"My love?" Shawn was looking down at her, and she gave him a small, weak smile.

"Can we never do that again?" She gave a small laugh as she pushed herself into a sitting position. Everything ached.

But it was starting to pass; the magic inside her was settling somewhat, but not much. It was still a building inferno, trying to break free from the last vestiges of whatever those bindings had done to her.

Shawn laughed and pulled her into his arms, holding her tightly. She sank into his warmth, wishing they had more time. He gave a small cry of pain when she squeezed him back.

"Oh gods, Shawn. You're hurt, I'm sorry I forgot." She pulled back, taking in the wounds up close.

"I'll be fine, A Chroi." He grabbed her hands and kissed her knuckles; she could feel his breath rattle against her skin.

Gods, he was covered in blood, both his own and that slimy black blood from the Shadow beasts. She could see the cuts more clearly now. The gash from his shoulder was definitely reopened and bleeding heavily, and the one she had seen happen on his side seemed to have slightly stopped, but it still looked terrible.

He *needed to be* healed.

"Lila? Can you heal him?" She turned to her best friend, only to see the look of horror on her face. Lila was looking beyond them. "What's wrong?" Her heart was racing as Lila lifted her finger to point.

In their quest to get the bindings off of Audelia, they had lost track of what Kage was doing. She had seen Shawn somehow send magic at him that had held him to the ground.

Her heart racing, she turned to where her best friend was pointing. The blue light of the magic that had been holding him was beginning to melt away, and Kage seemed to radiate red and black mist. It made her blood turn cold as he began to rise, not stand, but float from the ground he had been lying on.

She and Shawn struggled to their feet, leaning against each

other, as they watched Kage's body float wrapped in that mist. The wolf behind them snarled and began to hit the barrier in earnest; she could hear tiny cracks echoing from each hit.

He was breaking it. But she knew in her soul the wolf would not break it in time to stop whatever was about to happen.

She turned to Shawn; she saw he knew it too. Whatever was about to happen, they and Lila were on their own. He grabbed her hand, lacing their fingers together, and squeezed, and she squeezed back in reassurance.

Kage's body turned to shift him until he was standing, floating in the air. It was then that they saw what the mist was doing—it was *healing* him. More tendrils of black formed on his skin and seemed to pulse as the mist moved over him.

Oh, gods.

"He's healing...." Lila spoke softly, her tone giving away her disbelief at what she was seeing.

"Fuck." Shawn cursed.

"What do we do?" Audelia asked, looking back and forth at them. *How in the worlds could they stop him, if the fucker could heal?*

Lila looked at her and swung her gaze back to Kage, who was almost healed now, and the mist was starting to recede from his body.

The wolf behind them howled and rammed against the barrier again and again. She heard her uncle and Mathias call her name again. But she was too scared to look away from what was happening.

For a moment, when Shawn had started to cut the bindings, she thought they could win this. That what they had set out to do could happen. She could free her realm from the monster that had taken it all those years ago.

But, if this... *IF* this was what his agents were capable of? How could she ever hope to stop him?

Kage's body slowly lowered to the ground; every inch closer, she could feel her magic trying to surge again. It was slower than before, like those bands had suppressed too much of it.

Lila stepped forward, her hands beginning to spin in circles, her fingers moving as if she were forming letters in the air; she could hear her chanting softly under her breath.

Shawn handed Audelia back her blade, his own gripped firmly in his hand as they prepared for whatever may happen next.

Together. They would face it together.

Kage smiled at them. It was sinister and utterly inhuman; his skin looked as though more of those crawling shadows had taken over and were now visible beneath his skin. His eyes were, fuck they were deep crimson. Whatever humanity had been left in the bastard was gone. It made the power inside her swell, preparing to strike.

He was a complete monster now.

Lila screamed, sending a blast of her pearlescent power at Kage. From where Audelia stood, she could feel it pulse over her; it fueled the magic inside herself that rose to answer the call.

Audelia held her breath as she watched the waves of power head straight for Kage, but before they made contact, he raised his hand and smirked. The wave stopped, and with a flick of his wrist, he sent it away like he was swatting a fly.

"You shouldn't have done that." He leered. His smile turning more predatory.

Before Lila had time to protect herself, Shadows sprang from the ground around her in a circle, and she was encased in them. They held her suspended in the air, and Audelia could see her screaming in pain, but nothing came out.

Gideon screamed again, his shout full of heartache and rage, as he watched Lila continue to writhe and scream in silent agony, the shadowed cage around her growing darker by the minute. Magic burst from Gideon and struck the barrier, making it shake, and more spider-web cracks formed. It still wasn't enough. It would never break in time.

"Lila!" Audelia screamed and raced for her best friend. Not knowing what to do, but she had to do something.

Shawn screamed her name in warning and fear.

She turned in time to see Kage coming at her unnaturally fast, and before she had full time to raise her blade, his cold hand was around her throat, and the other was wrenching the blade from her hand.

"You are mine!" He snarled in her face; his breath made her stomach turn. It smelled of decay.

She fought against him, kicking and punching, as his grip tightened on her. Her magic started to swell, but it still struggled to break free all the way; whatever those binds had done, it seemed worse when she was this close to Kage.

If she could only get one of her blades free.

She felt what felt like a snake's grip around her wrists, holding them at her sides, so she kicked with everything she had.

His grip tightened, cutting off her air.

"I will never be yours!" She snarled at him and, for good measure, spat at him.

She relished the revolting look on his face as her spittle hit him.

But it was short-lived because he took one of his fists and punched her hard in the stomach, and she tried to cough but only gasped through her struggling breaths.

Her eyes darted around for anything. She could see the wolf nearby still breaking the barrier; it was chipping away more, but still not enough. She could see the fire in its eyes, the determination.

Lila was still stuck in the darkening bubble; she could barely see her now, except for small shadows of her trying to break free from the bindings. Gideon's scream was growing louder, his magic crashing against it in vain, his eyes never leaving Lila.

And Shawn—*wait, where was Shawn?*

She searched for him but didn't see him.

But she could feel him, whatever had awakened in him, she could sense it like a tethered line stretched from her to him. In it, she could feel the rage inside him. Before she could react to it, her vision blurred as Kage gripped her throat tighter. She felt his nails, which were usually kept short, were now like talons digging into her throat.

She thought if he gripped her any tighter, he would end up ripping out her throat.

"You will be...." his words are cut short as Shawn's appears behind him, yanking him away from Audelia, blue light seems to seep off of Shawn, his eyes were—*fuck they were glowing*, she noted as her body fell to the ground in a heap, making her gasp for air. She took in lungfuls of air as she watched the scene before her.

Shawn looked like an avenging god as he began to battle with Kage again. The two exchanged blow after blow, both hitting the mark, but it seemed like for every blow Shawn dealt, as Kage moved to deliver another, he seemed to heal. That strange mist was back each time.

Audelia watched in horror as Shawn, even with the glow coming from him, could tell his strength was waning.

The wolf that was behind her howled *like a call to war;* the other wolves answered its call. The glow around Shawn seemed to brighten for a moment, and Shawn screamed as it arced from him in a wave with enough force to push Kage away.

She sighs in relief as she watches Kage land hard on the ground.

But he smirks as he sits up, and her heart *drops.*

It all happened so fucking fast, one second, Kage was on the ground, seemingly defeated, and the next, he was on his feet directly in front of Shawn, plunging a black and red jagged-looking dagger straight into Shawn's heart.

Her blood runs cold as the glowing blue around Shawn sputters out, and he coughs up blood, leaning forward as Kage sneers something at him, his gaze swinging to Audelia in a large, sinister smile, like–like he has *won.*

She screams in rage as she climbs to her feet, and an inferno bursts from her chest right as Kage, at the same time, attempts another black barrier around them, and the one around Lila shatters as Kage is thrown to the ground and goes limp.

Shawn...

CHAPTER THIRTY~NINE

Everything felt off balance as she ran limping from the pain in her leg towards Shawn, where he had collapsed to the ground.

Her body felt so cold, even though she could still feel the flames that lapped at her skin. They were fading, but that ball of fire in her grew again as it fed on her agony, waiting to destroy whoever or whatever dared to hurt her next.

Shawn...please....

That thought kept running through her head as she took each step towards his body. He was so fucking still, and as she got closer, there was so much blood that the bright green grass around them was a deep black crimson.

Her heart surged into her throat as she dropped to her knees next to his body. She pulled him slightly to her; he groaned in pain. As much as she hated that she had hurt him with the movement, her heart lurched with the hope that he was still alive.

Which meant he just needed to be healed.

"Lila! I need you!" Her cry was broken as she yelled for her best friend. She knew Lila was probably weak after trying to break free from the hellish cage she had been placed in.

But she couldn't lose Shawn, not after he taught her to live. Taught her how love *should feel. He was hers, and she was his.*

Gods.

She could hear the running footsteps approaching her. But she couldn't look up from Shawn's battered body, from the blood, she had a hand on the biggest of the wounds, the last one.

Her stomach turned, and her heart was icy as she felt the blood well around her fingers. "Shawn....please, my love...wake up.... come back!" She pleaded. *You can't leave me here. Not now, please.*

His body shook slightly, as if he were fighting an internal battle; still, his eyes did not open. *Fuck, this can't be happening.*

She leaned down and kissed his forehead. He felt clammy, and she couldn't remember if that was a good or bad thing. Her brain just kept focusing on his breathing and willing the blood to stop.

"Oh *gods.*" It was Lila's voice. She sounded hoarse; her usual melodic tone was broken and raspy. Audelia barely registered Lila kneeling beside her; she just kept her head bent towards Shawn, whispering for him to wake up. Asking whatever fate that watched them, to allow her this. To not take Shawn.

"Lila...please...please heal him. "I....can't..." Her words stopped as sobs wracked her body, she couldn't get the words out. She hoped with as much in her heart as she could that maybe, just maybe, if she didn't voice the words, it wouldn't happen.

"I'm not sure if I can, Del... but...I'll try." Lila's voice shook a little, and Audelia looked up and saw how drained her best friend looked. She nodded at her friend. Hoping.

Audelia watched as Lila took several deep breaths to settle herself. Placing her shaking hands on Shawn gently, he stirred a little, but still, his eyes did not open, his breathing so damn shallow. Lila hummed softly, almost inaudibly, the light she had seen before glowing softly, but then sputtering for a moment. It took her a few agonizing tries before light came brightly from her and seemed to settle over the closest wound, the one by his hip. She watched as the skin tried to knit together, doing so slowly but then seeming to stall.

"Give me a moment.... I just need to focus a bit better..." Lila spoke softly; she sounded so defeated, and it made Audelia's heart race. She didn't speak, merely nodded, tears falling as she looked down at Shawn's greying features.

She heard other footsteps approaching them and the curses of several voices, one of which was female. Audelia hadn't even realized the barrier had collapsed when Kage was taken down.

Mara.

Her gaze swung towards her aunts; she was leaning against Bronn, and she looked okay, no visible injury, only tears brimming in her eyes. "Auntie?... Can you help? Please?" Her voice sounded so small. This could work. If Mara helped, then Shawn would be *okay*, and all of this would be in the past. They could finish this together. *Right?*

"I... I can try my dove." She looked at Bronn for a

moment, and he nodded. Audelia watched as Mara knelt beside Shawn and placed her hands on his body. She saw then that her aunts' hands were shaking as well, like she herself was reaching her limit. Audelia swallowed a lump in her throat.

"*Please*, Shawn, come back to me...you *promised*..." She whispered to him again as her aunt tried to get her magic to work.

A glow began, this one was softer, calming. It felt like a warm blanket, and Audelia watched as Shawn's eyes opened. Some of the grey pallor of his skin became slightly flushed, more like him than he had been when she came to kneel at his body and had seen him lying in pools of his blood.

Oh gods, it was working!

"Shawn? Baby?" Audelia's heart was racing, her aunt was still sending that warm glow over his wounds, but Shawn coughed, it was wet and painful sounding.

"It's okay, my love...take your time..." Her voice was soft.

He looked at her; his features seemed too pale, but she saw the remnants of that blue glow still sitting along the edges of the green in his eyes.

"Are you alright, A Chroi? Is anything hurt?" His eyes searched her face from where he lay next to her. He tried to shift so that he could see her better. He gave a cry of pain, and blood gushed from some of his wounds from the movement.

"Stop moving, you stubborn man, let them heal you. I'll be alright. I promise." She didn't care that her body hurt, that she was still bleeding herself. Only he mattered to her.

Him, *surviving* this.

"I'm sorry, I wasn't fast enough to stop him..." His fingers reached up; they shook as he traced the line of what she assumed was the beginnings of welts on her neck from Kage's grip on her.

"It's fine, my love. Just please.... let them heal you, okay?" The last words choked as she pleaded with him, leaning towards him, she gave him a gentle kiss on his lips.

Her heart stuttered, his usually warm lips, the ones that she always craved, they were so fucking cold now. Her gaze swung to where her aunt and Lila sat—*wait.*

They weren't touching him anymore. Why had they stopped?

"What are you doing? Why did you stop!" She yelled; her words wobbly as tears began to fall anew.

Before they could respond, a growl echoed around them. Audelia swung her gaze toward the sound, to see the wolves had formed a circle around them, like they—like they were protecting them?

But it was beyond the circle of the wolves that made her heart stop. Kage was standing again. He looked a little worse for wear, but the bastard was still alive even after those waves of flames had hit him.

He gave a smile, it was inhuman and made a shiver shoot down her spine as she watched several shadow beasts began to form again, fuck they were like damn cockroaches. These didn't seem to wait like before, no, these began to race toward the wolves and her cadre.

They seemed more vicious than before, like this was the last-ditch effort of a wounded animal.

"Mathias, stay with them, we will hold them off while they heal Shawn," Bronn ordered Mathias, who had been kneeling beside Audelia. She realized then that his hand had been on her back, rubbing soothing circles across it. She had been so lost in her worry; the touch hadn't even registered till now.

But it wasn't Mathias's comfort that had given her pause, no, it was her uncle's words—the way he had paused and seemed to want to say something else but had decided not to.

Before she could ask what was going on, Bronn had run off toward the others, the only one who had lingered besides Mathias was Gideon, who was looking at Lila with worry lining his eyes.

"Go, Gideon, help stop them. We'll be okay here." Lila's words were warbled like she was trying to hold back tears.

He opened his mouth to say something, then quickly closed it before nodding and heading towards the newly begun battle.

Shaking her head, she turned back to Shawn, who was growing paler again, but his gaze wasn't on her. She tracked his line of sight and took in the large, white, and moonlight-silver wolf stalking towards them.

Its eyes never wavered from Shawn's.

In the distance, she heard the other wolves and her Cadre engaging with the creatures Kage had sent again.

The wolf edged closer to them; she could barely see it through the tears. Its eyes were definitely on Shawn. There was this gleam of *agony* in its eyes. It was a brilliant contrast to the blood currently dripping from its great white maw.

"Mathias–" She whispered. Too scared to talk too loudly. Not sure what this wolf wanted, but she would fight it if it meant to harm the man she loved.

"I see it. But I don't sense...anything malicious," He breathed. His own eyes kept track of the wolf's movements.

When it had appeared a little while ago, she thought they were in even bigger trouble. Shawn was *dying*; she could feel it in her bones, and Kage was still there fighting other wolves currently. She would make him pay for what he has done. Her clothing was in tatters and drenched in blood, both her own and Shawn's. She looked and saw her aunt had moved to sit beside Lila, and they had linked hands, placing the linked digits on Shawn. A warm glow barely covered his body, but the wounds *weren't* stitching.

Her heart was pounding in her ears, the end was coming, one she wanted so desperately to deny.

She can't lose him.

Please don't take him. She begged to whatever god apparently found her life favourable to give her these gifts. She would *gladly* trade them for Shawn.

She wouldn't be able to go on *without* him.

Audelia watched as Shawn raised a shaky hand toward the wolf. She tried to pull him back, she wasn't entirely sure if the wolves had come to help or if they were merely buying time before killing them as well.

Shawn bleeding out before her was probably a damn buffet to that wolf.

But Shawn just kept reaching for it. Like he needed to touch the wolf, he groaned in pain, trying to move toward it.

Maybe the wolf could *help*? She didn't know much about where they were, but she did remember from the lessons with Gideon that Guardian Shifters tended to keep near portals. Many of them healers.

What if this wolf was a healer?

Gods, please be a healer.

She relented and watched as the wolf nuzzled Shawn's hand and whimpered. She could hear the heartbreak in that small whimper.

Her heart lurched.

No.

Please not yet

The wolf moved closer, lying beside Shawn, nudging him here and there like he was trying to tell him something. Audelia just watched them. *Why was this wolf here? What did it want with Shawn?*

Shawn had watched the wolf stalk to him, its movements were graceful and determined. Part of him, the one that didn't fully understand what was happening to him, was worried that this *very* giant wolf was going to kill him. Another, *older* part *knew* this wolf. Had always known him, yet it didn't make sense.

He couldn't understand how, but when they had entered The Glade what seemed like ages ago now, he had felt himself change.

It was slow at first, just this odd humming in his bones, but as they lingered, listening to the Druids chant, listening to Lila tell them who she really was, it had grown. Shawn could feel it thrum inside him like a calling.

It felt like coming home; it was warm and safe, just like how he always felt around Audelia.

Gods, Audelia.

He felt her still brushing her delicate fingers through his hair, whispering his name, asking him not to *leave* her. He saw that Mathias was just behind her, keeping watch over her. Good, at least one of them was still protecting her.

Gods, did he want to keep that promise. Ever since that power inside him had awoken, he had thought that maybe, just maybe, they could do this. That this was the answer they had needed. He wouldn't just be some weak human anymore; he had...*something*, and that something could help her. *Keep her safe.*

For a time, since, he thought it would work. It was still small and growing, but perhaps it would be just what he *needed*.

Until they were in the portal getting here, and somehow that fucking bastard had gotten the drop on him, and he felt that cold steel slice through his body.

He thought right there he had entirely failed her.

It had gutted him.

"Young one." A voice spoke, breaking him from his trailing thoughts. It was deep and foreign, but his gaze snapped back to the wolf prowling towards him.

He couldn't talk easily earlier when he had spoken to Audelia to try to reassure her. It had felt like it was taking everything in him *just* to say those words.

So, he just watched the wolf, both intrigued and confused, for the wolf had made no movement of its blood-covered maw. Just watched him with an eerie intelligence.

"Yes, just as you think. I spoke to you in your head, young one." Its brilliant violet eyes shone with what looked like worry and agony.

He stretched a painful hand towards the wolf; he didn't know why he did that, but something old and primal told him to do so. He felt Audelia try to keep him from reaching it, probably worried about what the wolf would do. But he felt it in his soul, this wolf would not hurt him or her.

It was closer now; he could feel its warm breath on his icy body. *Fuck*, dying was like being plunged into a lake in the middle of winter.

Because he was dying, wasn't he?

"Yes, I am sorry." The wolf nudged him then, its nose felt odd against his increasingly cold skin; its words sounded so remorseful.

"What is going on with me? Not the dying, that was my fault, I wasn't fast enough." His words were normal, his usual cadence back. Which was odd, because when he had talked to Audelia a moment ago, his words were wet and broken. He knew Lila and Mara tried as they might to heal the wounds, but the healing wasn't working. He knew it would never work.

"You do not speak from your lips; you speak from your heart. That is how we communicate with others like us."

"Like us? Like, I could be a wolf?" *What was happening?* He was racking his brain for stories his Sobo had told him years ago, but his mind felt fuzzy, like everything he could usually recall about those stories was somehow slipping away.

"Yes, it is how you called us. Do not strain yourself, young one. You are–I am sorry, but *more* hurt than just dying." The wolf whimpered out, nudging him again.

It felt comforting, just like Audelia's every soothing touch. Even with all the heartbreak he could feel from her, she was comforting, always had been; she was his *everything*. His soul was linked to hers; he had known that since they were kids.

His A Chroi.

He didn't want to *leave* her.

"I don't understand, I just—I just want to be able to protect her... I can't..." His words trailed off. It was becoming increasingly difficult for him to focus on what he wanted to say.

"She is your bonded." The wolf's gaze looked at her for a moment before looking back at him. He saw such sorrow there.

"Bonded?" Even the word sent a jolt of knowledge through him, one that fed his soul and made him want to fight harder, to always be there for her. The word was the answer to a question he never knew.

"*Yes*, you are a Guardian. An ancient line of protectors for those gifted with the magic of Gods. She is *your* bonded. It's like a mate, but you're not hers; hers is out there, waiting for her. You are whatever she needs at the time, friend, brother, lover, but above all, *protector*. You are linked."

Gods.

"She—she has a mate?" He didn't know why he focused on that, given everything that was happening, but it tore at him nonetheless.

"Yes, but she does not remember him. He is lost to her, and she to him. But he waits; I can scent him on her. It's an *old* scent, but still there. I do not say this to harm you, young one."

Shawn nodded.

His thoughts turned to the woman he loves. She'll be alone when he leaves her, *fuck*, he didn't want that. She would have Mathias, who would guard her like a hawk, but he didn't want her to be lonely.

She deserved to be loved, to have someone see her for who she is, not because of the crown that would sit on her brow one day or for the magic that he could feel now. The burning heat of it was making what he now understood to be his own stretching out to greet it. As if answering her magic's call. To help it build its power and *protect* it. To protect *her.*

"I don't want to leave her. What can I do? Can you heal me?" His voice was turning desperate, even in the fog of his mind, he knew one thing and one thing only.

Her.

He was hers, and she was his, no matter what. And she needed someone, even if that wasn't him anymore. That thought gutted him. He had *promised* her. Promised never to leave her side. Perhaps this wolf could do what he cannot. Be her bonded, *in his place.*

"I cannot. I am *your* Guardian; I have waited a long time for you. I was once your ancestor's protector in the mortal realm. When I failed, I came here. I knew nothing but the forests until I sensed you one day over *two hundred* years ago, when a link to that realm and this opened."

"But that opened *only* fifteen years ago?"

"It did not. Many things have occurred since she was spirited away for safety. This realm is not a safe place to be anymore. I fear she has a long, dangerous road ahead."

Over two hundred years since they left? *Oh shit.*

"Then help me! I cannot leave her if she is going to be in that much danger, please...." He begged, then realized he was begging someone, and he didn't even know their name. "Sorry, what is your name?"

"Faron, young one." Shawn could see the regret in his eyes.

Before Shawn could speak again, he felt a pulse race through his body, it felt like—like Audelia, he had never noticed it before, but it felt older, like it had always been there, and he had only just opened the door to it.

It smelled like cherry blossoms, black currant, and warm amber, with hints of something he couldn't quite place. But it was beginning to waver.

"What is *that*?" His voice shook; he knew—he could feel what it meant. It made his heart drop, and he wanted to be wrong about it. They needed more time.

"The bond is severing.... You do not have much longer...I'm sorry, young one." Faron whimpered, nuzzling against Shawn like even he wished he could stop it.

"Am I your bonded? Is that how this works? That's why you came?" His mind was racing; maybe just maybe, he could *still* protect Audelia when he was *gone*. At least until maybe she could find this mate. The one who truly could protect her, even if it made jealousy course through his veins. *She wouldn't be alone, though.*

"Yes, you are, and we answered because we felt your magic call us to war, many of the wolves here are from your family's clan, ones that came here a long time ago." Faron looked over briefly towards where the others were battling those Shadow beasts, and amidst them was Kage.

He was saying something toward Audelia amidst the carnage he was delving out with what he now knew was *borrowed* magic.

Seeing him fueled the rage inside him. He wanted to make the bastard pay for what he did to Audelia. In the past, and since he showed up with that strange power of his.

"Become hers, please. I'm not sure how it works, but please. I can't die knowing she will be alone. Be whatever she needs. Be someone who sees *her*. Please—I can't leave her like this. I love her with everything I am." He felt the tears falling now. His heart was fracturing.

Audelia shifted, crying harder now, and he knew why; he could feel it, his body going numb.

"You wish for *me* to become her bonded?" Faron cocked his head slightly, looking at her.

"Yes, please.... I need to know she has someone, someone not bound by the past, someone who can be what she needs to help her find her mate. Get her to him. So, he can do what I could not.... *please.*"

He felt cold and suddenly detached. It felt like something was pulling him away, but it didn't feel warm and comforting; it felt *malicious.*

"What is this feeling?" He felt like he was being pulled apart now, and he gave a scream of pain. This one was not in his head, and he heard Audelia sob, begging him not to leave her. *I'm sorry, my love.* He thought.

"You are not just dying.... Your soul is being *taken*; I am sorry. I wish I could stop it from happening...But I *can* offer you one thing of peace: I have seen how you feel in your memories, and I will *protect* her. Be who she needs, I will bond to her."

"Can—can I tell her goodbye? I *need* to tell her one more time.... I love her."

Faron nodded as a small pulse of magic spread across Shawn and Audelia; then he felt that small glimmer of the bond he had felt earlier, and it went quiet. And he felt so tired and alone as he looked at the woman he loved one last time.

CHAPTER FORTY

Audelia still didn't fully understand what was happening. She merely watched as Shawn and the wolf seemed to watch each other.

But it was the wet cough he gave that brought her out of her thoughts. He wasn't healing; if anything, the greying pallor was beginning to return, and he was getting worse. Yet, the glow was still coming from Lila and Mara's linked hands.

She looked to Mathias, hoping he had noticed, she was too scared to ask her aunt and Lila, worried it would break their shaky connection. But his eyes were fixed on the battle unfolding around them, his hand gripping the hilt of his blade, keeping him *prepared* in case. She took a moment to look as well.

It was *chaos*, utter chaos. She had been right when she said Kage was attacking again like a wounded animal.

There were ghouls and shadow beasts everywhere, somehow, between the wolves and her cadre, they were keeping them away from where she was. But part of her was terrified that it wouldn't last long. Kage seemed more haggard than before, but he also seemed frenzied, like he was no longer in control, that whatever magic he had been using was now using him.

One of the ghouls seems to notice them just beyond the fray and starts to run at an unnatural speed. Audelia gasps and starts to shield Shawn. Mathias curses and stands, raising his blade and running to meet it halfway, slicing through it with such ease that Audelia is shocked.

Others begin to notice, and soon Mathias is engaged in battle with several of them. A wolf nearby was making its way toward them to give him backup.

It's a fight of claws, teeth, and blades as Mathias and the wolf keep the creatures at bay. Her heart pounds, and she sent out a prayer to whatever god or goddess to protect him. She can't bear the thought of another being harmed while protecting her. It was *too* much.

Shawn groaned in pain; Audelia's heart sank as her gaze swung back to him. She noticed it then, more blood. He was bleeding too much.... too fucking much.

Fuck, did he have anything left. Why isn't he healing? Why is he getting worse?

Lila and Mara both curse. The hiss of the words brought a chill down her spine.

"What's wrong? Why aren't you healing him?! Please...I can't lose him." She knew she shouldn't yell at them but fuck, she was so angered at the world, at everyone, at herself for not being stronger to keep Shawn safe. Shawn, who was only here because of her. She pleaded and begged.

"I'm so sorry......Del... We can't heal him...I'm so sorry." Lila was crying now, folding her blood-stained hands around herself like she was trying to keep herself together.

Audelia's heart lurched into her throat.

"What.... What do you mean you can't heal him? What is the use of having the kind of magic you have if you can't heal the man I love!" She screamed.

She felt her magic yawn awake, felt it begin to pulse and curl.

Audelia was sobbing as she pushed hair from Shawn's face; his eyes were still trained on the wolf. Whatever was going on between them, she hoped it helped him—hoped that it would be the saving grace they needed.

"*Please*....Shawn...Don't leave *me*.... You *promised* my love.... *please*..." She whispered, every word making her heart fracture more and more.

Mara crawled on her knees and sat beside Audelia, placing a gentle hand on her shoulder before speaking, her voice soothing, even though there was a slight shake as she tried to fight back her own tears. "We *tried,* my dove...but there is *no* coming back from this. The blade that monster used...*fuck*..." Mara cursed, and it startled her for a moment. Audelia could not remember a single time her aunt had *ever* used that word; if she was using it *now*, she knew the following words would *shatter* her.

Her heart was in her throat, and she couldn't breathe. This wasn't happening; she couldn't lose him.... he can't...*no*...

"What do you *mean*? Why can't you fix him....Mara *please*....I can't be without him....*Please*." The tears were coming harder now, her vision was nothing but a blur as she looked at her aunt, she hadn't wanted to look away from Shawn, too scared that he would disappear, but she needed to see her aunt's face as she explained why she was doing this to her.

Why...

"The blade he used, it was black and red, jagged and felt off right?" Her words were slow, but Audelia recalled the look of the blade as she watched it plunge through the man she loved several times.

She wanted to throw up.

But she nodded at her aunt.

"It's called the *Tenguistwa*, it's an ancient infernal blade, one that—" Her voice trailed off for a moment, and she looked toward where Audelia knew Bronn was fighting. She saw the worry etch her aunt's face for a moment before she turned back to Audelia. "It's used to render one's soul from their body with a killing blow to the heart."

What.

She felt faint as she took in the words her aunt was saying. A blade that rendered the soul from the body? Her magic surged, and she felt it wisp over her skin; it wasn't hot, on the contrary, it felt cool to the touch. As if it needed to check her over, make sure she wasn't the one who had been harmed.

When the magic had finished, it retreated back into the ball inside her, but it had grown again; it was burning so much now that she tasted ash in her mouth from the expenditure.

She took a haggard breath. "What does that mean? Why is that preventing you from healing him? He isn't dead yet. Look! He is still breathing." She searched her aunt's eyes, her own pleading as the tears welled up again.

Mara lowered her head and reached out with a gentle hand, and drew her knuckles gently against Shawn's bruised cheek. Her eyes found Audelia's again. They were so fucking sad it was breaking her even more. "Once, someone is stabbed through the heart with the blade.... The process starts, and there is no stopping it; it would take a full-blown god or goddess to try and *stop* it. I don't know how Kage got that blade...but I'm sorry, my dove."

"What process? His—his *death*?" The words were wobbly as she turned back to look down at Shawn and curled her body closer to his. She needed to be closer, needed to feel more of him.

He *would* survive this...whatever he and the wolf were doing, it would help...it *needed* to help.

He was dying.... she was losing him.... she would be alone *again...*

"The process of their death...but also of their soul being taken...." Lila spoke now, her voice low, as if she didn't want to say the words; Audelia could hear the soft sobs in her voice. "*Taken*...and *placed* inside the blade that killed them, *forced* to watch as the blade takes more innocent lives, until—"

"Until what, Lila? What could be *worse* than that?" She snapped. Her soul was screaming in agony now at the image that gave her. Her sweet, loving Shawn would be forced to kill? To watch as the blade that killed him took more lives?

"Until it shatters *forever*. It will never leave the blade unless the blade can be cleansed before the soul shatters, but even then, his soul will *never* know peace.... You'll never see him in the after." Lila was sobbing now, and Audelia heard Mara shift, wrapping an arm around Lila to comfort her.

Oh gods....

That sounded like an unbearable hell.... Shawn... oh gods, my love. She thought.

"How do we stop that? I don't want him to suffer like

that.... *please, what do I do?*" She pulled Shawn closer to her, needing to feel him.

"We will have to cleanse the blade, but it's not that easy; we need a *god* to do it," Lila spoke, her voice breathy as she gulped for air between sobs.

This couldn't be happening.

Audelia sobbed.

A sinister voice boomed across the valley, and it sounded like Kage, but *not*. Like the thing controlling him finally made its appearance. "Look at the little whore, crying over the dying dog. Do you like my little present, pretty one? It's going to look so nice as it shatters, maybe I'll hold off on killing, leave him a little...intact and make his soul watch as a fuck you." He sneered, and she knew that it wasn't Kage anymore, and a part of her knew it was Lefrain speaking now.

Lila stood on shaky legs and screamed, sending a blast of pearlescent light in the form of daggers at Kage; they struck him, knocking him to the ground for the moment.

Lila collapsed into a heap, her breathing shallow, but from the look of relief on Mara's face, as she checked her pulse, she was alive, just at her full limit now.

She felt Shawn shift; he cried in pain, this time, it was guttural and tore through her very soul. His skin felt like ice. All the warmth she had ever felt from him all these years it was *gone.*

No... She wasn't ready.

Not yet.

"*Please,* baby.... don't leave me...*hold on....* We'll figure something out, okay? *Please....* Don't leave *me.*" She was breaking; she could feel it. This would *shatter* her.

His body shook, and he was crying in pain. But still, his gaze was fixed on the wolf.

The wolf whined and looked at her. She felt something warm slither over her for a moment, and then it was gone.

And she suddenly felt empty, as if something was *missing*, but she wasn't sure what it was; yet, it brought her great sorrow.

The sorrow filled her, and she felt the earth rumble below them.

Mara and Lila gasped for a moment so softly that she barely noticed it.

She closed her eyes; she couldn't do this. Couldn't envision a world where he wasn't with her, a world where he was trapped in a blade until his soul shattered from being forced to kill innocents?

The fire inside her swirled in answer, making her body shake. She felt warmer, as if she were going to burn from the inside out.

Not her Shawn, not the man who made her feel seen, the man who, as a boy, always went out of his way to make her smile when she was sad, the man who saved her when she almost died because of the very man, that feet away was trying to destroy everything again.

He was her guardian knight; he always had been. Always.

"Audelia..." Her gaze snapped open to meet Shawn's green eyes, they were so fucking pale now, all the usual love and light were gone, she choked back a sob.

"Shawn—please—please don't leave me." She shifted so she could place her forehead on his, he was so damn *cold*.

"I'm sorry, A Chroi. I'm sorry I can't keep my promise. I *failed* you, my love." His voice was hoarse and small. *Gods.*

"No—no you didn't fail. *I* failed—I shouldn't have let you come. You would still be *safe*, not here bleeding, and—and—" She sobbed, she couldn't say the words aloud. Couldn't put them out there, even though they were echoing in her soul.

The inferno in her raised its eyes in answer.

He leaned up, his body struggling to simply lift himself, but he fought through it and pressed his lips to hers. She felt his tongue prod at her, and she opened. Through the tears they both shed, they claimed each other in that kiss one *last* time. They rest their heads against each other, her tears mixing with his.

A cry fills the air, and a growl. They swivel their heads to see Mathias and the wolf fighting Kage, who had managed to somehow get closer to them. Her heart pounded.

"*Audelia*—my love," Shawn whispered to her again, making her look at him. Her heart was in a million pieces.

Everything had gone wrong. It wasn't supposed to be like this. He wasn't supposed to be on the ground bleeding out. He wasn't supposed to be *dying*.

It was her fault. She *did* this. Everything. It was *her* fault. She begged to whatever gods would listen, begged that she could take his place. Let it be *her*. Not him. *Never him.*

"I love you. So damn much, I think I have since the first moment I saw you in that little flower printed dress, and your Mary janes, your beautiful red hair in two braids, you were so *beautiful* even then." He coughed and cried out in pain.

"*Shhh*—don't talk, my love—It's okay—I love you too," she cried.

"*No*, I want you to know this. Know that no matter what happens next, I will *never* regret getting to love you. I wish we had had more time. *Promise me*—A Chroi promises me that you will find love again. *Find it*. And become the amazing Queen, I know you are going to be." He reached up a shaking hand to cup her cheek, and she leaned into his touch.

The inferno leapt in answer. It was going to consume her soon.

"Not without *you* with me—I need you to help me be a good queen—*I need you*, please—Shawn, don't leave me—I can't—I can't be alone again." She pressed into his hand and forehead, needing more of him. Needing this *not* to be real.

"You *can*—and you will when the time is right. And it's okay... I want that for you. You are my greatest happiness, and I need you to stay that way. I need you to find love again–" His voice started to trail off, his eyes were becoming duller, lifeless.

"Don't leave.... *please, I love you, Shawn*....please" She pleaded again.

No....not now.... no.

"*Trust* the wolf.... His name is Faron...He will be your guardian now.... I love you, my heart...." The wolf, now fighting with Mathias against Kage, gave a great, mournful howl.

She felt it then, the magic that had been pulsing softly from Shawn, it disappeared. Then she felt his body sag, and his firm, callused hand fell from her cheek with a soft thud to the ground next to her.

Her breathing was starting to become erratic as she pulled his limp body to her, and she rocked. She heard Mara and Lila crying nearby, but all she could focus on was Shawn's limp body in her arms.

Her magic started to rise to her call.

She started to *wail*; her cries ripped from her as her body was licked with flames as she began to mourn the man she loved.

Kage laughed darkly and sinisterly, as if he relished her pain, as if he had *won*.

Her wails became cries of pure agony, and she screamed.

The scream was pure *rage* and *anguish*; it echoed across the valley, and in its wake rose a maelstrom of raging fire, built from her body with every syllable of her scream.

It surrounded her and Shawn, never touching their bodies, even though she could feel the heat coming from the flames now. It was almost volcanic in its intensity.

She screamed again. This time, the maelstrom burst free from where it had cradled against her and Shawn. It raced in every direction around them in blistering waves. The ground-breaking fell apart as the waves went.

She watched as the waves of volcanic heat passed over her cadre, the wolves, Mara, and Lila, like it was a ghost, only to slam into the ghouls and shadow beasts.

One moment, they were there snapping and clawing at her allies, the next, they were melted heaps scattered around, the grass burned as well, yet the spots where her allies stood remained green.

The inferno hit Kage dead on. Watched as the flesh melted off his bones as he screamed in agony, and his bones melted into a molten pile that landed in the burnt grass.

The inferno kept burning around them. She and Shawn were wrapped inside it, as she cried, as she mourned, she had been unleashed by his death. So, she kept burning and screaming for Shawn to come back to her.

CHAPTER FORTY~ONE

Everything was fucked.

Mathias had been through a lot in the past several hundred years of his life, but this might just take the fucking cake of fucked.

It had taken four hours to finally get to Audelia. Mathias could still feel the raging inferno that had raged around her and Shawn. Try as he might, every time he got close enough, even using the soft shadows that he hadn't used in just over a decade, could not keep the heat from hitting him. His hands still slightly ached from trying to get through the inferno.

He had not known such fear in decades, not since he had come home to find his mate dead and his son being threatened by his own grandfather. But, seeing his flower, the girl who had brought light back into his world after he lost Neya and had to keep away from his son. Seeing her scream in such blistering agony from loss, and not being able to get to her.

To comfort her when she needed it? That had torn him apart. He had screamed, trying to break through to her, but no one could get her to listen. She just gripped Shawn's body tighter, like she thought we would harm him.

Mara had said she was lost to the magic, that having had it

suppressed for so long, and then to have all these intense emotions had caused a cataclysmic overload for her.

To make it worse, she told them that if they didn't get Audelia calm soon, her magic would begin to devour her, like it had Kage and his creatures.

That terrified him. He did not want to lose her. Not his flower. Not the first ray of fucking sunlight in dark cold world since he lost Neya and had to leave his son. *Gods, his son.*

He could remember *now*. Remembered the boy he failed. His son, who used to play in the garden with Audelia, the same one who had created the necklace she was currently wearing. His son, who had looked so much like his mother.

He always failed. He couldn't even free her from the inferno that almost killed her; *no,* it was the wolf that had done that; it had been able to link into her and had put her to sleep.

Mathias had watched as her body went slack, and she collapsed upon the grass, her arms still tightly around Shawn's dead body. He had wasted no time in reaching her and pulling her to him. It took Skye, Bronn, and Alaric to get Shawn's body away from her, even in sleep, she had kept such a godlike grip, they had been scared that they would hurt her trying to remove his body.

Gods, Shawn. He hadn't quite liked the young male at first, but when the boy had taken the blood oath to prove he would do anything for *their* Queen. Fuck, he had such respect for him, then as the days went on and Mathias had started to train him. He had insisted upon, because he wanted to make sure Shawn could truly protect Audelia, not just as the future Queen, but because he didn't see what happened with Mathia and Neya, happen for Shawn and Audelia, he wanted to know the girl he loved as his own, that she was always safe with the man who held her heart.

Shawn had delivered and more. The tenacity reminded him so much of his own son.

He had died saving her, given the lasts of himself to make sure that fucker Kage could never take her again.

Mathias had watched his brother grip Shawn in his arms, and Mathias had kept Audelia in his own. The brothers carried both to the spot where they now rested.

They had come upon the ruins of the once brilliant, abundant city of Aldanien, and it was there they had seen the truth of the wrongness of the sprite Lila, who was in Gideon's arms, Lila had expended herself too much for having been cut off from most of her eternal magic too long.

The wrongness Lila had felt?

It was this.

The ruins of a city, one he knew well. The same city that, it being early sunset, should be a bustle of traffic from all corners of the realm, full of visitors from some of the smaller realms, by way of the portal house near the edge of the forest.

Aldanien should be brimming with laughter and bright colors from foreign fabrics and dyes, his mouth should be watered by the smells of baked goods and spices from cured meats.

Instead, it was like someone had torched it to the ground, but that had been some time ago. How long they still weren't sure, but he had to guess, as they settled in what used to be the Fernleaf Inn, a time ago, had been at least a century or two.

Everything felt *older* and smelled even worse now that his fae senses had returned. The rot seemed to linger, even though it looked like no one had travelled through these ruins for some time.

Mathias looked down at the young woman who was now curled up against him on the pile of ragged, moth-eaten blankets they had managed to find from several houses nearby. The bulk of their supplies had been left behind in the rush. She was still asleep; it was beginning to worry him. It had been hours, and they hadn't exactly been quiet getting to the campsite they had decided to make here instead of outside, where the firelight could easily be seen.

She barely even moved. Mathias was constantly checking her breathing, making sure he hadn't failed her even more.

Because he had *failed* her. She was hurting, and he could smell the change in her, the earth-shattering heartbreak of losing someone you love in such a brutal way. That scarred a being. Something he had pledged all those years ago in the garden of the palace when they first met, that she would never have happen to her bright, beautiful soul.

His flower. He was worried what these wilts to her soul and heart would do to her. He would do everything he could to make sure it wasn't worse for her.

That had started with having Mara clean her up. Luckily, they had a change of clothes for her—courtesy of the bag Audelia had been wearing. Lila and Mara, even as tired as they both were, cleaned her and changed her into the clothes stained with Shawn's blood. No one wanted her to wake up and see his blood upon opening her eyes again.

He could still smell it on her, though Mathias wasn't paying attention to the chatter around the flames, they had been discussing doing the rites of the afterlife come dawn. So, Audelia could say one final goodbye to him.

"Can we even still do the rights considering?" Mara asked, her voice soft; he could still hear the heartache in the light tones of her speech. What did she mean?

"Mar. Why wouldn't we give him the Rites of Morana? He died as a *warrior*. He deserves for Morana, the Goddess of Endings, to bring him to the halls of conquest." Mathias's voice was a soft growl. He did not like the idea of them even considering doing that to Shawn, denying him his place. That it was coming from Mara shocked him.

He may not be a part of their world, but clearly, after everything, he was. Not just because of the oath to Audelia, but that magic that had been surging from him during the fighting, and the fact that the very magic had brought them the wolves.

Shawn had saved their fucking, sorry asses.

"Because his soul is *gone*. That bastard used The Tenguistwa." Lila spit out her voice, groggy despite the edge of it, and everything in Mathias went still. "His soul will never reach that hall."

The Tenguistwa? No, *how the fuck did Kage get ahold of the blade of soul-killing?*

Instinctively, Mathias cradled Audelia closer, like he could protect her from what was to come. The pain of knowing the man she loved would be tortured and forced to kill until the agony of each death would eventually *rip* his soul apart.

Fuck. He wanted to find the bastard and bring him back just to kill him again.

He ran his palm up and down her arm absently, wanting to soothe her like he did when she was little and would come to find him in the library. Where he tended to hide from people of the court. She would be crying because of something he never fully understood, and they would snuggle in the window seat while he read, and she would curl up against him.

Those moments always made him wonder if that was how life could have been if Neya hadn't been killed, and his son could have had a happy childhood.

A wolf howled nearby, and the entire group went still. The wolves had followed them into the ruins and had taken up positions to guard them. That was something he still needed to understand what was going on.

"Are we going to address the fact that we have a pack of Adrastos wolves surrounding us?" Skye asked, as always, his brother seemed to sense the questions he too thought, but unlike Mathias, he was *able* to voice them.

As if they had sensed the question, the enormous wolf from earlier in the valley emerged from the shadows where it had been keeping watch by Shawn's body. They had wanted him close but not too close for when she woke.

The sight of it stole Mathias's breath, and worried him some, so he angled his body slightly to keep himself between the still unknown wolf and Audelia. The way the firelight caught the snow-white fur and the tufts of silver moonlight on its coat, it looked like a great, vengeful god.

Which was apparently the wrong move because the great wolf swung its brilliant violet gaze toward him and gave a low growl. One that sent a shiver down his spine.

"I would be very wary of how you move, Mathias," Bronn spoke quietly as they all watched the wolf make its way further into the camp. Its gaze swung around, assessing but always returning to Mathias, where he held Audelia curled under a warm blanket.

He slowly moved his hand to the hilt of his sword. It was an awkward angle if he had to pull it, but if the wolf tried to hurt Audelia, he wouldn't mind a cut to his leg.

I smell her on all of you. A voice echoed in his mind, and he stiffened. He noticed quickly that they all did.

"What the fuck?" Alaric swore, from his spot on a bedroll by the fire, he was still eating the remnants of the stag they had taken down earlier while everyone settled into the camp.

"Well, I don't know what's creepier, that he is talking in our heads or that he says he smells Audelia on all of us," Skye spoke from his spot a few rickety beds over, still near Mathias, he was guarding Audelia's other side, so she was covered at all times.

"I think *both*," Lila spoke, and Mathias watched her curl slightly closer to Gideon, who had also shifted his body to protect her from whatever would happen next.

That had been a shocking development when they were preparing the camp, and a sudden burst of jasmine and cedarwood filled the encampment, the telltale sign of a mating bond recently formed, and all heads had immediately swung to Gideon and Lila as their scents began to blend into one another.

Mathia's heart had felt like it was going to explode when those first scents hit his nose. It pulled him back to when he and Neya had first felt the bond snap together.

Shaking away the thoughts, he turned his gaze back to the wolf currently stalking to a spot dangerously close to him and Audelia, who was now shifting in her sleep, gripping him tighter, like she was trying to cling onto something or maybe someone in her sleep.

"Tha mi air do ghlacadh, Del," he whispered to her in

Gaelic, placing a gentle kiss on the top of her head, and pulling the fur blanket they had found over her more.

You care for her. The wolf tilted its head, watching Mathias. It was odd; a part of Mathias wondered if the wolf cared for her as well, which would definitely be weird, considering they hadn't dealt with the Adrastos wolves in at least a century, if not longer.

They usually kept to the forests, usually near a portal, or deep in the mountains. *Unless* they had a bonded, then they were never far from them.

They were never far from their bonded.

The words played around in his head over and over, as he looked from the wolf to Audelia asleep in his arms.

Mathias let out a sharp exhale as the realization hit him. "Fuck."

"Mathias?" It was Bronn, his voice smooth, tilted with worry, who had angled himself in front of Mara during this odd standoff between Mathias and the wolf.

Faron, that is my name, not the wolf. You do not see me calling you, the meat sacks. There was a glint of annoyance in the wolf, *sorry* Faron's eyes.

"The wolf, Faron. He is—he is *bonded* to Audelia—How the hell is that possible? I didn't think she had one before we left here?" Mathias's mind was swirling with all the past discussions on how to *improve* her safety over the years since he had joined the guard. Naseria never mentioned seeking The Adrastos as a guardian for Audelia because she had the cadre, and eventually, her mate would protect her whenever he was found.

"No, even Waldrom said she didn't have one here; he made inquiries when we heard Lefrain was stirring," Mara spoke, her voice worried. *Was she thinking what he was? Had they* missed *the signs?*

No, *I was not always hers; I was another's. Before that, I had wandered for centuries, until two hundred or so years ago, when I sensed my bonded through a portal for the first time. I have remained in these woods ever since,* waiting.

Mathias was trying to keep his cool, but this damn wolf was talking in what seemed like riddles, and it was frustrating.

"What does that have to do with our Queen?" Gideon asked, his voice hoarser than its usual jovial, rich tone.

In a way, it does. In others, it had nothing to do with her. Faron made to step closer to Audelia. It made Mathias stiffen. He still wasn't sure about *this.*

Audelia was all he had left. He did not want to risk her, too. Not on the *whim* of an ancient magical wolf.

This is not some whim, dragon rider. I was asked by my bonded to become hers, and hers I shall remain, until death.

At that quip, his thoughts went straight to Tadan. He couldn't feel the bond in the way he remembered, but he could feel the warm ember deep down. But that wasn't his focus. He would find Tadan another night. This one, his focus was the young woman in his arms, the one Faron was claiming, *his* bonded had asked her to become *hers.*

That means—oh *gods, Shawn?*

Indeed. Faron let out a small whimper, the noise causing Audelia to stir, her arm slipping from behind the folds of the fur, and that's when he noticed it.

Blood.

Not hers, but Shawn's. He could smell the slight difference; it had his scent on it. But it wasn't on her skin. It was on the bracelet she wore.

His breath caught. It was on the jade-beaded bracelet he had seen Shawn give her before they left. One he intended as a ring till he could get her one. His heart broke and then roared in his ears.

He couldn't let her wake up and see the bracelet covered in her love's blood. He quickly moved his hand and, as gently as he could, slipped the bracelet off her delicate wrist. He would clean it in a basin in a moment. He slipped the delicate jade beads into his trousers pocket.

"Indeed, what? Can you talk *plainly* for; I don't know *once*? I get wolves are cryptic at the best of times, but we need to know how you became *our* Queen's bonded and if you truly mean to *protect* her." Skye snapped. His brother never could handle people who don't just speak outright.

Faron sighed. Mathias stifled a laugh because he had never in all his years heard a wolf, fucking sigh.

Faron spoke into their minds again. *What I was telling your brother, young one, is that I was bonded to Shawn, I felt him just over two hundred years ago when a portal opened to the mortal realm. He called for me when you all arrived, and I was too late to save him, however.* The grief and regret were heavy in his voice.

"Did you just say, *over* two hundred years ago? That's *impossible*. Waldrom opened a portal going on fifteen years ago." Bronn's words were soft, like he was still working out the details.

But he was right, something was wrong. It had only been close to fifteen years since that day in her room.

What is wrong, young ones, is that this is not the realm you left. When Lefrain took hold of the realm, he opened it to the Acheron. He tore this realm, unleashing the beasts and demons from that cold, dark realm. His realm. The Goddess Aurelia, the keeper of Light and

Protector of Realms, sacrificed her life to seal this realm off from all others. Time has moved faster here than in the other realms. It was the only way to keep him from her. Faron dipped his head at Audelia. *In her final moments, she also summoned an ancient line of protectors to keep her safe in that realm.*

"That's why the portal felt *off*. The reason it felt older—*Oh gods*—" Lila's words trailed off, like she was now lost in thought of what that could mean. She turned and buried her face into Gideon's chest, like the truth was too much and she needed his comfort.

What it meant was that he was wrong before, they were not just fucked, they were so fucked, that he wasn't sure they would make it out of this.

"What ancient line? She *only* had us keeping watch all these years." Gideon asked.

You truly are young, if you cannot even see what was in front of you these years. Faron sounded very annoyed at this point as he came around to Audelia and plopped down beside her.

Mathias wasn't sure they would get much more out of the wolf.

"*Shawn*," Mara whispered, like she couldn't even fathom what she had said.

"What?" Bronn's gaze whipped to his mate's face.

"That's *who* he is talking about, Shawn was *always* there. Whenever she needed someone, Shawn was there. He was her protector, and when he was dying...." Her words trailed for a second, and she sucked in a breath like she was fighting her grief. "He *transferred* that protection, didn't he, Faron?"

Yes. He asked that I bond with her and protect the woman he loves, so here I remain, and here I will gladly be —friend, brother, whatever she needs, I will give.

"So, let's get this straight, our Queen had a bonded we didn't know was her bonded, and now she has a new one, and to top all that batshit crazy off, it's been over two hundred years since we left?" Alaric asked, he had his daggers out now and had been cleaning the blood from the blades so they wouldn't damage the steel.

*The quickness of a young mind is quite—*adept.

Skye busted out, laughing his ass off. "I believe that Faron just called you *slow*." His laugh was cut off by Alaric throwing a bone from the stag at Skye, making the others laugh.

After that, they all fell silent, no one knowing what to say in response to this *unexpected* turn of events. Mathias continued to rub Audelia's back in a soothing gesture, hoping she would wake soon. She had to be hungry by now. But he did not want to disturb her sleep either.

She will wake soon. Faron spoke from his spot near her, his very large head resting just below her feet above the blanket. *However, she is not entirely herself. You must be careful with her.*

Mathias, not wanting to worry the others, as they all spoke around the fire. He focused and stretched a part of himself that had not been done in a very long time. He spoke down the precarious lines of a bond, this one shakier because Faron was not his bonded.

Because of her loss of Shawn? Earlier, you put her to sleep. Thank you for that. Mathias felt his shadows stretch now that he opened the channels of his magic. It felt strange to use them again, but it also felt good, like stretching an old muscle.

They glittered as spots of moonlight from above cast over them, reminding him of the first time Neya had seen them; she called them beautiful, more so when he used them to caress her cheek from across the table where they had sat.

Yes, and no. Their bond was strong; they loved each other. It is something that usually does not happen when a bonded has a mate. But he is lost to her. Still is. Faron whimpered softly as if the thought caused him pain.

She has a mate?

Yes. But she does not remember him. Nor does she fully remember you; something has blocked her, something bigger than us all.

Those words sounded ominous as fuck.

Wait, she can't remember anything? But the spell broke for the rest of us? Why not her? And also, since when did she have a mate? She was eight *when we left this realm.* Mathias looked down at her; she was stirring more, and a furrow had begun to form on her brow. Did she know yet? How on earth can they even start to help her if she *still can't* remember?

No, another being, possibly one of the gods, put a block on her memories; it blocked the first spell from completely unraveling. To protect her, she will retain her fae immortality but not *her memory.* Faron tilted his head at her, like he was sensing some change in her. *I am surprised you asked if she has a mate, considering she wears a part of him on her.*

Part of him on her? What the fuck did that mean, but it was there, a scent he had always smelled on her, it was softer than her main smells, but at one point, he recalled it was stronger.

She shifted again, rolling onto her back, and he saw it then; it glinted in the firelight.

The necklace.

The one his son had made her all those years ago, it danced in the firelight, the delicate gold wrapping around two stones, one a pearl color with a small cherry blossom encased, forever in bloom, and just below, he could see it swirling now, a dark blue almost black crystal where shadows swirled in its depths.

Wait—that means.

Yes, your son is her mate.

Before Mathias could say another damn word, he stopped, his body froze, and he saw Faron snap up from his spot from the corner of his vision.

His breathing sped up as he watched Audelia's eyes snap open. The blue irises were bright; aether seemed to dance just behind the blue.

Fuck.

CHAPTER FORTY~ TWO

Audelia's eyes snapped open, everything felt sharper like the film had been lifted from her eyes and her senses.

Everything felt stronger, but there was this crushing wrongness.

Shawn...

He echoed in her thoughts, feeling his body going cold in her arms. The inferno that had been burning around them, it had licked against them. At first, it hadn't hurt, but then it had become scorching, but she hadn't been able to turn it off, it just kept growing in strength. Audelia had prepared to let her magic *consume* her and Shawn.

She didn't know if she could face this new reality of her life *without* him.

But before the inferno of her rage and magic could take them both, a voice had echoed in her head. It felt different, not like when Waldrom would render her unconscious for their little chats.

No, this had felt older, softer, kind, and comforting. She had *leaned* into it, hoping it would take the grief away. Feeling everything go black around her, she had tightened her hold on Shawn before everything went dark.

She had given in to that dark, only now she felt that burning in her soul again, that *ancient thing* willing her to wake once more.

She felt a warm body beside her, as if she had curled against someone. Her first thought was Shawn, that maybe everything had been some horrible dream, and when she looked around, they would be in the room they had shared at Bronn's, and that she hadn't watched Kage kill the man she loved.

"Del?" It was Mathias's voice, it was drenched in concern, and like one would talk to a wounded animal, and it was extremely close. So close that she could feel the richness of his cadence beneath her ear.

She was lying against Mathias, she quickly jolted away, not wanting comfort, not wanting anyone but Shawn, but he was gone.

Because of her.

She looked around her; they were currently camped in the ruins of some building, a home, maybe? Considering the broken bits of bedding here and there.

What happened to this place? She thought.

Audelia took in the looks of worry on everyone's faces. It looked like everyone had made it, except for the twins and... and *Shawn.*

The thought had her heart sinking. The tears beginning to well again.

What surprised her, though, was the giant white wolf with specks of silvery moonlight on his fur and those beautiful, ethereal violet eyes. It watched her, its eyes brimming with grief that echoed her own.

Trust the wolf, Faron. Shawn's voice played in her head. The last words he had told her were to *trust* the wolf who had come. He had brought the others, who had saved them. *But why? Why was there a fucking giant wolf in their camp.* She had figured the wolves would have left the moment the battle had ended, before; she had laid *waste* to the valley.

Her eyes swept wildly; she felt her magic begin to surge again. Like, she couldn't get a handle on it. As if it wanted to consume her again.

It was feeding off her grief.

Breathe. You need to breathe, fire princess. The voice from earlier spoke again. It sent a chill down her spine, but then she felt herself take a giant gulp of air and then another.

Good girl.

Her gaze swung that time to the wolf staring at her, her mind barely registered that she had stood and had begun to back away. Everyone was coming closer to her. They were all too close, had too much sympathy in their eyes.

"How—How are you *in* my head?" she whispered, her voice shaking.

Because I am your new bonded, the wolf spoke, his voice was warm, inviting a balm to her chilled bones.

"Little one?" It was Bronn's voice that broke the raging thoughts going through her head. His voice was soothing as he used her childhood nickname, the one he told her about.

Wait, the nickname.

The ones that have been hurting every time he or another of them uses it. She searched for the memory. They had *told* her, even Lila had said, as soon as they passed through the portal, the spell Waldrom had put on them would be broken.

It would break. She *would* remember. Everything had been so chaotic before. She hadn't had time to focus on anything but staying alive and keeping the ones she loved alive. She had *failed* even at that.

Shawn's loss was like a dagger at her throat, even as hope bloomed at the idea of truly remembering herself.

She took a deep breath, just like the ones Bronn had taught her over the years, to center herself and focus on what she needed to.

So, she did, she traced through her mind. It felt like opening a map to her life; she could feel the pages unfolding, but where there should be a kaleidoscope of memories, those little core memories —everything that made her, *Audelia*. All she saw were fuzzy pages. *Nothing.* She gripped harder, maybe she was still too stunned by everything that had happened.

Maybe it would take a minute, so she pulled and grabbed and began to rip at those pages in her mind. But nothing. All that was left in its place was a ringing *hollowness,* where her life should have *been.*

"Little dove?" It was Mara this time, her voice closer as Audelia opened her eyes. Her aunt blurred before her as the tears fell heavily.

She couldn't remember.

It wasn't *there.*

Those words. The ones that should be soothing, especially

now, with Shawn's loss so fucking heavy on her. They felt like more daggers at her throat.

It *hurt.*

"Don't—don't fucking call me that!" She yelled; it came out choked. The magic inside her began to swell again. Raising to the call of her emotions.

Calm down, fiery one. Faron spoke in her mind again.

Gods, why won't they just leave her alone. Her world was imploding again. They were fucking liars again. They *promised.* They said that all they had to do was get through the fucking portal, and she would be herself again.

She would *wake* up. She *would* remember her parents, remember *all of them*, remember why she loved them so much. It wasn't that she *didn't* love them, but she loved who they had become to her, and she desperately wanted to feel......*attached.*

Now, all that existed was this *hollow* feeling; she could see the love in their eyes, but she couldn't feel it.

It rang so fucking hollow and the only one that never felt hollow. The one who turned her entire world, the one who saw HER. Not the lost queen, not the girl they raised—*just* Audelia.

He was *gone.*

Not just gone, *destroyed.*

The world spun for a moment, and she could hear their voices, but nothing seemed to register. Shaking her head, she cleared some of the grief enough to see that they were all coming closer to her.

Wanting to comfort her.

She didn't want it.

Not from them.

Maybe one day again. But right now, she didn't want to be near them. She needed to see Shawn.

Did they bury him? She didn't know what had happened after she killed Kage and his creatures. Had she gotten them all?

"She can't remember you idiots, *stop* fucking calling her those *names*." It was Mathias. He was yelling at the others. It warmed her a little. Of everyone besides Shawn, *he* had seen her, too. Had seen that the nicknames and the constant telling of stories about her as a kid had wrecked her. *Picked* away at her. Made all those insurmountable *expectations* seem unattainable.

Gasps came from all of them except him. Mathias, who always knew more than the others when it came to her. As much as she would enjoy his comfort, it would mean remaining, and she couldn't right now. He nodded. *He knew.*

She used that opportunity to back away toward the remains of what had once been an archway, hopefully to the outside. She needed to get out of this place.

It felt like the walls would fall on her and trap her in this hell.

This hell, where she still didn't fully know who she was. A hell where her body felt even more foreign than it ever had. Had she changed somehow? Everything had felt sharper, stronger than before.

Because your fae self has reawakened. Your immortal again, fiery one. Faron spoke again in her head, and she saw him take a step closer. She still didn't get what he meant by *bonded.*

Mara and Bronn took a few steps closer to her. She saw Mara move her hand into her pocket and the glint of a bottle in the firelight.

They were going to drug her and put her to sleep again as if she were some wild, untamed animal.

No. She didn't want that. She didn't want to sleep. She *wanted* Shawn. She needed to see his body, see that he was truly gone.

"Don't come near me." She sneered, her magic surged and skated across her body, not in flames this time, but in little dances of what looked like wispy hues of blues and purples of light.

"It's *okay*, we aren't going to hurt you, Audelia, we want to *help* you," Mara spoke again, her words sounded comforting, but Audelia didn't want them. Didn't want the damn pity she saw in each of their eyes.

It all felt so fucking hollow. She knew this wasn't fair to all of them; they loved her, and she loved them, but it was *too much* right now.

She watched all of them except Mathias take several steps closer, their hands up. It just angered her. Her magic swelled again; those little swirls of blues and purples shimmered over her, blasting out toward the people who loved her and sending them all flying back.

Tears streamed down her face as she whispered, *"I'm sorry."*

Then, she turned and ran through the crumbling archway.

The coolness of the night air caressed her heated skin, soothing her somewhat. Everything was dark; twilight was on the cusp of becoming total night, but the moon was providing plenty of light as she took in her surroundings.

They seemed to have taken refuge in what was the ruins of some large city. As she ran, she saw crumbling buildings. Down one road she chose were the molded woods of what looked like old stalls of some sort. Maybe this had been a trading outpost at one point.

It was *confusing*. She could have sworn Gideon's lessons had told her that many abundant cities lived near where most of the portals opened, including the great tree they had come out of. Maybe they had moved farther away just in case others came looking for Kage and his creatures.

Thoughts of him made shivers run down her spine. When he had talked as Shawn died, his voice hadn't been his. It was someone else's, and she did not want to come across who that was. Though a part of her knew it had to have been Lefrain using Kage as a puppet.

A shimmer of something *pulled* at her, breaking her thoughts. She started to run toward it, knowing she probably shouldn't; she had no idea what was going on right now, and her memory was still gone.

But the shimmer pulled at her more, begging her to follow, so she did. A part of her knew what was at the end, but she didn't understand how that was possible. However, the shimmer was identical to that of the last revenants, as if some string was binding them together. She had felt it briefly in the valley, but it had been stronger than it was now.

She stumbled over a few uneven spots in the cobblestone paths where roots had taken over. Righting herself, she pulled up short as she saw what looked to be the ruins of some large pillory. Where at one point in time, people would stand around listening to announcements or watching punishments.

But it was what she saw on it *now* that broke a sob from her chest.

There, with the moonlight pouring down upon it, was a body covered in a gossamer sheet. From here, it looked like the moon was kissing the body lying there, one final goodbye.

She knew it was *him*. Every fiber of her soul and heart screamed as she ran towards the body.

The shouts of the others, telling her to wait and that everything would be okay, made her falter in her steps. A small moment of relief hit her that she hadn't harmed them too much.

She ran faster, not caring if she fell, she needed to see. Needed to know what her heart and soul were screaming at her, that he was gone.

Her heart was pounding in her ears as she stood before the body. The shimmering feeling was stronger here as some last part of the magic she had felt from him had lingered, luring her here to say goodbye.

She didn't want to. She didn't want this to be the last time she saw him.

But she *needed* to see.

It hit her as she stepped closer. The scent she knew was his, a mix of mint and bergamot, with hints of some sort of woody leather she couldn't quite place anymore. The scents that had always brought her comfort were now cold—*broken*, slowly falling away.

No.

She rushed the final feet and, stealing her heart, she ripped away the sheet blocking his body from her and the elements...

She gasped.

He was gone. He really was gone.

Her hand shook as she reached out to touch his now-cold skin; all the warmth was gone. She sobbed as she traced the lines of his face. He looked *peaceful*, as if he were merely asleep.

Gods, she wished he were. That he would feel her touch and wake and tell her she was beautiful and that he loved her. But he didn't. Not a single flinch, as she looked over his body. Her heart was shattering.

"I'm so *sorry*, my love. I am sorry I couldn't stop this, that you died saving me. I wish I had been stronger for you. I know you would say that I don't need to be, to lean on you, that you could handle the weight. But who do I lean on now?" Her voice was soft as she leaned her forehead against his cold one.

Her tears fell heavily, her magic not far behind, but it was the raging inferno, or the one she felt earlier, *this* was different, softer. Like a part of her was waking up that she didn't understand.

The bright light was back; she could feel it. Her chest had become warm, despite how cold she felt kneeling beside her love's dead body.

She didn't want to be here. *She needed to leave.*

She screamed into the night, all her grief and frustration at failing Shawn. Failing everyone, she had seen it —the *cost* of it. Even in her wild state, she saw how tired everyone looked. Lila was as white as a ghost; her usually tanned skin was gone.

Her failures, all her shortcomings, everything, had led to *this*. This was her punishment for not being strong enough.

She could hear voices, but they sounded muffled, as if they were behind a wall. Looking up from where her body had rested over Shawn's, she saw her cadre: her aunt and uncle, and the wolf Shawn had told her to trust, *Faron*.

Some kind of barrier was blocking them from her; she felt it, it felt like parts of herself.

Had she done that?

She steps away from Shawn's body. Every step felt like more and more of herself was falling away. She was becoming a husk of her former self. Between the loss of him and this new, strange feeling body, she couldn't, she didn't *want* to think about anything.

She just wanted to leave.

She gripped the necklace around her neck, the one that always brought her calm when she was younger. "Audelia!" Mathias calls to her. His voice panicked.

He never panics; it hurts to hear it, but she can't. She needed to *leave*.

Leave.

I Can't be here.

The words play over and over in her head, and she decides in a split second that she truly can't remain. Not with these people who are strangers and yet not. Not even for Mara, Lila, and Bronn, whom she had known this whole time, could she remain. *It was too much.*

Shawn was gone, and she wanted to be gone too.

So, she turned and ran and kept going even as she felt the brilliance of the light in her chest expand and engulf her. Not as the smell of pine filled the air, replacing the musty smell of the decaying city she had been in.

CHAPTER FORTY~THREE

The scent of pine was everywhere. She didn't understand what had happened. One moment, she was in the ruins of some city the cadre had taken refuge in, and now, she could hear the crunch of grass on her boots and the smell of heavy forest around her as the wind picked up. The last remnants of her magic swirled around her.

Fuck, what had she done?

All she could remember as the swell of magic engulfed her was that she wanted the warmth and safety that Shawn used to give her.

She looked around the pitch-black around her, and she could see a little, which shocked her because the moon, where she currently was, barely made itself known through the thick overbrush of the trees, with too few pockets of silvery moonlight. Everything was cast in a never-ending darkness, yet she could see some.

It was slowly getting brighter as she ran, like a heavy moon-filled night. It was as if someone had placed a filter over her vision, granting her the ability to see in the dark; she could get used to *that*.

It felt like her body had been replaced, and she had been placed in a new one that felt like her own but didn't quite *fit* right.

Where the fuck was she?

A sudden sinking feeling filled her. She couldn't remember her life here, which meant she had no fucking clue where anything was, and now....

Gods.

Now, she was away from people she knew, people that she trusted, even if it felt like the betrayal that had only just buried itself away had clawed back to the surface, suffocating her in the process.

She was so *fucked.*

What did she do now?

Okay, okay, she could figure this out; she was smart. Gideon told her she had a keen eye for strategy. Surely, she could figure *this* clusterfuck out.

She stood motionless for a moment, the sudden stopping making the world spin. She had barely even realized she had *still* been running; it was as if her body was pulling her somewhere and hadn't wanted to stop.

She took a deep breath and listened around her, knowing that even if she still couldn't figure out where she was, she could at least see if she was *alone*. If she even had time to figure things out. *Please don't be some monster lurking in the dark.*

She took another deep breath for good measure and began to listen. Around her, she could hear the wind rustling the branches above her in gentle whispers into the night, the hoot of an owl nearby singing a balm to her heart. But other than that, she didn't hear the crunching of leaves or sticks, as if something of a good weight had trodden over them.

Good, she was alone.

Another thought quickly followed.

Fuck, she was alone in an unknown forest, in a realm she didn't know.

The panic started to rise again, but she shoved it down. She could do this. Shawn had believed in her.

Yeah, and then he died, because of it. Some dark, cold voice echoed through her head.

She shook it off; she couldn't dwell on it, as much as she wanted to curl into a ball and cry out all her grief. In this moment, she couldn't. For some reason, as she had fled for a moment to breathe, her magic had surged and sent her away.

Audelia began to look herself over; she needed to know what she had with her because she had run off without her bag, and honestly couldn't remember what she had on her in the moments that Shawn died.

A sob tore through her resolve, she threw a hand over her mouth to muffle the noise, hoping nothing heard her.

She shook her head again. She felt along the curves of her body, the clothes felt different than the ones she had put on this morning, or was that yesterday? *Fuck* she didn't even know how long she had been out for.

It didn't matter, the clothes fit, but they were tighter against her curves, clearly not made for her, probably Lila's they were similar in some spots of their bodies, just Audelia had thicker thighs and ass, and her breasts were larger than the lithe form of her best friend, but they fit.

She still had on her baldric corset, and Audelia sighed in relief that the two small daggers that Mathias had given her were still in their spots. Good, that's good, she had something to protect herself with, and possibly, if she could figure it out, hunt with.

Which she needed to do soon because she realized she was fucking famished.

Her braid had been redone, from what she felt, and she felt along the slope of her neck to wear the necklace with the two stones always rested just above her breasts. Good, she didn't know what to do if she lost that. It had been with her from the beginning and was the one thing in her life that always made sense.

She had never fully understood why, but touching it always grounded her; she felt at peace, *safe*. She felt it pulse under her fingertips. An answer. To what she didn't know.

Moving her hand lower, she felt the slight bulge of the coin purse Mara had given her on the walk to The Glade. It didn't have many of the coins used here, but hopefully enough that if she could find a town or somewhere, she could purchase food, supplies, and information.

Skye had told her that in this realm, if you were ever lost and in need of something, someone knew it, you just needed the right coins to get them to talk. Yet, she didn't know a single value of any of them.

She didn't feel pockets on the thick breeches she had been put in. They truly had changed all her clothes, then she supposed they would have needed to check for injuries, she had been covered in... in Shawn's blood.

Shawn.

Her hand immediately shot to her left wrist, where she

should have felt the cool, smooth stones of the jade bracelet he had given her the morning before everything changed. She felt nothing, just bare skin.

It was *gone.*

She had lost the bracelet, the one Shawn had given her as a token of his intentions to propose to her when things settled. It was gone like he was.

Had it broken during the battle? Had she lost it in her mad dash and transport here?

She turned around, debating if she could even find it here. She wasn't even sure what direction she had been running from.

In the dark of the forest, it all looked the same, and she had been so lost in her grief that she hadn't even noticed it wasn't there or which way she had been running. Shit.

In a wave, grief crashed over her as she gripped her bare wrist. Her knees gave out, and she felt the rough ground bite into her knees as she pulled her arms to her stomach and doubled over. Her forehead touched the cool blades of grass, and she cried.

It was gone, the last piece of Shawn she had.

She let the tears fall again. She gave herself over to it. She didn't care what happened. Didn't *care* that she was queen to people who probably needed her. She just let the grief wash over her.

The wind picked up around her like a small cyclone, fallen leaves swirled as she felt the familiar prickles over her skin, and she felt the heavy feeling pull her under.

She didn't hear the wind anymore, she heard nothing, just felt that familiar heavy dark. The one that meant she was on the ground unconscious, and she was in this strange plane again.

"Waldrom?" Her voice sounded so small, so fucking *broken.*

This time, he wasn't just a shadow; she gasped as she watched a man with sandy blonde hair walk into her line of vision. A small orb of light danced around above her head. He was handsome; he looked far younger than she had thought he would, tall and strong-looking. However, he had this regal air about his features, the sandy hair was pulled back from his face, but still half of it was down to her shoulders, he had beautiful hazel eyes, with specks of what looked like Aether dancing around the rims of the hazel, his eyes were keen and knowing. He had a soft, kind face and a trim beard. That seemed at odds with the rest of his face, like it aged him. He had a slightly crooked nose, as if someone had broken it, but it hadn't healed correctly.

He knelt in front of her just enough to help pull her up to her feet. "I'm here, my little star." His voice was softer, full of remorse, but still rich and honeyed as before.

She didn't know why, but with his words, she launched herself into his arms, holding tight to him. She felt him gasp in shock and then felt his arms band around her to hold her.

"I am so sorry, my dear. But we do not have much time. *Things* have happened." His voice sounded worried, and Audelia pulled away from him to look at him more closely, worry etched the lines of his face.

"What happened?" She asked. "Does this have to do with why my memories aren't back?"

"Fuck." His eyes searched her, and then his warm hands were at her cheeks as he looked at her more closely, as if he were seeing past her into her mind or maybe her soul.

"This—this was not from me. Audelia, things have become dire. I need you and the others to find me. I am in the Cave of Asida; my sister knows the location. Come find me. I will do what I can." He looked beyond her for a moment, like he was seeing something she didn't. "You can do this, my little star. I know everything has gone wrong, and I am so sorry for that. I did not predict a goddess shutting down the realms, or that so much time would pass. But please, my dear girl, *be safe*. I shall see you soon."

Before she could say another word, or tell him that she wasn't with Mara, or what the fuck her meant by more time had passed? He was gone, and she felt the world around her shift.

Audelia woke with a gasp, her head pounding, and the remaining embers of the light on her chest beginning to fade.

Well, shit.

That had been all of barely helpful, and she had the feeling that Waldrom didn't understand that talking cryptically when someone still didn't know her realm was probably not the best idea.

But she needed to carry on, and she would be cautious until she knew what he meant by that someone had sealed her memories in a way that wove over what he had initially done, that apparently a goddess had sealed off the realms?

It was all too much, she couldn't focus on it all, but she didn't know one thing; he had given her a destination, The Cave of Asida.

Sighing, she looked around as she stood again, picking the direction to her right, she started to walk, she knew she should find somewhere to rest, maybe climb a tree and hope she doesn't fall out, but she needed to walk, she didn't want to sleep even though her body felt like it had been pulled in a million directions and ached.

So, she walked. Letting her movements just become monotonous, tried not to really think about anything, just hoping that she would see the lights of a town or something. She needed to know where she was. Hopefully, her magic had helped *some,* and she wasn't too far from the cave she needed to reach.

Hopefully, she would also find her friends, she missed *them.* The hate towards them that had coursed through her like a tidal wave was drifting farther and farther away with every step toward the unknown.

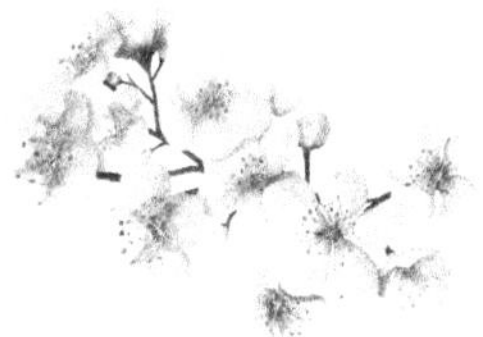

Audelia had walked for what had been hours. She wasn't even sure anymore. The constant blackness was driving her nuts. Wherever her magic had taken her, it had to be so far removed from civilization that she was beginning to fear it would be days or weeks before she saw another person.

She was so unbelievably tired, every muscle in her body was screaming from how much she ached, she wasn't sure if it was from walking or from battle earlier, probably both, if she were being honest.

She needed to find a spot to rest soon.

A little further down the way she had headed, she saw in the far-off distance a light, the soft glow of something; from this distance, she couldn't be sure if it was from a village, home, or maybe someone's campfire.

She weighed her options for a moment; she could head away from it to find somewhere to rest, or she could head as far as her body would take her toward it. It could be a village, where she could purchase a room, and hopefully some food, and in the morning get answers.

But could she really trust people? She was a lost Queen in a realm she couldn't recall, what if she walked to a foe?

Gods, she had been so fucking stupid in her needing to leave, in riding her emotions so fucking hard that her magic had done this.

Bronn was right. She needed to get a *better* handle on it. A pang of regret worked its way free at the thoughts of her uncle.

Something soft caressed her cheek. It felt feather light, comforting, which shook her to her core because as she turned toward the touch, there was nothing there.

No one. Had it been an illusion, her tired mind playing tricks on her? Or something more.

Whatever it had been, it was gone now. She was still alone, lost in some gods forsaken forest, heading toward a light that had at least grown brighter, but still some distance off.

She couldn't keep going. She felt her knees shaking. At this point, she was tempted to just drop to the ground and curl around herself till sleep came.

The leaves rustled to the left. She saw it then, a large oak tree with what looked like a good-sized knot indented at the base of its trunk. It would make the perfect place to rest. Her back would be protected. Only her front would be exposed. She could work with that.

Also, at this point, she didn't even care; she just needed to rest.

So, she trudged toward the tree. The closer she got, the more she noticed it was much bigger than it had been from where she had seen it. She would be able to curl into it, and as long as no one moved right in front of the trunk, they would not see her.

Perfect.

She could get a few hours of rest before dawn. The light she had seen was still in view as she looked behind her, so come dawn, she would make her way toward where it had been. *Hopefully*, finding help.

Audelia carefully crawled into the opening of the knot; it was more comfortable than she had figured it would be, although still certain parts dug into her skin. But she would get used to it.

It was only for a few hours, anyway. She hoped Gaios, the god of luck, whom Alaric loved bringing up, would be on her side.

So, she curled in to hold onto her warmth and removed one of her daggers just in case someone did come across her. She would be *ready*.

Sleep took her quickly, and she dreamed she was on the back of some great creature. It was scaled and radiated blue and green scales that shimmered in the sunlight. The wind whipped through her hair, and she realized she was in the clouds; she was flying. *Oh gods.* The head of the beast she rode turned slightly, and she took in the large head, the snout and scales, and the small horns that dotted its face. Its eyes were a deep red, with flecks of gold in them—familiar. And reptile-like.

Oh gods, she was on a dragon, wasn't she? A muffled voice broke through the revelry, but it didn't sound like hers. It sounded velvety and deep—a *male* voice.

Before she could try to say something, to figure out why she was dreaming about being on a fucking dragon, she was yanked by the arm roughly.

Audelia was startled awake and swiped out with her dagger as best she could, considering her arm was being held, and took in the three huge, inhuman-looking males standing before her.

They were disgusting. They looked human at first glance, but as her eyes adjusted, she took in the too-large eyes that were pitch black, the oddly angled faces, the protruding ears that seemed on the verge of beginning to flop, pointed teeth, and one of the men the less human of his counterparts had skin the color of moss colored tree bark.

The image before her sent shivers down her spine.

"Looks, what we found. A little rabbits caught in our traps. Shall we plucks it?" The one holding her spit, his voice was like nails against a chalkboard mixed with a growl.

"Lots of morsels she is. Let's have a taste." Another said, his voice garbled and soured. He was missing teeth, she noticed, as he opened his mouth and dragged a long-forked tongue across his cracked lips, and even from here, she could smell the rot coming from him.

"Let me go!" She yelled and began to fight with everything she had to break free. The three of them laughed, the sound raked down her spine.

"Ohs, looks like we got a fighter we haves. She'll fetch a

pretty-pretty copper." The one with the moss tree bark for skin sneered, his cheeks heated like whatever he had seen in her fight delighted him, in a way she did not want to find out.

The one holding her looked at his friend for a moment, and she used that to her advantage and threw her wait into a twist, her arm screamed in protest, but as she moved, she brought his body off-kilter, and she dropped the dagger out of her hand that couldn't move to drop it into the other, and fast as an asp she struck.

She landed the blow right between his ribs, or at least she hoped. She had no idea if he even had ribs. Regardless of it, had done the job, and he howled in pain and fell to the ground. Dropping his hold, she held her grip tighter, feeling the wetness from his blood.

And she bolted.

She raced as fast as her legs could carry her. She could hear the heavy footsteps of the other two giving chase. Fear coursed through her, and her magic rose to meet the feeling. She hoped it would send her to another place this time. Somewhere safer.

She didn't have that luck, as she tried to extend the magic in some way, she honestly wasn't sure what to do with the magic, but she twisted in her run and threw a handout toward the two chasing her, fuck, they were gaining fast.

The magic sputtered. Nothing came out; she could feel it in her veins, could feel where it slept, that it was writhing, waiting for her call. But even as she kept screaming in her head to do something, it didn't answer.

Fuck, she was probably too exhausted.

She slammed into the chest of someone or something, and before she could react, she was hauled up by her throat, and to her horror, an orange-skinned creature, like the ones who had found her, was staring up at her from where he dangled her in the air.

She gasped for air and kicked with everything she had. "Having trouble, boys? Foxy, you trying to cause trouble? I like the troublin' ones." The creature tilted its head, its beady, bulging eyes unnerved her, as did the tusk-like teeth coming from its mouth or the way it seemed to *hungrily* take her in.

"It's a good chase, Itti. We found good one. It fetch a very good price. Many will wants to taste it, use it, maybe eats it." One of them, who had chased her, said it sounded amused by her.

The thought of each thing it said made her want to throw up. Gods, what would they do to her, because she knew they weren't talking about just having her for a meal, it was worse than that by the gleam that now shown in the creatures' eyes, or the ripping of her clothing from behind her, she could feel the cool air hit parts of her skin. The scrape of nails from meaty fingers against her skin.

"Looks, like a unspoils ones too. All that pales skin. Oh yes, oh yes, pretty coppers." Another new voice leered.

Fuck, there were even more.

Think, *think*, Audelia.

An idea struck her, one she had learned from lessons with Bronn, about this very type of hold. With the thought in her mind, Audelia went limp. Forcing her entire body to go heavy.

It worked, but it didn't just lower her. She was tossed like a rag doll. She gasped as her body hit the trunk of a tree, and she watched as the creatures began to circle her.

Fuck, they were huge. It was as if they had grown, or her brain was scrambled from the hit and loss of oxygen. Her throat ached.

Audelia stood, her legs shaky, but she forced the magic in her to settle into her legs, hoping it would help her move, and she ran just as the one closest to her went to grab her.

She didn't make it far before she was yanked by her braid. She cried out in pain, the strands coming loose in the hold one of them had on her.

Gods, she was going to die.

No.

She wouldn't allow whatever these things were to kill her, she grabbed the still-sheathed dagger from her baldric and twisted hard, she felt some of her hair yank from her skull and the dull ache from it.

But she took her dagger and threw it at the one who had grabbed her hair. Before it could respond, she ran again.

Pushing as hard as she could, fighting the tears, fighting to break through. She wanted her friends, and she wanted Shawn. She wanted *someone*. Someone to protect her. Until then, she would fight and keep fighting.

The world around her went darker, like the light that even she could see by had disappeared and before she could do a damn thing, she felt thick muscled arms wrap around her waist, and a warm hand gripped over her mouth, cutting off any scream as she was pulled against the expanse of a large chest.

"Hush, fierce one, if you do not wish to die." The voice was thick, warm, and rich in its baritone, and screamed whispered promises in the dark. Her heart began to pound as the body twisted them, and she was slammed against the bark of a tree.

The man's body encased her from sight, and she looked up at him and was met with eyes of a deep green encased in midnight.

CHAPTER FORTY~FOUR

Kairos had been asleep against the thick upper trunk of the tree for a short while, his long legs stretched out over the branch. His shadows were currently keeping him both balanced and secure to the tree.

It had been a god-awful long night, a week, if he was honest. He had been tracking the flesh traders he had found a bounty on since he and Eirlys had parted ways so she could return home for a time. He fucking hated when she went back to Dharan to see her family. He never went; he wasn't welcomed, and he wouldn't take away her ability to go back home, not after it had taken so long for her even to be allowed back.

He wished he could. Wished he had a home. It was never the place he was forced to remain in by his father, never the barracks where he had been turned from a boy into the killer he is now.

No, his home was gone. All he had left was his mother to care for, and to save her from the *hel* she endured because of his father.

He didn't care if he had to destroy this whole damn realm if it meant ending the bastard who had created him and saved his mother from her torment.

He needed to save her; he couldn't fail, *not again.* Not like he did with *her.* The grief that had never fully settled rose toward the surface, and he pushed it back down again.

So, he did what he did best, he shut off his emotions. His focus became revenge, which is why he had taken the bounty from Aillard. He knew that his father routinely did business with flesh traders to get him whatever he needed for his sick desires. This group, he had seen before in the castle, knew they worked regularly with his father.

Which meant they had information on his father, information that could lead to, hopefully, some weakness he could exploit.

So he could kill his father.

His shadows pulled at him, breaking his thoughts, and then he heard it. The sounds of footsteps coming this way. They were light and swift, female from the soft breaths that his shadows picked up on from this distance.

"Looks like the fleshers found a new quarry, poor thing. But perfect for catching them." He whispered to himself as he began to climb down; he used his shadows to mask every noise he made.

He threw a wall of shadow over himself and began to walk towards the sounds of running, and as he grew closer to the poor soul who would die for running if he knew Itti, their leader, he would kill her for making him work at this late hour.

His shadows pulled at him again, making him change course, and as he did, everything emptied out of him.

Every thought, every plan, gone. As he took in the woman, the shadows had pointed out.

She was *glorious.*

And it both pissed him off to no end and intrigued him.

Kairos watched as the young woman ran through the forest, her steps sound, as if she had run these woods every day of her life, but that *couldn't* be. The forest of Semperion, since the dawn of the ages, had always changed its paths. If one didn't know the rhythms of her ever-changing branches, one would *die*.

Yet, as he watched her, the forest seemed to sing in her presence, halting the assault of the changing, like it wanted her to escape. Which was *strange*, usually, the forest relished in the lives taken. But not *her*. *Why?* He wondered.

His breathing picked up as a patch of moonlight cascaded down over her, illuminating her features. His breath caught as he saw her face, and he realized it wasn't the moonlight causing her to glow; it was *her*.

She was glowing as she ran, like the way the Goddess Kainda, the huntress. Her red hair was in a thick braided plait gliding behind her, and her delicate features had his heart racing again. He had never seen such a gorgeous woman, and he had bedded plenty in the past two hundred years of his life.

But she was.... *gods, she was magnificent.* He felt his own heartbeat surge in his ears.

He had taken a step towards her, before he had even registered, he had moved. His shadows were trying to pull away from him, towards... towards *her*.

Fuck, what was he doing?

He halted, shaking his head free from the thoughts swirling, telling him to go to her. The woman had somehow bewitched him; he shouldn't care about her. His goal was the flesh traders chasing her, the ones he could now hear screaming through the trees for her.

He took in the look of them, and fuck, they had seen better days. They looked like someone had beaten them within an inch of their lives, and from the fury in Itti's eyes as he chased the woman, Kairos had the feeling she had done that.

Which sparked his curiosity. Most women he knew were meek and malleable. Too few warrior women around anymore. The ones he did know. Fuck. They didn't look or act like this woman, who was currently running towards where he stood, just behind a tree.

His shadows began to seep out toward her, but he realized quickly that it wasn't him sending them out; he hadn't even decided what to do with her, yet here they were *leaving* of their own accord.

What the fuck?

He tugged at them, trying to force them back before he was seen. If Itti caught sight of him too early, he would use a send-stone and flee before he could get hold of him. If any of those fuckers knew anything, it was *Itti*.

He was just about to turn around and leave the girl to her fate when he heard the sob. It fractured away from her, and it was like it pierced straight through his cold, dead heart. His right hand immediately went to his left wrist and began to rub the piece of fabric there.

His heart began to scream as it pounded inside him, and he rubbed the fabric again. Trying to focus himself as he watched the running woman, taking in her rapid breathing, she was getting closer.

No.

He can't do this. He can't help; it could jeopardize everything. He couldn't fail his mother, not anymore, the last time he had seen her in the *prison*, she called her bedchamber, she had looked so...so gods damn *frail,* he had been terrified to even touch her. She wouldn't last much longer under the suffocating hate that was his father.

He shouldn't save this woman. He wasn't that kind of male, not anymore. Not for a very long time.

It was better just to let her die quickly than live the life she would probably have if the fleshers decided she was worth the trouble, which was *rare*, if Itti was angry.

Kairos felt a hum come from the fabric he was caressing; he always did when he needed to ground himself. He looked down at it. He could still remember the day she had given it to him and how she had looked that day. The memory pulled forth with every swipe over the ribbon.

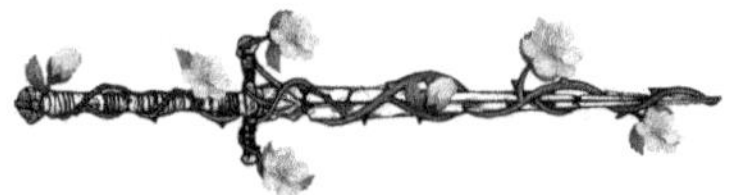

I t was the day he and his mother had left the royal palace where she lived. They had been there for several years, having sought out his uncle, who now stood behind her. The man scared him. He was tough-looking and practically snarled at anyone who got too close to her. But Kairos didn't care. He loved being around her, his firebird. She was his best friend, and even at the tender age of eleven, he knew he loved her. It was why he had made the necklace around her neck, why he had pledged to become her knight one day.

Even at seven, she was everything; she spun his entire world. The thought of having to leave her behind gutted him. She was crying, her cheeks splotchy from it, and he reached out to her with his hands, cupping her cheeks, and swiped the tears away. He didn't want her to cry, he thought. "What is wrong, my firebird?"

She hiccupped and leaned into his touch, her eyes fluttering closed as she took a deep breath. She was so strong, even when she was upset. She reopened them, the blues of her eyes still sparkling with tears, but there was this steadfastness that stole his breath.

"I have a bad feeling, please don't go, Kairos, please. Stay here. I'll tell Mama and Papa to add guards to you and your Mama. You'll be okay here." She pleaded, grabbing hold of his shirt, her little fist turning white from her tight grip. He reached and rested his hand over hers.

He gave her a sad smile, "I don't want to go, but Mama says we must, and it's okay. I'll go, and I can become a squire this year, and before you know it, I'll be a knight, and I can come back to protect you always. I promise." His little thumbs worked back and forth on her cheeks; her skin was so soft. With the redness, her freckles were more pronounced, and he counted each of them. Ten in total, each making her more and more beautiful. He sighed; he would miss her so much. The idea of leaving her was destroying him, but Mama needed him. He could protect her while he grew stronger to protect the girl he loved.

"Promise?" She whispered.

"I promise, firebird, I will come back and be the strongest knight you have ever seen, even stronger than my uncle. Then, you'll never have to be scared of anything." He grinned and looked at his uncle behind her; he wanted more than anything to be as strong as, if not stronger than, his uncle. His uncle, who usually only smiled for her, gave him a nod and a smile, one that said he would hold him to the promise.

She gave him a brilliant smile that brought a blush to his cheeks.

She moved and pulled her braid, which looked so intricate that it had to have taken her maid ages to do, and ripped the ribbon from it; the locks of red cascaded down her back, framing her delicate features. She looked like one of the celestials, and it took his breath away.

"Give me your wrist." She reached her small hand out for his, and he quickly obliged. Heat radiating off his cheeks, as she bit her cheek and began to tie the ribbon around his wrist. It was huge on his wrist, but she made she it was tight. "There, that will always protect you. So, you come find me, my warrior." She reached toward him and placed a kiss on his cheek, tears falling down her cheeks, before she ran back towards his uncle. Who pulled her into his arms, giving Kairos a look that said, come back, soon.

That moment had been the last he had ever seen her, the ribbon was now just the right size on his wrist, and he had sewn the end together to keep it safe on his wrist.

Then, he had paid a pretty penny for a preservation and cloaking spell to be placed on it, keeping the hues of blues and golds perfect, before he began his training. It looked exactly as it had the day she tied it on his wrist.

No one could see it except for him and the one it belonged to, which didn't matter because she was gone. The first one he ever failed. *His Firebird.*

He had promised her the world, promised he would come back and protect her. But he hadn't, had been too late to save her from the horrible death his father had made her have. It was the reason Kairos had given in. Let his father beat him, mold him, and turn him into the killer he was.

So that one day he could avenge her death and meet her again in the afterrealm. And drop to his fucking knees and beg for her to forgive him for failing. To tell her how much he had loved her all those years.

The hum felt stronger as another sob broke free from the running woman, no, not a sob, but a cry of *pain.* As his gaze snapped up, he watched one of the closer hobgoblins of the fleshers grab hold of her braid and yank her back.

His hand went to the blade at his side, and his shadows raised and posed to attack. He didn't understand why he was giving such a strong reaction, but everything in him had begun to scream.

Protect, protect, protect.

He took another step but faltered as he watched the woman twist in the hold, crying out as her hair broke free from the thick braid it had been in. The red curls falling around her made her look even more like the huntress Goddess. He let out a sharp gasp as the woman grabbed a dagger from her body and tossed it with such deadly precision that his cock stirred unbidden. *She was indeed one hel of a woman.*

Kairos watched as she ran before she even knew if the blow she had dealt had ended the bastard's life, which she had. A spark of pride coursed through him as she ran and ran. Her steps became more and more determined.

An idea sparked in his mind, one that would send him

further into the depths of hel, before the end. She *would* make excellent bait, clearly, Itti *needed* her, or the monster that he was would have killed her already. Which means there is a very powerful bidder out there looking for her.

One that might have connections to his father.

His shadows tugged again, sending a pulse towards him that he found odd. *They* wanted to protect her, to reach her, and *never* let go. Like some force was telling them, she was *important.*

Well, he wouldn't argue with that, but maybe not in the way the force deemed her important. *Right now, she was the perfect bait.*

With that final thought, he stepped forward in quick strides aided by his shadows, and once she was in grabbing distance, he shrouded the world around them both in midnight.

Kairos quickly grabbed her by her waist, which was thick and inviting, which seemed to infuriate him further. Because he itched to trail his fingers over every supple, thick inch, to feel what her skin felt like under his touch. So, like the logical male he was, he pulled her body toward his. Feeling her body against his, he suppressed his groan.

Fuck. He needed to bed a woman soon if he was this desperate. He quickly wrapped his other hand around her mouth, silencing her scream, and leaned forward. He was immediately hit with her scent of Cherry blossoms, peony, black currant, and amber, and something deeper, *richer* that felt so gods damn *familiar.*

His lips grazed the lobe of her ear, the delicate skin sending shocks down his spine. He needed to be away from her, and soon. He whispered, "Hush, Fierce One, if you do not wish to die." He had taken several quick strides to the closest tree and twisted their bodies, pressing hers against the trunk of the tree hard.

He could hear her heartbeat echoing into his very blood. He looked her over then, taking in the ripped clothes and the cuts all over her body, each one he saw more and more red.

His own breathing was becoming harsher as he fought every instinct screaming at him to kill them all, to take every single piece of their bodies and rip and rip until nothing was left. But he pushed it down. He had a *plan.*

She was bait, *gorgeous,* fierce bait.

Kairos felt his entire body go cold as he took in the deep red welt on her delicate throat, the size of two very large hands that had pressed tightly on her. He felt even his shadows rise in unending rage as he took in those marks—the brutality of it.

They hurt my woman. *Kill. Destroy.*

The thought caused him to jolt back a step. *Where the fuck had that come from.*

She squirmed a little, bringing attention back to her. His hand was still over her lush lips; he could feel her warm breath against his callused palm. "Don't *move,* sweetheart." He challenged, his voice dripping with annoyance. Her breath caught.

Then, he did something entirely stupid, he looked into her eyes. Took in the deep blue irises with flecks of honey gold in them, and every single thought eddied out of his mind.

Fuck me. He thought.

It wasn't even the fierce defiance in them or the way they seemed to see into his very soul and call forth his broken, dead heart. It was the aether that flowed at the edges. This woman, she was Gods *touched.* Something that hadn't been seen since before *she* died. Since the wizard went into hiding.

Whoever she was. She was *valuable*, which means he couldn't let Itti get a hold of her at all. But it also meant that he could leverage information for her. Then double-cross the bastard.

A plan formulated in his mind, as he watched his shadows slither around her gently, like they were seeking to comfort her.

Stop it, he scolded them in his mind. They didn't respond. Releasing a deep breath of annoyance. Kairos grabbed the woman and flipped her again, so she was now against his front.

Gods, he had to stop doing this to himself, every single curve of her was pressed into him, and he didn't know how much longer he could hide his attraction to her, even if he would rather be rid of her, she was trouble, he could smell it off her. And she was a fool for being out in this wild, with only two daggers and no supplies.

The sooner he could use her as bait and get the information he needed, the better.

He pulled his dagger as he let the shadows around them disappear, and they appeared before the charging fleshers, who halted and snarled.

He pressed the blade against her gentle throat, and he felt her gasp and then shudder in fear. His entire body seemed to rebel as the sounds worked their way through him. *What the fuck was wrong with him tonight?*

He had done far fucking worse. She was just some fucking woman at the wrong place and the wrong time. She didn't matter, only the information she could get him did.

But she does. Mine. *Protect her.* His thoughts raged. *He was fucking losing it.*

"Looking for this?" He drawled. He was already bored and annoyed having to deal with the hobgoblins, and they hadn't even spoken yet.

The woman tried to break free, but then whimpered in pain as she caused a cut on her arm to rub just right, and it began to bleed again.

The smell of her blood sent rage through him, the edge of his vision blurred red, and his shadows hissed as they crawled over her and pressed against the wound, trying to soothe her pain.

Itti smiled, watching the tears fall down the woman's cheeks. She was terrified now; he could feel her shaking. His heart was pounding as he looked down at her briefly. That need to protect her grew, licked like a shadowy flame against his soul.

Shit.

The look on her face, the terror, the hopelessness, it broke him. This fierce woman in his arms was breaking before him at the sight of the creatures before him, and because of the blade at her throat.

Kairos lowered his blade, surprising himself. He didn't understand what was going on with him; he never acted like this, never changed his plans so willy-nilly. But this woman was awakening a part of him that he thought he had lost ages ago.

She let out a soft gasp as the pressure left her skin, and he found himself pushing her behind him. His shadows had begun to curl around her, creating protection for her. *Fucking traitors.*

Itti snarled at him. "Lets it go. Ours, she is. We found her first. Ours." Itti growled again, this time deeper, and bared his gnarled teeth.

Kairos felt the woman reach up behind him for his jacket and clutched it, her hands shaking.

And a voice he had never heard before came out of him. It was thick and full of such venom that he surprised even himself as he spoke the words. "Which one of you touched *MY* woman?"

CHAPTER FORTY~FIVE

His woman?

What the hell was he playing at?

Audelia could not wrap her head around what was going on. First, having woken to those creatures grabbing at her and trying to kill or rape her, or whatever the fuck they had planned. Then, having been caught by this man. Her entire world was in a whirlwind.

She didn't know which way was up anymore.

Should she trust him? Her options were very *limited* at the moment. Yet, even when he had pressed the blade to her throat, she hadn't feared him.

That itself should send her running for it, especially now that he was occupied with whatever was going on in his mind. But she found herself keeping closer; something about him felt familiar and *safe*.

When the big one, Itti, had snarled at her, his beady eyes devouring her like he would enjoy the cries of pain he wished to reap upon her, she had reached out and gripped the man, who was now protecting her after his whole *my woman* bullshit.

Audelia didn't know if she would ever process that change in events or that when he said those words, and she heard the promise of death upon those who had harmed her, that her heart had done a flip, and butterflies, fucking butterflies had set to beat their wings in her stomach.

When all this was said and done, she needed to get away from him, this familiarity and safeness she couldn't trust it, couldn't trust *herself* with it.

The last time she had, she lost Shawn. She couldn't do that again.

So, as the creatures stared them down, and this stranger with death in his eyes demanded again, "Who did it? Who touched what is mine?" Audelia hardened her heart; she shored up every wall she could think of.

But maybe she could use him? He seemed to be slightly protective of her; she could perhaps at least get answers from him, maybe a way to the closest village or city. So she could find the Cave of Asida.

"Yous? No, we found her, if fleshy girl belongs to anys, its us." The one with moss-bark skin, snipped, each word sounding more and more garbled, it was as if he was chewing on the words. It made her stomach turn.

"Eggs is right. My boys and me found her. Nots you." Itti spit. He seemed to smile, like what he had said meant he had won this.

Audelia could feel it, the *shift* in the air, violence seemed to thicken. The shadows that seemed to cling to both him and her started to edge away, slithering like snakes in the grass.

This male did not like how they kept talking about her. The rage seemed to seep from him, yet they were none the wiser to the death they seemed to creep closer to.

"I don't think you, Itti, understand me. Not that it's that surprising. Hobgoblins, you are not the smartest bunch of creatures to have crawled out of the pit." The man snarled, his chest rising and falling like every breath he held back.

But she could feel it coming from him. That *malice* and a small part of her was leaning toward it. Wanting to see what he would *unleash* on those who had harmed her.

Wait... what? That's crazy, she isn't that kind of person. Yes, she wanted them to pay, but not in sheer violence, not when the most they had done was hurt her a little; she did more to them if she were honest. But, in this moment, her blood sang with the need.

Gods, she needed sleep.

She felt a shadow sweep over her cheek, as if it sensed her weariness, her worrying thoughts, and sought to comfort her. Audelia leaned into it, surprising herself. That was another thing she couldn't seem to wrap her head around.

These shadows.

They were entirely different from the ones she found earlier. They felt--honestly, she couldn't describe how they felt, just that she didn't *fear* them. Yet, not fearing them was scaring her.

She felt like she couldn't trust anything, but despite it all, something bigger than herself was telling her that she could trust this moment. It unnerved her, yet it also became an ember inside, begging for more. After everything that had happened over the past month, she wanted to lean into it desperately.

Itti growled at the man standing in front of her. "She mine, little man. You may have caughts it. But she *mine*. Fetch lots of money. Many will bid. Many, yes, worth not dead."

The male sighed, full of annoyance. "Fucking idiots."

She couldn't help but nod in agreement.

Suddenly, shadows jumped out, grabbing hold of two of Itti's men, wrapping around them, and squeezing. Audelia could hear muffled shrieks and the sound of bones and flesh crunching.

Her heart rate sped up as she watched. The man in front of her stepped slightly to block her view of the two currently dying in agonizing pain. Like he feared, she couldn't handle watching.

She merely skirted around him to see and caught the look of horror on their faces and the quick look toward Itti and moss-bark, the ones who had grabbed her, hurt her. But they couldn't talk, and just as quickly as the shadows had grabbed them, they disappeared as the bodies collapsed to the ground in heaps of lumped flesh.

She heavily swallowed and looked up at the man before her. She still couldn't fully see him; the moonlight had only hit certain spots on his face. At this current angle, she could see the cut of a strong jaw, high cheekbones, and the arch of a well-sculpted brow.

Audelia knew if she ever fully saw this man. That he would look carved from the ideas of what a god-given flesh should look like. It sent a chill through her, parts of her wanting to reach out and touch the lines of his face to see if his body would react to the touch. She shook away the thought.

And gods, he was tall, even in the shadows of the forest; she could tell when he had thrust her against that tree before, that he was well over a foot taller than her.

"They nots yours! She not either!" Itti bellowed. It was a roar that broke over her skin, making the fear she had been trying to tamp down resurface.

The male in front of her seemed to notice and reached back to push her behind him again, his touch gentle. Then, he gave her a reassuring squeeze on her forearm before his complete focus went back to Itti. She felt a shadow play with her hair in a soothing gesture.

"I really am getting tired of this. Which of you *touched* her? Which of you put your vile hands where they don't belong?" Each word was measured and laced with venom and a cataclysmic rage that had every hair on her body standing on end.

"I cut you ins. Gets bigs paysouts when she sold. How bout tat?" Itti's gasped out, his own nerves were starting to show after watching two of his men be killed like they were nothing.

The man in front of her just laughed. It was dark and cruel.

"Why would I want a cut when I could have it all? She is *my* woman. Maybe I'll sell her myself?" His sneer was cruel, and her heart dropped into her throat.

Gods, was that his plan? To sell her himself?

Fuck, she was a fool if that's the case. She could have gotten away, could have run while he was busy with these creatures, but instead, she remained.

Thinking herself *safe.*

Audelia took a soft step back, trying not to garner any attention from him while his focus was on Itti and his remaining cohort.

The man's gaze swung to her like he had known what she

was about to do. His hauntingly beautiful eyes of emeralds and dark midnight narrowed on her. "Don't even think it, sweetheart."

She gulped as he reached out an arm again and pulled her toward his back. She slammed against the strong lines of it, the warmth that radiated from him.

Her heart was beating wildly, her breaths heavy now. That fear, which she hadn't felt near him, had crept back into her, and she feared. Feared that what he had told Itti was entirely true.

That she had traded one evil for one that could be far worse.

"I am a reasonable man. I do nots know who you ares'. Buts, I promise you makes lots wit her if you let us go, I will help." Itti stood a little taller than before. *Was this creature really that stupid?*

"Besides, we caughts first, we gets first sample. I wants to touch mores.' Moss-bark spoke, his voice full of a slimy want.

He realized his mistake too late, as the man in front of her disappeared in a flash, only to appear before moss-bark, and Audelia watched as the blade she had seen in his hand earlier plunged through him like it was going through butter. "This, you, disgusting bastard. Is far *too* quick for the likes of *you*. For touching what belongs to me." She could barely hear the words; her heart was pounding so loudly in her ears, and she could have sworn the necklace resting against her skin pulsed at his words.

She screamed as Itti suddenly had her by the throat again. *Fuck*, she was so focused on what the man in front of her had been doing, and the justice served to moss-bark for harming her that she had forgotten the worst one of them.

Shadows surged out, trying to wrap around her to pull her free, but they could not get her free. She could feel their warm touch, feel what seemed like frustration vibrate from them. The promise of death for stopping them.

Something was preventing them from pulling her free. She tried to wrench free from the bulking hand, cutting off her air. Then she saw something in Itti's hand that glinted, it looked like some sort of gem, and he sneered as he brought her closer to his face. She tried not to vomit as the putrid stench of his breath blew against her face as he spoke. "Clever this things here. Blocks shadows from that one. You are mines pretti thang. Bet you taste reall good." And before she could flinch away, his large tongue lapped against her cheek, and she kicked out, trying to make contact with his skin.

A great *roar* broke through the air, causing her heart to skip a beat. In the dark of the woods around them, she caught just the slightest movement from behind Itti.

She tried to cry out to the male for help, but part of her wondered that, despite how he had been acting, he had decided she wasn't worth the headache of the effort. She kept pulling for her magic, but it had curled so deep inside her and was *refusing* to budge.

Fuck, she had the feeling it wouldn't rise for a time, she had used too much.

She swung her leg out and made contact with the large creature's stomach. She had thrown everything she had in that kick, and thank the gods for her training, because she struck true.

He howled in pain and let go of her, and she plunged to the ground hard. She gasped in both pain and renewed oxygen.

"You bitch!" He snarled and lunged at her, the glint of a

knife suddenly in his hands, and she quickly scrambled for her blades, only to realize they were no longer there.

Had the other man taken her blades? How had she never noticed? Where was he now?

Her body ached as she quickly searched for something to grab as Itti threw his body at her and pinned her to the ground. His weight crushed her, and she beat at him, trying to wrench him free.

She clawed and spat at him as he began to paw at her. *Gods.*

But, just as quickly as he had pressed against her, he was torn from her, the sudden loss of pressure had her gasping and her head pounding. Shadows converged on her again, they seemed to cradle against her, trying to check her for more injuries. She didn't know why she did it, but she whispered "Thanks" into the night air.

The sound of flesh being torn apart drew attention from the shadows to watch the man, who had used her as bait and then protected her, plunge a blade through Itti's large throat.

Her heart was racing, as she tried to stand but found her legs would not bear her weight.

Audelia watched as the shadows ran at Itti and began to tear at his body as the male stabbed him over and over, the great creature was not dying easily, even after having a blade pierce his throat. "I told you not to touch, *my woman*, Itti. For that, you die." The words sent a thrill down her spine. The *venom*, the *possession* in them.

She was transfixed as she watched the stranger, and the shadows gripped parts of Itti, and to her horror, she watched as they rendered every appendage from Itti's body, ending with his head—the sickening thud of each hitting the ground.

Now, she should run *now*.

Get as far from this man as she could. If he could do that, gods know what he could do to her, especially when she was weaponless, and her magic was so drained that she could scarcely get an ember to stir.

The moonlight shifted then, and she gasped, taking in her savior. She was right; he was huge. Almost seven feet tall from the looks of him, with deep, corded muscles over his body that seemed to cling to the tunic he wore. He was truly a work of art. Deadly art. He stood there, like *death incarnate*, drenched in the blood of those who had harmed her and sought to do worse.

She watched his chest rise and fall in heavy breaths, watched him crack his neck to the side, popping loose a muscle. She was mesmerized as she watched him sheath his blade and begin to stalk toward where she was still crumpled to the ground. Every move toward her was like a predator, yet she wasn't afraid, and maybe that made her the greatest fool that ever lived.

But some deep, *ancient* part of her said that this man before her, this death god, would not harm her.

Her breathing hitched as he crouched on his haunches before her, his large, thick fingers grazing her cheek so delicately it was at odds with the violence she had just witnessed.

The moonlight shown on his face more, and gods, her earlier assumption had been correct and then some, he was truly a work of an artist, the gods given mortal flesh, but he was not mortal, she saw in the moonlight the tips of ears, poking through the tendrils of his dark hair.

He was beautiful. The rounded almond eyes, still that stark breathtaking emerald surrounded by pools of dark midnight, a strong Roman-like nose, and lips that were full and perfect. If he had been from the world she knew, he would have been called an Adonis for how perfect he looked.

But there was also a hardness about him, in the furrow of that well-sculpted dark brow, the darkness that lurked in his eyes, not just because of the color, no, this was *more* than that. It was a dark promise hiding there. There was also a warrior's strength in how he held himself before her, but slightly unhinged like he was teetering on the edge of control as he looked her over.

She took several deep breaths, regretting it immediately because her head swam, and she felt the edges of her vision cloud over. The world spun, and she could have sworn the look of fear and concern crossed his expression, and he lunged for her before her body fell sideways, and everything went dark.

She could have sworn she heard him yell, "Fuck!" Before, everything was quiet in the dark.

CHAPTER FORTY~ SIX

OP!

SNAP!

Audelia jolted awake as the continuous snap and pop of a fire crackled near her. Audelia felt something warm envelop her; it settled over her body, making her feel safe, as the exhaustion once again caged in her senses. Deary-eyed, she looked just enough to see the flames dancing, casting shadows on some nearby trees. She curled into the warmth of whatever had been placed over her, lulling her back into an achy sleep.

She felt a brief touch over her forehead, and she whimpered, leaning into it. Sleep still weighed heavily on her. The touch had been whisper soft, gentle. She knew who it had been, who had covered her. He was always taking care of her.

In that brief, fleeting moment, borne of denial, she imagined that when she woke again, she would see Shawn lying beside her. His lopsided grin, making her heart melt. She would be safe, and he would pull her into his arms, whispering, "*A Chroi*," and everything would be *okay*.

Soft tears drifted down her cheeks, and she didn't *want* to acknowledge why her heart suddenly began to feel heavy again.

She heard the soft snores of someone nearby, and she sat with a start, the world coming back into stark contrast. She felt the softness of what appeared to be a pelt fall to her waist.

She looked to her side, and everything shattered again. No one was beside her, and she was alone. Audelia started to look around, taking in the shadows dancing over trees as the fire flickered in the soft breeze. They were outside, in some small grove.

Before she could look around more, the sound of a body shifting had her gaze swinging toward the noise, her body went taut as nerves settled deep. She took in the body, leaned against a tree, the form tall and thick, *not Shawn*, but the man from earlier. The panic settled a little at the sight of him. The one who had saved her or captured her. She still wasn't entirely sure.

Her heart dropped as reality came back to her. It wouldn't be Shawn; it would never be him again. She shook away the grief that threatened to consume her again.

So, instead, she focused on her would-be rescuer, still deciding if she could trust him.

He was now leaning against the bark of a tree, his features seemed so soft in what appeared to be sleep. It made him seem *younger*, as if in his dreams, he was freed from the burdens that plagued him during the day.

His voice, rich and thick, made her jump. "How are you feeling, Fierce one?" *Had he not been asleep?*

"I'm...fine. I think. What happened?" Her voice was hoarse, like she had swallowed sand. Her hands immediately went to soothe the ache at her throat, wincing as her fingers danced over the raised flesh from where Itti had grabbed her, her eyes had never left his, which had now opened, narrowing at her.

She watched as he tracked her movements, his nostrils flaring. In the dim edge of the firelight, his eyes had gone black, any trace of the green from earlier eclipsed.

Audelia's mind wandered to what she could remember, him grabbing her, his touch rough yet gentle. This male was a complete enigma. Then, she remembered him killing two of the creatures and moss-bark dying. Then, Itti, the large one, had grabbed her. In those moments, she honestly thought she was going to die. *Until* that man had ripped Itti from her.

She remembered watching him rip Itti apart, the thoughts of those deaths should *haunt* her, should *turn* her stomach, but she found she couldn't feel an ounce of sorrow, knowing they had planned to do far worse to her.

The question remained, though. *Was this male going to do the same?*

"You passed out, and I brought you to the camp our *generous* friends had left behind." He smirked, and Audelia took in the little camp around them. She had been right earlier. The camp was set in a small grove of trees that seemed to cradle around them. Adjusting her eyes to the dim edges of the fire-light, she saw leftover supplies and other bedrolls, and what looked like a large chest, one with speckles of dried blood across the front of it.

Her blood ran cold at what could possibly be in there or who had been in there. Then she thought of the soft pelts over her body, and she quickly shoved them away. She didn't want anything those bastards had used.

"Don't worry, those were *mine*." He told her as he leaned toward her more, and her gaze swung back to him. Now that the firelight was casting its glow against his features more, the emerald in his midnight eyes seemed to dance and almost glow, taking on an otherworldly quality.

She wished she were an artist; her fingers itched to paint them, to try to capture the colors. They were truly *beautiful*.

"Why did you help me?" A rustle of cool wind blew through the camp, and deciding to believe him about the pelts, she quickly covered her body with them. She let out a soft groan at the return of warmth.

If the area she was in was going to remain this cold, she would need warmer clothes. Supplies. Help.

He huffed. Then, she watched as he seemed to have a small war with himself, the muscle in his jaw flexing over and over, and he ran a hand through his dark curls.

"Well, if it's any consolation, thank you." Her words were soft, and she had truly meant them. She was grateful, but Audelia didn't know and didn't really *want* to think about what would have happened if he hadn't shown up.

"You wouldn't *need* to thank me if you hadn't been running around with only *two measly daggers* in the Forest of Semperion." He spat out, and she could hear the meaning in each word; he thought her an idiot.

Maybe she was. But it wasn't like she had planned to come to this place, wherever it was.

Suddenly, she realized, and maybe it was because the grief and danger were now fading somewhat, but she didn't know how much she should tell his male.

Parts of her *trusted* him, she had from the moment she looked into those eyes. It unnerved her, but something about him lured her in and made her want to trust him. For now, she would listen to that feeling, at least to get out of this place.

Trying a different tactic, she spoke softly. "What is the Forest of Semperion? I'm... *unfamiliar* with that name."

"Do you often go wandering in the dark, in forests meant to kill those who walk amongst their branches?" His brow lifted in challenge, as if he was baiting her, his growing irritation palpable with his deflection.

She took a deep breath, trying not to rise to the clear bait he dangled. She needed him for now. She was lost and had no clue about this world. He made for the perfect tool.

The idea of wandering a forest that he just said *likes to kill people* did not set well with her, even if she was getting vexed by his annoyance.

But her biggest worry, the one that kept running through her mind, *was how much she could divulge. She supposed if she kept the queen part out of everything, she could tell him some things— enough to get him to help.*

Hopefully.

"It was not *intentional*." Her mind raced, trying to think of how to word everything without revealing what she needed to hide. "I had accidentally transported myself here. I was walking, and next thing I knew, my magic *surged*, and I was here." Her heartbeat erratically as she watched him, waiting to see how he would react to that.

He seemed to pause at her words, the muscles in his jaw twitched. "Gods, did I get myself stuck with an absolute fool, so you not only cannot control whatever magic you have, which makes you as incompetent as a fucking child. You have no clue where you are? You have to be fucking kidding me!" He barked out. The shadows around him had started to gather, feeding off the growing anger.

The sight of shadows made her flinch, but her anger had risen too high at his words. He stood and began to pull at his hair, muttering something she could hear.

Fuck this shit.

"Well, that was fucking *rude.* It wasn't my plan to be running for my *life* in the middle of a dark wood. *Asshole."* She snapped back at him; well, so much for keeping calm, in order *to get him to help her.*

He stopped his pacing and swung toward her; his well-sculpted brow arched in surprise. Then, it shifted to something darker, making a shiver dance down her spine.

He moved in a flash; one moment, he had been feet away, and the next, he was crouched before her. He took her chin and gripped it, the grip punishing. Her heart started to race.

"Listen here, sweetheart. I will be as fucking rude as I wish to be when you fuck up my plans to get information out of those disgusting bastards." His eyes were full of malice.

Fuck, why did her smart fucking mouth have to show up now?

She gulped and tried to break free from the hold he had on her jaw. Her eyes swam with defiance as she looked at him. But he wasn't done yet.

"Gods, why? *Why* did *you* have to show up? When I was this fucking *close* to getting information from them? I should have just let them have you! Save myself the damn trouble." he yelled in her face. Each word made her flinch.

She hadn't feared him before, even with the blade at her throat, but now with him looking at her with such hate. She was *scared*.

A small whimper escaped her lips, and he gripped harder. The bite of his fingers on her skin made her eyes swim with tears. That only seemed to unhinge him more. Like he was treading a line, and her response was making it *worse*.

"Damnit!" Regret laced his tone, and he relented the hold slightly, his fingers still held her, but it didn't have the same bite as before. He looked at her, his eyes softened for a moment as he whispered the next words. "Are you here to torment me? Make me regret my choices?"

"*I'm no one*, I'm just *lost* in a place, I don't know." She gasped out between his grip. Hoping she could bank on those whispered words, that maybe he would see she was just someone lost.

For a moment, she thought they had won out. That he saw her for what she was. Just lost and in need of help.

Gods, she was wrong.

"Of course you are. Just a sweet, lost little rabbit, *weak* and *alone*. It's *pathetic*. I have to *ruin* my ENTIRE fucking plan for some pathetic female who is *lost* in the woods." He sneered, his words biting into her. His eyes sang in challenge, but the malice she saw there didn't fully meet his expression. He must have noticed that she caught on, because his face suddenly became devoid of emotion, as if a mask had slipped into place.

They made her feel so fucking small. He was right; she *was* weak and pathetic. Her actions had led to Shawn dying and her losing her family and her cadre. She had let her own cowardice destroy everything good in her life. She should let this male end her, just let him end it all.

She felt herself curl inside, felt everything inside her give in. Her body going limp in his hold. The grief of her failures crushed her.

It seemed to spark something in him; she caught a shift in his demeanor before he gripped her harder again, yanking her closer to his face. "Can't even respond now? Did the *pitiful* little rabbit *lose* all that fire? Pity." His eyes danced with anger as he took in her expression, her lack of resolve. Becoming everything he had said she was.

Maybe she had lost it, perhaps it had never been there.

Wait, no.

She may not remember who she truly was, but she did remember who she had been. Audelia had been raised by a strong woman and had taken step after step to get herself stronger. She didn't let shit get to her, even when she thought Kage had broken her. Audelia had taken that pain and humiliation, and she burned it to the fucking ground. Audelia rose from the ashes every time.

She felt her magic rise to the surface, just barely, but enough to let the spark rise again. Audelia used it to fuel her, to *ground* her.

She was taught to bow to no one, and she wasn't going to let some pompous ass of a male treat her like this for something she didn't mean to do. So, she did the only thing she could think of in the moment.

She shifted enough to throw her weight backward, and she broke free from his grip, feeling the pinch of his fingers trying to hold her, and then she threw her head as hard at him as she could, she bit back the cry of pain as her forehead made contact with what felt like his nose. She heard the sickening crunch of cartilage.

He screamed out, "Fuck!" Her vision swam a little, but she shook it off and rolled her body away from him. She threw the pelts at him for good measure.

She staggered to her feet and swung about, looking for something, anything. *Fuck! Where were her daggers?*

Audelia spotted something shining in the light of the flames, and she dove for it. Just as her fingers grazed the hilt of what looked like a short sword, she was yanked back by thick hands.

She gave a small yelp and was flipped onto her back. Her breathing picked up, her heart pounding in her ears, which made the ache in her head worse. But she kicked and screamed and fought with everything she could.

Above her loomed the man who had saved her; his eyes were blazing as he quickly grabbed her wrists and yanked her arms above her head. His legs pinned hers in place. She was entirely at his mercy.

She felt the shadows from earlier snake over her body, their touch *gentle*, entirely at odds with the anger radiating off the male above her.

"Will. You stop. Fighting. Me." He sneered. She could have sworn she saw the barest of smirks sitting in the corner of his lips. As if he had to stop himself from seeming amused as he spoke again. "There's that *fire*, Fierce one." The words were so soft she almost missed them.

She looked up at him with wide eyes, the firelight hitting every well-sculpted inch of his war god face. *Fuck he was gorgeous. Why did the crazy, possible killer have to be so damn attractive.*

Even with the cut across his nose, which she noticed in the light of the flame, had started to clot and seemed to be slowly stitching itself together again.

She wondered *what he was.*

Who he was.

"Well, maybe don't insult someone you just met?" Defiance laced every word; she snarled and tried to break free again.

He groaned and pulled away from her, bringing her with him in a fluid movement; she was sitting in front of him. She looked at him, confused.

"Gods, you are an infuriating female." He groaned as he dragged his large, tanned hand down his face in frustration.

"It's my best trait, I have been told." She shrugged, and her stomach growled.

"Somehow, I am not surprised by that fierce one." He smirked and let go of her. He stood and walked toward the fire, and she watched as he grabbed some sort of meat from what she could now see was an iron spit and began to place it in a nearby dish.

He returned to where she was still sitting, stunned by his sudden change in demeanor. "Here, you should eat." His words were suddenly kind as he held out a plate with chunks of meat and some bread with a three-tined fork.

"You are giving me whiplash." She muttered as she took the plate. The aroma of the meat and bread made her mouth water. She couldn't remember the last time she had eaten. *Had it been yesterday? The morning before?*

She stared at the food, debating if it was even safe to eat. His words in the forest earlier to Itti, playing through her head. *What if it was drugged? What if that body-sized trunk was for her?*

"It's not poisoned; I would not stoop to such petty ways to

harm a person." He huffed and snatched the plate back, annoyed, and took a bite of the meat and then a mouthful of the bread. "Not when a blade does an easier job. Less *mess*."

"Well, sorry for being cautious, today hasn't exactly been a good day for me. You are a stranger in a strange place whose name I don't even know." He handed her the plate back and watched her, his gaze softened for a moment.

Seriously, she was going to get whiplash from how he acts. It slightly reminded her of Mathias, how he treated other people. A pang of longing and regret drummed through her.

He seemed to weigh her words, and then, a shadow rolled toward them, bearing a plate, like his own personal servant. *She had to admit that was fucking clever.* He grabbed the plate and took a bite of his own meat. Audelia took a bite of her food and let out a moan as the flavors of the spices and meat exploded in her mouth.

Gods, this was amazing.

He stiffened for a moment and then shook his head, looking up at her again. His voice was thick, velvet dipped in rich chocolate. "Kairos."

As shiver and pulse ran down her body at his name. She rolled her shoulders, trying to shake off the feeling. Swallowing her mouthful of food, she spoke. "I'm Audelia."

Audelia could have sworn she heard him whisper, *beautiful*, but she shrugged it off. With how he kept looking at her in annoyance, she was clearly a little fuzzy in the head to even think he would say something like that.

They sat in silence for a while, just eating. She savored every bite, not just because it was delicious, but because she would have to leave here and travel alone, and wouldn't know when she would have a meal like this again.

"Thank you. For the food." She spoke softly, giving him a small smile. She watched him flinch like the smile had caught him off guard, then he quickly threw that same annoyed expression back on his face.

"It's nothing. I was hungry, and the deer I had caught earlier in the evening would have gone to waste otherwise." He dismissed her as if responding was a chore for him. *Ass.*

CHAPTER FORTY~SEVEN

He knew his words had pissed her off, but he didn't really care. When she had finally woken, he saw that raw vulnerability in her, the way it seemed to wrap as deeply around her as the grief he saw in her burning blue eyes. He hated how it had made his heart pound and his magic surge. Kairos knew he had to put as much distance between them as he could.

So, he acted like an asshole, a role he easily slipped into because that's what a monster like him excelled at. Kairos left her to her food and her thoughts. Standing, he wandered to the edge of their camp. Well, not their camp, but the fleshers, he could still smell the rotting corpse scent near certain areas.

Fleshers were disgusting not just for selling fae but because they usually ate those, they usually couldn't get a good deal for, after they did horrible things to them first. Those were the basics of why, when Aillard had sent him that missive about seeing Fleshers in the area hunting, he gladly jumped on it.

Anything to rid the realm of their ilk.

Once he was far enough at the edge of the camp, Kairos called his shadows from the depths of the forest, each one slithered back and curled around his body like a second skin. He was prepared for them to tell him someone or something was still out there; this was Semperion, after all. If the forest didn't kill you, then whatever ungodly things that roam these trees would.

Nothing.

Good, last thing he needed was more of Itti's men coming to find them when he was so fucking bone tired. He had been riding his magic earlier, *hard*. Kairos usually didn't like letting that part out to play. It had been necessary, he thought, Itti was well known for his tricks.

It was why, when he found their trail days ago, he had sent word to Aillard that the contact was right about Fleshers in the area and that it would be fruitful.

Fuck.

He would have to explain to Aillard why he had veered from the plan. Not to mention having to deal with the other Night-Shadows. They would be pissed that he had failed to capture Itti, Hel he was pissed at himself for it.

The plan had been simple. Take out his crew and subdue Itti, and then utilize the skills that the monstrous part of himself loved to use to gather information on what he was sent for. Simple. So *fucking* simple.

But then he had seen Audelia, and everything had gotten so complicated in ways that still made no sense.

Now, the plan was gone, and he was left with a female who seemed to *pull* at him. In more than just lust. It was encompassing, and it had only been a few hours.

Kairos turned from his spot in the shadows of the encampment's edge. She was currently huddled close to herself, her long, shapely legs pulled up, her cheek balanced on a knee, as Audelia stared off into the dancing flames.

He took half a step before he even realized he had, like his very soul, wanted to seek her out. Find out what was going on in that mind of hers and why it left such a haunted look on her beautiful features.

Kairos fisted his hands tightly, so tightly that he could feel the pinch of his nails digging into his flesh. He used the pain to focus again. If he was going to use her, he needed to get a fucking grip on himself. Kairos prided himself on his self-control. Especially lately, control was how he kept the darkest parts at bay.

So, he started to walk the perimeter, stopping every so often at the torches placed every few feet, he spoke in soft tones to the shadows curled around the tiny flames. His sprites. They were shy, so he knew they would not reveal themselves around a stranger, so he simply reassured them and walked to the next.

After feeling that they were still secure here, Kairos walked back to his place at the trunk of a cypress tree. His nature skills had come in handy in this forest, and he knew that the tree wouldn't try to swallow him whole in the night like others would.

He should probably decide whether to pretend to help this female or leave her to her own devices and follow at a distance to see who seeks her out.

The latter sat like acid in his stomach.

"I'm sorry to be a bother, but..." Her soft, ethereal voice broke through his thoughts, tugging at his soul, and even his shadows rose at the tilt of it.

Shit. He was fucked. So, gods damn fucked.

"Out with it. It's late, and dawn comes sooner than the dark of this place would make you think." He snapped; it was probably a little harsher than needed, but he had to keep his distance. Had to.

She flinched at his tone, but it was over in an instant; instead, a blaze of determination and challenge seemed to blaze behind her vibrant blue irises.

"My apologies. But I am currently lost in an unknown world. I was hoping that some shred of kindness existed in you. That per—perhaps you would help me." The confidence in her wavered at the end of her request, and it tugged at a part of him, he thought long since dead.

Dead with his *Firebird*.

Kairos sat in silence for a time, weighing his options. Being her savior could prove fruitful. If he could gain her trust. Then, when he needed to use her, it would be so easy she wouldn't even realize she had been tricked. But to gain her trust, they would have to grow closer. That he knew would be dangerous, even deadly.

The snap of the fire broke his thoughts, and then part of what she had said registered; he stiffened.

Wait, lost in an unknown world? What the hell did that mean?

"What do you mean, unknown world?" he tilted his head in question. He remembered her saying earlier that she was lost, but he assumed she meant she was lost in the *forest*. Kairos had been lost in his handling of his emotions at the time. Still believing she was here to torment him. Which, in truth, was probably the case. Urdr, the god of all fates, was probably laughing at all of this.

Fucking Fates.

Audelia stilled then, and he watched the war in her, how

she debated what to say next, she was hiding something. If the scent of fear that crossed over to him was any indication, the fact that she remained quiet for far too long was. Well, that made two of them.

"Nothing. Turn of phrase. My magic. It's fickle. I was upset before, and while trying to get away. I managed to travel farther than I thought possible." She chewed on her plump lip, making the already reddened hue darker, making him wish he could trap that lip between his own teeth.

Kairos cleared his throat, trying to push his attraction to her away. The last thing either of them needed was him trying something stupid, as *tempting* as that felt. Audelia had shifted and tucked her errant curls behind a delicately arched ear. She was Fae.

She seemed young. Hopefully, she didn't scent his desire for her, or was too lost in whatever grief and other emotions that it didn't register.

He decided he wasn't in the mood to fight with her, even if part of him had relished the idea. Kairos decided he would be kind *briefly*. Hoping he wasn't about to fuck everything more than it was currently. "I see. Well, as long as you can hold your own, you can come with me to the edge of the forest for now. I am not going to fucking hold your hand. So, if you can't keep up, then you're as good as dead."

"I'm not some weak woman. I can handle myself." The fire was back in her eyes, and fuck if it didn't make her breathtaking. He mulled over her calling herself a woman; she spoke it as if she didn't know she was a fae female. Strange.

"Then it's settled. Get some sleep. We leave at first light." Kairos turned away from her then and began to settle into his spot, using his arm to pillow the rough edges of a root.

He could hear her huff in annoyance and turn over toward the embers of the campfire. Usually, he would be closer to the warmth, especially in Semperion, where the nights could become ice-cold. However, in his current state, he didn't quite trust himself. Especially not around this female.

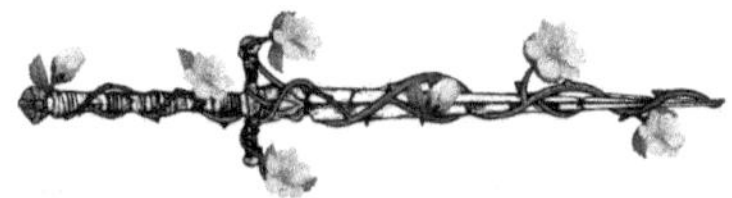

Sleep did not come easily for Kairos; it never usually did. But tonight, it was worse. Not only because of the female feet from him currently whimpering in her sleep. No, this unease, causing his insomnia, was one he dreaded with everything he had.

The curse.

Kairos could feel it under his skin. It crawled just under the surface and called to him. The scent of sulfur and metallic tang of blood filled his senses as it always did. He needed to get to his dragon soon. Hopefully, the effects will hold off till they reach the end of the forest. Struggling to sit up without grunting out in pain, Kairos pulled at his tunic, exposing his chest and the beginnings of the scales on his skin. They felt cool against his now fevered skin.

Swallowing the dryness in his throat, he reached out in his mind as his fingers curled gently against Eirlys' scales.

Eirlys? He called out into the void of their bond.

Her honey-dipped voice did not fill his head, and dread filled him.

If she was too far—if he couldn't even reach her in thought.

Kairos wasn't sure he would make it to the forest's edge. The curse dug deep, making him swallow a scream.

Staggering to his feet, using the rough bark of the cypress as support, Kairos stood. He needed to get away from the camp. If the pull became too much, he would be lost to the monster, and with the whimpers coming from Audelia. He feared what that dark part of him would do about it.

On shaky legs, Kairos walked from his spot on the tree, using his shadows to stabilize himself. He sent a few who went with hints of glee toward Audelia to watch over her. He may not like the situation, but if he were lost to *this* tonight. He would ensure that he harmed no other innocent fae or being.

Maybe she wasn't innocent, a dark thought scored through his mind.

He shook it away. No, she radiated pureness. If the Fleshers had been hunting her, it wasn't for anything other than evil things.

As he staggered away, Kairos reached into his pocket for the Astarothian stone he had pulled off of Itti's corpse after Audelia had passed out. Coming to a stop a reasonable distance from the campsite, he leaned against a nearby rock, patches of moonlight making their way through the thicket of the branches above his head.

The beams illuminated the onyx stone in his hand as he rubbed a thumb over the veins of writhing silver. The stones were *rare*, so rare that the owners of most of them hoarded them like fire drakes. So, for Itti to have been entrusted with one was worrisome indeed.

Aillard would have answers about that, he was sure. Hopefully, when he reached Noxia, his friend would be there with news of his own. It had been ages since he had been to Noxia, a tiny town in the middle of the Gloomfrost valleys. Aillard was from there and had found Kairos, in what seemed to be a lifetime ago.

That night was the hardest, most liberating moment in his life. He owed his friend everything. If it weren't for his magic of melding, Kairos would still be that fucking monster's puppet. Both of them.

As if the curse knew he was thinking of being free again, a sharp pain burst from him. It felt like his bones were going to snap, and he knew they would. If the change came.

Kairos? Kai?

Urdr must be watching him tonight, as Eirlys' honeyed voice full of worry filled his mind. Just hearing her seemed to ease the beast inside. Kairos looked up at the boughs of evergreens and cypresses around him, hoping that maybe, just maybe, he would see the shadow of her wing soaring above him.

I'm here. Shit, even in his mind, he sounded on the edge.

It's okay. I promise I will be back soon. Talk to me. Kairos leaned into her voice, using it to center himself.

About what?

Anything. I sensed something earlier, but the connection was shaky.

Kairos thought for a moment, had she sensed his shift when he saw Audelia? His dark gaze looked back toward the dim light of the camp, tugging on the shadows a little.

They responded with a tingle, meaning all was well.

I met with—an issue.

An issue? The fuck does that mean?

Wondering how to respond because, in truth, even Kairos wasn't sure still. The female in his camp was a complication for sure, but that pull. He couldn't ignore that pull. Deciding not to talk about it with the curse still looming over him, he chose distraction.

What are you up to? Distract me. Kairos stroked the scales on his upper shoulder; he could feel the curse and the beast he could become eased. With the connection open, that feverish feel was beginning to cool.

Really? Kairos, what happened earlier? I could feel your heart rate from The Cove. Eirlys's voice had turned stern, and all he could do was laugh in his mind. Even hundreds of miles away in Dharan, the dragon's home, she would still try to boss him.

She knew him too well, fuck that meant he would have to mention the female in his camp and everything.

Are you close enough for me to send you my memory? Sometimes, if a bonded dragon and their rider had a strong bond, they could share memories, but they needed to be a certain distance, too far, and it wouldn't work.

Kairos felt the shimmer of green that brushed against his mind's eyes. She was close enough. *Thank fuck.* He sent her everything.

Kairos showed her his hunt for Itti and the fiery goddess that the Fleshers had chased, and he even revealed his lapse in judgment when he referred to the female as his own. The brutality of the kills, what they made him feel as he protected her, and how his shadows have been acting. Then, the fact that Itti had an Astarothian Stone.

Silence greeted him for a while, and Kairos just stared up at the patches of moonlight. He could still feel the curse, but it had lessened to a dull ache in his bones.

Why do I always miss the fun? Just be careful, idiot. I'll be at the edge of the forest in six days. Kairos felt the connection between them slip away. He wished she could have remained longer, but he knew that The Cove kept their magic sealed tight, so more than likely, she was soaring just outside the shield wall.

Kairos stayed against that rock for a while longer, and he wanted to make sure the curse remained dormant before he walked to the camp again. She had been through enough in the past several hours. The worry for her gave him pause as the warm feeling settled in his soul; he really needed to get a hold on himself.

After a time, he felt his bones ache with fatigue, and Kairos pushed off the rock, his shadows curled around him as he walked back to the camp. Just as he reached the boundary of it, Audelia cried out in her sleep.

Kairos went stock still as she cried out. It was pure anguish, and he could have sworn small flames curled around her body like his shadows did. "Shawn…" She whimpered out, and her voice was so damn small that it broke parts of him.

He walked closer to her, standing over her body as she cried in her sleep. Kairos felt an odd surge of jealousy at the sound of another male's name on her lips. *Odd.*

Shaking it off, he leaned down and brushed some of her hair from where it stuck to her feverish body. A snap of electricity coursed through his body at the touch and his shadows. They sang at the feel.

He snapped back up, his heart pounding in his ears as he marched back to his spot at the tree, but before he let sleep claim him, he whispered into the firelight night. "I have you, I promise." Kairos fell asleep watching her, his shadows swirling around him and reaching for her in comfort.

CHAPTER FORTY~ EIGHT

She dreamed of warm touches, whisps of shadows that felt like stardust at midnight, and deep green eyes. *I have you, I promise.*

Audelia stretched her body out from the spot on the bedroll she had been sitting on last night. She didn't remember falling asleep; the last thing she could recall was staring into the flames of the fire and trying not to fall back into her grief.

As she worked a kinked muscle in her shoulder from sleeping on the hard ground, she realized the grief was still palpable, but she felt like she could focus just a hair more than last night. As if some of the weight of it had been lifted in her sleep. It filled her with regret and shame.

The sound of movement to her right broke her train of thought.

Audelia watched as Kairos moved around the camp, gathering supplies. She still didn't know what to make of him. He had moments last night where he was kind and almost thoughtful, but then a switch seemed to click, and he became cold and abrasive again.

She couldn't entirely blame him, from what little he had revealed after the encounter with the creature Itti and his fleshers, that's what Kairos had called them. Whatever that meant, she didn't want to think too much about what that meant. Thankfully, he had saved her, and she understood his behavior. Kairos had needed them alive. Audelia had destroyed that.

She was noticing a pattern; everything she touched lately turned to ash and ruin. Maybe she was cursed. It would explain why her memory was still gone. Why, just as she finally got the love of her life, she had to watch him *die*. Die, and not be able to stop it.

She had all this power, power that, according to Bronn and her aunt, was from a damn goddess, yet she couldn't stop his death—*her fault*.

Everything was her fault.

Trying to stop the spiral, Audelia refocused on Kairos. She watched how he moved. He was a sight. Now, in the shafts of orange sunlight, the forest was thick here, so that even in the early hours of what she assumed was dawn, only small shafts of light illuminated the space. But between the shafts and the glow of the still-burning firelight, which he must have restocked in the night, Kairos's features look even more god-like. Like some ancient craftsman had carved his cheekbones and almond-shaped eyes in honor of the god they worshipped. He was tall, the same height as Mathias, she thought, and of a similar build, huge and imposing. Honestly, even his facial features reminded her of him, just darker than her friend and protector.

Kairos was dressed in black leather that seemed to hug every well-toned muscle of his body. Audelia wasn't sure if it was the same one he had worn the night before or if he had changed. But the lack of blood from Itti and his fleshers made her think Kairos had at least bathed somewhere. She watched how every muscle shifted as he gathered supplies and placed them inside two packs. He had a sort of lethal elegance, one honed from years of battle. He was a warrior through and through.

She had thought so when she had met him last night, just from his eyes, she knew. Knew that the male who held her forcefully but gently was a male you did not mess with. Watching how he took out Itti and his ilk was another clue. But seeing him doing something as mundane as packing bags? He even made that look deadly; her mouth went dry watching him.

As if he had sensed her eyes on him, Kairos turned toward Audelia. For a moment, she caught softness, but the hardness that she had captured last night returned to his Adonis features. As if that gentle beast side of him had never even occurred. He was such an enigma.

"If you're awake, then you should be helping break camp. Or is this how our travels together will go, princess?" His warm chocolate tone took on a mocking jilt as his dark eyes bunched in annoyance.

Audelia flinched at him calling her *princess*. He didn't know how true those words were. He may mean them as a taunt, but they felt like a dagger to the heart.

She was royalty, she was a queen no less, but in this

moment, being scolded by the man who saved her? She felt small and weak.

"I don't know, do you plan on being an insufferable ass the whole journey?" She quipped as she stood, feeling grateful that the rest had returned her jelly legs back to their usual form. The last thing Audelia wanted was for him to think her weak. Even if she did feel it, his words solidified it.

However, she would not let him know that. Over the years, Audelia had gotten good at pretending she was strong and had her shit together, even if she felt dead inside.

So, she squared her shoulders and lifted her chin in defiance of his words. Audelia reached down, grabbed the bedroll, and began to roll it. It was a little harder to roll than a nylon sleeping bag, but the concept was similar. "You said it would be a few days until we reached the edge of the wood? How big is this forest?"

She barely remembered running through the thicket last night, but she did remember the heavy feeling of the vastness of the dark around her.

"The Semperion takes up about three-thirds of the upper kingdom. Luckily, you landed in the east most end closest to the mountain ranges of Ghanta." He scoffed, annoyed with her naivety.

Three-thirds? She wanted to ask how big the kingdom was or if they were even in her kingdom. But she didn't want him to think her more stupid than he already did, and she didn't fully trust him yet. What if he worked for Lefrain? What if he was *worse* than Lefrain?

After that, they worked in silence, breaking the rest of the camp. Kairos said they wouldn't take much, as the forest was too dangerous for horses, so they would have to walk until they reached the small farmstead, where he had left his horse. So, an hour later, Audelia stood by the last remnants of the fire with a pack strapped to her; it felt heavy.

It wasn't just supplies in the pack; no, it was as if fate had decided to strap all the things weighing her soul down to it as well. She would give anything to have Shawn with her, to have Mathias and the rest of her friends. Audelia missed them all so terribly much.

Oh gods, what had she done? She had just wanted time to breathe, not to be sent, gods know how far, from the people who loved her.

"Are you coming? Or do you plan on remaining?" Kairos growled from a distance. Audelia snapped her gaze to where he stood at the edge of the little grove their camp had stood in. He looked so damn imposing, standing with a pack on his back and two massive swords strapped just behind the pack, nestled against the expanse of his broad shoulders.

Kairos had pulled his dark locks back into a half-bun. Usually, she made fun of males who used a bun, but with him, it just added to the dark, warrior-like look. Not to mention the additional two daggers strapped along his belt. Shadows writhed around him like a cloak.

Speaking of weapons, Audelia looked around the camp for them, and she hadn't seen them when she was packing. Had she dropped them in the forest last night? No, cause even the baldric that had been across her breasts was gone.

"Can I have my weapons back, please?"

Kairos huffed and turned toward the darkness of the trees before them. "Earn them back. Let's go, Fierce One." With apparent dismissal, Kairos began to walk into the tree line, the shadows around him cloaking him more.

Fucking asshole.

Audelia ran after him, not wanting to lose sight of him in the dark, even with the occasional shaft of daylight, it was still hard to see more than twenty feet in front of her. She had noticed, though, as she trailed behind him, that everything she did see was sharper. Audelia was used to walking through a dark forest, and she could barely count the number of times she wandered the trees back home at The Glade. Those times, she could see but barely, if it was dark enough, some pockets were so dark that she had to move by instinct.

This, though, was strange; it was dark, but it was like someone had added just a hint of light to everything, just enough to make out the shapes and some details of the bark or Kairos walking ten feet from her.

Was it the magic of this place?

Audelia contemplated what could be causing this enhanced ability to see in the dark, if it was the magic of this place. A part of her wondered how much more of her birthplace was like this.

As she walked, Audelia could have sworn every so often,

light brushes of shadow curled around her legs and occasionally brushed her fingers.

It should scare her, after everything that had happened in those moments with Kage and Shawn's death, just a touch from a shadow should fill her with a deep fear. But these didn't; these *felt* different. She had noticed it before, but now that her head was a little *clearer?* Audelia had been right; the shadows currently touching her were gentle and comforting. The total opposite of the male they answered to.

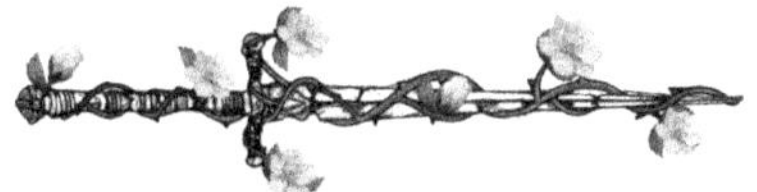

Kairos, walked through the forest on edge. Not because of his surroundings, which were still oddly tranquil, which set his teeth on edge waiting for the *shift*. For the darkness that was Semperion to awaken and consume them both.

No, his vexation was in the form of the redheaded temptress walking behind him. He prided himself on being calm under pressure, but something about this female shattered everything.

She was dangerous, and he didn't even think she was aware of the pull she held. That if she were to say just the right words, he might just *burn* the world at her command, and that thought terrified him.

So, fucked.

As they had gathered what meager supplies they could carry together, he kept seeing a deep sadness creep over her features, and his shadows responded in kind. They kept trying to curl around her, offering her solace, just as they had done for him when his own inner turmoil was exposed.

It also didn't help that she was such an oddity, she appeared fae in every aspect, but how she held herself? It was like she didn't even know she was Fae, which was impossible because she looked at least a few decades old. Young, yet still well into her years, from the way she held herself. She wasn't some *faeling*.

"This is so *strange*. Is this the magic of this place?" She spoke so softly that if it hadn't been for his acute hearing, he would never have heard her. He glanced back at her, she was currently waving her hand in front of her, and she looked so fucking beautiful with the serene, amazed look on her features.

"What magic?" His voice was rough as he came to a stop so abruptly that she rammed straight into his chest. He caught her in his arms, her slender frame fitting so damn well that he practically dropped her like she was covered in acid. Kairos couldn't afford those thoughts.

She gasped and looked hurt at his shoving her away, but she quickly fixed her features back into that strong, determined set of the jaw. "How am I able to see so well in this darkness? I'm no novice when it comes to the dark of a forest, but it's like a soft glow is all over the place. It's...*beautiful and magical*." Audelia blushed then as her deep blue eyes met his.

"Semperion has been called many things, but beautiful is definitely not one of them." He couldn't help but laugh. Was she serious? Was she playing some game? Acting like a damsel that seems to not know a damn thing about this realm, about herself? To what end?

"Well, with the fact that I can see in the dark, crazy far, I would call it beautiful. Clearly, you don't get around much if you can't see it." She huffed and began to walk ahead of him. Kairos just watched her, watched her luscious form as she strode through a forest that would devour her in a second if it decided it was hungry.

"This place *kills* Audelia, it is darkness and a monster worse than some that prowl around this realm. *Worse,* because at least the demons that hunt the beings of this plane have a reason for it. *This place?* It just devours because it can. It becomes a monster and enjoys it." He hoped his voice didn't catch at the end of his snapping at her. Because as he spoke, Kairos realized that he spoke more of himself than the trees and the death magic they held, because when the curse took him? He killed and killed and ravaged the realm for no reason other than the bastard holding his leash telling him to.

She turned again and smiled; she smiled so damn brightly she seemed to glow as she spoke. "Sometimes, even the darkness can be beautiful. It can be worth so much more, without the dark, we can't have light. Even living in the dark, you should still look for the bits of light trying to find you." Audelia looked up as small shafts of daylight broke through and rested about her.

She reminded him of hope and the goodness in the world. Kairos felt himself taking a step toward it, wanting to wrap himself in that warmth and heal himself with it. Devour her light so his darkness could be snuffed out.

To make her his. *She already is.* A voice spoke in his mind, one he had heard before when he was trying to break himself free from the curse; it reminded him of the wizard his mother knew. The one that drove his uncle crazy, but was always so kind to Kairos. He had told Kairos that he was meant to protect, that he would be the one to protect—To protect his *Firebird*. But he failed then. He would always fail.

He was a monster, and monsters don't deserve the light.

Even if that flaming brightness that was the female standing before him was one he craved deeply. He would only destroy her and relish in it.

She would be his damnation.

She *was* his damnation; it was only a matter of the form she would take.

CHAPTER FORTY~ NINE

They barely spoke the next several days as they traveled the half-dark of Semperion. Several times, Audelia could have sworn that just off in the distance, the trees would shift. Whenever she asked Kairos, he just brushed her off with a growl and a look of disdain.

Five days.

Five days and she still hated him, even in the brief moments when he seemed softer. He would recalibrate, and that dark, cold façade would return, and he would become even more distant than before.

Audelia was keeping her usual steady pace behind him as she noticed the beginnings of daylight just ahead. It was like a beacon of hope as the trees lessened around it—*the end of the forest,* she thought, as she picked up her pace.

Finally, after days of darkness, she would *finally* feel the warmth of the sun on her skin again.

She was so caught up in her excitement that she hadn't even noticed that Kairos had stopped walking or that the air around them had gone heavy, like the forest had given pause. Audelia turned to look back at him, to see why he had stopped, when something heavy slithered around her calf and gripped. The pressure made her gasp as she looked down at the obsidian vine that was traveling up her leg like a python.

"Kai—" before she could finish his name, she was yanked back, her face slamming into the hard path, loose stones and broken branches tore at her face as she was pulled into the looming dark. If he had shouted, she couldn't have heard over the deafening ringing in her ears.

Audelia's heart was pounding as she searched for her magic; she had felt it the past few days, a small ember flickering in and out as the days wore on.

As she reached for it now, hoping that she could use it to lash out, burn away the vine, pulling her further into the dark, faster and faster. It wouldn't answer; she felt it flicker out again as panic surged. She tried to get a grip on the ground, hoping maybe, just maybe, an errant root would fall into her path that she could grab and hold on.

Nothing, but dirt and grass buried into her nails as she was pulled. Chancing a look up, she didn't see him. He wasn't there. Had he decided this was the perfect moment to be rid of her? Briefly, she had thought *maybe*, just maybe, they had a chance of being friends when they had their last full conversation, but it had barely lasted. His coldness leached into everything. Now, it had fully won out, leaving her for dead in the hands of whatever was dragging her.

She could still see, so at least she had some bearing, even if the forest was beginning to feel heavy and evil. There was truly something *evil* lurking here. Was this what Kairos had meant by the forest killed? Was this her fate?

She had survived whatever Kage had become, lost the love of her life, her friends, only to die here *by* a forest?

Audelia was suddenly pulled up, the world shifted as she dangled upside down, her braid fell to her chin as she screamed. Heart racing, she tried not to let the panic consume her. Kairos might now come to save her, but she was Audelia Elide fucking Ferelith, she would not let this happen again. She could save herself; she *would* save herself.

She took a deep, steadying breath, closing her eyes. She let the sounds of the forest settle around her. It was quiet, too quiet, whatever had grabbed her would appear or return, but she still wasn't entirely sure what was happening. So, she needed to move fast.

Audelia twisted herself and saw the trunk of a gnarled oak nearby. If she could swing enough, she might be able to grab one of the knots, and if she got lucky, she could yank hard enough to break the vine or at least move to a branch nearby and try to cut it away, hopefully with one of her blades.

Deciding it was truly her best option, Audelia started to swing. It was slow going at first, but soon, the more she curled toward herself and then pushed with every outward curl of her body, she gained the momentum she needed. She tried to grab a low-hanging branch to pull herself to the trunk. But she kept getting just a small grip that her fingers lost, and was met with the bark tearing at her hand with every pull of her weight.

Thinking fast as she heard rustling coming from the dark depths nearby, Audelia reached up. Swung again and again, and reached for something, hoping that maybe one of her blades hadn't fallen; her fingers trailed over nothing.

Fuck.

Still, she tried to grab the branch to pull herself to safety. Over and over, she got the grip, and the weight and speed of her momentum tore her away before she could steal her grip.

Just a little more...

She curled as tight as she could and sprung herself toward the tree again, she felt the power inside her rise just a touch, it had been so damn quiet lately, but it seemed to push her harder, with a rush of fiery heat down her spine, Audelia managed to grip the branch.

The rustling got louder as Audelia began to pull herself onto the branch as close to the trunk as the vine holding her would allow. It gripped her tightly as she struggled to maneuver herself on the branch.

The air around her grew colder, so cold it felt like ice was forming on her skin that even the fire that had burned in her for a moment seemed to *shrink* from it. Audelia pulled at the vines, gripping and trying to untangle herself; the shadows seemed to deepen around her.

One moment, she could see in front of her, and the next, the shadows had become so *dark* that it was as if a patch of pure midnight had sat on the branch next to her. Audelia's heart was pounding so hard in her chest that she felt it might burst at any moment.

She wasn't sure which was worse —the frost that seemed to be coating the area around her or the patch of midnight shadow that was moving closer to her. Closing her eyes for a moment to think, she needed not to panic, even if that was exactly what she wanted to do.

She remembered what Mathias had told her a few weeks ago when she managed to get him to train her.

"Remember, Shadow flower, when faced with two dangers or even more, do not panic. I know it seems to be the better option, but my dear girl, you do not need to panic. You are so fucking capable of sheer power that those dangers will bow to you. I know you don't remember, but you hold the fire of ancient gods within your very soul. You make them bow. You look within, and you use it. Make it bleed or bow. Then you burn the other to ash."

Stealing her breath, Audelia looked again at the patch of midnight before her, and she realized that it didn't feel wrong. Not like the patches of ice forming around her, as the cold grew in strength, she felt another presence. This one felt older, almost as ancient as the power curled within herself.

That can't be good.

Taking a gamble that this patch wasn't a threat and could possibly help her before whatever was causing the torrent of ice showed up, Audelia sat up a little straighter and went to open her mouth.

But before she could even speak a word, the midnight shadow crashed into her, engulfing Audelia in its inky blackness. It curled around her in thick tendrils, and within that darkness, she spotted tiny specks of deep phthalo emerald that seemed to watch her, gauge her reaction. Heart pounding, she could have sworn she knew those emeralds. Knew them in her soul, and they called to her.

As if in answer, they lurched for her in the inky black, she screamed or would have if it wasn't for the crush of large, callused hands pressing over her mouth as the form of Kairos began to form in front of her, his features blending so perfectly with the shadow she wasn't entirely sure it really was him.

It made him look like beautiful, lethal, pure death incarnate.

"Don't make a fucking sound." His voice was by her ear as he harshly whispered. She went still as he curled toward her, his body still part shadow, blocking her from sight. She fought against his hold, not wanting to put herself in that position again. Not needing to be saved.

She had this handled; Audelia had gotten herself into this tree, even with her still trapped by the vines. Vines seemed to grip tighter as she tried to get out from Kairos's hold.

"Stop moving, or you will get us both killed." His command was a growl that settled deep in her belly.

"Let go of me." She mumbled into his hand, and she tried to move to get her mouth some leverage so she could bite his fucking hand, to get him to relent.

He pressed her tighter, pushing her back against the bark of the tree. She felt the rough bark digging into the blouse of her shirt, having shed her leather jerkin earlier because it had felt stifling. Now, she regretted it as the bark tore into her skin through the fabric.

She felt trapped as he held her tightly against the trunk of the tree; her magic seemed to curl inward as ice suddenly burst everywhere. One moment, they were within the lush greenery of the forest, and the next, they might as well have been transported into a frozen tundra.

Before she could try to say a word to him about what the fuck was happening. A woman walked into the clearing. Audelia had just been hanging in. She was—fuck she was beautiful.

The woman was tall and willowy, with elegant curves and raven-black hair that cascaded to the ground in wispy curls.

Audelia watched through the thin veil in the shadows that encased her and Kairos from view. The woman was dressed in a slightly tattered evening gown, reminiscent of those seen in Medieval movies and stories. In the shafts of light that seemed to glow around the woman, she looked no older than Audelia, yet seemed to possess a regality befitting a queen, with her high cheekbones and pillowy lips. Her eyes, *gods*, her eyes were sharp, pale ice blue, almost like the ice around her had taken on the look of her eyes in homage.

"I know you are here, my dear. I can *feel* your burning passion. Come out, come out." Her voice was a soft melody, each note striking something deep within Audelia, making her want to get closer, to kneel before this ethereal woman.

She hadn't even realized she had been starting to move until Kairos growled in her ear and shoved her even harder into the tree. She cried out into his hand in pain.

"Come out, dear. I know you are here. My vines still sing of you. Please, my dear, I only mean to help you." The woman's icy eyes roamed around the trees and the bushes around the clearing. She hummed as she began to walk around the area. With each step, she seemed to glide.

Audelia met Kairos' blazing eyes; they had gone so dark with every step the woman took in their direction. She watched as he looked at the vines still holding her captive.

"Fuck." Quick as an asp, Kairos pulled out a small dagger and began to saw at the vines, which in turn made them squeeze her harder. Tears were falling from her eyes now at the sheer pain of each squeeze.

A honeyed voice broke both of their concentration on him, cutting the vines in vain. "Oh, you *naughty* thing. Trying to cut my vines?" Both of them stilled at her words. Kairos pressed closer to Audelia, trying to shield her more from the woman walking closer.

Ice began to crawl up the tree now, thick and sharp. "Come out, dear. I promise I mean no harm, unlike that *beast* with you now." Audelia looked at Kairos again. He flinched at the woman's words, and she felt her blood run cold.

It didn't seem logical even as she felt her body moving, or the purring of the vines as they realized she was giving in. She shouldn't be listening to what this woman was saying, even with her sweet, endearing words; something seemed off about her. Yet, Audelia felt her power rise just enough to shove at Kairos; she felt like she wasn't herself in those moments. She pushed at him using just a little of the flame that lived inside her, and she watched his eyes go wide before he adjusted and shoved her against the tree again, harder.

"*Don't* listen to her words. It's a trick. Don't be so fucking *stupid*, Fierce One." His eyes went entirely black, and his beautiful, carved face took on a nightmarish glow, one that had a shiver of fear run down her spine. In all the days she had been with him, she hadn't feared him, but at that moment, she did.

He seemed to notice the fear undoubtedly in her eyes because his softened for half a heartbeat before he used his shadows to hold her still harshly, but it felt less of a bite than before. Just enough to hold her. To hope she would listen.

"Don't," He whispered again; her heart was pounding in her ears. She didn't know who to believe, the strange male before her or the ethereal woman who held herself with such ancient regality that it stole Audelia's breath.

"I can sense you, dear. You seem so *scared*. Come to me, and I'll make it all better." Her words were becoming increasingly sickly sweet, and a voice deep inside her screamed for her not to listen. However, something about her voice drew Audelia in, and her body began to go numb.

She wasn't even aware of when she gently grazed her fingers over the vines like a lover's caresses. Her body trembled as she did so; she felt them pull stronger in that moment, a sense of their—*her*—satisfaction flooding her just before the vines tightened and wrenched her and Kairos out of the tree.

She felt Kairos grab her around the waist and pull her to him, where she landed on top of him with a heavy thump. Audelia stared down at the male, surprised he had saved her from the heavy landing. Before she could say thank you, she was yanked up into a standing position by the vines.

She gasped as new ones coated in thick ice grabbed her arms, pulling them out to her sides, barring her from proper movement. Audelia watched as Kairos summoned his shadows, but they were blocked by a wall of ice that encaged him before melting away into thick ice chains, holding him to the ground where he had moved into a kneeling position.

Audelia watched as the woman walked to where Kairos knelt; he was now thrashing in the ice chains. The woman leaned down and gripped his chin. Her beautiful features twisted in disgust as she looked him over. "You truly are an abomination, aren't you?"

"Go fuck yourself, hag." He growled and was rewarded with ice shooting from her hands to coat his mouth.

"Such bad language in front of a young female." She tsked and shoved at him one last time, and Audelia watched the burning rage in his eyes. They looked at her, and she could see the war of anger and worry in those dark irises.

Audelia's attention shifted to the woman walking toward her, every step leaving an icy footprint behind. As she approached Audelia, she felt that odd calm once again drench her body.

She went lax as the woman reached out a delicate hand and brushed icy fingers against Audelia's cheek. She wanted to flinch instead. Audelia screamed in her head to move away from the pain, but something stopped her. Even the fire within seemed to pause again. Not wanting to reveal too much to this woman.

"Look at you, *precious*. I haven't smelled this kind of ancient magic since the days of beginnings." The woman leaned in closer as Audelia took in her features. She had looked beautiful from a distance, but now with her directly in her sight. Audelia had never seen anyone like this woman; every feature in her face was sharp and soft at the same time, and her eyes were truly the lightest, almost white-blue. Everything about this woman screamed beauty and calm.

Yet something deep inside her screamed not to trust it, not to trust the almost sickly sweetness of this woman.

Audelia reached deep again as the woman began to play with the loose strands of her fiery curls. The touch from someone who seemed kind should feel soothing, like a mother's touch, but it burned. Audelia was surprised her body wasn't giving out from the icy touch. Her magic flickered as if to tell her to *hold on*.

"Where have you been all these years? Why are you with this monster?" She pulled back slightly to look Audelia over, her head tilted at an angle like she was trying to see into Audelia's soul.

"Wh—who are you?" She struggled to get each word out as the woman before her stared deeply; it was becoming too much.

The woman laughed, and each soft note grated on Audelia so much that when she dug deep again, she felt her magic rise just a little.

"Oh dear, how *rude* of me." The woman gave Audelia a wolfish smile. "My name is Melantha, and yours, my darling?"

She didn't want to say, didn't want this woman, Melantha, to know her name. Audelia tried to look at Kairos to see if he was still there, still okay. As if in answer, she felt it then.

A few tendrils of shadow wrapped themselves around her wrist. She felt them before the night she met Kairos, remembered how they felt, and she felt them again now. They remained in her line of sight but just out of sight from the woman in front of her. If she could, she would have sagged at the sense of safety they brought her.

She took a deep breath, still not answering the woman. Melantha watched her, every feature still beautiful and kind, in complete contrast to how she was making Audelia feel.

"You are being *rude*. I have given you my name, and I have *saved* you from that *beast*. Yet, you still look at me harshly and refuse to give your name?"

Audelia felt a nudge from a tendril that had snaked into her hair, and she could have sworn she heard a voice. It was soft and truly gentle. *Lie, tell her a fake name. Do not let her have yours. She is dangerous, Audelia.*

"Penelope—My name *is* Penelope." She used the name of the heroine from the last fantasy novel she had read before all of this had happened. She put as much inflection as she could muster into the name. *Willed* herself to believe that it was her name.

Please believe me.

Melantha seemed to pause, then she seemed satisfied with

the answer. Audelia felt some of the ice begin to thaw from their hold on her arms. Then it was gone. Her arms fell at her sides, and if it weren't for the strangling vines still around her body. She would have collapsed at the relief from the stinging pressure.

"Now, tell me, my dear Penelope. How did you come to possess the fire of the Phoenix?" The words were harsher than before, like some of the sickly-sweet façade had fallen away.

"I—I don't know what you're talking about. I'm—I'm just a traveler." She whimpered the words, hoping the woman would believe it. All the while, Audelia dug deep, begging the fire inside to please answer her, for Waldrom to hear her. Someone to help her.

Melantha walked closer again and cupped Audelia's cheek. She still couldn't *move*. When the woman was too close, that numb feeling would creep back in, accompanied by an odd calm that made her stomach turn.

"I promise you are safe with me. I will not allow a monster like that abomination to hurt you. The power you possess, it once belonged to a very dear *dear* friend of mine." The shadow at her neck rubbed up and down, and she swore this time she heard Kairos in her head.

Just a little more, Fierce one. I've got you. Keep lying, don't let her know. You are doing so well.

"Don't look at that thing, girl." Melantha's voice was suddenly deeper, harsher. Audelia hadn't even realized she had looked over at Kairos, still trapped in the ice chains, but she could see that just under the surface of the cool blue were dark whisps.

His shadows.

"Sorry... I am still not sure what you are talking about.

Garren is my *friend;*" She hoped her voice was steady with the lie of his name, no way would she give her power over him. "we were just traveling to reach town." Her heart was pounding as she felt her magic begin to rise.

Melantha laughed again, this time, it rang out into a cackle, one that set Audelia's teeth on edge as she tried to move. She needed to get away from this woman. Whatever she was, whatever relationship she had with The Phoenix Queen, however long ago. Something told her it was not a good friendship.

"Your *friend?* Do you have a tendency to make *friends* with monsters, dear? I would think Eudora would have made sure her magic went to someone sensible. Pity."

At the sound of the Phoenix Queen's name being used, Audelia felt her magic rise in a wave. The cold that had seeped so deeply into her bones thawed and was replaced by brimstone.

"The observation could be made that you are the monster, Melantha. After all, you attacked me and my friend for what? A chat?" The brimstone in her bones steeled her spine. It was time to stop playing this woman's games.

"What a mouth on you." Melantha smiled this time, her mouth stretching so wide that the edges reached each ear; it was unsettling as her features shifted for a moment and then returned to the serene, beautiful woman.

But she had seen it—the truth behind the façade.

Caldumim Ina Tutunmi, say it under your breath. Trust me.

His voice was velvet-soft in her mind, and if they weren't currently faced with danger, she would love to hear him talk like that more often.

"Caldumim Ina Tutunmi," She spoke softly, hoping

Melantha wouldn't hear it as the woman had started to pace in front of her, lost in whatever debate she was caught in.

Audelia felt it then, a soft hum under her feet. Then, slowly, shadows started appearing from where she stood, and she watched out of the corner of her eye, not daring to completely look away from Melantha as the woman slowly became more and more unhinged. As those shadows moved like fog on the ground toward Kairos.

She watched as they slowly seeped into the ice holding him. Hope sparked in her heart as they started to melt slowly.

"Pity indeed. I am sorry, my dear, but you are leaving me little option. But I am a very considerate goddess, even stuck here in this mortal cage. If you kill the monster, *the abomination*, I will spare you, and you can become my faithful. And I shall give you unimaginable power." Melantha stood before Audelia again in a flash, her features had darkened, and Audelia's power rose from within, finally. She felt that brimstone turn into a raging inferno. Felt the depth of what her magic could be, and it eclipsed the one before her.

Audelia smiled then, and she watched as Melantha thought she had won. That Audelia would willingly kill Kairos. A male who yes, she barely knew, but she did know one thing. She trusted him; she couldn't explain it, but something in her soul told her to trust him. That even when he was being an asshole, that he could be trusted.

So, she closed her eyes for a moment, grounding herself, when she opened them again, she watched as Melantha's eyes widened in shock, and she knew that the woman or whatever she was, would see the fire burning in her eyes she had felt the tidal wave of her magic awaken fully and with it. She submitted to the fire, surrendering to her power.

"I think I'll pass. Et Fiero utno visia." With the spell spoken that had been whispered to her over and over as the brimstone had flowed through, burning the traces of the ice, Audelia watched as blue fire burst from her body, burning away the vines and shoving Melantha across the clearing into the trunk of a tree with a sickening crash.

CHAPTER FIFTY

Audelia ran to Kairos' side, flames still licking at her body as she pulled at the melting chunks of ice that had held him still. Her body was starting to tremble from the exertion. It wasn't until she had seen him thrown and ensconced in ice that she had begun to realize she cared about him. Even when he had been cruel and cold towards her, she had cared. In a way, that scared her.

"Are you okay, Kairos?" Her words were a whisper; she didn't know if she had managed to kill Melantha or not, and she was scared to draw too much attention to them.

His gaze turned to her, and she saw the worry reflecting in his own, and she felt her heart skip a beat, before she shook the feeling away. His hand broke free, and he reached to grasp her shoulder before the other broke free and ripped the ice from his lips away.

She winced as blood trickled from where the ice had dug

into his chin. This was her fault. If she had been paying better attention to her surroundings, she wouldn't have been grabbed by those fucking vines, and they would have reached the edge of this forest.

Before she could ask him again or even try to stand, a growl broke through the silence of the clearing, and a wall of adamant shadow blocked a spark of bright green aiming for them. It splashed against the wall, and Audelia could hear the hiss of it burning into the shadow.

"YOU LITTLE BITCH!" Another bright green flash slammed into the wall as Audelia and Kairos stood holding onto each other. Audelia chanced a look at Kairos, and he looked pale.

Audelia swung her head to face where Melantha had landed, only to gasp as she took in the woman who had been holding them hostage.

Gone was the visage of a beautiful woman; in her place was something that lay in nightmares. The form before her had bile rising to Audelia's throat. "Oh gods, what is she?"

Melantha stood taller than before, her height nearly double what it had been before; her elegant curves were replaced by lumpy, emaciated flesh with boils and missing bits of flesh. Audelia had never seen anything so horrifying. The high cheekbones and supple lips were gone, and in their place was a wide-set, thin smile that bordered from each ear with missing, rotting teeth. Even from where they stood, Audelia could smell the reek of her—the rot of both body and magic.

Melantha's bulbous eyes, still that stark ice blue with a milky hue, now narrowed at Audelia. She felt herself take a step back as Melantha took one forward on gnarled legs with chunks of flesh slapping against exposed bone.

"She is a Ciannait Hag. I've heard stories about them, but

I've never *seen* one before. We need to get out of here *now*." Kairos's words were rushed, and Audelia noticed then that even he was shaking now.

What the hel was a Ciannait Hag?

He took a step in front of Audelia, blocking her from Melantha's sight, who was just watching them. Her head tilted at an odd angle with the clumps of loose, dried hair with bones woven within it falling to her humped shoulder with exposed bone. Audelia looked away to take in Kairos; he was becoming more and more tense by the second.

"What is a Ciannait Hag?" She knew they needed to move, but she needed to know what the fuck that thing was, and she feared a little at the fact it knew what she was, *who* she was. She needed to remain hidden until she found the others. Even with the trust she held for Kairos, it was tentative at best.

She could also feel a pulse from him, similar to the one she felt in her own bones, but different; hers was the warmth of a flame, and his felt cool and dark like the shadows that moved at his command. Audelia wanted to lean into that feel, fall into it.

"She is an ancient being, once a minor goddess, usually the maiden of a goddess's temple, corrupted by their want of true power. I thought they had all died out long, long ago at the time of the Dragon Knight and his mate, The Phoenix Queen." His words were whispered as he pulled out his blades from their spots across his back.

"How do we kill her then?" Audelia was growing worried by the minute. *How were they supposed to kill something so powerful?*

"Luck. If we could find its heart on the astral plane, we could ensure it remains dead. But, unless you can find it when she ends up conjuring, well, let's hope Urdr likes us." He said with a manic grin.

He swung them in an arching motion as he dropped into a defensive position, as he nudged her back toward the dark forest behind them. She complied, but not before she reached forward and yanked one of the blades on his hip free, flipping it in her palm to test the feel in her hands.

Not too bad, she could handle this if it came to that. Finding this thing's heart would be another challenge.

Kairos looked back at her, his eyes filled with anger, but she merely shrugged and turned her gaze back to the hag before them. But she wasn't there anymore. The spot she had been moments prior was now *empty*. "Kairos! She's gone!"

Kairos swung his gaze back and quickly stepped closer to Audelia, guarding her tightly as his gaze swung from side to side. But nothing was in the clearing with them. Audelia's chest rose and fell in quick movements as her breathing picked up and fear crept up her spine.

"Fuck, where did that thing go?" Shadows rose around them, locking them into another wall of dark adamant.

But he didn't get them up fast enough before a shot of green struck him in the side, and he went flying from her sight, Audelia called out to him, but he didn't move, and she turned toward where the green came from to see Melantha standing off the side emerging from the shadows of the trees.

Wait. No, not the shadows of the trees, because Audelia watched in horror as Melantha shed the bark of the trees that had been her flesh moments before; she had never left the clearing but had somehow camouflaged herself from their sight.

Fuck, how on earth could they fight something that could blend like that?

With flame, little star, call on your fire. Waldrom's voice filled her head, but it sounded faint, filtered, and more distant than usual.

But she nodded, he had never steered her wrong yet, even if she was annoyed by the cloak and dagger of not just fucking telling her things.

Shaking the thought, knowing it was useless, and she had a literal monster standing before her, leering at her. Audelia took a deep breath and then another, and she began to plunge into the fire that curled deep inside her. Luckily, it was not too far from her, having stretched itself on and off all day.

"Such a *foolish* girl. You could have had everything you could have dreamed of." Melantha's voice had lost that melodic tone, and now it was the throaty voice of an ancient crone, sending shivers of fear down Audelia's spine.

"I think I came out the better end if your so-called *everything*, ends in my looking like that. I'm not vain, but damn. Hard pass." Audelia dug deeper within herself, feeling the flames begin to lick up her arms, but they were weaker than before, and she felt her body going heavy.

Fuck. She wouldn't last like this for long. Audelia squared her shoulders and gripped the blade in her hand a little harder, preparing to lunge at the hag.

"I shall enjoy feasting on your flesh; you are older than I prefer to eat, but I have coveted that power in your veins for millennia. With it, I shall rule the worlds and make them bow." Melantha laughed, the sound grating as she raised her hands at her sides, and the ground around Audelia erupted in spikes of ice and hewn rock. She jumped out of the way before one of those spikes tore her apart.

She hadn't moved fast enough before part of that spike tore through her leather pants. Audelia cried out as she felt the warm blood well against her skin. Limping, she retreated toward where Kairos had landed, hoping that he was still alive.

Another round of spikes began to quake the ground, but something inside of Audelia rose, and she felt the words just before she yelled them into the space around them. "Liat un Grie!" The words foreign, but something deep within purred with satisfaction at their release.

As the words left her lips, Audelia watched as violet sparks spread from her fingers and shot out toward the spikes breaking through the ground before, each one reduced to ash in moments before she stumbled backwards, tripping over a knotted root.

Before she could move to stand, blackness descended upon her, and she felt his warmth and his scent of smoke and citrus coil around her. "Kairos?" She whispered into the dark before it receded a little, and she saw him kneeling before her, his dark phthalo green eyes simmering with unchecked rage.

He didn't answer before standing and running toward where Melantha stood, seething at Audelia's escape.

Audelia watched as Kairos summoned shadow-like flame around his blade as he charged at the hag and gasped as Melantha summoned her own sword, one hewn of stone wrapped in spiked vines, each a green color that seemed to drip and hiss. Poisoned?

"Look out!" She shouted as she watched Melantha swing the blade like a skilled swordsman, but Kairos parried in time and twisted his body to narrowly miss the tipped spikes of her blade. He swung his sword at her, and the blow landed into her arm. Audelia's blood ran cold at the sound that came from Melantha's lips.

She watched as they both traded blow after blow, both with blade and magic. It was breathtaking to watch as sparks of onyx and vibrant green seemed to blend with their blades. After a while, she could tell Kairos was growing tired, either from the blow earlier or because he was facing what Audelia had gathered was an immortal, possibly another ethereal. Regardless, he was beginning to falter, and it had her body humming with fear.

Fear that one more blow and he would not get back up.

She couldn't allow that.

Not again. Not as the image of Shawn taking that final death blow to save her. She fought the grief and tears from falling as she started to rally in her heart.

Audelia could not let another die for her, not another she had grown to care for deeply. She wouldn't allow it. She would burn the world before allowing another to die for her.

Audelia stood on shaky legs, grabbing a discarded sword from the ground near her. One, she assumed Kairos had left for her in case he failed, and took several deep breaths before she ran into the fray. She reached them just in time to block a blow that would have cleaved his shoulder in two.

She grunted at the force of the swing but held steady. All those years of sword lessons in the dojo coming to the surface. She was not a master swordsman, but when it came to protecting those she cared for? Audelia would be unstoppable; she swung the blade in her hand in a steady arch toward Melantha.

Melantha, caught off guard by Audelia, didn't have time to

block the arch, and Audelia felt the splatter of warm blood hit her face as she managed to lacerate Melantha's side.

Not wasting time, she moved into another swing, this time, it was blocked by a wave of deep green magic that would have hit her dead on if not for the sudden wall of black wispy shadows taking the brunt of it.

Adrenaline pumped in her veins as she looked briefly at Kairos and nodded a thanks, and he did the same in return. "So, touching, how you are both going to die together." Melantha cackled before a burst of vibrant orange and green rushed out from her body.

Kairos rushed at her and pulled her into him as they were both propelled back by the magic. Audelia cried out as the orange and green seemed to seep into her skin and burned like ice. They landed in a pillow of black shadows that curled around them, reminding Audelia of a bean bag.

"Are you okay?" Kairos's voice was soft, far softer than she was used to; it was laced with pain and worry and made her heart race.

Not able to talk around the pain radiating in her body, she merely nodded. He reached over and cupped her cheek gently in an uncharacteristic way. "Let's finish this." She nodded again as she leaned into his touch.

Together, they stood and turned back toward Melantha, whose skin was taking on a darker shade of decay as she began to move her hands in different movements, as if preparing for another casting of magic.

But Audelia saw it then, it was just a flicker at first, but in between each movement, something in Melantha shifted. Then, she saw it. There, in the odd shift, was a green and red beating heart. Melantha's heart. Gone and visible in quick successions, but in a pattern if one were to look closely.

Audelia grabbed Kairos by the wrist, halting his forward movement. "*Look there.*" She said softly, pointing as best she could with her eyes. He caught her line of sight, and she watched as he grinned when he turned back toward her.

Audelia held back as gasp when she felt the soft caress of star-flecked midnight brush against her mind. It felt like home. It felt right as she let it in, and wasn't surprised when, a moment later, Kairos's melted chocolate voice filled her head.

You are truly brilliant, Fierce one. You found her weakness. If we can time our magic just right, we can end the bitch.

Hoping her next words were in her head and not out loud, Audelia spoke, *I don't know how to control my magic. The times you saw. I'm not sure how I managed those things; it was like instinct, but I'm not sure how to control it.*

Kairos watched her taking in the words in his head and nodded. Seemingly understanding and not judging her for it. There would be time to analyze *that* later.

Melantha's cruel voice broke through the sudden quiet of the clearing. "Any last words? Pleading always tastes so *delicious.*" Audelia watched as Melantha continued the movements with her hands unbidden.

Kairos and Audelia began to walk closer to Melantha, acting as if they were going to attack with their blades again. *I'll distract her. She wants me anyway.*

Audelia moved away from Kairos and felt some of his shadows curl around her shoulders like they had before, but this time, they seemed to be more alive, like asps ready to strike if need be.

"I'm not going to plead to a creature like you." Audelia

sneered, hoping her tone belied her terror because she was terrified they would fail. This hag before them, everything about her screamed at Audelia to run, that this was a battle she would lose.

She wasn't entirely sure if that was her instincts or something deeper telling her that. But she did know she no longer wanted to cower if she was to become what she was meant to be. She had to do this. Face the impossible, and hope like hel she succeeded.

"Oh, and what will you do, dear? *Kill me*? Ha!"

"Even the mighty eventually fall." Audelia dug deep inside her again, feeling the well of power begin to surge at her words as if they called to them. She hoped that, like before, she could keep Melantha from noticing the rise of heat from her magic, as she squared her shoulders and raised her blade.

Melantha laughed again as she spoke softly, and a figure appeared, blocking Melantha from sight. The vine-like humanoid figure stood in that spot with its spiked blade and raced at Audelia before she had time to react fully. She only barely managed to parry the spiked blade.

"Audelia!" Kairos called out to her as another vine figure sprouted up and began to charge at her. The shadows that had been resting on her shoulders shot out toward the incoming figure. Audelia watched in a brief moment as those shadows became a thousand small daggers that began to plunge into the vine's figure as Audelia twisted herself to slice at the one in front of her.

I think I can do it now, but I'm going to need you to try to use your magic too, Fierce one.

Audelia didn't respond, only dug deep, willing the flames to gather in her very blood and spread out. Her heart raced as she gave in to the inferno. The blade in her hand was engulfed in flames as she let the magic ride her. As she arched her blade again in a riposte.

The vine figure burst into brilliant flame and collapsed into a pile of ash as Audelia turned back toward Melantha. The hag continued to make the strange movements over and over, as if in a trance.

Audelia felt it then, the sudden shift in the air. Everything was suddenly colder, so frigid that even the fire that was a burning inferno inside her seemed to shy from it.

Kairos. Whatever we are going to do, it needs to be now.

I know.

She felt his star-flecked midnight caress her mind before it disappeared.

Kairos materialized out of pure shadow a second later, standing beside her as she faced Melantha, who had begun to smile sinisterly. Audelia felt the shadows around Kairos build into a torrent of black, and her heart pounded in her ears from the force of it.

Audelia watched as Kairos sent onyx straight for the spot that kept appearing, containing Melantha's heart. Without thinking, Audelia closed her eyes and focused on her own fire, willed it from her, as every flame left her body. She watched as it formed into a flaming arrow that cut straight through the onyx torrent of shadows that had engulfed Melantha.

With bated breath, she watched as the arrow shot straight through the pitch black and straight into the green and red beating heart of the hag.

As the flame and shadow made contact, everything in the air shifted and slowed as they watched the heart shrink and shrivel into ash. Moments later, time seemed to speed up as

Melantha screeched as her decayed flesh imploded in an explosion of greyish skin and moss-green blood. Kairos pulled Audelia back and shot up a wall of black shadow just as the chunks of flesh and blood reached them. Nearly gagging on the scent of what had been the hag.

But before they could celebrate, a blast of wind knocked them both back, and they slammed into a nearby rock with a heavy thunk. It blasted over and over, preventing them from getting back up, and as suddenly as the odd wave of wind had occurred, the world around them stilled.

Leaving Audelia lying in Kairos' arms as silence settled around them.

CHAPTER FIFTY~ONE

Silence settled heavily around them, so stark that Audelia's ears were ringing as loud as her heartbeat that still roared. She was still in Kairos' arms and knew she should extricate herself from his warmth, but after what just happened? She was a little reluctant to lose the safety she felt.

Kairos' arms felt beyond safe; he was stirring things in her that terrified her, but in this moment, she was clinging to them. During the fight, she had realized how much she had grown to care for him in ways that were beginning to defy logic or words.

He was a stranger, *yet* a kernel of doubt set in that he truly was. Could he be someone she knew long ago, before this all happened?

Kairos looked at her, his own breathing heavy as his eyes trailed over her body, checking for injuries. It wasn't until she felt his hands move to grip her hip and slightly squeeze that she saw the unbidden lust burning in his green eyes, making her breath hitch. Part of her wanted to chase, even knowing it was just the adrenaline talking because she was still swimming in her grief and wanted to chase something that would erase the damning numbness that had filled the past several days. Wanted to feel something, *more*.

Audelia looked him over, trying not to think of the hand at her hip and the burning warmth of it. Instead, she checked him for injuries; she could see that the cuts from the ice over his mouth had stitched back together, leaving only dried blood. She wondered if she had hurt her head more than she thought, as the sight of him covered in blood did strange things to her.

She felt an unmistakable pull to this male, and it was beginning to terrify her. *It's the adrenaline, that's all this is.*

Kairos opened his mouth to say something, but then closed it as she shifted from her perch in his lap. The groan that left his lips she felt deeply in her core; even as a sick feeling of guilt settled like a lodestone in her heart and belly. The pull was stronger than it all. Audelia held her breath as Kairos began to lean forward, his hand moving from her hip to her lower back, caging her in.

She didn't know what to do. She should have pulled away; she was grieving, and she didn't know this male. But something deep in her gravitated toward it. Something powerful.

His lips were inches from hers, and she could feel the heat of his breath and the intensity of his eyes, which had her heart galloping. She felt her magic answer in kind. Audelia felt right away that it wasn't rising as if to protect her; no, she felt a deep yearning from her magic, as if it wanted to curl into his and take root.

Suddenly, her magic and his own surged, and she felt a shock course through her body. As she watched swirls of red and blues reach toward the star-flecked midnight that she had come to know as his magic. Audelia watched as his eyes flared with an emotion she couldn't place, but had the feeling reflected in her own. Then, it was gone in a flash, and Kairos was shoving her away with a frustrated growl as he got to his feet and began to pace back and forth. Leaving her sprawled on the damp earth, confused as hel.

"I'm sorry." She whispered, unsure why she was apologizing exactly, or if the apology was entirely for him and not for the stark feeling that she was betraying what she and Shawn had held together.

Gods, she was a horrible person. She had just lost the love of her life, and here she was, almost kissing another male barely two weeks later.

Kairos stopped pacing, and his phthalo green eyes bore into hers with flashes of different emotions before she watched as all expression seemed to freeze over, and the return of that pure dark was back.

She felt herself swallowing hard as Kairos stared at her with predatory intent. No trace of the previous lust left, as if he had turned a switch back to his usual self.

"Let's go. We need to get out of this gods damned forest before something worse than a Ciannait Hag appears." His voice was harsh and cut through her like a blade, and she found herself flinching at the tone.

Kairos barely even acknowledged her as he stormed out of the clearing after grabbing the rest of his fallen weapons. Audelia remained glued to the ground for a moment, trying to process what had just happened.

Kairos stopped at the edge of the clearing and turned back toward her, as he must have realized she had not followed and growled at her so harshly that the hairs on the back of her neck rose. "Let's fucking *go*."

Not wanting to anger him further, and still confused as fuck by his constant hot and cold attitude towards her. She felt like she was going to get whiplash from this continuous back-and-forth. Audelia stood, grateful once again that her legs didn't buckle under her just from his heated stare alone.

She nodded and, grabbing the blades she had lost earlier, she placed the last one back into the bandelier across her chest that Kairos must have grabbed on his way to find her.

To save her.

The question was why he had even bothered when he clearly hated being near her.

They moved in a blur as they ventured back into the silent dark of the forest. Before long, Audelia felt her movements increase in such a preternatural way that she was confused at first until she noticed Kairos' feet in front of her moving just as quickly. That was when she saw it. That was when she saw it - the shadows had gathered around them both, presumably propelling them through the last remains of the forest.

With every step closer to where the last of the sun lingered at the growing edge of the forest. Audelia could feel the rage coming off Kairos in waves. So strong that her magic had risen again, this time in protection, like it wasn't entirely sure what would happen when Kairos finally gave in to his rage.

The tension becoming stifling.

After what felt like ages, even with Kairos' shadows lending them speed, they finally reached the ridgeline of trees.

Audelia could have wept as she saw open space before them and felt those last blissful rays of the evening sun.

Even when they reached the precipice of the forest, his anger had not let up. If anything, Audelia was sure that if he felt any more anger, he was likely to combust into a pile of ash. She still wasn't entirely sure why he was so angry with her. Only that with every glare he gave her way when he deemed to see if she was still there. One thing resounded for her as the cause. *Audelia.*

Asshole.

They kept walking, even when they had reached a point where the shadows of the forest didn't even reach them anymore. Audelia wasn't sure if she was smart for just continuing to follow the male before her, whose shadows had travelled up his back and formed a shroud around him as they walked, making him even more menacing than he had been before. Or if it would be wiser to use this moment, when he wasn't paying attention to her, to go their separate ways.

The idea caused Audelia to look around the flat landscape around them, she had barely noticed that they had entered an open valley with some spots that dipped out of sight, and smaller patches of tree line. The world was beautiful, *her* world, she reminded herself, was breathtaking. The greenery seemed to chase the horizon as they walked.

A pang of loss travelled through her at the thought of being alone again. As much as his brooding was beginning to worry her, she feared being alone more. She didn't trust herself anymore. Didn't know the world she was in; everything was tentative for her.

Audelia didn't even know if her friends, her guards, would even bother to find her, not after what had occurred to the twins before they had even left the mortal realm. Or if they could even *find* her.

Deciding she was going to at least stop and get some answers from him, she found herself slamming into his thick back. She had been so lost in thought that she hadn't even noticed he had stopped walking. Audelia fell back onto her ass and groaned.

"We will make camp here tonight." She could feel the violence in his words. Audelia moved to stand as she noticed him storming off to what looked to be the ruins of a stone barrow near a small outcrop of trees and a small brook. Audelia might not know a lot about certain things, but she had gone camping frequently growing up with Bronn, and he had taught her some survival skills.

Including where to make camp that kept one blocked from others traveling, with a pang, she realized he had been teaching her how to survive what was to come.

Audelia was still so damn angry with him about the lies, but it warmed her heart to know that even if he couldn't tell her who she was and who he was to her, Bronn still made sure she would be prepared for what fate would bring.

The evening was fast approaching, and she felt a chill in the air, and as she noticed, Kairos had begun to check the small inside of the barrow that formed a small cave. Audelia hoped nothing still lingered inside. Deciding she should do something other than standing around. Without proper camping supplies, Audelia couldn't do much. However, she could at least ease some of his anger by making a fire.

Audelia turned on her heel and walked to the small outcrop of trees that surrounded the east side of the barrow and started collecting brush.

After a few minutes, she had a decent amount for at least a small fire. Audelia picked a spot near the opening of the barrow, figuring that if it got cold enough, they could huddle inside with the fire just in front of them, keeping them warm and warding off anything that might grab them directly.

She piled the sticks and loose needles into a decent little mound, one that would hopefully burn all night. Taking some of the bigger loose rocks lying around, Audelia made a barrier to keep the wind off the embers. Smiling at her campfire, Audelia grabbed two more rocks she had found during her search for the ones around the wood to ignite a fire.

Audelia wasn't sure why she was surprised to find limestone here in this world, but she was grateful for it. She began to strike the rocks together over the perfect spot, swiping in the motion that should activate the flint. She tried over and over, but still couldn't make a big enough spark.

She was just about to give up and ask Kairos if he had something to start the fire with when a voice filled her head. It was soft and familiar. *Et Fiero.*

Trusting the voice like she had earlier with the hag, Audelia spoke the words out loud. "Et Fiero." As the last syllable left her lips, she felt a warmth spread over her body, and then suddenly, before her, was a beautiful fire. Audelia felt such pride as she watched the dancing flames before her.

She felt him first, moments before Kairos appeared at her side and dropped two small rabbits beside her. She hadn't even realized he had left their little campsite.

But she was grateful as her stomach growled. She felt her cheeks redden as Kairos looked over at her. He began to dress the rabbits with such speed that she was in reverent awe of his skill. Clearly, he spent a considerable amount of time in the wilderness. Then again, she doubted this world had grocery stores.

A while later, they sat in torturous silence, eating their rabbits. She didn't care for small game, but after days of barely eating more than stale bread and cheese that they had found in the stores at the Fleshers' camp. The game was a feast, and she had to admit Kairos could cook very well.

She felt ashamed that she couldn't really help him with the dressing and preparing of his kill. But, while he had cooked, she had gathered fresh water to fill their skins from the brook he had mentioned near the south side of the outcrop of trees. She was laying out their bedrolls when the rabbit had finished.

"Thank you, again." If she hadn't been looking at him, she wouldn't have noticed how rigid Kairos had become at her harmless words. But even seeing the sudden shift, she hadn't been prepared for him to slam her to the ground by the throat.

There was such hate and accusations in his eyes that parts of her heart broke at the sight. She felt tears well up and fall as she observed him, watching and wondering if this was it. He had finally run out of use for her and would end her.

"*Who*. Are. You." Each word was sharp and bit into her skin. She tried to push away from him, to create some distance so that she could think. Her movements seemed only to anger him more.

Yet, she still didn't fear him. Not really.

It was strange; she could feel the rage and violence pouring off him, but her soul didn't fear. Maybe she was more broken than she thought. Because even faced with possible death, she didn't fear him. Didn't fear what was to come.

"I—already—told—you." She choked out every word through the limited breaths she could get out from his grip.

His face loomed closer, his hot breath against her face as he snarled. "I don't believe you." His grip tightened, and she knew there would be bruises later. "Now, fucking tell me the truth."

She pleaded with her eyes for him to see reason, to lessen his grip. She knew she needed to tell him the truth. But it wasn't that she didn't trust him. It was that she was beginning to trust him too much. Those she trusted tended to either betray her in some way or they died for her.

He pressed her harder into the ground, the bite of loose stones digging into her spine as his body engulfed her own. She was trapped. But she wasn't defenseless; she had her magic, it was temperamental, but it was there, and she had been trained by Bronn and Mathias.

She could do this. At least so she could speak better, think more clearly, and help Kairos see why knowing her truth could get him killed.

"Kai—ros, pl—ease." She choked out as she reached for her magic. It rose quickly, this time as if it sensed her desperation.

Help me.

In answer, her magic surged in a wave, shoving Kairos from her. She screamed as she felt his grip rip harshly from her throat as he landed feet from her. Before he could stand again, Audelia stood on shaky legs and coughed as she gasped for fresh air. "Kairos—I promise; I am not a threat to you... please."

She screamed as shadows slammed into her, throwing her into the crumbling wall of the barrow. She saw the dark green of his eyes moments before he stepped from the wall of shadow. He looked like a death god coming to claim his prize.

"Not a threat to me? Ha." His voice was thick, death incarnate, even his features had shifted, taking on a darker, deadlier edge. He almost looked demonic. It sent a shiver down her spine.

"I'm not, I swear." She spoke softly, gasping as she felt the press of a blade against her throat.

"Who are you, Audelia? Because a nobody, a lost female, doesn't attract the things you keep seeming to. First Itti and his flesher who were hunting with a gods damned Astarothian Stone, and then with a fucking Ciannait Hag?" He pressed the blade harder into the soft flesh of her neck, and she felt the sickly warmth of her blood as it trailed down her throat.

"I promise. Who I am isn't a threat. I—just—I—can't tell you, please. Trust me." She was sobbing now.

This was it; she was going to die. Die, and she wouldn't even be able to see Shawn again, not while his soul was stuck in that fucking blade.

She wanted him to trust her, even if him trusting her scared her so fucking much, she didn't want to see another good male die because of who she was. If she could take away her destiny, she would, but until then, she would do her damnedest to ensure others wouldn't fall as she completed it.

Especially not Kairos. It had been such a short time, but she was growing to care for him more and more as the days wore on. Shawn's face flashed before her mind's eye, and she cried. Cried for the man she had lost, for the love they had shared, for what her destiny had stolen from him.

"*I love you, Audelia...*" Her heart cracked open, and grief began to swallow her as she heard Shawn's last words play over in her head.

Suddenly, the pressure on her neck was gone, and she opened her tear-filled eyes to see Kairos standing before her. The rage was gone, but she could still see frustration in his dark irises, and what she could have sworn was heartbreak, as he turned and stormed off into the darkness of the trees.

Audelia collapsed to her knees, relief flooding through her, but also a deep grief that slammed into her as she leaned against the stones of the barrow. Her eyes felt so unbelievably heavy as the last of the adrenaline vanished from her body.

Audelia fell asleep as visions of Shawn dying over and over played in vivid detail.

CHAPTER FIFTY~TWO

Kairos needed to get away from her.

He had never lost his shit so severely as he did just now, it was why even though it was gods freezing tonight, he had stormed away from the warmth of the fire. Needing to think. To gain clarity.

Yet, the images of the day refused to budge from his thoughts and all those feelings they seemed to stir in his soul.

It was beginning to piss him off.

Because when those vines had gripped Audelia and yanked her from his sight. He had been filled with such deep-seated fear. Not for himself, *no*, it had all been for *her*.

That control? The one he spent his entire life building snapped.

Suddenly, all those plans he had cultivated, even when he had needed to restructure because of Audelia. They *disappeared* at the sight of those blue eyes widening in shock and fear as those vines yanked her from him.

He only paused because of the war inside of himself. The one that had been filled with both terror and relief at her disappearing from sight.

Yes, he was planning on using her as bait. To garner favor with his father's allies. It been fucking perfect. Yet, the longer he remained around her, the more those plans fell like sand in the wind. The night before, when the light of the fire had hit her and made her look like a goddess given life. His heart pounded as she seemed to glow, the fire feeding the flame in her very soul. It had been breathtaking.

He just wanted to lose himself in it, to forget who he was. To make the look of grief that seemed to pass over her eyes become some forgotten thing. To make her his, and damn everything he had ever planned. Luckily his own grief had pulled his head out of his ass and he managed stopped it.

Yet, it hadn't entirely left in that moment. Nor had it since.

Then the logic settled in for a moment, reminding him that he needed to continue his promise. That he needed to end his father, the curse on his soul, to avenge his Firebird. Her absence was a blessing, he had thought.

Then he heard her scream in the dark of the Semperion. The sound filled him with a profound feeling of loss, and he shook off his logic and ran. Ran toward the female he didn't want to care for—the remnants of his plans shredding apart with every step.

Walking further from the camp, Kairos thought of everything that had happened after he had crossed that threshold.

First, he found her blades. That had filled him with rage. Not that she let herself lose them, but because it would mean she would have to face whatever had dragged her into the dark, alone, weaponless, and if the drops of blood along the path were any indication. Injured.

When he reached that damn clearing, the bitter cold that had filled him was nothing compared to the current icy wind whipping at his clothes. She was struggling to get away from where she hung like a sack of meat for whatever had wielded those vines. The sight had him seeing red.

His shadows surged, and he quickly found himself on the branch above her, just as she had managed to get a grip. He been so fucking proud of her, but still that terror that had sent him to her aid had yet to let go. She wouldn't be safe til whatever grabbed her was gone. That protectiveness that routed so deep in him, *fuck,* it still *unnerved* him.

In such a short time, Audelia had shifted so much of who he was that Kairos wasn't sure if he would ever be able to gain control of how she made him feel.

Looking back now, he should have left. The moment had been there, before he had used his shadows to protect her again, he could have left her to whatever Urdr planned for her. But then, visions of another set of blue eyes and fire-red hair filled his vision, and he knew. Knew that regardless of what this female did to him, the plans that she shattered. He couldn't leave her to that fate. Wasn't sure if he ever would be able to.

He had decided even as the danger remained clothed in the dark of the forest, that he would *not* fail again.

Thinking through the battle that occurred after his promise to himself, Kairos made his way back toward the camp, having been walking in a circle around the perimeter, sending his shadows out here and there to check they were safe.

He still couldn't believe it had been a *Ciannaint Hag,* and that they had fucking *won.*

How her eyes had shown with such wonder, that even now his knees felt weak at how just gods damn beautiful she had looked in that heat of victory—his Fierce One.

He had felt the pull, the one that had been building for

days, it had gone taut as their eyes had met. She had been on top of him from where they had sprawled after that blast had sent them flying, Kairos taking the brunt of their landing. Suddenly, the heat of battle shifted to a different kind of heat.

He had found himself giving in; it still bothered him how much he had wanted to let everything go. How badly he craved the way she made him feel. Audelia had the power to destroy him, and in that moment, with her warmth seeping into him. Kairos hadn't given a damn.

Taking in the female shivering in her sleep near the fire, he was again in that moment when all that heat, all that feeling of taking what he wanted had snapped. One moment he had been seconds away from claiming those plump lips that had been distracting as fuck the past several days.

When an errant thought from her had slammed into him. In his moment of revelry, he had forgotten to reaffirm his mental barrier, the one that had dropped during battle so they could speak and plan. Gone was the growing lust for her as the thought swirled around him. It was becoming intolerable with the swirling feelings this female was constantly plaguing him with.

Yet he had kept wanting more, still did. Even with how things had changed, as those feelings she was feeling had flooded him.

He felt everything shift in such a cataclysmic way that he didn't know if he could ever get her back to this point. She had pulled away, and he had felt the grief well up inside her, that bitter taste of it embedded into his senses. It had settled deeply and changed everything.

It fucking pissed him off. How dare this other male take this from him?

He had felt jealous of a fucking dead male. The male, who was encompassing what had been passing between them. Before he could grasp onto that, the jealousy moved on to fear. Fear that if he let himself feel something for her, he would give in to the pull. That he would get her killed.

So instead, he let himself slip into the dark and pushed her away. It had broken him to act like that towards her, but it was for the best.

But as he let the dark build, he reinforced that black adamant wall in his mind from her. He let the anger and rage build. Not just at who she might be that had caused Itti to track her or for the Hag to have found her, but the power he had felt during the fight was like nothing he had ever felt before, even now standing at the edge of the camp, he felt it, it was dimmer, but it was still such an ethereal power. One that made him want to devour the world for her, to fall to his knees and worship her.

Audelia was—fuck she was power, and beginnings and endings. She was *everything*.

That last part had echoed in different ways through his mind as they had made camp, all more terrifying than the last. Then, when she had *thanked* him.

Showed such gratitude toward him after everything that had happened. He had acted brash and horrible towards her, and she had *thanked him*?

That had sent him over the edge. Kairos felt himself riding the dark abyss of power he was cursed with. Felt the monster just below his skin. It found satisfaction in the growing fear in her eyes and relished it even more as she tried to fight most of that fear.

But then, sometime during his attempt to get her to reveal

who she truly was, he saw everything in her mind as it flashed past her thoughts. He squeezed her throat, reveling in the feel of her erratic pulse and gasps for air. It was one thought that had set a chill to his fevered skin.

She didn't *fear* him.

That had given him pause, and he pulled more at the monster's leash as he saw how she feared herself, feared what telling him the truth would cause him. Audelia had worried *for* him. *Why? Why did she care?*

The thought even now had him trudging back into the small forest around them. Needing to find that clarity again, because she was a maelstrom, one that was constantly pulling him into her waves into the chaos of her.

Even with the monster starting to run the show more and more, it wasn't until the trickle of blood ran down her throat that he realized the monster had been unleashed too much.

The sight of her life force trailing down the slender neck he dreamed of licking and nibbling had filled him with such horror and self-loathing. So much that his stomach rolled, and he slammed into the monster within and pulled just in time to see the thoughts in her head slam into him as he yelled at her again.

Kairos felt her affection for him, radiating from her like the first rays of sun in spring, and he felt his heartbeat thunderously in his chest.

Then, he heard the words. Heard the love the male she grieved held for her.

Felt *everything* she had felt.

Then he faltered. He couldn't kill her, even if every sensible part of him screamed that her being around would cause nothing good. He shoved it down deep like he did the monster that lurked in his soul.

He let go of her and ran.

Ran hard as he felt her grief wash over him again, fighting the urge to go back and pull her into his arms and never let go.

After he punched the trunk of an oak near the brook, roaring into the night, he walked back in silence. He heard her cry out, heard her call for the male who died saving her.

Kairos didn't fight it in those moments, as he sent his shadows to cradle her.

He pulled her suddenly frail body into his arms, lending her comfort even for a short while.

After her body calmed and she fell into a deep slumber, he laid down beside her. He knew in that moment they would need to part soon, or he would give into the feelings that pulled at him—that engulfed him—would burn around him, as long as it meant she would remain at his side.

As sleep took him, he wondered why that would be a bad thing if it meant Audelia would be safe.

CHAPTER FIFTY~THREE

Audelia awoke to the soft warmth of a fur pelt covering her body where she was curled on the bedroll, which was strange because she had fallen asleep with a wool blanket covering her. Her teeth had chattered well into the night as a cold wind had filtered into their camp. Her first thought was Kairos. That he had yet again done such a kind and loving thing, she wanted to express her gratitude to him. But she knew that his mood changed like a breeze in a storm; she didn't want it to change, just yet.

So, instead, she smiled to herself even as the last of the nightmares haunted her. They had eased at some point, feeling more distant, as if something had placed a balm over the harshness. Whatever it had been, she was grateful.

Hoping she had woken before him and could do something nice for him, she rolled only to see his spot was empty. The bedroll was still lying there, so he hadn't been gone long or left without her, at least.

She stood and stretched out her tight muscles and looked around with her hands on her hips, wondering where Kairos had gone. He was nowhere that she could directly see, so she assumed that he had gone to fill their skins or maybe to scout the area.

Making herself useful, Audelia walked around the edge of the barrow and found several berry bushes. Her mouth watered as she began to pluck several berries from the stems. Audelia reached into the pocket of her dark leathers and pulled out a handkerchief that sent a dull ache through her. Mara.

As she plucked more berries, placing them on the delicate cream cloth, she thought of her aunt. She missed Mara so much, missed their talks about romance books or just sitting around watching trashy reality shows. Above all, she just missed the comfort of being with the woman who, for all intents and purposes, was her mother.

She missed all of them. So terribly much, it had been plaguing her lately, if she would ever find them again. Audelia hoped that when she reached the cave that Waldrom had wanted her to find, maybe *he* would know how to find them.

Audelia just prayed to whatever gods watched over this world that they would watch over them all and that the people she loved would forgive her for leaving like this.

Gathering the last of the berries, Audelia turned back towards camp and walked to where the last of their food stores were just inside the mouth of the barrow. She pulled out the last of what tasted like cheddar cheese to go with the berries. They would really need to find something for the rest of their journey. Bronn had taught her to hunt with a bow, but she wasn't the best shot with smaller animals.

If she could happen across some animal, she might be able to help with procuring more than the meager berries she had, currently staining the kerchief in her hand.

Perhaps she could ask Kairos to teach her how to use the bow more effectively; she would likely need to hunt for her food as she journeyed to the Cave of Asida.

At least, she hoped he would, after last night, she wasn't entirely sure if he would be willing to help her past his first agreement.

Audelia wanted to tell him desperately, but she still wasn't sure if she could fully trust this unexplainable pull she felt towards him.

As if thinking of him had summoned the male himself, Audelia sensed him moments before he stepped into the camp. His hair looked wet, the dark curls framing the sharp, rugged features of his face. Now that they were out of the dark of the forest and she could see him in the sunlight, he was beyond handsome. Her first assessment of him —looking like a Greek God—was wrong; *no,* Kairos was more than godlike in his features, he was what the gods would aspire to be. He was breathtaking, even when his features darkened as he watched her looking at him.

Audelia turned away, suddenly embarrassed for her ogling of him. She was sure that if he ventured closer, her cheeks would look as hot as the rest of her body felt. Taking a centering breath, she looked at him again and smiled gently before extending the kerchief in her hand.

"I found some berries, they looked like blackberries from

my home, so I am really hoping I didn't just pick something poisonous." She laughed a little, her voice feeling shaky.

Kairos just nodded and grabbed the kerchief full of fruit from her, popping a few into his mouth. She almost missed the slight upturn of his lips at the taste of the berries, but she had seen it, and it warmed her heart that she had done at least something good.

He passed them back to her and turned toward their packs. "Finish packing. We're leaving as soon as possible." *Straight to the point again,* she thought.

They quickly broke camp and headed to the east. This time, now that Audelia wasn't so lost in her damn head, took in everything around her as she easily kept pace with Kairos, who, for once, wasn't entirely brooding.

This world was truly beautiful. It was still early morning, so the sun had cast a soft, orange and pink glow over the world, making the mists appear like fairy dust rolling over the hills and valleys that surrounded them.

"This place is—it's breathtaking," Audelia said after hours of walking and taking in every single detail of her world as her mind would allow. The sun had reached its peak in the sky, making the world around her even brighter.

"For the most part, but don't let its beauty fool you. We haven't had true peace in this world for over two hundred years." Kairos' voice seemed tinged with regret as he nodded and continued to walk. Audelia stopped in her tracks at his words, though, her heart beginning to pound in her ears.

Did he just say—two hundred years?

"What—what do you mean two hundred years?" That wasn't right. *No,* Gideon was a walking history book for their world. He told her that the world had been mostly peaceful, but Lefrain had only just begun his destruction in the two decades before she was born. This was not something he would have just forgotten to tell her.

The world felt like it was spinning as she stood there. It took a moment for Kairos to notice she had stopped walking. Audelia thought through every conversation she had with him and with the twins about this place. Thoughts of the twins being skewered before her as they left had her swallowing the sob as she pushed past to think of the timeline of events they had taught her.

It had only been fifteen years since Waldrom sent them through the portal in The Glade. So, maybe she had misheard him. Audelia gasped when she felt calloused fingers grip her chin and lift it.

Audelia looked up to meet Kairos' dark eyes, the green of them seeming to simmer amongst the black like wildfire. "It's been just over two hundred years since the portal to the Archeron opened. How do you not know that?" His words held suspicion as his grip tightened on her.

Two hundred years? What the hell happened?

If it's been that long, then—she needed to tell him. Maybe not *who* she is, but that she hasn't been here for a very long time. But one thing was for sure, Audelia was fucked.

Audelia watched him for a moment, the dark green in his eyes drawing her in, making her heart race. "Kairos—"

"Yes, Fierce one?" His tone brokered no room for anything but the truth.

But she still didn't know how to say the words, say what she had been dying to tell him since he saved her from the Ciannait Hag in the forest. *If it had been two hundred years, he would think she was mad, delusional. Or perhaps hate her and wish her harm for abandoning everyone for so long, while she lived a simple, happy life.*

His grip tightened, and he moved closer to her, his large frame looming over her. She swallowed hard as she fought the words.

"Are you going to tell me who you are finally?" He stepped closer, his grip becoming more punishing, as if he were getting closer to losing his hold on his temper. Audelia shifted in his hold. "Or do I need to have some fun with you first? Because I *will* get answers." A shiver ran down her spine at the threats and veiled promises in his words.

She had to tell him; she *needed* to trust him. Even if she was scared, too. Terrified that if she trusted him, she would somehow lose him. Audelia was so damn tired of losing people.

Those you lost are your fault. A voice like poison filled her head; she had heard it before, and just like the first time, it filled her with dread.

"What just happened?" Kairos' voice filled her senses; the harshness was gone, and in its place was the deep, melted chocolate tone that made her toes curl in her boots. "One moment, you were fine, and then you were suddenly distant. Audelia, don't pull away from me, talk to me." His thumb skated across her jaw in a soothing motion, easing some of the grief.

"Nothing—just remembering something. It's fine." The look he gave her told her he didn't buy that shit for one moment, but he had bigger concerns. Like who she was.

She couldn't take the silence anymore; it seemed to press in on her. "Kairos, I promise, just like I did last night, I am not a threat to you. But I was born here, but I haven't been in this realm for a very long time." Audelia hoped her voice had sounded as sure as she had hoped it would.

Kairos stared at her for a moment, and she saw the war in his eyes. Weighing the decision of whether he trusted her words. Then he shocked the hell out of her by asking in a soft tone. "How long?"

Taken aback for a moment, Audelia cocked her head as much as his grip—which had not wavered—would allow. "For me? Fifteen years, but if what you are saying is true, then it's been since the portal opened to the Archeron." She could taste ash in her mouth as she spoke the words.

Did her family know? Did Mathias and the rest of her cadre? What the fuck had happened that time had become so jarred?

Kairos let go of her as if holding her had burned him, and he just turned away and began to walk. *What the fuck?*

Audelia was stunned by his sudden brush-off, but not wanting to trail too far behind now that she knew everything would be even harder to accomplish without help. How was she supposed to unite her people if, to them, she had been gone for *two centuries?*

They walked again in silence, traveling until the sun had begun to dip behind the distant mountains, a sight Audelia had glimpsed sometime after noon during their excursion.

Audelia had tried all day to get him to talk, to get some sort of answer about their world, but Kairos had shut down again. She had seen the walls forming around him as the day went on.

Finally, as they made camp that evening, Audelia couldn't take any more. "What is wrong?" she snapped. Audelia was so damn tired of feeling like they had gotten closer, become tentative friends, only for him to pull back and build that wall. Tonight, that would change. She needed it to change in a way that tore at her soul with deep desperation, that she was sure was stemming from the grief still heavy in her heart.

At first, he ignored her as he had all damn day, but Audelia wasn't going to let him, and she shoved her way into his path. "What the fuck is *wrong?*" Audelia gripped the front of his tunic, forcing him to remain when he tried to move away from her again.

"*What is wrong?*" His words were sharp and accusatory as he pushed against the hand she held against his chest; Audelia stumbled back a step before she locked her stance a little better. "What is wrong is that you are still keeping secrets and just casually dropped the bomb that you haven't been in this world in over two hundred years." His heart pounded against her palm as he spoke.

He was in pain. She could feel it; she wasn't entirely sure how she knew he was in pain, but something deep within her could feel it coming off with every word thrown at her.

"I'm sorry. It's not something that is easy for me to talk about. Hel, I don't even really remember who I am." The words were out before she even realized she had said them. Audelia gasped and tried to pull away, to run. But Kairos's hand snapped up and gripped her wrist and held her hand to his chest. Trapping her in his hold as he took a step closer.

Audelia's eyes widened at the sight, and she trailed her eyes up to his face. She expected him to be angry, to see that darkness clouded over his features. But it wasn't there; instead, she saw a sort of sorrow pass over him as he watched her. Then he spoke, his words were tender, and they made her heart flip. "What do you mean, Audelia? What happened to you?" He took half a step toward her, shifting his hold on her wrist.

He hadn't used her full name before in this way, the only times he did use it in the past few days were when he was pissed at her and looked murderous. Audelia didn't know how to deal with the emotions coursing through her at him using it in such a tender way.

But she felt the words tumbling forth unbidden, yet she felt lighter as she spoke them. "I don't know who I am, at least not *really*." She paused, trying to get the words out. *How did she explain this to him?* "Two months ago, my entire life was turned upside down. I was told things—things that I still can't wrap my head around." She tried to pull away again, needing the space, but he held firm, and she latched onto that. Gaining the courage to finish. "But they led me *here*. To the world, I was born too. To the world, *I* need to save." Her eyes burned as she struggled to hold back the tears, and her voice softened as she pleaded with him. "*Please*. Kairos. Will you help me?" She felt tears fall as she watched his expression.

She knew with even what little she had just spoken; she could have doomed herself and this world. But she needed to tell him at least this part. Needed him to know it.

She couldn't explain it, but that pull deep inside her had screamed it, and she had felt her power uncurl as each word spilled forth.

Audelia held her breath as she waited for the killing blow, waited for the end. Waited for him to decide she wasn't worth it, to leave her cold and alone in this strange place.

She felt his thumb work its way back and forth across her inner wrist in soothing motions, and it set her blood aflame.

Every sweeping motion, Audelia allowed it to anchor her as she waited for him to speak, finally.

Kairos' eyes heated for a moment as he watched her like a predator watches its prey, then just as quickly, the heat was gone, and his usual distant façade returned, and her heart lurched. Audelia felt vulnerable under his heavy gaze.

She was going to lose him; this was it. She would be alone again, and right at that moment, Audelia wasn't entirely sure if she could handle it if he rejected her plea for help.

"I will help you get to the next town, but that is the extent of my help." With that, Kairos pulled away, leaving Audelia feeling suddenly achingly cold.

What had just happened?

The rest of the evening, Audelia spent at the edge of the fire, away from him, watching him cook. The only solace was that, maybe, just possibly, she had a chance in the next several days to change his mind. Was that he set a plate of some meat and bread by where she sat—a silent offering.

She merely nodded and ate quietly; when she finished, she pushed the plate away and laid down, turning away from him. As sleep took her, Audelia could have sworn she felt his stare burning into her back and the caress of shadows.

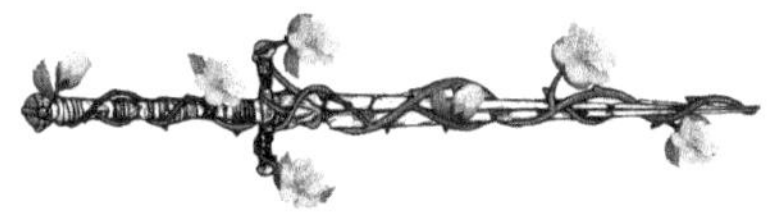

He was in hel.

That's what it felt like for the next few days as he and Audelia traveled across the Gloomfrost valley. Luck was on their side as they traveled, and it was the time of year when only the occasional nomad traveled through these valleys.

His only worry was whatever Archeron's might lay in wait between here and Noxia. Crawlers and werbeasts were the usual. But with everything that had happened in recent days, Kairos was on edge. He worried that the magic that seemed to settle and pulse around Audelia would lure in something bigger than the vermin that plagued near valley towns and villages. Something possibly worse than the hag.

He wouldn't let them get near her.

That thought resounded through him as a steady rhythm in time with his heartbeat.

The days wore on as Kairos watched the ever-altering scenery around them, as the open valleys started to turn into freshly plowed fields around them that he knew in a month's time would be abundant with crops and the sounds of people.

But even with the scenery and the ever-growing worry of what could find them, his thoughts and sight always traveled back to Audelia. She stole his every waking moment in maddening circles. Back to that night, when she had revealed that she had no knowledge of who she truly was, only that she was meant to *save* this world.

Everything in him had stopped. Then a rising call had thundered through him at the importance of her words.

He had wanted so desperately to pull her into his arms and tell her that he would never let anything happen to her and that he would gladly stay by her side. To be her shield.

But then his thoughts traveled to the last female he had said those words to. His Firebird.

Kairos knew, with his growing feelings for this female, that if he failed her, like he did the girl he loved, it would destroy him.

So, he pushed her away. Pushed away her warmth, pushed away what they could be.

It was the only way to protect her.

He only wrought destruction.

Kairos knew that the pull he felt towards her was growing every day as he breathed in her scent, a mix of cherry blossom, amber, and fruity black currant that seemed to have seeped into even his shadows. That he wasn't sure he could hold out much longer.

He had already begun to give in. The night after he had pushed her away, they had been set upon a small benderrat that was in no way truly small, considering the rodent was the size of a stock pig. He had watched her struggle with using her magic. His Fierce One could fight, and damn did she, but Kairos could see she struggled using both.

So, like the fucking fool of a male, he was Kairos offered to teach her every evening at camp how to fight and use magic at the same time. She had told him the magic she did know seemed to come in the form of whispered words from what she said sounded like her aunt's voice in her head.

Audelia had become so sad in those moments as he watched the regret and grief wash over her, and it took everything in him not to kiss her and hold her till those feelings left. He hated seeing that fire in her go out.

For the past few nights, after they ate whatever he had caught that evening, Kairos taught her how to fight demons and use her magic. She was fucking breathtaking to watch as she moved through the motions. Audelia held such power and grace with every twist and thrust with the daggers and short sword he had given her. Each was like an extension of herself. Whoever had trained her, had done a damn good job.

They broke camp that night, and as she went through the newest technique, adding more minor battle spells to each movement. Kairos watched her fiery red hair glow in the firelight, and his mind wandered to his Firebird. He wondered if she would be like this if she had lived, if he hadn't failed her.

Everything in him knew she would be, and for a moment, he forgot she was gone; instead, Audelia and his Firebird blended into one as she twisted into a repose by the firelight. The image stopped his heart.

"That's enough for the night. Get some rest. We reach Noxia tomorrow evening." He said gruffly before he darted for the trees.

He needed to get away from her.

He was too enraptured by his Fierce One.

No, *not* his. Fuck. She wasn't even *his*. Audelia was still mourning the man whose name she cried out to in her sleep. It was becoming less and less, but still, she called out for him.

They had chosen the ruins of an old watchtower that had fallen when his father took power to set up their camp. It was overgrown but situated on a large, cliff-like hill. It was secure, and he had used his shadows to block them from any traveling at night along the roads that led into town.

She was safe.

Knowing she was, Kairos walked some distance from the camp, sending some of his shadows to watch over her, including one of his Shadow-sprites, who had grown accustomed to Audelia. Lettie had even begun sitting on Audelia's shoulder during travel. However, she remained in her lightest form because she was still shy, so he doubted Audelia even *knew* she was there.

Their actions warmed his heart, knowing that one of them protected Audelia directly. Shadowsprites may be little, but if one was to ever fuck with them or those they care for, that being would find themselves burned in Shadowfire. A rare form of magic. Powerful and godlike, it was why he was protective of the sprites, making sure they hid in the shadows around natural flames.

As he reached the edge of the small cliff, he swung his legs over the edge and tugged on the bond with Eirlys.

He hadn't heard from her for a few days and was starting to get worried; she hadn't met them at the edge of the forest. The last message down the bond was, *Don't wait up, dummy.*

Kairos knew that meant something had come up, but she was okay.

Still, they had been apart for too long; he had felt the slips and knew she needed to reach them soon, or she would fall into The Whist or deep sleep until he could reach her.

Eirlys?

A moment later, Kairos felt that shimmer of green against his stardust midnight wall in his mind. Her voice filled his head a moment later, and he sighed with relief.

Hey Kai.

You going to be coming soon? Or did you decide that you were that bored with little ol' me? He teased.

Well, now that you mention it, maybe I'll fall into The Whist. I could use a good nap.

You would miss my dumbass too much, and you know it.

True, your stupidity is entertaining, especially around females. Speaking of. How are things with the redheaded? What was it you said? Goddess-given flesh? Her bemused huff echoed in his mind.

He laughed at that, even though it was true. Audelia was— there were no words that could ever properly encapsulate her beauty. Still, he didn't want Eirlys to know how much she truly had embedded in his very soul lately.

They're fine. We are almost to Noxia. Would have been there sooner if someone had been at the edge of the forest, like she said she would.

Someone's touchy. Maybe you should get the pretty female to touch you, so you lighten up, buttercup.

Kairos rolled his eyes.

Anywhoo. I will be there, hopefully, by tomorrow evening, unless the wind shifts too much. BUT. You will never guess why I am running late. Playful excitement ran down the bond between them.

Fine, I'll bite. Why are you so late?

Tadan.

Everything in Kairos's head emptied, and he felt cold, so cold that his body shook. He hadn't heard that name in over two centuries. Not since his uncle died, and his dragon had gone into The Whist. None of the elders in The Cove could explain why he went into it after his bonded had died instead of dying himself.

But Taden was old as shit. Older than most of the Elders still alive in The Cove.

Is—is he gone then? Kairos braced for it, for Eirlys to tell him that the last links to his uncle were gone. He knew his uncle was gone, knew that Mathias would never willingly leave the princess, his Firebird. If she was gone, then so was his uncle. But the thought of losing Tadan? It was killing him.

He couldn't lose another connection to everything he had loved. Even having Eirlys, who was Tadan's youngling, conceived before the fall of everything, didn't count; she didn't know her father. She had hatched fifteen years *after* Tadan had taken to The Whist.

No. Kai. *I can't explain it, but I was on my way to you. When I felt this surge of power pull at me, and I* knew—*knew it was my father. So, I turned back and raced for the cave he slept in. Kairos, he is* stirring.

What? *How is that possible? The Elders said—*

I know. But Kai. He is waking *up, I heard him in my head when I reached the den. All he said was, "Fire will rise again; She will rise again." I don't know what that means, but I might actually get to meet my dad!*

Kairos was about to respond when he heard rustling coming from the edge of camp. He stood quickly, calling to his shadows for the location and what it was. None responded.

Eirlys, I need to go. Just get here soon, okay? We'll talk more then. I am happy for you. Kairos shut down the connection and placed his full focus on whatever had entered their camp.

Audelia.

The thought of her in danger had him racing the short distance to where she lay, curled up under the blanket of her bedroll. Kairos let out a breath he didn't even know he had been holding at the relief of her sleeping soundly.

He heard the rustling again, and this time, his shadows ran for him, curling around his arms as they whispered *wolf.* Kairos couldn't even focus on the words because the rustling had shifted, this time closer to where his Fierce One lay.

Kairos took a step forward, only to halt as he took in the large pair of bright violet eyes watching him through the bushes.

672

CHAPTER FIFTY ~ FOUR

Wake Audelia.

That voice—

Audelia hadn't heard that since—since Shawn died in her arms. How is he here? Her heart started pounding in her ears so much that they had begun to ring.

But she still remembered it all the same.

Faron.

She was jolted awake as the familiar voice filled her head. She was terrified to open her eyes as she lay there, too nervous to move. Were the others with him? Gods, she didn't know if she could face them after everything that had happened.

Wake, girl. There is danger.

Her first thought was Kairos. Was he okay? If there was danger, then he was either hurt or about to be hurt. Faron doesn't know Kairos, so he wouldn't know how important he was to her. She needed to warn him, needed to know he was okay. Even a part of her worried about the wolf, who was a piece of Shawn. She knew deep in her bones that he was there because of Shawn. That thought had tears forming.

Shaking away the overwhelming grief of hearing his voice again, and what it brought back to the surface. Audelia opened her eyes and sat up, gasping as she took in the scene around her.

The moon cast a heavy glow in the sky, illuminating the large wolf as it bared its teeth at Kairos. He was inching his way towards her, blades drawn and reflecting the firelight. His shadows were around him in a storm of stardust midnight as he watched the wolf.

Fuck.

She needed to stop this before they killed each other. Audelia went to stand, but her legs gave out under her. Before she could catch herself, she fell against a warm, broad chest, the daggers strapped to his bandelier dug into her back as he curled his arm around her.

"I've got you, Fierce One." His breath was warm, and with the sultry tone of his voice, a shiver ran down her spine.

She shook away the feeling; she needed to focus. Needed to keep these two from killing each other. Both were very much 'kill first, ask questions later' types of males. As Kairos righted her, his grip didn't lessen as he started to move her from where she had been. He was trying to protect her from the wolf. It warmed her and made her heart race. Words knotted in her throat as she tried to speak; the grief from seeing Faron was pounding in her ears, mixed with the realization that Kairos was being this dark knight toward her, and everything suddenly felt twisted.

Which Kairos must have taken as fear, for she was suddenly behind him. His shadows curled around them both as a shield against danger.

Against Faron.

"Kairos, he isn't—" Fuck she couldn't get the words out; how did she explain this?

Faron, clearly not liking that he couldn't fully see her, bared his fangs in a snarl that sent a shiver down her spine. She hadn't heard that snarl since—since Kage went to attack her again in the glade, since she lost Shawn.

Kairos was pushing her further back, trying to maneuver them into a path so he could whisk her away to safety.

But he didn't get it; they were safe. *Beyond safe.* Faron would never hurt her. But he would hurt Kairos, it was then that she realized the danger Faron spoke of—was Kairos

She could feel the malice washing over Kairos, the pulse of it bore into her skin where he held her. The darker edge that Audelia had noticed during their time together seemed to pull at the leash he kept it on.

Audelia opened her mind toward Faron like Kairos had been teaching her. He had said it was simple magic, but it was easier if the other end wished for you to enter. She had hoped that Faron was open to her words.

Faron, calm down. Please.

Audelia watched as Faron cocked his head as the words registered, but he still wasn't standing down as his gaze swung toward Kairos again, whose shadows had started to thicken.

She knew if she didn't diffuse this, it would be catastrophic, and she would lose two beings that she cared deeply for. Would lose one of the final parts of Shawn.

"Kairos, it's okay. I know him." *What if he didn't listen like*

Faron clearly wasn't? Speaking of how *did* he find her? From what she figured, as Kairos had taught her about this world, she had been leagues away from where they came through the tree.

I can find you anywhere, Audelia. Faron's gaze bore into hers again.

Okay, we'll table that *for later. But seriously, calm the fuck down. He is my friend.*

He smells—wrong. Faron growled and made to move toward her again. Kairos sent shadows out at Faron that he jumped away from and swatted away like they were no more than flies.

Damn. This was about to become catastrophic fast if she didn't get one of them to calm down. She tried to reach Kairos in his mind, but found her way blocked by deep star-dusted midnight adamant walls. He had told her that speaking mind to mind was easier in battle, but he seemed too lost to whatever this was to let her in. Fuck. She redirected back toward Faron, hoping to get him to relent.

He smells fine. Why are you here? Why did you even bother looking for me? The number of questions she had was overwhelming. *Where are the others?* She needed to know if they were here, too.

No reply.

Realizing she would need to take drastic action before this situation worsened, she came up with a plan.

Audelia tried to step towards the wolf again, hoping that maybe if she stood between the two alpha holes, that she could get them both to back off. Just enough so she could tell them together that things were fine.

But just as she managed to get a step from the shadows and in front of Kairos, she was yanked back again by his arm.

As much as she was enjoying his warmth in the cool night, this shit had to stop.

"Kairos, he means us no harm. Both of you. Fucking stop." On the last words, Audelia had twisted her fingers in a motion Kairos had taught her; the movement was for amplifying, and she had hoped she used it right.

Both were suddenly quiet, even the shadows had dampened, but Kairos hadn't lessened his hold, and she noticed now that he was trembling a little. As if he were barely holding on to his unchecked anger.

Audelia pushed back so that she could fully stand between them, but she felt Kairos wrap his hand around her wrist like he needed to have some contact with her in case this went south. Her gaze traveled from where he held her still to his face, and she watched the warring emotions cross his handsome features. But he nodded. Nodded as if he trusted her judgment, even if it worried him.

The gesture made her heart race as she looked from him to Faron, who had stopped his leering but still refused to look away from Kairos.

"Seriously, *stop*, Faron." Audelia rolled her eyes and moved a little more in front of Kairos, hoping that maybe if she blocked the male from the wolf's gaze, he would calm some.

"Audelia—you know this wolf?" The last word came out more than just a question of knowing him; she also had the sense that Kairos knew there was something more about this particular wolf.

Guardian. That's what he had called himself the evening she awoke after the battle that had cost her Shawn.

Not just a Guardian, fiery one, yours.

Realizing Faron was listening into her mind, Audelia shot

up her mental defenses like Kairos had taught her, the wall of flaming adamant barring both males from entry until she deemed it.

"I'd like it if you stayed out of my head for the time being. Can you talk out loud?" Audelia stared Faron down; she would let him in just enough if she had to, but she wanted Kairos to be a part of this conversation. She owed him that much.

Faron dipped his head toward her, then both Kairos and Audelia watched in abject horror as Faron's body shifted, fur receding to give way to olive-toned skin, the crunching sound of bones reshaping, and a groan that seemed to shift from canine to male in the flash of an eye. Until standing before them was a very tall, very naked male.

Audelia blushed as she took in the male before her, then her heart shattered. Because as her eyes wandered from the chiseled chest of the olive-toned male, it was his face that had waves of grief, making her knees buckle, Kairos was there to catch her as she fell to the ground.

Faron looked like he could be an older version of Shawn; the sharp jaw, the high cheekbones, and almond-shaped eyes that were the same bright violet the wolf had, but every feature was Shawn's.

It felt like a dagger to her heart, and she had to look away, burying her face into Kairos' chest, who wrapped his arms around her and held her as she cried.

"Audelia—Fierce One, what's wrong?" His voice was soft in her hair as he pulled her closer to him, his touch gentle and protective. She shouldn't be leaning into him, shouldn't be gaining comfort from this male, the one who had become so deeply embedded in her soul that she was dreading parting from him tomorrow.

"Who are *you*?" Kairos growled as he tightened his hold, his shadows curling around her like a blanket in comfort.

"It's—" Gods, she couldn't get the words out. She didn't want to say his name out loud; she didn't want this—this reminder of who she had lost. *Why does he look like him?*

Faron, seeming to have picked up on her discomfort, spoke softly, his voice gravely, as if he had not spoken aloud in a very long time, but Audelia sagged in relief when he didn't sound like Shawn—small mercy, she supposed.

"I am sorry, Audelia, I have not been in this form for over a thousand years, I did not realize—until I saw your face and felt your grief. Of whom I look like."

His apology just made things worse, and she found herself burying her face more. She couldn't look, couldn't see what Shawn would have had the chance to become if...if...if she hadn't gotten him killed.

"I will ask you once more, and if you continue to upset her, I swear to all the Gods. I will gut you even if she named you *friend*." Kairos' words were like blades that cut through the night. "*Who are you?*"

"My name is Faron. I come from the planes of Delmira. I am *hers*—guardian, friend, whatever she needs of me. I do not wish her distress, but until both of you allow me into your minds, this is the only way." His voice softened, gentler than she had expected, and her body sagged in relief a little. He was right; she had asked this of him. But how could she have known—known he would share so many similarities with the man she lost and loved? The man whose very soul was still trapped in the fucking blade. "Who might *you* be, one who has the flames of Archeron etched upon their soul? You seem familiar to me *yet*—not."

Kairos stiffened under Audelia at Faron's words. What did he mean by that? Audelia pulled away to look up at Kairos. His gaze swung to hers, and she saw there, in the dark green that swam with the endless darkness was, shame, disgust, and worry. But even with all the darkness that she saw, she wasn't scared of him. Whatever Faron was talking about, she knew without a doubt that Kairos was good.

As much as her protector, as the wolf said he was.

She turned to look at the wolf, and this time, his features did not bring on the wave of grief. She still saw Shawn, but different now that the shock was gone. She noticed the slight differences now that the shock had worn off—the dimple in his chin, the specks and streaks of white in the rich black of his long hair, the long ears with tips of fur the same shade as his coat.

She honed in on those differences until the grief settled, and she fully shifted out of Kairos' hold, still holding onto his hand as if she still needed to be close to him and he to her.

Faron tracked the movement, and then his gaze swept between them a few times before a small smile played on his lips before returning to the thin line they had been before.

Kairos finally spoke as if a spell had been broken on him. She supposed he needed a moment, but she wasn't sure, just that he needed a moment. "You're—a Guardian? *How*? I thought you all died out eons ago?"

"We hide from those who do not need us, dragon rider. I came to her when she needed me most. To her side I will remain until I fall in my duty. Then my spirit shall pass to the beyond, and if needed, another shall take my place. Perhaps it will be *you*." Faron cocked his head at Kairos. His gaze assessing. Something passed over his features, gone, and then the same impassive look returned. *What had that been?*

Kairos opened his mouth to say something, but Audelia cut him off, hoping to kill whatever thought was in Kairos' head. She asked Faron. "How did you find me?"

She knew she was deflecting, but Audelia was scared that his words would undo her. That they were the mirror image of the ones screaming in her head, the ones that had told her, in the moments that the grief didn't have her in its grip. That Kairos was *hers*, and she was *his*.

"I told you, I will *find* you wherever you go. However, I was waylaid by carrying your belongings. I am many things; a pack mule is not one of them, but the tall, dark one insisted I take these to you." *Mathias,* she could picture him staring the wolf down as he demanded that he take her belongings with him. She suppressed a smile as his words registered.

"My—things?" Her hand snapped to her bare wrist. Every time the grief had taken hold of her over the past several days, it was made worse by the fact that she had *lost* the bracelet of Jade that Shawn had given her. *Did he have it with him? Was it truly not lost?*

Faron nodded and turned back toward the bushes he had come from, his bare ass shining in the firelight, they really needed to get him clothes.

Kairos must have thought the same because he growled and tossed a nearby blanket at the wolf, who caught it just in time as he turned, saving Audelia from getting another eyeful of the male's cock.

Audelia stood immediately, disentangling herself from where she had been half in Kairo's lap. Her eyes searched for the bracelet that she needed to see again. Needing to know if it wasn't lost, however, when the firelight caught on the sapphire and rubies on the hilt of the blade, still in its scabbard, that he now held in his hands.

Her mother's sword.

She closed the distance in a flash, ignoring Kairos, calling for her to be careful. She couldn't focus on anything else, not as she took in the blade that seemed to call for her. Audelia may not fully remember herself or her parents, but she had known from the moment Bronn had handed her this very blade in his office.

That it was her mother's, and now hers.

Audelia grabbed the scabbard from Faron, the rest of her things forgotten as she needed to see the blade in full. She couldn't explain it, but she *had* to see it, hold it.

It seemed to sing a song, an answer to a question that sat deep in her soul.

Holding the scabbard in one hand, Audelia gripped the hilt with her other hand and pulled; the sword came free with ease.

Her heart raced as every inch of the beautiful blade, with its intricate carvings on the silver, seemed to glow in the embers of the fire.

She raised it above her head, and a sense of utter calm washed over her.

The blade glowed incandescently as the moonlight hit the blade, and Audelia could have sworn she felt magic surge from the moon itself into her body through the blade. It filled her like a well in a storm, and she felt it thrum within.

A voice filled her head; it was ethereal and full of unsung power as it spoke to her.

Welcome home, daughter of fire, sister of moonlight, bringer of the eternal light. Rise from the Ashes and claim your birthright.

PRONUNCIATIONS

<u>Names: (In order of appearance)</u>

Audelia Elide Ferelith: Auh-del-ia Ill-eed F-ehr-uh-lith
Bronn Ferelith: Brah-n F-ehr-uh-lith
Mara Ferelith: Mar-uh F-ehr-uh-lith
Mathias Tenebris: Mah-THAY-ahS TEN-uh-bress
Naseria Ferelith: Nah-sey-reAH F-ehr-uh-lith
Garrik Ferelith: Gar-rick F-ehr-uh-lith
Skye Tenebris: Sky TEN-uh-bress
Waldrom: Wahl-drum
Tadan: Teh-dawn
Gaios: Gae-oS (God of luck)
Morena: Mo-Rin-a (Goddess of death)
Ezreal: Ezreah-el
Micah: Mic-ah
Lila: Lye-la
Gideon: Gid-eon
General Fartail: Far-tall
Lefrain: Leh-fraun
Sobo: So-bo
Ichiro: ee·chee·row
Flontis: Feh-lan-tus (God of tricks & oracles)
Neya: Neh-ah
Farais: Far-Ah-is
Faron: Fair-en
Tenguistwa: Ten-gu-ist-wah
Adrastos wolves: Ah-dras-tos

PRONUNCIATIONS

Aurelia: Auh-rel-ia (goddess of light and protector of the realms)

Kairos: kai·ruhs

Eirlys: AIR-lis

Aillard: Ail-lard

Urdr: Ur-dear (God of Fates)

Melantha: Me-lan-tha

Ciannait Hag: kyah-nait

Eudora: y-oo-d-AW-r-uh (The Phoenix Queen)

<u>Places:</u>

Dragsnic: Drahg-ss-nicK

Atentan: Ah-tin-ahn

Aldanien: Ahl-dawn-ien

Acheron: Ach-ehr-on

Caves of Asida: Ah-cee-dah

Dharan: DAH-ran

Semperion: Sem-per-ion

Noxia: Nox-iah

Gloomfrost Valley

Ghanta: Gah-an-tah

<u>Shawn's term of Endearment</u>

A Chroi: ah-CHREE the CH makes a loch noise

<u>Magic phrases:</u>

Et Fiero: At Fey-roH

Cadalium nito: Ca-Doli-um Nee-toh

Ento: Ehn-toe

Cal dara ut mirama: Cah-l dar-A ut Mir-Ama

Beatiu Unti Pateounce: Be-ati-uh UHN-tee Pateh-unCe

A sheanairean nan còmhnardan, fosgail do chridhe do na rìoghachdan, agus thoir air ais sinn gu rìoghachd teine agus sgàil:

Ut Tala Nach: uht Tah-la nah-oct

Caldumim Ina Tutunmi: Cal-dumi-mn In-ah Tut-un-mi

Et Fiero utno visia: At Fey-roH UHN-o Vis-ia

Liat un Grie: Li-at uhn Gr-ieh

<u>Magic Items</u>:

Astarothian stone: As-tah-roth-ian

ACKNOWLEDGMENTS

First off, I would like to thank my husband, Richard, for putting up with my crazy as I wrote this story. My writing a novel has been a long time coming, and I don't think he realized the depth of which I would fall as I wrote, lol. But he took it all in stride and made sure to keep our four beautiful kids out of my hair when I needed the quiet to just write or go over edits from my alpha. He was always there to hear me rant for hours about the most minor of issues that had nothing to do with our reality and everything to do with the tribulations of my characters. I don't think I can count on two hands the number of times I yelled out, "What are you doing?!" only for my husband to be at my side, worried that something happened or he did something. Only for me to mumble incoherently about so and so doing something crazy. Pretty sure he thought I was losing it, and that might still be the case. But I digress. Thank you so much for being my rock through this, I love you.

Second to my Alpha reader and my best friend, Devon. Thank you so much for encouraging me every step of the way even when I know my grammar was driving, you nuts. Luckily, it has gotten better-ish; I can weave a world from scratch, but have me put commas, tenses, and more where they should be, and well, my brain breaks. I will treasure our mom lunches where we annoyed whatever waiter was lucky enough to serve us for hours at Olive Garden as we talked on and on about our own novels. So, damn proud of you for sticking with and finishing your own novel Of Wind and Shadows (Seriously, go check it out!). You will forever be my partner in crime, and I look forward to more years of us sending chapter after chapter to each other even when we become famous because it works for us. Love you for always being the one friend that remained through all my own issues and always telling me I could do this. I will never be able to fully repay you for all of this.

To my parents, thank you so much for always encouraging me growing up to continue to tell my stories. For going to every drama and choir event I participated in and for ignoring my weirdness as I walked in circles with magazines, toys, and whatever I could use to fuel my little stories. Now, here I am about to publish my first novel, all those odd moments amounted to this. So, thank you both so much, and I love you.

To my HfSD girlies. Thank you so much for coming into my life because of our shared love of shadow daddies, for continuing to encourage me to write my story, for letting me blow up chat about the most random things, and for reading this story after I finished. I will forever be grateful to each of you, wonderful women. I miss you all.

Finally, to my high school English and Creative Writing teachers for always encouraging my voice and giving me the tools to make this journey even possible. I know I wasn't always the best student but your steadfastness in helping me will remain with me forever. Thank you.

ABOUT THE AUTHOR

Jade Jones is a mom of four amazing kids and three fur babies that keep her constantly on her toes, proving that life is an ever-changing adventure. When she isn't juggling following her passion of being a writer and weaving worlds together and motherhood, you can find her on the couch with her husband Richard of seven years, watching one of the many fantasy movies and shows that they love to binge over and over.

When she isn't bingeing comfort watches or writing, you can find her either gaming on her computer playing RPGs & MMOs, or she might be diving into the next fantasy or romance read that has caught her heart.

Creating worlds has always been the biggest dream for Jade and getting to finally show the world a taste of the worlds she can create brings such fierce joy, she hopes that you fall in love with the characters, their strife's and that maybe you will find your own fire and become the heroine/hero of your own story.

Happy reading!

www.ingramcontent.com/pod-product-compliance
Lightning Source LLC
Chambersburg PA
CBHW062057290726
48975CB00001B/19